NORTHERN PROVINCE

43 44
Louis Trichardt

40
39 42
Tzaneen
41

KRUGER NATIONAL PARK

38
37 36
35 Sabie

• Waterval-Boven

33
GAUTENG
• Pretoria
Johannesburg•

NORTH-WEST

34

EASTERN TRANSVAAL

FREE STATE

• Newcastle

Marquard•
31 32
Fouriesburg
30
Bloemfontein•

KWAZULU/NATAL

29
St Lucia

28
27 26
LESOTHO
25
24 23

• Durban

OUTH AFRICA

CAPE

EASTERN CAPE
• Umtata

Port Edward

22
21
20

17 • Cradock

19
18 • King William's Town
East London

Indian Ocean

10
• Oudtshoorn
George•
11 13
15 16
Knysna 12 14
• Port Elizabeth

Beaufort West•

PE

HIKING TRAILS
OF SOUTHERN AFRICA

WILLIE AND SANDRA OLIVIER
HIKING TRAILS
OF SOUTHERN AFRICA

SOUTHERN
BOOK PUBLISHERS

ISBN 1 86812 514 9

First edition, first impression 1995

Published by
Southern Book Publishers (Pty) Ltd
PO Box 3103, Halfway House 1685

Photographs by Willie and Sandra Olivier
Line drawings by Christina Walters, Lesley Coombes and Dr Jack
Maps and contour profiles by CartoCom, Pretoria
Climate graphs by Sandra Olivier
Cover design by Wim Reinders
Designed by Wim Reinders & Associates, Cape Town
Set in Baskerville (old style) 9/11 pt by Wouter Reinders, Cape Town
Reproduction by Hirt & Carter, Cape Town
Printed and bound by National Book Printers,
Drukkery Street, Goodwood, Western Cape

CARTOGRAPHER'S NOTE

Although every care has been taken to ensure the accuracy of location maps and contour profiles/trail maps, these are intended only as visual aids. This is particularly so with regard to contour profiles, where the quality of available trail maps varies considerably. I wish to express my gratitude to the National Hiking Way Board for permission to reproduce contour profiles where available and the Government Printer for authority to use official maps as a basis for location and trail maps/contour profiles.

Information from official maps is reproduced under Government Printer's authority 8547 of 8 July 1986 and the Office of the Surveyor-General of Namibia.

KEY TO LOCATION MAP

Trail route and direction

Beginning point/
Ending point of trail

Road route numbers

Boundaries of nature reserves and national parks

KEY TO DAILY CONTOUR PROFILES

Beginning point

Distance covered

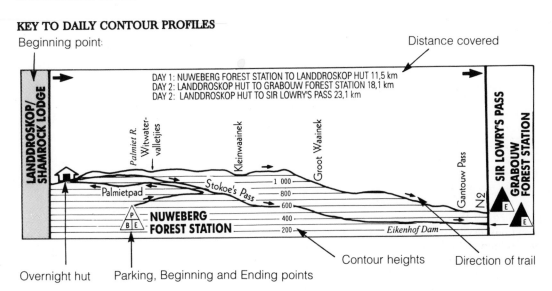

DAY 1: NUWEBERG FOREST STATION TO LANDDROSKOP HUT 11,5 km
DAY 2: LANDDROSKOP HUT TO GRABOUW FOREST STATION 18,1 km
DAY 2: LANDDROSKOP HUT TO SIR LOWRY'S PASS 23,1 km

Overnight hut   Parking, Beginning and Ending points

Contour heights   Direction of trail

CONTENTS

Introduction 1
How to use this book 2

BEFORE YOU GO
Trail terminology 4
Planning your outing 5
Food 5
Equipment 7
Packing your backpack 12
Kitlist 13
Hiking hints 14
General hints 15
Trail ethics 16
·First aid 17

THE TRAILS

NAMIBIA
Waterberg 23
Naukluft 31
Fish River Canyon 41
Other Namibian trails 49

NORTHERN AND WESTERN CAPE
Klipspringer 50
Oorlogskloof 56
Cederberg 63
Boland 74
  Limietberg 78
  Hottentots-Holland 82
Swellendam 88
Swartberg 96
Outeniqua 104
Harkerville 113
Other Northern and Western Cape trails 118

EASTERN CAPE
Tsitsikamma 125
Otter 134
Gonaqua 142
Alexandria 147
Mountain Zebra 154
Amatola 160
Kologha 168
Transkei 173
  Coffee Bay to Mbashe River 180

Port St John's to Coffee Bay 184
Msikaba to Port St John's 189
Other Eastern Cape trails 194

KWAZULU/NATAL
The Natal Drakensberg Park 199
  Giant's Cup 207
  Mzimkhulu 213
  Mkhomazi 217
  Giant's Castle 221
  Mdedelelo 225
  Cathedral Peak 229
Mziki 233
Other KwaZulu/Natal trails 239

FREE STATE
Koranna 245
Brandwater 250
Rhebok 256
Other Free State trails 262

NORTH-WEST, GAUTENG AND EASTERN
TRANSVAAL
Rustenburg 271
Suikerbosrand 276
Uitsoek 282
Fanie Botha 287
Prospector's 295
Blyderivierspoort 302
Other North-West, Gauteng and Eastern
  Transvaal trails 309

NORTHERN TRANSVAAL
Magoebaskloof 319
  Dokolewa 324
  Grootbosch 327
Wolkberg 330
Giraffe 337
Hanglip 342
Mabudashango 348
Other Northern Transvaal trails 354

REFERENCES
Glossary 357
Bibliography 360
Index 367

INTRODUCTION

In the seven years since the publication of *The Guide to Hiking Trails,* the number of hiking, backpacking and guided wilderness trails has grown phenomenally and today outdoor enthusiasts have a choice of well over 200 overnight trails. Many of the original trails have undergone significant changes, while the number of new trails is increasing every year.

Although the emphasis of hiking, backpacking and guided wilderness trails differs fundamentally, these activities have much in common and have therefore been included in a single volume. Most of the route descriptions and the information on the flora, fauna, history and geology of the trails described in *The Guide to Hiking Trails* have been completely revised and updated, and some have been omitted, while several new trails have been included.

Owing to space limitations it is not possible to provide a detailed description of all overnight trails and, in addition to the comprehensive chapters on 44 trails, concise descriptions of over 120 other trails have been included.

In instances where it came to our attention that a trail authority practises racial discrimination those trails have been omitted, at the expense of making the book as comprehensive as possible. This does not necessarily mean that all such instances came to our attention, nor does it imply that those trails not included in this book were omitted because they practise racial discrimination.

The authors have taken every care to ensure the correctness of all information, particularly in respect of trail descriptions. However, trails are sometimes redirected or changed and the authors do not accept any responsibility for inconvenience, injury or death arising from hiking any trail.

With the consolidation of the conservation authorities in South Africa's new regions, information regarding permits, etc. is likely to change in several instances, while telephone numbers are constantly changing.

Over the past 16 years numerous officials of conservation bodies, experts and friends have been called on to assist us with information and to answer questions. This book would not have been possible without their assistance and we would like to thank them most sincerely. A special word of thanks to Theuns van Rensburg of the National Hiking Way Board, Trevor Dearlove of the National Parks Board and Elna Haasbroek of Safcol at Sabie, as well as all staff members of Southern Book Publishers involved in the production of this book.

Trailing takes on special significance when the purely physical motivation is replaced by an aesthetic and spiritual consciousness. There is the joy of listening to the melodious song of a bird obscured by dense foliage or the distant roar of a lion. The changing kaleidoscope of colours at sunrise and sunset, the aromatic smell of the Karoo after a thunderstorm and the murmur of a crystal clear stream are other precious moments you will reflect on long after the trail is over.

The information we share in this book is the result of thousands of kilometres of hiking and backpacking and 16 years of research. We hope that this book will take you, the reader, on many exciting and rewarding journeys of discovery and that the knowledge we share with you will lead you to a greater love and appreciation of the many beautiful, unspoilt areas in southern Africa.

Willie and Sandra Olivier
Windhoek
Namibia

HOW TO USE THIS BOOK

BEFORE YOU GO

Essential information on equipment, trail food, planning a trail, safety and first aid are discussed here – although briefly. Seasoned hikers will be acquainted with most of the information supplied and this section is therefore a common-sense guide specifically for the novice.

THE TRAILS

The trails are arranged in a logical geographical sequence, starting in Namibia, continuing down through the Cape and in a semi-circle along the eastern part of the country to the Northern Transvaal. A map indicating the positions of all the trails described can be found on the front endpaper.

A brief summary of trailing opportunities not described in detail in this guide is included at the end of each region under the heading Other Trails. A map indicating the positions of these trails can be found on the back endpaper.

TRAIL PLANNER

Distance: For many of the trails various options are available but generally the maximum length and duration are given, except in the case of wilderness areas where the number of options makes this impossible.

Grading: The degree of difficulty of each trail is indicated by a grading:
- A is very easy.
- A+ is easy.
- B is moderate.
- B+ is moderate with some demanding sections.
- C is difficult.
- C+ is an extremely difficult trail.

The grades are based on a person of average fitness, hiking under ideal conditions, but it should be borne in mind that your level of fitness, mental preparedness and the prevailing climatic conditions could place a trail in a completely different grade.

Reservations: It is essential to obtain a permit and/or make a reservation well in advance. The name, address, telephone number and fax number (where available) of the relevant authority, as well as how long in advance reservations are accepted, are given. Remember that these details, particularly telephone numbers, may change.

Group size: The minimum and maximum number of people allowed on each trail is supplied.

Maps: You should not set off on a self-guided trail without a comprehensive map of the area. While some trails have high quality full-colour maps, others only provide a sketch map.

When trails are well marked a sketch map will suffice, but when this is inadequate the Government Printer's topographical map numbers are provided. These maps are available from the Surveyor-General's offices in Cape Town, Pretoria, Bloemfontein and Pietermaritzburg.

Facilities: Accommodation and other facilities provided on the trail are described under this heading.

Logistics: When planning your trip you will need to know whether the trail is circular or linear. If it is linear, suggestions regarding transport arrangements are included.

Overnight facilities at the start and end of the trail are described where they are available.

Relevant information: Specific information which you should be aware of is brought to your attention here. Therefore this section is **essential** reading.

How to get there: Brief directions on how to get to the starting point are given. A location map is also provided.

Climate: Where reliable data are available, rainfall and temperature figures are represented graphically, so that the expected conditions in any month can be seen at a glance.

However, *average* figures were used in these graphs and often the weather stations are at lower altitudes than the trail area. Because of this, conditions experienced could vary and the data supplied should be used as a guide only. In instances where reliable data are not available a brief outline of the climate is supplied instead.

TRAIL ENVIRONMENT

Flora and fauna: These are described in an attempt to make you more aware of your surroundings, and will assist you in choosing a trail according to your interests.

For the sake of uniformity the following reference works have been used throughout:

Flora: Scientific plant names follow those of Gibbs Russell (1984). The *National List of Indigenous Trees* (1986) was used for the common English names of trees.

Fauna: In the case of mammals the common English names and statistical data come from *The Mammals of the Southern African Subregion* (Smithers:1983) and the conservation status of mammals follows the *South African Red Data Book – Terrestrial Mammals* (Smithers:1986); reptiles and amphibians follow

McLachlan (1978). The common English bird names are according to *Roberts' Birds of Southern Africa* (Maclean:1993). The conservation status of birds is according to the *South African Red Data Book – Birds* (Brooke:1984). The common names of fishes are according to *A Complete Guide to the Freshwater Fishes of Southern Africa* (Skelton:1993).

History: In order to provide a better understanding of the area in former times, a brief history is outlined. In some cases a clear picture is still emerging and the information provided may become outdated.

Geology: Where geological features are obvious and likely to be of interest, they are discussed briefly.

TRAIL DESCRIPTION

This section contains either a detailed day-by-day description of each hiking trail or suggested routes in wilderness areas. Special features to look out for are noted.

The contour profiles for each day's hike will assist you in planning your day. However, on certain trails the variations in altitude are minimal, making a contour profile unnecessary.

In such instances a sketch map showing major features of the trail is provided. In wilder-

ness areas you are free to blaze your own trail and an area map is provided for these areas.

In some instances (e.g. Magoebaskloof and the part of the Eastern Cape formerly known as Transkei) much of the information relating to trails in the same area is so similar that this is dealt with in an introduction to the area.

BEFORE YOU GO

The novice is likely to be confronted by a bewildering array of questions, such as: Where can I hike? What equipment will I need? How fast should I walk in an hour? to mention just a few. This section therefore gives information and advice which will culminate in a successful hike for the first-timer, as well as providing useful tips for seasoned outdoor enthusiasts.

TRAIL TERMINOLOGY

The proliferation of hiking, backpacking and guided wilderness trails since the opening of the Fanie Botha Hiking Trail in 1973 has brought about a bewildering array of terms. Our own introduction to "do-it-yourself" trails was on the Otter Hiking Trail in 1976. In those days it was not nearly as popular as it is today and the Afrikaans name *wandelpad* conjured up visions of an easy ramble through forests and along the coast. Our illusions were soon shattered when we encountered rather steep ascents, were forced to camp next to a river coming down in flood and had to swim across the Lottering and Bloukrans rivers!

This experience illustrates the importance of correct terminology so that outdoor enthusiasts immediately realise what they are in for.

A **hiking trail** is a continuous, well-defined route through a natural or man-made environment on which the user carries gear and food in a back-pack. There are specific overnight stops at the end of each day and accommodation ranges from campsites to wooden chalets. The route is usually indicated by painted footprints but other methods are also used, for example stakes.

With the establishment of the National Hiking Way Board in South Africa in 1975, a network of trails stretching from the Soutpansberg in the northern Transvaal to the Cederberg in the western Cape was envisaged. However, as a result of the transfer of large areas of state land administered by the Department of Environmental Affairs to the respective provincial authorities in 1987 and

the subsequent commercialisation of the Forestry Branch, this ideal has been abandoned.

State, municipal and conservation authorities, as well as private landowners, have established hiking trails.

Backpacking trails are not along designated footpaths and you are free to blaze your own trail. No overnight facilities are provided and one sleeps in caves, under the stars or in a tent carried by the backpacker, although in a few instances patrol shelters can be used. The term "backpacking" is usually used for trails in wilderness areas where man has in no way scarred the landscape, except for paths and tracks established for management of the area. No footprints guide you in the right direction and there are no distance indicators. Backpacking trails are not recommended for the novice and it is essential that you are well prepared and have good mapreading and navigation skills before venturing into a wilderness area.

Guided wilderness trails are conducted under the supervision of a trails officer in natural and wild areas such as national parks and game reserves. These trails are ideal for the novice as heavy backpacks are not usually carried and distances covered each day depend on the group's fitness and the weather. The trails officer will not only guide you but will also share a wealth of knowledge of the area with you. Do not confuse these trails with game-viewing tours – often less game is encountered on foot as animals will tolerate vehicles at closer range. In addition, you cannot approach dangerous animals too closely on foot.

Both hiking and backpacking opportunities are described in this guide, while a summary of guided wilderness trails is provided.

Interpretative trails are usually no more than a few kilometres long, and they emphasise education and the interpretation of the environment. A comprehensive booklet is supplied to guide you and at intervals along the route numbered markers draw your attention to interesting features which are explained in the booklet.

Day walks offer an ideal opportunity for those wanting to stretch their legs without having to don a heavy backpack. In most major tourist areas, for example the Drakensberg, southern Cape and the Cape Peninsula, there are ample opportunities for day walkers and guidebooks are available. Fatalities do occur among day walkers and it must be stressed that this activity should not be taken too lightly. It is essential that you are appropriately dressed and adequately equipped with rain gear, water, snacks and a map.

PLANNING YOUR OUTING

Once you have decided you would like to attempt a trail, you cannot simply pull on your boots and set off. One of the best ways of familiarising yourself with hiking is to join a hiking club where you will learn from those with years of experience. For a list of these organisations write to the Hiking Federation of South Africa, P O Box 1420, Randburg 2125, Telephone (011) 886-6524, Fax (011) 886-6013.

In addition several books dealing with equipment and trails are listed in the bibliography and are well worth consulting. A monthly South African travel and outdoor magazine, *Getaway*, regularly includes comprehensive articles on hiking trails and provides updates on new developments. Equipment is also occasionally featured. *Great Outdoors* is another South African magazine specialising in the outdoors.

Without careful planning a trail can easily end up in a disaster, so do spend some time planning your trip. Keep the following in mind:
■ Choose a trail to suit your level of fitness. Your first outing should ideally be a short, weekend trail. Always bear the weakest member of the party in mind and ensure that all party members are fit.

■ Obtain the necessary permit from the authority in charge.
■ Consider the climate. This factor is vitally important as it will determine what equipment, clothing and food you will take.
■ Obtain the necessary maps. On most hiking trails the map supplied will suffice but in wilderness areas you should obtain the 1 : 50 000 topographical maps as trail routes are not indicated with route markers and, with the exception of the Cederberg Wilderness Area and the Drakensberg, special trail maps are not available. Moreover, make sure that you know how to use the maps and familiarise yourself with the use of a compass.
■ One of the golden rules is never to set off alone. Three people is the minimum, but four is a safer number.
■ Check your equipment beforehand and ensure that it is serviceable, especially your boots.
■ Obtain a weather forecast before setting off.
■ Always inform someone of your intended route and expected time of return. Where a mountain register is provided it should be completed correctly and in detail.

FOOD

A considerable amount of effort usually goes into planning your trail meals. Weight plays an important role here and can dampen the budding gourmet cook's enthusiasm. Most supermarkets, however, stock a wide range of instant, dehydrated soya-protein meals, dehydrated vegetables, instant mashed potatoes, and instant

soups and desserts. Soya-protein meals are often frowned upon by outdoor enthusiasts but by adding one fresh ingredient and a few spices and herbs you will be surprised how much the taste of soya-protein meals can be enhanced. They are also easy to prepare.

Outdoor stores usually carry a fairly wide

The following **three-day menu** caters for three people and is designed to help you plan your own. It can easily be adjusted to suit personal tastes and trail conditions. Always consider the facilities at the overnight stops. If wood is provided you could consider vacuum packing fresh meat for a braai.

Weights given are average and will vary according to the product brand.

	Breakfast		Lunch		Supper	
DAY 1	muesli	300 g	6 slices rye bread	375 g	3 cups instant soup	35 g
	3 rusks	60 g	6 cheese wedges	100 g	curry soya mince	120 g
	1 orange	300 g	1 mini salami	200 g	rice	150 g
	3 sheets		½ pkt dried figs	125 g	chutney	75 g
	crispbread	95 g	peanuts & raisins	150 g	1 banana	100 g
			3 apples	500 g	coconut	60 g
			1 l isotonic drink	80 g	1 pkt instant pudding	100 g
					coffee/tea/hot chocolate	
DAY 2	oats	150 g	6 sheets crispbread	190 g	3 cups instant soup	35 g
	3 rusks	60 g	3 hard-boiled eggs	190 g	instant mashed potato	112 g
	1 grapefruit	300 g	1 tin sardines	106 g	1 tin tuna	185 g
	3 slices rye		1 fruit roll	80 g	1 small green pepper	100 g
	bread	90 g	3 crunchie biscuits	60 g	dehydrated onion	25 g
	coffee/tea		1 l isotonic drink	80 g	dehydrated peas	50 g
					1 chicken stock cube	10 g
					custard powder	100 g
					milk powder for custard	100 g
					coffee/tea/hot chocolate	
DAY 3	muesli	300 g	6 sheets crispbread	190 g	3 cups instant soup	35 g
	3 rusks	60 g	6 cheese wedges	100 g	macaroni	200 g
	stewed fruit	200 g	1 tomato	200 g	Bolognese soya mince	120 g
	coffee/tea		small tin pâté	100 g	Parmesan cheese	50 g
			½ pkt dates	125 g	1 chocolate slab	200 g
			peanuts & raisins	150 g	coffee/tea/hot chocolate	
			3 apples	500 g		
			1 l isotonic drink	80 g		

MISCELLANEOUS

peanut butter	250 g	18 tea bags	54 g
jam	300 g	hot chocolate	100 g
milk powder (4 l)	400 g	3 pkts teatime	
sugar	500 g	biscuits	600 g
6 coffee bags	75 g	salt, pepper, herbs	25 g

range of lightweight foods, including freeze-dried meals. These meals are not only very palatable, but are also extremely light and in some instances require no cooking. Disadvantages are that they are expensive and you may find the portions too small if you have a healthy appetite.

Although everyone's kilojoule intake varies, men on average burn up 17-21 000 kJ (4-5 000 cal) and women 13-17 000 kJ (3-4 000 cal) a day. About 4 185 kJ (1 000 cal) a day should be added for a trail averaging 15 km a day or when you're hiking in cold weather. Also remember that you will need about two and a half times as many kilojoules to gain 300 m in altitude than to walk on level terrain for an hour!

You do not need to be a dietician to ensure that you are well nourished on the trail. The following is a rough guide of the average person's daily nutritional requirements:

■ two servings of milk products or milk (one serving is 250 ml milk, 60 ml milk powder [dry], 45 g cheese)

■ two servings of protein-rich food (one serving is 80 to 250 ml nuts, 60 ml peanut butter)

■ four servings of fruit and vegetables (one

serving is a piece of fruit, 125 ml cooked dehydrated vegetables)
■ four or more servings of bread or cereal (one serving is one slice of bread, 125 ml cooked cereal, 125 ml cooked pasta or rice).

Also remember the following:
■ When planning your menus, cater for about 1 kg of food per person per day, bearing in mind that in cold weather you will have a bigger appetite.
■ If you are hiking in a particularly arid area, include a few fresh items such as cucumber, tomatoes and carrots. They are worth the extra weight.
■ Each member of the group should have their own supply of snacks such as glucose

sweets, fudge, nuts, dried sausage and dried fruit.
■ Those who enjoy a sundowner or nightcap will have to decide whether it is worth carrying the extra weight. Remember to decant the contents of glass bottles into plastic bottles. If carrying the foil bag from a box of wine, ensure that it is well positioned in your pack and will not be pierced by a sharp object.
■ Always carry an extra day's emergency rations of high energy foods such as chocolate, nuts and raisins and glucose sweets. Don't be tempted to eat the rations before completing the trail!
■ Pack your cooking utensils and food sensibly so that all items needed for quick tea stops are kept together and food for lunch is easily accessible.

EQUIPMENT

Nowadays there is a wide range of scientifically designed, lightweight equipment to choose from. By the time you consider investing in your own equipment, you will probably have had the opportunity to try out borrowed equipment, in which case you will have formulated a few personal preferences.

Following is a discussion of essential items of specialist equipment. The designs and features of equipment are changing continuously and only the general features and principles are discussed here.

Golden rules when buying equipment
■ Carefully consider your requirements. It would serve very little purpose, for instance, to buy a lightweight artificial-fibre sleeping bag suitable for caravanning if you intend to hike in the Drakensberg during winter.
■ Before buying your equipment spend some time talking to fellow backpackers, browse through manufacturers' catalogues and consult some of the literature available on equipment.
■ Shop assistants in specialist backpacking stores constitute another invaluable source of information.
■ Unless you know what your exact requirements are, do not be tempted to buy equipment from supermarkets. It might be cheaper, but in most cases their staff simply do not have the expertise to advise you.
■ Always buy equipment with a reputable brand name. Some manufacturers of backpacks,

for instance, guarantee their products for life. This does not, however, mean that you have to buy the most expensive equipment in the store.
■ Buy what is comfortable and practical, not what is fashionable. Over the last few years equipment has tended to change frequently. What you buy should ultimately be dictated by your requirements and your personal taste.
■ Finally, decide on the price you wish to pay. Be realistic but never compromise quality for price.

Footwear
On any trail comfort starts at ground level – your feet. Few things can spoil a backpacking trip as much as blistered and aching feet. Backpacking footwear can be divided into four basic categories:
■ lightweight footwear suitable for casual rambling over easy terrain
■ medium-weight boots suitable for hiking and backpacking trails
■ mountaineering boots suitable for hiking and backpacking in rugged mountainous terrain and snow
■ specialist rock climbing boots.

In recent years there has been a worldwide move towards lightweight footwear and in South Africa the use of Alpine-type mountaineering boots – once the norm – has to a large extent become restricted to winter backpacking trips in the Drakensberg.

This was brought about partly by the lower quality and poorer performance of leather boots as the cost of leather soared and partly because of environmental considerations.

Taking general trailside conditions in southern Africa into consideration, medium-weight boots are probably the most suitable for hiking and backpacking.

When buying boots the most important considerations are size, comfort and protection. To ensure a good fit you should wear your hiking socks when trying on a pair of boots. Before tying the laces, push your foot as far forward as possible, until your toes are rubbing against the toecap. If you can still manage to squeeze a finger down the inside of your heel you know that you have the right fit. This extra room is necessary to allow your feet to expand and to prevent your toes from rubbing against the end of the boot on downhill stretches. Do up the laces firmly – not too tightly – and ensure that the boots do not constrict the broad part of the foot and that there is sufficient room for your toes to move freely. Walk up and down in the shop and check that your heels are held firmly in the back of the boots. If they rise more than about 6 mm you should try a smaller size.

Always try boots on both feet. Most people have one foot slightly bigger than the other and although a boot might fit one foot perfectly, you could find that the other boot of the same size is either too big or too small!

Once you have the right pair of boots it is important to give them a chance to adjust to the shape of your feet before embarking on your first trip. The time it will take you to break in your boots will depend on the stiffness of the sole and the leather or fabric. Begin by wearing the boots around the house and on day hikes until you are satisfied that they are properly worn in.

Boots have become increasingly expensive and should, therefore, be cared for properly. One of the most common mistakes is to dry wet boots in front of a fire. This causes shrinkage which could make the sole separate from the uppers. Wet boots should be aired as much as possible and then walked in until they are dry.

In the course of your travels your boots will be subjected to a great deal of hard wear, rain and sunshine. To revitalise the unique qualities of leather boots – breathability, suppleness, strength and durability – you should occasionally treat your boots with boot polish or Dubbin.

This will waterproof your boots, without affecting their breathability. Contrary to popular belief, Dubbin does not cause stitch-rot. However, remove all dirt, especially in seams, before applying. After treating your boots, ensure they are dry, stuff them with newspaper and store them in a dry place.

Backpack

After footwear, your backpack is the piece of equipment most crucial to your enjoyment of a hiking or backpacking trip. Comfort is once again of the utmost importance.

It is important to select the correct size backpack, i.e. the correct length of backpack or frame. This is, however, not as simple as it sounds. For instance, just because you are tall does not mean that you should buy a long-frame pack – the size of the frame/pack must be related to your torso size. Most good quality internal frame packs have a self-adjusting system, making it possible for people of varying heights to use the same pack. However, if you opt for an external frame pack make sure that the frame is the correct length.

Try on the pack and fasten the hip belt so that the top edge is just above your hipbone. Adjust the shoulder straps until the pack fits snugly against your back. The top harness point should not be more than 5 cm below your high prominent neck bone.

Ask a shop assistant or friend to help you gauge this position correctly. Because the sizes of packs and frames vary, you might have to try several times before finding the correct fit.

Another major consideration is the capacity of the pack, i.e. the cubic capacity measured in litres, and here the old adage applies: if it's a large pack, fill it up, if it's a small pack, it will not fit in. Considering general weather and other conditions in southern Africa packs with a capacity of 70 l and 55 to 60 l can be considered to be adequate for men and women respectively.

As for the type of backpack you should buy – internal or external – this is a matter of personal choice. Backpack designs are changing continuously and the last few years have seen some revolutionary designs appear on the market.

Ask yourself the following questions when deciding on a new backpack:
■ Are the hip belt and shoulder straps well padded?
■ Are the shoulder straps easily adjustable?

■ Does the hip belt have a quick-release buckle?

■ How many side pockets are there?

■ Is there a sac extension?

■ On external frame packs, is there a mesh backband to allow for ventilation?

■ Is the zip covered with a flap to make it showerproof?

Sleeping bag

When choosing a sleeping bag your choice will be between a down-filled bag or an artificial-fibre bag. Once again there are several factors you should consider: weight, packed size, design, warmth and finally price. Your final choice will be determined by how these factors relate to the circumstances under which you intend using the sleeping bag.

Down sleeping bags have the advantage of being light, compact and warm, but on the negative side, lose their insulating properties when wet and are expensive.

As a result of extensive research the quality of artificial-fibre sleeping bags has increased tremendously in recent years and some artificial-fibre bags compare favourably with down bags with respect to warmth. Advantages of artificial-fibre bags include the ability to retain their insulating properties when wet and their price. On the negative side, they are generally heavier and bulkier than down bags.

Two basic styles of sleeping bags are available: mummy-shaped and rectangular. If you are likely to spend long periods of time in cold weather conditions a mummy sleeping bag makes good sense, as the body-contoured shape of these bags provides the most satisfactory warmth-to-weight ratio.

The bag should have a well-shaped hood or cowl which can be drawn over your head, and a drawstring. In very cold weather conditions the cowl can be drawn over your face so that just a breathing hole remains open. In this way heat loss from the head, neck and shoulders – the body's major sources of heat loss – is prevented. Mummy bags usually do not have full zips, but some long styles have a short zip. Another feature of a well designed mummy bag is a circular, insulated foot-piece which not only provides added warmth but also gives better foot space.

Rectangular bags are the most popular sleeping bags in South Africa. They usually come with a full zip which gives you the advantage of being able to control the temperature. On a warm evening you can unzip the bag to reduce the temperature and in cold weather you can zip two bags together for extra warmth. At home the bag can be used as a duvet. Ensure that the bag has a down-filled draught tube behind the zip to prevent heat loss.

Although waterproof sleeping bags made from Goretex and Vent-x are widely available overseas, most sleeping bags in South Africa are at best shower resistant. However, you should never try to waterproof your sleeping bag as this will destroy its breathability and you will wake up in an uncomfortable pool of sweat.

A properly cared for down sleeping bag will see you through many warm, comfortable nights.

How to care for your sleeping bag

■ Keep your bag dry. If it does get wet, dry it out in the open as soon as possible. Gently squeeze out excess water, but do not wring out. Handle the bag with care to prevent the baffles from being damaged.

■ Never expose your bag to excessive heat such as direct sunlight or a fire, as this could lead to a hardening of the down.

■ Store your bag loosely – preferably by hanging it up when not in use. If the bag is compressed for extended periods the natural resilience of the filling will be strained.

■ Keep your sleeping bag as clean as possible both inside and out. The use of an inner sheet and a sleeping bag cover will not only keep your bag clean, but will also give added warmth, although they will add about one kilogram of weight.

■ Down sleeping bags should always be hand-washed. Fill a bathtub with enough lukewarm water to cover the bag and add special down soap. Gently wash the bag, avoiding harsh twisting or wringing. Drain the tub, and gently rinse in fresh water. Repeat this process until all the soap is removed. Press down gently onto the bag to squeeze out as much water as possible before lifting it out by supporting it from underneath. Dry the bag carefully in in a warm place, away from direct heat. Gently massage down lumps into individual plumules. Alternatively, down sleeping bags can also be dried in a tumble drier set on a low temperature. To prevent the down from clumping, a few tennis balls should be placed in the drier with the bag.

Closed-cell groundpad

To prevent cold creeping up from the ground you will need some form of insulation. Before closed-cell groundpads were available backpackers used alternatives such as vegetation (e.g. renosterbos), newspaper or airbeds for insulation.

First time out you might find your groundpad a bit hard, but in terms of comfort, weight and size (rolled) it is superior to both open foam and airbeds. Some high-quality closed-cell groundpads with a thickness of 9 mm are suitable for temperatures as low as -10 °C!

For backpackers who are prepared to forego lightness for the sake of comfort, a self-inflating mattress is the answer. These ingenious mattresses are ideal for backpacking – they are lighter than conventional airbeds, more compact and you do not need to waste time inflating them. Their disadvantages are that they are heavier than groundpads, more expensive and tend to puncture easily.

Emergency blanket or sportsman's space blanket

The emergency blanket is an extremely light (70 g) sheet of thin aluminium foil, one side of which is highly reflective. It takes up hardly any space, is relatively inexpensive and can be used for a variety of purposes such as extra insulation or an emergency shelter against rain or sun. It does not stand up to rough handling, however, and should not be used as a ground sheet, except in emergencies.

The sportsman's blanket is a more durable all-purpose "blanket" which can be used as a ground sheet. It is heavier (310 g) and more expensive.

Waterproof garment

The selection of rain gear is bound to be problematic unless you are prepared to delve deep into your pocket to buy a garment made of Goretex or Vent-x.

Conventional rain garments are generally either showerproof or waterproof. Showerproof garments have the advantage of breathability and perform satisfactorily in light rain. However, on trails where adverse weather conditions can set in for prolonged periods these garments are totally inadequate.

Waterproof garments, on the other hand, provide a sealed shell which is unable to breathe. Large volumes of warm, humid air are released by the body and being unable to escape through the waterproof material, they form water vapour when making contact with the cold surface of the garment.

Rain jackets with a full zip are versatile as you can unzip the garment to improve ventilation without removing the jacket. At the same time a zip has the disadvantage of being vulnerable to leakage.

The answer to these problems is the development of Goretex and Vent-x, fabrics which are 100 per cent waterproof, but breathable and virtually impenetrable by wind. Overseas these fabrics are used for a wide range of equipment, e.g. rain gear, sleeping bags, tents and sports and leisure outerwear. Since these fabrics are not manufactured in South Africa, but imported, Goretex and Vent-x equipment is unfortunately expensive, but well worth the money spent.

Backpacking stove

It is always advisable to carry a backpacking stove. Not only is it convenient for a quick mug of tea but you could find firewood stocks depleted at huts where you have been told to expect it.

There are three main types of backpacking stoves, classified according to the type of fuel they use: alcohol (methylated spirits), unleaded petrol (benzine), and gas (butane or propane). Various types of stoves are available, each with their own advantages and disadvantages, so your choice will largely be dictated by personal taste. The most important factors you should consider are efficiency, ease of operation, fuel economy, cooking capacity, size/mass, and price.

Benzine stoves rate high on efficiency and fuel economy and, in addition, they burn cleanly. Their main disadvantages are that they have to be pre-heated and are difficult to refuel (both somewhat cumbersome operations).

Methylated spirit stoves (alcohol) are easy to erect and operate, and are efficient. They perform well in windy conditions, and their wide base makes them stable. A set of pots, frying pan, potgrip and (with some models) a kettle are supplied with these stoves. These accessories pack into a compact unit. On the negative side, they have a low fuel/heat ratio. On a short weekend outing this is not a problem, but on longer trips you will need a large supply of fuel, adding to your weight and taking up space.

Another negative factor is that pots are blackened during cooking.

Compared with other makes, **gas stoves** are considerably cheaper and clean burning. When shielded from the wind they are reasonably efficient, but perform poorly in windy conditions, at high altitudes and in cold weather. In some models the centre of gravity is high, making them unstable, while empty gas cartridges have become a major source of pollution.

Tent

On some trails you have to be totally self-sufficient, and this includes accommodation. Never depend on caves being vacant – always carry a tent.

In years gone by most tents were single-skinned, which meant that if you accidentally touched the side of the tent when turning over in the night you were rudely awakened by a shower of water, caused by condensation. This problem was largely solved by the double-skinned tent, or a tent with a flysheet, as it is more commonly known. The inner tent is made of either an absorbent cotton or a breathable nylon fabric which is suspended from the tent poles in such a way that it does not come into contact with the outer tent. Vapour passes through the breathable fabric of the inner tent and condenses when it comes into contact with the cold outer sheet. At the same time the air trapped between the inner tent and the flysheet acts as an effective insulator.

Features of quality backpacking tents to look out for are a waterproof, sewn-in groundsheet with fairly high "walls", mosquito netting and a bell on either side. The latter are useful for storing packs in and as an entrance/exit.

The most common tent style is the A-frame, but dome tents have become increasingly popular. The main advantages of these tents are that they are easy to erect, more spacious and can be pitched without guy-ropes. Because of their domed shape they can withstand high winds.

Clothing

Unless you intend doing regular winter backpacking trips into the Drakensberg you are likely to have most of the required clothing.

Ensure that your hat will give you adequate protection against the sun. If you are trailing in an area where cold temperatures can be expected it is wise to pack a balaclava or a woollen cap which can be pulled over your ears, as

about 30 per cent of the body's heat is lost from the head.

In summer short-sleeved shirts or blouses are more suitable than T-shirts, which provide little ventilation and tend to cling to one's body. Cotton shirts, on the other hand, are more airy and have the added advantage of a collar that can be turned up to protect your neck from the sun.

In the winter it is advisable to pack a long-sleeved woollen shirt for extra warmth. You will also need a warm jersey or a densely knitted, fleece-lined hooded tracksuit top. Avoid leisurewear tracksuits, as they generally do not keep the cold out. Wool is in all cases preferable to other fabrics on account of its excellent insulating qualities.

Even in wet, cold conditions shorts are preferable to long trousers which can cause discomfort and chafing once they are wet. Never wear jeans – they are heavy (and even heavier when wet) and take ages to dry.

Generally your normal underwear should be sufficient, although cotton garments are more comfortable. For winter trailing thermal underwear is recommended. Some people prefer to hike with a string vest, whatever the time of the year, as it facilitates ventilation in warm weather, and during winter it is a surprisingly effective insulator. You do not need to take a change of underwear for every day's hike as it is usually possible to wash or rinse underwear on the trail.

A general rule to prevent loss of body heat is to cover the body with several layers of thin clothing rather than a single, thick layer. This is because heat is prevented from escaping by the layer of dry air trapped between the different layers of clothing.

When it comes to socks there is no substitute for wool and although a wool/fibre mixture is acceptable you must ensure that the percentage of wool predominates. Avoid nylon socks as they will overheat your feet and cause blisters. Most hikers prefer to wear two pairs of socks – a thin inner pair of either wool or cotton, and a thick woollen outer pair. This reduces the likelihood of blisters considerably as the socks absorb the chafing that would normally occur on your skin.

Miscellaneous items

Although there are several torches available on the South African market, none is particularly suitable for hiking. The well-organised hiker will, however, have little need for a torch and the small torches are best. They not only take up very little space, but are also light, as are the spare batteries.

A 2-litre water-bottle or two 1-litre bottles are essential on any trail. Plastic water-bottles are most commonly used, but have the disadvantage of giving water a plastic flavour when exposed to the sun for long periods of time.

Some plastic water-bottles available in backpacking stores have a felt covering which helps to keep water cool when kept damp.

A plastic, dish-shaped bowl or a plate with a definite rim is preferable to a flat plate. You will seldom have need for a fork on a trail, but take a sharp knife and a dessert spoon from your kitchen drawer, rather than buying a "special" cutlery set.

PACKING YOUR BACKPACK

Here are some hints to assist you in packing your backpack.

■ Limit the weight. Your pack should never exceed a third of your body weight. Ideal weights are 20 per cent of the body weight of women and children and 25 per cent of the body weight of men.

■ Before packing, line your backpack with a large garbage bag or a sac liner. This will ensure

that the contents remain dry should you hike in rain for an extended period. Although most good quality backpacks stand up to their claim of being waterproof, water does sometimes seep through seams and zips. A sac liner has the advantage of durability and can, therefore, be used several times.

■ Pack systematically to ensure that unnecessary items are not included and that you do not

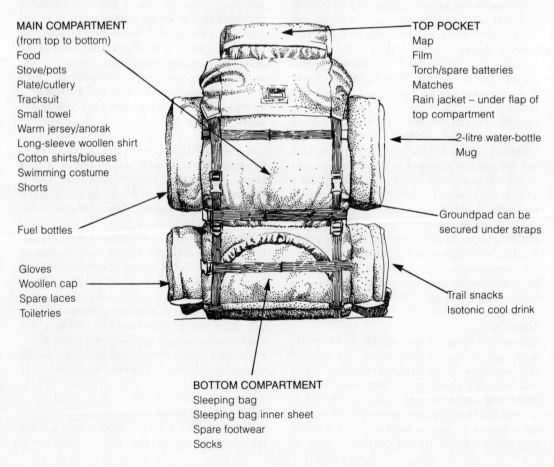

MAIN COMPARTMENT
(from top to bottom)
Food
Stove/pots
Plate/cutlery
Tracksuit
Small towel
Warm jersey/anorak
Long-sleeve woollen shirt
Cotton shirts/blouses
Swimming costume
Shorts

Fuel bottles

Gloves
Woollen cap
Spare laces
Toiletries

TOP POCKET
Map
Film
Torch/spare batteries
Matches
Rain jacket – under flap of
top compartment

2-litre water-bottle
Mug

Groundpad can be
secured under straps

Trail snacks
Isotonic cool drink

BOTTOM COMPARTMENT
Sleeping bag
Sleeping bag inner sheet
Spare footwear
Socks

KITLIST

Item	Approx mass in grams	E = Essential O = Optional C = Check relevant info	Item	Approx mass in grams	E = Essential O = Optional C = Check relevant info
Backpack			backpacking		
backpack with hip belt	1 800	E	stove ⎫ always		
internal frame			pots ⎬ be	2 000	E
external frame			pot grip ⎪ self-		
spare clevis pins	10	O	fuel ⎭ sufficient		
pack cover	25	O	matches	15	E
			pot-scourer	20	E
Sleeping gear			dishcloth	80	E
sleeping bag	1 800	E	trail snacks	50	E
inner sheet	500	O	trail food for 5 days	5 000	E
mattress/closed-cell			emergency rations	50	E
groundpad	400	C	2-litre water-bottle (full)	2 075	E
ground sheet	720	C			
tent	3 000	C	**Toiletries**		
			tissues	10	O
Footwear			toilet paper & trowel	10	E
boots/walking shoes	1 800	E	small towel	250	E
spare bootlaces	50	E	biodegradable soap	25	E
spare footwear	750	E	toothbrush & paste	45	E
woollen socks (2 pairs)	400	E	comb	15	E
cotton socks (2 pairs)	200	E	sunscreen cream	120	E
gaiters	150	O	lip salve	20	E
			insect repellent	50	E
Clothing					
woollen cap/balaclava	125	C	**Miscellaneous**		
sunhat	75	E	first aid kit	300	E
2 cotton shirts	400	E	emergency blanket	70	E
1 woollen long-sleeved			litter bag	25	E
shirt	250	E	torch, spare		
jersey	700	E	batteries & bulb	115	E
2 pairs shorts	300	E	candle	60	O
3 pairs underwear	150	E	camera & film	1 000	O
thermal underwear	300	O	compact binoculars	400	O
sleepwear	300	O	map	50	E
tracksuit	700	E	compass	100	O
gloves/mittens	100	O	permit	7	E
waterproof rain gear	600	E	passport/visas	40	C
swimming costume	150	·O	waterproofing bags	50	E
			survival bag	240	C
Cooking & food			cord (5 m, thin nylon)	50	E
cutlery	50	E	notebook & pencil	50	E
plate & mug	110	E	whistle	10	E
can opener	20	E	field guides	–	O
			walking stick	–	O

leave anything behind. There is nothing as frustrating as discovering on the trail that you have forgotten to pack something!

■ Items you are likely to use often during the day and your rain gear should be easily accessible.

■ To conserve energy when walking the bulk of the weight in your pack should be in line with your centre of gravity. This is best achieved by packing heavier items in the top half of the pack, closest to your back, leaving the bottom half for lighter items.

Use the illustration on page 12 as a guide to packing your backpack.

The kitlist supplied on page 13 is for a five-day trail. Do not follow it religiously, but use it as a guide and adapt it to suit the trail type, trail length and your personal needs.

Obviously if the trail has overnight huts you will not lug a tent along! However, even if the trail brochure states that firewood is supplied at each overnight stop, it is advisable to carry your own stove.

HIKING HINTS

Safety is of the utmost importance and disregard for a few commonsense rules can turn a trail into a tragedy. In most cases where fatalities or serious injuries have occurred on trails they could have been avoided.

Bear the following points in mind – they will not only ensure pleasant hiking, but could also save lives.

■ The party should always be led by the most experienced person.

■ Plan each day carefully. Start off as early as possible if you have a long day ahead of you, if the terrain is difficult or unfamiliar to you or in hot weather.

■ Keep in mind that there is considerably less daylight in winter than in summer.

■ Large parts of southern Africa receive rain in the summer and thunderstorms are common in the afternoon. Try to reach your destination before the rain sets in.

■ Hike at a steady pace. Three kilometres an hour is a good average. For every 300 m you gain in altitude an hour can be added. On steeper sections it is advisable to shorten your stride slightly, while maintaining your hiking rhythm. Avoid frequent long breaks – rather have short rest stops and use the opportunity to appreciate your surroundings.

■ Keep the party together. A member lagging behind is an almost sure sign of trouble, exhaustion or exposure. Establish the cause of the problem, assist the person by spreading the weight of his/her pack among the other members of the party and keep him/her company. In large groups it is advisable to appoint someone to bring up the rear. If you do this you will always know who the last person is.

■ Keep your energy level up by eating snacks –

peanuts and raisins, glucose sweets, chocolate and dried fruit – between meals.

■ If you encounter bad weather or if the route proves too demanding physically, do not hesitate to turn back if you have not reached the halfway mark of the day's hike by midday.

■ Misty conditions occur frequently at high altitudes. If mist sets in seek a suitable shelter and stay put until it has cleared.

■ If you are hiking in the mountains and snow falls, seek shelter and move off the summit at the earliest opportunity to avoid being trapped if conditions deteriorate.

■ Be aware of the dangers of flash floods. Never cross a flooding river. Fortunately most South African rivers soon return to their normal flow after flooding. Either wait until the flood has subsided or make a detour.

■ Some routes necessitate frequent river crossings. At times it might be possible to boulder-hop across, but avoid long jumps with a heavy pack which could result in a slip, and not only a soaking, but also injury.

■ If you are uncertain about a river's depth always probe it without your pack. If the river is shallow undo the hip belt of your backpack and loosen shoulder straps for quick off-loading.

■ Float packs across deeper rivers.

■ Avoid crossing rivers near the mouth unless there is a definite sandbar. These rivers are more likely to be shallow and slower where they are wide. Steer clear of bends, where the water is usually deeper and the flow stronger.

■ Avoid the dangers of lightning by staying clear of prominent features such as trees, ridges, summits, shallow caves and large boulders. Find an open slope, sit on a groundpad or a backpack, preferably on a clean, dry rock, with your knees drawn up, feet together and hands in your lap. If you are in your tent during an electric storm, sit in a crouching position and avoid touching the sides.

■ Always carry a 2-litre water-bottle. Remember that smaller streams are often dry during the winter months in summer rainfall areas and dry during the summer months in winter rainfall areas. Unless ample water is available along the route it is advisable to ensure that you always keep a reserve supply of water.

■ Water-bottles should always be filled from safe, fast-running streams above human habitation. Water below human habitation should be regarded as unsafe and should not be drunk before it has been boiled.

■ Water suspected of being infested by bilharzia, cholera or other waterborne diseases should be boiled for at least five minutes. This method is preferable to using commercially available chemicals. Strain water through a handkerchief to remove debris before boiling it.

■ In the event of a veld fire, try to find shelter in a kloof or ravine rather than going up a slope. Avoid waterfalls and take care and time to minimise unnecessary risks.

■ Always carry a whistle. It can be used to attract attention should you get lost. Remember the international SOS – three short, three long and three short whistles.

GENERAL HINTS

Few things can be as frustrating as arriving at the end of a hard day's hike in the rain only to discover that your matches are soaking wet or that the batteries of your torch have run down. As you gain more experience of the outdoors you will learn how to avoid these annoying mishaps and turn a good trip into a memorable one. Here are a few basic, commonsense hints:

Good **waterproof rain gear** is essential on any outing, whether it is a day ramble or a week-long expedition. In the mountains and at the coast the weather can change rapidly from beautiful and sunny to violently stormy. The authors have even experienced a thunderstorm in the Fish River Canyon in mid-winter! Your raincoat will be of little use in a sudden downpour if it is safely packed away in the bottom of your pack, so do keep it in a handy place.

To avoid that feeling of despair when you switch on your **torch** and nothing happens, turn one of the batteries the wrong way round when not in use. Remember to take **spare batteries** and a **spare bulb along**.

Waterproof matches can be bought at specialist backpacking stores, but are unjustifiably expensive. Take a **cigarette lighter** along, as well as keeping some matches and a small piece of striker in an empty film container – it is 100 per cent waterproof when closed properly!

A **potgrip** will allow you to move your pots without getting your fingers burnt, or even worse, watching your meal end up on the ground. Also useful is a **long-handled spoon**.

Avoid glass bottles – they are not only heavier, but also break easier than plastic ones. Decant all liquids into screw-top **plastic bottles** or **aluminium containers**. Some aluminium containers are available in different colours to ensure that you do not confuse your water and fuel bottles. Don't use aluminium containers for acidic liquids.

A very handy container for substances like honey, jam, peanut butter and condensed milk is a **squeeze tube** filled from one end and then sealed with a sliding clamp. It is re-usable, but remember not to turn the screw top too tightly or it will crack.

Where large, wide rivers have to be crossed take along a **survival bag** – a large orange heavy-duty plastic bag – to float equipment across. As the name implies this bag has numerous other uses and although somewhat sweaty, it can also be used as a bivvy bag.

Although each group should have a well-equipped **first aid kit** it is advisable for each person to carry their own plasters.

A common complaint on trails is sore feet. An extra pair of **light footwear** – running shoes, sandals or towelling slippers – will give your feet a much needed rest after a hard day's hiking.

A 5 m length of thin **nylon rope** is useful for emergency situations, repairs and as a washing line.

Always remember to take **precautions against the sun** – sunhat, sunscreen lotion, etc.

Remember to **pack all food away** before going to sleep or you might discover in the morning that mice or small predators have made off with your provisions.

A **Swiss army knife** is useful on a trail. It is light, compact and most models have all the gadgets needed on a trail – tin-opener, knife, tweezers and scissors. Attach it to your pack with a piece of string.

TRAIL ETHICS

The following suggestions on how to help conserve the natural environment you're enjoying have been divided into five headings.

Land

■ Do not litter. Tissues tucked into sleeves or under watch straps inevitably fall out and are one of the most common forms of litter in the outdoors. Cigarette ends, plastic sweet papers and toilet paper are also a nuisance. Even orange peels, commonly regarded as biodegradable, should not be discarded as they can take up to five months to decompose. The following are estimates of how long it can take for litter to decompose under ideal trailside conditions: plastic-coated paper: 1 to 5 years, plastic bags: 10 to 20 years, plastic film: 20 to 30 years, nylon fabrics: 30 to 40 years, aluminium cans: 80 to 100 years and glass: indefinitely.

■ Carry a refuse bag and pick up litter along the way.

■ Never bury litter. In most cases it will be uncovered by the elements or animals such as baboons. This is not only unsightly, but broken glass and tins with sharp edges can cause injuries to fellow hikers and animals. Remember: carry out what you carry in.

■ Avoid shortcuts. If hikers take shortcuts the trail's gradient and consequently its erosion potential is increased. The steeper gradient also demands greater exertion.

■ Step over erosion bars, not on them, and avoid kicking up stones.

■ Avoid areas with little or no vegetation. They are extremely susceptible to erosion and can take up to 25 years to recover after human trampling.

■ Avoid scree and talus slopes for the same reasons. Hiking on them can cause miniature rockfalls which destroy vegetation that has become established under difficult conditions.

■ Never roll rocks down slopes or over cliffs. This may injure other people, cause fires and erosion and destroy vegetation.

■ Disturb the area as little as possible when setting up camp where there are no developed campsites. Pitch your camp on level ground, not only for your own comfort, but also because sloping ground erodes easily once the vegetation is compacted.

■ Keep your backpack as light as possible. This will not only lighten your load and thereby increase your enjoyment of the trail, but will also reduce compaction and erosion.

Water

Many of the rivers and streams of southern Africa are the habitat of rare and endangered aquatic life which can easily be destroyed by carelessness. Keep the following in mind:

■ Avoid camping closer than 60 m from any water body, wherever possible.

■ Do not use soap directly in streams or rivers – a good swim is normally sufficient to clean up – and don't brush your teeth directly in the rivers or streams. Cooking and eating utensils should be washed away from the water.

Air

One of the main reasons people go trailing is to seek solitude. Noise pollution is as objectionable as littering.

■ Avoid shouting, yelling and whistling – it decreases your chances of seeing wildlife.

■ If you smoke, take care, especially in dry grasslands. Never smoke while you are hiking. Stop, sit down and relax. Use a flat rock as an ashtray and remember to put the filter in your litter bag.

■ Smoke from campfires also causes air pollution. Where fires are permitted, keep them small.

Flora and fauna

■ Do not pick flowers.

■ Avoid shortcuts which could destroy sensitive or endangered vegetation.

■ Fires are generally not permitted in wilderness areas. Where they are permitted, remember the following:

– If an old fireplace is available use it rather than making a new one.

– Choose a level spot where the fire will be protected from the wind.

– Don't make fires near vegetation or on the roots of trees – clear the area around the fireplace of all leaves and humus.
– Keep the fire small – it is more comfortable to cook over, more intimate, easier to control and you will also conserve wood.
– Use only dead wood and do not break seemingly dead branches off trees; it is not only unsightly but often the branches are merely dormant.
– Never leave your fire unattended; keep water handy.
– Extinguish your fire properly before going to sleep or breaking up camp; douse it with water, stir the coals and douse again.

■ Do not cut vegetation to sleep on – carry a groundpad.
■ Disturb animals and birds as little as possible, particularly those with young or in nests, as well as seemingly lost or injured animals or birds.
■ Do not feed animals and birds. Some animals, especially baboons, soon learn to associate humans with food if they are fed and later become aggressive scavengers. In addition you may pass on harmful bacteria to animals.

General
■ Where toilets are not provided human waste can be disposed of by the "cat method". Select a flat, screened spot at least 50 m from the footpath and open water. Dig a hole no deeper than 20 to 25 cm to keep within the biological disposal layer and after use fill the hole with loose soil and trample lightly over it. Alternatively loose stones can be used to cover human waste. Toilet paper should preferably be burned.
■ Do not sleep in caves with rock paintings, except where this is expressly permitted, and never tamper with or spray water over the paintings.
■ Leave all archaeological sites untouched. In terms of the National Monuments Act it is an offence to disturb such sites in any way.
■ Your enjoyment and appreciation of the outdoors will be considerably enhanced by reading more about the area beforehand. There are numerous pocket-size field guides on flora and fauna that can be taken along on your outings.

FIRST AID

Most emergency situations are either related to extremes of weather or to a physical injury or disability. It is therefore essential that every hiker should understand the principles of preventative measures and the methods of first aid. It is strongly advisable to read some of the many authoritative publications available on this subject or to enrol for a course in first aid. Unless you are medically trained you can give only emergency first aid and hopefully prevent any deterioration in the condition of the patient until a rescue party arrives.

The three most serious physical injuries or disabilities are cessation of breathing, bleeding and shock. All of these situations will call for immediate action and the following general directions should be followed:

Take control. The leader of the party must take control of the situation immediately. If it is the leader who is injured, the next most experienced member of the party must take control. Remain calm, assess the situation and direct the other members of the party to improvise equipment or construct a shelter.

Approach safely. In the event of a serious fall on difficult terrain, care should be taken not to cause rockfalls or to endanger the lives of other members of the party. If the casualty cannot be reached safely or the necessary equipment is unavailable, help should be summoned without delay.

Apply emergency first aid procedures. If the casualty can be reached, assess the person's condition and if the injury appears to be related in any way to the spinal column, avoid any movement.

Check for breathing. Lick your fingers and hold them in front of the injured person's mouth or nose; put your hand on the chest or stomach. If you cannot feel breathing or movement, apply artificial respiration, first removing any obstruction to the air passages.

Check the pulse. If there is none, apply cardiopulmonary resuscitation.

Check for serious bleeding. Internal bleeding

may be indicated if the casualty is pale, clammy and restless. Try to stop fast or heavy bleeding by applying direct pressure, using a pad of folded cloth and if possible elevating the wound. In addition, use a tourniquet for a fast-bleeding wound on a limb. Use a belt or a strip of material (*not* thin rope) twisted tightly with a stick. Be sure to loosen it every half hour for a few minutes.

Treat for shock. After any major injury, be on the lookout for signs of shock which can cause: paleness, clammy skin, fast weak heartbeat, quick breathing, dizziness or weakness.

After loosening tight clothing, lie the patient down with feet higher than the head. Reassure and keep the patient comfortable and warm, covering him without allowing him to get too hot. If possible, give small sips of warm sweet tea or sugar water.

Check for other injuries and give first aid treatment. Start with the head and work your way down, examining all areas of the body for bleeding, sensitivity, fractures, pain or swelling.

Planning what to do. Your plan of action will depend on whether the casualty can carry on unassisted, whether evacuation by the party is possible or whether outside assistance is required.

Take the following into account: the patient's injuries, the time of day, weather conditions, the terrain, the availability of shelter, the size and physical condition of the group and the availability of outside help.

Execute the plan of action. If the situation requires evacuation with outside help, at least two members of the party should be sent. They should preferably be stronger members of the party and must follow a predetermined route from which they should not deviate. They should have the following information:
■ where, when and how the accident occurred
■ the number of casualties as well as the nature and seriousness of the injuries
■ what first aid has been administered, what supplies are still available and the condition of the casualties
■ the distance between the casualties and the closest roads and the nature of the terrain
■ the number of people at the evacuation scene
■ what type of equipment might be necessary.

While waiting for help to arrive the remaining members of the party can make shelters and prepare hot meals and drinks for the casualty and themselves.

Prevention and cure. About 90 per cent of all ailments experienced on trails are related to foot and leg problems. The best first aid is prevention and avoidance. Make early decisions and treat any wounds or ailments medically or

---

FIRST AID KIT

A well-equipped first aid kit should always accompany a hiking party, even on a short weekend outing. When assembling your kit, bear in mind that space is limited and that it is always possible to improvise. Hikers suffering from a chronic ailment such as diabetes, asthma, allergies or weak ankles or knees should ensure that they have sufficient medicine or equipment to take care of themselves.

The kit should contain the following:

antibiotic	malaria tablets
anti-diarrhoea pills	mosquito repellent
anti-histamine: cream and tablets	nail scissors
anti-inflammatory gel	needle and thread
antiseptic: cream and solution	painkillers
bandages: wide crepe & narrow gauze	plaster: zinc oxide & sealed individual
cotton wool	safety pins
eardrops: antiseptic, analgesic	throat lozenges
eye bath	surgical gloves (for Aids control)
eyedrops	tweezers
isotonic drink	wound dressing

behaviourally as soon as they occur, before the condition worsens. Common injuries and health hazards all hikers should be aware of are discussed briefly below.

Bilharzia: This disease, which is fairly common in large parts of Africa, is caused by a snail-borne parasite which attacks the intestines, bladder and other organs of its hosts. Bilharzia is unlikely to occur in streams and rivers above 1 200 m in altitude because of the unsuitability of fast-flowing water as a habitat for snails. It is also less likely to be found in any water body mixed with sea water.

Human habitation is usually associated with bilharzia, so avoid drinking, swimming or washing in water downstream from any human settlement. If bilharzia is suspected, boil water for at least five minutes before use. Water temperatures of 0 °C for three to four nights are sufficient to kill snail hosts, while water temperatures of over 28 °C for several days are also poorly tolerated by snails.

Bites and stings: For the majority of spider bites as well as bee, scorpion and wasp stings discomfort can be relieved by applying an anti-histamine lotion and taking anti-histamine medication. If the patient has an allergic reaction to a sting, arrange for evacuation. Thick-tailed scorpion (*Parabuthus*) stings and button spider bites could be dangerous, in which case urgent medical assistance is essential.

Blisters: Blisters are the most common cause of discomfort and should be treated before they form. If certain spots on your feet are prone to blisters, cover these areas with a dressing and a broad strip of plaster before putting on your boots. A potential blister can usually be detected when a tender "hot-spot" starts to develop. Cover the affected area immediately with a dressing and zinc oxide plaster. If a blister forms and you have not completed your trip, it is best to pierce the blister with a sterilised needle or a pair of scissors. Take care, however, to avoid infection. Gently press out the fluid, dab the blister with antiseptic and then cover it with a dressing and zinc oxide plaster. This should, ideally, be done once the day's backpacking is over. Check the affected spot regularly for infection. If you have completed your trip, preferably leave the blister unpricked and uncovered to heal by itself.

Bruises: You can minimise swelling from a bad bruise by holding the affected area under cold running water, and keeping it elevated and still.

Burns: Besides blisters, sunburn (classified as a first-degree burn) is probably the most common ailment suffered on trails. Prevention is better than cure, so wear a sunhat and apply sunscreen lotion frequently, especially on the nose and face. Turn up the collar of your shirt (one of the reasons why a button-up shirt is preferable to a T-shirt) to prevent sunburn to your neck.

Scalds and minor burns should be treated by holding the affected area in cold water until the pain subsides. Do not apply greasy ointments, and do not prick burn blisters. If available, cover the burn lightly with a gauze dressing held in place with a plaster: burns heal better if left exposed to the air.

Burns of a more serious nature should not be immersed in water. Instead, cover the area immediately with a sterile dressing or clean cloth. If clothing sticks to the burn, leave it on. Treat for shock and give the patient plenty of water or isotonic drink. Help should be summoned as soon as possible.

Cramps: Muscular cramps are caused by a shortage of either salt or water or both, combined with physical exertion. Allow the person suffering from cramps to rest, keep the affected area warm and gently massage. Administer an isotonic drink and avoid further strenuous exercise until full recovery.

Diarrhoea and vomiting: For both complaints the patient should be rested and given frequent doses of isotonic drink mixed to half strength. Diarrhoea is a natural body mechanism to dispose of bacteria and should preferably not be treated with commercial anti-diarrhoea medication. Obviously, if time pressures demand that the patient must hike, you will have no alternative but to administer anti-diarrhoea medication.

Stomach pains and biliousness without diarrhoea and vomiting might be serious if accompanied by persistent fever. The patient should rest, be kept warm and a high fluid intake should be maintained. Evacuation might be necessary.

Dislocation: The symptoms of dislocation are visible deformity and severe pain. It is important to obtain skilled help quickly, because the dislocated joint will soon begin to swell. Do not attempt to push it back into place unless you are medically trained, as this can damage blood vessels and nerves or cause fractures. Wrap the joint in wet cloths, keep it still (use splints if necessary) and get the injured person to a doctor as soon as you can.

Ear infections: Earache can be treated with an oily, antiseptic, analgesic eardrop such as Aurone. Middle ear infections are far more serious and can affect one's balance. If you are more than 12 hours away from help and the person has a temperature a wide-spectrum oral antibiotic should be administered.

Foreign bodies such as insects can usually be floated out with warm water or oil. Heat a little oil in a teaspoon (testing a drop on the back of your hand to ensure it is not too hot), pour into the ear and leave for five minutes before letting it run out. Take care not to push the object deeper into the ear in an attempt to get it out. It is better not to try to get a smooth, hard object out as you will more than likely push it in further.

Exhaustion: Avoid exhaustion by not over-exerting yourself, eating trail snacks between meals and maintaining a healthy water intake. If the condition does set in the patient should be allowed to rest at a comfortable temperature and given water and food with a high glucose content.

Eye injuries or infections: Foreign bodies should only be removed if you are able to take them out easily. Any objects that are partially embedded in the eyeball should not be removed. In such cases cover the eye with a doughnut bandage held on with another bandage and evacuate the patient.

In most cases, however, natural watering of the eye will dislodge and wash away small objects. Bring the upper lid down over the lower eyelid for a second or two – the tears resulting from this may wash the object away. If this does not have the desired effect, let the person blink into an eye bath or apply eyedrops into the inner corner of the eye. Carefully lift the lid by the lashes and let the drops run over the eyeball. Blinking during irrigation might help. You could also try lifting the object out with the corner of a piece of moist sterile gauze.

Eye infections should be treated with a sulphacetimide eye ointment and covered with a light bandage.

Fever: Normal human oral temperature is 37 °C. A temperature which drops below 35 °C should be regarded as serious, whereas up to 39 °C indicates a mild fever and over 40 °C a high fever. Rest and a large fluid intake is essential. Cool the patient off by removing any hot clothes or bedding, wiping with a wet cloth and fanning; administer aspirin too. If there is no obvious cause and the fever persists, evacuation should be seriously considered. Check for malaria symptoms as described on page 21.

Heat exhaustion: Heat exhaustion is caused either by exposure to a hot environment or by overheating as a result of physical exertion. Symptoms are nausea, dizziness, thirst, profuse sweating and headaches. Lie the victim down in a cool, shady place with feet higher than the head, loosen clothing and cover lightly. Administer frequent doses of isotonic drink.

Heat stroke or sunstroke: Heat stroke is more serious than heat exhaustion as it affects the nervous centre that controls your body temperature. This condition can set in very rapidly and occurs as a result of failure of the sweating process and other body heat regulatory mechanisms.

Symptoms are an excessively high body temperature, dry red skin, headaches, irrational behaviour, shivering, cramps, dilated pupils, and, finally, collapsing and unconsciousness. Cool the patient down immediately by moving into the shade, taking off tight clothing, pouring water over or wiping him down with wet cloths, and fanning. If the patient is conscious, administer fast-acting aspirin and plenty of isotonic drink. Get medical help urgently.

Hypothermia: The lowering of the body's core temperature to the point where the heat lost exceeds the heat gained, results in hypothermia. It is usually a result of a combination of unfavourable weather, inadequate food intake and unsuitable clothing, as well as over-exertion. One or more of the following symptoms may be present: weakness, slowing of pace, shivering, lack of co-ordination, irrationality, blue skin colour, difficulty in speaking, decreased heart and respiratory rate, dilated pupils and unconsciousness.

Prevent further heat loss and keep the patient moving while looking for a suitable shelter. If a suitable shelter is not found within a few minutes, erect the best possible shelter. Remove wet clothing and immediately replace with warm, dry clothes. The patient should then be zipped into a pre-warmed sleeping bag, or warmed up between two people, well covered with sleeping bags. If the patient is able to eat, warm food and drink (sugar/glucose water, chocolate and soup) should be taken. Do not give any alcohol, coffee or any other stimulants. Do not rub the victim to restore circulation, or put him near a fire – direct heat is dangerous.

Further exertion should be discouraged as this will deplete essential energy.

Lung and throat infections: A sore throat without fever can be treated by gargling with salt water or an antiseptic solution, or by sucking throat lozenges. A sore throat with fever will require antibiotics and the patient should be kept warm and be rested.

Bronchitis can be serious and the patient will need rest, warmth and a wide-spectrum antibiotic. If fever persists, the patient should be evacuated.

Malaria: A bite by an infected *Anopheles* mosquito can transmit microscopic blood parasites, resulting in malaria. In certain areas (endemic areas) there is always the risk of contracting malaria. Other areas where there is usually only a risk during summer are called epidemic areas. However, it is advisable to take anti-malaria precautions when visiting both kinds of areas, even if only passing through. Consult your pharmacist to find out which brand of preventative tablet should be taken.

As mosquito bites are normally unpleasant, take a few simple preventive measures. After sunset wear long trousers and long-sleeved shirts. Apply a mosquito repellent to bare areas and remember to reapply every two hours as it does evaporate.

In its early stages malaria is easily cured, so it is essential to consult a doctor immediately should you develop any of the symptoms. These are vomiting, general body ache and severe fever.

Nosebleeds: Changes in altitude, increased activity and cold temperatures are the main causes of nosebleeds. Fortunately, most nosebleeds are minor and can be stopped by applying direct pressure firmly against the nostril or pinching the tip of the nose for 5 to 10 minutes. If bleeding persists, pack the nostril with gauze or cotton wool, pinch for 10 more minutes, then leave the dressing in for two hours or so. Remove carefully. Do not blow your nose for at least four hours after a nosebleed.

Pain: Treat general pain with the painkillers in your first aid kit, taken with plenty of fluid. If the pain persists and there is no obvious cause, seek medical treatment.

Snakebite: Your chances of being bitten by a snake are extremely small and only about 16 of the 160-odd South African snake species are deadly. Once again, it is wise to take preventative action. Keep your eyes open, especially where the path is overgrown. If you carry a stick,

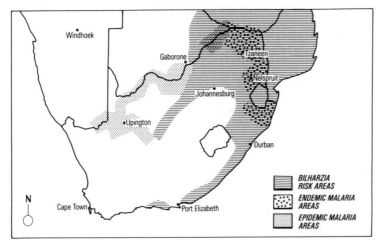

Present distribution of bilharzia and epidemic and endemic malaria in southern Africa

swish it in the grass in front of you. Considering that 75 per cent of all bites are inflicted on the leg, ankle, foot and toe, wear stout boots and gaiters if you anticipate bundu-bashing. About 15 per cent of snakebites are inflicted on the hand and finger, which means it's wise to look before placing your hand behind a rock. Similarly, look under and around a log or rock before sitting down on it. Do not overturn logs or rocks; step onto them, not over them.

Except in unusual circumstances, the life of a snakebite victim will seldom be in immediate danger. The venom of a puff adder, which is responsible for most bites, is seldom life-threatening within 10 hours of the bite, while cobra bites take about two to four hours to cause distress symptoms. Although mamba bites can seriously affect breathing within one or two hours, there is no question of dying within five minutes as is popularly believed. Boomslang venom is extremely poisonous, but bites from this back-fanged snake are extremely rare as the snake is not aggressive. Berg adder bites are never fatal, with patients showing an improvement within three to four days of being bitten.

In the event of a snakebite, the following first aid treatment must be given:
■ Immobilise the victim, as any unnecessary movement will increase the heart rate and consequently the spread of the venom. Keep the bite below heart level.
■ Immediately apply firm finger pressure above the bite.
■ Thoroughly disinfect the bite area.
■ Reassure the victim and administer a painkiller if necessary. Do not allow the intake of alcohol.
■ For mamba and cobra bites on a limb, apply a crepe bandage or torn strips of cloth firmly (but not too tightly) from just above the bite to the top of the limb. **Do not use a tourniquet.** Cold wet cloths (ideally an ice-pack) applied to the bite will further slow down the action of the poison.
■ For adder, viper or boomslang bites, do not bandage or use a tourniquet. Immobilise the victim and apply cold water or cold wet cloths to the bite.
■ If attacked by a spitting snake (cobra or rinkhals) immediately wash the eyes out with plenty of water, for at least 10 minutes. Lift the eyelids up so that the water washes under them too. Further treatment should not be necessary but if irritation occurs, see a doctor. Do not

attempt to wash the eyes out with diluted antivenom.
■ If the snake cannot be identified, clean the affected area and wait 10 to 15 minutes to see if symptoms develop. If there are no symptoms, keep the victim immobilised and under observation for two to three hours.
■ Two members of the party should get help and alert the nearest doctor or hospital, giving the identity of the snake if possible.

Old-fashioned beliefs that should *not* be applied include cutting the skin, sucking out the poison and killing the snake for identification – in this way a second person could be bitten. In addition, antivenom should only be administered by people who have been medically trained.

Sprains and strains: Sprains are caused by either tearing or stretching ligaments or a separation of muscle tendon from the bone and are most common in the ankle, wrist, knee and shoulder. The symptoms are extreme pain and severe swelling caused by fluid or blood accumulating in the tissues. Elevate the injured limb, and lightly apply cold water or wet cloths. An anti-inflammatory gel can also be used. This will reduce the swelling and also minimise deep bleeding. If you are skilled, bind the joint with a long crepe bandage. Take a painkiller if necessary. Keep the sprained joint as still as possible in a resting position. After 24 hours change over to heat treatment: warm the sprained joint by the fire or in the sun, or soak it in hot water three or four times a day.

It is often difficult to differentiate between a sprain and a fracture and, if pain persists, splint the affected limb and obtain medical help. Other signs of fractures are a floppy foot or hand, or difficulty moving the fingers or toes.

Strains are caused by overextending or tearing muscle fibre and are usually less serious than sprains. Treat as for sprains.

Tickbites: Do not attempt to pull the tick off if it does not come off easily. You may leave its head behind. Rather make it fall off by covering it with any thick oily substance, like Vaseline, or holding a lighted cigarette at close range.

Disinfect the area well and, should any signs of infection or fever appear within 10 days, visit a doctor.

NAMIBIA

WATERBERG

Situated on a plateau which is like a lush island in the surrounding thornveld, the Waterberg Hiking Trail offers you the opportunity to discover this interesting game park on foot. Although the trail is over easy terrain, hikers take the risk of an unexpected encounter with a rhino or a lone buffalo and have to be prepared to take quick evasive action. Fascinating sandstone formations and sheer cliffs, both coloured by numerous colourful lichens, are other outstanding features of this trail. Distances covered each day are short, allowing plenty of time for bird-watching and relaxing.

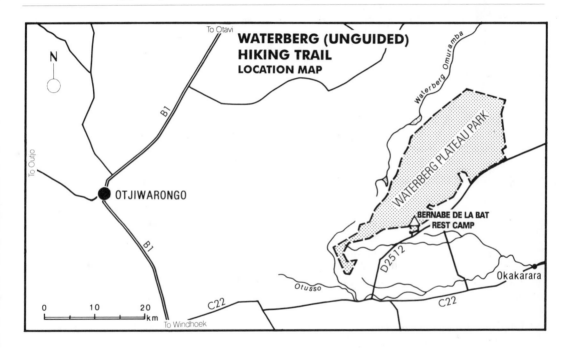

TRAIL PLANNER

Distance 42 km; 4 days

Grading A

Reservations The Director of Tourism, Private Bag 13267, Windhoek, Namibia, Telephone (061) 23-6975 (reservations), (061) 23-3875 (information), Fax (061) 22-4900. Written reservations can be made 18 months in advance, but are only con-firmed 11 months before the trail date when telephone and personal reservations are accepted. It is important to specify that you are booking for the *unguided* hiking trail to avoid confusion with the guided wilderness trail.

Group size Minimum 3; Maximum 10
Only one group is allowed on the trail each week.

Maps A sketch map is included in the information leaflet on the trail which is forwarded with your receipt and permit. The area is covered by 1 : 50 000 topographical map numbers 2017AC, 2017AD and 2017CA.

Climate

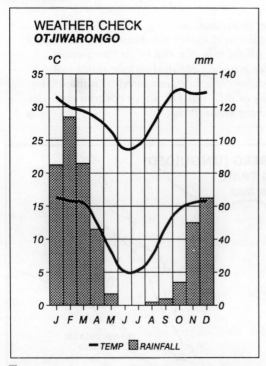

WEATHER CHECK
OTJIWARONGO

°C · mm

— *TEMP* ▨ *RAINFALL*

Facilities Hikers are accommodated in basic stone shelters without any bunks or mattresses. Water and pit toilets are provided, but no fires are allowed.

Logistics Circular route. There is no hut at the start/end of the trail. Accommodation in the Bernabé de la Bat rest camp where the trail starts/ends ranges from campsites

to bungalows. There is also a shop, licensed restaurant and filling station.

Relevant information
■ South African citizens require a valid passport when entering Namibia, while other nationalities travelling from South Africa should check on visa requirements.
■ Owing to the high summer temperatures, the trail is only open from 1 April to 30 November, starting every Wednesday and ending on Saturdays.
■ Hikers undertake the trail at their own risk and must complete an indemnity form before setting off.
■ Children under 12 years old are not permitted on the trail.
■ Despite the undemanding terrain, you should be fit and agile to take evasive action in the event of an unexpected encounter with buffalo or black rhino.
■ The possibility of being confronted by rhino or buffalo can be reduced by walking at a leisurely pace, especially in densely vegetated areas, and by staying alert at all times.
■ Under no circumstances should you deviate from the trail to follow rhino spoor or for any other reason.
■ All refuse must be carried back to the start of the trail as no refuse bins are provided at the overnight shelters.
■ Backpacking stoves are essential as fires are not permitted on the trail.

How to get there The turn-off to the park is signposted about 29 km south of Otjiwarongo along the B1. Follow the C22 towards Okakarara for about 41 km before turning left onto the D2512, a gravel road. The entrance gate to the Bernabé de la Bat rest camp is reached about 17 km beyond the turn-off.

TRAIL ENVIRONMENT

Flora The park lies at the south-western limit of the tree savanna and woodlands of the northern Kalahari and to date some 480 flowering plants have been identified. The vegetation is characterised by grasslands with trees and large shrubs in dense or open clumps of varying sizes.

You are bound to notice the enormous common cluster fig trees growing in the vicinity of

the springs on the lower slopes above the rest camp. Among the trees and shrubs you will see as you ascend the slopes to the Mountain View are sandpaper raisin with its characteristic square stem, common wild pear and leadwood. Namaqua fig and Namib coral tree are seen at the base of the cliffs, while the orange, green and grey lichens clinging to the cliffs are espe-

WEEPING WATTLE

In Namibia this species occurs in dry forest, as well as thorn tree, mopane and mountain savanna north of Otjiwarongo. Also known as the African wattle, it grows as a small to medium-sized tree of 5 to 10 m high and is particularly attractive between September and December when the tree is covered in showy sprays of bright yellow flowers.

The weeping wattle is one of the "rain trees" of Africa and derives its name from this unusual feature. The "rain" is produced by the larvae of spittle bugs (*Ptyles grossus*) which frequent the trees in summer, and occurs just prior to the start of the summer rains. After piercing the bark with their sucking mouth parts, the larvae produce a frothy substance by bubbling air through the juices which they extract from the tree. This foam protects the insects against the sun and insect-eating species. At times the larvae produce such large quantities of the frothy substance that the excess drips from the tree, sometimes forming pools of "water" on the ground. This phenomenon has, however, not been observed in Namibia.

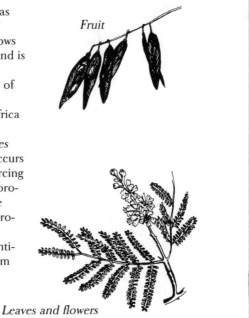

Fruit

Leaves and flowers

---

cially eye-catching. Over 140 species have been identified in the park.

The outward route winds mainly through the rocky outcrop community which occurs in a belt several hundred metres wide along the edge of the plateau. A species unlikely to escape your attention is the laurel fig which is often seen clinging to rocks with its exposed roots. Other conspicuous trees include wild seringa, weeping wattle and lavender fever-berry, as well as hairy red and common (Rhodesian) bushwillows.

The return route passes through the bush savanna on the plateau which is dominated by the silver cluster-leaf. Also occurring here are the wild seringa, Kalahari apple-leaf, peeling plane and common (Rhodesian) bushwillow.

If you are unfamiliar with the flora of the Waterberg, be sure to obtain a copy of *Waterberg Flora, Footpaths in and around the Camp* by Patricia Craven and Christine Marais. Some 40 species are illustrated and described in the guide, which is small enough to fit into your backpack.

Fauna The Waterberg lies at the centre of the home range of Namibia's eland population and the park was originally established to protect this species.

Other large antelope occurring in the park are blue wildebeest, gemsbok, kudu, red hartebeest, tsessebe and impala, as well as the rare black-faced impala. Roan were translocated from the Okavango region and sable from western Caprivi and the park is an important breeding nucleus for both species. Smaller antelope include the dimunitive Damara dik-dik, steenbok, common duiker and klipspringer. The park is also the home of Namibia's only foot-and-mouth disease-free population of buffalo. The founder population was translocated from the Addo Elephant National Park in the eastern Cape in 1980. In 1985 the population was supplemented with 36 animals from Addo and the Willem Pretorius Game Reserve in the Orange Free State in exchange for 12 black rhino which were reintroduced into the Augrabies Falls and Vaalbos national parks.

White rhino were translocated from Natal, while black rhino were reintroduced from Etosha and Damaraland in 1989. To deter poachers, it was decided to dehorn the park's white rhinoceros population in 1993. Although there is always the possibility of seeing rhino along the trail, you are more likely to become familiar with their large spoor on the path, as well as their dung. By having a closer look at the dung you will be able to determine the species – white rhino are grazers so their dung consists of grass, while black rhino are browsers and

*Outline of heads of (a) white rhinoceros and
(b) black rhinoceros*

their dung is consequently coarser. Carnivores include aardwolf, brown hyaena, leopard, caracal, bat-eared fox and black-backed jackal, as well as several mongoose species.

Other mammals you may spot include warthog, giraffe, rock dassie and chacma baboon. Lesser bushbabies are sometimes seen at dusk in the dense vegetation above the rest camp.

The park is the habitat of some 250 bird species, including several near endemics and the only breeding colony of the Cape vulture in Namibia. Of particular interest to birders are Hartlaub's francolin, Rüppell's parrot, Bradfield's swift, Monteiro's hornbill, Carp's black tit and rockrunner. Also of interest, but more widely distributed in Namibia, are rosyfaced lovebirds and shorttoed rock thrush.

Booted and African hawk eagles, as well as bateleur and gabar goshawk have been recorded.

On the scree slopes and rocky outcrops you might see crested, redbilled and Hartlaub's francolins, swallowtailed bee-eater, scimitarbilled woodhoopoe, Monteiro's hornbill and pied barbet. Also to be found here are cardinal woodpecker, Carp's black tit, shorttoed rock thrush, rockrunner and brubru.

The cliffs provide ideal nesting sites for black eagles and seven pairs are known to breed in the park.

THE CAPE VULTURES OF THE WATERBERG

The cliffs of the Karakuwisa Mountains are the habitat of the northernmost colony of Cape vultures in southern Africa. In the late 1930s the colony numbered more than 500 birds, but by 1985 they numbered less than 13. One of the most important factors that contributed to their decline is bush encroachment on the farms surrounding the Waterberg. The Cape vulture is adapted to open savanna habitats, but as a result of bush encroachment the birds' ability to see carcasses has been seriously reduced and access to carcasses is impossible in many areas. In addition, vultures have to run to take off after feeding, which requires ample open ground. As a result of the bush encroachment, however, the birds do not have sufficient "take-off areas".

Another cause of their decrease was the indiscriminate use of poisons on some farms surrounding the park to control problem animals such as black-backed jackal, caracal and cheetah. Understandably, just one poisoned carcass could have a severe impact on the vulture colony.

To save the vultures from becoming extinct the conservation authorities initiated various strategies, including controlled burning, an extensive educational programme aimed particularly at farmers and supplementary feeding of the vultures. Considerable success has been achieved and by the late 1980s the decline was reversed and the colony is slowly on the increase again. A vulture hide was opened to the public in 1993 and accompanied tours are conducted on Wednesdays. Other vultures to be seen at the hide include whitebacked, lappetfaced and whiteheaded vultures.

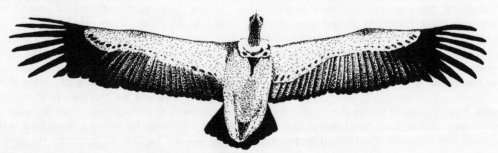

The distinctive flight pattern of the Cape vulture

The cliffs also support 14 pairs of peregrine falcons – one of the highest densities in Africa. Other cliff-breeding species include rock kestrel, rosyfaced lovebird, Bradfield's swift and palewinged starling. Species occurring on the plateau include Coqui francolin, purple and lilacbreasted rollers, fawncoloured lark and shorttoed rock thrush. White helmetshrike occur in small flocks and can easily be identified in flight by their conspicuous white wing flashes.

History Engravings of animal tracks on the rocks in the wilderness area and the accounts of early travellers and explorers provide evidence of the inhabitation of the Waterberg by Later Stone Age people and the San.

In more recent times the pastoral Herero settled in the area, and called the mountain *Omueverumue* or the "narrow gate" – a reference to the narrow nek between the Omuverume Plateau in the south-east and the Waterberg. When the Rhenish missionary Carl Hugo Hahn visited the Waterberg in 1871, the area surrounding the Waterberg was inhabited by large numbers of Herero under their well-known chief, Kambazembi.

The first whites to visit the Waterberg were Francis Galton and Charles Andersson, who passed by in 1851. Of the Otjozondjupa fountain above the rest camp, Andersson wrote: "Its source was situated fully two hundred feet above the base of the mountain, and took its rise from different spots; but, soon uniting, the stream danced merrily down the cliffs." Otjozondjupa is the Herero name for calabash, a reference to these gourds which were cultivated here.

In November 1873 the Rhenish missionary Heinrich Beiderbecke arrived at the Waterberg, two years after Hahn's visit, and established a mission station. It was, however, destroyed during a clash between the Damara and the Herero in 1880 and was only rebuilt 11 years later when the missionary Wilhelm Eich arrived at Otjozondjupa. The ruins of the mission station can be seen along Mission Way, one of the walks in the rest camp.

On 11 August 1904 the deciding battle between the Hereros and the Germans took place at the Waterberg. Fear of losing their land when large areas were allocated to white farmers and the German policy of gradually impoverishing the blacks caused the Herero to rise in 1904 while the German *Schutztruppe* were engaged in quelling an uprising by the Bondelswarts, a Nama tribe, in the south.

German forces were rushed from abroad and although the first shots between the Germans and the Herero were fired in January 1904 it was not until August that year that the Herero were finally defeated. The German force consisted of 96 officers, 1 488 soldiers, 30 cannons and 12 machine guns, while the number of armed Herero has been estimated at between 5 000 and 6 000.

Following their defeat, large numbers of Hereros, including their chief Samuel Maherero, fled into the wastelands of the Omaheke (Sandveld) and further east into present-day Botswana, while smaller groups fled to northern and north-western Namibia.

The graves of the German *Schutztruppe* killed in the battle of the Waterberg, as well as a few Herero graves, can be seen in the cemetery at the end of Mission Way.

In 1907 the mission station was leased to the *Landespolitzei*, and was temporarily used as a depot until the police station was built. The *Rasthaus* was completed in 1910 and was used as a police station until 1932 when it was vacated. It was subsequently used as a guesthouse, but closed down in 1966. During the construction of the rest camp it was extensively renovated and now serves as a restaurant.

Covering some 40 549 ha, the Waterberg Plateau Park was declared a game park in June 1972 for the protection of its eland population, as well as the breeding of Namibia's uncommon game species for restocking of other suitable areas. A wilderness area covering some 18 600 ha was set aside on the plateau in 1984.

Geology On account of the mountain's unique character and spectacular Etjo Sandstone formations, the Waterberg was proclaimed a national monument in 1956.

The plateau is about 48 km long and varies from 8 to 16 km in width. The highest point of the Waterberg (1 885 m) is at Omuverume in the south-west, while the Karakuwisa Mountain (1 878 m) is the highest point on the plateau.

The Waterberg is renowned for its fascinating column-like rock formations which have been sculptured by countless aeons of extremes of temperatures, wind, rain and lichens. With the exception of the northern side, the mountain is capped by sheer cliffs 70 to 75 m high. Towards the north, the plateau becomes more broken and lower and is approximately the same height at the north-eastern side as the surrounding plain.

The Waterberg is an erosional relic of a sandstone casing which covered a large area of Namibia millions of years ago. It consists of sedimentary rock of the Karoo Sequence and from the base upwards can be divided into two sections. The lower Omingonde Formation consists of reddish-brown mud-, silt-, sand- and gritstone, as well as conglomerate, and was probably deposited by rivers in a shallow lake.

The upper Etjo Formation is composed of brown sandstone which forms the perpendicular cliffs below the crest. This formation was shaped by windblown sand which gradually settled in the lake. Two factors are mainly responsible for the elevated position of the mountain. Millions of years ago the Karoo layers south of an imaginary line between Grootfontein and Omaruru

were lifted in a north-west/south-east direction as a result of pressure in the earth's crust. In addition, the resistance of the Etjo sandstone to weathering prevented the erosion of the mountain. The flexing of the earth's crust resulted in pillar-like seams developing in the Etjo Formation. Rainwater on the plateau flows into the seams and seeps downwards until the impermeable Omingonde Formation forces it to the surface, giving rise to the numerous springs at the base of the Waterberg.

Millions of years ago the Waterberg was inhabited by dinosaurs such as Melanosaurus, Tritylodon, Massopondylus and Pachygeneles – all herbivores – and Gryponyx, a carnivore. Although these animals disappeared from the face of the earth more than 100 million years ago, their tracks have been preserved in the mudstone and can be seen in the south-eastern part of the park.

TRAIL DESCRIPTION

Day 1: Bernabé de la Bat Rest Camp to Otjozongombe Shelter Setting off from the rest camp on the Mountain View Walk, you will gain some 120 m up to the plateau. On reaching the base of the cliffs, the trail levels off and you will admire the variety of lichens adding splashes of colour to the reddish rocks. After a while you will scramble up a short gully where two plaques commemorate mountaineering accidents at Waterberg in 1957 and 1975. On reaching the plateau edge your progress is obstructed by two stiles which prevent game from making their way down from the plateau. A large noticeboard here informs you that only hikers with the necessary permit may venture beyond this point. Before scaling the second stile, however, make a short detour to the Mountain Viewpoint from where you will have a bird's eye view of the rest camp and the flat thornbush savanna to the south.

A few minutes beyond the second stile, you will pass a magnificent cliff covered in orange lichens. It is believed that some lichen species help to erode the rocks into their characteristic shapes. The trail winds past rock pillars, egg-shaped rocks and domes and about an hour from the Mountain Viewpoint you will cross a jeep track. Here you must take the right-hand fork – the return route joins here on day four.

Continuing through the labyrinth of rocks near the cliff edge, the Omatako Viewpoint is reached about an hour beyond the jeep track. From here you will identify the Omatako Canal cutting through the surrounding farmlands and, if visibility is good, the Omatako Mountain with its twin peaks.

For the next hour you will continue to wind through sculptured sandstone formations, remaining fairly close to the cliffs. A short way beyond the appropriately named Sandstone Buttresses the trail swings away from the cliffs and 30 minutes later you reach Beacon Koppie (1 616 m). This is one of the few places on the trail where you are elevated above the dense bush.

From Beacon Koppie it is about an hour along a fairly sandy path to the shelter. Soon after setting off again the trail takes you past some natural rock pools which are filled by rain during the summer months and about 30 minutes later you will pass the Three Sandstone Pinnacles. The usually dry Ongorowe River is passed a short way on and from here it is a 20-minute walk to the first overnight stop. The shelter is a short distance from the plateau edge overlooking the Otjozongombe Valley and towards sunset it is worthwhile heading for the edge to watch the cliffs as they take on a fiery

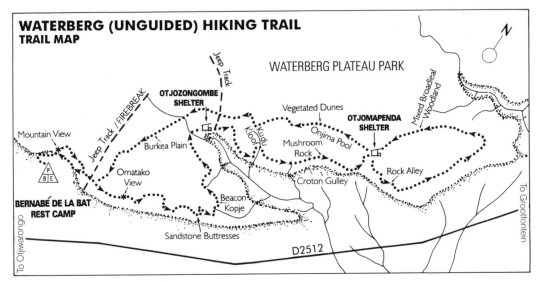

WATERBERG (UNGUIDED) HIKING TRAIL
TRAIL MAP

WATERBERG PLATEAU PARK

N

Jeep Track

OTJOZONGOMBE
SHELTER

Vegetated Dunes

OTJOMAPENDA
SHELTER

Mixed Broadleaf
Woodland

Jeep Track / FIREBREAK

Mountain View

Kudu Kloof

Onjima Pool

Mushroom
Rock

Burkea Plain

Omatako
View

Rock Alley

Croton Gulley

P
B E

Beacon
Kopje

BERNABÉ DE LA BAT
REST CAMP

To Ojiwarongo

Sandstone Buttresses

D2512

To Grootfontein

orange hue. The day's hike covers about 13 km and is usually hiked in six hours.

Day 2: Otjozongombe Shelter to Otjoma-penda Shelter As this day's hike is only 7 km and requires no more than 3 hours' hiking, even at a relaxed pace, a leisurely morning can be spent at the shelter. Most of the day's route winds through eye-catching rock formations near the edge of the plateau. Ten minutes after setting off you will dip through Klipspringer Kloof and after about half an hour pass through Kudu Kloof. Further along you will pass through Decora Gully, which takes its name from the specific name of the Namib coral tree and a short way further you will reach Croton Gully, named after the lavender fever-berry which grows abundantly here. The trail then briefly takes you close to the edge of the plateau with views of the dramatic cliffs and the plains below.

Mushroom Rock, passed about 90 minutes after setting off, is unlikely to be missed. True to its name, the 4 m-high rock formation resembles a mushroom. Here there is a short detour to Jane's Cave and although more of an over-hang, it is a cool resting spot and worth making the detour. During the hacking of the trail, the cave was noticed by the daughter of park chief Treigue Cooper, and named after her.

With less than an hour's walk remaining from Mushroom Rock, you can take your time. Shortly before reaching the shelter you will pass an enormous boulder which has been fractured into squares, providing ideal holds for ferns and laurel figs resembling bonsais. The square

blocks splashed with blotches of orange lichens look as though they could have inspired Pablo Picasso and other Cubists.

Situated amongst a jumble of rocky outcrops, sandstone pillars and eroded domes, Otjomapenda Shelter is smaller than Otjozongombe and hence has a more cosy atmosphere. A massive boulder forms the back wall of the shelter which comprises two sleeping areas and a central eating area. Trees close to the shelter have been tagged with name plates which can be useful if you are unfamiliar with them.

Day 3: Otjomapenda Loop Although you may be tempted to leave your backpack at the shelter, this could be risky as there are baboons on the plateau who might decide to have a closer look. Fortunately only 8 km are hiked, so your pack will not be too much of a burden. Once again the trail winds past rocks draped in laurel figs and you should take the time to stop and follow the path of their roots clinging tenaciously to cracks and crevices.

Just before swinging away from the cliffs you will pass a small rock arch on your left. After this the number of rocks gradually diminishes with the path becoming more and more sandy as you make your way across the vegetated dunes. The walking here is fairly taxing.

For the remainder of the day you will walk through mixed broadleaf woodland where species such as weeping wattle, Kalahari apple-leaf and silver cluster-leaf are dominant. Since the scenery is not as varied as along the plateau edge you could be tempted to stride out the last few kilometres, but take care – rhino do occur in the area. Check the path carefully for signs of their large spoor.

Quite unexpectedly you will notice rocks towering above the trees ahead of you. The overnight shelter is close by and after passing through Dassie Alley the path winds around some large rock formations back to the shelter.

Day 4: Otjomapenda Shelter to Bernabé de la Bat Rest Camp The final day's hike covers 14 km and if you have not seen any game yet, you should consider an early start. Perhaps you will be lucky!

About 10 minutes after setting off you will reach Onjima Pool, a natural rock pool which holds water well into the dry winter months. You are bound to be surprised by the variety of spoor in the mud – it is a popular drinking place.

From here the trail continues through the vegetated dunes for about 90 minutes and once again the spoor in the path will provide sufficient evidence of game. Klipspringer Koppie is a good place for a break and half an hour further the jeep track giving access to Otjozongombe Shelter is crossed. After crossing through the usually dry Ongorowe River, the trail winds across Burkea Plain which takes its name from the abundance of wild seringa trees.

About 90 minutes after crossing the Ongorowe River you will join the trail where it split off on day one. However, a few minutes after crossing the firebreak, you will branch off to the left towards the plateau edge. The final section of the trail takes you through spectacular rock formations for some 30 minutes.

Probably not more than five hours after setting off you will be back at the Mountain Viewpoint and from here all that remains is the descent to the rest camp, along the outward route followed a few days previously.

NAUKLUFT

Situated on the edge of the Namib Desert in Namibia, the Naukluft massif contrasts sharply with its surroundings. Rising some 1 000 m above the plains, the Naukluft Mountains are characterised by deep ravines, rolling hills and an extensive plateau where game is often encountered. On account of the rugged terrain the trail should not be attempted if you are inexperienced or unfit, but those who do take up the challenge will be rewarded with spectacular views, dramatic mountain scenery and crystal-clear pools near the end of the trail.

TRAIL PLANNER

Distance   120 km 8 days; or 58 km 4 days

Grading   C+ 8-day option; C 4-day option

Climate

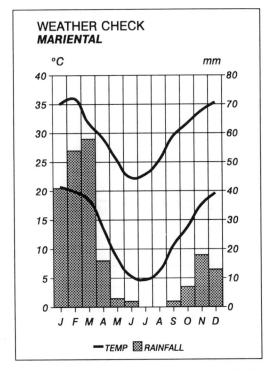

WEATHER CHECK
MARIENTAL

— TEMP ▨ RAINFALL

Day temperatures averaging about 20 °C can be expected during winter, but evenings are cool and temperatures of below freezing point are not uncommon at night. Light snowfalls occur occasionally during winter, especially at high altitudes. The average annual rainfall for Naukluft is 193 mm, but is extremely variable, ranging from 46 mm to 545 mm a year. Most of the area's rainfall occurs between December and April as thunderstorms.

Reservations   Director of Tourism, Reservations, Private Bag 13267, Windhoek, Namibia, Telephone (061) 23-6975, Fax (061) 22-4900. Written reservations can be made 18 months in advance, but are only confirmed 11 months prior to the trail date when telephone and personal reservations are accepted.

Group size   Minimum 3; Maximum 12

Maps   A full-colour trail map with useful information on the history, flora and fauna of the area on the reverse is available. One free copy of the map is forwarded with your receipt and permit.

Facilities   The Hiker's Haven at Naukluft and Ubusis Hut are equipped with beds and bunks with mattresses, running water, showers and flush toilets.
The other overnight shelters are basic structures consisting of a three-quarter stone wall with a roof. Sleeping is on the ground and water, pit toilets and stone tables and benches are also provided. Refuse bins are provided at all huts.

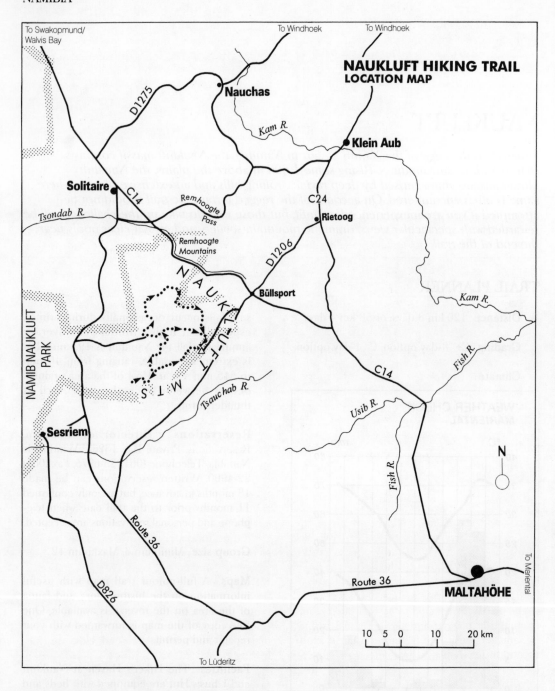

NAUKLUFT HIKING TRAIL
LOCATION MAP

To Swakopmund/
Walvis Bay

To Windhoek

To Windhoek

Nauchas

Kam R.

Klein Aub

D1275

Solitaire

C14

Remhoogte Pass

C24

Rietoog

Tsondab R.

D1206

Remhoogte Mountains

Büllsport

Kam R.

N A U K L U F T

NAMIB NAUKLUFT PARK

M T S

Tsauchab R.

Usib R.

Fish R.

C14

Sesriem

Route 36

D826

Fish R.

To Mariental

Route 36

MALTAHÖHE

N

10 5 0   10   20 km

To Lüderitz

Logistics The eight-day route is circular. Hikers can drop off supplies beforehand at Tsams Ost, the halfway mark, where there is a large steel cupboard. Vehicles are parked at the Naukluft office and the first and last nights of the trail can be spent at Hiker's Haven. There is also a four-day circular option which follows the first three days of the trail to Adlerhorst before returning to Naukluft.

Two vehicles are essential for the four-day linear option since the end point is about 21 km from the Solitaire-Sesriem road and the chances of hitching a lift back to the Naukluft campsite are extremely slim.

Relevant information

■ South African citizens require a valid passport when entering Namibia, while other nationalities travelling from South Africa should check on visa requirements.

■ Only eight groups are permitted to set off per month.

■ The entrance gate to Naukluft is open between sunrise and sunset.

■ The trail is only open between 1 March and 31 October because of the excessively high summer temperatures.

■ Hikers are not permitted to start the trail at Tsams Ost without informing the office at Naukluft.

■ A backpacking stove is essential as fires are not permitted on the trail, except at Hiker's Haven. Here you must, however, provide your own wood or buy it from the office.

■ Stout boots should be worn as the terrain is extremely rugged.

■ Since there is very little overhead cover on the trail, hikers should take precautions against the sun.

■ Prevent dehydration by drinking plenty of water when it is available. Set off each day with a full 2-litre water-bottle and use it sparingly until reaching the next water point.

■ Winter temperatures can drop to freezing point, so be prepared for extremes.

■ Hikers with an acute fear of heights should not attempt the trail as there are two sections where chains have been secured to assist hikers in scaling several sheer waterfalls, the largest being 28 m high.

■ No soap, not even biodegradable soap, should be used in the springs.

■ Water is provided at each overnight stop.

How to get there

Approaching from the south along the B1, take the C19 to Maltahöhe, just south of Mariental. From Maltahöhe, follow the C14, a gravel road, for about 116 km to just before Büllsport. Turn left onto the D854 to reach the entrance gate about 10 km further. Alternatively, travelling along the B1 between Kalkrand and Rehoboth, you must turn onto the C24 about 3 km south of Rehoboth. At Rietoog, turn onto the D1206 which is followed for 28 km to Büllsport where you will join the C14. Turn left there and a short way further, on the right, onto the D854. The entrance gate to the park is reached about 10 km onwards, with the park office 12 km beyond the gate.

TRAIL ENVIRONMENT

Flora The Naukluft complex lies in the transitional zone between the Namib Desert in the west and the dwarf shrub savanna in the east and, consequently, has an interesting variety of plants and trees. Three of the five plant communities occurring in the Naukluft complex can be seen along the trail.

The massif is dissected by several deep kloofs draining the plateau and the perennial springs in some of these kloofs support dense **kloof communities**. A highly aromatic herb growing in some of the riverbeds is the wild mint (*Mentha longifolia* subsp. *wissii*). The banks of the kloof communities are dominated by large trees including common cluster fig, sweet thorn and karree, while ebony trees occur higher up the banks. Hardy trees and shrubs, including quiver tree, blue-leaved corkwood, *Euphorbia virosa* and *E. mauritanica* grow on the rocky valley slopes. A conspicuous species growing at the base of the sheer cliffs is the Namaqua fig which

is easily identifiable by its white roots clinging to the rocks.

The **mountain communities** occur on the steep, sparsely vegetated mountain slopes and are characterised by small trees and shrubs. Conspicuous on exposed slopes is the resurrection bush (*Myrothamnus flabellifolius*) which grows in large communities. For most of the year this bush, with its dry brown branches curving inwards, appears to be dead. However, following rain it expands, unfolding soft green leaves within an hour, hence the name.

As you traverse the massif you will notice that the northern and eastern slopes are more sparsely vegetated than the southern and western slopes, the reason for this being that the latter are in the rain shadow. Characteristic trees and shrubs of the northern and eastern slopes are the shepherd's tree with its conspicuous white trunk, mountain thorn, Namibian resin tree, small-leaved guarri, driedoring (*Rhigozum trichotomum*) and the trumpet flower (*Catophractes alexandri*). Dominant species on the western and southern slopes include quiver tree, phantom tree, blue-leaved and white-stem corkwoods, as well as the paperbark milkbush.

The vegetation of the **plateau communities** is dominated by herbs with a Karoo-like character. Among these are kapokbos (*Eriocephalus ericoides*), skilpadbossie (*Zygophyllum*) and everlastings (*Helichrysum* spp.), as well as several *felicia* and *senecio* species. Trees and shrubs are generally absent, the mountain thorn being the most conspicuous, while scattered shepherd's trees and Namibian resin trees also occur.

Situated in an arid area, the massif is the habitat of a large variety of succulents. In addition to the quiver tree, other aloes found here include *Aloe karasbergensis*, *A. hereroensis* and *A. argenticauda*, a species favouring dolomitic soils. Also occurring here is the rare *A. sladeniana* which favours rock crevices and is mainly restricted to the Naukluft and Zaris mountains.

Other noteworthy succulents are cobas, elephant's foot (*Adenia pechuelii*), *Hoodia currori* and *Lithops schwantesii*, a stone plant which is restricted to southern Namibia and has yellow flowers.

Fauna The mountainous terrain of the Naukluft complex provides an ideal habitat for Hartmann's mountain zebra and the park supports a healthy population of this species. They occur throughout rocky areas of the mountain complex in family groups of between three and 12, bachelor herds and solitary stallions. Although you are likely to see them during your hike, they blend in exceptionally well with their surroundings and are difficult to spot unless they are on the run. They are very alert and once they take flight usually retreat to a safe distance before stopping to investigate the disturbance.

Pairs or small family groups of klipspringers are common in the rocky areas of the massif, which is also the habitat of several troops of chacma baboons, numbering up to 40 individuals, and rock dassie.

The area also supports a healthy kudu population which is largely confined to the densely vegetated kloofs and river washes. Your best chance of spotting this species is during the early mornings and late afternoons when they can be seen along the mountain slopes.

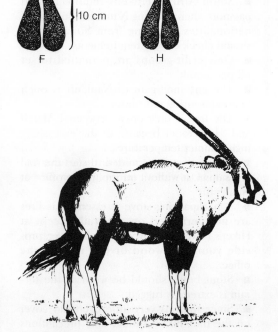

Gemsbok – a typical species of arid areas such as the Namib Desert

Other antelope species you might see are steenbok, springbok and gemsbok.

Leopard have been sighted on a number of occasions by park officials and judging by the numerous kudu and mountain zebra skeletons in the kloofs, the park supports a healthy leopard population. Other predators recorded in the park include black-backed jackal, Cape and bat-eared foxes, as well as several mongoose species. Aardwolf, African wild cat and caracal also occur.

To date some 204 bird species have been recorded at Naukluft of which 98 species are resident, 35 migrant and 19 nomad. The number of species is, however, closely linked to climatic conditions, fluctuating between 116 in dry years and 152 in wet years.

Noteworthy species to keep an eye out for include Rüppell's korhaan, Monteiro's hornbill, Herero chat, rockrunner and whitetailed shrike – all of which reach the southern limit of their distribution here. The massif also lies at the northern extremity of Karoo species such as the Karoo robin and cinnamonbreasted warbler which use the Fish River as a flyway to penetrate this far north into Namibia.

The rocky slopes and hillsides are the habitat of shorttoed rock thrush, as well as mountain and familiar chats, both of which are common. The Herero chat is a rare resident and your best chances of ticking it are in the Ubusis area. Here you might also see rockrunner, a species which has also been recorded at Tsams Ost.

Species attracted to the cliffs include black eagle and rosyfaced lovebird, both of which are common, and augur buzzard. Bradfield's swift visits the massif infrequently, mainly during the summer. Black stork, a rare resident, have been recorded at Naukluft, as well as the Tsams Ost and Lemoenputs Valleys on the western side of the mountain.

Ludwig's bustard is an occasional visitor to the plateau and the plains surrounding the massif, while Rüppell's korhaan is a common plains species. The plains west of Naukluft also provide a habitat to whitebacked and lappetfaced vultures.

Typical species of the plateau are Namaqua sandgrouse, swallowtailed bee-eater, Karoo chat, chat flycatcher and bokmakierie.

The Arbeid Adelt area attracts several species which usually do not occur elsewhere on the massif, including purple roller, Monteiro's hornbill, groundscraper thrush and crimsonbreasted shrike.

Unlikely to escape your attention is the sociable weaver which occurs commonly throughout the area. Although these medium-sized birds are quite inconspicuous, they can easily be

Rosyfaced lovebirds have a characteristic shrill metallic shreek call

identified by their enormous communal nests and their characteristic "chip chip" call.

History Rock paintings, stone implements and other artefacts have provided positive evidence of the presence of Stone Age people in the Naukluft for thousands of years, while pastoralists were also attracted to the massif during the last millennium.

In more recent times, however, Naukluft was closely linked to the resistance of the Witbooi Nama to German colonial rule. Reminders of the fierce clashes which took place here include the grave of a German soldier.

Following the attack on Kaptein Hendrik Witbooi's settlement at Hoornkrans by Major Curt von Francois in April 1893, the German *Schutztruppe* were involved in several inconclusive skirmishes with the Witboois. In one of these clashes a 25-year-old cavalryman, Richard Kramars, was killed and his grave near Hiker's Haven serves as a reminder of this bloody period. Von Francois was replaced in March 1894 by Theodor Leutwein who concluded a two-month truce with Kaptein Hendrik Witbooi, while waiting for the arrival of more troops. Witbooi refused to acknowledge German sovereignty and on 27 August 1894 Leutwein launched a three-pronged attack on his main camp at Naukluft.

The camp was seized by that afternoon and the Witboois then headed up the Naukluft to Gams on the plateau where they clashed with the Germans on 30 August. From here they made their way southwards and on 2 and 3 September the two sides clashed at the head of the Gurus Kloof, the Khoi name for what later became known as Ubusis Kloof. The Witboois retreated down Gurus Kloof and headed southwards, only to be forced back northwards by the *Schutztruppe*.

Both sides were exhausted by then and although the number of Witbooi casualties is not known, the German losses were 17 dead and 24 wounded. While Leutwein rested his men on 5 and 6 September the Witboois headed for the only water hole which was still accessible at Tsams Ost.

A few days later Kaptein Witbooi sent a message to Leutwein, offering a conditional surrender. Realising that a military victory over Witbooi was unlikely, Leutwein accepted the offer and a peace treaty was concluded at Tsams Ost on 15 September 1894.

In terms of the treaty Witbooi accepted the paramountcy of the German empire and agreed to the stationing of a garrison at Gibeon. Witbooi, however, retained his territory and jurisdiction over his people and the Witboois were allowed to keep their arms and ammunition.

Geology The Naukluft massif has an interesting geological history and if you keep a lookout on your hike you will be able to see some of the geological features.

The Naukluft Mountains were formed some 500 to 550 million years ago when large sheet-like units of fractured and folded sedimentary rocks were placed into their existing positions along fault or fracture planes known as thrusts. These nappes form the uppermost geological formation of the Naukluft Mountains and consist mainly of grey dolomites and limestones. The contorted layers of quartzite and dolomite in the cliffs to the north of Ubusis Hut provide a striking example of the forces which accompanied these movements.

The porous, creamlike deposits in several of the streams draining the plateau are unlikely to escape your attention. Known as tufa, fountain stone or waterfall limestone, these formations occur throughout the Naukluft Mountains. They are formed by the evaporation of calcium-rich water which seeps from an underground drainage system and their deposition is promoted by waterfalls and vegetation. Formations such as those in the Naukluft River are still active, but several enormous relict tufas reflect periods of higher rainfall in the past.

The Naukluft Nappe Complex is underlain by sedimentary formations of the Nama Group, consisting mainly of black limestones which were deposited into a vast shallow sea some 600 million years ago.

The Nama sediments rest on a much older basement of metasedimentary and volcanic rocks, gneisses and granites. Known as the Rehoboth-Sinclair Basement Complex, these formations date back to between 1 000 and 2 000 million years ago. This formation is mainly seen on the western side of the Naukluft Mountains and forms the scattered inselbergen on the plains at the edge of the Namib.

TRAIL DESCRIPTION

Day 1: Hiker's Haven to Putte Shelter The first section of the day's hike follows a track down the Naukluft River over easy terrain. After about 5 km the trail turns off to the right, ascending steeply up Elephant Skin Path which takes its name from the rough texture of the dolomite rocks exposed on the slope.

From the Panorama Viewpoint you will have an expansive view towards the west. Over the next 1 km the gradient of the trail is more gen-

tle, but you will soon lose altitude to Fonteinkloof where there is a small spring.

From Fonteinkloof the trail ascends steeply along the appropriately named Heartbreak Pass and you will gain about 200 m in altitude to the Zebra Highway. Judging by the width of the track, the path must have been in use for countless years by the mountain zebra inhabiting the Naukluft. Once you have accomplished the ascent you can relax as the remaining few kilo-

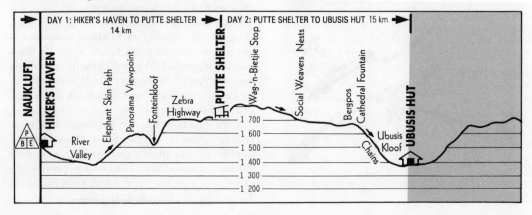

metres of the day's hike follow an easy gradient with magnificent views of the Tsauchab River valley and the Zaris Mountains to the west.

A short distance beyond the second viewpoint of the day you will pass Crassula Corner, named after the abundance of pig's ear (*Cotyledon orbiculata*), which belongs to the crassula family. This species has pendulous or hanging, tubular pinkish-orange flowers in mid-winter.

Putte Shelter lies in a small basin and takes its name from a well about 150 m west of the shelter. The well is equipped with a hand pump and it is possible to have a shower here. The hut is usually reached about six to seven hours after setting off.

Day 2: Putte Shelter to Ubusis Hut The day's hike starts with a short, uphill stretch along an indistinct track. The route is well marked, however, and after about 2 km you will join a rough track where a clump of buffalo-thorn trees provides welcome shade.

From here the trail follows the track across the undulating hills and along this section you will pass a large sociable weaver nest. Bergpos is reached about four hours after setting off, but do not count on filling your water-bottle here as the borehole was closed several years ago. The trail then begins to descend into Ubusis Kloof and about 2 km beyond Bergpos you will reach Cathedral Fountain, which takes its name from the cave nearby with its domelike roof. Water is usually available here throughout the year.

Downstream of Cathedral Fountain the kloof becomes a narrow ravine hemmed in by steep orange cliffs. Through the centuries large potholes have been scoured into the white dolomite riverbed which has been polished smooth by the swirling water. Chains have been anchored at several difficult sections to assist hikers, one along the right-hand wall of the gorge to help you get past a deep pothole which holds water for several months after good rains.

Further on you will have a choice of two routes to scramble down a waterfall, and near the deepest end of the ravine you will have to negotiate a high waterfall. A tufa formation on the side suggests that the water of Cathedral Fountain might have reached the waterfall during a wetter period.

Below the waterfall the kloof widens, but the boulder-strewn riverbed makes for difficult hiking. Ubusis Hut used to be a holiday cottage before the farm was incorporated into the park and is a complete surprise with luxuries such as a flush toilet and a cold-water shower and bunks.

Day 3: Ubusis Hut to Adlerhorst Shelter The third day's hike is a relatively short 12 km. From Ubusis the trail heads back up Ubusis Kloof and if you keep an eye out you may see some large black eagle nests on the face of the sheer cliff, while African black duck are sometimes seen at Cathedral Fountain. The fountain is fed by water seeping from the seam between the underlying quartzites and shales and the overlying grey dolomites.

At Bergpos the trail swings north, following a rough mountain track for about an hour. Hiking along the track, one cannot help but admire the perseverance of the early farmers in their efforts to make the area accessible. The trail then turns off to the right, following a dry river course for about 2 km before rejoining the track, and along this section another communal nest of sociable weavers can be seen.

The final 2 km of the day's hike follows the track across a wide plain, descending gradually to the overnight shelter, which comes into view with about 500 m of the day's hike left. The name Adlerhorst was given to this area by the pioneer farmers who sunk a borehole here to provide water for their livestock. Adlerhorst means eagle's nest and was probably named after the presence of eagles in the area or because of its lofty position high up in the mountains. Unlike the other trail shelters which are square, Adlerhorst is round since a disused cement dam was used as its base. Keep an eye out for kudu which are occasionally spotted in the vicinity, especially early in the morning and late in the afternoon.

Day 4: Adlerhorst Shelter to Tsams Ost Shelter Initially, the trail follows an easy route along a mountain track before gaining height steadily. You then follow a river course along Zebra Kloof before joining a tributary of the Tsams River.

Over the next few kilometres you follow the winding course of a dry riverbed until your progress is blocked by a high waterfall. The only way of bypassing this obstacle is to take the steep ascent up the right-hand slope of the valley, but before doing so take off your pack and continue down the river for about 100 m to the lip of the waterfall. The steep climb is followed by an even steeper descent and once you are down in the valley, take another short detour to the base of the fall where there is a pool.

A short way further you will pass an enormous phantom tree with a circumference of close on 4 m on the left-hand side of the valley. The riverbed is rather rocky and since this section can be quite tiring it is advisable to take your time and appreciate the scenery. Continuing further downstream, the valley becomes more densely vegetated and among the dominant species growing here are common cluster fig, sweet thorn and ebony tree. Shortly before reaching the Tsams Ost Campsite the trail passes several delightful small springs.

At the campsite the trail joins a gravel road which is followed for about 2 km to the Tsams Ost Shelter which is situated amongst a clump of acacia trees to the right of the road. The well with its large waterwheel at the turn-off to the hut dried up shortly after the trail was opened in May 1989, but following good rains the water level is likely to rise again.

Water can, however, be drawn from a well about 80 m west of the shelter. Close to the shelter is a large steel cupboard which can be used by hikers doing the full eight-day trail to store provisions, making it possible to carry only four days' rations on each leg.

Day 4: Optional return route from Adlerhorst Shelter to Hiker's Haven To simplify logistics for hikers doing only four days of the route, a route is available back to Naukluft. It is a fairly long day's walk and an early start is advisable.

Day 5: Tsams Ost Shelter to Die Valle Shelter The day's hike begins with a steep

climb up Broekskeur, an Afrikaans expression for "tough going". Some 200 m is gained before you reach the crest of the ridge from where you descend gradually to an old mountain track, much of which has been washed away.

Once again you will ascend steeply to a nek before winding along Euphorbia Kloof, which takes its name from the abundance of gifboom (*Euphorbia virosa*) growing on the rocky slopes. After dipping down, the trail gains height once more, passing Quiver Tree Ridge where numerous quiver and phantom trees are conspicuous on the slopes. The trail then winds downwards to Fonteinpomp, where you can stop for lunch since the remainder of the day's hike is through open country without overhead cover.

During dry years the borehole may be dry, so use your water sparingly during the first section of the trail in case you are out of luck here.

For the rest of the day you will follow a track for 11 km, and this is without doubt the most monotonous stretch of the entire trail. Keep an eye out, however, for the paperbark milkbush which is often mistaken for corkwood trees. Although the light yellow papery bark resembles that of the blue-leaved corkwood, the paperbark milkwood belongs to the euphorbia family.

Shortly before reaching the hut, the trail joins the access road to Die Valle which is followed for a short way to the hut situated in unsurpassed surroundings. When the water table is high, water is pumped to the tank by means of a solar-powered pump and it is even possible to have a shower. During dry periods, however, water has to be carted in and should be used sparingly.

Day 6: Die Valle Shelter to Tufa Tavern From the overnight shelter you will follow the

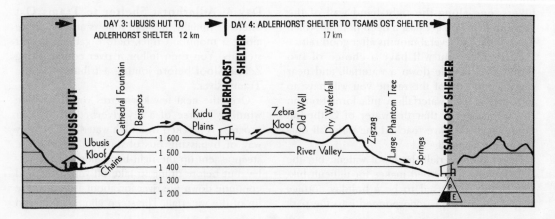

course of the Valle River upstream for about 1 km before climbing steeply up the left-hand slope of the valley. Before starting your climb, walk about 300 m to the base of the waterfall, passing a fountain on the way. The detour is well worth it! The ascent seems almost vertical in places and you will gain some 200 m in altitude up Groot Hartseer ("Great Heartbreak") before joining a contour path.

After following the contour path for about 1,5 km you will drop down into the Valle River. A short traverse downstream will bring you close to the top of the falls and at some of the difficult sections chain handholds have been provided. Just above the falls you will have to make your way past several large potholes which hold water for several months after good rains.

From the lip of the falls you will have magnificent views of the valley some 200 m below.

A spring and a large tufa cave are passed a short distance above the falls and for the next few kilometres the trail follows the meandering course of the river upstream. A conspicuous feature along this section of the trail is an enormous Namaqua fig with its white roots extending over a distance of some 40 m.

Further along, the trail reaches the plateau, passing Quartz Valley, before dropping down to Arbeid Adelt, the name given to the farm which was incorporated into the park. The plateau is sparsely vegetated but a clump of buffalo-thorn trees close to the trail provides welcome shade and a good lunch stop.

The final section of the day's hike is along a rough track which, in years gone by, provided access to the stock kraal on the plateau. From here you will lose about 350 m in altitude to Tufa Tavern, which takes its name from the nearby tufa formation.

The shelter is situated to the left of the jeep track amongst a clump of umbrella thorn trees. Water is obtainable from a bricked-in spring fitted with a hand pump, about 70 m south-east of the shelter.

Day 7: Tufa Tavern to Kapokvlakte Shelter

An early start is advisable since the trail gains some 500 m in altitude. After following a track for a few kilometres, the trail heads for the steep-sided Arbeid Adelt Kloof, ascending steeply along the river course.

A short way up the kloof your progress will be blocked by a high waterfall where water is available for most of the winter following good summer rains. Since the slopes on either side of the waterfall are too steep to negotiate without exposing hikers to danger, a 28-m chain has been anchored at the waterfall to help you overcome this obstacle. When the trail was being laid out in 1988 the head of the Naukluft Section of the Namib-Naukluft Park, Peter Bridgeford, suggested scaling the waterfall without the assistance of a chain or rope and this daunting section was unofficially dubbed Peter's Folly. Bridgeford was the driving force behind the construction of the trail and despite limited manpower and funds he persevered, using his ingenuity to obtain material for the shelters.

Above the falls the trail continues up the kloof, gaining height steadily until reaching World's View where you will walk along the edge of the cliffs overlooking the farm Blässkranz, some 500 m below. The final section of the ascent follows an easy gradient to Bakenkop, at 1 960 m the highest point of the trail. Looking almost due west from here is the highest point of the Naukluft massif (1 988 m).

The remaining few kilometres of the day's

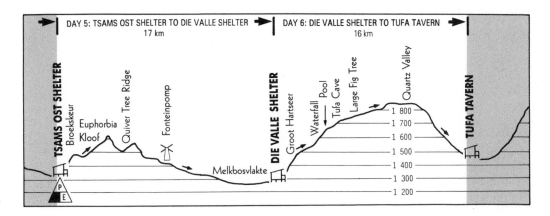

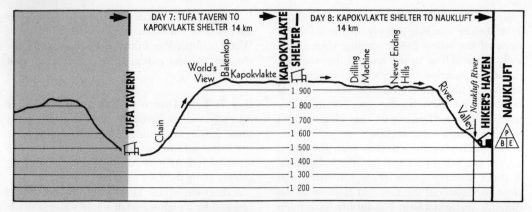

hike traverses easy terrain on Kapokvlakte, which takes its name from the kapokbos (*Eriocephalus ericoides*). The name is derived from the white, woolly flowers which reminded the early colonists of *kapok* ("snow").

Kapokvlakte shelter is shaded by an enormous buffalo-thorn and water is provided in two 200 *l* drums.

Springbok and Hartmann's mountain zebra are often seen on the plateau, while gemsbok tend to migrate into the area during dry periods.

Day 8: Kapokvlakte Shelter to Hiker's Haven

The first few kilometres of the day's hike follow a rough mountain track and, shortly after setting off, you will pass an area which has been fenced off. This has been done to enable researchers to compare the vegetation of areas which have not been grazed with those utilised by game.

Continuing across the flat plateau, the trail turns off the track about 3 km further on. Looking across to the left you will see the remains of an old water drilling machine which was dragged up onto the plateau in 1947, again showing the determination of the early farmers

to succeed in these arid areas. From here the trail follows the watershed of the Naukluft River, before dropping steeply into its tributary. The riverbed is scattered with large round boulders, requiring some boulder-hopping, and shortly before joining the Naukluft River you will see another magnificent Namaqua fig clinging to the cliffs on the left-hand side of the gorge.

After joining the Naukluft River the trail follows the kloof downstream, passing several inviting pools. Especially impressive is a large tufa waterfall which cascades into a crystal-clear pool near the bottom of the kloof and even on a cool day it is hard to resist the temptation to take a quick dip.

Provided you have made an early start, this magic spot can be reached by lunchtime and since the end of the trail is a mere 20 minutes away, there is no need to rush.

From here you will continue along the left-hand bank of the river, passing several enormous common cluster fig trees, before crossing over to the right. A short distance further on you will cross over to the left once more by way of a weir, joining a well-defined path to the ending point, a few hundred metres onwards.

▲ 1
2 ▼

1 Mushroom Rock passed on the second day of the Waterberg Unguided Hiking Trail
2 Otjomapenda Shelter provides accommodation on the second and third nights of the Waterberg
Unguided Hiking Trail

▲ 4

▲ 5

▲ 6

3 The Waterberg Unguided Hiking Trail winds across the plateau of the Waterberg Plateau Park
4 Die Valle Shelter, the sixth overnight shelter on the Naukluft Hiking Trail
5 Quiver trees and hikers, Die Valle, Naukluft Hiking Trail
6 View over the Fish River Canyon, the second largest canyon in the world

7 Descending over 500 metres from the northernmost viewpoint into the Fish River Canyon
8 River crossings are a frequent occurence on the Fish River Canyon Backpacking Trail
9 Rock sculptures, Waterberg Guided Wilderness Trail
10 Approaching the plateau of the Brandberg, the highest mountain in Namibia

▲ 7   8 ▼

13 ▲

11 Part of the second day's hike of the Klipspringer Hiking Trail follows the course of the Orange River

12 Some 40 000 rock paintings have been recorded in the Brandberg – frieze from *Felsenzircus*

13 Augrabies Falls at the start of the Klipspringer Hiking Trail

▲ 14

15 ▼

14 The Kransduif route meanders through several rock arches and caves eroded into the sandstone formations in the Oorlogskloof Nature Reserve
15 Looking across the plains from the escarpment in the Oorlogskloof Nature Reserve

▲ 16

17 ▼

16 The 20 metre high Maltese Cross in the Cederberg Wilderness Area
17 The Wolfberg Arch in the Cederberg has been sculptured by centuries of wind, rain and extremes of temperature

FISH RIVER CANYON

On this trail in southern Namibia you will follow the winding course of the Fish River Canyon, the second largest canyon in the world, for about 86 km. With a depth of over 500 m in places, the canyon is one of Africa's greatest natural wonders, formed over aeons by titanic forces from below and the erosive action of water. The trail winds through total wilderness and during the late afternoon you will be amazed by the transformation of the harsh and desolate surroundings into beautiful rich golden-orange shades, later fading into soft pastels.

TRAIL PLANNER

Distance 86 km (approximately); 4 or 5 days

Grading C

Climate

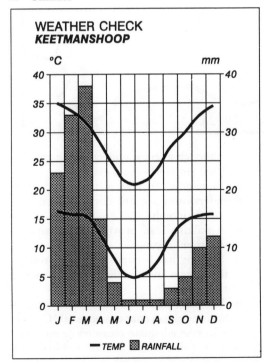

WEATHER CHECK
KEETMANSHOOP

- TEMP ▓ RAINFALL

Reservations The Director of Tourism, Private Bag 13267, Windhoek, Namibia, Telephone (061) 23-6975 (reservations), (061)

23-3875 (information), Fax (061) 22-4900. Written reservations can be made 18 months in advance, but are only confirmed 11 months before the trail date when telephone and personal applications are accepted.

Group size Minimum 3; Maximum 40

Maps A full-colour trail map with useful information on the history, flora, fauna and geology on the reverse is available. One free copy of the map is forwarded with your receipt and permit.

Facilities There are no facilities whatsoever on the trail and you can sleep wherever you choose.

Logistics Linear route, requiring two vehicles. It is usually not too difficult to arrange a lift with tourists from Ai-Ais to the main viewpoint to collect your vehicle after you have completed the trail. Hobas, about 10 km from the starting point, has a number of shaded campsites, ablutions and a swimming pool. Accommodation at Ai-Ais, where the trail ends, varies from campsites to bungalows and luxury flats. Amenities include an indoor thermal pool, outdoor swimming pool, shop, licensed restaurant and filling station.

Relevant information
■ South African citizens require a valid

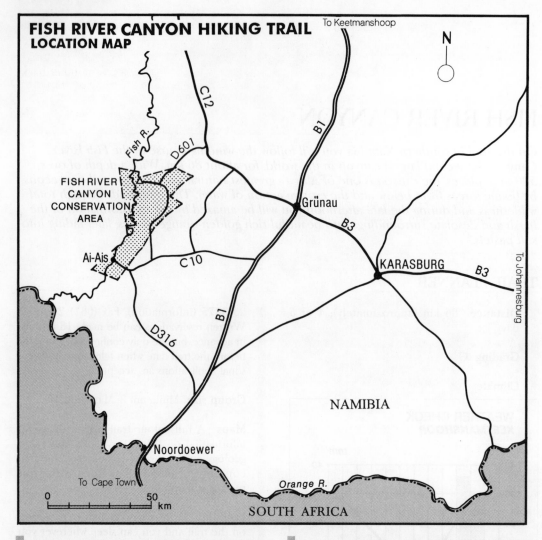

FISH RIVER CANYON HIKING TRAIL
LOCATION MAP

To Keetmanshoop

N

C12

Fish R.

D601

FISH RIVER
CANYON
CONSERVATION
AREA

Grünau

B3

Ai-Ais

C10

KARASBURG

B3

To Johannesburg

B1

D316

NAMIBIA

To Cape Town

Noordoewer

Orange R.

0   50 km

SOUTH AFRICA

passport when entering Namibia, while other nationalities travelling from South Africa should check on visa requirements.

■ Owing to excessive summer temperatures and the danger of flash floods, backpacking is only permitted from 1 May to 30 September.

■ On making a reservation a medical form will be forwarded to you which must be completed by a doctor not earlier than 40 days prior to the hike. The certificate must be produced at Hobas before you commence the hike.

■ The trail should not be attempted by those with weak ankles and knees.

■ Sturdy hiking boots with good ankle support are essential, while canvas or running shoes are useful for river crossings.

■ Although a tent is unnecessary, a ground-pad and groundsheet are essential.

■ Remember to take a light raincoat as thunderstorms are not uncommon during the winter months.

■ A walking staff provides extra support during river crossings.

■ Littering has become a serious problem in the canyon and all refuse must be carried out to Ai-Ais.

■ Even during the cooler winter months temperatures can soar to above 40 °C so be sure to take adequate measures against sunburn. A wide-rimmed hat and a shirt with a collar that can be turned up will be useful.

■ During periods of excessive heat, walking should be restricted to between first light and 11:00 and after 15:00 Namibian Winter

Time. When planning the distance to be covered each day remember that camp must be made before 17:00 Namibian Winter Time as it gets dark very quickly in the canyon.

■ The water is generally safe to drink, despite its muddy colour. Water obtained from stagnant pools when the river is not flowing should be purified or boiled. Do not pollute the water with soap or shampoo, but use biodegradable soap and wash away from the river.

■ Look out for scorpions and spiders when collecting firewood and shake out your boots before putting them on in the morning.

■ This is one of the few backpacking areas where you are allowed to make a fire. However, as driftwood is scarce on the first section of the canyon it is advisable to take a backpacking stove along. Do not make fires under a tree or on tree roots, use only driftwood and never break off seemingly dead branches from trees. Keep other backpackers in mind and use wood sparingly.

How to get there Approaching from the south, the turn-off to Ai-Ais is reached 37 km north of Noordoewer on the B1. Follow a gravel road for 71 km to a T-junction where you turn left to Ai-Ais, 10 km further on. The starting point near Hobas is reached by turning right at the T-junction and continuing for about 65 km along a well signposted road.

Approaching from the north, Hobas is best reached by turning onto the C12 at Grünau. About 60 km further you must turn left onto the D601 which is followed for 30 km before you turn right to Hobas.

TRAIL ENVIRONMENT

Flora The vegetation of the area is a dwarf shrub savanna which is characteristic of the arid regions of southern Namibia, reaching its northernmost limit near Rehoboth.

With the exception of reeds (*Phragmites australis*) and rushes (*Juncus arabicus*) which grow in the riverbed, the vegetation in the canyon is mainly restricted to the river banks. The most common tree species are camel- and sweet thorns, karree, buffalo-thorn and ebony tree, while the Namaqua fig is characteristically associated with rocks.

Shrubs include shepherd's tree, wild greenhair tree and the wild raisin. A species you are likely to identify easily is the wild tamarisk with its needle-like grey-green scaly leaves. It grows as a small to medium-sized tree and favours dry riverbeds and river banks in and on the fringes of desert areas.

During May and June the white, trumpet-like flowers of *Datura innoxia*, a poisonous member of the potato family, can be seen in bloom. It is an alien from South America which was introduced into the country in contaminated fodder and has invaded many of Namibia's rivers.

Scattered on the barren slopes are ringwood trees, quiver trees, *Euphorbia mauritanica*, *E. virosa* and *Aloe gariepensis*.

Fauna The pools in the canyon are usually well populated with fish. Five species have been recorded: smallmouth yellowfish (*Barbus aeneus*) largemouth yellowfish (*Barbus kimberleyensis*), sharptooth catfish (barbel) (*Clarias gariepinus*), carp (*Cyprinus carpio*) and Mozambique tilapia (*Oreochromis mossambicus*). You must, however, obtain a permit at Ai-Ais if you intend fishing.

The pools are also the habitat of water monitors (leguans) (*Varanus niloticus*) which sometimes reveal their presence when they take to the water with a splash.

Three mammals you are likely to see on the rocky slopes are klipspringer, rock dassie and chacma baboon. Klipspringer are usually seen

pods

Leaf form and flowers

The sweet thorn is the acacia with the widest distribution in South Africa

Kudu usually occur in well-wooded areas

in pairs or small family groups and they will often startle you with their high-pitched alarm call before making off with great agility over the rocky terrain. Their characteristic spoor, two small oval prints, is frequently seen in the damp sand on the edge of the river. There are a number of chacma baboon troops in the canyon, and at the start of the backpacking season when they are still fairly shy, you are more likely to hear the warning bark of the sentinel than to actually see them. However, as they become used to more backpackers passing through, they become less concerned about people and, later in the backpacking season, are often seen at close range.

The canyon is also the habitat of kudu, leopard and several smaller mammals such as the ground squirrel and the dassie rat.

Although the Fish River does not flow throughout the year, it has several large permanent pools in the middle reaches which make it an important transit route for birds moving further north to Hardap Dam and the Naukluft Mountains. Birds you are most likely to see are those attracted to the open water and the river banks such as the grey heron and the hamerkop, which is easily identified by its distinctive hammer-shaped head. It is a uniform dark brown and is usually seen hunting in shallow water, where it feeds on frogs and other aquatic animals. The Egyptian goose can be identified by its "honk-haah-haah" cry, which is often heard early in the morning or in the late afternoon. When disturbed it will fly a little ahead of you, escorting you away from its territory. Another common species here is the threebanded plover.

Birds of prey include the black eagle which is sometimes observed soaring overhead, the African fish eagle which perches in trees near the river and the rock kestrel.

Among the species commonly seen are pied kingfisher, rock martin, redeyed bulbul, moun-

HARTMANN'S MOUNTAIN ZEBRA

Hartmann's mountain zebra (*Equus zebra hartmannae*) are seldom seen and often the only indications of their presence are droppings, spoor or rolling places. They are very wary animals and normally only come down from the plateau above the canyon at night to quench their thirst.

Their distribution in Namibia is restricted to the mountainous transitional zone between the Namib and the inland plateau. In the south they occur in the Fish River Canyon and the Huns Mountains and after a break of about 400 km in their distribution, they recur in the Naukluft Mountains and the Khomas Hochland further north. A small, isolated population inhabits the Erongo Mountains south-west of Omaruru. They also occur in a narrow strip from the Ugab River northwards to Kaokoland and south-western Angola and eastwards to farms in the Outjo district.

At first glance Hartmann's mountain zebra appears similar to the Cape mountain zebra (*Equus zebra zebra*), but it differs in a number of respects:
■ It is slightly larger than the Cape mountain zebra, with a shoulder height of 1,5 m as opposed to 1,3 m and bears closer resemblance to a horse in build.
■ The stripes are more widely spaced, with the result that the pale stripes are either the same width or slightly wider than the black stripes.
■ The legs are almost equally banded black and buff, and the mane is well developed.

Hartmann's mountain zebra occur either in family groups, consisting of a stallion, mares and foals, or in bachelor groups, while solitary stallions are occasionally encountered. Most foals are born between November and April after a gestation period of 12 months.

They feed mainly after first light and between mid-afternoon and sunset, resting in the hottest part of the day in summer.

tain, familiar and sicklewinged chats, Cape wagtail, fiscal shrike and palewinged starling.

Should you do any bird-watching in the reedbeds near Ai-Ais, you might spot African black duck, purple gallinule, moorhen and Cape white-eye. Cape and Karoo robins have been recorded in the riverine bush, with the Karoo robin preferring the more open areas.

History The Fish River Canyon, with its relatively abundant resources of water, fish and game, was an oasis to the early inhabitants of this otherwise arid region.

Twenty-seven archaeological sites have been located along the trail and from these sites it is apparent that the size of the settlements increased as the canyon widens towards Ai-Ais.

To its early inhabitants, the Fish River Canyon had a supernatural significance. According to a San legend, the canyon owes its meandering course to the serpent, Kouteign Kooru, who made the place his lair in the distant past. He was relentlessly pursued by hunters and to escape from them he retreated into the desert where he carved deep scars into the earth.

The southern and central parts of Namibia were also inhabited by the Nama, a nomadic Khoikhoi race. They never practised agriculture but herded cattle, fat-tailed sheep and goats and supplemented their diet by hunting and gathering. In 1903 one of the Nama tribes rebelled against German rule, but was defeated four years later. It was during this period that Ai-Ais was used as a base camp by the German forces. Grim reminders of this almost forgotten war are seen at Gochas Drift in the lower reaches of the canyon where you will pass the grave of a German soldier, Lieutenant Thilo von Trotha.

When South Africa invaded the territory in 1915, wounded German soldiers found a safe refuge at Ai-Ais and recovered from their wounds. After World War I the spring was leased to a Karasburg businessman, who provided basic facilities for visitors. In 1962 the Fish River Canyon was proclaimed a national monument and six years later a game reserve. The rest camp was officially opened in March 1971 and almost a year later the Fish River came down in flood with a magnitude which happens only once in 10 000 years, and almost everything except the main building was washed away.

Geology One of the most interesting aspects of the 160-km long canyon is its geology. Looking across the canyon from the main viewpoint you will see the various geological layers which have been exposed by centuries of erosive action. The steep slopes leading from the riverbed originally comprised sediments and lavas which were deposited 1 800 to 1 000 million years ago.

Some 1 300 to 1 000 million years ago the Namaqua Metamorphic Complex developed when these deposits were subjected to phases of folding, metamorphism, and the intrusion of granite. Later dolerite intrusions can be clearly seen in the form of dark wall-like dykes which run to the top of the Namaqua Metamorphic Complex but not into the overlying rocks of the Nama Group. This indicates that the intrusions must have taken place post-Namaqua but pre-Nama, and are thought to have occurred about 880 million years ago. At first glance these dykes are often mistaken for basalt reefs.

About 750 to 650 million years ago the southern part of Namibia was inundated by a shallow sea and sediments from higher areas

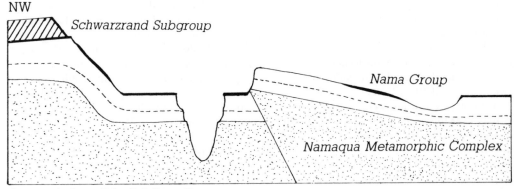

NW

Schwarzrand Subgroup

Nama Group

Namaqua Metamorphic Complex

Geomorphology of the Fish River Canyon

washed into this basin. These sediments now form the flat-lying Nama Group which is composed of several layers. The small pebble conglomerate at the base of the group is only a few metres deep and is referred to as the Kanies Member. This is followed by a 150 to 200 m thick layer of carbonates, grits, sandstone and quartzite known as the Kuibis Subgroup. Overlying these two groups is a 10 m band of dark limestone, shale and sandstone of the Schwarzrand Subgroup.

About 300 million years ago the early valley, which had developed about 200 million years previously as a result of a system of north-south running fractures which facilitated erosion, was deepened by southward-moving glaciers during the Gondwana Ice Age.

This was followed by another period of fracturing which produced faults that allowed water, heated deep in the earth, to flow to the surface as springs, the best known being those at Palm (Sulphur) Springs and Ai-Ais.

At a later stage incision by the Fish River gave the canyon its present morphology – the most striking features having developed mainly during the past 50 million years.

TRAIL DESCRIPTION

The trail starts at the northernmost viewpoint and since there are no set overnight stops along the trail you can set your own pace and select your own camping spots. Depending on your level of fitness, the trail is usually completed in four or five days.

Gazing over the canyon from the starting point at the northernmost viewpoint, you will notice that the canyon is in fact a canyon within a canyon. While the upper canyon was formed as a result of crustal movements, the lower canyon was incised deeply into the floor of the upper canyon.

The descent into the canyon is rather steep, but fortunately there are chains to hold on to as you begin your descent. It can take anything between 45 and 90 minutes to reach the canyon floor and you are well advised to take your time over this section. Once at the bottom you should not miss the opportunity to cool off in the enormous pool awaiting you.

Between the northernmost viewpoint and Palm Springs the canyon reaches its greatest depth and this is undoubtedly the most spec-

Hydrology The Fish River is the longest river in Namibia and from its source in the Nauchas Mountains in western Rehoboth it follows a course of more than 800 km to its confluence with the Orange River, 110 km east of the Atlantic Ocean. For the first few hundred kilometres the river runs with hardly any incision, but south of Seeheim it starts descending and at the junction of the Gaub River the incision reaches a depth of approximately 50 m. A few kilometres south of the Gaub River it drops in quick succession over two waterfalls and enters the canyon proper.

With the exception of Namibia's boundary rivers it is the only river in the country which usually has permanent pools in its middle reaches outside the rainy season. The flow of the river varies with the rainfall, which occurs from the middle of November to the end of March, but since the construction of the Hardap Dam near Mariental in 1963 flooding of the river has depended on its tributaries south of the dam. When in flood the Fish River becomes a raging torrent, moving at a speed of between 12 and 14 knots and flowing more than 100 m wide in places.

tacular section of the hike. The route follows the left-hand bank of the river and on account of the large boulders interspersed with stretches of soft sand your progress will be relatively slow.

The sheer cliffs of the Nama sediments are especially impressive and you will probably notice that the contact between the sediments and the underlying basement rock is virtually horizontal. This phenomenon is known as an unconformity and represents a break in the geological record during which the basement rocks were eroded to a plane surface before sedimentation resumed.

You will also pass several dolerite dykes which are often mistaken for basalt. Although dolerite is genetically related to basalt, it differs in that the magma (molten matter) intruded into the surrounding rocks without reaching the surface.

About 2 km before Palm Springs the emergency exit to the Palm Springs Lookout is seen on the left-hand bank of the river. Faint wafts of sulphur usually indicate that you are close to your destination, but you will only see the palm trees at the last minute.

Despite the pungent odour of the spring, Palm Springs is a popular overnight stop and wood is often scarce here. The trees at the spring are not indigenous to southern Africa and their presence has given rise to several theories, the most popular being that they grew from date stones discarded by two German prisoners of war who escaped from the internment camp at Aus during World War I. One of them was said to have suffered from skin cancer and the other from asthma, but after bathing in the sulphur spring for two months both were miraculously cured. This story is often confused with that of the two Germans who fled into the Kuiseb Canyon during World War II to escape internment and whose experiences have been immortalised in the book *The Sheltering Desert*.

The hot spring is caused by surface water filtering down cracks and fissures in the rocks to a depth of about 1 000 m before it is forced back to the surface at a flow estimated at about 30 litres per second and a temperature of about 57 °C. It is rich in fluoride, chloride and sulphate.

The hot water from the spring flows down the slope into shallow pools at the edge of the river where it mixes with cold water. From time to time reeds encroach on the pools, making access difficult, but after heavy floods the reeds are washed away.

From Palm Springs the boulders give way to stretches of sand, round river stones and later gravel plains which make progress considerably easier. Downstream of Palm Springs the canyon widens and the route cuts across the inside of the wide river bends, necessitating several river crossings. Depending on the level of the river, you can either hop across without so much as getting your feet wet or you will have to wade through.

Table Mountain, a familiar landmark, is passed about 29 km from the start. The campsite opposite the spot marked "Sand Against Slope" on the trail map is reached a few kilometres further on and is another popular overnight stop with some delightful pools.

Lower downstream the river meanders vigorously and there are several shortcuts, the first being just before the formation known as the Three Sisters. This shortcut is situated on the right-hand bank of the river, with a clump of wild tamarisk trees almost blocking its entrance. From the river you will ascend Kooigoedhoogte

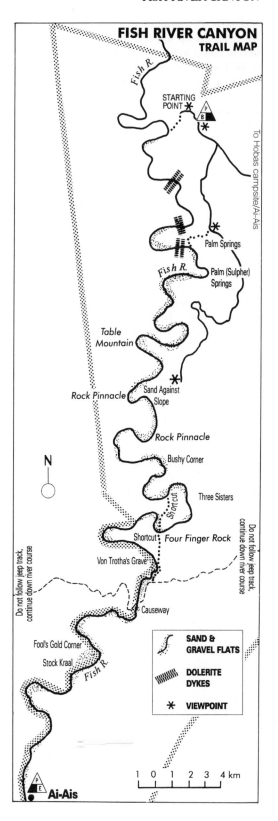

FISH RIVER CANYON
TRAIL MAP

Fish R.

STARTING POINT

To Hobas campsite/Ai-Ais

Palm Springs

Fish R.

Palm (Sulpher) Springs

Table Mountain

Rock Pinnacle

Sand Against Slope

N

Rock Pinnacle

Bushy Corner

Shortcut

Three Sisters

Shortcut   Four Finger Rock

Von Trotha's Grave

Do not follow jeep track, continue down river course

Do not follow jeep track, continue down river course

Causeway

Fool's Gold Corner

Stock Kraal

Fish R.

	SAND & GRAVEL FLATS
	DOLERITE DYKES
*	VIEWPOINT

1 0 1 2 3 4 km

Ai-Ais

47

and once the summit is reached Four Finger Rock looms up ahead. The route then meanders across a gravel plain and, shortly after you pass a seep surrounded by white mineral deposits, the river comes into view on your right. However, you will continue straight ahead to rejoin the river at the end of this 2,5 km shortcut, immediately below the Four Finger Rock which marks the end of the deepest part of the canyon.

Do not continue along the river here, but wade across and follow the jeep track up the slopes, before descending into a valley to reach another well-known landmark, the German Soldier's Grave, about 2 km further on. Lieutenant Thilo von Trotha was shot from behind here by a Bondelswart Nama who suspected him of being a decoy during a raid by the Germans to recover stolen cattle. Ironically Von Trotha was on a mission to negotiate peace with the Bondelswarts. The grave has been packed with stones and a metal plaque placed on it, but blends in so well with its surroundings that it is easily missed. It is situated on the western edge of the valley leading from Four Finger Rock, so keep to the right of the valley rather than following the dry river course.

Cross the river and continue along the right-hand bank for about 1 km where there is another popular overnight stop with some deep pools. The canyon now widens considerably and the Nama sediments give way to deeply dissected mountainous terrain of basement rock.

Ai-Ais is a good day's walk further south of here and shortly after setting off you will cross over to the left-hand bank of the river. A short distance further you will join up with the only other emergency exit on the trail. The emergency route follows the jeep track to the left which eventually joins up with the road between Ai-Ais and Hobas.

The route to Ai-Ais crosses the river at the causeway and you will follow the jeep track for a short way before turning off to the left. Be sure not to miss this turn-off as the jeep track continues westwards to the rugged Huns Mountains.

Further along you will pass Fool's Gold Corner where there is another fairly long shortcut to an old stock kraal. Continuing downstream, the river is crossed several times before you pass a pump station and, a little further ahead, the measuring wall just above the rest camp. Here you will join a track which is followed for less than 1 km to Ai-Ais where you can soothe your aching muscles in the thermal waters.

Ai-Ais is a Nama word meaning "scalding hot", a reference to the thermal spring which has a temperature of about 60 °C, and you will have a choice of relaxing in the indoor thermal pool or the swimming pool. The spring is said to have been "discovered" in 1850 by a Nama shepherd searching for stray stock, although it is likely that the spring was known to the early inhabitants of the area thousands of years ago.

OTHER NAMIBIAN TRAILS

BRANDBERG

Distance Various options; 4 days or longer

Reservations No permits required (August 1994)

Group size No limit on maximum number of hikers

Facilities No facilities

Description Covering some 750 km², the Brandberg rises abruptly from the surrounding plains in central Damaraland, about 170 km west of Omaruru. It is a harsh and inhospitable mountain with deep ravines choked by massive boulders which take on a deep, orange glow in the late afternoon. On account of the extremely rugged terrain, extremes of temperature and the unpredictable water supply, the Brandberg should be attempted only by fit and experienced backpackers after careful preparation. Königstein, with a height of 2 573 m, is the highest point in Namibia. Besides being spectacularly scenic, the mountain is also a treasure-house of rock paintings and to date more than 43 000 individual paintings have been recorded.

UGAB RIVER

Distance Guided wilderness trail, 50 km (approximately); 3 days

Reservations The Director of Tourism, Ministry of Environment and Tourism, Private Bag 13267, Windhoek, Namibia, Telephone (061) 23-6975.

Group size Maximum 8

Facilities Sleeping is in the open and hikers must provide their own equipment, including backpacks and sleeping bags, as well as food.

Description This trail affords the opportunity to discover one of the most fascinating deserts in the world on foot. Trails depart from the entrance gate to the Skeleton Coast National Park, 200 km north of Swakopmund, on the second and fourth Tuesday of the month throughout the year. The trail is not confined to a specific route, and it alternates between the gravel plains, the well-vegetated Ugab River with its impressive canyon slopes and the granite plains. Although game such as gemsbok, Hartmann's mountain zebra and springbok occur in the area, the emphasis is on the fascinating smaller creatures which are adapted to live in these harsh conditions and the interesting flora which includes the *Welwitschia* and numerous lichen species.

WATERBERG GUIDED WILDERNESS TRAIL

Distance Guided wilderness trail, no set route or distance; 3 days

Reservations The Director of Tourism, Ministry of Environment and Tourism, Private Bag 13267, Windhoek, Namibia, Telephone (061) 23-6975.

Group size Maximum 8

Facilities The trail camps are equipped with mattresses. Other amenities include water, washing facilities (cold water only), a toilet and firewood.

Description The Waterberg Plateau Park with its fascinating sandstone rock formations lies about 60 km east of Otjiwarongo and is a sanctuary to several rare species of game. The trails are conducted in the 18 600 ha wilderness area set aside on the plateau and trailists could encounter white and black rhinos, buffalo, sable, roan, giraffe and blue wildebeest. Birding can be rewarding too, since the mountain is the habitat of several Namibian "specials". Trails are conducted on the second, third and fourth weekends of every month between April and November, starting on Thursday afternoon and ending early on Sunday afternoon. Backpacks, water-bottles, cooking and eating utensils are supplied, but trailists must supply their own sleeping bags and food.

NORTHERN AND WESTERN CAPE

KLIPSPRINGER

This three-day trail in the Augrabies Falls National Park in the northern Cape winds through an arid but fascinating area which is usually not considered ideal for hiking. Starting near the renowned Augrabies Falls, the trail traverses almost primeval scenery which at times is reminiscent of a lunar landscape. A sharp contrast is created by the refreshing section along the sandy banks of the Orange River and the flat plains. The fairly short distances covered and some unexpected surprises make this a most enjoyable route.

TRAIL PLANNER

Distance 40 km; 3 days

Grading A+

Reservations The Director, National Parks Board, P O Box 787, Pretoria 0001, Telephone (012) 343-1991, Fax (012) 343-0905 or P O Box 7400, Roggebaai 8012, Telephone (021) 22-2810, Fax (012) 24-6211. Reservations are accepted up to a year in advance.

Group size Minimum 2; Maximum 12

Maps A sketch map is included in the

information leaflet on the trail, which is forwarded with your receipt and permit.

Climate

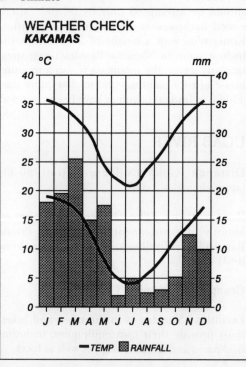

WEATHER CHECK
KAKAMAS

°C / mm

J F M A M J J A S O N D

━ TEMP ▨ RAINFALL

Facilities Two huts, with bunks and mattresses and a central cooking area, provide accommodation on the trail. Other facilities include drinking water, fireplaces, a pot and

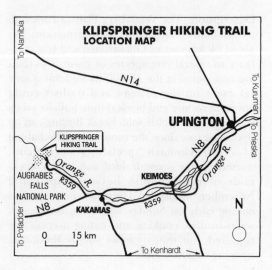

KLIPSPRINGER HIKING TRAIL
LOCATION MAP

To Namibia
N14
To Kuruman / To Prieska
UPINGTON
N8
KLIPSPRINGER HIKING TRAIL
Orange R.
Orange R.
AUGRABIES FALLS NATIONAL PARK
R359
KEIMOES
N8
KAKAMAS
R359
To Pofadder
0 15 km
N
To Kenhardt

kettle and flush toilets. Firewood is supplied, but there are no lamps or showers.

Logistics Circular route. There is no hut at the start/end of the trail. Facilities at the Augrabies Falls Rest Camp range from campsites to self-contained chalets. There is also a shop, restaurant and a filling station.

Relevant information
■ The trail is closed from mid-October to 31 March on account of the excessive summer temperatures.
■ You are advised to take anti-malaria precautions.

■ On account of currents, swimming in the Orange River can be dangerous and it is advisable to keep to shallow water.
■ Even during winter adequate protection must be taken against the sun.
■ Since there is no water between the huts on the first and third days, you must set off with a full water-bottle on these days.

How to get there The park is reached by turning right 8 km west of Kakamas onto the R359. About 24 km further on the park is signposted to the right and the entrance gate is about 5 km further on.

TRAIL ENVIRONMENT

Flora Although the park is situated in a low-rainfall area, the vegetation is characterised by a rich variety of plants, including several succulent species adapted to arid conditions.

Seventeen vegetation communities have been identified in the park, but only those you are likely to encounter are briefly discussed here.

The first section of the trail passes through riverine scrubland comprising trees such as sweet thorn, white karree, buffalo-thorn and wild tamarisk. Shrubs include river bush-cherry, Karoo bluebush and honey-thorn.

Characteristic among the cracks in and around the pink gneiss domes is the Namaqua porkbush, an odd-looking waxy succulent shrub. In the depressions between the gneiss domes the vegetation is dominated by black thorn, while stink-bush, jacket-plum and honey-thorn also favour this habitat.

On the first day's hike the trail passes through several large drainage lines where the dominant small-leaved Karoo boer-bean can be seen growing on rocky banks.

The vegetation along the Orange River consists mainly of honey-thorn bushes and wild tamarisk, while white karree, narrow-leaved spike-thorn, buffalo-thorn and ebony trees occur along the lowest reaches of tributaries of the Orange River.

The quiver tree is particularly abundant in the vicinity of the Swartrante, while species such as blue neat's foot and karree corkwood can be seen among the black boulders on the slopes of the Swartrante. They occur mainly on slopes with a north-westerly aspect, as these slopes are usually warmer than those with a south-easterly aspect, which are favoured by the rosyntjiehout (*Rhus populifolia*).

Fauna As it is situated in such an arid area, the main attraction of the park is not the game, although some 47 mammal species occur here. In July 1985 six black rhinos from the Etosha National Park in Namibia were reintroduced into the Augrabies Falls National Park, nearly 150 years after the last black rhino was shot in the area. The founder population has adapted extremely well and the first calf was born in October 1987. Since they are in the section of the park north of the Orange River you need not fear an unexpected confrontation.

The rock dassie is one of the most common mammals found in the park and will often surprise hikers with its shrill whistle before scuttling away to the safety of a rocky lair. Ground squirrel are also frequently sighted. Chacma baboon occur in the rocky koppies while vervet monkeys are attracted to the riverine bush.

In 1981 a small herd of springbok was reintroduced and populations now occur in the southern and northern sections of the park. Kudu migrated naturally into the park and small groups and individuals have established themselves successfully. Among the less frequently seen antelope are common duiker and steenbok, which prefer the open grassy areas.

Two rare species inhabiting the park are the aardvark and the aardwolf. Although it is seldom seen, the presence of the aardvark is evident from the numerous burrows. The aardwolf

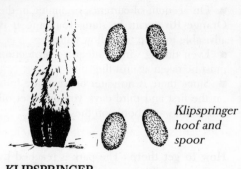

Klipspringer hoof and spoor

KLIPSPRINGER

The trail takes its name from the agile klipspringer. They usually occur in small family groups but are difficult to spot because their thick, bristle-like hair, which is speckled yellow and brown, blends in well with the surroundings.

The klipspringer's narrow, oval-shaped hooves are adapted to enable it to move with ease over difficult terrain. The legs appear unusually long because the animal walks on the tips of its blunt, rubbery hooves.

Klipspringer are often seen balancing daintily on sharp rocks

As they are principally browsers of various small shrubs, klipspringers can go for extended periods without drinking water, obtaining sufficient moisture from succulent greens.

---

appears to have increased since the proclamation of the park and is sometimes seen in the vicinity of the Swartrante.

Predators such as leopard, caracal and the black-backed jackal naturally control the rock dassie, baboon and rodent populations.

To prevent predators from leaving the park and preying on domestic stock on adjoining farms, the entire boundary fence of the park has been electrified.

In addition to the abovementioned mammals, a further 27 smaller mammal species have also been recorded.

To date some 195 bird species have been recorded in the park including *Red Data* species such as black stork, Ludwig's bustard and rosyfaced lovebird.

The African fish eagle is regularly seen along the river, while the black eagle nests in the gorges below the falls.

The broken veld is the habitat of species such as sabota, longbilled and spikeheeled larks, as well as grey-backed cisticola. Also represented are the chats, including tractrac, Karoo and anteating chats.

The riverine bush is the richest habitat for birds, supporting more than a quarter of the total number of species. Birds you are likely to see here include whitebacked mousebird, pied barbet, redeyed bulbul, dusky sunbird, masked weaver and whitethroated canary.

Species you may be lucky enough to tick along the Orange River are hamerkop, Egyptian goose, blacksmith plover, swallowtailed bee-eater, brownthroated martin and red bishop.

The park is also the habitat of no less than 33 gecko, agama, skink and lizard species. Among these is the red-tailed rock lizard (*Platysaurus capensis*) which can be seen on the rocks at the edge of the gorge. The females are a uniform grey-green, while the males can be identified by their red tails. Another species to keep an eye out for is the rock agama (*Agama atra*) with its distinctive blue head during the breeding season.

The sharptooth catfish (*Clarias gariepinus*) is the most numerous of the 14 fish species found in the Orange River. Its diet consists mainly of other fish and you will be able to spot it near the surface of the water from the viewpoint at the falls. It grows up to 2 m long and weighs up to 60 kg. It is likely that its enormous size, long whiskers and frightening appearance gave rise to the local legend of the water monkey, a mythological creature that is said to inhabit the depths of the river gorge.

A species of particular interest is the endangered Namaqua barb (*Barbus hospes*) which occurs only downstream of the Augrabies Falls.

History Several Middle and Later Stone Age sites have revealed the presence of very early inhabitants in the park. The area was also inhabited by the Khoikhoi and the last of their leaders to rule in the area was Klaas Lucas, after whom the island on which the rest camp is located was named.

The falls derived their name from the Nama word *Aukoerabis*, meaning "Place of the Great Noise". The early Khoikhoi knew the river as the *Gariep*, which means "river", and believed that this was the home of the legendary water monkey.

The first white person to see the falls was the Swedish soldier Hendrik Jacob Wikar, who deserted from the garrison at the Cape in 1775. Three years later, on 6 October 1778, he saw the *magtige groote waterval* ("the mighty waterfall") which tumbled down a cliff "... 2 maal zo hoog als't casteel" ("twice as high as a castle"). The name Aukoerabis was first recorded by Colonel Robert Gordon, the deputy commander of the garrison at the Cape.

Following Wikar's directions Gordon located the falls and in 1777 he renamed the Gariep River the Orange River, after Prince William V of Orange.

In 1824 the English traveller George Thompson named the falls the "Catheract of King George" and he was erroneously credited as having "discovered" the falls − a misconception which persisted until 1916 when Wikar's diary was published.

The first steps to conserve the falls were taken in 1954 when the Upington Publicity Association asked the National Parks Board to proclaim the area a national park. Several obstacles, including a diamond prospecting concession and the inclusion of the area as part of the Orange River Project, threatened the proclamation of the park, but it eventually took place on 5 August 1967.

In June 1988 the park was enlarged from 9 415 to 82 415 ha following the proclamation of the Riemvasmaak area as South Africa's second contractual national park. In terms of the agreement, Riemvasmaak will remain a military training area, but its conservation will be managed jointly by the South African National Defence Force and the National Parks Board.

The SANDF subsequently withdrew from the area, paving the way for the resettlement of the Riemvasmakers who were removed from the area in 1972 and resettled in Namibia and Ciskei.

Geology The Augrabies Falls is amongst the largest in the world and an excellent example of the weathering of granite by water.

Although the Augrabies landscape has been fashioned over the past 1 400 million years, the falls were formed some 1,8 million years ago when an upthrust of the subcontinent caused the river to flow more rapidly. The falls were originally at the lower end of the gorge, but over the millennia they have gradually eroded their way to their present position.

The Orange River drops some 90 m over a series of cataracts and rapids before plunging 56 m over the main falls. Rumours abound that the huge pool at the bottom of the falls, estimated to be 130 m deep, is a treasure-house of diamonds which have been trapped there over countless aeons.

In the vicinity of the falls you will see numerous river courses which are usually dry. Geological research has shown that the Orange River mainly follows a system of master joints where it has eroded faster than along the subordinate joints. In this way water is "stolen" from slow-forming channels, a geological process known as river piracy.

Below the falls the river flows for about 15 km through a narrow gorge with an average depth of 240 m. During normal flow the river has an average depth of 2 m, increasing to 8 m when the river is in flood. The average volume is 45 m³/second, but during the 1974 floods this increased to an incredible 7 000 m³/second, cutting off the park headquarters on Klaas Island for 14 days.

Most of the rocks in the park are composed of coarse-grained red biotite gneiss or pink gneiss. It resembles granite closely and contains the same main constituents, namely quartz, microline and albite-oligoclase, with subsidiary iron ore and biotite. When weathered, the gneiss rocks form large rounded domes, typically orange and brown in colour, and are characteristic of the scenery in the park.

The Swartrante, formed by erosion between 1 000 and 700 million years ago, are typical *inselbergen* (isolated "island" mountains).

TRAIL DESCRIPTION

Day 1: Rest Camp to Fish Eagle Hut The trail starts at the western corner of the camping/caravan site and is marked with the silhouette of a klipspringer on a yellow background and small klipspringer emblems and arrows painted on rocks.

The first part of the trail winds fairly close to the edge of the ravine, crossing several seasonal streams and rivers which split off the main stream just above the falls to form eight islands of different sizes and shapes, before merging below the falls.

About 2 km from the start the viewpoint at Arrow Point is reached and here you will have a magnificent view over the gorge and the Twin Falls. From here the trail swings away from the gorge to skirt the deep side canyon which has formed Arrow Point and crosses the channel further upstream to pass the potholes a short way further on. A detour to the potholes, marked "Maalgate" on the trail map, is worthwhile. Through the ages the swirling action of water has eroded these interesting potholes.

The trail then winds through pink gneiss rock formations which have been carved into fascinating shapes by wind, water and extremes of temperatures – huge boulders balancing on delicate pinnacles, isolated columns, deep crevices and small caves which offer shelter to small mammals, birds and reptiles.

Looking to the south, the scenery is dominated by a huge, dome-shaped boulder, aptly named the Moonrock. On the last day of the trail the route will take you up and over this familiar landmark.

You will then cross four fairly deep river valleys, including the Kurasie Seep, and about two hours beyond the potholes you will reach the Ararat Viewpoint where you will once again have a breathtaking view of the Orange River Gorge.

About 30 minutes further you will reach Afdak – a shelter which has been built on the edge of the gorge. Do not count on enjoying the scenery in solitude as the viewpoint is accessible by car and popular with visitors to the park. Stone tables and seats under cover provide a comfortable escape from the heat with the added attraction of a superb view of the river. Although the hut is close by, this is a good lunch spot.

The final kilometre to Fish Eagle Hut is along a jeep track and is easily completed in 15 minutes. The hut is situated on the northern end of the Swartrante and the area is littered with quartz and semi-precious stones. Tempting though such booty may be, remember that it is an offence to collect rocks or any other objects in a national park. Leave the stones untouched, therefore, for other hikers to enjoy.

As the afternoon is usually spent at leisure at the hut, it is a good idea to follow the next day's route down to the river for a refreshing dip.

Day 2: Fish Eagle Hut to Mountain Hut From the hut the trail follows a well-cairned route along a drainage line, passing through an area where diamond prospecting took place during the late 1950s. The river is reached after about 30 to 40 minutes and here the smooth granite walls of the gorge give way to a deeply dissected landscape. Although on a much smaller scale, the descent and scenery are reminiscent of the Fish River Canyon.

The first section along the river is fairly rocky and is not well marked, but since the trail follows the course of the river downstream, there is no possibility of getting lost. After about 0,5 km the river swings abruptly north only to swing west again 1 km onwards at Echo Corner.

The river bank becomes more sandy, making the going more difficult, and after about 90 minutes' walk through the sand you will reach Witkruiskrans, named after the nest of black eagles nearby.

Leaving the river, the trail follows Diepkloof, a dry river course. This section is particularly attractive, especially after rain when the water seeps over the smooth rock banks in the riverbed. After a while the route swings east, following another wide drainage line for about 30 minutes, before swinging south into another river course to reach the mountain hut 10 to 15 minutes later. The hut is situated amongst a jumble of large rock piles and the scenery is especially attractive towards late afternoon.

Day 3: Mountain Hut to Rest Camp From the hut the trail follows a jeep track across a wide grassy plain where you may see springbok. After branching off to the left you will ascend steadily up the slopes of the Swartrante and from the top of the ridge you will have an expansive view over the park. The black rocks

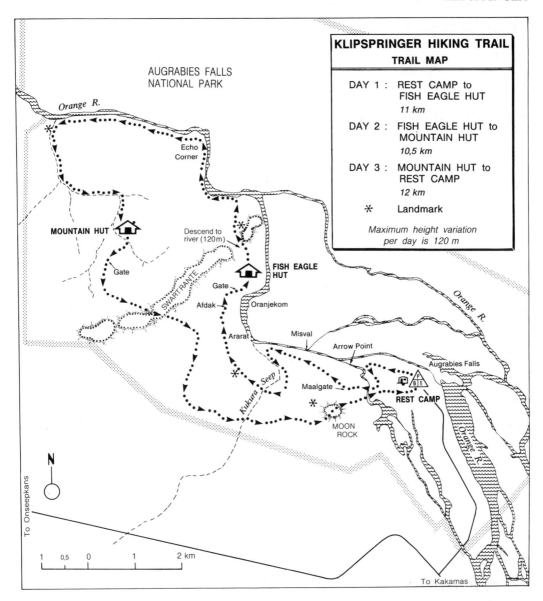

AUGRABIES FALLS
NATIONAL PARK

Orange R.

Echo
Corner

KLIPSPRINGER HIKING TRAIL
TRAIL MAP

DAY 1 : REST CAMP to
FISH EAGLE HUT
11 km

DAY 2 : FISH EAGLE HUT to
MOUNTAIN HUT
10,5 km

DAY 3 : MOUNTAIN HUT to
REST CAMP
12 km

✳   Landmark

*Maximum height variation
per day is 120 m*

MOUNTAIN HUT

Descend to
river (120m)

Gate

**FISH EAGLE
HUT**

Gate

SWARTRANTE

Afdak

Oranjekom

Orange R.

Ararat

Misval

Arrow Point

Augrabies Falls

Kukura Seep

Maalgate

REST CAMP

MOON
ROCK

Orange R.

N

To Onseepkans

1   0,5   0   1   2 km

To Kakamas

of the Swartrante are often mistaken for dolerite, an igneous rock, but consist of quartzite-rich granulite. Granulite is a metamorphic rock which is white on freshly broken surfaces, but becomes black with weathering.

The trail then winds down the eastern slopes of the Swartrante and traverses another grassy plain dotted with quiver trees. A short way further on you will cross the road to Afdak before joining the main tourist road which is followed until you reach the turn-off to the Moonrock.

From the parking area the trail leads up and over the Moonrock and from the crest you will have a 360-degree view of the park surroundings. Here you will see the continual exfoliation process − large slabs of rock flaking off in layers. This is caused by extreme temperatures. While the temperature of the inner rock remains fairly constant, the outer rock is heated up during the day. At night the exterior cools down more than the interior, causing the rock to crack and flake. From the Moonrock it is about 3 km to the end of the trail, with the route passing mainly through sandy veld.

OORLOGSKLOOF

The relatively unexplored Oorlogskloof Nature Reserve near Nieuwoudtville on the Bokkeveld escarpment offers you a choice of a three- or four-day route; or alternatively you can blaze your own trails. The trails wind through an interesting variety of plants and reveal dramatic scenery – deeply dissected valleys hemmed in by sheer cliffs, sandstone formations sculpted into fascinating arches and expansive views. Unlike most other hiking trails, there are no overnight huts and you will sleep under the stars.

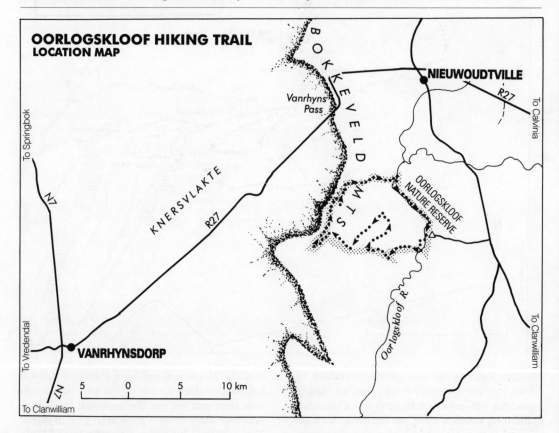

OORLOGSKLOOF HIKING TRAIL
LOCATION MAP

TRAIL PLANNER

Distance Kransduif route: 46 km; 3 or 4 days

Grading B+

Reservations The reserve is administered by the Cape Nature Conservation Department. Only telephonic reservations are accepted, Telephone (022) 921-2289. On 1 February reservations open for March to June, on 1 June for July to October and on 1 October for November to February. Enquiries about the trail can be made at (02726) 8-1159.

Climate

Average daily maximum summer temperatures at Oorlogskloof range between 27 °C and 31 °C, while minimum temperatures are generally low. During winter day temperatures are moderate, but nights are cold, with the average minimum temperature for June being 4 °C. Oorlogskloof lies within the winter rainfall region and most of the area's annual rainfall of 500 mm is recorded between April and August. June and July are the months with the highest rainfall.

Group size Minimum 2; Maximum 12
Three groups of 12 are allowed per day.

Maps The trails are marked on a photocopy of the 1 : 50 000 topographical map, sections 3119CA and 3119AC. It is useful, though, to carry the topographical maps, especially if hiking the wilderness option.

Facilities Only basic campsites with pit toilets and water are provided on the trail.

Logistics Circular route. A basic campsite is available at the Populierbos, also known as Driefontein, about 10 minutes' walk from the car park. Two wooden huts, accommodating 10 people each, are planned.

Relevant information

■ At the end of summer many of the streams will be dry, making it essential to confirm water points with the officer in charge at Nieuwoudtville, Telephone (02726) 8-1159.

■ Backpacking stoves should be carried as fires are not permitted along the trails.
■ Since no overnight shelters are provided on the trails hikers should consider carrying a backpacking tent during winter and spring when rain can be expected.
■ As the terrain is fairly rugged, stout footwear – preferably boots – is recommended.
■ Precautions against mosquitoes are advisable.
■ After heavy rains, crossing the Oorlogskloof River on the first day can be a problem. A series of pole bridges without handrails span the river and hikers with a fear of heights could find this rather daunting. Usually, however, it is possible to boulder-hop across the river.
■ At the end of the first day on the Kransduif Trail and on day two of the Geelbekbosduif Trail there is an emergency route. You must follow the path to a jeep track where you turn right, continuing for 10 km to the nearest farmhouse. The jeep track passes Brakwater Camp.

How to get there Travel to Nieuwoudtville and leave the town along Voortrekker Street, joining a gravel surface road. About 16 km after leaving the town a signboard indicates the turn-off to the Oorlogskloof Nature Reserve on your right. Pass through the farm gate, keep left at a split after 2 km, drive over the dam wall and continue past the farmhouse to reach the parking area about 7 km after turning off the main road.

TRAIL ENVIRONMENT

Flora Since the area lies in the transition zone from mountain fynbos and mountain renosterveld to the flora of the Karoo, an interesting variety of plants is encountered along the trail.

The vegetation in the reserve, which lies at the northernmost limit of distribution of mountain fynbos, is dominated by mountain fynbos. The fynbos occurs mainly on the top of the plateau and in the west of the reserve the percentage of reeds and rushes is significantly higher than in the east.

Between July and September numerous flowering bulbs add a blaze of colour to the fynbos, but their flowering times are influenced by the

rainfall. Among these are the mauve *Moraea tripetala*, which flowers between August and December, as well as a wide variety of gladioli, watsonias and red-hot pokers (*Kniphofia* spp.).

Among the protea species occurring are wagon tree, Clanwilliam sugarbush, laurel sugarbush and real sugarbush. Other representatives of the protea family include *Leucospermum calligerum* which has globose, creamy-yellow flowers between July and January, *Leucadendron procerum* and *L. sheilae*.

The sprawling *Aloe mitriformis*, which reaches the northern limit of its distribution here, is unlikely to escape your attention. The thin stems are too weak to support the heavy clusters of densely spiralled leaves and the stem usually lies on the ground.

Fynbos trees and shrubs include nana berry, real wild currant, kuni-bush, rock candlewood, sand olive and sea guarri.

Short, dense mountain forest communities occur in river valleys with perennial water. Dominant species here are Breede River yellowwood, rock candlewood, Cape saffron, spoonwood and wild olive.

The Karroid shrub veld occurs on shale and mudstones in kloofs and is dominated by renosterbos (*Elytropappus rhinocerotis*), kapokbos (*Eriocephalus ericoides* and *E. africanus*) and botterboom (*Tylecodon paniculatus*). Other conspicuous species include geelmelkbos (*Euphorbia mauritanica*), as well as several pelargonium species. An interesting species to keep an eye out for is the elephant's foot (*Dioscorea elephantipes*), which has a partly exposed, roughly textured rootstock measuring up to 60 cm in diameter. The best example of the Karroid shrub veld community occurs in the Kobee Valley.

Fauna Antelope you chance seeing are common duiker, klipspringer, steenbok and grysbok, as well as grey rhebok.

Small predators occurring in the area naturally include aardwolf, caracal, African wild cat and small-spotted cat. Bat-eared and Cape foxes have also been recorded, while leopard pass through the area occasionally. In the river valleys the numerous scats of the Cape clawless otter betray their presence.

Other species recorded include chacma baboon, honey badger, striped polecat, small-spotted genet, suricate, aardvark and rock dassie.

Among the 138 bird species recorded to date in Oorlogskloof and the Kobee area further south are the rock pigeon and the rameron pigeon, after which the Kransduif and the Geelbekbosduif routes respectively have been named. Four main habitat types have been identified: riverine, bush, fynbos and Karoo.

Species attracted to the open pools in the Oorlogskloof include hamerkop, black stork, Egyptian goose and South African shelduck, as well as African black and yellowbilled ducks. In the adjoining riverine vegetation keep an eye out for olive thrush, European reed, African marsh and African sedge warblers, as well as grassbirds and Levaillant's cisticola.

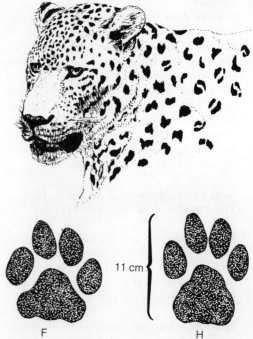

Leopard – classified as rare – occur in the Oorlogskloof Nature Reserve, but are rarely seen owing to their secretive nature

The bushy valley slopes and patches of kloof forest are the habitat of speckled, whitebacked and redfaced mousebirds, as well as Cape robin, titbabbler, barthroated apalis, Cape batis and yellowrumped widow.

Species you could see in the fynbos on the plateau are Cape sugarbird, as well as malachite, orangebreasted and lesser doublecollared sunbirds.

The Karoo habitat attracts species such as Ludwig's bustard, Namaqua sandgrouse, longbilled lark, greybacked finchlark, southern grey

Yellowbilled duck are attracted to open pools in the Oorlogskloof

tit and Karoo chat. Also recorded in this habitat type are sicklewinged chat, Karoo robin and rufouseared warbler.

Among the birds of prey you might see are blackshouldered kite, black, booted and martial eagles, as well as steppe and jackal buzzards. Lanner falcon, rock and greater kestrels, black harrier and gymnogene are other possibilities.

The pools in the lower reaches of the Oorlogskloof River are the habitat of three fish species which are endemic to the Olifants River System. The sawfin (*Barbus serra*) is considered vulnerable, while the Clanwilliam yellowfish (*Barbus capensis*) and the Clanwilliam sandfish (*Labeo seeberi*) are classified as rare. The chubbyhead barb (*Barbus anoplus*), which has a much wider distribution extending to Natal and the Transvaal, also occurs.

History The abundance of water throughout the year in an otherwise arid area, wild fruit and game, attracted Stone Age people to the area. Several rock painting sites have been identified in this area, which also attracted Khoikhoi pastoralists.

By the early 1700s the northern frontier of the Cape Colony had expanded north of the Olifants River, resulting in several clashes between the white settlers, the San and impoverished Khoikhoi who had reverted to a hunter-gatherer lifestyle. In one such clash in the northern Bokkeveld, a kraal belonging to Jantjie Klipheuwel was attacked by a commando on 25 September 1739. Thirteen Khoisan were killed and a number wounded, while the rest surrendered. A total of 162 cattle, 209 sheep, three horses and five rifles were captured. During the attack, which took place at dawn, an officer, Captain Hendrik Debes, was wounded in the head, while a Khoi soldier was killed. This skirmish gave rise to the Afrikaans name of the river - *oorlog* means "war".

One of the earliest explorers in the Bokkeveld Mountains was Carl Thunberg, who travelled through the *Bokkeland* in 1774, describing it as extremely bare with only a few farms and Khoi herders. He was followed by William Patterson, who descended the northern slopes of the Bokkeveld Mountains in August 1778, while John Barrow explored the eastern foothills of the range in 1798.

The small settlement of Nieuwoudtville was established on land bought from the Nieuwoudt brothers by the Dutch Reformed Church in 1897. During the late 1920s/early 1930s farmers started settling in the Oorlogskloof area and some of the stone structures which they built can be seen in the reserve.

Covering some 5 570 ha, the Oorlogskloof Nature Reserve was established during the International Year of the Plant in 1983. The Southern African Nature Foundation played a leading role in this regard by providing the necessary funds for the purchase of the land.

TRAIL DESCRIPTION

KRANSDUIF ROUTE

Day 1: Driefontein to Doltuin Camp From the car park you will head south and less than 10 minutes after setting off you will drop down into a poplar grove. A basic campsite, which is ideal for hikers arriving in the late afternoon, is reached a short way further on. Braai places are available here.

Quite suddenly you will start descending steeply into the Oorlogskloof River Valley, scrambling down the cliff face. You will then traverse just below the base of the cliffs to reach a cairn after a while. Keep left here since the trail to the right is the return route on the last day. A pleasant surprise awaits you a little way further on - a small seep has been dammed up, providing a welcome drink. Another seep is passed 30 minutes later and shortly thereafter several large stone structures dating back to the days of the pioneering farmers, known as Kameel se Gat, are reached. Kameel was a black farmworker who lived here towards the end of the 1800s and the early 1900s.

You will lose some 100 m in altitude going down to the river and, depending on how agile you are, the descent can take up to an hour. Unless the river is in flood, it is easily crossed and the inevitable ascent commences immediately. Fortunately the gradient is not too punishing and about 45 minutes after leaving the river you will reach the base of the cliffs. Here you can quench your thirst under an overhang where a small cement dam retains water seeping slowly through the rocks.

Next, a chimney of a few metres has to be negotiated but two well-secured ropes assist

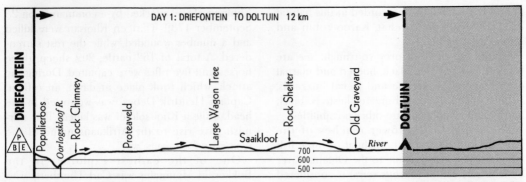

DAY 1: DRIEFONTEIN TO DOLTUIN 12 km

DRIEFONTEIN · Populierbos · Oorlogskloof R. · Rock Chimney · Proteaveld · Large Wagon Tree · Saaikloof · Rock Shelter · Old Graveyard · River · DOLTUIN

700
600
500

hikers up this otherwise tricky section onto the plateau. Keep to the left here as this is where the Geelbekbosduif route branches off to the right.

The walking is relatively easy now with the path winding through impressive stands of proteas and other typical fynbos plants. Towards the 4 km mark you will descend through a small kloof where you will no doubt be impressed by the enormous wagon trees. For the next few kilometres the trail skirts the broken edge of the plateau and dips through some small valleys with the rugged rock formations adding an interesting variety to the trail. In a few places the geological history is revealed to hikers and you are sure to notice bands of quartz pebbles in the sandstone.

Between the 5 and 6 km markers a pulpit-shaped rock is descended via a well-positioned ladder and a stream, running well into summer, is crossed a short way further on. There are many suitable lunch stops along this section but one worth waiting for is reached less than 20 minutes after the 6 km mark, where the trail leads through a cool rock shelter.

After the 7 km mark the trail veers away from the cliffs and the walking pace again quickens as you cross the plateau with stands of proteas flanking the path in places. Donkeys which ran wild many years ago are often seen here. You will descend gently from about the 9 km mark, passing a few graves under wild olives to the left of the trail. From the graves it is just over half an hour's walk along the river valley to the Doltuin Camp. The word "Dol" comes from the Afrikaans for "digging up", a reference to the small patches of cultivated fields where the early farmers established small-scale farms. These areas are now extensively invaded by renoster-bos (*Elytropappus rhinocerotis*).

The camp is well shaded by a few tall laurel sugarbush trees and if the stream close to the camp is dry, water can usually be obtained by following the emergency exit route to the base of the cliffs, a few minutes' walk away.

Day 2: Doltuin Camp to Pramkoppie Camp
The first few kilometres continue in a south-westerly direction, ascending at the head of the valley. Ten minutes after passing the 3 km mark you will pass through the first of ten rock arches encountered on this day. After the 4 km mark the trail levels out and meanders along the edge of the plateau, passing some interesting sandstone sculptures, and about 2 km further the route forces you to crawl through a narrow passage.

A few minutes after passing the 8 km mark a signboard indicates a 2,6 km detour to Arrie se Punt. Backpacks can be left here as you will return to this point. About half an hour after setting off on the detour, another signboard directs you to a viewpoint 200 m onwards. At 915 m this is the highest point on the trail and the detour is certainly worthwhile as you are rewarded with a magnificent panorama. On a clear day you will see the flat-topped Gifberg and Vanrhynsdorp.

Returning to the start of the detour, you will skirt the edge of the escarpment with the sheer cliffs dropping away at your feet. Along this section, rockpools have been weathered into the sandstone and must be attractive after rain.

After rejoining the main trail you will cross a nek and then descend to traverse the plateau dotted with proteas. After 1 km of easy walking you will descend into a small kloof known as Kouekloof, crossing a seasonal stream. Returning to the edge of the plateau, you will have expansive views of the almost desolate plains some 600 m below and then wind down through a rocky section. Close to the 15 km mark you will pass through two large caves before rounding Pramkoppie, named after its

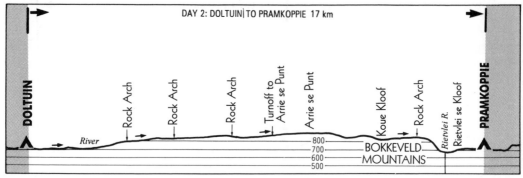

DAY 2: DOLTUIN TO PRAMKOPPIE 17 km

DOLTUIN — River — Rock Arch — Rock Arch — Rock Arch — Turnoff to Arrie se Punt — Arrie se Punt — Koue Kloof — Rock Arch — Rietvlei R. — Rietvlei se Kloof — PRAMKOPPIE

800 — 700 — 600 — 500 — BOKKEVELD MOUNTAINS

resemblance to a breast, and then descend steeply into the valley where the overnight camp is situated.

You will turn right onto a jeep track which is joined a few minutes beyond the 16 km mark. A mere 5 minutes further you will reach the delightful camp tucked away under a clump of shady wild olive trees, a haven for bird-watching. After good rains, water is available from a stream just behind the campsite.

Day 3: Pramkoppie Camp to Brakwater Camp From the overnight camp you will follow a jeep track for about 10 minutes before the Klein Heiveldvoetpad splits off to your left. Be sure to take this trail and do not continue along the jeep track! A forested kloof is reached a few minutes further on and after ascending steadily for about 10 minutes the shady forest is left behind.

Another 30 minutes of hiking brings you to the top of the plateau and from here it is a short walk to the 250 m detour leading to another viewpoint. Once again you are rewarded with expansive views of the Knersvlakte which stretches from Vanrhynsdorp in the south to Bitterfontein in the north, with the Sandveld forming the western boundary. Various explanations of the name have been suggested, one being that early travellers gnashed on their teeth

when they crossed the hot, dusty, waterless plain. It has also been suggested that the area was originally known as the Knecht's or Servants' Vlakte after the early tenants who were known as *knecht van de staat* ("servant of the state"). Looking north you will see the 8 km-long Vanrhyn's Pass which was originally built by Thomas Bain.

For the next few kilometres the trail traverses the plateau with the Rietvlei River Valley constantly in view and then dips in and out of a small kloof where you might find water in winter.

Almost two and a half hours after leaving the camp the trail winds away from the plateau edge to take you to Spelonkkop past an old stone leopard trap, another relic of the early farmers. A short way further on the trail seemingly comes to a dead end at a sheer cliff. However, after careful inspection you will notice a chimney with a ladder to your right. The section that follows is quite taxing – you have to make your way slowly over, around and past a jumble of enormous boulders. It is easy to wander off the trail here, so keep a sharp lookout for the trail markers. After emerging from this maze you will have a 2 km downhill walk to the Brakwater Camp, which is also beautifully shaded by wild olive trees.

You can almost always count on a swim at the

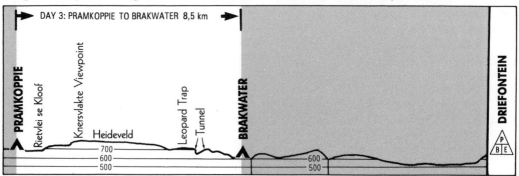

DAY 3: PRAMKOPPIE TO BRAKWATER 8,5 km

PRAMKOPPIE — Rietvlei se Kloof — Knersvlakte Viewpoint — Heideveld — Leopard Trap — Tunnel — BRAKWATER — DRIEFONTEIN

700 — 600 — 500 — 600 — 500

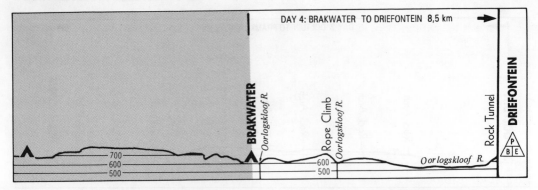

DAY 4: BRAKWATER TO DRIEFONTEIN 8,5 km →

Brakwater Camp as it is situated alongside the Oorlogskloof River.

Day 4: Brakwater Camp to Driefontein Car Park

From the camp you follow the jeep track through the river and continue steeply up the slope called Jakkalskop. Not more than 15 minutes after setting off you will join a path leading off to the right. The path ascends steadily to the base of the cliffs and shortly after the 2 km mark you will be able to quench your thirst with ice-cold water from a seep which has been dammed. Ten minutes beyond the seep a ladder and a rope will help you onto the plateau to avoid an otherwise impassable stretch.

After a short three-minute detour you will scramble down to below the cliffs again and close to the 3 km mark you will descend steeply to the river along a section with loose shale. Quite soon, however, you will reach the river where some delightful pools make this a good tea spot.

For the next few kilometres the trail undulates slightly, remaining close to the river and mainly under cover of the riverine bush. Shortly before the 7 km mark you will emerge from the bush and ascend until reaching the cliff base at the 8 km mark. About 10 minutes further on you will crawl through the final rock tunnel of the trail behind a waterfall, so watch out for the rocks which are very slippery. A short distance further on the downward route of the first day is joined. From here it is about 20 minutes to the car park.

Although days three and four can be done in one day this is not advisable because of the demanding terrain.

ALTERNATIVE ROUTES

The Geelbekbosduif route covers 37,5 km and can be hiked in three or four days. Hikers are also free to blaze their own trails.

CEDERBERG

Few mountain regions in southern Africa can boast the magnificent scenery of the Cederberg. Centuries of wind and rain have sculpted extraordinary rock formations out of the soft sandstone and gnarled cedar trees seemingly grow from the rocks on the highest peaks, while several rare plant species such as the snow protea and the rocket pincushion can be found only in this range. The Cederberg is criss-crossed by an extensive network of well-maintained footpaths and today it is one of the most popular backpacking and climbing areas in South Africa.

TRAIL PLANNER

Distance A large number of routes are available to backpackers. Options range from day excursions from a base camp to weekend and week-long trips.

Grading B and C, depending on the route taken

Climate

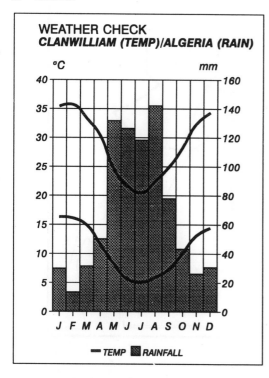

WEATHER CHECK
CLANWILLIAM (TEMP)/ALGERIA (RAIN)

— TEMP ■ RAINFALL

Reservations The wilderness area is administered by the Cape Nature Conservation Department. Only telephonic reservations are accepted, Telephone (022) 921-2289. On 1 February reservations open for March to June, on 1 June for July to October and on 1 October for November to February.

Group size Minimum 2; Maximum 12
The wilderness area has been divided into three zones: the northern zone, which includes Pakhuis and Skerpioensberg, the central area extending southwards to the Wolfberg and the western and southern part which includes Sneeuberg, the Maltese Cross and the south-western extremity of the wilderness area. A maximum of 50 people per day is permitted into each zone, including privately owned property.

Maps The 1 : 50 000 map of the Cederberg, published by the Forestry Branch, is the most detailed map of the area. Paths, huts and rock formations are clearly indicated as well as interesting features such as an old leopard trap, an old cedarwood station and two blockhouses.

Facilities Stone huts without any facilities, originally built for rangers patrolling the area, are available at Boontjieskloof, Middelberg, Crystal Pool, Sneeukop, Sleepad and Sneeuberg. They are occupied

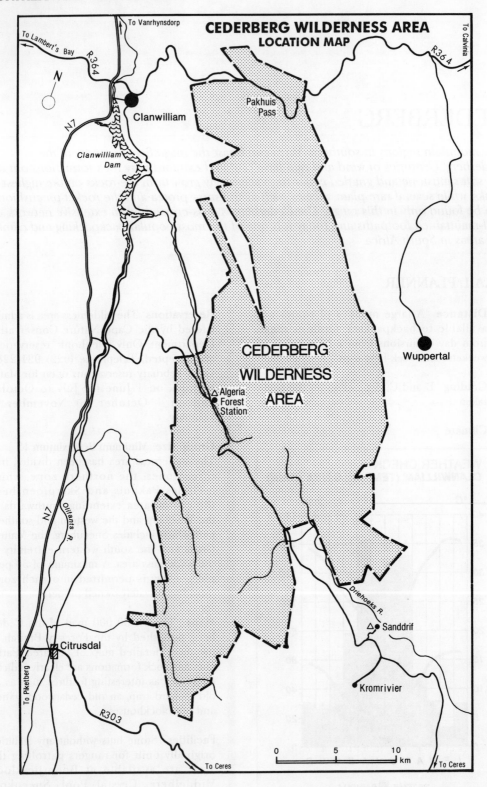

CEDERBERG WILDERNESS AREA
LOCATION MAP

To Vanrhynsdorp

To Lambert's Bay

R364

To Calvinia

R364

N

N7

Clanwilliam

Pakhuis
Pass

Clanwilliam
Dam

Wuppertal

CEDERBERG
WILDERNESS
AREA

Algeria
Forest
Station

Olifants R.

Driehoeks R.

Sanddrif

Citrusdal

To Piketberg

Kromrivier

R303

0   5   10
km

To Ceres

To Ceres

on a first come, first served basis, but conservation officials enjoy priority. Alternatively, you may camp wherever you wish in the wilderness area.

Logistics In many instances circular routes are possible. However, when traverses are tackled two vehicles are necessary because of the remoteness of some of the starting/ending points.

The campsite at Algeria Forest Station has ablutions with hot and cold water, fireplaces and picnic tables and there is a beautiful swimming pool in the Rondegat River. A smaller campsite is available at Kliphuis in the Pakhuis Pass.

At Uitkyk, 5 km south of Algeria, there are two restored farmhouses, accommodating seven and 14 people respectively. They are equipped with bunks with mattresses, a shower, toilet and fireplace. You must supply your own firewood, cooking utensils, crockery and cutlery and bedding.

Reservations for Algeria, Kliphuis and Uitkyk should be made when obtaining your permit.

Sanddrif on the farm Dwarsrivier, 30 km south of Algeria, has campsites, as well as cottages equipped with beds, a stove and fridge, hot and cold water and flush toilets. Reservations can be made with Messrs

Nieuwoudt, Dwarsrivier, P O Cederberg 7341, Telephone (027) 482-2825. The Cederberg Tourist Park on the farm Kromrivier, about 6 km further on, has campsites and bungalows. Reservations must be made with the Cederberg Tourist Park, Private Bag Kromrivier, P O Citrusdal 7340, Telephone (027) 482-2807.

Relevant information
■ Fires are strictly forbidden in the wilderness area and it is essential to carry a backpacking stove.
■ Since huts are occupied on a first come, first served basis, it is advisable to carry a tent, especially during winter when snow could occur.
■ During summer many of the streams and pools could be dry.
■ A daypack is useful for day trips up Cederberg, Tafelberg, Sneeuberg and to the Maltese Cross.

How to get there The main entry point is along the provincial road which branches off the N7, 26 km north of Citrusdal. You follow the road for about 17 km before you reach Algeria. From Algeria, the road continues over the Cederberg Pass to Welbedacht, Eikeboom, Dwarsrivier, Kromrivier and finally Ceres.

TRAIL ENVIRONMENT

Flora The vegetation consists of mountain fynbos with a rich variety of species endemic to the Cederberg range.

One of the most striking proteas, the snow protea (*Protea cryophila*), is endemic to the Cederberg. The specific name means "fond of the cold", a fitting description, for these plants are often completely covered in snow during the severe winter months. They are limited to the highest mountain summits between altitudes of 1 750 and 1 900 m, stretching for about 25 km from Sneeukop to Sneeuberg. The immature pure white flowers resemble a fluffy snowball but when they open during February, they reveal their red inner surfaces.

The striking rocket pincushion (*Leucospermum reflexum*) is also endemic to the Cederberg, occurring only in the north-east of the range. The name is derived from the crim-

son-red flowers which curl outwards to resemble a pointed rocket-head. *L. reflexum* var. *luteum* with its exceptionally beautiful pale yellow flowers also occurs but is less frequently found.

Several other members of the protea family

The crimson-red flowers of the rocket pincushion create a spectacular display between July and December

CEDAR TREE

The range takes its name from the Clanwilliam cedar which grows only in the Cederberg range from Pakhuis Pass in the north to the Maltese Cross in the south.

As a result of exploitation by early woodcutters and uncontrolled fires, these trees are confined to scattered populations on rocky outcrops and mountaintops at altitudes between 1 000 and 1 650 m. The Clanwilliam cedar belongs to the cypress family and is therefore not related to the cedar trees of the Middle East and North Africa, which belongs to the pine family. The closely related Willowmore cedar also has a very limited distribution and is restricted to the Baviaanskloof and Kouga mountains in the eastern Cape. The mountain cypress has a much wider distribution, occurring as far north as Mount Mulanje.

Bleached skeletons of cedar trees are a familiar sight in the Cederberg

It normally grows between 5 and 7 m high but trees in protected places can reach up to 20 m in height with a trunk diameter of up to 2 m. The massive, gnarled old trees are a characteristic sight, as are the bleached skeletons of trees devastated by fires. The leaves of the young trees are needle-like in contrast to the adults' scale-like leaves which grow up to 4 mm long.

occur in the Cederberg. The wagon tree grows as a gnarled tree usually reaching up to 5 m, although old specimens reach up to 7 m tall and 1 m in diameter. Some fine specimens can be seen in Sederhoutkloof.

The common name was given to the tree because it provided wood for wagon making and brake blocks.

Other proteas include *Protea punctata*, the Cederberg protea (*P. acuminata*), *P. laevis* and the dwarf green protea (*P. acaulos*).

Among the ericas growing on the slopes and among the rocky outcrops are the pink *Erica eugenia*, *E. inflata* and *E. junonia*, while the large white *E. monsoniana* and the red and yellow Malay heath (*E. thunbergii*) can also be seen.

During February masses of red disas (*Disa uniflora*) create a spectacular display along the stream banks, while the dry fynbos between 730 and 990 m is the habitat of *Disperis macrocorys*, which is endemic to the Cederberg. This orchid grows up to 17 cm tall and the slender plants bear a single pale yellow flower during September and October. A more common orchid to be on the lookout for on dry mountain slopes between 300 and 1 000 m is *Disa filicornis*. Flowers varying from white to deep pink can be seen from October to December.

Two plants of considerable economic impor-

tance also occur in the Cederberg. Rooibos tea (*Aspalathus linearis*) bushes grow as multi-branched erect shrubs of up to 2 m high. The leaves and stems of the plant are harvested and dried and are then ready to be used for brewing tea. This species occurs naturally in the Gifberg near Vanrhynsdorp and the Calvinia and Clanwilliam areas where it is cultivated commercially. The last harvest of rooibos tea in the wilderness area took place in 1969, before which some 4 000 kg were harvested annually.

The sale of buchu (*Agathosma betulina*) was also an important source of income. During the last two decades of the 1800s and the beginning of this century more than 45 000 kg were harvested annually in the western Cape. It grows as a compact shrub about half a metre high although it can reach up to 1,5 m. The leaves have a distinct aroma, and are used for making buchu brandy, vinegar and buchu oil.

Fauna The mammals of the Cederberg are similar to those occurring in the mountains of the south-western Cape, but because it borders on the Karoo, certain Karoo species are also found here.

Mammals you are most likely to see are rock dassie, chacma baboon and klipspringer which inhabit the rocky areas, while grey rhebok favour the mountain plateaus. Grysbok and common duiker also occur but are less frequently seen.

In 1991 the first leopard sanctuary in South Africa was set aside in the Cederberg, one of the last few areas in the Cape with a sizable leopard population. Covering some 2 300 km², the sanctuary comprises the wilderness area, adjoining farmland and water catchments, and has an estimated population of 30 to 40 adult leopards. Research has shown that leopards occur mainly below the 1 200 m contour in the Cederberg, with home ranges varying from 40 to 69 km².

Other predators include African wild cat, caracal, bat-eared and Cape foxes, as well as aardwolf – a species listed as rare, but seldom seen on account of its nocturnal behaviour. Among the numerous smaller mammals is the spectacled dormouse, locally known as the namtap. Despite its wide distribution, relatively little is known about this nocturnal rodent which is considered to be rare.

Some 200 bird species have been recorded in the Clanwilliam district, while at least 81 species have been identified in the Cederberg. The cliffs and gorges are the habitat of species such as rock pigeon, black swift, rock martin and red-winged starling.

Species you are most likely to see on the rocky slopes include ground woodpecker, Cape and sentinel rock thrushes, mountain and familiar chats and the Cape rockjumper.

Among the birds of prey, black eagle and rock kestrel are the most common. Other raptors include the blackshouldered kite, steppe buzzard and the African marsh harrier.

Greywing and Cape francolins inhabit the fynbos scrub and often you only become aware of their presence when they scurry out from the fynbos alongside you. Typical fynbos species include Victorin's warbler, Cape sugarbird, orangebreasted sunbird, Cape siskin and protea canary.

History The area between Citrusdal and Clanwilliam is rich in rock art dating back to the Later Stone Age, with a large concentration in the Pakhuis Pass, while the plains surrounding the Cederberg were inhabited by groups of pastoral Khoikhoi who preferred the more grassy areas.

The first recorded contact between whites and the San was in 1655 when an expedition of Jan Wintervogel encountered a San party and described them as "... of very small stature, sub-sisting meagrely, quite wild, without huts or anything in the world, clad in skins like the Hottentots and speaking almost as they do".

The first trekboers settled along the banks of the Olifants River at the beginning of the 1700s. Trouble soon arose when the farmers intruded upon the traditional hunting domains of the San, who retaliated by raiding farms. To counter the raids a commando system was initiated in 1715 and during the last commando raid in 1772, over 500 San were killed and 293 captured between Piketberg and the Sneeuberg north of Graaff-Reinet. It therefore appears unlikely that the San inhabited the area after the turn of the eighteenth century.

The earliest reference to cedarwood was made in 1700 by Governor Simon van der Stel, who described the wood as suitable for use by farmers wanting to settle in the area. The missionary-traveller Charles Barrow listed it as one of the usable trees of the Cape in his work of 1796 and the German naturalist Henry Lichtenstein described it as good timber wood.

In October 1805 the Livestock and Agricultural Commission reported that people living in the Cederberg made their livelihood by cutting timber in the forests which they calculated to be about "four hours long and half an hour wide". They predicted that the forests would soon be destroyed if the felling continued and extracted a promise from the woodcutters that they would sow seeds in the kloofs during April each year. This was the first attempt to regenerate the forests by human agency.

In 1836 the British geographer Sir James Alexander visited the cedar forests and complained bitterly about the wanton destruction and uncontrolled burning. Eight years later the German traveller W von Meyer visited the area and voiced similar complaints.

A forest ranger was appointed in 1876 to exercise control over the Cederberg, but since he was stationed at Clanwilliam it was impossible for him to do this effectively. Although only dead trees were allowed to be exploited from 1879, the Superintendent of Woods and Forests wrote in his annual report of that year that about 1 000 poles were ready for use as telegraph posts. Five years later it was reported that cedarwood had been used as telegraph posts between Piketberg and Calvinia. Assuming one pole was used every 40 m, 7 250 poles would have been required over the distance of 290 km.

The French forester who was appointed Superintendent of Woods and Forests of the Cape Colony in 1880, Count M de Vasselot de Régné, visited the Cederberg in 1882. Earlier in his career he had worked in North Africa and the Cederberg apparently reminded him so much of the Atlas Mountains that he suggested the name Algeria for the forest station. George Bath was appointed the first forest ranger in 1905 and gave the station the name suggested by De Régné.

During the 2nd Anglo-Boer War (1899-1902) several skirmishes between the Boers and the British took place in the Cederberg. To limit the movement of the Boer forces across the Cederberg the British built blockhouses to guard narrow passages, the remains of which

can still be seen at Krakadouwpoort in the northern Cederberg and at Boskloof near Citrusdal.

The grave of Lieutenant G V W Clowes, also known as the Englishman's Grave, in the Pakhuis Pass is another reminder of the war. Clowes, a member of the 1st Gordon Highlanders, was riding well ahead of his scouting party when he ran into a Boer commando. He was gunned down when he charged the Boers with his sword drawn and was buried near the spot where he fell on 30 January 1901.

The Cederberg Wilderness Area, 71 000 ha of state forest land, was proclaimed on 27 July 1973 and was the third such area to receive this status in South Africa.

TRAIL DESCRIPTION

The Cederberg lends itself to creating a large variety of routes, ranging from short weekend outings to more extensive backpacking expeditions lasting several days. A few of the more popular routes are described here and these can be combined to create a variety of longer trails. Times and distances are approximate.

ALGERIA, CRYSTAL POOL AND UITKYK CIRCUIT

This is a popular weekend excursion which offers a number of options, depending on the fitness of the group.

Day 1: Algeria Forest Station to Crystal Pool
After passing through the gate at the top end of the campsite, you will cross a tributary of the Rondegat River and follow the path leading up the right-hand side of Helsekloof. Fortunately, the ascent is not as formidable as the name (Hell's Ravine) suggests, with the path following a gradual zigzag. About 30 minutes from the start the trail passes through a cedar plantation, established between 1896 and 1919. The plantation was established with the financial assistance of the railways with a view to obtaining wood for sleepers and was originally known as the Railway Plantation.

About halfway up the kloof a eucalyptus belt is reached and a detour to the left here leads to a beautiful waterfall which is particularly impressive after rain. During February red disas (*Disa uniflora*) can be seen clinging precariously

to the damp rocks. You then continue through cedar plantations and you should reach the plateau about two hours after setting out, with Middelberg huts being reached a short way further on.

The huts were built in 1903 for patrolling purposes and cedarwood was used for all the woodwork. The nearby stream with its small pools is a welcome resting spot on a hot day. The distance from Algeria to Middelberg is about 5 km and is usually covered in about three hours.

The route to Crystal Pool is joined immediately south of the huts and follows a gradual zigzag up to the Geelvlei Plateau. Further along Cathedral Rock with its fluted towers and crenellated spires is seen on your right. The path winds across Grootlandsvlakte and you will pass several turn-offs to the right which should be ignored. The first two lead to Uilsgat Needles, while the third continues to Sleepad Hut.

After continuing across the plain for about 1 km the path swings north and follows the Wildehoutdrift for about 1 km before reaching Groot Hartseer, where you will gain about 150 m in altitude over a short distance. Once the plateau is reached it is about 30 minutes' easy walk to Crystal Pool. Several striking burnt-out cedar trees are passed and the route snakes vigorously to avoid numerous large boulders.

Crystal Pool is idyllically situated in a small amphitheatre and if the weather is fine you can camp among some huge boulders along the

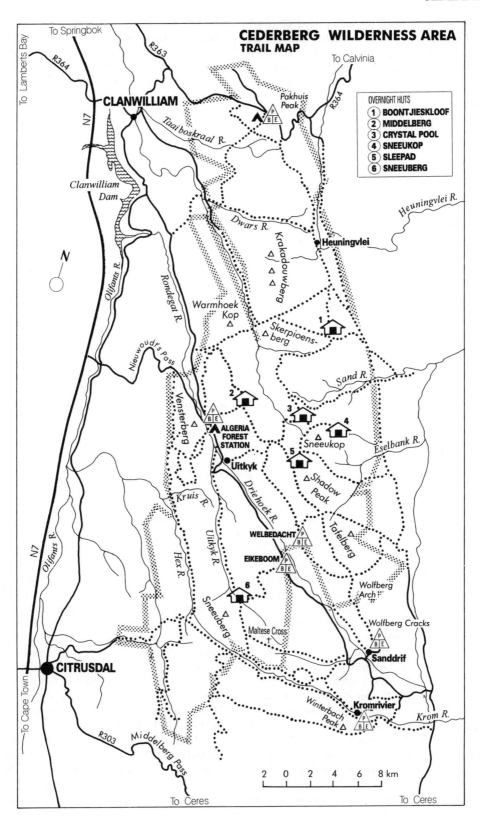

CEDERBERG WILDERNESS AREA
TRAIL MAP

To Springbok
To Lamberts Bay
R363
To Calvinia
R364
N7
CLANWILLIAM
Taaiboskraal R.
Pakhuis Peak

OVERNIGHT HUTS
1 BOONTJIESKLOOF
2 MIDDELBERG
3 CRYSTAL POOL
4 SNEEUKOP
5 SLEEPAD
6 SNEEUBERG

Clanwilliam Dam
Olifants R.
Heuningvlei R.
Dwars R.
Krakadouwberg
Heuningvlei

N

Warmhoek Kop
Skerpioens-berg
Sand R.
1

Rondegat R.
Nieuwoudt's Pass
Vensterberg
2
ALGERIA FOREST STATION
3
4
Sneeukop
Eselbank R.

Uitkyk
5
Kruis R.
Driehoek R.
Shadow Peak
Tafelberg

Hex R.
Uitkyk R.
WELBEDACHT
EIKEBOOM
6
Wolfberg Arch
Wolfberg Cracks

N7
Olifants R.
Sneeuberg
Maltese Cross
Sanddrif

CITRUSDAL
Winterhoek Peak
Kromrivier
Krom R.

To Cape Town
R303
Middelberg Pass

2 0 2 4 6 8 km

To Ceres
To Ceres

stream at the head of the valley. Red disas are prolific along the stream in mid-summer and the large pool close to the campsite is an excellent place for a refreshing dip during summer.

Should bad weather force you to seek shelter, you first have to cross Klein Hartseer before reaching the hut. Since there is no water at the hut during the dry summer months, it is advisable to fill your water-bottles before ascending Klein Hartseer as the closest water to the hut is about 10 minutes' walk beyond the hut. About four hours should be allowed to cover the 11 km leg between Middelberg and Crystal Pool.

Day 2: Crystal Pool to Algeria via Sleepad Hut and Uitkyk

From Crystal Pool you have the option of either retracing your steps and descending to Uitkyk or you can continue to Sleepad Hut before descending to the Grootlandsvlakte and then to Uitkyk.

Although the day's hike covers about 20 km the extra effort required on the latter alternative is well worth the effort. The route is, however, not recommended for the unfit!

From Crystal Pool you continue in a north-easterly direction for about 10 minutes (ignore the turn-off to the left) before reaching Engelsmanskloof, where you turn right. Over the next 1,5 km you will gain about 200 m in altitude, passing spectacular scenery – massive red cliff faces, rock formations towering like baroque castles, lichen-clad overhanging rocks and a rock balancing precariously on the edge of a precipice.

A jeep track is joined at the shale band (locally known as Die Trap – "The Step") below Sneeukop about an hour after setting off and you will follow this in a southerly direction for roughly 45 minutes before you arrive at Sleepad Hut. During November the mountain slopes are covered with masses of watsonias and in February large clumps of red disas can be seen flowering along the streams.

The view from the hut is magnificent with wide panoramas of the greater part of the Cederberg range. If you decide on a more leisurely trail and overnight here, the late afternoon is particularly spectacular when the harsh grey rocks slowly change colour – first to a golden yellow, then orange, blue and mauve, finally melting away with the darkness of the night.

Water is obtainable from a stream close to the hut and it is possible to have a refreshing shower under a small cascade just below the hut.

Sleepad (Sledges' Way) was named after the route taken by ox-drawn sledges that were used to drag the equipment of the British astronomer Thomas Mann up to the shale band. Mann set up his station on Sneeukop in 1843 to measure the arc of the meridian.

From Sleepad you will descend steeply to Grootlandsvlakte, losing about 200 m in height, and you will then follow the path to Algeria for a short while before branching off to the left. After about 1,5 km you will turn right onto the path which winds down Die Gat to Uitkyk for the next hour. The route provides stunning views, but it is advisable to make an early start as the afternoons in Die Gat can be very hot. From Uitkyk it is about 90 minutes' walk along Van Der Merwe's trail to Algeria.

WELBEDACHT TO SANDDRIF

This route takes you through some of the most spectacular scenery in the Cederberg, including Cederberg Tafelberg, the Wolfberg Arch and the Cracks. Although two vehicles are required for this traverse it is possible to extend the trail by another day by returning along the jeep track to Welbedacht.

Day 1: Welbedacht to Tafelberg

Welbedacht is reached by taking the left turn-off to Driehoek farm about 14 km south of Algeria. Follow the road for a short distance before turning left onto the road to the old forest station post. From the parking area you must walk along a track through a pine plantation and after crossing Driehoeks River continue to the old homestead.

Behind the old homestead the path zigzags steadily up the kloof and you will see some fine specimens of the Clanwilliam cedar. Shortly before reaching the top of the kloof (about two hours after setting off) a track leads off to the right to Welbedacht Cave, also known as Die Klipgat. The cave can accommodate about 15 people but it is unsuitable in winter as the north-westerly wind drives rain straight into it. Water can usually be obtained from the stream in Welbedacht Kloof.

This is an ideal base camp for an ascent of Cederberg Tafelberg, the second highest peak in the range. From the cave it is a short climb to the jeep track where you will turn right, following the track for about 1 km to a cairn marking the turn-off to Tafelberg. Head for the saddle between Tafelberg and Consolation Peak and then for the top of the gully between Tafelberg and the Spout.

Keep an eye out here for a gully branching off to the left, following it until your progress is blocked by a chimney which is quite smooth, but easily accomplished provided you do not suffer from vertigo. Cederberg Tafelberg is only 60 m lower than Sneeuberg and from the summit you will have a magnificent view over the Cederberg range and the Tanqua Karoo to the east.

Head back along the same route you used for the ascent to reach Welbedacht Cave about five to six hours after setting off.

Day 2: Welbedacht Cave to Wolfberg Arch
Returning to the jeep track, you will initially follow the route of the previous day. However, do not take the detour at the cairn to Tafelberg, but continue along the jeep track which follows the contour. As you start descending slightly you will notice the kloof draining the shelf between Consolation Peak and Tafelberg, as well as Corridor Peak on your left. A few minutes later you will cross the appropriately named Waterkloof Stream.

Continuing over easy terrain, you will remain on a contour below Corridor Peak for another 1 km before dropping down to a stream. With about 2,5 km remaining the track descends steadily to Die Rif, which is about 8 km from Welbedacht Cave.

During the hot summer months the cool shade of the oak trees at Die Rif provides a most welcome rest stop. Before setting off, remember to fill your water-bottles as you are unlikely to find any water until you reach the Wolfberg Arch.

The small cedar forest at the foot of Gabriel's Pass is one of only five places in the Cederberg where the Clanwilliam cedar – which normally grows on the Peninsula Formation – occurs on the Nardouw Formation above the shale band.

From Die Rif the path zigzags to the top of Gabriel's Pass, from where you have a magnificent view of Sneeuberg to the south-west and the Tanqua Karoo to the east. After a short descent the path leads off to the right and you will ascend to the plateau along a well-cairned route. The section between Die Rif and the Wolfberg Arch is normally covered in one to one and a half hours.

The impressive Wolfberg Arch is most imposing when approached from this direction, standing isolated like the portal of a ruined cathedral. Centuries of wind, rain and extremes of temperatures have carved a nearly symmetrical archway of about 15 m into the soft sandstone. Looking through the arch you can gaze down over the Tanqua Karoo and the Bokkeveld Mountains in the hazy distance.

From the arch you will follow a well-marked route through rocky terrain in a south-easterly direction and looking back you will have a completely different perspective of the arch. You can look for water at the stream draining the plateau, but it should not be relied on.

Day 3: Wolfberg Arch to Sanddrif via Wolfberg Cracks The Wolfberg Cracks are about one and a half to two hours further south along a route which winds past fascinating rock formations. At times the formations create a lunar landscape in which human figures, faces and animals seem to leer at you.

You should take care when approaching the cracks as there are two far less spectacular cracks lower down to the right and you must be sure to follow the cairns.

The cracks consist of a vertical cleft 30 m deep which has been forged through the sandstone of the Wolfberg. In one place the cracks are so narrow that you have to squeeze feet first through a tiny passage blocked by huge chockstones and in another place it is necessary to hang onto a ledge in order to drop 2 m down to a lower level. This might sound a bit hairraising, but it is quite manageable.

Once you have overcome these obstacles, the cracks widen considerably and you will see one of the most spectacular formations in the Cederberg – two enormous natural rock arches with spans of 29 m and 20 m respectively.

Another fascinating feature of the cracks is the spectacular colours that glow on the vertical stone walls in various shades of orange, ochre, yellow, rust brown and deep red, depending on the time of day.

The final stretch once again forces you to crawl along a narrow passage and finally, about an hour after first entering the cracks, you emerge into the open. Straight ahead the tapering Cederberg range is framed by an enormous archway, while to your right you can enjoy a breathtaking view of Dwarsrivier, framed by 30 m high cliffs. After passing through the arch the path descends to the right, traverses a narrow ledge and then seemingly comes to a dead end. At this point you have two options. You can either descend via a chimney at the far end of the ledge or you can scramble down the far end of the ledge where there are a number of good hand- and footholds. On your right is the wider, second crack which is normally used as a return route by backpackers exploring the cracks only.

From here the descent is steep and it is necessary to take care, especially after rain. You will lose about 350 m in altitude during the descent which takes 45 minutes to an hour.

At the bottom of the descent you will join up with a jeep track with the route to the right leading to Sanddrif a short way further on, about 9 km after setting off from the arch.

The Wolfberg Cracks are on private property and the necessary permit must be obtained from Messrs Nieuwoudt of the farm Dwarsrivier.

EIKEBOOM TO SNEEUBERG HUTS AND CEDERBERG PASS VIA DUIWELSGAT

This is another enjoyable weekend trip but unfortunately it requires either a two-car party or arrangements with "fetchers" as the starting and ending points are about 11 km apart.

Day 1: Eikeboom to Sneeuberg Huts The start of this route is about 17 km south-east of Algeria on the main provincial road to Ceres and can easily be recognised by the clump of oak trees on the right-hand side of the road.

The Maltese cross, one of the fascinating rock formations of the Cederberg

The route follows the jeep track up Sederhoutkloof and after about 1,5 km passes a well preserved stone leopard trap. About half a kilometre further you will pass through one of the finest stands of waboomveld in the western Cape. The route ascends steeply along the southern slopes of the valley, passing a deserted farm, Hoogvertoon, on the plateau.

Looking north-west some of the best preserved specimens of Clanwilliam cedars can be seen among the crags and outcrops of the Koerasie Mountain. On the plateau the road covers fairly level terrain and after about 2 km a fairly indistinct shortcut leads off to the right. After ascending a small ridge the terrain once again levels out, with Sneeuberg dominating the scenery straight ahead.

About 2 km further the track ends at the Sneeuberg Huts, roughly three hours after setting off. The huts are situated at the foot of the mountain from which they take their name and one of them is an ingenious shelter built amongst the boulders directly behind the first hut. The huts are an ideal base camp for exploring the Maltese Cross and Sneeuberg itself.

The Maltese Cross is situated about 5 km south-east of the huts and is reached in about one and a half to two hours. You must join the path immediately behind the huts and after about 10 minutes you will ascend to the shale band at the base of Sneeuberg, gaining about 100 m in altitude. The remainder of the route covers fairly easy terrain.

The 20 m-high formation, a pillar broadened at the upper end to form a cross, is also known as the Cross of the Cedars. The cedars have long since disappeared and the Maltese Cross now keeps a lone watch over the area.

In rock climbing terms the Maltese Cross is graded as F3 and has been described as a serious pitch with bad protection. The first ascent was made in 1949 by two climbers, Goodwin and Bacquiere. In their account they reported: "It was then that we found traces which we decided could only be made by baboons ... Evidently, then, baboons are more than a match for man in the most delicate rock-climbing...". A more likely explanation is that the droppings were those of eagles, possibly the black eagle.

More adventurous and fitter backpackers will find the ascent of Sneeuberg a worthwhile excursion. The ascent not only reveals spectacular views, but Sneeuberg is also one of the best localities to see the magnificent snow protea

(*Protea cryophila*) which flowers during late January and February.

Setting off from the Maltese Cross you will retrace your steps towards the Sneeuberg Huts for about 1,5 km. Midway along Sneeuberg a turn-off to your left is marked with a cairn close to where the trail makes a short descent to a stream. Turn left and continue up the gully, which is well marked with cairns. It should not take you more than two hours to reach the nek just below Sneeuberg and by that time you will have gained some 400 m in altitude.

The final ascent to the summit is also well marked along the south-eastern side of the peak and involves two rock scrambles which most backpackers should manage. You will gain some 200 m in height and about 45 minutes should be allowed for the ascent and 30 minutes for the descent. From the highest peak in the Cederberg (2 027 m) you are rewarded with indescribable vistas of the Cederberg range and on a clear day you can even see Table Mountain, some 150 km away. Across the valley is Cederberg Tafelberg, which is only 60 m lower than Sneeuberg, the Wolfberg and the wide fertile valley of the Dwars River. Looking south-east you can see Citrusdal, the Olifants River Valley and Boskloof, which used to be a popular access point to the southern Cederberg in years gone by. To the north-east the landscape is dominated by the majestic Krakadouw Peaks.

You will return along the same route, turning left when you reach the path on the shale band which is followed for about 45 minutes to the huts. The round trip from the Sneeuberg Huts takes between seven and eight hours.

The Maltese Cross is on private property and the necessary permit must be arranged in advance with Messrs Nieuwoudt of Dwarsrivier.

Day 2: Sneeuberg Huts To Cederberg Pass via Duiwelsgat From the huts the path leads north-west across easy terrain for about 3 km before descending towards Duiwelsgat along Noordepoort. The path clings to the western slope of Koerasieberg and takes you past some of the most spectacular scenery in the Cederberg. The route mainly follows the 1 100 m contour, with magnificent views of the rugged Duiwelsgatkloof on your left, before ascending at the head of the kloof. Some fine cedar trees are passed on the ascent and later on you will

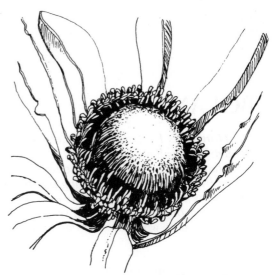

The snow protea – a species endemic to the Cederberg

pass an old cedarwood station on your left, where logs were stored before being taken down the mountain.

At Slangvlei the path levels out before dropping down to Klein Duiwelsgat, where a steep descent awaits you. You will initially follow the course of the Uitkyk River and the path then drops down into the kloof formed by Smalberg on your left and Uitkyk se Piek to the right.

Roughly five to six hours after setting off, the path ends at the hairpin bend on the Cederberg Pass, about 6 km from Algeria. If a vehicle has been left at Algeria you can either follow the road back to Algeria or hike up Cederberg Pass, and descend along Uitkyk Pass, following Van der Merwe's Trail back to Algeria for about an hour. Although the latter route is longer, it is a worthwhile deviation, time permitting. The descent along the old Uitkyk Pass starts at the summit of the Cederberg Pass, about 3 km from the hairpin bend.

Before the construction of the Cederberg Pass in 1969 the old pass had the distinction of being one of the steepest passes in South Africa – with a gradient of 1:10, it climbs some 300 m in just over 3 km.

From the old Uitkyk Forest Station at the bottom of the pass you can continue to Algeria either along the gravel road or along Van der Merwe's Trail, which winds along the Rondegat River.

BOLAND

The Hottentots-Holland and Limietberg sections of the Boland Hiking Trail take you through deep valleys, past high challenging mountain peaks and across amber-coloured mountain streams. Situated in the heart of the Cape Floral Kingdom, the trails are characterised by a profusion of flowering plants. Although winter and spring are the most colourful seasons, every season presents its own floral display. The trails are conveniently close to Cape Town, offering a choice of several two- and three-day options on the Hottentots-Holland section, while the two-day Limietberg section further north links two well-known passes.

Aspects common to both sections of the Boland Hiking Trail are discussed in this general introduction.

TRAIL ENVIRONMENT

Flora The vegetation of the Limietberg and Hottentots-Holland mountains has been classified as mountain fynbos, the collective name for the richly varied fine-leaved vegetation of the mountains of the western and south-western Cape. Mountain fynbos occurs in a 40 to 150 km-wide belt from Nieuwoudtville to the Cape Peninsula, stretching eastwards for 800 km to Port Elizabeth, with isolated patches occurring as far east as Grahamstown.

Although covering only 0,04 per cent of the world's land surface, this vegetation type is so rich that it has earned itself the status of one of the six floral kingdoms in the world. Research of comparative land areas has shown that fynbos is three times richer than its nearest competitor, with more than 1 300 species per 10 000 ha as against 420 for its nearest rival in Central America.

There are at least 8 550 species of flowering plants in the Cape Floral Kingdom, which covers a mere one per cent of South Africa's total land surface. It is dominated by the erica (605 species), protea (300 species) and restio (reeds and rushes) families. The monocotyledonous families are represented by over 1 336 species, of which some 625 species belong to the iris family. Sadly, nearly 65 per cent (more than 1 300 species) of all endangered plants in South Africa occur in fynbos.

Some 1 150 fynbos species have been recorded in a 45 km² area at Jonkershoek, while several hundred other species have been recorded elsewhere in the Hottentots-Holland Nature Reserve.

The ericas are represented by more than 150 species. Among those easily identifiable are the green heath (*Erica sessiliflora*) with pale green tubular flowers and the showy orange-red *E. curviflora*, which flowers between March and June. Also striking is the beautiful four sisters heath (*E. fastigiata*) with its pink star-shaped flowers which can be seen between August and January.

In spring the pink, bell-shaped flowers of *E. sitiens* create a spectacular display on the southern slopes near Landdroskop.

Seventeen protea species, as well as several other members of the protea family, have been recorded in the reserve. The attractive Kogelberg silver bottlebrush, which has been chosen as the trail emblem, occurs in small, scattered populations from the Franschhoek/Hottentots-Holland mountains, extending eastwards to the Riviersonderend Mountains. It grows up to 1,5 m tall and during a slight breeze its silky hair presents a striking display. The flowers, a combination of red, silver and a touch of yellow, can be seen during April and May.

The uppermost slopes are dominated by

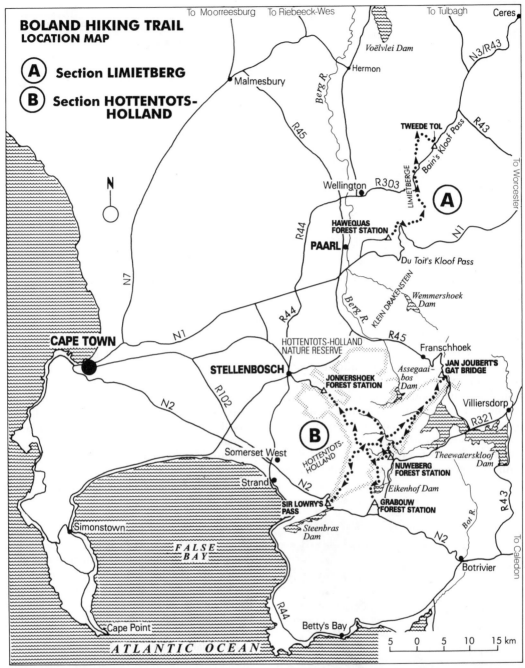

BOLAND HIKING TRAIL
LOCATION MAP

Ⓐ Section **LIMIETBERG**

Ⓑ Section **HOTTENTOTS-HOLLAND**

restios such as *Elegia grandis* and the russet brown *Restio bifarius*, while the brunia family is represented by several brunia, berzelia and nebelia species.

Among the orchid species you are likely to see are the red disa (*Disa uniflora*), which flowers between January and March, and *D. tripetaloides* which flowers between November and January.

Other flowering species likely to attract your attention include the red crassula (*Crassula coccinea*), which produces bright crimson flowers in mid-summer, the white and yellow inkblom or white harveya (*Harveya capensis*), which turns black when damaged, and the dainty gay-faced blue lobelia.

Although the flora of the Limietberg is similar to that of the Hottentots-Holland Mountains,

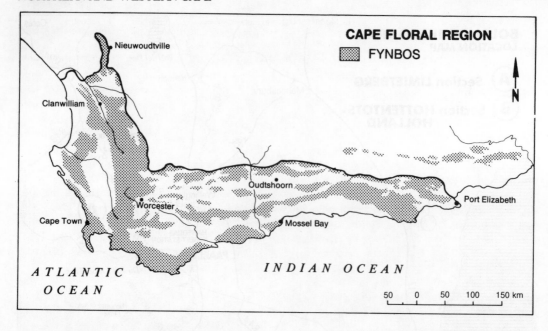

CAPE FLORAL REGION

FYNBOS

the veld is generally sparser, with fewer dense stands of Proteaceae and Bruniaceae. Keep an eye out, however, for the beautiful mountain protea (*Protea nana*), which rarely grows taller than 1 m. The nodding wine-crimson flowers are best seen between mid-winter and late spring. Also keep an eye out for *Leucospermum lineare*, a species which is restricted to the mountains from Bain's Kloof to Jonkershoek.

Another eye-catching species is the katstert

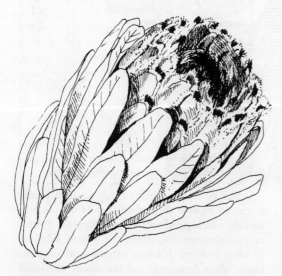

The scientific name of the bearded sugarbush (Protea magnifica) *refers to its magnificent flowers*

(*Bulbinella frutescens*) which creates a spectacular display on the Suurvlakte in spring with its bright yellow flowers.

The banks of the Wit and other rivers are densely vegetated by lance-leaved myrtle and water white alder, while good stands of rockwood, sand olive and false ironwood occur towards Tweede Tol.

Those interested in the flora of the area will find Lee Burman and Anne Bean's *Hottentots Holland to Hermanus* wild flower guide useful.

Fauna As in other Cape mountains, the fauna of the Boland mountains is neither spectacular nor plentiful. Animals which you are most likely to see are chacma baboon, grey rhebok and rock dassie. The grysbok favours densely bushed areas at the lower elevations, while you could chance upon klipspringer in rocky areas of the higher slopes.

The smaller mammals are represented by several rodent species, including Cape spiny mouse, Smith's rock elephant-shrew and the striped mouse. Porcupine also occur, but since they are nocturnal you are unlikely to see them. Discarded porcupine quills or the occasional holes they dig in search of bulbs often betray their presence.

Leopards occur, but because of their stealthy and nocturnal habits they are seldom seen. Other predators include black-backed jackal, caracal, Cape clawless otter, small grey mongoose and small- and large-spotted genets.

The birdlife of the Boland mountains is considerably poorer than that of the savanna and Transvaal Lowveld areas and about 100 species occur regularly in the fynbos areas.

Typical fynbos species include Victorin's warbler, orangebreasted sunbird and protea canary. The Cape siskin occurs on the rocky slopes, while the Cape sugarbird has a preference for proteas and migrates with the seasons. In winter and early spring it is usually found on the lower slopes where it feeds on the nectar of blue and real sugarbushes. In summer and autumn, however, it is found on the higher peaks where species such as the Hottentot white sugarbush and the peach protea (*P. grandiceps*) occur. The rocky areas provide a habitat for black and Alpine swifts, ground woodpecker and Cape and sentinel rock thrushes. Also to be found here are mountain and familiar chats, Cape rockjumper and bokmakierie.

Birds of prey of the rocky areas include black eagle, jackal buzzard and rock kestrel.

A reptile of particular interest is the Hawequa flat gecko (*Afroedura hawequensis*) which was only discovered in 1985. Occurring from Bain's Kloof to the Franschhoek Mountains, its distribution is centred on the Hawequas Mountains. The body is covered by six dark brown transverse bands, with yellow spots at the edges of the bands. It inhabits narrow cracks in sandstone rock, but since it is nocturnal you are unlikely to see it.

History Archaeological research in the Jonkershoek Valley has confirmed the presence of Early Stone Age people in the region about 90 000 to 150 000 years ago.

In more recent times the Boland mountains and surrounding areas were occupied by the San, who were known to the Khoikhoi as the *Obikwas*. The name was originally interpreted to mean "murderer" but is nowadays understood to mean "fishermen". One of the mountains passed near the end of the first day's hike of the Limietberg still bears the name Obiekwaberg.

The valleys and plains below the mountains were inhabited by groups of Khoikhoi who arrived at the Cape with their sheep about 2 000 years ago and acquired cattle later.

The name Hottentots-Holland dates back to a visit to the area by three farmers in June 1657 to buy cattle from the Peninsular Khoikhoi. According to an inscription in the diary of Jan van Riebeeck, the Khoikhoi regarded the area as their "Holland" or "fatherland". On 3 May 1672, the Hottentots-Holland and False Bay areas were ceded to the Dutch East India Company by the Chief of the Peninsular Khoikhoi, Kuiper.

The rugged mountain range between the Cape and the interior was once considered the limit of civilisation and was promptly called the Limietberg by the early settlers at the Cape.

The Berg and Olifants river valleys were the home of the Cochoqua Khoikhoi who followed a seasonal migration route with their livestock. This route took them to Table Bay around November/December from where they would cross the Cape Flats, arriving in what is today Stellenbosch in January. They then continued to the Paarl area and along the Berg River to where Wellington is today, swinging westwards to complete the circle.

Before the arrival of the first white people the gigantic granite domes above Paarl were familiar landmarks to the Khoikhoi, who camped in the summer at the foot of what was known to them as the Tortoise Rocks.

In October 1657 the fiscal, Abraham Gabbema, set off on an expedition to the interior to buy cattle. He was the first white man to set foot in the Berg River Valley and on 22 October his party saw two gigantic domes which sparkled like gems in the rising sun, inducing him to name them "the Paarl and the Diamant". These domes are now known as Gordon and Bretagne rocks.

LIMIETBERG

This popular weekend hike winds along the Hawequas and Limiet mountains, linking the Du Toit's Kloof and Bain's Kloof passes. Situated close to Cape Town, the trail winds through typical fynbos with spectacular mountain scenery. Junction Pool, a longstanding favourite with Cape hikers, invites the weary hiker for a refreshing dip towards the end of the first day. The second day offers uninterrupted views of the patchwork of farmlands and the large natural pools at the end of the trail are most welcome on a hot day.

Aspects common to both sections of the Boland Hiking Trail are discussed in the general introduction which should be read in conjunction with this chapter.

TRAIL PLANNER

Distance 36 km; 2 days

Grading B +

Climate

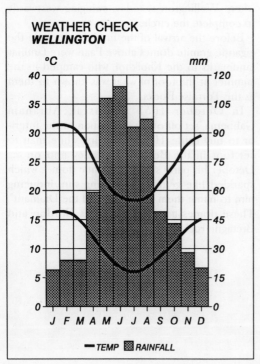

WEATHER CHECK
WELLINGTON

— TEMP ▨ RAINFALL

Reservations The Reservations Officer, Private Bag X1, Uniedal 7612, Telephone (021) 886-5858, Fax (021) 886-6575. Reservations are accepted up to a year in advance.

Group size Minimum 2; Maximum 12

Maps The trail is indicated on a photocopy of the 1 : 50 000 topographical map and is forwarded with your receipt and permit.

Facilities Overnight accommodation along the trail consists of a wooden hut with bunks and mattresses, water, refuse bins and toilets.

Logistics Linear route without any public transport, necessitating two vehicles. There is no hut at the start of the trail, but Tweede Tol, where the trail ends, has excellent camping facilities. The campsite is, however, closed between June and September.

Reservations are essential and should be made through the Hawequas office.

Relevant information
■ As the trail winds through open fynbos with hardly any shade, protection against the sun is advisable.

■ Fires are not permitted at the hut, so you will need a backpacking stove.

■ There is little water on the second day's hike and it is advisable to fill water-bottles before leaving the pass, especially in the dry summer months.

■ The second day's hike is fairly demanding and should not be attempted in bad weather.

■ A permit is required to use facilities at Tweede Tol where the trail ends.

How to get there The start of the trail at the Hawequas Conservation Area office is reached by taking the R101 turn-off on the N2 north of Paarl. Turn left at the stop sign and continue to the route signposted to Hawequas.

TRAIL DESCRIPTION

Day 1: Hawequas Forest Station to Limietberg Hut The trail commences at the Hawequas office, ascending steadily through an area which used to be under pine plantations. After about 5 km the Du Toit's Kloof Pass is reached and here you will join a tarred road leading off to the left.

The mountains to the south-east were named after a French Huguenot farmer, Francois du Toit, who settled on the farm Kleinbosch, close to the start of the trail, in 1692. In the early days the pass was nothing more than a track used by animals as a migration route. The first efforts to improve the route to the interior were made in 1824, but it was only 1949 that the Du Toit's Kloof Pass was completed. Most traffic now uses the Huguenot toll tunnel, which was completed in 1988 and is nearly 4 km long.

From the top of the pass you will follow the tarred road which provides access to a post office tower until just beyond the 8 km mark. Here the trail branches off to the right to wind across Suurvlakte. After skirting New Year's Peak (1 327 m), the trail swings north and descends gradually along the eastern slopes of the Hawequas Mountains. Dominating the scenery ahead is Groot Wellington Sneeukop

(1 685 m), the second highest peak in the Slanghoek Mountains.

Close to the 14 km mark you will reach Junction Pool which is at the confluence of the Wit River and a tributary between New Year's Peak and Krom River Peak. Like most rivers flowing through fynbos vegetation, the water of the Wit River is brown, which makes the name somewhat incongruous. The river is in fact named after the white river stones and the white effect created by the numerous rapids, waterfalls and cascades.

The remaining 4,5 km of the day's hike follows the Wit River in Paradise Valley which is named after Paradise Kloof, a precipitous valley carved into Klein Wellington Sneeukop. About 2 km before the hut the trail joins a jeep track and a short way further on you will pass over a furrow in the rock by means of a small concrete bridge. While assisting his father in the construction of Bain's Kloof Pass, Thomas Bain conceived the idea of redirecting water from the Wit River to the Berg River Valley, which was experiencing a drought. The furrow, known as the *Boerevoor* or *Die Witrivier Grip*, was constructed by a local farmer in 1856.

To the left of the track is Hugo's Rest, built

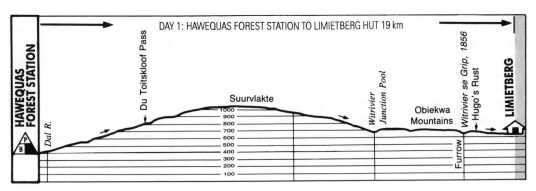

DAY 1: HAWEQUAS FOREST STATION TO LIMIETBERG HUT 19 km

The orangebreasted sunbird is often seen extracting nectar from watsonias and proteas

by P J Hugo and notorious for the stories of bad luck surrounding it. Hugo died before he could occupy the house and in 1949 a veld fire destroyed the building. After a couple had been murdered there by an escaped convict in 1978, the ruins were demolished and the site is now barely visible. Also nearby is a large flat tombstone marking the Hugo family grave.

About 1 km further is a memorial to a student and three would-be rescuers who drowned in 1895 during an outing to Klein Wellington Sneeukop by students and teachers of the Huguenot College in Wellington. One of the students, Lettie de Jager, was marooned after a flash flood, causing her death and that of her three would-be rescuers.

The Limietberg Hut is situated about 100 m from the Wit River in the appropriately named Happy Valley. Late in the afternoon you can enjoy the scenery as Deviation Buttress and Klein Wellington Sneeukop fade into the darkness. The beautiful swimming pool close to the hut is particularly appreciated on a hot summer's day.

Day 2: Limietberg Hut to Tweede Tol The trail continues along the jeep track to reach Bain's Kloof Pass after about 2 km. It is advisable to fill water-bottles here as water is usually not available until one starts descending Wolwekloof.

The pass is named after Andrew Geddes Bain who was born in Scotland in 1797 and came to South Africa at the age of 19. He established his reputation as a road builder after helping a group of people build the Onderberg Pass and then voluntarily supervising the construction of the Van Rhyneveld's Pass. In 1837 he was appointed by the Royal Engineers to build roads in the eastern border areas and his first assignment was to build a road from Grahamstown to Fort Beaufort.

Bain explored the area in 1845 and construction of the Bain's Kloof Pass commenced in 1849, to be completed in 1853. Convict labour was used and the unmarked graves of 21 prisoners who died during the construction of the pass are situated a short way off the trail in Bain's Kloof Village.

After crossing the road, the trail starts to climb eastwards into the Limietberg, which was considered to mark the limit of civilisation by the early settlers at the Cape. The trail then levels off as you continue northwards on the slopes below Limietkop. Presuming you have made an early start, a rewarding breakfast stop with a wide uninterrupted view of the area is reached after about 6 km. To the south lie Simonsberg and the Franschhoek Mountains and in the distance Table Mountain can be seen on a clear day. Dominating the foreground are the massive granite domes balancing above Paarl, while to the north you will see Voëlvlei Dam and across the Swartland as far as Piketberg.

In the vicinity of the 6 km mark you will be surprised to see the Breede River yellowwoods growing on the exposed slopes – not in their usual kloof habitat. After a short level section, the trail descends gradually for about 2 km until the grinding ascent up *Pic Blanc* (1 049 m) – the "White Peak". Once again your efforts are well rewarded by the expansive views, which include Waaihoek Peak above Ceres and the start of the Hex River Mountains.

Finally the trail swings eastwards, descending sharply to reach the top of Wolwekloof near the 13 km mark. Now you can relax as the most demanding section of the trail has been com-

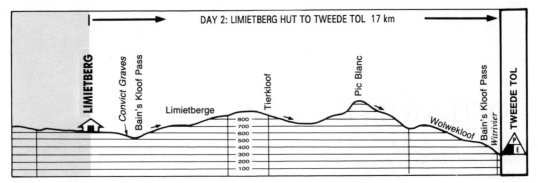

DAY 2: LIMIETBERG HUT TO TWEEDE TOL 17 km

pleted and you will find yourself descending the final 4 km to Tweede Tol.

While descending along the northern slopes of the wide, deep Wolwekloof, the Slanghoek Mountains can be seen across the valley carved by the Wit River. The large natural pools in the Wit River are most welcome at the end of the trail.

HOTTENTOTS-HOLLAND

Winding its way through the 26 000 ha Hottentots-Holland Nature Reserve, the Boland Hiking Trail with its panoramic views and its profusion of wild flowers can hardly be matched for scenic beauty anywhere in the world. The trail winds through the heart of the Cape Floral Kingdom and between July and September you will see the proteas at their best, while masses of ericas blanket the slopes during spring and summer.

Aspects common to both sections of the Boland Hiking Trail are discussed in the general introduction which should be read in conjunction with this chapter.

TRAIL PLANNER

Distance 40 km; 3 days (various other 2-day options are possible)

Grading B; B+

Climate

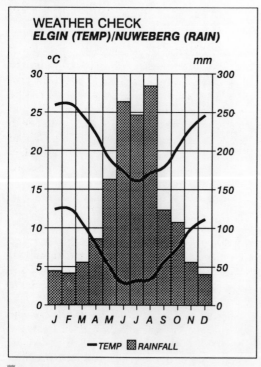

WEATHER CHECK
ELGIN (TEMP)/NUWEBERG (RAIN)

— TEMP ▨ RAINFALL

Reservations The Reservations Officer,

Private Bag X1, Uniedal 7612, Telephone (021) 886-5858, Fax (021) 886-6575. Reservations are accepted up to a year in advance.

Group size Minimum 2; Maximum 12
The maximum number of hikers permitted on each trail is based on the nature and sensitivity of the area and zoning for the type of outdoor experience.

Maps A photocopy of the National Hiking Way Board map is forwarded to you with your receipt and permit.

Facilities Accommodation on the trail consists of two huts with bunks and mattresses at each of the two overnight stops. Water, refuse bins and toilets are also provided.

Logistics The Nuweberg to Jonkershoek and Nuweberg to Franschhoek Pass routes are linear, requiring transport arrangements. All other routes are circular.

Relevant information
■ During bad weather the trails can be closed at short notice. A taped message on telephone number (0225) 4301 will inform you what the current position is.
■ Hikers terminating their trail at Jonkershoek or Jan Joubertsgat must make

prior transport arrangements in the event of the trail being closed when they arrive.

■ The entire trail system is closed in July and August because of the extreme climatic conditions during these months and for trail and hut maintenance.

■ During the rainy season Boegoekloof is inaccessible because of the high level of the river, and as a result the Boegoekloof circuit is closed from the beginning of April to the end of September.

■ Owing to the fire hazard in the dry summer months, the Jonkershoek Traverse is closed from September to the end of March. Since Jonkershoek does not fall under Cape Nature Conservation, hikers should contact the Department of Water Affairs and Forestry in Stellenbosch, Telephone (02231)

5715 for permission to exit between April and the end of June.

■ The latest starting time for Boesmanskloof/Aloe Ridge huts is 09:00, while hikers headed for Landdroskop/Shamrock Lodge must start before 13:00. The earliest starting time for all routes is 07:00.

How to get there The only entry point is at Nuweberg which is reached by following the N2 over Sir Lowry's Pass. Take the first turn-off to the left into Grabouw and continue through the town to the R321 to Villiersdorp and Franschhoek. Turn left here and continue for about 11 km to the signposted turn-off to Nuweberg to the left. The starting point is reached a short distance further on.

TRAIL DESCRIPTION

The Hottentots-Holland Hiking Trail has a complex network of trails, enabling you to hike at least seven different routes.

NUWEBERG TO LANDDROSKOP/ SHAMROCK LODGE
Day 1: Nuweberg to Landdroskop/Shamrock Lodge From the parking area, follow the road to the forestry village and Nuweberg Dam for about 500 m before turning right onto a plantation road. Over the next 3 km the trail ascends steadily through pine plantations before emerging into a strip of fynbos separating the Nuweberg and Grabouw plantations. A short way further on you will join the original descent from Nuweberg to Eikenhof and Grabouw.

You will gain some 200 m in altitude over the next 1,5 km before the trail levels off along the 1 000 m contour. About 6 km from the start you will pass the Sphinx to your right with Nuweberg towering some 300 m above you to the left. Keep an eye out along this section for the Hottentot white sugarbush which has beautiful creamy-white to pink flowers in autumn.

With about 3,5 km left to the hut you will cross a tributary of the Palmiet River and about 500 m further another tributary.

The trail then continues along the Palmietpad which takes its name from the river of that name.

About 1 km from the hut the trail is joined by the route via Stoekoe's Pass and a short way fur-

ther you will pass the route to Jonkershoek and the Boegoekloof Circuit. Landdroskop is reached after a short downhill stretch.

The Landdroskop Hut is a stone structure, built around a central room with the sleeping-quarters leading off. Shamrock Lodge, a wooden hut, is situated nearby, but has a better view.

JONKERSHOEK TRAVERSE
Day 2: Landdroskop/Shamrock Lodge to Jonkershoek From Landdroskop Hut the trail leads west, skirting the slopes after which the hut is named. The trail ascends gradually and after 1,5 km crosses a stream and continues to rise, crossing several scree slopes. After about 4 km you will pass below Somerset Sneeukop (1 590 m), the highest peak in the Hottentots-Holland range.

During late January the slopes here are covered in masses of blood-red flowers of the peach protea (*Protea grandiceps*) and the path to the summit has been aptly named Grandiceps Path. A detour to the summit is rewarded by the breathtaking view of the Cape Peninsula, as well as the Groot Drakenstein and Franschhoek mountains.

After passing the Triplets the trail loses some 200 m in height and near the 8 km mark the Boegoekloof Circuit turns off to the right. About 2 km further you will pass Pic Sans Nom (Peak Without Name) and after a short, level stretch the trail begins its arduous descent down

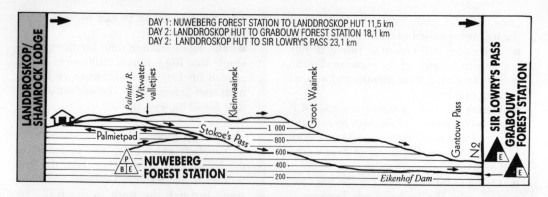

Swartboskloof. It is a steep descent and you will lose some 700 m in altitude over the next 3 km.

Near the 13 km mark the trail crosses the shady Swartboskloof Stream and here the trees and running water make a welcome resting spot. The route then descends through stands of mountain cypress and blue sugarbush, while yellowwoods, wild almond and red alder are encountered lower down at Sosyskloof.

Shortly after the 14 km mark the trail joins the Jonkershoek Circular Drive which is followed for about 3 km to the gate at the forest station.

The first white settler in the Upper Jonkershoek Valley was a German ensign in the service of the Dutch East India Company, Jan Andriessen. He settled here in 1682 and, since Dutch ensigns were known as "jonkers", he became known as Jan Jonker, hence the name Jonkershoek. By 1717 108 land grants had been made in the area, resulting in heavy exploitation of the forests in the valley and on the slopes above Somerset West.

BOEGOEKLOOF CIRCUIT
Day 2: Landdroskop/Shamrock Lodge to Nuweberg via Boegoekloof From Landdroskop the trail follows the Jonkershoek Traverse

for 8 km before branching off to the right. Over the next 2 km the trail descends steeply to Kurktrekkernek where you will have a magnificent view over Jonkershoek to the north-west and Dwarsberg (1 523 m), Victoria Peak (1 589 m) and Emerald Dome (1 510 m) to the east. The last two peaks were originally known as Groot- and Klein Sneeukop, but as there were so many peaks with those names they were renamed at the beginning of this century.

From Kurktrekkernek the trail follows a tributary of the Riviersonderend for about 1 km before dropping into Boegoekloof. Over the next 1 km the river is crossed several times and at about 12,5 km you will reach Dwarsbergpoel, an enormous swimming pool set in unsurpassed surroundings. The pool is hemmed in by steep cliffs on both sides with a 25 m-high waterfall cascading down the slopes of Dwarsberg.

The kloof takes its name from the abundance of buchu (*Agathosma*) growing here and just before the 13 km mark you will pass the site of an old buchu camp. Certain species of buchu were used for medicinal purposes by the Khoikhoi and were much in demand by the early settlers for treating kidney diseases and other ailments. Even today the plant has commercial value: essential oils are extracted from

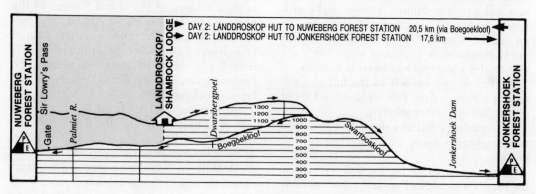

the leaves for pharmaceutical use, while it is also used in buchu brandy. The flowers vary from white to pink and mauve to bluish-purple.

After the 13 km mark the trail crosses the river once again and remains on the right-hand side of the valley until it joins the Boesmanskloof Route at Red Hat Crossing. The trail ascends gradually with spectacular views of the valley far below and two more waterfalls, before losing about 100 m in altitude at Red Hat Crossing.

Turn right here and after about 1 km you will reach Eensbedrogenpoel, an inviting swimming pool situated in another tributary of the Riviersonderend. A little further you will pass the connecting route from Landdroskop on your right and a short way further the jeep track between Landdroskop and Nuweberg is reached. Here you will turn left and after 3,5 km of downhill walking you will arrive at Nuweberg.

BOESMANSKLOOF TRAVERSE
Day 2: Landdroskop/Shamrock Lodge to Boesmanskloof/Aloe Ridge
From Landdroskop the trail descends along a jeep track and shortly after the 3 km mark the Boesmanskloof route turns off to the left, with the jeep track continuing to Nuweberg, some 4 km further.

A short way further on you will join the route starting at Nuweberg and here you may meet up with hikers doing the two-day circuit via Boesmanskloof or the Franschhoek Pass Traverse, starting from Nuweberg.

From the junction the trail leads over level terrain and after about 1 km reaches the Riviersonderend where you can stop for a swim in the Eensbedrogenpoel. You will cross the river a short distance further and the trail then traverses around a spur into Boegoekloof before descending sharply to cross a tributary of the Riviersonderend by means of a wooden bridge at Red Hat Crossing.

The trail climbs steeply out of Boegoekloof to Stoney Nek past a stand of Stokoe's proteas (*P. stokoei*) and Kogelberg bottlebrush. About 1,5 km beyond Stoney Nek you will reach Zoetenhoopkloof and here you can cool off in Pootjiesglypoel before attempting the long uphill slog ahead of you. The last stream before the hut is crossed just over 1 km onwards and it is advisable to fill your water-bottle here.

The trail then climbs gradually over the next 3 km to Pofaddernek, from where you have a magnificent view over the Theewaterskloof

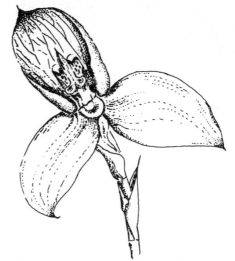

The beautiful red disa is a delight along streams in January and February

Dam, the Franschhoek range and Boesmanskloof far below.

The first 2 km of the descent are fairly steep and can be unpleasant after heavy rains. Proteas along this section include the wagon tree and *Protea cordata*, the latter being easily identified by its distinctive heart-shaped leaves.

The distance to the huts is deceptive and you will probably despair of ever reaching them when, quite suddenly, the Boesmanskloof Hut appears on your left. You will cross the river by means of a neatly constructed suspension bridge before reaching Boesmanskloof Hut. Aloe Ridge Hut, which is named after the fan aloe, is a short way further on. The fan aloe is restricted to the Franschhoek Mountains in the south and the Roodezand Mountains in the north and the common name is derived from the strap-shaped leaves which are arranged in an erect flat fan. Fan aloes grow on rocky slopes and their scarlet flowers are seen at their best between August and October.

After unpacking you can cool off in the inviting swimming pool a short way upstream of the suspension bridge.

ALTERNATIVE ROUTE
Day 1: Nuweberg to Boesmanskloof/Aloe Ridge
The trail starts at the Nuweberg office, following a level forestry road through pine plantations and reaching a pleasant picnic spot shortly before emerging into the fynbos.

On leaving the plantations you will enter the

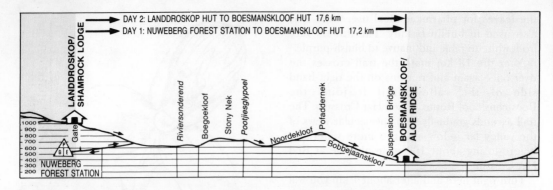

Hottentots-Holland Nature Reserve and the going is fairly level for another kilometre. Shortly after crossing the Palmiet River the gradient steepens and after the 3 km mark you will reach a nek where the Boesmanskloof route turns off to the right, while the jeep track continues to Landdroskop. The remainder of the route to Boesmanskloof is described in the Landdroskop to Boesmanskloof Section.

BOESMANSKLOOF/ALOE RIDGE TO NUWEBERG CIRCUIT

This trail takes you back to Nuweberg and, depending on your route, this will either be your second or third day on the trail.

Boesmanskloof to Nuweberg

Covering about 12 km, this is an easy return route to Nuweberg. First thing in the morning you will retrace your steps, crossing the suspension bridge and continuing for about 250 m along the previous day's route.

A pair of yellow footprints marks the turn-off

The brown-bearded sugarbush occurs in the mountains of the south-western Cape

to the left and after a gradual climb the trail levels off, following an easy route with fine views over the orchards in the valley below and the Theewaterskloof Dam.

About three hours after setting off you will drop down into the Riviersonderend where a weir takes you across to the other side. The pools here are inviting and with most of the day's hike behind you this is a good lunch stop.

The deep canyon carved by the Riviersonderend further upstream is a popular one-day kloofing trip. Covering about 16 km, the route has two compulsory jumps, one being about 7 m high. But if this is not exciting enough there is Suicide Gorge with its four waterfalls, the highest jump being about 14 m! Both routes are only open during the summer and should not be attempted by those afraid of heights.

A fairly steep climb awaits you to Nuweberg and you will gain over 300 m in altitude from the river to the office. From the Riviersonderend you will pass through a patch of pines before emerging into fynbos, ascending steeply before following a contour for about 500 m. After passing through another patch of pines you will join the road to the Nuweberg office.

FRANSCHHOEK PASS TRAVERSE

Depending on your route this will either be your second or third day on the trail.

Boesmanskloof/Aloe Ridge to Jan Joubertsgat Bridge This section of the trail covers about 11 km and you should allow for four hours. Initially the trail traverses easy terrain along the lower slopes of the Franschhoek Mountains dominated by Bushman's Castle (1 350 m) and Franschhoek Peak (1 406 m). The trail winds in and out of several kloofs

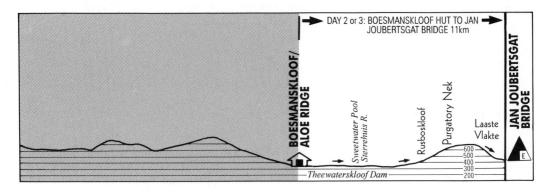

formed by streams originating higher up the slopes of the Franschhoek Mountains.

Shortly after the 6 km mark you will start ascending and about 1 km further you will reach the appropriately named Rusboskloof. From here the the trail rises steadily for about 2 km, gaining some 300 m in height to Purgatory Nek. This name originated around 1823 when the Royal African Corps was involved in the building of the Franschhoek Pass. They found the work and living conditions so unbearable that they felt they were being purged of their sins. Like many other early passes into the interior, the original route across the Franschhoek Mountain was nothing more than a game track – in fact the old Elephant Pass lies just to the right of the trail. Simon van der Stel described this route as "... wide and broad, yet ... extremely narrow on the side of that steep mountain ... having below it an alarming depth, and cannot be negotiated by a wagon because it is so narrow." The first pass across the mountain was built by a farmer named S J Cats and became known as the Cats Path. The pass was completed in 1819, but could not be used by

heavy wagons and in 1822 it became impassable after heavy floods.

Construction of the existing pass began in 1823 under the supervision of Lieutenant Mudge. Work was completed in 1825, making the Franschhoek Pass the oldest pass in South Africa.

Shortly after the 9 km mark the trail branches off to the right. The original route used to continue across private land for about 4 km to the U-bend on the Franschhoek Pass. Permission to hike across this land was withdrawn a few years ago when ownership of the land changed, necessitating a change in the route. After following a level course for about 1 km the trail drops steeply into the valley carved by the Jan Joubertsgat River, losing some 250 m in altitude over the final 2 km. The river was named after a farmer who apparently drowned there, while the bridge of the same name was built in 1823. The 5 m-high single arch bridge has a span of 5,5 m and is considered one of the best examples of dressed stonework, as well as one of the oldest bridges in South Africa. It was declared a national monument in 1955.

SWELLENDAM

This imposing trail traverses the 11 000 ha Marloth Nature Reserve in the Langeberg
Mountains above Swellendam, offering options of a six-day, five-day or weekend route. An
outstanding feature is the floral wealth which changes with the succession of the seasons.
Your efforts will be rewarded with magnificent mountain scenery and views of the patchwork farmlands on the plains below and the Little Karoo. The trail was opened in June
1979 and was the first circular trail of the National Hiking Way System.*

TRAIL PLANNER

Distance 81 km; 6 days
(2- and 5-day options are possible)
Grading B+ (except first day which can be
classified as C)

Climate

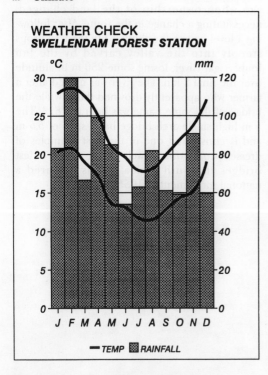

Reservations The Officer-in-Charge,
Marloth Nature Reserve, P O Box 28,
Swellendam 6740, Telephone (0291)

4-1410, Fax (0291) 4-1488. Reservations are
accepted up to a year in advance.

Group size Minimum 2; Maximum 16

Maps A full-colour trail map with information on the history, flora and fauna of the area
on the reverse is available. One free copy is
forwarded with your receipt and permit.

Facilities The six overnight huts are
equipped with bunks and mattresses. Other
amenities include water, refuse bins and pit
toilets while fireplaces are provided at the
Koloniesbos and Wolfkloof huts only.

Logistics Circular route. The first overnight
hut, Koloniesbos, is accessible by car, but
cars may only be parked at the reserve
office, 4,3 km from the hut.

Relevant information
■ Entry into the Marloth Nature Reserve is
only allowed between sunrise and sunset
unless prior arrangements have been made.
■ On arrival at the reserve office you must
sign the register and indicate which huts you
will use. On completion of the trail you must
indicate your safe return in the register.
■ A lightweight stove is essential as fires are
not permitted at the Boskloof, Goedgeloof,
Proteavallei and Nooitgedacht huts.
■ The Vensterbank route should be avoided in rain, mist and strong wind and by
those afraid of heights.

■ Snow can be expected between June and December and it is essential to take suitable clothing and rain gear. The summer months can be extremely hot and it is important to take precautions against the sun.

How to get there In Swellendam, turn off Main Street into Andrew Whyte Street. Keep left at the Y-junction and ·continue along the road signposted Swellendam State Forest/Swellendam Conservation Area.

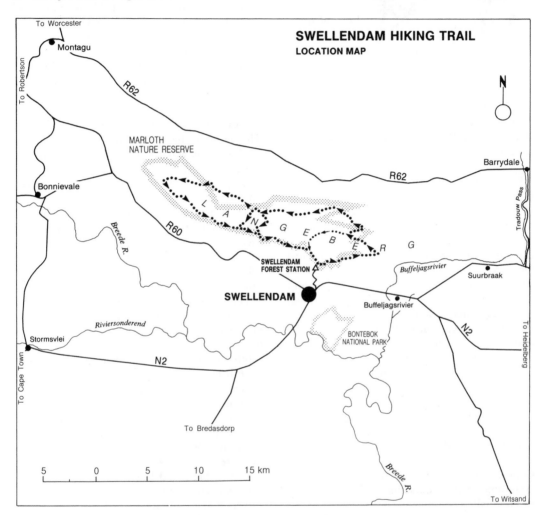

TRAIL ENVIRONMENT

Flora The trail winds mainly through mountain fynbos, which dominates the vegetation of the Langeberg range, while isolated patches of remnant indigenous forest occur in the kloofs on the southern slopes of the range.

When you cross the range it will immediately become obvious that the northern slopes are not only warmer and drier than the southern slopes, but also lie within the summer rainfall area. As a result the vegetation of the northern and southern aspects differs remarkably.

In the vicinity of the appropriately named Proteavallei more than half a dozen protea species can be seen. Among these are broad-leaved, long-bud, blue, real and brown-bearded (*P. speciosa*) sugarbushes. The king protea (*P. cynaroides*) occurs in two colour variations – the rare white and a beautiful dark pink. Large concentrations of the peach protea (*P. grandiceps*) create a spectacular display when they are in flower between September and January in the vicinity of Dwariganek, west of Proteavallei.

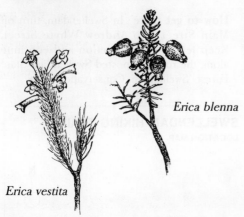

Two of the Erica *species occuring along the trail*

Some 30 erica species occur along the trail, including the Riversdale heath (*Erica blenna*), which is restricted to the Langeberg range between Swellendam and Riversdale. It is one of the most striking ericas with yellow urn-shaped flowers with green tips between July and October. Other eye-catching species include *E. vestita* which occurs on the lower slopes and has dark red to white tubular flowers between August and May, and the pink form of *E. curviflora*. Keep an eye out in damp areas along the lower slopes for the attractive bright pink flowers of *E. cubica*.

Other fynbos species which deserve mention are the Caledon bluebell (*Gladiolus rogersii*), which flowers between July and November, suurkanol (*Watsonia pyramidata*), which presents a beautiful display during October and November, and whip rush (*Bobartia indica*), also known as biesroei, which are common on the slopes, especially after fires. The strawberry everlasting (*Syncarpha eximia*), which grows up to 1,5 m tall, is conspicuous in summer.

Trees and shrubs of the fynbos include members of the protea family, mountain cypress, fountain bush, iron martin, willow currant, rock candlewood and wild olive.

The indigenous forests on the southern slopes of the Langeberg were a ready supply of timber for the early settlers and very few forest areas remain. Today they are restricted to small patches in river gorges and rugged ravines such as Doktersbos, Koloniesbos, Duiwelsbos and Wamakersbos. Typical species to be seen in these forests include Outeniqua and real yellowwoods, red alder, candlewood, Cape beech and Cape gardenia.

Fauna Compared to the savanna and grassveld areas of southern Africa, the fynbos vegetation does not support a great variety of larger mammals. This is partly due to its low grazing potential, the dense growth form and a lack of trees that bear berries and fruit. Many species of game have, however, disappeared as a result of farming, the exploitation of the indigenous forests and hunting.

The last bluebuck was shot near Swellendam at the beginning of the nineteenth century and there is not a single specimen in a South African museum. Another antelope which almost suffered the same fate was the bontebok. The future of this species was, however, secured in the 1830s when a group of farmers in the Bredasdorp district realised that they were endangered. In 1837 Mr Alexander van der Byl enclosed about 2 500 ha on his farm and stocked it with 27 animals. Other farmers followed and in 1931 the Bontebok National Park was established near Bredasdorp. In March 1960 most of the bontebok were caught and relocated in the present park, 7 km south of Swellendam.

The usual fynbos fauna occurring along the trail include klipspringer, grysbok, grey rhebok, chacma baboon and rock dassie. Predators include caracal, striped polecat and the large-spotted genet, as well as leopard which are frequently heard in the vicinity of Nooitgedacht.

Porcupine quills are often encountered along the trail, while areas where they have foraged for bulbs and roots are also seen frequently.

In terms of diversity and density the birdlife of the fynbos areas is considerably richer than the forests of the southern Cape, but poorer than the Transvaal bushveld, and about 101 species occur regularly in fynbos. Research has shown that mountain fynbos supports about 200 to 431 birds per 100 ha, compared to 925 to 1 600 per 100 ha in the Transvaal acacia woodlands.

The birds most closely associated with the open fynbos are Cape sugarbird, malachite, orangebreasted and lesser doublecollared sunbirds, as well as protea canary. Other fynbos birds include Karoo robin, neddicky, spotted prinia and bokmakierie.

Birds of prey you could see are black eagle and the jackal buzzard.

Species of the more wooded areas include rameron pigeon, Cape turtle dove and the Piet-my-vrou or red-chested cuckoo, a common breeding migrant whose characteristic call is usually heard between September and February. The paradise flycatcher is a summer migrant (September to April), while the bluemantled flycatcher is a resident species.

History Before the arrival of the whites, the area around Swellendam was inhabited by small groups of San and the Hessequa Khoikhoi who inhabited the coastal plains up to the Gouritz River.

The arrival of the white settlers during the first half of the 1700s resulted in conflict between the San and the new arrivals. By the late 1740s the San were hunted like animals by commandos of white settlers and it was not until 1792 that the commandos were disbanded.

In 1743 the Governor-General of the Dutch East India Company, Baron Gustaaf Willem van Imhoff, ordered the establishment of a district in what was known as *De Colonie in de Verre Afgeleegene Contreije* ("the Colony in the remote regions"). Initially four civilian councillors were appointed and, with an assistant magistrate and a secretary, they were to serve under the magistrate of Stellenbosch. This system proved unsatisfactory and in 1745 a magistrate was appointed. Work on the Drostdy started the following year and was completed in 1747. The new district was named Swellendam, after Governor Hendrik Swellengrebel and his wife Helena ten Damme.

As a result of the San raids and dissatisfaction with what was regarded as the ineffective government at the Cape, the Drostdy was occupied by 60 armed burghers (civilians) on 17 June 1795. The magistrate was dismissed and a free republic declared. Independence was short-lived, however, as three months later the Cape was occupied by Britain. The burghers hoped for better conditions under British rule and voluntarily handed back the keys of the Drostdy to the magistrate, who resumed his official duties.

TRAIL DESCRIPTION

Day 1: Swellendam Forest Station/Koloniesbos Hut to Boskloof Hut Depending on your starting point, the first day's hike covers either 16,1 km or 11,8 km and is usually completed in five to six and a half hours. Some 800 m is gained in altitude within the first 7,5 km from Koloniesbos, making this the most strenuous section of the trail, and an early start is advisable.

From the office you will follow a gravel road for about 1 km before the trail turns off to the right. The remaining 3,3 km to the two-roomed wooden Koloniesbos Hut follows easy terrain, mainly through pine plantations.

From Koloniesbos Hut the trail initially ascends steeply through pine plantations and after about 1 km branches off to the right to descend to Wamakersbos. The left-hand fork is the return route of the two-day hike via Ten o'Clock Peak. The forest was a ready source of timber for the wagons of the early settlers, hence the name. The route descends to the Wamakersbos River where water-bottles should be filled during dry periods as the next water is likely to be at Hoekrus, some 5,5 km further on.

From the river the trail ascends steeply to emerge into the fynbos near the 2 km mark.

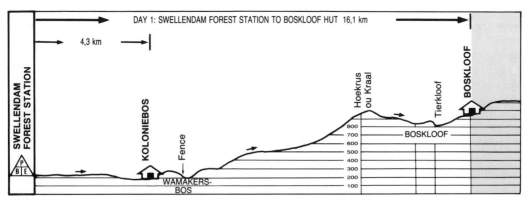

Over the next 5 km the trail gains altitude steadily for most of the way and, as you climb, you will be rewarded with magnificent views over Swellendam and the surrounding wheat-fields, with Buffeljags Dam to the east. The final kilometre to Hoekrus is a steep haul and, judging by the flattened vegetation, this is a favourite resting place with a delightful waterfall a short distance downstream.

From here the trail continues to ascend for a short way and towards the east the Langeberg range can be seen disappearing in the hazy distance. During October and November these slopes are covered in masses of white everlastings (*Helichrysum*). The route then descends and you will see your destination about 4 km away at the head of Boskloof. After crossing a small stream near the 9 km mark, you will pass the turn-off to Ten o'Clock Peak just after the 10 km mark. Shortly afterwards a river with an inviting pool is crossed in Tierkloof by means of a wooden bridge.

From the river you will ascend once again, gaining about 200 m in height before reaching the hut which is beautifully situated next to a river with fine swimming pools a short way upstream.

Day 2: Boskloof Hut to Goedgeloof Huts
This relatively easy 10 km hike commences with a steep zigzag. For the first kilometre you will hike along Drosterspas ("Deserter's Pass") to Vulture's Rock, which resembles these birds which have almost become extinct in the western Cape. From here you will continue to climb to Knuckle Rock, but don't neglect to take the short deviation to the viewpoint overlooking Boskloof and the hut far below.

A short way onwards the trail drops down to the Langkuile River, where a profusion of ericas can be seen, followed by a stiff climb to Het Goedgeloof Nek and an even steeper descent. Over the final 3 km the trail loses some 500 m in height and it is important to take your time. Along this section you are treated to a panoramic view of the colourful patchwork of farmlands in the Montagu/Barrydale Valley, both towns being visible on a clear day.

The stone huts at Goedgeloof were originally built for patrol purposes and the natural stone blends in well with its surroundings. Additional accommodation is provided in the cooking shelter adjacent to the huts.

Swimming is prohibited in the nearby dams, hence the showers at the huts, and you should not make a nuisance of yourself at the farms in the vicinity.

The spectacular sunsets from Goedgeloof never fail to impress. In the late afternoon the tall yellowbushes on the slopes behind the huts are transformed into a glowing golden-yellow sea and looking north you will see a kaleidoscope of pastel shades, fading into the darkness.

Day 3: Goedgeloof Huts to Proteavallei Hut
From the Goedgeloof Huts the trail descends to the Warmwater River and just over a kilometre further crosses a small stream, the last water up to Proteavallei Hut. From here the trail winds steadily upwards for about 1,5 km to Warmwaternek and you will gain nearly 500 m in just over 1,5 km. Two dominant species occurring here are the tall yellowbush and *Leucospermum calligerum*, which has globose, creamy-yellow flowers between July and January. The nek is usually reached after about two hours and with only 5 km remaining you can take a well-earned rest. Dominating the scenery to the south is Misty Point (1 710 m), the highest peak in the Langeberg range, while

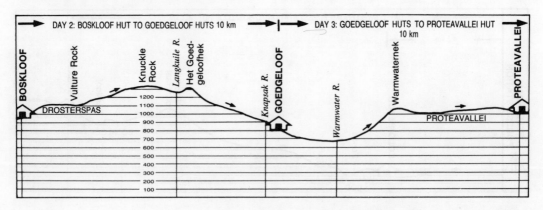

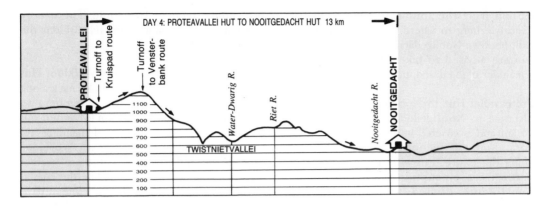

Leeurivierberg (1 628 m), the second highest peak, is prominent to the west.

The remaining 5 km is over easy terrain, much of it level, and it will be worth your while to hike this section at leisure so that you can enjoy the spectacle created by masses of flowering proteas. Especially attractive between January and June are the dense stands of long-bud sugarbush.

Shortly before reaching the hut there is a junction, the trail to the right being the route to Vensterbank and Nooitgedacht, while the route to the hut and Kruispad turns off to the left.

Proteavallei lies in a basin enclosed by two mountain ridges. The hut is similar to Boskloof Hut and is situated alongside the delightful Protea Stream. From the balcony of the hut you will enjoy a magnificent view of Misty Point, which as the name suggests is often shrouded in mist.

Day 4: Proteavallei Hut to Wolfkloof Hut or Nooitgedacht Hut
Depending on your destination, you have a choice of three routes. Two of the routes, a 7 km route via Kruispad and a 12,5 km route via Vensterbank, cross the range

to Wolfkloof, while the third route continues to Nooitgedacht.

Proteavallei Hut to Wolfkloof Hut via Kruispad
From the hut the trail ascends almost immediately for about 1 km. This is followed by a steep descent along Kruispad and after 6 km the trail joins the contour path between Nooitgedacht and Wolfkloof (for the remainder of the description refer to Day 5).

Proteavallei Hut to Wolfkloof Hut via Vensterbank
Although this route to the hut is about 5 km longer it is far more spectacular. From the hut the trail follows the Nooitgedacht route for about 2 km, ascending steadily to Dwariganek. The Vensterbank route turns off to the left here, and you will continue to climb for just over 1,5 km to Vensterbank which is named after the sheer cliffs which are reminiscent of a window-frame. After a short but steep climb, the trail starts to zigzag steeply downwards and along this section you will have spectacular views of the Swellendam wheatlands ahead of you and Leeukloof on your left.

The trail loses some 900 m in just over

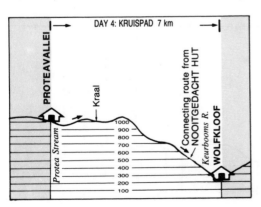

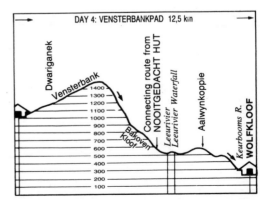

3,5 km from the spur extending from the Leeurivierberg to where it joins the contour path between Nooitgedacht and Wolfkloof and you are advised to take your time (for the remainder of the description refer to Day 5).

Proteavallei Hut to Nooitgedacht Hut The distance to Nooitgedacht is approximately 13 km and is covered in about six hours. The flora along this section is amongst the best along the entire trail with an abundance of wagon trees, pincushions (*Leucospermum*), rooistompie or red mimetes (*Mimetes cullulatus*), cone- and yellowbushes (*Leucadendron*) and blushing brides (*Serruria*).

After retracing your steps for about 400 m you will join up with the main trail to Nooitgedacht. As happens so often on this trail, you then start to climb almost immediately to reach Dwariganek after 2 km. Here the Vensterbank route branches off to the left while the main trail continues in a westerly direction. From here the trail descends sharply to the Twisnietvallei ("Do Not Quarrel Valley"), losing some 600 m in altitude in just 3 km, before ascending again for a short distance. It then continues to descend to the Water Dwariga River only to climb steadily for 2 km to Luiperdnek.

The final 5 km of the day's hike winds downhill along the slopes of Middelrivierberg and Klipspringerkop. Shortly before reaching the hut a signpost indicates the trail to Wolfkloof Hut, 21 km away. The route to Nooitgedacht Hut turns off to the right here and shortly before reaching the hut you will cross the Nooitgedacht River. The hut is similar to the Goedgeloof Hut; it was built about 30 years ago, also for the use of rangers patrolling the area. It is tucked away in a small kloof and consists of

two rooms sleeping 16 people. The nearby swimming pool offers welcome relief during the summer months.

Day 5: Nooitgedacht Hut to Wolfkloof Hut From Nooitgedacht the trail doubles back along the southern slopes of the Langeberg to Wolfkloof. Approximately 21 km is covered, but the terrain is generally not too demanding and it takes about eight hours to reach Wolfkloof. An early start is therefore advisable.

After ascending for a short while the coastal plains come into view for the first time in days. To the west lies Robertson, the farms of Bonnievale and the hazy Riviersonderend Mountains, while the farm Jan Harmsegat lies at the foot of the slopes.

Near the 10 km mark the Middel River, which was originally identified as the site for another hut to break this long section into two shorter days, is reached. A stiff climb out of the Middel River Valley awaits you before the trail levels out for about 2 km. Shortly before the 14 km mark the route dips down to a stream and after a short but steep ascent winds down to Bakovenkloof.

After 15 km the Vensterbank route joins up with the main trail. Kleinhoutbos, with its four beautifully shaded ravines, is normally reached around lunchtime and is a pleasant surprise to the weary hiker. Especially welcome is the swimming pool above the Leeurivier Waterfall which drops into a narrow, deep ravine.

The trail then climbs for a while, before descending to Aalwynkoppie. A little further on it is joined by the Kruispad shortcut, less than 2 km from Wolfkloof. The final stretch of the day's hike drops steeply to Wolfkloof.

The hut is larger than the other huts and can accommodate 30 people. It is built at the bot-

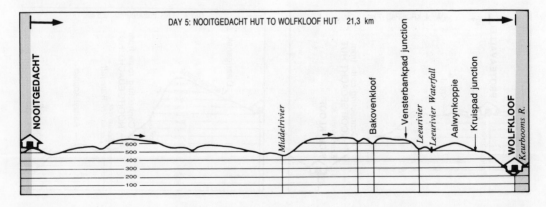

DAY 5: NOOITGEDACHT HUT TO WOLFKLOOF HUT   21,3 km

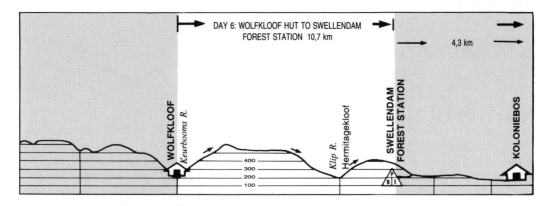

tom of the Wolfkloof Valley on the slope over-looking the Keurbooms River and there is an inviting swimming pool opposite the hut.

It is possible that Wolfkloof is named after the hyaena which were often called wolves by the early pioneers and travellers. James Backhouse reported numerous "wolves" when he passed through Swellendam on his tour of mission stations in the Cape in October 1835. He did, however, use the correct scientific name of the spotted hyaena when referring to wolves.

Day 6: Wolfkloof to Swellendam Forest Station The final day's hike covers 10,7 km and is usually completed in four hours.

First thing in the morning a wooden bridge takes you across the Keurbooms River, named after the keurboom or blossom tree which grows in profusion in the river gorge. The common Afrikaans name means "choice" tree, an apparent reference to its exquisite floral beauty. The sweet-scented purple to white flowers are borne in long sprays during spring and on clos-er examination of the flowers it will become obvious that this tree belongs to the pea family. After crossing the Keurbooms River the trail ascends steeply out of Wolfkloof before follow-ing an easier route along the 500 m contour on the slopes of One o'Clock Peak. It then

descends to the Klip River in Hermitage Kloof where picnic facilities are provided for day visi-tors. On the opposite bank the trail climbs sharply out of the kloof along the slopes of Twelve o'Clock Peak.

Looking at the map, you will probably have noticed the series of peaks named after the hours of the day. These names were given because they were used by the early settlers as enormous "sundials". Perhaps you will be able to check how accurate they are!

You will join a forestry road shortly after the 8 km mark, passing through Doktersbos, a small patch of indigenous forest named after the Swedish botanist Dr Carl Thunberg, who explored this forest in 1772. During his explo-ration of the forests above Swellendam and Grootvadersbos, Thunberg was assisted by a local farmer, a certain Mr Rothmann. In one of these forests Thunberg discovered the Cape gardenia and in appreciation for Rothmann's assistance named it *Rothmannia capensis*.

The final 2,5 km of the trail to the reserve office follows a forestry road through pine plan-tations.

ALTERNATIVE ROUTE

A two-day circular trail via Ten o'Clock Peak covers 19,4 km.

SWARTBERG

This trail offers you the opportunity to discover the rugged Swartberg, which separates the Little and Great Karoo, on foot. Winding through dramatic mountain scenery, the trail takes the hiker through Karoo and fynbos vegetation types, revealing contorted rock formations and deep kloofs. Your efforts will be rewarded with spectacular views of the Little Karoo with its patchwork of farmlands and the vast Great Karoo plains stretching northwards. There are several options, enabling hikers to plan outings ranging from a two-day to a five-day hike.

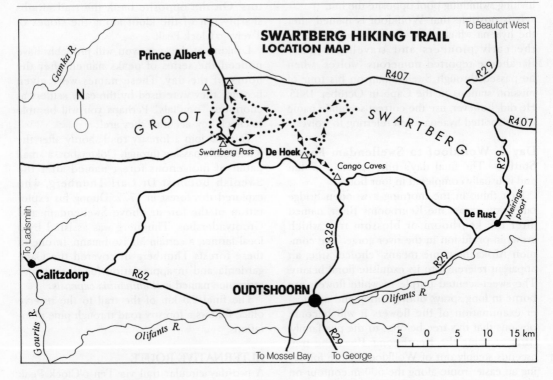

TRAIL PLANNER

Distance 65,1 km; 4/5 days (shorter options possible)

Grading B+

Reservations The State Forester, Swartberg Conservation Area, Private Bag X658, Oudtshoorn 6620, Telephone (0443) 29-1739, Fax (0443) 22-8110.

Group size Minimum 2; Maximum 30

Maps A full-colour trail map with useful information on the history, flora and fauna of the area on the reverse is available. One free copy is forwarded with your receipt and permit.

Facilities The three overnight huts are

96

equipped with bunks with mattresses. Other amenities include water, cold water showers, fireplaces, firewood, refuse bins and toilets.

Climate

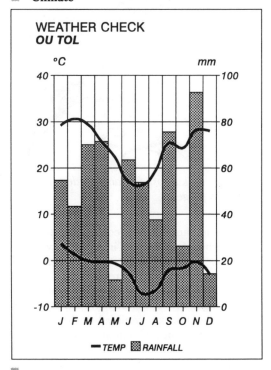

WEATHER CHECK
OU TOL

— TEMP ▧ RAINFALL

Logistics Circular route, with linear options. Ou Tol is the only starting/ending point with a trail hut. Accommodation at the De Hoek Resort starting/ending point ranges from campsites to self-contained cottages and must be reserved through *Places*, P O Box 1266, Oudtshoorn 6620, Telephone (0443) 22-8214, Fax (0443) 29-1931.

As the parking area of the Malvadraai starting point is directly alongside the Swartberg Pass, it might be risky to leave vehicles here unattended. Hikers setting off from Scholtzkloof will have to make transport arrangements as this is a linear route.

Relevant information
■ It is essential to set off each day with 2 litres of water.
■ The Crest route between Ou Tol and Bothashoek should under no circumstances be hiked in inclement weather.
■ As there is no overhead cover along the entire trail, precautions should be taken against the sun.
■ Since the trail is in an all-year rainfall area, keep rain gear handy and your pack waterproofed.
■ Always be prepared for cold weather, as snow has been recorded in mid-summer.

How to get there From Oudtshoorn take the R328 towards Prince Albert. About 25 km beyond Oudtshoorn the road forks with the right split continuing to the Cango Caves, one of the starting/ending points of the trail. Continuing along the R328, signposted to Calitzdorp and Prince Albert, the turn-off to De Hoek is indicated about 5 km further with the entrance gate some 2 km further on.

Approaching from the north, travel to Beaufort West along the N1. From here you must turn south onto the R29 passing through De Rust after 58 km. Keep to the right at De Rust and continue along the R29 for 32 km to Oudtshoorn. From here you continue as described above.

TRAIL ENVIRONMENT

Flora The vegetation of more than 80 per cent of the Swartberg consists of various mountain fynbos communities, while Karoo veld types occur on the dry, lower southern and northern slopes of the range.

The mountain fynbos is dominated by protea shrublands which have been divided into six communities ranging from summit communities to wet and dry communities of the northern and southern slopes and waboomveld.

Much of the vegetation along the trail was

destroyed by a fire which raged for several days in the Swartberg in February 1992. Only small patches of vegetation in sheltered places and a 10 km stretch between Gouekrans and Ou Tol did not burn down, but the vegetation has shown a remarkable recovery.

The composition of the fynbos is similar to that of the southern Cape mountains with a rich variety of restios, bush tea (*Aspalathus*), everlastings, watsonias and gladioli. Among the ericas are the fire heath (*Erica cerinthoides*), which is

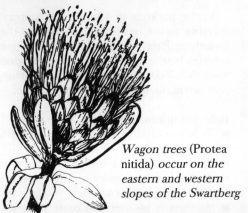

Wagon trees (Protea nitida) *occur on the eastern and western slopes of the Swartberg*

The Cape rock thrush favours boulders, cliffs and rocky gorges

especially prolific after veld fires. Two ericas which favour the drier inland mountains are *E. andreaei*, with its white urn-shaped flowers and *E. eustacei*, which has white to pale pink flowers. Both species can be seen in flower between August and October.

The proteas are, however, the most conspicuous members of the fynbos flowers. Among the several proteas occurring in the range is the strap-leaved protea (*Protea lorifolia*), which has been chosen as the trail emblem. The brownish-pink to off-white flowers of this compact shrub are enclosed by strap-shaped leaves and are not always obvious at the first glance. It is widely distributed throughout the drier, inland mountains of the southern and south-eastern Cape.

The most dominant protea is the water white sugarbush which has pink or white flowers between late summer and autumn. Other proteas occurring along the trail include the wagon tree, which forms dense stands in Scholtzkloof, the broad-leaved sugarbush and the real sugarbush, as well as several cone- and yellowbushes.

The Karoo veld types consist of a mosaic of sparse shrublands with a rich diversity of succulents. The southern and northern foothills of the Swartberg are characterised by patches of spekboomveld, dominated by porkbush and yellow pomegranate. Mountain renosterbosveld occurs in the vicinity of the Cango Caves and in Scholtzkloof and among the conspicuous species are renosterbos (*Elytropappus rhenocerotis*), bitter aloe and porkbush.

Fauna Although some Karoo species occur, the mammals of the Swartberg are similar to those occurring in the southern Cape mountains and rock dassie and chacma baboon are the animals most likely to be seen.

Of the six antelope species recorded in the

area you are most likely to come across the grey rhebok which is often seen in the vicinity of the Bothashoek Hut. It has an estimated density of four animals per 3 km², increasing to nearly five per square kilometre in recently burnt areas. Klipspringer are occasionally seen in rocky areas, while kudu are confined to the northern slopes of the range. Common duiker, grysbok and steenbok also occur, but are seen infrequently.

Predators include leopard, caracal, serval, black-backed jackal and several smaller species. Most of the mammals are, however, either small or nocturnal and are easily overlooked or hardly ever seen. Among those recorded in the Swartberg are porcupine, honey badger, Cape and scrub hares, antbear and Cape clawless otter.

Most of the 150 bird species recorded in the area to date are associated with the fynbos. Especially conspicuous when the proteas are in flower is the Cape sugarbird, while the orange-breasted sunbird are attracted to the ericas. Other sunbirds recorded include the malachite, as well as lesser and greater doublecollared sunbirds.

Other species you might tick include greywing and Cape francolins, Karoo robin, spotted prinia and Cape siskin, as well as Cape and protea canaries.

Be on the lookout for ground woodpecker, Cape rock thrush, familiar chat, Cape rock-jumper and Victorin's warbler on the rocky slopes and kloofs. The cliffs attract species such as black eagle, rock kestrel, rock pigeon, several swifts and redwinged starling.

Raptors recorded in the area include black-shouldered kite, booted and martial eagles, as well as peregrine and lanner falcons.

History Rock paintings in the entrance to the famous Cango Caves and near De Hoek testify to the inhabitation of the area by Later Stone Age people thousands of years ago. These paintings are concentrated in the foothills of the range and are mainly found between Meiringspoort and the foot of the Swartberg Pass. The plains below the Swartberg were inhabited by pastoral Khoikhoi, known as the Attaqua. These pastoralists grazed their herds from Attaquas Kloof near the Gouritz River, eastwards to the Gamtoos River.

The first white person to set foot in the Oudtshoorn district was the Dutch East India Company official, Izak Schrijver, who was sent on an expedition by Simon van der Stel to barter for cattle with the Khoikhoi. Schrijver reached the area in January 1689 after travelling through the Attaquas Kloof, returning to the Cape with over 1 000 head of cattle and a large number of sheep.

White settlement of the Oudtshoorn district dates back to the 1730s and many of the early trekboers settled in the foothills of the Swartberg. Oudtshoorn was established on the farm Hartenbeestenrivier which was surveyed in 1847 and was proclaimed a village in August 1863.

White settlement north of the Swartberg dates back to the 1760s. One of the earliest farms in the area, Kweekvallei, was acquired in 1762 as a loan farm by Zacharias de Beer. Prince Albert was laid out on the farm in 1842.

For more than a century after the foundation of settlements to the north and south of the range the Swartberg presented a formidable barrier. Work on the 25 km-long Swartberg Pass started in 1881, but was taken over by Thomas Bain two years later and completed in December 1887. About 240 prisoners, mainly from George and Knysna, provided the labour for the construction of the pass and were kept at convict stations near Ou Tol and at the Blikstasie on the northern slopes of the pass. The pass was opened in January 1888 and a toll house was opened at Ou Tol in May that year. The pass was the last of the 23 built by Thomas Bain, son of Andrew Geddes Bain, the engineer who built Bain's Kloof Pass over the Drakenstein Mountains in the western Cape.

TRAIL DESCRIPTION

The Swartberg Hiking Trail has a network of routes, enabling you to hike various combinations. A five-day circular route starting/ending at De Hoek is described here.

Day 1: De Hoek Resort to Gouekrans Hut
Set off from the northern end of the resort, initially following the De Hoek circular day route. As you leave the resort a stream is crossed and almost immediately it becomes obvious that a strenuous climb lies ahead. Looking across the valley to your left you will notice the homeward route on the final day.

Do not count on covering the first 3,8 km in a mere 60 minutes as indicated on the trail map. One and a half to two hours is more realistic as some 500 m is gained in altitude. Surrounded by interesting sandstone sculptures, the Ysterpuisie ("iron pimple") junction at the 3,8 km mark is a good place for a tea break.

At the junction the circular day route returning to De Hoek branches off to the left and the route to Gouekrans to the right, continuing steeply upwards around Perdekop. After about 1 km the path more or less levels out, making for much easier walking with the path flanked by grassy vegetation with the bright red flowers of *Erica cerinthoides* prominent along this stretch.

Between the 4 and 5 km markers you will turn right onto a wide jeep track which was never completed. The walking along here continues at an easy gradient, allowing you to enjoy the view down Grootkloof. The tapestry of farmlands in the Little Karoo, hemmed in by a low mountain range with the Outeniqua Mountains purple in the distance provide lovely scenery. Ahead of you is the gnarled-looking Plooiberg (Afrikaans meaning "folded mountain"), testifying to the tumultuous forces which shaped these mountains.

Half an hour after joining the track, you will cross over a saddle onto the northern side of the mountain. A footpath is joined here and initially the path is fairly level. As you start

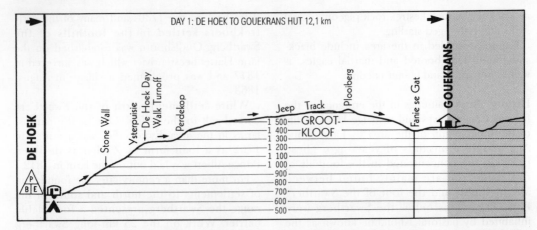

DAY 1: DE HOEK TO GOUEKRANS HUT 12,1 km

descending, the hut, although only a small white dot on the opposite side of the valley, comes into view. At this stage, the hut is still about an hour away.

A steep descent awaits you towards Fanie se Gat, one of the few swimming pools on the trail. The pool is not large, but is adequate for a refreshing dip. With the hut less than 15 minutes away, it is worth relaxing here and although there is not a large flat area to spread out on, resting alongside the stream above the pool is pleasant.

Below the pool you will turn right onto a jeep track which is flanked by patches of tall proteas. The turn-off to the hut is bound to take you by surprise. Nestling behind large rocks, the hut is neatly tucked away and invisible from the track.

The hut consists of four rooms in a row with a covered braai/eating area with tables and benches at one end and will remind you of a stable. You will be impressed by the ingenuity of the hut-builders who used enormous boulders as the back wall of the hut. From the hut, which is situated on the edge of a steep cliff face, you will have a magnificent view of the surrounding mountains.

Day 2: Gouekrans Hut to Bothashoek Hut
Covering just less than 13 km, the entire day's hike is along a jeep track and although there are a fair number of strenuous uphills, the hut can be reached before lunch. Once again the time of three hours given on the trail map is cutting it a little fine.

Initially you will backtrack along the final stretch of the previous day's route on the jeep track which is flanked by dense strands of broad-leaved and real sugarbushes. The trail ascends steadily and near the 4 km mark you will look down Grootkloof, with the Great Karoo stretching out to the north.

After dipping down, the jeep track ascends steadily once again, winding its way between a prominent koppie with a radio mast and Blouberg (1 921 m) to the right, before levelling off slightly. You will then head for a nek between Witberg (1 858 m) to the right of the jeep track and an unnamed koppie.

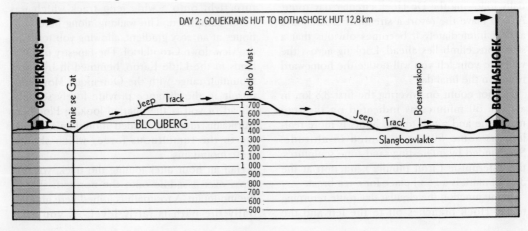

DAY 2: GOUEKRANS HUT TO BOTHASHOEK HUT 12,8 km

Near the 11 km mark you will look down onto the Bothashoek Hut and as you descend, the scenery to the left of the trail is dominated by Boesmanskop (1 886 m). Since the jeep track meanders, the hut appears deceptively close and it will be at least 45 minutes before you can relieve your shoulders of your backpack.

Bothashoek, originally a farm, was demarcated as part of the Swartberg State Forest in 1912. The hut is built of natural stone and consists of four rooms, one of which has a small wood-burning stove and a loose-standing cooking shelter. After unshouldering your pack you can investigate the possibility of a dip at Daantjie se Gat which is a few hundred metres further on along the jeep track. However, do not count on finding water here during dry periods.

Day 3: Bothashoek Hut to Ou Tol Hut

Depending on how energetic you feel you can choose between the direct route of 13,3 km along the jeep track or the 18,5 km option via Malvadraai and the Swartberg Pass. If opting for the shorter route, you should reach the hut well before lunchtime. The longer route is worth the extra effort and is described here.

From the hut the two routes continue along the jeep track for 2 km, gaining some 100 m to Luiperdnek. On reaching the nek you will notice the jeep track stretching all the way to the Swartberg Pass. You will also see the road continuing westwards to Gamkaskloof, also known as Die Hel, as well as three small patches of pine trees, Ou Tol Hut being at the patch in the middle. Here the route via the Swartberg Pass splits off to the right onto a path which is initially somewhat indistinct.

The path ascends to just below the crest of a koppie and then continues along a ridge with magnificent views to your left. You will be able to distinguish the stark white Swartberg Pass and later you will be amazed by a deep, rugged gorge with ochre, orange and light-coloured gnarled rock formations. Near the 5 km mark you will start descending along a spur, zigzagging in places, to join up with a deep valley carved by a tributary of the Dorps River.

The trail sticks to the northern side of the valley and although the path undulates around small kloofs, it is mainly downhill with awe-inspiring scenery and some enormous wagon tree proteas. Soon after entering the valley you will notice the Swartberg Pass snaking up the mountain. It is, however, more than an hour before you will join up with it. For the final kilometre you will hike alongside the Dorps River, crossing it twice, and although its gurgling sound is refreshing you are unlikely to find a pool suitable for a dip. You will probably reach the river before midday and the shady trees make this an ideal lunch stop.

Keep a lookout for the attractive pinkish purple flowers of the tree pelargonium (*Pelargonium cucullatum*). A member of the geranium family, it is known as the wilde malva in Afrikaans, hence the name of the bend.

After joining the road at Malvadraai you will turn left and commence the 7,4 km ascent, gaining more than 600 m up the Swartberg Pass. Unless it is the peak tourist season you are unlikely to find the dust churned up by passing vehicles too much of a hindrance.

About half an hour after setting off you will notice the Blikstasie just above you on the right. Take a short scramble to inspect the ruins of this now derelict stone jail which housed the convicts who built the pass.

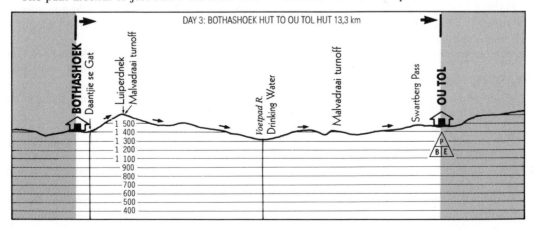

DAY 3: BOTHASHOEK HUT TO OU TOL HUT 13,3 km

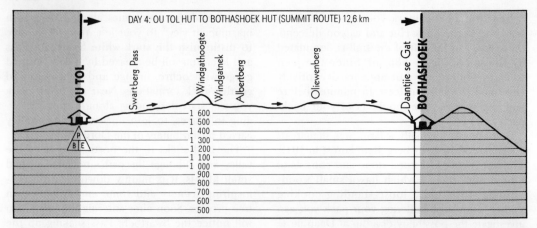

Making your way up the pass you will have plenty of time to admire the skilful work of Thomas Bain. The stone walls retaining large sections of the pass are perfectly packed. Dramatic mountain scenery is also a feature of the pass with the valley dropping steeply to the Dorps River to your left, while the close-up views of the gnarled rockfaces above also demand your attention. At certain times of the year flowering ericas, proteas and leucadendrons will delight you.

The distances indicated on the trail map and the distance markers do not quite correspond, but after rounding the final bend in the pass at Teeberg the hiking is at a more relaxed gradient and Ou Tol Hut is about 45 minutes further on.

On passing through the gate you will notice a Voortrekker memorial on your right. The hut is screened from the road by tall pine trees which were planted in 1943 to determine the suitability of the Swartberg for afforestation. Their heights vary from 37 to 43 m and their diameters from 794 to 1 372 mm.

Ou Tol is a comfortable house with three bedrooms, a bathroom and a cosy kitchen which has a wood-burning stove. There is also a covered braai area outside the back door.

Day 4: Ou Tol Hut to Bothashoek Hut The 12,6 km summit route is the highlight of the Swartberg Hiking Trail, but be warned: you are totally exposed to the elements on this route and it should therefore not be attempted if there is the slightest doubt about the weather. You are unlikely to find suitable shelter if foul weather sets in.

Setting off behind the hut, your muscles are immediately warmed up with a steep climb to

the top of the Swartberg Pass. Here you will cross the road and a short distance further on you are faced with a daunting sight – the trail zigzagging up the crest of the mountain. After accomplishing this taxing ascent the trail eases off as you cross Windgathoogte and, shortly after the 4 km mark, Windgatnek. Both these names are warnings of the gusty winds which can lash these mountains.

The trail follows a gently undulating route, winding from one side of the mountain to the other, and at times you will skirt sheer cliffs, but the path is never dangerous. The views are stupendous with simultaneous panoramas of both the Little and Great Karoo with Oudtshoorn to the south and Prince Albert in the north. You will notice the influence of the harsh climate along the summit with the vegetation much sparser – even the ericas appear stunted.

As you pass below Oliewenberg (1 857 m) close to the 8 km mark, the trail starts descending, levelling out as you round a koppie, and then descends for 2 km to join the jeep track at Daantjie se Gat. At Daantjie se Gat you will turn right, backtracking the few hundred metres to the hut along your outward stretch on the previous day.

The last leg of the trail from Bothashoek Hut to De Hoek Resort is 8,7 km and fit hikers with time constraints will be able to complete it on day four, provided an early start is made from Ou Tol.

Day 5: Bothashoek Hut to De Hoek Resort Taking the path behind the hut, you will follow a kloof up to Bushman's Nek where you will cross over to the southern side of the mountain. From here you will enjoy an expansive view of the Little Karoo with the Outeniqua Mountains

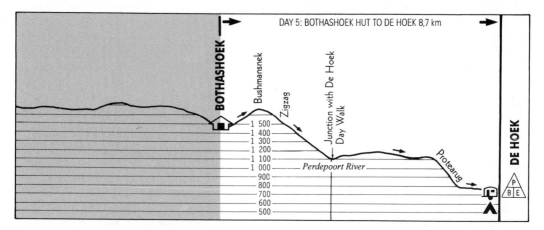

DAY 5: BOTHASHOEK HUT TO DE HOEK 8,7 km

BOTHASHOEK · Bushmansnek · Zigzag · Junction with De Hoek Day Walk · Perdepoort River · Protearug · DE HOEK

1 500 · 1 400 · 1 300 · 1 200 · 1 100 · 1 000 · 900 · 800 · 700 · 600 · 500

in the distance and De Hoek in the foreground. The path initially zigzags down the steep slope and then meanders around rocky outcrops along a spur, joining the circular De Hoek Day Walk close on 5 km after setting off.

With the Perdepoort River carving a deep valley to the left, the trail passes through proteaveld along a spur which has been appropri-ately named Protearug. The distance markers for the last few kilometres are a little confusing as those of the circular day walk are indicated in the opposite direction to the main trail.

After descending almost 900 m in 7 km from Bushman's Nek to De Hoek you will enjoy the final few hundred metres of level walking back to the resort.

OUTENIQUA

The Outeniqua Hiking Trail in the southern Cape alternates between stretches of pine-scented plantations and towering indigenous forests characterised by glades of ferns, moss-covered tree trunks and tranquil streams. Part of the trail leads past the deserted goldmining village of Millwood, once the scene of frenzied prospecting during the Knysna gold rush, and through the area where the few remaining Knysna elephants still roam. When it was first opened, the Outeniqua Trail gained the reputation of being the toughest hiking trail in South Africa, but the route has since been changed considerably, making for more pleasant hiking.

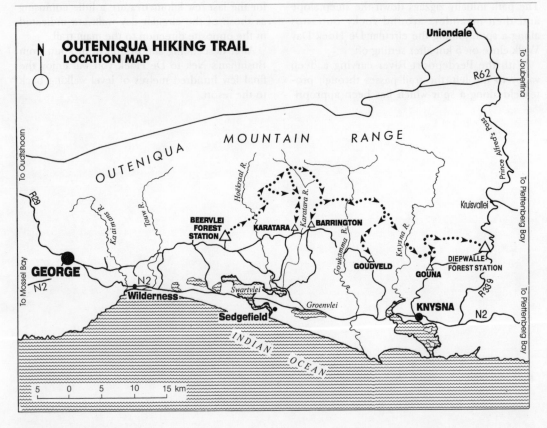

TRAIL PLANNER

Distance 105 km; 7 days (shorter options possible)

Grading B+

Reservations The Regional Director,

Southern Cape Forestry Region, Private Bag X12, Knysna 6570, Telephone (0445) 82-5466, Fax (0445) 82-5461. Reservations are accepted up to 12 months in advance.

Group size Minimum 2; Maximum 30

■ **Climate**

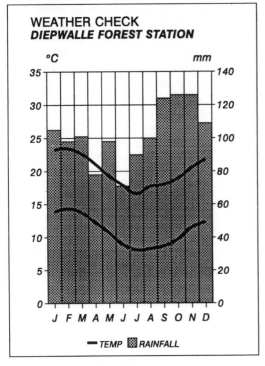

WEATHER CHECK
DIEPWALLE FOREST STATION

°C — mm

— TEMP ▨ **RAINFALL**

Maps A full-colour trail map indicating the route between Witfontein and Diepwalle (as at February 1988) is available, although the section between Witfontein and Windmeulnek is no longer in use. The map contains useful information on the history, flora and fauna of the area and one free copy is forwarded with your receipt and permit. The first day's route between Beervlei and Windmeulnek and the last two days' route from Diepwalle to Harkerville are indicated on a photocopy of the 1 : 50 000 topographical map.

Facilities The seven overnight huts range from old forestry houses to wooden huts. They are equipped with bunks with mattresses, fireplaces, firewood, water, refuse bins and toilets.

Logistics Linear route without public transport. Since the starting and ending points are on back roads, two vehicles are required. Overnight huts are provided at the start (Beervlei) and end (Harkerville) of the trail. Hikers commencing the trail at starting points other than Beervlei must set off before 12:00 to ensure that they reach the first overnight hut before nightfall. The only exception is Platbos Hut which is less than 2 km from the starting point at Farleigh.

Relevant information
■ Since the trail is in an all-year rainfall area, a waterproof jacket and warm clothing are essential. Packs should also be waterproofed.
■ After heavy rains the swollen rivers could be dangerous. Cables span the Karatara and Knysna rivers, but you should not take any unnecessary risks.

How to get there From Wilderness you must continue towards Knysna along the N2 for about 4 km, turning left onto the Hoekwil road to join the Old Passes road 5 km further on. Turn right here, passing the Bergplaas turn-off 5 km onwards and continuing for about 4,5 km to the signposted turn-off to Beervlei Forest Station. Turn left here to reach the starting point a short way further.

TRAIL ENVIRONMENT

Flora The vegetation of the Outeniqua Mountains has been classified as Knysna forest and mountain fynbos. Except for the second day's hike, which is mainly through open fynbos, the trail alternates between indigenous forests and pine plantations.

The indigenous forests of the southern Cape are considered to be temperate and constitute the largest natural forest in South Africa. Covering about 60 000 ha, they stretch discontinuously along the narrow coastal strip between

Mossel Bay and Humansdorp, extending inland to the lower slopes of the Outeniqua and Tsitsikamma mountains. About 42 000 ha of the forests are protected on state forest land, while the remainder is in the hands of private landowners.

The southern Cape forests are composed of about 125 woody tree and shrub species, which is about half the number of species occurring in the eastern Cape and just over one-third of the number of species occurring in Natal.

Three main forest types have been identified in the southern Cape forests. Ranging from dry to moist and wet, they cover 36, 48 and 16 per cent of the total area covered by indigenous forests respectively, and their composition is determined by factors such as altitude, rainfall, soil type and aspect.

The **dry forest** has a scrub-like appearance and reaches a maximum height of 15 m. It occurs mainly along the coast and very steep slopes.

The **moist forest** reaches heights of 15 to 30 m and is commonly known as "high forest". It is found on the plains and hills and along the foothills of the mountains. The moist forest is the most productive and commercially valuable of the tree types, containing species such as Outeniqua and real yellowwoods, stinkwood and ironwood. The forest floor is densely vegetated and black hazel is common here.

The **wet forest** is found in the deep, perennially wet ravines and sheltered mountain kloofs. This forest is generally about 15 m high and includes species such as red and white alders, stinkwood, Cape holly, Cape beech and tree fuchsia.

Two interesting species found in the Knysna forests are the Terblanz beech and the black bird-berry, both of which occur as isolated populations in the Lilyvlei area of the Gouna Forest.

Some of the trees along the trail have been marked according to the *National List of Indigenous Trees* and can be identified by referring to the list on the reverse of the map. Dr F von Breitenbach's *Southern Cape Tree*

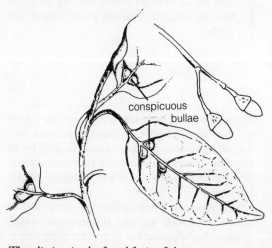

The distinctive leaf and fruit of the stinkwood

Guide illustrates 116 trees and small shrubs of the southern Cape forests and its handy size makes it worthwhile taking along.

Fynbos occurs mainly on the higher mountain slopes and is considerably poorer than that of the winter rainfall region further west. The erica family is represented by several species including *Erica densifolia* with its distinctive red or white tubular flowers with green tips and *E. glomiflora* which bears white, pink or purplish-red flowers between April and December. Also growing here is *E. triceps*, a species named after the three flowers at the end of each stem.

Several members of the protea family have been recorded in the Outeniqua Mountains, including the king protea (*Protea cynaroides*), *Mimetes pauciflorus*, grey conebush and tall yellowbush.

The iris family is represented by species such as the Riversdale bluebell (*Gladiolus rogersii*), the large brown Afrikaner (*G. liliaceus*) and *G. carneus*, flames (*Anapalina caffra*) and watsonias, varying in shades from salmon pink to terracotta.

Other typical fynbos species include knoppiesbos (*Brunia intermedia*), finger bush (*Stoebe alopecuroides*) and blombos (*Metalasia*).

A few isolated patches of fynbos, generally referred to as fynbos islands, occur within the indigenous forests. One of these islands, Die Mark, is passed on the first day's hike between Beervlei and Windmeulnek Hut.

It was initially believed that these islands were man-made, either as a result of the activities of the Outeniqua Khoikhoi or the woodcutters and hunters who exploited the area later. However, recent research suggests that these islands are relics of a more arid period when the fynbos covered a much larger area. Evidence for this theory includes the presence of fynbos ants and ant-dispersed plants, as well as fynbos rodents which do not occur in the surrounding forests. During a subsequent wetter phase the forests encroached on the fynbos, reducing it to isolated patches.

You will find Audrey Moriarty's wild flower guide *Outeniqua, Tsitsikamma and Eastern Little Karoo* a useful guide to many of the species occurring in the area.

Fauna Little remains of the game which once roamed the coastal plains and forests of the Outeniquas. As early as 1775 Anders Sparrman

KNYSNA ELEPHANTS

The Knysna forests were once the home of an estimated 400 to 500 elephants, but during the Millwood gold rush they were relentlessly hunted for their ivory and between 1870 and the turn of the century their numbers declined to a mere 50. British royalty also contributed to their demise when Prince Alfred, second son of Queen Victoria, shot two elephants at Buffelsnek in 1867.

In 1920, the famous elephant hunter Major P J Pretorius obtained a permit to shoot one elephant to determine whether the Knysna elephants were a distinct subspecies or not. Pretorius actually shot five elephants but the question of whether they were the largest of the African elephants and a distinct subspecies remained unresolved. By this time there were only 13 elephants left.

Between 1920 and 1970 the composition and size of the population remained unchanged at between 11 and 13 animals. After 1970, however, the population decreased rapidly and when a census was conducted in 1979 only three elephants − a bull, a cow and a calf − could be tracked down.

Over the years various recommendations to protect the remaining few elephants and to boost their numbers by introducing elephants from the Addo Elephant National Park were turned down by the government. Then, in 1991 it was announced that five young elephants would be translocated from the Kruger National Park in an effort to establish a viable population.

Problems surrounding insurance claims in the event of the elephants damaging private property delayed the translocation for nearly three years. However in July 1994 three six-year-old elephants captured in the Shingwedzi area of the Kruger National Park were moved to their new home in the Knysna forests. After being kept in a boma for three months the elephants were released into the forest, but in October one died of pneumonia and exhaustion. If the project is successful further relocations will be considered.

The elephants are still seen from time to time in the Gouna and Diepwalle forests, so be on the lookout!

observed that lion no longer lived there permanently and that the elephants had taken refuge in the forests.

The forests are the habitat of bushbuck, bushpig, blue duiker, vervet monkey and leopard, which also occur in the mountainous areas. Species you could encounter in the mountainous areas include klipspringer, grey rhebok, chacma baboon, and rock dassie.

Several genet and mongoose species, as well as other predators, also occur but because they are largely nocturnal they are seldom observed.

The southern Cape forests are the habitat of some 40 typical forest birds. Several species, however, have the southern limit of their distribution here, including cuckoo hawk, crowned eagle, buffspotted flufftail, tambourine dove, crowned hornbill and scalythroated honeyguide.

One of the most interesting birds is the Narina trogon which was named by the traveller Francois Le Vaillant in 1781 in honour of a Khoikhoi girl whom he admired. Because of its habit of sitting motionless in the shade of trees it is not easily seen, but can be recognised by its distinctive call − "Hoot, hoot, hoot hoot hoot hoot hoot hoot", gradually dying away. However, you are unlikely to hear its call during the winter months and your best chances of doing so are between October and January.

The Knysna lourie, another attractive forest dweller, is easily identifiable during flight when the crimson wingtips are clearly visible. It has a loud "kok-kok-kok" call, which rises and then slowly fades away.

Among the songsters are chorister robin, which often imitates other forest birds, as well as Cape and starred robins.

Forest floor feeders include the terrestrial bulbul and the olive thrush.

Birds frequenting the fynbos can broadly be divided into those of the open fynbos and those of the rocky areas. Open fynbos species include greywing francolin, ground woodpecker, spotted prinia and the Cape sugarbird.

The rocky areas are the favoured habitat of rock kestrel, rock pigeon, Alpine swift, Cape rock thrush and Cape rockjumper.

History Indications are that Middle Stone Age people inhabited the Outeniqua Mountains about 12 000 years ago. They were succeeded by what has become known as the Wilton culture of the Later Stone Age some 3 000 years later. The descendants of the final Wilton culture began specialising in a marine economy and adopted a coastal way of life. It is likely, however, that the coastal caves were occupied on a seasonal basis by the Wilton people, who migrated from their winter settlements on the coast to the interior during the summer months.

The area was also inhabited by the Outeniqua Khoikhoi and it has been suggested that the name Outeniqua means "people carrying bags" or "people carrying honey in bags". This is an apparent reference to their crossing the mountain range to barter honey with other Khoikhoi tribes in the Langkloof.

Exploitation of the indigenous forests started as early as 1711 and was accelerated after the botanists Carl Thunberg and Anders Sparrman publicised the forests as an asset to be exploited commercially.

The first woodcutter's post was established near George in 1777 and from that date persistent devastation of the forests continued for more than 150 years. In 1778 Governor Joachim van Plettenberg expressed concern about the lack of control and proposed the establishment of a control post and harbour at Plettenberg Bay. Johann Meeding was transferred from the Swart River woodcutter's post midway between George and Knysna to Plettenberg Bay where he built a timber store. The woodcutters entered into contracts with Meeding and delivered timber to the shed. The

first shipload left for Cape Town in August 1788 in Meeding's ship *Meermin*. The remains of the 61 m-long building was declared a national monument in 1936 and can be seen on the outskirts of Plettenberg Bay.

Trees were felled to provide timber for the settlement at the Cape, and after the establishment of George in 1811 the demand became even greater. At the start of the Great Trek in 1835 there was an unprecedented demand for timber for wagon building. During this period control of the forests was entrusted to local magistrates, postmasters and justices of the peace. These officers had other full-time occupations and had neither the time nor the inclination to curtail the wanton destruction. The Great Fire of 1869 had also helped to open up the forests, making exploitation easier.

In 1874 Captain Christopher Harison became the first full-time Conservator of Forests of the George, Knysna and Tsitsikamma areas, but he was able to exercise very little control over the large number of woodcutters who had by then settled in the forests.

The discovery of diamonds at Kimberley in 1869 and the opening of the Millwood goldfields in the late 1870s accelerated the destruction of the forests. The Cape government's appointment of Count M de Vasselot de Régné as Superintendent of Woods and Forests for the Cape in 1880 was an important milestone in the history of scientific forestry in South Africa.

Following the discovery of gold on the Witwatersrand in 1886 and the construction of a railway line to the Rand, however, the demand for timber increased even further and the recommendations made by Thomas Bain and Captain Harison in 1867/68 that only mature trees be felled was completely ignored, resulting in the total collapse of their proposed conservation policy.

Large numbers of woodcutters continued to exploit the forests until the Forestry Act of 1913 was passed. The Act made provision for the registration of all woodcutters while allowing no new additions to the registration list. In 1939 the last few independent woodcutters were placed on pension and the exploitation problem was finally solved.

MILLWOOD

In 1876 a gold nugget was picked up in the Karatara River by a farmer of the Knysna district, James Hooper. Diggers and prospectors began flocking to the area and in 1880 the first Mining Commissioner was appointed.

In 1885 rich alluvial gold was discovered by C F Osborne and within a short period more than 600 diggers were panning gold along streams such as Forest Creek, Golden Gully and Jubilee Creek, named after Queen Victoria's Jubilee. A total of 2 360 oz of registered alluvial gold, then valued at £11 020, was recovered from the works by mid-1886.

The discovery of reef gold by John Courtney in 1886 provoked a rush, at the height of which Millwood had three newspapers, the *Millwood Sluice Box*, the *Millwood Eaglet* and the *Millwood Critic*. In addition to about 75 wood and corrugated iron buildings, the village boasted six hotels, a post office and a police station by 1887.

Some 27 reefs were mined by over 40 syndicates, but the reef gold proved to be uneconomical and the mining companies soon ran out of capital. After the discovery of gold on the Witwatersrand the focus shifted north and by December 1893 the population of Millwood had decreased from over 1 000 to 74. The ramshackle tin and iron houses were soon reclaimed by the forest and all that remains of the romantic Knysna Gold Rush era are the mine shafts, an old boiler, Monk's Store and a few gravestones in the cemetery.

TRAIL DESCRIPTION

Day 1: Beervlei Hut to Windmeulnek Hut

The trail initially follows a gravel road before turning off into the Beervlei indigenous forest where you will cross several tributaries of the Klein Wolwe River.

Further along you will join a plantation road which passes through an area known as Die Mark and then descend along a ridge to the Wit River. The road ends a short way beyond the Wit River and from here you will continue along a forest path, dropping down steeply to the Hoogekraal River. The trail then ascends steeply up the slopes of Corneliskop through indigenous forest and you will gain nearly 200 m in altitude. After traversing a spur you will join up with plantation roads once more, ascending steeply up Corneliskop before following an easier route along its upper slopes.

Shortly before reaching Windmeulnek Hut the trail winds around Perdekop, skirting pine plantations before emerging into open fynbos. Windmeulnek Hut is reached 16 km after setting off from Beervlei and you will gain nearly 500 m in altitude. The wooden hut is situated on a sheer ridge, the name being derived from the swirling effect of the wind and mist on the ridge.

Day 2: Windmeulnek Hut to Platbos Hut

The day's hike starts with a short climb before you descend to the Karatara River. After about 3 km you will reach the river for an early morning swim, although the icy water is likely to deter all but the very brave. *Karatara* is a Khoikhoi word meaning "deep and dark" and the pools live up to this description. The descent is followed by a 4 km climb along the slopes of Spitskop (1 003 m) and you will gain

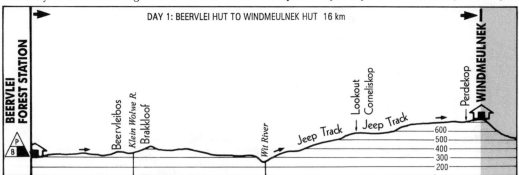

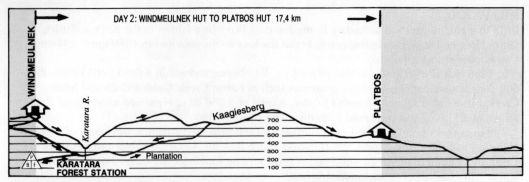

about 400 m in altitude before dropping down to the Plaat River where there is an inviting swimming pool.

Just before the 10 km mark the trail is joined by the supplementary route from Karatara Forest Station. From here you will ascend gradually along the slopes of the Kaagiesberg before descending to Farleigh Plantation. Near to the 14 km mark the trail passes into pine plantations and shortly before reaching the hut you will pass through a patch of indigenous forest.

Situated on the edge of the indigenous forest, the hut consists of three rooms, a kitchen with a table and benches, fireplace and a cold-water shower, as well as an outdoor cooking shelter.

The original hikers' hut at Farleigh is now used as forestry offices. One of its rooms has been decorated with murals of proteas and springbok and in one corner of the room is a beautiful painting of a lake and reindeer. The murals were painted between 1943 and 1945 by an Italian prisoner of war, but unfortunately the artist is unknown.

Day 3: Platbos Hut to Millwood Hut From Platbos Hut the trail leads through pine plantations and after about 2 km passes the site of an Italian prisoner-of-war camp dating back to World War II. Farleigh was one of the forest stations where prisoners of war worked in the

plantations and constructed buildings between 1943 and 1945. Teams of prisoners also worked at Gouna and Buffelsnek forest stations.

You will come to the Homtini River about 3 km further on and although it will probably be too early for a swim, the beautiful pool suggests itself as a good breakfast spot. The river is usually crossed easily, but if it is flowing strongly you can hold onto a cable strung across the river.

A short, steep ascent awaits you on the opposite bank and the trail then follows a forestry road through pine plantations for about 3 km before entering Jubilee Bush. You will hike through this beautiful indigenous forest for about 3 km until you reach Jubilee Creek Picnic Site. The trail to Millwood disappears into the forest on the far side of the bridge which is also the start of the Jubilee Creek Walk, a 4 km ramble through this historic area. Along this section you will pass several relics of the heady mining days – an alluvial gold digging site, a water furrow and blue gums (*Eucalyptus globulus*) planted by the early miners.

A short way further on a stream is crossed, with the Outeniqua Trail continuing to the left while the Jubilee Creek Walk continues for a short way to a magnificent waterfall which cascades into a large pool.

Near the 13 km mark you will be tempted by

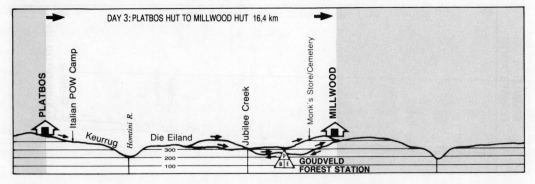

a large pool in Millwood Creek and the trail then ascends sharply along a fire-break before winding through the area which was once the bustling village of Millwood. The names of some of the old streets and the market place are displayed and shortly before reaching the hut you will pass the old cemetery and Matteroli – the only building from the Millwood era remaining in situ. Also known as Monk's Store, the building now houses an information centre on the gold rush era. The name Matteroli is said to be a corruption of "Mother Holley", the affectionate name of an owner of a boarding house during the gold rush era.

Millwood Hut, formerly a forestry house, is situated on the edge of Streepbos, a small patch of indigenous forest.

Day 4: Millwood Hut to Rondebossie Hut

The original route used to wind through pine plantations, but was subsequently redirected through the Lawnwood and Virgin indigenous forests. The day's hike starts with a gradual ascent along forestry roads first alongside pine plantations and then through fynbos at Portland Heights. From here you will have an uninterrupted view of the indigenous forests and pine plantations and, looking westwards, you will see the previous day's route.

About 4,5 km from the start the trail descends into a forest with a low canopy, Lawnwood Forest, and over the next 4,5 km you will drop down steeply to the Knysna River, losing some 500 m in altitude. The name Knysna is derived from a Khoikhoi word and there are several interpretations of its meaning. It has variously been translated as "hard to get there", "straight down", "there is wood there" and "place of ferns".

Once again a steel cable spans the river to assist hikers when the river is flowing strongly. The Knysna River is followed upstream for about 1 km, but do not expect an easy hike. You will have to scramble over boulders and at some difficult sections wooden ladders have been provided to help you along. An inviting swimming pool is reached near the 10 km mark and suggests itself as a good lunch stop.

A steep climb awaits you out of the deep valley carved by the Knysna River and you will gain some 200 m in altitude in less than 1 km before the trail levels off. You then pass through Lelievleibos, named after the striking George lily (*Cyrtanthus elatus*) which was once abundant in the area. At the 12 km mark the path joins a gravel road which is followed through the Virgin Forest for about 3 km, ascending gradually. Shortly after the 15 km mark the trail turns off to the right onto a path which is followed for about 1,5 km through the indigenous forest to Rondebossie Hut.

The hut is an old forestry house, consisting of a common room with a fireplace and several rooms which have been decorated with names of hikers carved or burnt into pieces of wood. There is also an outside cooking shelter. A swimming pool, situated about 1 km from the hut, is well worth a visit on a hot day.

Day 5: Rondebossie Hut to Diepwalle Hut

For 2 km you will follow roads through indigenous forest and alongside pine plantations. Near the 2 km mark you will cross the Rooiels River and about 1 km further an old steam-driven engine, used to haul logs from the forest nearly a century ago, is passed. A short way further on there is a turn-off to the right leading to the Witplek River – the only water point for the next 8 km.

Over the next 3 km the trail ascends steeply along the northern slopes of Jonkersberg where extensive patches of kystervaring (*Gleicenia polypodiodes*) are found. From Jonkersberg there is a fine view over the Gouna Forest and

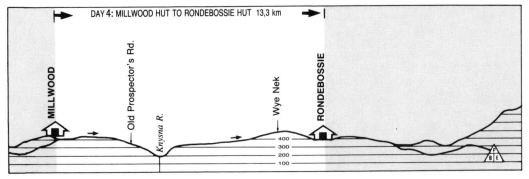

DAY 4: MILLWOOD HUT TO RONDEBOSSIE HUT 13,3 km

MILLWOOD Old Prospector's Rd. Knysna R. Wye Nek RONDEBOSSIE

400
300
200
100

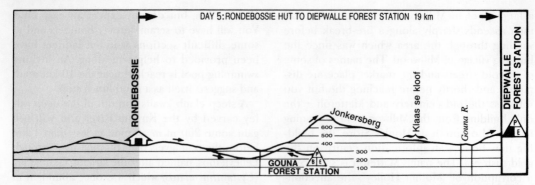

the sea with landmarks such as the Knysna Heads and Lagoon and the Robberg Peninsula near Plettenberg Bay clearly visible, as well as the mountains further inland.

Near the 9 km mark the trail passes into Vanhuysteensbos with its impressive forest tree ferns, following a forest track along Klaas se Kloof. A short way beyond the 11 km mark you will join up with one of the alternative routes of the Elephant Walk which starts at Diepwalle Forest Station. The full route covers 18,2 km, but trailists also have a choice of two shorter routes.

Shortly after the 12 km mark you will descend into Muiskloof where water is usually available and a short way further on you will cross a tributary of the Gouna River. A few minutes later the Rooi River with its eye-catching forest tree ferns is crossed with the Knysna/Uniondale road being reached a short

way on. Diepwalle Hut is reached about 500 m further after a short climb. The hut, a double-storey house built from stone and lined with wooden panelling upstairs, is a complete surprise.

Diepwalle was originally known as "Deepwalls" and earlier in this century timber was transported from here to Knysna by rail. The terminal of the 35 km narrow-gauge railway line was at Ysterhoutrug, a short way below Diepwalle. The line was in use from 1904 to 1949.

Day 6 and 7: Diepwalle Hut to Harkerville Forest Station The trail was extended in 1994 by two days. From Diepwalle the route continues through indigenous forest for 16 km to Fisantehoek, while the last day's route to Harkerville Forest Station is 11 km. From Harkerville it is possible to link up with the Harkerville Hiking Trail.

HARKERVILLE

Scenery ranging from tranquil indigenous forest to rugged coastline has made this two-day trail in the Sinclair Nature Reserve in the southern Cape extremely popular. The coastline is characterised by small coves separated by rocky headlands which provide some challenges and although the hiking here is taxing, it is also exhilarating. Delightful rock pools invite you for a dip during the summer months, and if it's too cold to swim you can spend an interesting interlude just exploring them. The Sinclair Hut is perfectly positioned on the edge of the coastal plateau with fynbos stretching down to the cliffs.

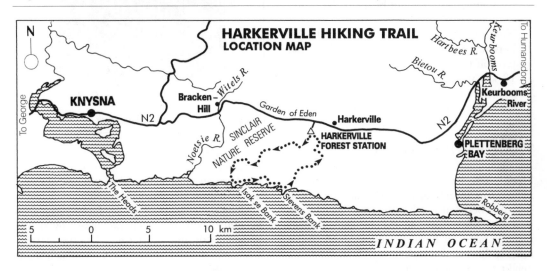

TRAIL PLANNER

Distance 26,6 km; 2 days

Grading B+

Reservations The Regional Director, Southern Cape Forest Region, Private Bag X12, Knysna 6570, Telephone (0445) 82-5466, Fax (0445) 82-5461. Reservations are accepted up to one year in advance.

Group size Minimum 2; Maximum 12

Maps The trail is indicated on a black and white printed map with information on the geology, flora and fauna of the area, which is forwarded with your receipt and permit.

Facilities The two trail huts are equipped with bunks with mattresses, while drinking water, fireplaces, firewood and refuse bins are provided. The huts have toilets.

Logistics Circular route. At the start/end of the trail hikers are accommodated in the Harkerville Hut, a converted forester's house sleeping 24. The hut has electric lighting, a cold-water shower, flush toilet and a wood-burning stove, as well as braai facilities.

Relevant information

■ Hikers afraid of sheer drops could experience difficulties at some of the coastal sections. Several narrow rocky ledges have to be negotiated, while ladders and wooden bridges are provided at other difficult obstacles.

■ Backpacks should be kept as light as possible and packed well to prevent the pack from unbalancing you along precarious sections. In addition, nothing which could catch on jagged rocks should be lashed onto packs.

■ If possible, time the coastal section to coincide with low tide. Consult a tide table.

■ During inclement weather extreme caution should be exercised on the coastal section as the wet rocks are slippery.

■ In 1994 the Outeniqua Hiking Trail was extended to link up with the Harkerville Hiking Trail. Hikers can combine the two trails, although it will not be a circular route.

How to get there Travelling along the N2 between Knysna and Plettenberg Bay, the turn-off to the Harkerville Hut is signposted 13 km west of Plettenberg Bay. Follow a gravel road to reach the hut 1,5 km on, ignoring two deviations to the right.

Climate

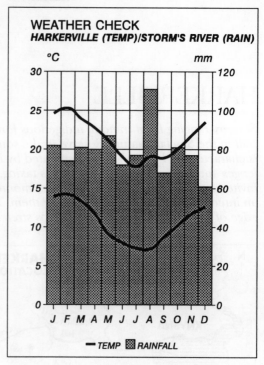

WEATHER CHECK
HARKERVILLE (TEMP)/STORM'S RIVER (RAIN)

— TEMP ▒ RAINFALL

TRAIL ENVIRONMENT

Flora The trail winds mainly through the indigenous forests of the Tsitsikamma which stretches between the Keurbooms River in the west and Krom River in the east, while short sections take you through fynbos. Much of the route is through dry, high forest which reaches a height of between 10 and 18 m. Among the common trees found here are Outeniqua and real yellowwoods, stinkwood, Cape holly, candlewood, white pear, assegai, Cape beech and forest elder. Also occurring are false ironwood, kamassi, tree fuchsia and wild pomegranate. Sagewood and forest num-num grow in the rel-

The showy, tubular, orange and brick-red flowers of the tree fuchsia are usually obscured by leaves

atively open understorey while clumps of forest tree fern grow along stream banks.

Along the coast the high dry forest is replaced by a dry scrub forest characterised by sparse undergrowth and short trees. Dominant trees are candlewood, Cape and common saffron, as well as white milkwood.

An interesting species of the scrub forest is the Cape wild banana which is restricted to the coast between Knysna and Humansdorp. It is closely related to the crane flower (*Strelitzia reginae*), as well as the Transvaal and Natal wild bananas. With leaves of 1 to 2 m long, this small tree reaches a height of up to 8 m.

Flowering plants to be seen along the coast include krantz aloe, the blue agapanthus (*Agapanthus praecox*) and gazanias (*Gazania rigens*).

The fynbos of the coastal plateau comprises species such as the blue sugarbush, tall yellowbush, the red, tubular *Erica versicolor* and several everlastings (*Helichrysum*). There is also a variety of bulbs and corms such as watsonias and babartia (*Bobartia spathacea*), which is especially conspicuous after veld fires with its bright yellow flowers.

There are also several fynbos islands in the Harkerville forest, but they are mainly overgrown by climbing ferns (*Gleichenia polypodioides*). Among these are Die Mark, Grooteiland and Kleineiland. It was initially suggested that these islands were the result of man-made disturbances of the forests. However, more recent research has provided evidence that they are remnants of fynbos which have been invaded by the forests.

Fauna The forests are the habitat of blue duiker, bushbuck, bushpig and leopard, but the animal you are most likely to see or hear in the forests is the chacma baboon. Rock dassies inhabit the rocky coastline, while Cape clawless otter occur near streams along the coast, but are seldom seen.

Although the famous Knysna elephants once seasonally migrated from the Gouna and Deepwalls forests to the coast in the Harkerville area, there has been no evidence of them crossing the national road since 1979. During a survey conducted in 1969-70 by Nick Carter on behalf of the Eastern Cape Branch of the Wildlife Society, elephants were even observed digging in the fynbos above the coastal cliffs, close to where the Sinclair Hut is today. The eastern limit of their range along the coast was the Kranshoek Viewpoint.

The elephant skeleton on display in the Knysna Publicity Association office was found in the Garden of Eden in 1983. The elephant was estimated to have been between 60 and 65 years old when it died in the early 1970s. A more detailed account of the Knysna elephants can be found in the chapter on the Outeniqua Hiking Trail.

Other mammals recorded in the area include vervet monkey, honey badger and porcupine, while the Cape grysbok occurs in fynbos areas.

Seals, dolphins and whales are sometimes seen from suitable vantage points on the cliffs.

The birdlife of the area is similar to that occurring along the Otter Hiking Trail with forest, fynbos and sea and shore birds being represented. The forests are the habitat of some 35 typical forest species including greenspotted and cinnamon doves, Knysna lourie, Narina trogon, redbilled woodhoopoe and Knysna woodpecker. Also occurring are terrestrial bulbul, starred robin, Cape batis and bluemantled flycatcher, while forest canary occur in the forest margins.

In the fynbos patches you chance ticking Knysna and Victorin's warblers, Cape sugarbird and orangebreasted sunbird.

Among the species you are most likely to see along the rocky shore are African black oystercatcher, turnstone and kelp gull. Other species to keep an eye out for include whitebreasted cormorant, while Cape gannet occurs offshore.

History Exploitation of the southern Cape forests was initially concentrated on the forests west of Knysna. A control post was established at Plettenberg Bay in 1788 and Johann Friedrich Meeding was appointed as superintendent of the forests of the Knysna/Plettenberg Bay area. Meeding is regarded as the first forester in South Africa and during his term of office effective control and conservation measures were enforced.

Because of the potential value of the forests as a source of wood for the Royal Navy, control over the Knysna/Plettenberg Bay forests was transferred to the navy in 1812. However, when the Royal Navy lost interest in the forests in 1825, the area was once again opened up to wanton destruction.

The Harkerville area is named after Major Robert Charles Harker, who came to the Cape with the 152nd Regiment. After arriving in Cape Town in 1823, Major Harker established himself at Woodville near George where he unsuccessfully tried his hand at farming. In 1826 he was appointed Government Resident at Plettenberg Bay, a position which he held until 1848 when the post was abolished.

By the mid-1850s woodcutters started exploiting the Tsitsikamma forests from the east, opening up vast tracts. In 1874 Captain Christopher Harison was appointed the first full-time forester of the George, Knysna and Tsitsikamma forests and implemented a new forestry conservation policy. However, as a result of the discovery of gold in the Knysna forests in 1876 the policy virtually collapsed.

Scientific control of the forests was implemented following the appointment of Count M de Vasselot de Régné as Superintendent of Forests in the Cape Colony in 1882 and the first Forestry Act was passed in 1888.

In 1939 the axes of the woodcutters finally fell silent when their exploitation rights were cancelled by the Annuities for Woodcutters Act which made provision for the payment of a small pension. For the next 28 years only windfalls and dead trees were exploited and in 1970 the first multiple use management system was introduced.

Geology The geology of the rocky coastline is dominated by hard sandstones of the Table Mountain Group which were deposited some 500 million years ago.

In the distant past pressures in the earth's crust tilted the sediments steeply, in some places almost vertically. Over countless centuries the bashing waves, salt-laden mists and temperatures have eroded the cliffs into what must be one of the most rugged coastlines along the southern African coast.

TRAIL DESCRIPTION

Day 1: Harkerville Hut to Sinclair Hut The trail immediately enters the enchanting indigenous forest, initially following the same route as the Perdekop Trail, an educational trail for youth groups visiting the Harkerville education centre. Keep the tree list on the map handy as trees along the section are numbered according to the *The National List of Indigenous Trees*. You will be impressed by some enormous Outeniqua yellowwoods and the stinkwoods are easily identifiable by their cylindrical trunks dappled with patches of white and orange.

The trail traverses easy terrain and after the 4 km mark you descend gently, passing some forest tree ferns, to cross the Wit River which is sometimes only a trickle of water. Some 10 minutes on a forestry road is crossed and between the 6 km and 7 km markers the trail takes you through pine plantations. A short way on you will reach a stand of enormous Californian redwood trees (*Sequoia sempervirens*). They were planted in 1925 as one of a few experimental plots in South Africa and although the 33 m-high specimens are impressive, they do not nearly match those in their natural environment on the west coast of the United States of America where they attain heights of up to 100 m.

You turn right here and after a short, gentle

uphill stretch along the road you re-enter the indigenous forest, continuing over easy terrain. As you approach the 10 km mark you will notice the forest becoming lower and more scrub-like – a warning that you are nearing the coast. Some 15 minutes after the 10 km mark you emerge from the forest with a magnificent view over the sea and rugged coastline. Initially the descent is extremely steep but wooden stairs with railings make this otherwise impossible section quite manageable. The remainder of the descent requires careful footwork and takes longer than expected.

The coast is characterised by several small coves separated by rocky headlands with steep cliffs. Unfortunately the beaches are not covered in sand but with loose round rocks which are taxing on the feet, ankles and knees. At the end of the first bay you will face your first challenge of the day – a sheer rock cliff above a deep gully. It is, however, not as daunting as it appears at first as the chain handholds are firmly secured to the rocks and there are sufficient footholds.

The stretch along the coast is only 3 km, but depending on how agile you are, could take you as long as the first 10 km. Along this section there are a number of wooden ladders and you will have to ease yourself along narrow ledges.

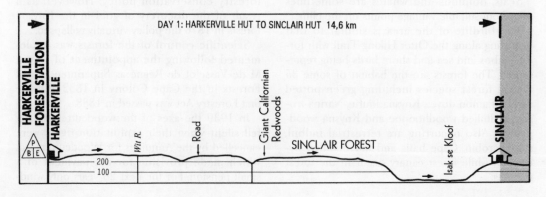

DAY 1: HARKERVILLE HUT TO SINCLAIR HUT 14,6 km

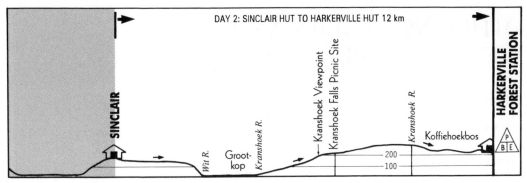

DAY 2: SINCLAIR HUT TO HARKERVILLE HUT 12 km

SINCLAIR · Wit R. · Groot-kop · Kranshoek R. · Kranshoek Viewpoint · Kranshoek Falls Picnic Site · Kranshoek R. · Koffiehoekbos · HARKERVILLE FOREST STATION · 200 · 100

At the end of the coastal section you ascend steeply to the plateau, initially passing through coastal scrub forest where blue agapanthus add a touch of colour in summer, before you emerge into fynbos near the edge of the plateau.

The final kilometre to Sinclair Hut is sheer bliss as it is along an almost level path. The hut consists of two rooms separated by a central cooking area and is picturesquely positioned at the edge of a bluegum plantation. From the wooden deck in front of the hut hikers are rewarded with superb views of the fynbos stretching down to the cliffs and the sea far below.

Day 2: Sinclair Hut to Harkerville Hut The first 30 minutes are pleasant walking along the coastal plateau through fynbos to a forested kloof where you start descending. Soon, though, the trail emerges into the fynbos again and you descend quite steeply along a ridge to the Kleineiland River. This is a good breakfast spot as the river has soft grassy banks and the pools are inviting for an early morning dip.

Once again the coastal section is about 3 km and the scenery is as exhilarating as the first day. Particularly striking are the steeply dipping sandstone formations of the Table Mountain Group which have been eroded into jagged cliffs by the constant washing of the waves, salt-laden mist and rain. Orange lichens cling to the rocks while cheerful yellow gazanias grow in rock crevices surprisingly close to the sea.

Once again the coastal section is characterised by several small coves separated by rocky headlands where rock scrambling is inevitable. There is one particularly nerve-racking section where a near vertical cliff directly above the sea has to be traversed, without the assistance of any chains. Fortunately, though, there are sufficient natural hand- and footholds.

Near the 4 km mark you pass through a rock arch and further along you ascend steeply to avoid an impassable stretch of the coastline. The trail then descends down a scree slope where steps have been constructed and looking back towards the headland you will see an enormous rock arch. A short way on a ladder without a handrail spans a deep gully at a rather awkward angle and after a final rock scramble you can heave a sigh of relief as there are no more tricky sections.

At the end of the final beach of the day you meet up with the Kranshoek Walk where an information board explains the origin of the ankle-twisting, boulder-covered beaches. The inevitable ascent follows and within 20 minutes you are likely to meet up with envious tourists at the Kranshoek Viewpoint where you will be rewarded with a magnificent view of the rugged coastline.

From the viewpoint you follow a route close to the edge of the deep gorge carved by the Kranshoek River and about 15 minutes later you reach the Kranshoek Falls which are impressive after rain, but no more than a few damp seeps after a dry spell. This marks the halfway point of the trail and the picnic tables on the lawn above the falls are quite suitable for lunch.

Since there is no water on the homeward lap of the trail water-bottles should be filled above the falls. From the falls the trail continues across the road and soon you are meandering through the forest. There are no landmarks in the forest and although there are a few gentle uphills and downhills, the last 6 km is undemanding. About 90 minutes after setting off from the falls you turn right onto the forest road which gives access to the Kranshoek Falls and Viewpoint. A mere 10 minute walk will take you back to the Harkerville Hut.

OTHER NORTHERN AND WESTERN CAPE TRAILS

NORTHERN CAPE

ORANGE VIEW

Distance 41,5 km; 2 days

Reservations Prieska Municipality, P O Box 16, Prieska 8940, Telephone (0594) 6-1002.

Group size Minimum 2; Maximum 10

Facilities There are no facilities at the overnight stop, which is an overhang at the end of the first day's hike.

Description The trail has been laid out in the Rooihoogte Mountains north-west of Prieska. The area is characterised by mountainous terrain with several deep gorges. The first day's hike covers 8 km, but can be extended by undertaking two optional excursions of 6 and 4 km respectively along two gorges. The turning point on the second day's hike is reached 8 km beyond the overnight stop and is a mere 200 m from the Orange River. From the vantage point hikers are rewarded with magnificent views of the Orange River, some 250 m below. The return leg covers 15,5 km and is over relatively easy terrain with the first and last sections retracing sections already covered.

POFADDER

Distance 76 km; 4 days

Reservations Pofadder Municipality, P O Box 108, Pofadder 8890, Telephone (02532) 46.

Group size Minimum 3; no maximum

Facilities Only basic campsites at overnight stops.

Description This trail north of Pofadder gives backpackers the unique opportunity of discovering this relatively unexplored part of South Africa. The trail, laid out in a figure eight,

stretches between Onseepkans and the old mission settlement at Pella and can be hiked in either direction. Two days of the four-day hike follow the course of the Orange River, while the other two days traverse the Bushmanland plains and rugged mountains. A highlight of the section along the river is the 30 m Ritchy Falls, also known as the Verkeerdomvalle (Back to Front Falls) because of the sudden change in the direction of the Orange River. Shorter options are also possible. The trail is only open between 1 May and 30 September.

SEEKOEIRIVIER

Distance 25 km; 2 or 3 days

Reservations Seekoeirivier Hiking Trail, P O Box 147, Colesberg 5980, Telephone (051) 753-1378.

Group size Minimum 2; Maximum 10

Facilities The overnight camp consists of two rondavels, accommodating eight people. Amenities include beds, mattresses, a kitchen equipped with a gas stove and fridge, hot and cold water, bathroom, toilet, fireplaces and firewood.

Description This trail near Colesberg offers trailists an opportunity to discover the natural beauty of the Great Karoo and to experience life on a Karoo farm. The trail traverses rugged terrain with interesting rock formations and beautiful views over the surrounding area. The first day's route to the overnight stop on the banks of the Seekoei River covers 5 km. Swimming is permitted in the river and hikers can also try their hand at fishing. The second day's hike follows a circular route of 15 km in the mountains and only a daypack needs to be carried. The third day's route is a short 7 km back to the starting point. Interesting features along the trail include an old stone leopard trap and rock paintings.

TRANSKAROO

Distance 42 km; 3 days

Reservations Ms E Van Der Merwe, Transkaroo Hiking Trail, P O Box 105, Noupoort 5950, Telephone (04924) 2-2112 or (04926) 2-1506.

Group size Minimum 2; Maximum 12

Facilities At the Wilgefontein base camp and the two overnight stops accommodation is provided in comfortable huts equipped with stretchers, a kitchen, shower, toilet, fireplaces and firewood.

Description Situated in the Upper Karoo, this circular route traverses a 10 500 ha farm near Noupoort. The trail winds through typical Karoo scenery varying from boulder outcrops to hilly terrain and table-top peaks. About 15 km is covered on the first day's hike and highlights along the route include interesting rock formations, a beautiful rock pool and panoramic views. The second day's hike covers 19 km and from Beacon Hill there is a 360 degree view of the surrounding countryside. The final day's route covers 8 km, passing interesting rock paintings, some of which are estimated to be about 500 years old. Animals occurring in the area include mountain reedbuck, grey rhebok, baboon and rock dassie. A shorter, two-day option over 25 km is possible.

WESTERN CAPE

ARANGIESKOP

Distance 20,9 km; 2 days

Reservations Robertson Municipality, P O Box 52, Robertson 6705, Telephone (02351) 3112.

Group size Minimum 2; Maximum 23

Facilities At the starting point accommodation is provided in a cottage, while an overnight hut is available at the end of the first day's hike. Amenities include hot and cold water and bunks.

Description This circular route in the Langeberg traverses the mountains with their sheer cliffs and deep gorges north of Robertson. The trail winds through fynbos characterised by ericas and proteas, while disas present a colourful display during summer. Among the animals hikers might surprise are chacma baboon, klipspringer and grysbok, while the birdlife is typical of the fynbos areas of the south-western Cape. On the first day's hike of 9,5 km the trail gains some 1 100 m in altitude, but hikers are rewarded with far-reaching views over the patchwork of farms in the Breede River Valley, Robertson and the Koo region between Montagu and Matroosberg. The return route covers 11,4 km.

ATTAQUASKLOOF

Distance 34,7 km: 2 days or 39,3 km: 3 days

Reservations Outeniquas Conservation Area, Private Bag X6517, George 6530, Telephone (0441) 74-2671.

Group size Minimum 2; Maximum 12

Facilities Accommodation at the end of the first day's hike and day two (if the optional circular route is hiked) is provided in a renovated farmhouse. Bunks with mattresses, a wood-burning stove, paraffin lamps, a cast iron pot and kettle, as well as hot and cold running water and a fireplace are provided.

Description The steep upgrades and descents of this trail dictate that it should only be tackled by very fit hikers. Situated in the 10 000 ha Attaquaskloof Nature Reserve, the trail traverses the rugged mountains west of the Robinson Pass which connects Mossel Bay and Oudtshoorn. The reserve lies in the transition zone between the winter and all-year rainfall areas and as a result the fynbos is not only exceptionally beautiful, but also very interesting. The first day's hike covers 15,5 km while the second day's hike is an optional 4,6 km loop. On the third day the trail partly follows the historic Attaquaskloof Pass, the earliest route into the interior, before traversing the southern slopes of the Skurweberg from where spectacular views can be enjoyed.

BESEMFONTEIN

Distance 29,6 km; 2 days

Reservations Towerkop Nature Reserve, Private Bag X216, Ladismith 6885, Telephone (028) 551-1077.

Group size Minimum 2; Maximum 30

Facilities Hikers are accommodated in two huts at the start of the trail at Besemfontein. Amenities include bunks, gas stoves and refrigerators, pots and kettles. A stone shelter is available at Uitkyk on the trail.

Description The rugged northern slopes of the Klein Swartberg Mountains north-west of Ladismith are characterised by high peaks and deep gorges. The first day's hike covers 19,4 km and affords hikers spectacular views of the Karoo and The Hell (Gamkaskloof). The highlight of the second day is the inviting pool at the base of a series of waterfalls in the Verlorenhoekskloof.

Since Besemfontein lies within the mountain fynbos to Karooveld transition zone, the trail winds through an interesting variety of plants, including the endemic Ladismith protea. Game to be seen include klipspringer and grey rhebok.

BLOUPUNT/COGMANSKLOOF

Distance 27,7 km; 2 days

Reservations The Public Relations Officer, Information Bureau, P O Box 24, Montagu 6720, Telephone (0234) 4-2471.

Group size Minimum 2; Maximum 16

Facilities Klipspringer Cabin at the start of the trail is equipped with 12 beds, as well as a wood stove, showers with hot and cold water, toilets, fireplaces and firewood. Dassie Cabin at the car

park has four beds, electricity, hot/cold water showers, toilets, a fireplace and firewood.

Description These two-day trails have been laid out in the 1 200 ha Montagu Mountain Nature Reserve west of Montagu. The routes wind through spectacular rock formations with vegetation ranging from succulents to fynbos.

The Bloupunt Trail of 15,6 km leads to the 1 000 m peak of that name from where trailists can enjoy expansive views of Ashton, Bonnievale, Robertson, McGregor and Montagu. The return leg passes close to three magnificent waterfalls.

The Cogmanskloof route is 12,1 km long and except for the first 2 km beyond Klipspringer Cabin which is rather steep, traverses easy terrain. Despite the lower altitude trailists will nevertheless enjoy magnificent views of Montagu and the surrounding mountains.

BOESMANSKLOOF

Distance 15,8 km (linear); 31,6 km (return)

Reservations The Manager, Vrolijkheid Nature Reserve, Private Bag X614, Robertson 6705, Telephone (02353) 621.

Group size Minimum 2; Maximum 15

Facilities There are no overnight facilities along the trail, but private accommodation is available at either end of the trail.

Description This popular trail between McGregor and Greyton winds through the Riviersonderend Mountains, following what was once the only direct route between the two quaint villages. Attractions along the route include the Oak Falls – a series of waterfalls and inviting pools – spectacular mountain scenery and a rich variety of fynbos plants, including two endangered erica species. Although the trail can be commenced from either side, hikers usually set off from Die Galg, walk to Greyton where accommodation is available at several establishments, and return along the same route the following day. On the return leg hikers will gain about 450 m in altitude to the highest point of the trail, followed by another steep climb (about 150 m) at Die Galg.

▲ 19

20 ▼

18 *(previous page)* The Wolfberg Cracks in the Cederberg form a vertical cleft of 30 metres deep and in some places just 2 metres wide
19 Red Hat Crossing over the Riviersonderend, Hottentots-Holland Hiking Trail
20 Sleepad Hut, one of several basic stone shelters in the Cederberg Wilderness Area

▼ 21   ▲ 22   23 ▼

21 Red disa, Hottentots-Holland Hiking Trail
22 Boskloof Hut, the second overnight stop on the Swellendam Hiking Trail
23 Glimpse of the patchwork of farmlands from the Swellendam Hiking Trail

24 Looking towards Gouekrans Hut, the first overnight stop on the Swartberg Hiking Trail
25 The Kruispad route on the Swellendam Hiking Trail offers magnificent views of the Swellendam wheatfields

▲ 26

▲ 27

28 ▼

26 The Gouekrans Hut lies in a secluded valley on the Swartberg Hiking Trail
27 Relaxing along an amber-coloured stream on the Outeniqua Hiking Trail
28 Matteroli or Monk's Store is one of only two buildings dating back to the gold rush at Millwood

29 *Mimetes*, Groot Winterhoek Wilderness Area
30 Rugged coastal scenery on the first day of the Harkerville Hiking Trail
31 Sections of the Harkerville Hiking Trail traverse near-vertical rockfaces

▲ 29   ▼ 30   31 ▶

▲ 32

32 Backpacking through fynbos in the Groot Winterhoek Wilderness Area
33 Relaxing alongside one of the inviting pools in the Groot Kliphuis River, Groot Winterhoek Wilderness Area

33 ▼

34 The historic residence at Geelbek where trailists are accommodated on the
Strandveld Educational Trail
35 View over Langebaan Lagoon from the Waterklip on the Strandveld Educational Trail

▲ 36   37 ▼

38 ▼   39 ►

36 Helderfontein Huts, Boosmansbos
Wilderness Area
37 The Springbok Hiking Trail traverses the
Nuweveld Mountains which are often snow-
capped in winter
38 View of the Karoo National Park from the
plateau
39 Deep valley carved by the Duivenhoks River,
Boosmansbos Wilderness Area

40 Staircase Falls, passed on the first day's hike of the Tsitsikamma Hiking Trail
41 Descending to the Bloukrans River on the second day's hike of the Tsitsikamma Hiking Trail
42 Peak Formosa seen from the top of the Rushes Pass on the Tsitsikamma Hiking Trail

▲ 41   42 ▼

43 Skilderkrans, passed on the second day's hike of the Otter Hiking Trail, offers magnificent views of the Tsitsikamma coastline
44 Groot River Lagoon, starting point of the Tsitsikamma Hiking Trail and ending point of the Otter Hiking Trail
45 Robinson Camp, the overnight hut at the start of the Gonaqua Hiking Trail
46 The rugged Tsitsikamma coast with Bloubaai in the distance as seen on the second day's hike of the Otter Hiking Trail

▲ 43   44 ▼

47 Kettlespout Falls, Hogsback Hiking Trail
48 Hiking in one of the deep kloofs carved by
the fast-flowing rivers draining the area traversed
by the Gonaqua Hiking Trail

▲ 47

48 ▼

BOOSMANSBOS

Distance 27 to 74 km; 2 days or longer

Reservations The Officer-in-Charge, Boosmansbos Wilderness Area, P O Box 109, Heidelberg 6760, Telephone (02934) 2-2412.

Group size Minimum 2; Maximum 12

Facilities Only basic overnight shelters (without any facilities) are provided in the wilderness area.

Description The Boosmanbos Wilderness Area in the Langeberg Mountain range is characterised by imposing mountain peaks, high krantzes and deep ravines. Access is via the Grootvadersbos State Forest north-west of Heidelberg. The vegetation is dominated by mountain fynbos and in spring the southern slopes are blanketed in magnificent pink ericas while the northern slopes become a yellow sea of leucadendrons. The most popular route in this 14 200 ha wilderness area is a 27 km, two-day circular trail to Helderfontein huts. The two-day route can be extended by continuing to the Klein Witbooisrivier huts, a route which leads over Grootberg (1 637 m), the highest peak in the area.

BRANDVLEI DAM/ KWAGGAKLOOF

Distance 42 km; 2 days

Reservations Worcester Publicity Association, 75 Church Street, Worcester 6850, Telephone (0231) 7-1408.

Group size Minimum 2; Maximum 18

Facilities Accommodation at the end of the first day's hike comprises two huts equipped with beds and mattresses, kitchen, cold water showers and outside fireplaces.

Description This trail takes its name from the two dams south of Worcester around which it winds. The first day's hike is an easy 18 km along the banks of the Brandvlei Dam and a highlight on this stretch is a hot water spring. A rather long 24 km is covered on the second day's hike and the terrain is slightly more demanding, but despite the relatively long distances the route is suitable for beginners and family outings. The trail starts and ends at Nekkies Holiday Resort at Brandvlei Dam just outside Worcester.

DASSIESHOEK

Distance 38 km; 2 days

Reservations Robertson Municipality, P O Box 52, Robertson 6705, Telephone (02351) 3112.

Group size Minimum 2; Maximum 35

Facilities Accommodation for 20 people is available in a cottage at the start of the trail, while 35 people can be accommodated in the Dassieshoek overnight hut on the trail. Hot and cold water and bunks, mattresses and fireplaces are provided.

Description Winding along the southern slopes of the Langeberg, this circular trail starts at the Silverstrand Resort near Robertson and then heads towards the Dassieshoek Nature Reserve. The trail leads through fynbos with a large variety of proteas and ericas, while disas are conspicuous during February and March. The first day's hike is a long (16,6 km) uphill slog and the trail gains some 500 m in altitude before dropping down to the overnight hut. Along this section the route passes through several delightful kloofs. The second day's hike covers 15 km, returning via Droëberg to the starting point. Along the route hikers will be rewarded with stunning views of the patchwork of farmlands in the valleys, the Breede River Valley and Robertson.

GAMKA

Distance 23,5 km; 2 days

Reservations The Reserve Manager, Gamka Mountain Nature Reserve, Private Bag X21, Oudtshoorn 6620, Telephone (04437) 3-3367.

Group size Minimum 2; Maximum 10

Facilities A tented trails camp is provided at the end of the first day's hike.

Description This two-day trail traverses the rugged terrain of the Gamka Mountains, an isolated range between the Swartberg and the Outeniqua mountains, south-west of Oudtshoorn. The vegetation of the 9 428 ha reserve varies from succulent Karoo to dry mountain fynbos and renosterveld and includes a number of rare plant species such as the golden mimetes. The reserve was proclaimed in 1974 to protect the small population of Cape mountain zebra which survived in the mountains. Other mammals include eland, klipspringer, baboon, grey rhebok and grysbok, while some 115 birds have been recorded to date.

GENADENDAL

Distance 25,3 km; 2 days

Reservations The Manager, Vrolijkheid Nature Reserve, Private Bag X614, Robertson 6705, Telephone (02353) 621.

Group size Minimum 2; Maximum 14

Facilities Overnight facilities are available at the start of the trail, as well as on the farm De Hoek at the end of the first day's hike. Fireplaces and firewood are provided.

Description Winding through magnificent mountain fynbos, this tough circular route rewards hikers with breathtaking views of the Riviersonderend Mountains and the surrounding countryside.

The trail starts at the Moravian Mission Church in Genadendal, west of Greyton. On the first day's hike of 14,3 km some 600 m is gained in altitude before the trail descends to De Hoek on the northern side of the mountain. On the second day's route of 11 km the trail crosses back to Genadendal. Once again there is a steep climb (the trail gains 800 m in altitude to the nek below Uitkykkop) before dropping down to Genadendal.

The trail traverses private property and the Riviersonderend Conservation Area.

GROOT WINTERHOEK

Distance 45 km; various options

Reservations The Officer-in-Charge, Groot Winterhoek Wilderness Area, P O Box 26, Porterville 6810, Telephone (02623) 2900. Guided weekend and four-day trails are conducted from Cape Town by the Wilderness Leadership School, P O Box 24046, Claremont, Telephone (021) 64-4532.

Group size Minimum 2; Maximum 12

Facilities Basic shelters (without any facilities) are provided at Weltevrede, De Tronk, Perdevlei, Groot Kliphuis and Die Hel.

Description Covering some 30 600 ha, the Groot Winterhoek Wilderness Area lies in the mountains south-west of Porterville. The area is renowned for its interesting rock formations, profusion of wild flowers and beautiful mountain scenery. The inviting swimming pools in the Groot Kliphuis River and the magnificent waterfall and pools at Die Hel, a deep gorge carved by the Vier-en-Twintig Riviere, are added attractions. Other popular areas include Groot Kliphuis and Perdevlei. Backpackers are not restricted to the footpaths and the more adventurous can tackle an ascent of the 2 077 m Groot Winterhoek Peak.

KRISTALKLOOF

Distance 25,5 km; 2 days

Reservations The Manager, Tourist Camp, P O Box 29, Riversdale 6770, Telephone (02933) 3-2420.

Group size: Minimum 2; Maximum 8

Facilities Basic campsites are provided at the end of the first day's hike.

Description An outstanding feature of the Langeberg range north of Riversdale is the profusion of fynbos plants. Between September and November the bulbs and orchids create a spectacular display while masses of everlastings are especially eye-catching in November. Two endemic pincushions, *Leucospermum mundii* and *L. winterii* occur in the area. The circular route starts at the Toll House in Garcia Pass and winds eastwards around Kampscheberg. The first 3 km of the hike ascends steeply to Wildehondekloofnek, while the remaining 6 km of the day's hike to the overnight stop at Boegoekloof is downhill. The second day's hike is an easy 16,5 km, the last section being along Garcia Pass.

ROOIWATERSPRUIT

Distance 24,5 km; 2 days with an optional third day

Reservations The Manager, Tourist Camp, P O Box 29, Riversdale 6770, Telephone (02933) 3-2420.

Group size Minimum 2; Maximum 14

Facilities Two overnight huts, sleeping six and eight people respectively, are provided at the end of the first day's hike.

Description This route traverses the Langeberg range west of Garcia Pass and can be started at either end of the trail, at the Toll House or the Korentevetterivier Dam. From the Toll House the trail gains some 600 m over the first 5 km to Nekkie, where there is an optional 3 km out-and-back detour to the Sleeping Beauty which offers one of the most spectacular views of the Langeberg range. After passing below Aasvoëlkrans the trail descends to the overnight shelters along the Rooiwaterspruit with its inviting pools. The second day's route is an easy 9 km hike which initially follows a fire-break before winding through and alongside pine plantations to the Korentevetterivier Dam. The trail can be extended to a four-day route by combining it with the Kristalkloof Hiking Trail.

SPRINGBOK

Distance 26,5 km; 3 days

Reservations The Director, National Parks Board, P O Box 787, Pretoria 0001, Telephone (012) 343-1991 or P O Box 7400, Roggebaai 8012, Telephone (021) 22-2810.

Group size Minimum 2; Maximum 12

Facilities Two huts equipped with bunks and mattresses, a fireplace and an iron pot. Firewood, water, chemical toilets and refuse bins are also provided.

Description This circular trail in the Nuweveld Mountains north-west of Beaufort West offers hikers an opportunity to explore the floral wealth and scenic beauty of the Great Karoo on foot. Situated in the 32 795 ha Karoo National Park, the trail takes its name from the large herds of springbok which once roamed the Karoo plains. Other mammals occurring in the park include Cape mountain zebra, gemsbok, springbok, black wildebeest and red hartebeest, while 183 bird species have been recorded. The first day's hike covers a mere 4,5 km, while the second day's route of 11,5 km is a steep climb to the overnight hut on the plateau. On the third day the trail descends along Fonteinkloof back to the rest camp.

STRANDVELD

Distance 30 km; 2 days

Reservations Geelbek Environmental Centre, West Coast National Park, P O Box 25, Langebaan 7357, Telephone (02287) 2-2798.

Group size Minimum 2; Maximum 12

Facilities Accommodation at the historic Geelbek homestead, which serves as a base, is inclusive of all meals. Amenities include bunks with mattresses and hot and cold water showers.

Description On this route trailists are introduced to various facets of the West Coast – strandveld, dunes and the coast. Some 30 interpretive sites have been marked and are explained in a detailed brochure. The first day's hike covers 14 km, while the second day covers 16 km. Since trailists return to Geelbek at the end of each day's hike there is no need to carry a backpack and a daypack will suffice. The programme stretches over three nights and two days and trails can be commenced on Mondays, Tuesdays or Fridays.

TIERKOP

Distance 30 km; 2 days

Reservations Outeniquas Nature Reserve, Private Bag X6517, George 6530, Telephone (0441) 74-2671.

Group size Minimum 2; Maximum 30

Facilities Tierkop hut consists of five rooms equipped with bunks and mattresses. Other amenities include a cold water shower, outside fireplace supplied with a grid, firewood and an axe, as well as cast iron pots.

Description Starting at Witfontein Forest Station just outside George, this semi-circular trail alternates between mountain fynbos, pine plantations and indigenous forests along the southern slopes of the Outeniqua Mountains. The first day's hike of 17,5 km ascends steadily before dropping down to the old George Dam and over the last 4,5 km climbs steeply once again to the overnight hut at Tierkop. Highlights on the second day's hike (12,5 km), an easy downhill stretch, include a magnificent waterfall

and Pepsi Pools, while the final section winds alongside the Garden Route Dam.

VAN STADENSRUS

Distance 25 km; 2 days

Reservations The Resort Manager, The Pine Forest Recreation Resort, P O Box 44, Ceres 6835, Telephone (0233) 2-1170.

Group size Minimum 3; Maximum 12

Facilities There are no overnight huts on the trail, but camping is permitted at Van Stadensrus, the halfway mark on the trail.

Description This circular trail traverses the Skurweberg west of Ceres. The route passes through an interesting variety of fynbos species and hikers are rewarded with panoramic views of the fertile Ceres Valley with its mosaic of farmlands. From the Pine Forest Resort the first day's hike leads in an anti-clockwise direction to the Van Stadensrus campsite on the banks of the Koekedou River. On the second day the trail passes Cascade Pools and then climbs steadily towards Ceres Peak, which can be done as an optional ascent, before dropping down to a viewpoint with magnificent vistas. From here it is a pleasant walk to the Pine Forest Resort.

EASTERN CAPE

TSITSIKAMMA

The trail traverses the slopes of the Tsitsikamma Mountains in the opposite direction from the coastal Otter Hiking Trail, crossing streams which later become rivers as they enter the sea. Much of the hiking is through open fynbos which will make you appreciate the small forests with their cool, leafy fern glades and the colourful fungi which create fairytale scenes. The attractive wooden huts are scenically situated, offering panoramic views. For those with limited time, shorter options of the trail can be hiked.

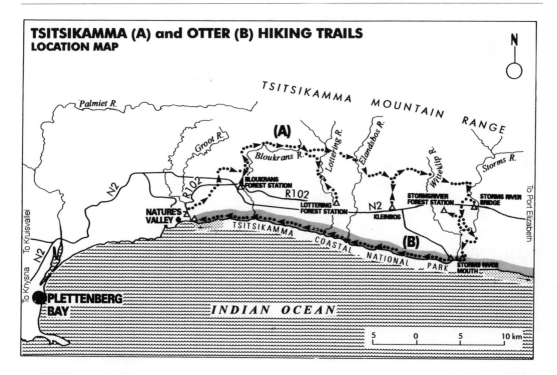

TSITSIKAMMA (A) and OTTER (B) HIKING TRAILS
LOCATION MAP

TRAIL PLANNER

Distance 57 km or 72 km; 5 days (shorter options possible)

Grading B

Reservations The Regional Director, Southern Cape Forest Region, Private Bag X12, Knysna 6570, Telephone (0445) 82-5466, Fax (0445) 82-5461. Reservations are accepted up to a year in advance.

Group size Minimum 2; Maximum 30

Maps A full-colour trail map with useful information on the history, flora and fauna on the reverse is available and one free copy is forwarded with your receipt and permit.

Facilities The overnight huts along the trail have bunks and mattresses. Fireplaces, firewood, water and pit toilets are provided.

Climate

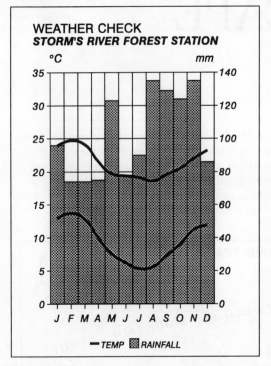

WEATHER CHECK
STORM'S RIVER FOREST STATION

− TEMP ▨ RAINFALL

Logistics Linear route. Arrangements can be made with Nature's Valley Guest House to assist hikers with transport at a reasonable charge. Telephone Mr and Mrs Bond on (04457) 6805. Kalander Hut, at the Groot River campsite, is conveniently situated at the start of the trail.

Hikers ending at Storms River Bridge can camp at the Tzitzikama Total Village, Telephone (04230) 910, Fax (04230) 954.

Those continuing to Storms River Mouth can either camp or stay in the self-contained chalets. Reservations are essential and should be directed to the Chief Director, National Parks Board, P O Box 787, Pretoria 0001, Telephone (012) 343-1991, Fax (012) 343-0905, or P O Box 7400, Roggebaai 8012, Telephone (021) 22-2810, Fax (021) 24-6211. There is a licensed restaurant, shop and coin-operated laundry.

Relevant information

■ After heavy rain river crossings can be difficult, demanding careful negotiating.

■ Extensive stretches of the trail are through open fynbos, so it is essential to take precautions against the sun.

■ Because of limited parking space, hikers terminating the trail at the Storms River Mouth Rest Camp are not allowed to leave their vehicles at the camp.

How to get there The trail commences at the Groot River Camp about 0,5 km east of the turn-off on the R102 to Nature's Valley.

TRAIL ENVIRONMENT

Flora Although towering yellowwoods and other forest giants are usually associated with the Tsitsikamma, 56 per cent of this trail passes through mountain fynbos. Situated towards the eastern limit of its distribution in an all-year rainfall area, the fynbos of the Tsitsikamma range is considerably poorer than that of the western Cape. The mountain slopes are most interesting from October to January when various erica, leucadendron and helichrysum species are at their best. To familiarise yourself with the fynbos, keep the trail map handy as species have been numbered on the map where they occur and these numbers correspond with the list at the bottom of the map.

Proteas are represented by the king protea (*Protea cynaroides*), tall yellowbush, white sugarbush, blue sugarbush, *Leucadendron salignum* and *L. spissifolium*. The critically rare *Leucospermum glabrum*, a medium-sized, rounded shrub with conspicuous bright orange-red flowers in spring, grows on moist south-facing slopes.

Between May and November several erica species transform the mountain slopes into a blaze of colour. Among these are the beautiful *Erica formosa* with its white, urn-shaped flowers which can be seen between July and November. Also attractive are the plumes of pale rose to white, cup-shaped flowers of *E. sparsa*, seen between May and November. Keep an eye out for the two-toned flowers of *E. densifolia* between September and March. The tubular flowers are usually red with green tips, but are occasionally white with green tips.

Other flowering plants include *Bobartia spathacea*, a tall rush-like plant with bright yellow flowers, the delicate lobelia, eulophia and

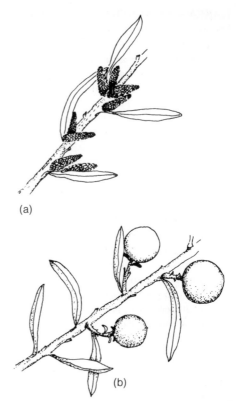

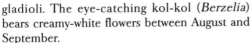

Outeniqua yellowwood with (a) catkins on male tree and (b) fruits on female tree

gladioli. The eye-catching kol-kol (*Berzelia*) bears creamy-white flowers between August and September.

The fynbos is generally treeless but mountain cypress, wild clove-bush, blossom tree, water blossom pea, fountain bush, iron martin and water white alder occur occasionally, either in clusters or singly.

If you are keen to learn more about the flora of the area, don't forget to slip a copy of Audrey Moriarty's wild flower guide, *Outeniqua, Tsitsikamma and Eastern Little Karoo* into your backpack.

Stretching between Keurbooms River in the west and the Krom River in the east, the indigenous forests of the Tsitsikamma region cover about 14 400 ha. More than half of this area falls within the Bloukrans and Lottering state forests.

Only 25 per cent of the trail passes through indigenous forest with extensive patches on the first day and last day (Sleepkloof to Storms River Mouth). The forests of the southern Cape are remnants of the extensive tropical forests which occurred thousands of years ago along the coastal areas to the southern Cape. During a subsequent arid phase the tropical forests retreated to the equatorial zones, but as a result of the favourable climatic conditions here, large tracts survived.

Although the forests have a basically tropical character, they are not truly tropical and have been classified as temperate forests. Of the more than 300 tropical species occurring in Natal and the former Transkei only about 130 are represented in the southern Cape forests. Temperate forests surviving outside the southern Cape are those in the Amatola, Katberg and Winterberg Mountains in the eastern Cape.

Among the trees you will find Outeniqua and real yellowwoods, stinkwood with its distinctive lichen-encrusted, dull-white boles, candlewood, white pear and assegai. Clusters of forest tree fern are common along stream banks and in moist forests.

The montane forest patches at higher elevations (Benebos, Keurbos and Mostertsbos) are remnants of the forests which once covered the

HAKEA – AN AUSTRALIAN INVADER

Sections of the trail pass through dense stands of *Hakea*, which belongs to the protea family and was introduced to South Africa in the 1830s. It was commonly used as a hedge plant and for firewood, and was once considered for dune stabilisation on the Cape Flats.

In the absence of effective competition from other plants and without any natural enemies hakea spreads quickly, colonising vast mountain areas and choking the surrounding vegetation. The dense masses require vast quantities of water, reducing the natural water flow as a result of water loss through transpiration. Old stands constitute a fire hazard and often the heat of the fire is so severe that the indigenous flora is completely destroyed.

It normally grows as a single-stemmed, multi-branched plant 2 to 3 m high, but in dense vegetation it can grow up to 5 m in height. The needle-shaped leaves are dark green and the fruit are about the size of a walnut.

The silky hakea (Hakea sericea) *has invaded large tracts of fynbos*

coastal plateau between the sea and the Tsitsikamma range. These isolated forests are restricted to the larger kloofs and consist mainly of species such as red and white alders, blossom tree and tree fuchsia.

The forest floor is the habitat of some 25 fern species, as well as numerous lilies, orchids and herbaceous plants. Among the climbing, twining and scrambling plants you will find traveller's joy (*Clematis brachiata*), climbing saffron, common forest grape, and David's root (*Melorthia punctata*), a fine liana with tuberous roots often seen enveloping the stems of trees in open areas and along forest edges. Characteristic of the exposed crowns of yellowwoods are the drooping beard lichens (*Usnea*).

Some of the common trees have been numbered according to the *National List of Indigenous Trees* and you can identify them by referring to the reverse of the trail map. You will also find the *Southern Cape Tree Guide* by F von Breitenbach useful. The guide describes 116 indigenous trees and tall shrubs of Outeniqualand and the Tsitsikamma and also contains a leaf-key.

Fauna Forty-six mammal species have been identified in the De Vasselot section of the Tsitsikamma Coastal National Park at Nature's Valley. Rodents account for more than half of

this number. The forests are the habitat of bushbuck, blue duiker, bushpig and vervet monkey. Leopard occur both in the forest and the mountains but owing to their shyness they are hardly ever encountered. Other members of the cat family include caracal and African wild cat.

Grysbok occur in dense scrub, often near the base of hills, while the grey rhebok prefers flat mountain plateaus.

Although rarely seen, klipspringer occur on the upper elevations in rocky areas. Rock dassie and chacma baboon also inhabit the rockier, more mountainous areas.

The Tsitsikamma region supports a richer birdlife than the fynbos areas further west. This is mainly due to the more varied habitat created by the indigenous forest and the fynbos, and more than 217 species have been recorded in the area.

Thirty-two species occurring in the forests and forest margins are listed on the reverse side of the trail map. In the forest it can be difficult to spot birds and very often their calls are the only way of positively identifying them.

The rameron pigeon can be identified by its low, hoarse "kroo-ku" note followed by stuttering bursts of "du-du-du-du" notes. Knysna lourie, Narina trogon, redbilled woodhoopoe and Knysna woodpecker also have distinctive calls. The last-mentioned species occurs from the Breede River mouth in the south-western Cape to Oribi Gorge in Natal. You are also reasonably likely to hear the onomatopoeic "meitjie, meitjie" call of Klaas's cuckoo between October and March.

Knysna and Victorin's warblers, two South African endemics with a fairly limited distribution, have been recorded in the trail area.

When the proteas and ericas are in flower there is continual activity by sugarbirds and sunbirds, including the Cape sugarbird, malachite and orangebreasted sunbirds, as well as lesser and greater doublecollared sunbirds. Other fynbos birds you might add to your list are greater honeyguide, Cape rock thrush, familiar chat and palewinged starling.

Among the birds of prey recorded in the forests are cuckoo hawk, tawny eagle and redbreasted sparrowhawk, while blackshouldered kite can be seen in fynbos areas.

History The San and Khoikhoi were amongst the earliest known inhabitants of the Tsitsikamma. Open areas outside the indigenous forests were preferred by the Khoikhoi as they provided grazing for their cattle and sheep, while the San kept to the more mountainous areas.

There are various forms of the word Tsitsikamma – tSietsikkamma, Sitsi Kamma, Tsitzikamma and Sietikamma – but according to P E Raper the name is derived from the Khoikhoi words *tse-tsitsa* and *gami*, meaning "clear" and "water" or alternatively "place where the water begins".

Among the early explorers to visit the region were Thunberg (1772) and Sparrman (1775). In 1782 the French traveller Le Vaillant was forced

to retrace his steps after being unable to find a suitable route northwards between the mountains and the sea because of the rugged nature of the surrounding mountains and the impenetrable forests.

Exploitation of the southern Cape forests started in the Knysna region but the stretch between the Storms and Keurbooms rivers was initially spared because of its inaccessibility.

Gradually the Tsitsikamma forests were worked from the eastern side and in 1867 a commission was appointed to investigate the condition of the forests. Thomas Bain, inspector of roads in the southern Cape, and Captain Christopher Harison undertook the investigation and compiled the first map of the Tsitsikamma forests. It was not until the Great Fire of 1869, which destroyed large tracts of forest between Swellendam and Uitenhage within six days, that the warnings of these pioneer conservationists were heeded. In 1874 Captain Harison was appointed as the first full-time forest conservator of the George, Knysna and Tsitsikamma forest. His headquarters were in Knysna and because of the vast distances involved it was difficult to exercise control. The situation was aggravated after the discovery of gold at Millwood in the Knysna forests and on the Witwatersrand, and the consequent industrial development which increased the demand for timber.

During 1880 the Cape Government intervened and appointed the Count M de Vasselot de Régné as Superintendent of Woods and Forests for the entire Cape Colony. He was a sylviculturist of international repute and he established scientific control and development of the remaining forests.

TRAIL DESCRIPTION

Day 1: Kalander Hut to Blaauwkrantz Hut
You will set off from the Kalander Hut, named after the Outeniqua yellowwood which is also known as the *kalander*. The name is apparently a corruption of *Outeniqualander*, – an "inhabitant of the Outeniqua region". The kalander is the famous "Big Tree" of the Knysna forest and several of these giants can be seen in the Knysna-Tsitsikamma forests.

After crossing the Groot River at the road bridge the trail returns to the forest east of the

old national road and winds through beautiful indigenous forest. After about 2 km it turns sharply left and climbs steeply to Douwurmkop. The hill takes its name from a small rounded shrub with silvery foliage and blue flowers (August to November) which grows here, *Lobostemon fruticosus*. In earlier times the leaves were said to be used as a cure for ringworm, known in Afrikaans as "douwurm". Here you have an excellent view over the Groot River lagoon and, further west, of Nature's Valley. The

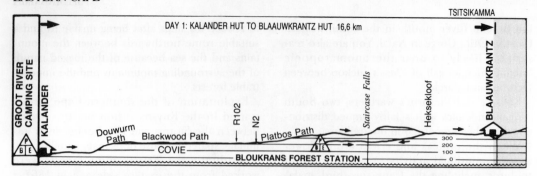

DAY 1: KALANDER HUT TO BLAAUWKRANTZ HUT 16,6 km

trail then follows a track over level terrain for about a kilometre before swinging left and returning to the forest.

After a while you will pass the settlement of Covie, and two and a half to three hours after the start you will cross the R102 near the Covie picnic spot. The trail continues along a forestry track through Platbos for another kilometre before passing beneath the N2 motorway. Shortly afterwards the trail turns right and follows a forest path for about 1,5 km to Staircase Falls, a good lunch stop. The falls cascade about 20 m over a series of ledges before dropping into a deep pool.

The trail then climbs steeply for a short distance through a damp forest with huge forest tree ferns and continues through pine plantations until it meets the jeep track leading up from the Bloukrans Forest Station. The final 2,6 km of the first day's hike follows the jeep track through pine plantations. From the hut you will have a magnificent view of the Bloukrans River gorge and Peak Formosa (1 675 m) commanding the range in the distance.

To cool down after your day's hiking, venture down to the Tolbos River which boasts a beautiful waterfall and several rock pools. An indistinct path on the northern slope skirts the waterfall, and this is the way to the pool below.

A shorter route, about 7,5 km, to Blaauwkrantz Hut leaves from the Bloukrans

Forest Station. The supplementary route is not as enjoyable though, and you will miss the Staircase Falls and the indigenous forests.

Day 2: Blaauwkrantz Hut to Keurbos Hut

After descending to the Tolbos River a steep climb awaits you for the next 2 km, after which you pass through Buffelsbos, so named because of the large herds of buffalo which once roamed the area. Despite attempts made by Captain Christopher Harison to protect them, the last buffalo was shot at Bloukrans in 1883.

The trail descends gradually for about 1,5 km to the Bloukrans River, which is usually reached after about two hours' walking. Waterwitelsgat, a deep pool just below the point where you cross the river, is one of the most inviting pools on the trail with the characteristic brown colour of the water caused by plant colloid and certain acids.

From the Bloukrans River the trail winds steeply out of the gorge and then ascends gradually along *Ouveldrug* ("Old Veld Ridge"). A signboard further along this section indicates that the hakea in the area is being controlled biologically.

Benebos, a beautiful indigenous forest, is a welcome change after the two-hour walk from Bloukrans River through open fynbos. If you decide on having lunch before reaching the hut, this is the best spot. Relaxing alongside one of

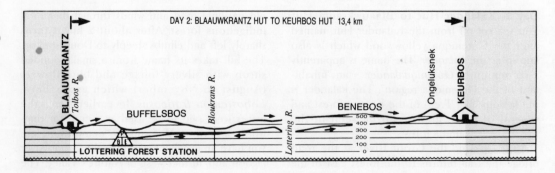

DAY 2: BLAAUWKRANTZ HUT TO KEURBOS HUT 13,4 km

the streams under the forest tree ferns you will be able to appreciate this fairyland of virgin forest, colourful fungi, mosses and ferns.

After leaving the forest the trail joins a forest track which is followed most of the way to the Keurbos Hut. The hut is named after the abundance of blossom tree or keurboom in the vicinity. Blossom trees usually occur in forest margins and play a significant role in the ecology of forests. It is a so-called pioneer species because of its ability to grow rapidly in forests denuded as a result of fire or other causes.

Unfortunately there is no swimming place close to the hut and swimming is not permitted in the Lottering River as the water is used for domestic purposes lower downstream. However, you can freshen up under the shower provided at the hut.

Day 3: Keurbos Hut to Heuningbos Hut

Initially you descend gradually along Ystermartiensrug, which is named after the iron martin which is abundant in the vicinity. This small tree or shrub is restricted to the mountain slopes between Swellendam and Van Staden's Pass, west of Port Elizabeth. After about 1,5 km you will reach the Lottering River and from here it is a long climb up the Rushes Pass to the nek between Klipbokkop and Elandskop. The nek offers a magnificent view over the valleys below and Peak Formosa.

Peak Formosa (1 675 m) is the highest peak in the Tsitsikamma range and was originally named *d'Estralla de Formosa* – "The Beautiful Mountain" – by early Portuguese navigators. Elandskop, south of the trail, is another name which recalls former times when the hills beyond the forests were a home to eland.

The trail then descends sharply to the Elandsbos River, which is reached after about three hours. From here you will follow Mangold se Pad, a road dating back to 1834 when a cer-

tain Mangold built it to facilitate the exploitation of the forests.

Indigenous trees were felled, trimmed to railway sleeper size and then transported to Storms River Mouth and lowered by a cableway to the river. Here they were loaded onto the 200-ton coaster *Clara*.

You will remain in pine plantations until just before the 11 km mark when you enter a small patch of indigenous forest – Heuningbos. With less than 2 km of the day's hike remaining, the hut comes into view on the eastern bank of the Kleinbos River. It appears to be closer than it really is, however, and it will be another half hour before you can unshoulder your pack – about six hours after setting off. Once again swimming is not permitted in the Kleinbos River as the river supplies water to the Boskor settlement downstream. The hut is well positioned, allowing you to relax with pleasant views of the forest, plantation and mountain peaks.

Day 4: Heuningbos Hut to Sleepkloof Hut

From Heuningbos the trail ascends along the Splendid Pass to Mostertshoogte. The pass takes its name from the silver mimetes (*Mimetes splendidus*) – a rare member of the protea family which grows here. Although it has a fairly broad distribution, from the Langeberg Mountains at Swellendam to the Storms River in the Tsitsikamma range, it is not common and the total population is less than 500 plants. Most populations are very small and seldom comprise more than five plants; only six populations of between 20 and 50 plants have been recorded. The tall shrubs (1,5 to 2 m high) are restricted to the cool, moist southern slopes and can be seen flowering between July and September, when the top leaves change to pale orange and yellow.

It is a long steady uphill to Mostertshoogte, with some 350 m gained in altitude since set-

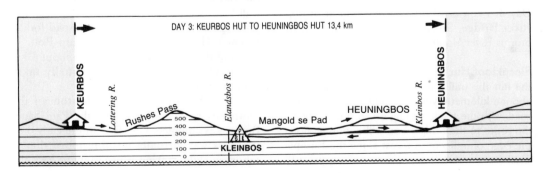

131

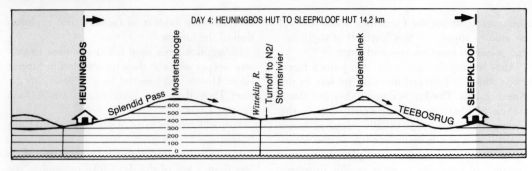

DAY 4: HEUNINGBOS HUT TO SLEEPKLOOF HUT 14,2 km

ting off from the hut. Amongst the flowers to distract you while ascending are strawberry everlastings (*Syncarpha eximia*), kol-kol (*Berzelia intermedia*) and king protea (*Protea cynaroides*). Mostertsbos and the Witteklip River are reached about three hours after setting off and this brief respite from the open fynbos is appreciated during summer.

At the 7 km mark the trail splits, the right-hand fork leading to the N2 and Stormsrivier Forest Station. The main trail, however, winds along the northern slopes of Stormsrivierpiek (1 019 m) to Nademaalnek (740 m) which is the highest point on the trail. With the uphill of the day over, you now descend along Teebosrug, named after the bush tea (*Cyclopia subternata*), a small shrub about 1 m tall. Pea-like, deep yellow flowers which turn orange or tan as they age, are produced in spring and early summer. The leaves and twigs are fermented, dried and used as honeybush tea which also has medicinal properties.

On the steep descent pause to drink in the beautiful view over Storms River gorge and you should see the Sleepkloof Hut far below. The final 1,5 km of the day pass through a delightful patch of indigenous forest with numerous forest tree ferns. The hut is situated on the slopes of Stormsrivierpiek (1 019 m) alongside Sleepkloof, overlooking the nearby forest and the Storms River gorge.

Day 5: You can terminate the trail at Storms River Bridge, Stormsrivier Forest Station or Storms River Mouth.

Sleepkloof Hut to Storms River Bridge From the hut the trail follows a forest road and after about a kilometre you will come to a fork in the road, with the track leading off to the left being the route to the bridge. You will continue along the edge of indigenous forest along the Bushpig Trail for about 0,75 km. Further along you will

join up with the Tree Fern Trail which is followed to the Storms River Bridge complex. This section is only 3,2 km long and, as it only takes about an hour to complete, you can reward yourself with a hearty breakfast at the restaurant.

Sleepkloof Hut to Stormsrivier Forest Station This route is just under 6 km and takes about 2 hours. Initially you will follow the same route as the one terminating at the bridge. However, where the trail splits at the 1 km mark, you will continue along the forest road, following part of the Bushpig Trail for 2 km. Shortly before crossing the N2, a track on your right leads off to the famous Big Tree, an enormous Outeniqua yellowwood which is well worth a visit.

You will cross the N2 just before the 3 km mark and a little way on the Skuinsbos picnic site is passed. Shortly thereafter the trail divides with the right-hand trail following Skuinsbospad for about 1 km and shortly after the 4 km mark turning right along Oubrugpad ("Old Bridge Road"). Stormsrivier Forest Station is less than 2 km further along this road.

As an alternative route to Storms River Mouth you turn left where Skuinsbospad joins Oubrugpad and drop down to the Oubrug via the Stormsrivierpas. Here you will meet the usual route to Storms River Mouth.

Sleepkloof Hut to Storms River Mouth This trail follows the same route as described in the previous section until the Skuinsbospad fork is reached. Here you will turn left onto Roth se Pad and descend through forest for about 3 km to the Oubrug picnic spot; it usually takes about two hours.

The bridge, which is at the bottom of the Stormsrivierpas, was used until the Paul Sauer Bridge was completed in 1956. In the early days the pass was virtually nothing more than a toboggan slide, making it necessary to lock the

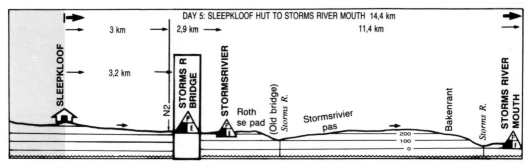

back wheels of the wagons to prevent the oxen from being overrun. It took almost a full day to negotiate the pass and, once it was completed, travellers would set up camp at the site of the Tzitzikamma Forest Inn. The picnic spot was the original site of Mangold's Sawmill, which was later moved to the bluff overlooking the Storms River.

From the bridge the trail ascends along the old pass for about 1 km, before winding through De Vos se Bos. Shortly after the 9 km mark the trail passes through pine plantations of the Blueliliesbush State Forest and then follows a forestry road along the edge of the plantation.

You will reach Bakenrant after 12 km and here you will have a magnificent view of the Storms River Mouth Rest Camp and the rugged Tsitsikamma coastline. Here you will join the Mouth Trail, one of several skilfully laid out walks in the Tsitsikamma Coastal National Park. After a steep descent you will reach the Storms River, which is crossed by means of a suspension bridge.

A short way further on you will come to a site display in a cave which was once the home of Khoisan with either seasonal or permanent patterns of coastal exploitation. The trail then skirts several rocky bays, ending at the rest camp about 1 km onwards. This section covers 14,4 km and is normally hiked in about five hours.

OTTER

Twilight forests of Outeniqua yellowwood, stinkwood and white milkwood, huge waves crashing against the rugged coastline, coastal plateaus covered with ericas and proteas – this is the changing kaleidoscope of the Otter Hiking Trail, the first official hiking trail to be opened in South Africa. Stretching between Storms River Mouth and Nature's Valley, this five-day route is without doubt one of the most popular trails in southern Africa.

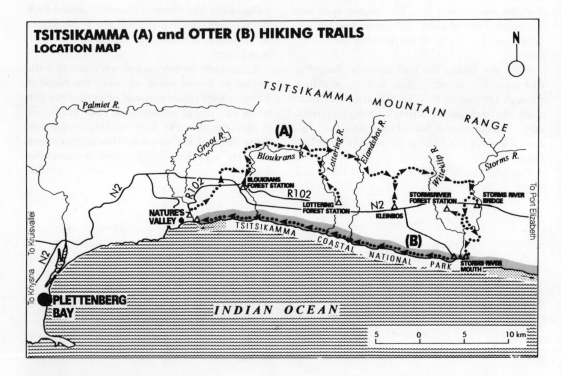

TRAIL PLANNER

Distance 41 km; 5 days

Grading B

Reservations The Chief Director, National Parks Board, P O Box 787, Pretoria 0001, Telephone (012) 343-1991, Fax (012) 343-0905 or P O Box 7400, Roggebaai 8012, Telephone (021) 22-2810, Fax (021) 24-6211. Reservations are accepted up to a year in advance.

Group size Minimum 2; Maximum 12

Maps A full-colour trail map with useful information on the history, flora and fauna on the reverse is available, but must be purchased separately.

Facilities At each of the overnight stops two wooden huts with bunks and mattresses are provided. Other facilities include fireplaces, firewood, water and chemical toilets.

Accommodation at Storms River Mouth Rest Camp ranges from campsites to self-contained cottages. There is a licensed restaurant and a well-stocked shop. Facilities at Groot River just outside Nature's Valley are limited to basic campsites served by ablution blocks.

Climate

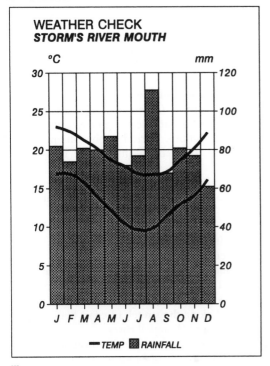

WEATHER CHECK
STORM'S RIVER MOUTH

— TEMP ▦ RAINFALL

Logistics Linear trail. Depending on transport arrangements, vehicles can be parked at the start of the trail or the Groot River Campsite near the end of the trail. Alternatively, Nature's Valley Guest House transports hikers back to Storms River Mouth at a reasonable charge. Arrangements can be made by contacting Mr and Mrs Bond at Telephone (04457) 6805.

The first overnight hut is only 2 hours' walk from the rest camp so it can easily be reached if a late start is made.

Relevant information
■ It is advisable to plan your hike to cross the Bloukrans River approximately 30 minutes after low tide. Swimming across should not be attempted at high tide unless you are a strong swimmer. Although the Lottering River usually does not present any problems, you might have to swim at high tide. A survival bag is useful for floating your pack across these rivers.
■ River crossings can be dangerous after heavy rains. Rather than risking your life, return to the previous hut or stay put on the path until the river has subsided.
■ Medical escape routes are provided just beyond Ngubu and Scott's huts, while escape routes in the event of flooding rivers or inclement weather are provided before the Kleinbos, Elandsbos and Bloukrans rivers.
■ Wood is sometimes unavailable and you are advised to carry a backpacking stove as it is an offence to collect wood, including driftwood, along the trail.
■ Water at the huts should be used sparingly as it is dependent on rain. If the rain tanks are empty, usually only towards the end of summer, water will have to be collected upstream of the closest river. Expandable water containers are handy for this purpose.
■ Remember to take litter bags as all litter must be carried out.

How to get there The turn-off to the starting point at Storms River Rest Camp is signposted about 9 km west of the Storms River bridge on the N2. From the turn-off it is about 9 km to the rest camp.

TRAIL ENVIRONMENT

Flora Although some large trees can be seen along the trail, the forest of the coastal belt is typically a dry forest with a scrub-like appearance. This forest type seldom exceeds 15 m in height and white milkwood and wild camphor bush are among the most common species. Other species to be seen include Outeniqua yellowwood, stinkwood, red alder, small-leaved saffron and Cape beech.

The dry coastal forest generally lacks the luxuriant undergrowth of the high forests further inland, but the rivers and streams are often fringed with verdant fern glades. Between December and February the scarlet, funnel-shaped flowers of the scarlet Knysna lily (*Cyrtanthus elatus*) are unlikely to escape your attention. It belongs to the amaryllis family and favours streams in indigenous forests.

Patches of fynbos also occur and it has been suggested that some of these communities were connected to those on the mountains in the past. However, as a result of natural veld fires, farming and forestry the coastal communities became isolated.

Several protea species, including the king protea (*Protea cynaroides*) and the blue sugarbush, have been recorded in the park. Another conspicuous family is the ericas which create patches of white, pink and orange-red when they flower, mainly between August and December.

One of the most spectacular orchids occurring along the trail is *Disa racemosa*. It grows in marshy areas and has deep pink flowers in November and December. Keep an eye out also during these months for the spider orchid (*Bartholina etheliae*) in the dry fynbos near Oakhurst Huts. Favouring damp localities is the bloumoederkappie (*Herschelia venusta*) which can be seen flowering near André's Huts in January.

In winter the powder puffs (*Brunia nodiflora*) with their large sprays of creamy white flowers are especially eye-catching, while several watsonia, gladiolus and other bulbous species can be seen flowering in spring and early summer.

A species unlikely to escape your attention is the cheerful gazania (*Gazania rigens*) which grows amongst the rocks along the coast. The yellow flowers with a white spot at the base of each petal can be seen from October to December.

Fauna Mammals inhabiting the forests include caracal, leopard, vervet monkey, bushbuck and bushpig while chacma baboon and rock dassie are found in rocky habitats.

A shy inhabitant of the park is the rare blue duiker. Research has shown that the park supports about one animal per six hectares, which is seven times lower than the density of the species in the Kenneth Stainbank Nature Reserve in KwaZulu/Natal. The blue duiker reaches the south-western limit in this vicinity and it has been suggested that the lack of a suitable habitat and therefore food is probably responsible for the low population density.

Often the trail follows the cliff edge and, from this excellent vantage point, be on the lookout

because several whale and dolphin species have been recorded along the Tsitsikamma coast. Large schools of Indian Ocean bottlenosed dolphins can often be seen frolicking offshore. Smaller schools of humpback dolphin also occur in the shallow water, but are generally less playful. The common dolphin prefers deeper water and large schools are frequently seen along the coast.

Some 210 bird species have been recorded in the park, of which 175 abound within the land borders and 40 species are associated with the sea and shore. The more common species are listed on the reverse side of the trail map.

Of the 35 true forest species, the striking Knysna lourie and the elusive Narina trogon deserve mention. Other forest species to look out or listen for include the greenspotted dove, terrestrial bulbul, starred robin, bluemantled flycatcher, olive bush shrike and the forest canary.

In the fynbos patches along the trail you might spot Jacobin cuckoo during the summer months, Victorin's warbler and the Cape sugarbird. Sunbird species recorded include the malachite, orangebreasted, greater and lesser doublecollared sunbirds.

Among the raptors recorded in the park are crowned eagle, forest buzzard and redbreasted sparrowhawk, while gymnogene have been observed along the stretch of coast between the rest camp and Waterfall River.

The marine habitats can be divided into the rocky shoreline, the area within and just beyond the breakers, offshore and deep-sea.

The rocky coastline is the habitat of African black oystercatcher, turnstone and kelp gull, while the zone within and just beyond the breakers is favoured by whitebreasted cormorant. Several tern species, including the endangered roseate tern and the rare Caspian tern, have been recorded here.

The offshore birds include the Cape gannet – which is often seen diving for fish in large flocks – petrels and skuas, while the deep-sea zone is the habitat of some four albatross species.

The Tsitsikamma coast falls within the warm temperate south coast marine faunal province which is influenced by the southward-flowing, warm Agulhas Current and the cold Benguela Current. Although the tropical fauna is less prolific and smaller than that of the east coast, several species are endemic to this transitional zone.

OTTER

The trail takes its name from the Cape clawless otter which occurs commonly along the Tsitsikamma coast. Based on research conducted along a 59 km stretch of coastline, the number of otters east of Nature's Valley has been estimated at 31.

Because of their acute sense of smell and hearing and their nocturnal habits, these otters are very seldom seen although you are likely to come across their characteristic hand-shaped spoor in wet sand or mud. You do, however, stand a chance of seeing this elusive animal if you sit quietly downwind of a holt, which is mainly found where a stream enters the sea, between 16:00 and sunset.

Although they usually occur along perennial rivers and marshes, the otters occurring along the coast at Tsitsikamma and in the vicinity of Port Elizabeth also frequent the intertidal zone and the sea. They forage mainly along submerged rocky ridges near the shore with red and brown rock crab, octopus and suckerfish accounting for about 80 per cent of their diet.

Right hind foot

One of South Africa's most popular hiking trails is named after the Cape clawless otter, which has webs on the hind feet only

Distances between the trail huts are short so you will have ample time to explore the intertidal zone which includes all those areas that could possibly be exposed with the changing tides. Its limits are determined by the high and low water marks at spring tide, with the zone above the high water mark known as the **Splash Zone**. No true marine flora or fauna occur here and it is mainly flotsam and jetsam which are of interest. The **Littorina Zone**, which is covered for a few hours during spring tide only, is fairly barren and is characterised by hundreds of little dark snails or periwinkles, the most common being *Littorina knysnaensis*. Other species to be found here include the false limpet (*Siphonaria capensis*), hermit crab (*Paguristes gamianus*), which adopts shells of various molluscs, and the black spiny ribbed limpet (*Helcion pectunculus*).

More frequently under water is the **Balanoid Zone**, which is named after the acorn barnacles (genus *Balanus*). It is subdivided into an upper and a lower zone, the latter being submerged for longer periods. Species do overlap but those usually only associated with the upper Balanoid Zone include the volcanic barnacle (*Tetraclita serrata*), star barnacle (*Chthamalus dentatus*), spiked limpet (*Patella longicosta*) and the armadillo (*Dinoplax gigas*).

Many species of the upper zone also occur in the lower Balanoid Zone. Brown mussels (*Perna perna*), commercial oyster (*Crassostrea margaritacea*) and false cockle (*Thecalia concamerata*) are found among the barnacles. A variety of

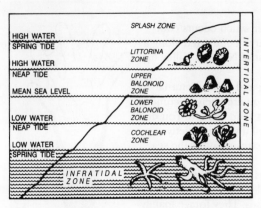

Zones and tide levels

worms, including the dark brown bootlace worm (*Lineus lacticapitatus*) and the phosphorescent worm (*Chaetopterus varieopedatus*), is also common in this zone.

The inhabitants of the **Cochlear Zone**, which takes its name from the pear limpet (*Patella cochlear*), cannot withstand exposure for long periods. A variety of limpets, including those common in other zones, are abundant in this lower intertidal band. The giant limpet (*Patella tabularis*) and the delicate-looking slipper limpet (*Crepidula porcellana*) are two other limpet species found here. The greatest variety of marine life of the intertidal zone is found in this zone and other species commonly found are Venus ear (*Haliotis spadicea*) and abalone (*Haliotis midae*).

The zone below the low water mark at spring tide is known as the infratidal zone and is only exposed under exceptional conditions. For visitors wanting to explore this fascinating world there is an underwater trail in the vicinity of the Goudgate at the western end of the rest camp. An SAUU third class diving certificate is, however, required.

To date some 80 bony fish and 12 shark, skate and ray species have been identified along the Tsitsikamma coast. To prevent over-exploitation of the park's marine resources bait collecting is strictly prohibited while angling is restricted to the 2,9 km stretch of coastline between Goudgate and the Waterfall.

History The coastline between Knysna and

Cape St Francis was once the home range of Khoisan people, loosely termed Strandlopers. Their diet consisted mainly of shellfish, supplemented by fruit, berries, roots, wild honey and meat from animals. Evidence of these Stone Age people can still be seen at a site display in a cave at the Storms River Mouth and Guano Cave which is passed on the first day of the Otter Hiking Trail.

In 1907 excavations at the Coldstream Shelter near the mouth of the Lottering River led to the discovery of 17 burial sites covered by flat stones, three of which were painted. Archaeological evidence suggests that the custom of covering burial sites with flat stones originated with the Khoisan people of the south-eastern Cape coastal belt in about 6000 BC. Some 2 000 years later they began practising the custom of decorating the stones with figures and one of the Coldstream burial stones is believed to be the most beautiful and best preserved stone found yet.

The area was also inhabited by the Outeniqua Khoikhoi who lived between Mossel Bay and the Gamtoos River. The name Tsitsikamma is derived from the Khoikhoi words *tse-tsitsa* and *gami*, which are translated as "clear water", an obvious reference to the numerous streams of clear water in the area. Another interpretation of the name is "place where the water begins".

The history of the wanton destruction of the Tsitsikamma forests is described in detail in the chapter on the Tsitsikamma Hiking Trail.

When the Tsitsikamma National Park was proclaimed in 1964 it was not only the first marine national park in South Africa, but also the first in Africa. The original boundaries of the park stretched for about 80 km along the rugged coastline between the Groot River at Oubosrand near Humansdorp and the Groot River estuary at Nature's Valley. The offshore boundary extended about 300 m seawards, while the inland boundary roughly follows the 200 m contour.

In 1983 the offshore boundary was extended to 5 km into the sea and four years later the De Vasselot Nature Reserve was incorporated into the park. As a result the land area of the park increased from about 1 612 ha to 4 172 ha, while the offshore area covers about 30 000 ha.

TRAIL DESCRIPTION

Day 1: Storms River to Ngubu's Huts The trail starts about 2 km west of the restaurant where a car park is provided for hikers. Shortly beyond the oceanettes, you will pass the Goudgate where claims were pegged after the gold rush at Millwood during the 1880s. An underwater trail has been laid out here for those wanting to explore the underwater world of the Tsitsikamma coast.

The trail initially traverses along the edge of the coastal forest and after about 1,5 km you will pass Guano Cave, with a large midden almost blocking its entrance. The midden is an accumulation of shells and bones which coastal Khoisan people discarded on the floor of their rocky home.

Once past the cave you will have to scramble over rocks where white arrows and otters painted on the rock indicate the route. Although this part is not difficult, progress is slowed down considerably and during rainy weather the rocks can be quite slippery. About 30 minutes beyond the cave you will reach Waterfall River with its beautiful waterfall cascading down the sheer cliff into a huge pool. Day visitors are allowed to walk up to this point and you might meet up with them here.

Since Ngubu's Huts are less than 2 km away this is an ideal resting spot and on a hot day the icy water of the pool is irresistible. The onward route requires a hop across a narrow gully where the pool cascades into the sea. The crossing is easily accomplished unless the river is in flood or during stormy seas when care should be taken.

After a short climb through indigenous forest the trail descends to the valley where the huts are situated below Olienboomkop. The huts are named after the park's first Game Ranger, Sergeant Petrus Ngubu, who helped with the planning and construction of the trail.

The huts are situated in a clearing in the for-est close to the sea where there are beautiful rock pools waiting to be explored.

Day 2: Ngubu's Huts to Scott's Huts First thing in the morning the trail ascends sharply to Olienboomkop Hill, passing through beautiful indigenous forest before emerging onto the coastal plateau.

The stiff climb is followed by a level section through fynbos and from Skilderkrans, a prominent quartzite outcrop, you will enjoy an impressive view over the sea some 100 m below. Keep an eye out for dolphins and if you are hiking the trail between July and October you might see a southern right whale.

Looking west from Skilderkrans you can see the white sands of Bloubaai in the distance. A short way beyond Skilderkrans the trail descends to a stream before ascending once again and after a level stretch drops down steeply to the Kleinbos River which marks the halfway mark of the day's hike.

On its way to the sea the Kleinbos River has carved a deep, narrow gorge and the series of pools and waterfalls upstream of where the trail crosses the river are well worth exploring. The gorge is in the shade for most of the day and as the river is usually reached early in the morning the water is ice cold.

From the river the trail climbs steeply for about 1 km through indigenous forest before levelling out on the plateau only to lose height again. Keep an eye out here for an indistinct track leading off to the left to Bloubaai, one of the few sandy beaches along this rugged coast. Bloubaai offers excellent swimming and with less than 3 km of the day's hike remaining is a good lunch stop.

After retracing your steps back to the main trail from Bloubaai, a steep climb awaits you and further along you will enjoy expansive views of Bloubaai far below, Skilderkrans and the

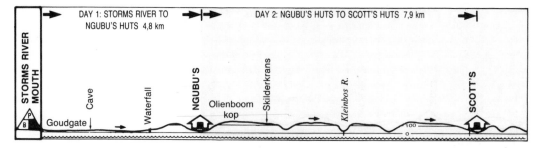

139

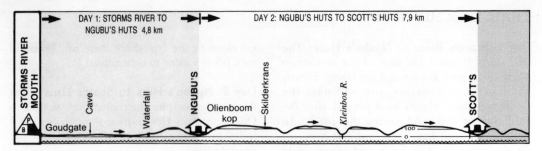

rugged coastline further east. The final kilometre of the trail descends through indigenous forest to reach Scott's Huts on the banks of the Geelhout River just short of 8 km after setting off.

The huts are named after Popo Scott, the first mate of the National Parks Board patrol vessel, *Natpark*, who also helped with the construction of the trail. The hut is situated close to the sea and the cove is ideal for swimming. Alternatively, you can cool off in the icy pool upstream of the hut.

Day 3: Scott's Huts to Oakhurst Huts From Scott's Huts the trail winds up the slopes through indigenous forest but soon returns to the rocky shoreline rounding Flip se Baai. Here the trail ascends steeply once again before dropping down to the Elandsbos River about 2 km from Scott's Huts. The Elandsbos River mouth is one of the most scenic spots along the trail and offers excellent swimming, as does the river further upstream. From here it is less than three hours to the Oakhurst Huts so you have ample time to enjoy the magnificent scenery.

The trail then follows an undulating course alternating between stretches along the coast and the forested slopes. After about 5,5 km you will ascend steeply to the coastal plateau. The trail winds through fynbos for about 1 km and quite unexpectedly you will look down on the Oakhurst Huts on the western bank of the Lottering River.

Since it is impossible to cross the river at the

mouth, the route winds slightly inland, descending steeply. At low tide it is possible to hop across some stepping stones, but at high tide you might be in for a swim. After crossing the river it is a brisk 20 minute walk to the huts, which are named after the homestead on the plateau just outside the park boundary. The house was originally built by one of the oldest families in the Tsitsikamma, Mr C J Whitcher, owner of a sawmill at Coldstream.

Day 4: Oakhurst Huts to André's Huts Although this is the longest stretch of the trail, the terrain is fairly undemanding and about six hours should be allowed for the 13,8 km stretch.

From Oakhurst the trail gains altitude steadily until it descends to the Witels River which is reached after about two hours. Over the next 6 km the trail follows its usual undulating course, alternating between stretches along the shore and through the indigenous forest before it drops down to the Bloukrans River, shortly before the 10 km mark.

Arriving at the river at high tide can delay your progress and it's a good idea to consult a tide timetable and plan the day's hike accordingly. During high tide the waves push far into the wide river mouth and a crossing should not be attempted unless you are a strong swimmer. The various routes across the river are clearly illustrated on the reverse side of the trail map. Packs should be waterproofed and can be floated across in survival bags. Once across you will

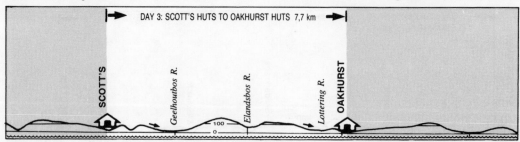

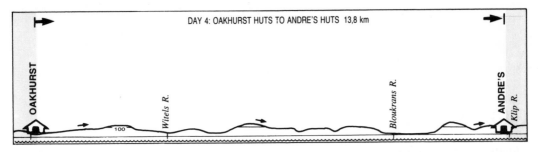

have to scramble back towards the river mouth along the rocks.

André's Huts are about one and a half hours away. The trail follows the coast for about 1,5 km before climbing steeply to the coastal plateau where the route winds through fynbos. Along this section there are some excellent views of the bays and the coastline. After passing the turn-off to the game ranger's house, which can be seen in the distance, the trail descends sharply to the Klip River where André's Huts are situated. The original hut was named after André Kok, who was camp manager at Storms River Rest Camp when the trail was laid out and who helped to build the original hut.

Day 5: André's Huts to Nature's Valley After crossing the Klip River the trail ascends sharply through indigenous forests before reaching the plateau, which affords splendid views of the Klip River Mouth and the rugged coastline. This section passes mainly through fynbos with species such as powder puffs (*Brunia nodiflora*), king protea (*Protea cynaroides*), blue sugarbush, red-hot pokers (*Kniphofia*) and several erica species. The trail then winds inland, descending to Helpmekaarkloof where you will pass through a patch of indigenous forest. After a short climb you will continue through fynbos along the clifftops to The Point, with more spectacular views of the coastline.

From here you will look down onto the golden beach at Nature's Valley. The descent along the cliffs is not easy, though, and during rainy weather it is fairly slippery – so do take care. The trail officially ends at the base of the cliffs, but after crossing the Groot River Estuary a 3 km hike to the Groot River Campsite awaits you.

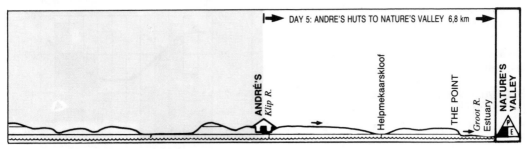

141

GONAQUA

Situated conveniently close to Port Elizabeth, this two-day circular trail traverses the rugged slopes of the Elandsberg, the easternmost extension of the Baviaanskloof Mountains. The route winds through deeply incised ravines with inviting pools and also takes you up steep ridges to reveal expansive views stretching to the coastline. The vegetation varies from pine and eucalyptus plantations to open fynbos, indigenous scrub and riverine forests, while succulents add an interesting dimension.

TRAIL PLANNER

Distance 30 km; 2 days

Grading B+

Reservations The Regional Director, Tsitsikamma Forest Region, Private Bag X537, Humansdorp 6300, Telephone (0423) 5-1180, Fax (0423) 5-2745.
0422 910 393

Group size Minimum 2; Maximum 18 (Robinson Camp) and 25 (Loerie Hut)

Maps The trail is indicated on a black and white printed map with useful information

on the history, flora and fauna on the reverse and is forwarded with your receipt and permit.

Climate

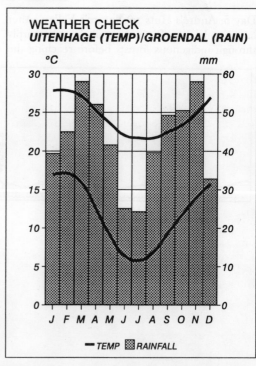

WEATHER CHECK
UITENHAGE (TEMP)/GROENDAL (RAIN)

Facilities Robinson Camp is equipped with bunks and mattresses while iron beds with mattresses are provided at Loerie Hut.

GONAQUA HIKING TRAIL
LOCATION MAP

Other amenities include water, cold water showers, fireplaces, firewood, refuse bins and toilets.

Logistics Circular route. Vehicles are not permitted at Robinson Camp which is situated about 500 m from the car park.

Relevant information
■ Both Robinson Camp and Loerie Hut can be used as the starting/ending point.
■ The Loerie Dam Nature Reserve is open between 07:00 and 18:00.
■ The trail lies within an all-year rainfall area, necessitating waterproofing of your pack, irrespective of the month you are hiking in.
■ After heavy rains river crossings could present a problem and caution should be exercised.

■ Swimming is permitted in the pools along the route, but on account of the indigenous fish inhabiting the rivers no soap should be used.

How to get there Approaching from the west along the N2, take the R102 off-ramp some 30 km east of Humansdorp and continue to Loerie. After passing through Loerie, turn left onto the Hankey road and a short way further, turn right onto a gravel road, signposted Loerie Dam Nature Reserve and Geelhoutboom. The parking area at the Environmental Education Centre is about 4 km further.

When approaching from Port Elizabeth, exit the N2 at the Thornhill interchange, joining the R331 to Hankey/Loerie. Upon reaching Loerie, continue as described above.

TRAIL ENVIRONMENT

Flora The vegetation of the area is dominated by mountain fynbos, while patches of indigenous scrub forest occur in the sheltered river valleys and ravines.

The trail lies near the eastern limit of the distribution of mountain fynbos and the diversity of species is consequently considerably poorer than the fynbos of the western Cape. Among the members of the protea family occurring are the tall yellowbush, broad-leaved, blue, white and real sugarbushes, as well as the king protea (*Protea cynaroides*). A striking member of the protea family which grows in the Otterford State Forest is *Paranomus reflexus* with its distinctive

Male and female cones of the tall yellowbush

greenish-yellow, spiky flowers. Among the ericas is *Erica pectinifolia*, which grows up to 1,8 m high and bears tubular white to pink flowers between November and May. Other typical fynbos species include brunia (*Brunia nodiflora*), several reeds and restios and a variety of bulbs such as watsonias.

Since the eastern Cape lies at the convergence of four floral regions, several species of the other floral regions are to be seen along the trail. Among these are the Suurberg cycad, concertina crassula (*Crassula perforata*), haworthias and euphorbias.

The indigenous forests are generally a low scrub forest, comprising species such as horsewood, coalwood, silky bark, common spikethorn, kooboo berry, white milkwood and forest num-num.

In the deep river valleys and kloofs the forests are taller and more dense. Dominant species here include Outeniqua and real yellowwoods, broom cluster fig and white ironwood.

Fauna The forests are the habitat of blue duiker, bushbuck and bushpig, while grysbok, common duiker and grey rhebok inhabit the fynbos. The predators are represented by leopard and several smaller species such as caracal, while aardwolf have also been observed.

Other species recorded include honey bad-

The timid aardwolf occurs singly or in pairs

F

(Half size)

ger, porcupine and vervet monkey, while the Cape clawless otter is present in the rivers and streams.

Among the birds attracted to streams and rivers are darter, hamerkop, Egyptian goose, yellowbilled and African black ducks, pygmy goose and brownhooded kingfisher.

Typical fynbos birds you chance ticking include rednecked francolin, Cape sugarbird and orangebreasted and lesser doublecollared sunbirds. Possibilities in rocky areas are rock kestrel, rock pigeon, Cape rock thrush, bokmakierie and redwinged starling.

Keep an eye out in the forests for crowned eagle, forest buzzard, Knysna lourie, redbilled woodhoopoe, olive woodpecker, olive thrush and Cape batis. Between October and April you are likely to hear the unmistakable call of the redchested cuckoo, while paradise flycatcher occur between September and March.

The streams and rivers of the area are the habitat of three indigenous species of fish – the Cape kurper (*Sandelia capensis*), longfin eel

(*Anguilla mossambica*) and the Eastern Cape redfin (*Pseudobarbus afer*). Two exotic species, the Mozambique tilapia (*Oreochromis mossambicus*) and banded tilapia (*Tilapia sparrmanii*) have also found their way into the rivers of the area.

The Elandsberg Mountains are the habitat of an extremely rare frog, Hewitt's ghost frog (*Heleophryne hewitti*), which has only been recorded in four streams in the area. This medium-sized frog is light to olive brown with dark brown spots and can easily be identified by the large friction pads on its finger and toe tips. It favours fast-flowing perennial streams with rocky beds.

History The trail is named after the easternmost group of the Cape Khoikhoi, the Gonaqua, whose territory extended as far east as the Keiskamma River. Initially the Gonaqua and the Xhosa coexisted peacefully and as a result of interaction between the two groups a new tribe, the Gqunukhwebe, emerged within the Xhosa during the late 1600s. However, as the Xhosa expanded westwards the Gonaqua were pushed back and by 1777 the two groups were divided by the Fish River. At the same time the Gonaqua came under increasing pressure as the Cape Colony was expanding rapidly eastwards. The only option was to migrate northwards, but here they came into conflict with the San and were gradually assimilated into other ethnic groups and ceased to exist as an independent Khoikhoi group.

Conservation of the Elandsberg dates back to 1896 when the mountains were managed as the Hankey Catchment Area. Afforestation started in 1918 when war veterans returning from World War I were employed as forestry workers, while the workforce was subsequently increased when large numbers of people who were unable to find work on the mines on the Witwatersrand were settled at Otterford.

TRAIL DESCRIPTION

Day 1: Robinson Camp to Loerie Hut The trail starts behind the hut, ascending immediately through fynbos before passing through a delightful patch of indigenous forest with a wooden bridge. After ascending steadily for about 1 km the trail drops down to Grootkloof

and then ascends steadily towards Windnek where you will pass through dense stands of blue and real sugarbushes.

The trail then descends to the Geelhoutboom River and a short way past the 4 km mark you will pass through scrub forest. Shortly after the

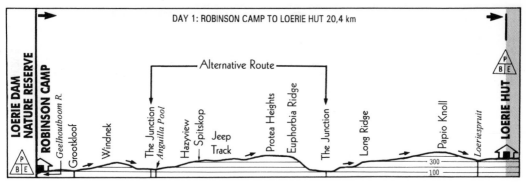

DAY 1: ROBINSON CAMP TO LOERIE HUT 20,4 km

— Alternative Route —

LOERIE DAM NATURE RESERVE · ROBINSON CAMP · Geelhoutboom R. · Grootkloof · Windnek · The Junction Anguilla Pool · Hazyview – Spitskop · Jeep Track · Protea Heights · Euphorbia Ridge · The Junction · Long Ridge · Papio Knoll · Loeriespruit · LOERIE HUT

300
100

5 km mark you will reach a tributary of the Geelhoutboom River where the shorter route to Loerie Hut turns off to the right. The route via Spitskop is a wide loop. You can leave your backpacks in the wire cages provided and collect them on your way back again. The route via Spitskop crosses the river several times and if you keep your eyes open you will notice the Enon conglomerates on the left hand side of the river bank. The round river stones and pebbles of varying sizes were deposited in the Great Gamtoos River basin million of years ago and were subsequently consolidated into conglomerate.

Near the 6 km mark the trail leaves the river and over the next 1,5 km you will gain height steadily. Fortunately the forest provides some protection against the sun. Leaving the shade of the forest, the trail levels off following a ridge and from Hazy View you will enjoy spectacular views of the Gamtoos River Valley to your left and the Elandsberg to your right. Looking westwards, the Cockscomb is a conspicuous landmark in the Great Winterhoek range.

At Spitskop a jeep track is joined and about 1 km further on the trail turns off to the right, heading for Keurkloof before winding up the aptly named Protea Heights. For the next 1 km you will drop steeply down to Sandelia Ford and there are magnificent views of the deep gorge carved by the Geelhoutboom River. Along Euphorbia Ridge several clumps of euphorbias, as well as crassulas will attract your attention and further along the descent is steep with loose shale, requiring careful footwork.

After a refreshing walk of just under 1 km along the river, the intersection with the more direct route to Loerie Hut is reached shortly before the 13 km mark. If you have to collect your pack, continue straight ahead for a few hundred metres, and then backtrack to The Junction.

From The Junction the trail ascends steeply through indigenous forest to the Long Ridge and after about 1 km you will emerge from the cover of the forest. A plantation road through pine plantations is followed for the next 2 km and at Papio Knoll, which is named after the generic name of the chacma baboon, you leave the road, descending through fynbos. At the 17 km mark the trail splits, with the next day's route to Robinson Camp continuing straight ahead, while the trail to Loerie Hut turns off to the left, passing through tall eucalyptus trees. After crossing a stream you will once again join plantation roads, continuing initially through eucalyptus plantations before emerging into pine plantations to reach the hut about 30 minutes beyond the split.

Accommodation at the overnight stop consists of two buildings, formerly used as a compound for forestry workers, as well as a cooking shelter nearby.

Day 2: Loerie Hut to Robinson Camp First thing in the morning you will have to retrace the last 2 km of the previous day's hike. Shortly after crossing a tributary of the Loeriespruit, the second day's route branches off to the left and then winds steadily uphill through open fynbos. Just below the old lookout you will pass through some dense stands of white sugarbush.

With a height of 559 m, the old lookout post is the highest point on the trail and from here you will descend steeply along a spur with expansive views of the Loeriespruit, Loerie Dam and the coastal plains further south. About 5,5 km after setting off, the trail descends into a patch of scrub forest and over the next 1 km you will lose some 160 m in altitude.

At the bottom of the valley you will join a tributary of the Loeriespruit and after following the course of the river for about 10 minutes you will reach the turn-off to Gonaqua Cave. The

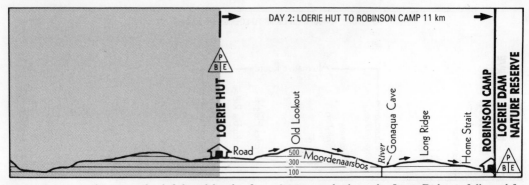

cave, a large overhang on the left-hand bank of the river, is reached about 10 minutes further downstream. It seems likely that the cave was used by the early San inhabitants of the area and the remains of a San, covered in skins, were discovered in the cave.

Returning to the junction, you will ascend steeply through scrub forest and you will gain about 100 m in altitude before the trail levels off.

A jeep track along the Long Ridge is followed for about 15 minutes and, shortly before the 8 km mark, the trail turns off to the left. For the remaining 2 km the trail descends through open fynbos with expansive views over Loerie Dam and the surrounding countryside. Just before reaching Robinson Camp you will join the onward route of the first day's hike and all that remains is a short but steep descent to the hut.

ALEXANDRIA

Situated in the Alexandria Conservation Area about 100 km north-east of Port Elizabeth, the Alexandria Hiking Trail winds across one of the most impressive coastal dunefields in the world, along high coastal cliffs and unspoilt beaches. Sections through the indigenous forest with its low canopy are a bird-watcher's delight. The wooden overnight hut is tucked away amongst white milkwoods and from the balcony you have a view over the sea where there is a good chance of seeing dolphins in the surf.

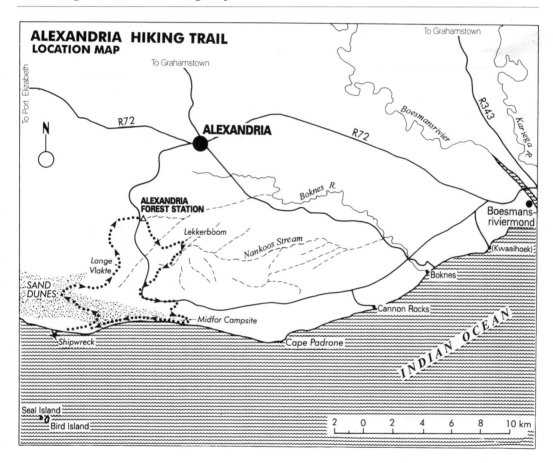

TRAIL PLANNER

Distance 2 days; 37,5 km

Grading B+

Reservations The Officer-in-Charge,

Alexandria Conservation Area, P O Box 50, Alexandria 6158, Telephone (046) 653-0601, Fax (046) 653-0302. Reservations are accepted up to one year in advance.

Climate

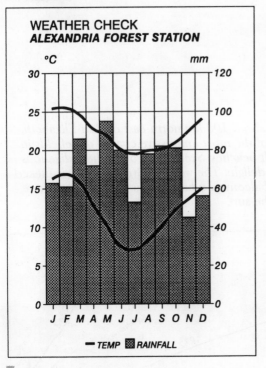

WEATHER CHECK
ALEXANDRIA FOREST STATION

— TEMP ▧ RAINFALL

Group size Minimum 2; Maximum 12

Maps The trail is indicated on a photocopy of the 1 : 50 000 topographical map that is forwarded with your receipt and permit.

Facilities Both overnight huts are equipped with bunks with mattresses, while drinking water and toilets are also provided. Fires are only permitted at the Langebos Hut at the start of the trail.

Logistics Circular route. Hikers are accommodated in an old forestry cottage, Langebos Hut, at the start of the trail.

Relevant information
■ Fires are not permitted at the Woody

Cape Hut, therefore a backpacking stove is necessary. However, fires are allowed on the beach between the high and low water marks. Only driftwood may be used, but this may not always be available.
■ Both huts are kept locked and you must therefore report to the office to collect the keys. For those arriving outside normal office hours, the keys can be collected from the keybox at the office.
■ The section of the trail across the dunes can be unpleasant on windy days and it is advisable to keep your sunglasses handy.
■ Be on your guard for ticks.
■ No refuse bins are provided at Woody Cape Hut and all litter must be carried back to the end of the trail.
■ Water at the Woody Cape Hut must be used sparingly since it is dependent on rain. Spring water is available at the base of the cliffs, but can only be obtained at low tide and should be used for washing only.
■ On both days an early start should be made because the wind is at its strongest between 12:00 and 18:00 and can make hiking unpleasant.
■ Before leaving Woody Cape Hut, the taps of the water tanks and the doors must be locked. Remember to return the key to the office on completion of the trail.
■ A tide table will be useful when deciding which route to take to the hut at the end of the first day.

How to get there Take the turn-off signposted to the conservation area, Karba and Grootvlei a few hundred metres west of Alexandria on the R72. After about 5,5 km the road forks. Take the left fork, signposted Alexandria Forest Station, and about 2 km further turn right to reach the forest station a short way on.

TRAIL ENVIRONMENT

Flora Five distinct plant communities have been identified in the Alexandria Conservation Area. The composition of the **coastal forests** extending along the coast from the Keiskamma River to about 10 km west of Woody Cape and between Port Elizabeth and Jeffreys Bay is so

unusual that a separate veld type, Alexandria Forest, has been named after it. These forests are best developed at Kei Mouth and Alexandria and vary from low (10 m high) forests to dense thickets.

Characteristic species of the seaward-facing

slopes include white milkwood, coastal red milkwood and coast silver oak. Among the more common species occurring on the leeward slopes are small knobwood, candlewood and kooboo-berry. Other species to be seen include white stinkwood, sneezewood, Cape ash and Cape gardenia.

The trees provide a habitat for several epiphytic orchids, including the beautiful yellow *Polystachya pubescens*. Although the Alexandria Forest is classified as a low forest, the valleys support several impressive Outeniqua yellowwood and coast coral tree.

The undergrowth is dominated by several kissing leaves species such as *Dicliptera*, *Siphonoglossa tubulosa* and *Justicia petiolaris*. Flowering plants of the forest floor are the small white iris (*Dietes*), the blue *Commelina benghalensis* and *Streptocarpus*.

Secondary grasslands are encountered at Midfor on the first day and at the farm Langevlakte on the second day. These grasslands have replaced the original forest which was cleared for farming, hence their name.

The vegetation of the younger stabilised dunes closer to the sea is characterised by **coastal or dune thickets** dominated by small to medium trees and shrubs. Typical species include Karoo boer-bean, bush boer-bean, red currant, dune sourberry, common pock ironwood, dune olive and septee tree. These species are well adapted to coastal conditions and although the vegetation is in a relatively early stage of development, it could develop into forest proper.

The **coastal or dune fynbos** occupies a narrow belt between the shifting sand and the dune thickets. Plants and shrubs of this community include pioneer species such as blombos (*Metalasia muricata*), gonnabos (*Passerina rigida*) and the bush-tick berry. Other typical Cape fynbos species are east coast heather (*Erica chloroloma*), slangbos (*Stoebe plumosa*), Christmas berry (*Chironia baccifera*) and waxberry (*Myrica cordifolia*).

The **dwarf thicket and fynbos** community is restricted to Woody Cape and has evolved as a result of wind, salt spray and the low level of soil nutrients. The effect of these factors is best illustrated by the white milkwood, a species which grows up to 10 m further inland but mature trees seldom exceed 20 cm in height at Woody Cape. Particularly conspicuous on the

cliffs near Woody Cape is the gousblom (*Gazania rigens*).

In addition to these five communities, the observant hiker will also see bush pockets, pioneer vegetation on recently formed dunes and the vegetation along the edge of the beach. The mobile dunes move between two and five metres a year and are, therefore, unable to support any permanent plant communities. Particularly interesting are the bush pockets which occur amongst the dunes on the landward side of the dunefield. Ranging from one to over five hectares in size, these dense pockets consist of small trees such as Cape sumach, dune crow-berry, sea guarri, dune olive, forest silver oak and bush-tick berry. Other species include waxberry (*Myrica cordifolia*), blombos (*Metalasia muricata*), gonnabos (*Passerina rigida*) and Christmas berry (*Chironia baccifera*). Sand movement along the landward edge of the dunes is almost parallel to the dunefield, reducing its movement to about a quarter of a metre a year. Since the plants living here are adapted to grow ahead of the encroaching sand, they play an important role in the stabilisation of the dunes.

The vegetation of recently formed dunes consists of pioneer species such as the seeplakkie (*Scaevola*), a creeper with yellowish-green succulent leaves, and *Ipomoea*, a perennial creeper which has been introduced to the east coast by sea currents from Mozambique.

Fauna The forests are the habitat of bushpig and bushbuck, with the latter also occurring in bush pockets in the dunefields. Common duiker, grysbok, vervet monkey and tree dassie inhabit the dune thickets, although some of these animals occasionally venture into the dunefield. Quite surprisingly, bushpig are known to scavenge on stranded fish and birds along the beach.

Larger predators include caracal and leopard, while smaller predators such as large-spotted genet, yellow mongoose, small grey mongoose and black-backed jackal also occur.

Among the smaller mammals occurring are the hairy-footed gerbil, vlei rat, Saunders' vlei rat, striped mouse, porcupine and Cape hare.

Several tropical forest birds inhabiting the east coast of South Africa reach the southern limit of their distribution in the eastern and southern Cape forests. Among these are the

The rare Damara tern is a summer visitor to the coast of Alexandria

tambourine dove, as well as the trumpeter and crowned hornbills.

The variety of habitat types – forest, grasslands, fynbos and the sea and seashore – attracts a large number of species and birders will find the checklist appended to the trail pamphlet useful. Knysna lourie are often seen in the low forest, which is also the habitat of the elusive Narina trogon, chorister robin, Cape batis and forest weaver. Starred and brown robins occur, but are less frequently observed, while the trumpeter hornbill is easily identified by its raucous call which varies from laughing to wailing or trumpeting.

Unless you hear the grating "churr" of the terrestrial bulbul, it is easily overlooked. While these bulbuls forage on the forest floor, the more common sombre bulbul is mainly restricted to the upper branches of trees, while the blackeyed bulbul favours the forest edge. Other species to look out for in the forest fringes include crowned hornbill and dusky flycatcher.

The grasslands at Midfor and Langevlakte are favoured by cattle egret, white stork – a summer visitor – large numbers of hadeda ibis, Stanley's bustard, forktailed drongo, bokmakierie and pintailed whydah.

Typical fynbos species include glossy starling, grey sunbird and collared sunbird.

The dense vegetation of the dune pockets attracts a large number of species including redfronted tinker barbet, black cuckooshrike, whitebrowed and Karoo robins, as well as barthroated apalis. Also to be found here are spotted prinia, Cape batis and southern boubou, as well as greater doublecollared and collared sunbirds.

At least ten bird of prey species, including the rare peregrine falcon, have been recorded. Raptors of the forest include cuckoo hawk,

crowned eagle and African goshawk, while longcrested eagle and forest buzzard might be spotted along the forest edge. Species favouring the grasslands include the peregrine falcon and martial eagle.

The dunefields of Alexandria are the habitat of the most easterly breeding colony of the rare Damara tern. This summer (November to March) migrant is more common along the Namibian coast where numbers are estimated at about 5 700 birds. Along the South African coast a number of breeding sites occur in the north-western, southern and eastern Cape and their numbers were estimated at 240 in 1992. Nests are a simple hollow scraped on gravel or shell slacks between coastal dunes and breeding sites should not be disturbed.

Another species utilising the dune slacks for breeding is the African black oystercatcher, which also occurs along the shore where you chance seeing whitefronted plover, as well as sanderling, a summer migrant. Bird Island is the habitat of a large breeding colony of Cape gannet, while Cape cormorant also breed on the island.

History Artefacts discovered at Woody Cape and elsewhere along the eastern Cape coast provide evidence that Middle and Later Stone Age people inhabited the coastline for thousands of years. These early inhabitants exploited the marine resources and middens consisting mainly of sand mussels (*Donax serra*) occur between the dunes of the Alexandria dunefield.

The area is also of more recent historical interest. At Kwaaihoek the first seafarer to round the Cape, Bartolomeu Dias, erected the Cross of St Gregory after his crew forced him to turn back in the vicinity of the Keiskamma River. A replica of the limestone cross or *padrão* erected on 12 March 1488 can be seen on the rocky promontory 4 km east of the small seaside resort of Boknes.

Situated on the north-eastern boundary of the conservation area is the farm Glenshaw where Nongqawuse was buried in 1898. In 1856, she had a vision which prophesied that if the Xhosa killed all their cattle and destroyed their grain, the whites would be swept into the sea by a strong wind. An abundance of grain and cattle, as well as wagons, clothes, guns and ammunition would then appear miraculously. It was believed that Xhosa heroes would rise from the dead and that youth would be restored to the elderly. This enormous sacrifice resulted in mass starvation by February 1857. Some relief was provided by the mission stations, but between 20 000 and 40 000 people died, while more than 150 000 were displaced.

The town of Alexandria, originally known as Olifantshoek, was named in honour of a Scottish minister, Alexander Smith, in 1873. Smith came to South Africa to take charge of the Dutch Reformed parish in Uitenhage from where he regularly conducted services in the Alexandria district.

The first attempt to establish control over the Alexandria Forest was in 1866 when Captain Johann Baron de Fin was appointed as Conservator of Forests. However, with only two rangers and six foresters to assist him, it was impossible to patrol the vast areas under his control effectively. These areas included the magisterial districts of Keiskammahoek, Stockenström, East London, Victoria East, Thembuland and Alexandria, as well as King William's Town. It is, therefore, easy to understand how the settlers in the area were able to obtain as much timber as they needed from the forests. The Alexandria State Forest was proclaimed in 1896.

Patches of indigenous forests were also cleared for agriculture, especially chicory, and Alexandria is the largest chicory producing area in South Africa.

It is uncertain when the pine plantations were initially established, but they were re-established in 1913 and today cover about 330 ha.

Geology Covering about 110 square kilometres, the Alexandria dunefield is not only the largest coastal dunefield in southern Africa, but also one of the most impressive in the world. It is comparable in size to the Australian coastal dunefields and also matches the coastal dunefields along the Oregon coast of the north-western USA.

The dunefield stretches in a two to three kilometre wide strip for 50 km from Sundays River Mouth to a few kilometres east of Woody Cape, reaching heights of up to 140 m. Estimated to be some 6 500 years old, the dunefield has been forming since the sea rose to its present level after the last Ice Age.

Sand and silt carried eastwards by the longshore drift are deposited on beaches and blown inland by the dominant, strong south-westerly wind to form barchanoid and transverse dunes. It has been estimated that about 170 000 m^3 of sand, or about 800 bakkie loads a day, accumulate each year. During summer the dunes are also influenced by the east winds and the dunes at Woody Cape are reversing barchanoid dunes.

Two fossil dunefields on the landward side of the Alexandria dunefield have tentatively been dated at 120 000 and 220 000 years, while the Kaba fossil dunefield, south-west of the town of Alexandria, has provisionally been dated at between one and three million years. The Nanaga fossil dunefield north-west of Kaba is even older with an estimated age of four million years.

Research has shown that these fossil dunefields were formed during periods when the sea level was much higher than at present. The dunes were subsequently consolidated into limestones and stabilised by vegetation and are no longer recognisable as dunes.

Also impressive is the aeolinite or dune rock underlying the Alexandria dunefield. These rocks were formed when the calcium carbonate-rich sand was compressed and cemented by calcite and are exposed as outcrops in the dunefield. The aeolinite can also be seen along the coast where it is exposed as sheer cliffs of up to 10 m high, stretching for several kilometres along the coast.

TRAIL DESCRIPTION

Day 1: Langebos Hut to Woody Cape Hut

From Langebos Hut the trail ascends along forestry roads and tracks, mainly through pine plantations, before descending for about a kilometre.

The descent is followed by another climb and the route then winds down to the Lekkerboom which is reached about 5 km from the start. This large Outeniqua yellowwood with a hollow in the base of its trunk is also known as the Waterboom and was a favourite resting place in years gone by. Early travellers en route from Alexandria to Nankoos used to cool their refreshments in the water which collected in the hollow trunk during rain, hence its name.

From the Lekkerboom the trail climbs gradually and along this section a few large Outeniqua yellowwoods and a magnificent coast coral tree can be seen. The trail then ascends gradually to reach a small clearing in the forest where log seats have been provided for the weary hiker. From here you will also have your first glimpse of the sea.

After descending gradually for about 1,5 km the trail joins the Alexandria/Cannon Rock road which is followed to the left until you reach the Midfor T-junction. The trail turns right here and continues along the road until the Midfor campsite is reached. Here the route passes through the campsite and leads to a wooden staircase which has been erected to protect the vegetation and to prevent disturbance of the sensitive dune.

For the next 5,5 km the trail follows the coastline before you have a choice of continuing along the coast or along the top of the cliffs. The first option is, however, impossible at high tide as the sea washes right up to the sheer cliffs. On closer inspection of the cliffs you will

notice the patterns of fossilised dunes. At Die Leer a ladder marks the end of the "low route" and provides access to the top of the cliffs.

The "high route" initially passes through a 0,5 km stretch of sand dunes before continuing through fynbos close to the edge of the cliffs. Along this section you are afforded splendid views of the impressive coastline, as well as Bird Island with its lighthouse, Seal Island and Stag Island about 8 km off the coast.

From the junction of the two routes it is a short walk to the wooden overnight hut which is tucked away amongst white milkwoods. It comprises two bedrooms, a kitchen and a dining room with a table and benches, as well as a balcony.

Day 2: Woody Cape Hut to Alexandria Forest Station

From the hut you will retrace your steps until reaching the junction with the first day's route. Here the trail turns left, passing through dense dune thicket until it reaches a ladder which has been constructed to prevent damage to the sensitive dune vegetation.

The trail winds across the sand dunes in a north-westerly direction for about 2 km before swinging north-east for about 1 km. Beacons have been placed strategically, but since the sand dunes move the beacons should be used as guides only.

Shortly before the 6 km mark the trail enters the dune fynbos before emerging into grasslands where the route is indicated by posts placed at 200 m intervals. After passing through a gate the route joins a vehicle road. Take a short break here and look back for a last view of the sea and Stag, Seal and Bird islands. Along this section water can be obtained at a windmill.

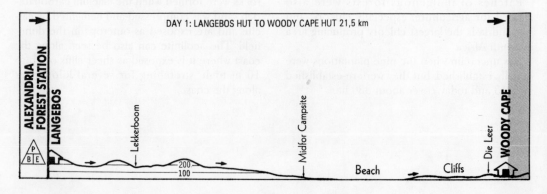

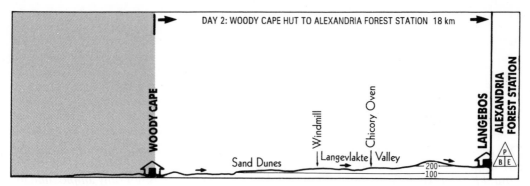

DAY 2: WOODY CAPE HUT TO ALEXANDRIA FOREST STATION 18 km

A short way beyond the 11 km mark you will pass an old chicory oven, used in the 1920s, and a restored farmhouse with its original yellowwood panelling. The trail soon branches off to the left, ascending gently through indigenous forest along a footpath before descending.

The final 2 km follow a vehicle track through the forest and the opening up of the forest canopy makes bird-watching easier.

Keep an eye out here for the Knysna lourie. The starting point is reached soon after crossing the divisional road to Boknes.

MOUNTAIN ZEBRA

This trail in the Mountain Zebra National Park offers hikers the opportunity of viewing the rare Cape mountain zebra, as well as other animals typical of the Cape Midlands, in their natural habitat. With fairly short distances hiked each day, there is not only ample time for observing the game but also for bird-watching. The route winds past weathered rock clusters, through kloofs and across shrub-covered slopes to just below the summit of the Bankberg and a spectacular panorama of the surrounding countryside.

TRAIL PLANNER

Distance 25 km; 3 days

Grading B

Climate

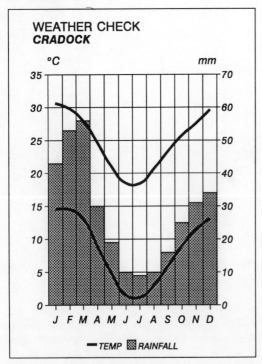

WEATHER CHECK
CRADOCK

— TEMP ▨ RAINFALL

Reservations The Chief Director, National Parks Board, P O Box 787, Pretoria 0001, Telephone (012) 343-1991, Fax (012) 343-

0905 or P O Box 7400, Roggebaai 8012, Telephone (021) 22-2810, Fax (021) 24-6211. Reservations are accepted up to a year in advance.

Group size Minimum 2; Maximum 12

Maps A sketch map of the trail is included in the information leaflet on the trail which is forwarded to you with your receipt and permit.

Facilities The two overnight huts are equipped with bunks and mattresses, lamps, a pot, pan and kettle. There is also a fireplace and firewood, a shower, chemical toilets and refuse bins.

Relevant information

■ It is advisable to carry at least two litres of water per person on the first two days, especially during the dry winter months.
■ Summer temperatures can be unbearably hot with little overhead cover, while extremely cold temperatures are recorded in winter when snow is not uncommon.

Logistics Circular route. There is no hut at the start of the trail. Accommodation in the park consists of fully equipped chalets and caravan/camping sites. There is also a shop which stocks groceries, meat and liquor, a filling station and a licensed restaurant.

How to get there The park is reached by taking the Graaff-Reinet road turn-off on the Cradock/Middelburg road, 5 km north of Cradock. The turn-off to the park is clearly signposted some 5 km along this road and from the turn-off it is a further 12,5 km to the park.

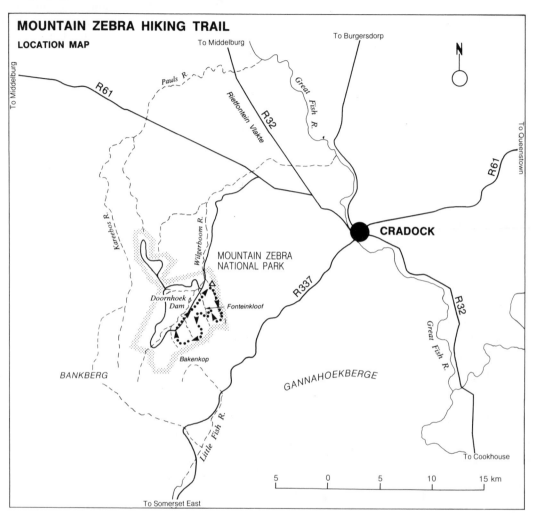

MOUNTAIN ZEBRA HIKING TRAIL

LOCATION MAP

TRAIL ENVIRONMENT

Flora The vegetation is typical of the Cape Midlands and represents a transitional zone between the dwarf shrublands of the arid Karoo in the west and the more temperate grasslands to the east, with both veld types being present. To date more than 350 plant species, representing 70 families, have been identified. The distribution of vegetation is closely linked to factors such as aspect, topography and soil.

Dense riverine bush dominated by sweet thorn and karree is characteristic of the vegetation of the Wilgerboom River, Fonteinkloof and Boesmanskloof. Other species found here include Karoo bluebush, wild olive and sagewood.

The pediments along the Wilgerboom River Valley are dominated by dwarf shrublands and open woodlands. Typical Karoo bushes found here include karoobush (*Pentzia incana*), mountain globe karoo (*P. sphaerocephala*) and wild aster (*Felicia filifolia*).

Karoo bushes and grass are typical on the

155

steep lower slopes of the Bankberg. Shrubs found here include glossy currant, sand olive and cross-berry. Dominant species of the dolerite outcrops include white stinkwood, mountain cabbage tree and *Aloe striata*. The leaves of this aloe are characteristically striped, hence the name *striata*. They are thornless and the Afrikaans common name, blou-aalwyn, refers to the colour of the leaves and not the flowers which are bright coral red and seen in winter and early spring. Grassland dominated by suurpol (*Merxmuellera disticha*) replaces shrubveld on south-facing slopes above 1 400 m.

The Rooiplaat plateau in the north-western corner of the park supports sweet grassveld and is an important grazing area, while the vegetation of the Bankberg plateau consists largely of sour grassveld and fynbos elements.

Fauna One of the main objectives of the park is the preservation of a viable, genetically pure population of the Cape mountain zebra (*Equus zebra zebra*) in balance with their environment. These animals were once plentiful in the Cape, inhabiting the mountainous areas of the province south of the Orange River and eastwards to the Gamka and Kamanassie mountains.

A close relative of the Cape mountain zebra, Hartmann's mountain zebra (*E. zebra hartmannae*) occurs in the coastal strip and the subcontinuous chain of mountains from southwestern Angola to the Orange River in Namibia.

Another conservation priority is the mountain reedbuck which favours mountainous regions where it has little competition from other larger grazers for the sweet grass it prefers.

Cape mountain zebra and spoor

The Cradock district appears to be the optimal area within its distribution range and the park supports what is believed to be the highest concentration of this species within its natural range. Prior to the introduction of measures in 1974 to control their numbers in the park the population stood at around 1 000, but is now maintained at between 500 and 600 animals.

When the park was proclaimed in 1937 the only large mammals in the area were Cape mountain zebra, mountain reedbuck, common duiker, steenbok and klipspringer. Restocking of species previously found in the area started soon after the proclamation of the park and included springbok, blesbok, black wildebeest, red hartebeest and eland. Kudu found their way into the park during the late 1970s.

Reedbuck were also introduced but did not establish themselves, while gemsbok, which were thought to have occurred in the northern parts of the Cradock district, did not settle down well either. Small numbers of grey rhebok once occurred naturally in the park, but their numbers declined to such an extent that they are no longer seen.

To date a total of 57 mammal species have been recorded in the park of which 35 are nocturnal.

Birdlife is relatively abundant and some 206 species have been recorded here. Uncommon species occurring in the park are booted eagle, a migrant which visits the park between August and April, black harrier and Cape eagle owl which you are likely to hear from the trail huts.

Typical species of the acacia veld include redfronted tinker barbet, cardinal woodpecker, forktailed drongo and fiscal flycatcher.

In the hillside scrub you chance ticking Karoo robin, titbabbler, neddicky, spotted prinia, longbilled pipit and dusky sunbird.

Among the resident species you are likely to see in the riverine bush are speckled and whitebacked mousebirds, olive thrush, Cape robin, fairy flycatcher and southern boubou.

Species you might spot on the rocky slopes and along the upper elevations of the Bankberg include black eagle, jackal buzzard, rock pigeon, ground woodpecker, rock martin and whitenecked raven. Also occurring here are mountain, buffstreaked and familiar chats, as well as stonechat and rock pipit.

Twenty-two snake species have been recorded in the park including the rare plain mountain adder (*Bitis inornata*), known from only

DIFFERENCES BETWEEN CAPE MOUNTAIN ZEBRA AND BURCHELL'S ZEBRA

Cape mountain zebras differ from Burchell's zebra (*E. burchelli*) in a number of ways:
- They are smaller and more compact.
- "Shadow stripes" are absent on the hindquarters.
- The stripes do not meet ventrally.
- The stripes on the legs extend clearly down to the hooves and encircle the legs.
- A definite dewlap is present.
- The stripes form a characteristic "grid-iron" pattern on the rump.

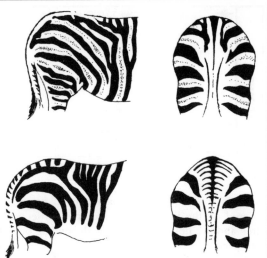

Burchell's zebra (above) and Cape mountain zebra (below)

12 specimens collected in South Africa. It is one of the rarest snakes in South Africa and inhabits a restricted area of the southern Karoo from Matjiesfontein in the west to Albany in the east.

History From the number of rock paintings discovered in the region it is clear that the area was once the home of the San. Twenty-seven of the 30 archaeological sites which have been recorded in the park are open sites, primarily along the river valleys. The oldest artefacts are representative of the Middle Stone Age, but most of the sites are dominated by scrapers of the Later Stone Age.

The park was proclaimed in 1937 when it became clear that the Cape mountain zebra was doomed to extinction. The government bought the farm Babylon's Toren, including its mountain zebra population of five stallions and one mare. In 1939 the mare produced a filly, but died the following year, while the filly died six years later without foaling. By 1950 only two rather old stallions remained and these were shot and given to the Transvaal Museum.

In the same year Mr J H Lombard of the neighbouring farm Waterval donated five stallions and six mares to the National Parks Board.

By 1964 the population had increased to 25 and the park was enlarged to 6 536 ha when four adjoining farms and a portion of a fifth farm was purchased by the state. One of the farms, Doornhoek, had a population of 30 animals, increasing the total to 55.

Since then the population has expanded rapidly and today a population of about 200 Cape mountain zebras is maintained in the park.

Over 200 surplus animals have been translocated to areas where they occurred historically, including the De Hoop Nature Reserve, the Karoo National Park, the Karoo Nature Reserve at Graaff-Reinet and the Tsolwana Game Park.

Small populations have also managed to survive in the Gamka Mountain Nature Reserve near Calitzdorp and the Kamanassie Mountains near Oudtshoorn, and the total world population of the Cape mountain zebra stood at about 680 in 1993.

In 1970 a studbook was introduced for the Cape mountain zebras and a detailed record of each zebra in the park is kept. The studbook is one of only two internationally recognised records for wild populations in the world and enables researchers to study aspects such as population dynamics, sex ratios and breeding.

TRAIL DESCRIPTION

Day 1: Rest Camp to Olien Hut The trail, clearly indicated with a black mountain zebra on a yellow background, begins at the caravan park in the rest camp. Before setting off, though, report to the park office and fill up your water-bottle as water is not always available from the

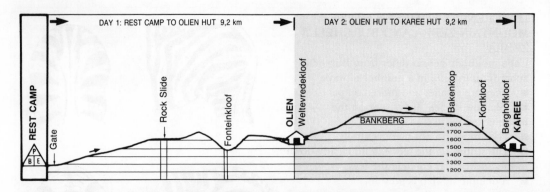

spring in Fonteinkloof. Approximately 9,2 km is covered on the first day and requires between three and five hours to complete, depending on your pace.

The first section follows a jeep track up Grootkloof to the foot of the Bankberg. At the end of the jeep track the trail crosses the Grootkloof River, continuing in a south-westerly direction. Soon you will pass a massive boulder with an estimated mass of 6 000 tons which, as a result of weathering, broke loose from the mountain in 1976. The clump of shrubs and trees nearby attracts large numbers of birds and is one of the highlights of the trail.

From here the trail rises steadily to Kwaggarif, the spur separating Grootkloof and Fonteinkloof, and from the ridge there is a superb view of the old homestead of Babylons Toren. The trail then drops down to a jeep track in Fonteinkloof before crossing the river. If water is available, top up your water-bottle before tackling the steep climb out of the kloof. The trail rises steeply to a plateau and here you will find yourself looking down onto the Weltevrede homestead. Once on the plateau, a jeep track is followed for a short distance before you branch off to the right to the first overnight stop.

The last 2 km of the day's hike is a fairly

steep descent to Olien Hut which is named after the abundance of wild olive trees growing in the vicinity.

The hut consists of two rooms, each accommodating six people, and a kitchen with a fireplace. Wood and coal are provided and water can be heated by means of a rudimentary geyser tucked away in the chimney. There is also an outside fireplace shaded by a clump of large wild olive trees.

On a hot day it is a good idea to follow the road down the kloof to the semi-natural pool in one of the streams above the Weltevrede homestead.

Day 2: Olien Hut to Karee Hut Remember to fill your water-bottle before setting off as there is no water along day two's route. A steep climb awaits you out of Weltevredekloof as you initially have to retrace your steps to where the route to the hut branched off the previous day. From here the trail ascends steadily along the slopes of the Bankberg and you will easily identify the mountain cabbage tree. You will gain some 400 m in altitude before levelling off below Bakenkop (1 957 m), the highest point in the park. Along this section you will be rewarded with splendid views of Weltevredekloof and

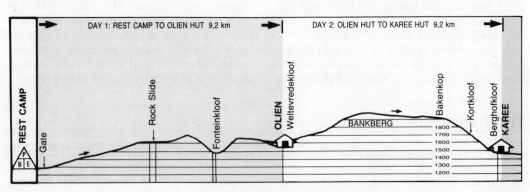

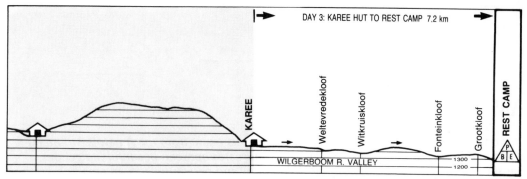

the surrounding countryside. During summer this section is best completed in the coolness of morning so an early start is advisable.

After traversing above the sheer cliffs below Bakenkop the trail descends steeply along a spur which separates Kortkloof on your left from Berghofkloof to your right, passing large weathered dolerite outcrops. These smooth, dome-shaped outcrops and clusters of boulders are remnants of a dolerite sheet which intruded the Karoo sediments and was subsequently exposed.

The trail then cuts across the spur before finally descending into Berghofkloof where you will join a vehicle track for a short distance. The trail takes you over a nek before dropping finally down to Karree Hut which is similar to the Olien Hut. This hut takes its name from the large karree trees growing here.

The day's hike covers about 9,2 km and takes between three and five hours to complete.

Day 3: Karee Hut to Rest Camp The final day's hike covers a mere 7,2 km, following an easy route along the Wilgerboom River Valley. From the hut the trail follows the jeep track down the valley, crosses the circular tourist drive and then continues along the course of the Wilgerboom River. The fairly dense riverine bush is the habitat of species such as sombre bulbul, Cape robin, southern boubou and common waxbill.

After about 2,5 km you will cross the tourist road again, passing first through Weltevredekloof and then, about 1,5 km further, through Witkruiskloof. From here the trail climbs steeply out of Witkruiskloof to skirt Rondekop, a prominent landmark. To the left lies Doornhoek Dam which attracts species such as dabchick, reed cormorant, goliath heron, sacred ibis and South African shelduck.

Overlooking the dam is the old Doornhoek farmhouse which dates back to the 1830s and is an excellent example of an early eastern Cape farm complex. The building was restored in 1984 and declared a national monument two years later. It has been furnished with antiques and can be hired by visitors to the park.

The route continues across Volstruisvlakte and, after passing through Fonteinkloof, crosses Springbokvlakte to reach the rest camp about 1,5 km further.

AMATOLA

Few trails can compare with this trail, which takes its name from the Amatola Mountain range in the eastern Cape. The six-day route alternates between beautiful indigenous forests, grasslands and patches of pine plantations and passes through an area rich in history. Outstanding features of the trail are the numerous waterfalls and inviting swimming pools tucked away in the enchanting forests. Although there are some strenuous climbs, efforts are always well rewarded with stupendous views. There is also a choice of two circular two-day trails and two day walks.

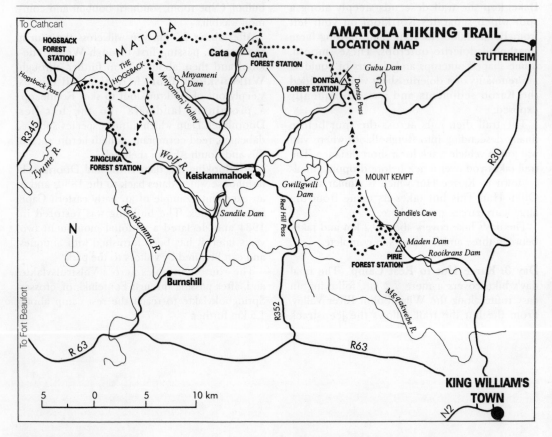

TRAIL PLANNER

Distance 105 km; 6 days (shorter options possible)

Grading C

Reservations Contour, P O Box 186, Bisho

5608, Telephone (0401) 95-2115, Fax (0401) 9-2756. Reservations are accepted up to 12 months in advance.

Group size Minimum 2; Maximum 12

Climate

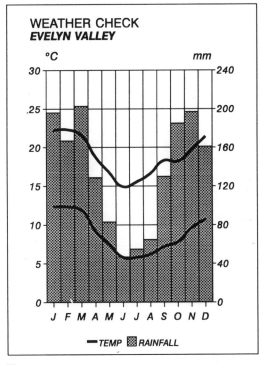

WEATHER CHECK
EVELYN VALLEY

°C   mm

J F M A M J J A S O N D

—TEMP ▨RAINFALL

Maps A full-colour trail map with useful information on the flora, fauna, history and ecology on the reverse is available, but must be purchased separately.

Facilities Amenities at the five overnight stops include bunks with mattresses, fireplaces, firewood, water and toilets.

Logistics No transport arrangements are necessary if you are hiking the two-day Evelyn Valley Loop at the start of the trail or

the Zingcuka Loop near the end of the trail. The six-day trail between Maden Dam and Tyume River is, however, a linear route, requiring a second vehicle – or you could rely on local taxis if not pressed for time.

Relevant information

■ During the winter months it is advisable to set off with a full water-bottle each day since many of the streams could be dry. All year round it is especially important to carry water on the second day since there is very little water along this stretch.

■ During the winter months the dry vegetation and the hot berg winds create a serious fire hazard. Hikers should refrain from smoking where there is a danger of fire, while fires at the overnight huts should be kept small and be extinguished.

■ Be prepared for rain between October and March, while dense mist is common in spring and summer. Snowfalls are possible during the cold winter months.

■ Some sections of the trail traverse traditional grazing land and you should be courteous to the local people at all times.

How to get there From the centre of King William's Town, follow Alexander Road northwards, and continue along Reserve Road. Follow the R30 to Stutterheim for approximately 10 km before turning left onto the Rooikrantz/Maden Dam road. You will then follow a gravel road for about 7 km before crossing the Rooikrantz Dam wall. Maden Dam is about 2 km further and the trail starts at the information kiosk at the end of the road.

TRAIL ENVIRONMENT

Flora The vegetation of the Amatola Mountains falls within the Dohne Sourveld consisting of indigenous forests, grasslands and fynbos.

The forests in this part of the eastern Cape are situated in the transitional zone between the southern Cape forests and the more subtropical forests of the northern part of the eastern Cape and Natal. Many of the subtropical species growing in the eastern Cape do not occur in the forests of the southern Cape. While the southern Cape forests comprise

some 125 woody species, the eastern Cape forests are the habitat of about 250 species. Among the trees which reach the southern limit of their distribution in the eastern Cape are lemonwood, coast coral tree, red beech and coffee pear.

Dominant species include Outeniqua and real yellowwoods, white stinkwood, Cape chestnut, red currant, Cape beech and forest elder.

The indigenous forests of the Amatolas reach up to 25 m in height and are an excellent example of the high forests typical of the east-

CAPE PARROT

The Cape parrot is also known as the redshoul-dered or green parrot. However, the Afrikaans name, Knysna papegaai, is a misnomer as this species does not occur in the Knysna area, but is confined to the forests from Alexandria east-wards. Its general colour is green, but its striking red forehead, chin and shoulders are distinctive. These birds are normally found in parties of five to 30 birds in the highest, coldest and wettest parts of the mountain forests, at altitudes of between 1 000 and 1 200 m. They feed on berries and the fruits of yellowwoods, wild olive and wild plum. As a result of illegal trading and the destruction of their habitat their numbers are declining and they have been classified as vulnerable.

The Cape parrot's diet includes wild plum

ern Cape. In contrast to the southern Cape forests with their luxuriant undergrowth, there is very little or no undergrowth in these forests. This is because of the dense canopy and sub-canopy which excludes sunlight from the lower layers. Competition for sunlight and survival is, consequently, strong. The lemonwood has adopted an interesting survival technique: where the vegetation is less prolific regeneration takes place by coppicing from old stumps, forming dense stands which restrict other trees.

At higher elevations the forests are replaced by dense sour grassveld which has been invaded by fynbos, giving rise to a mixture of fynbos and grassland vegetation. Typical fynbos species include the common sugarbush which grows mainly on the lower slopes while the Hottentot white sugarbush occurs higher up.

Fauna The forests and plantations are the habitat of several species including bushpig, bushbuck and leopard, which also occur in the more mountainous areas. Two species which reach the southernmost limit of their distribution here are the samango monkey and the tree dassie.

The tree dassie is similar in appearance to the rock dassie, but its coat is a darker brown with a creamy-white dorsal crest. As a result of the fragmentation and destruction of their forest habitat their numbers have declined significant-ly and they have been classified as rare. Their distribution is determined by suitable forest habitats and in South Africa they occur along

the coast from the eastern Cape to south-west-ern KwaZulu/Natal. The tree dassie grows up to 50 cm in length and has a maximum mass of 4,5 kg. It is a nocturnal animal and particularly noisy at night. Its call is described as "an alarm-ing raucous call, which ends in a sudden scream".

The rocky areas are the habitat of chacma baboon and rock dassie, while common duiker favour scrubs along the forest edge.

Other mammals occurring in the area include vervet monkey, spotted-necked and Cape claw-less otters, caracal and porcupine.

The Pirie Forest is also the best-known habi-tat of the giant golden mole, which is listed in the *International Red Data Book* as endan-gered. No more than 100 specimens are found in museums throughout the world and hardly anything is known about their biological and ecological needs. They are restricted to the forests of the eastern Cape.

Your best chances of seeing this 230 mm-long mole is after rains when it emerges from its burrow in search of insects and earthworms.

Another species which lives mainly under-ground is the giant *Microchaetus* earthworm. With a reputed length of up to 7 m, they are the world's longest earthworms, although lengths of 2,5 m are more common. They are seldom seen, however, as they only appear at night or after penetrating rain.

Two interesting amphibians occurring in the area are the Amatola toad (*Bufo amatolica*) and the Hogsback frog (*Anhydrophryne rattrayi*).

The Amatola toad was first discovered in 1925 and is confined to the Amatola Mountains, occurring in grassveld on the upper slopes and summit of the range. It is a uniform grey or olive-brown colour with a pale line down the centre of its back. Owing to its limited distribution and fears that its range could be reduced by afforestation, it has been classified as rare.

The Hogsback frog is restricted to altitudes higher than 1 100 m above sea level, favouring forested areas with damp leaf litter near streams. It is a small coppery brown to almost blackish frog and to date it has only been recorded in the Hogsback Mountains, Keiskammahoek and Katberg.

An interesting fish occurring in the area is the Border barb (*Barbus trevelyani*). This small minnow first became known to science in 1877 when it was discovered in the Buffalo River. Forty years later another specimen was caught in the same river near East London, but a search initiated in 1958 proved fruitless and it was feared to be extinct. A few years later a former curator of the Kaffrarian Museum in King William's Town, Mr C J Skead, had the stomach contents of a trout caught in the upper reaches of the Rooikrantz Dam analysed. The trout's meal was identified as a Border barb and this led to the discovery of a small population of these rare minnows in the shallow stream below the Maden and Rooikrantz dams.

At present the Border barb is confined to the upper reaches of the Keiskamma and Buffalo river systems and is considered a vulnerable species. The major threat to this species is habitat destruction, although the introduction of exotic angling species into the river systems also poses a threat to their survival.

Numerous bird species occur in this area, but because visibility is limited in the forests, their loud and penetrating calls are often the only means of identification.

Interesting winged inhabitants of the forests include cuckoo hawk, crowned eagle, Knysna lourie, Narina trogon and crowned hornbill. The more common species include rameron pigeon, olive woodpecker, chorister robin and terrestrial bulbul, while the redchested cuckoo is a common summer migrant.

Species you might tick in the fynbos-grassveld include olive and Cape rock thrush, stonechat, Cape robin, orangethroated longclaw and southern tchagra. Cape and Gurney's sugarbirds, as well as four sunbirds – malachite, lesser dou-blecollared, greater doublecollared and black – have been recorded.

History   Archaeological excavations in the vicinity of King William's Town and Stutterheim have confirmed the presence of Early and Middle Stone Age people in the region, while excavations near Maden Dam have provided evidence of Later Stone Age people. Indications are, however, that the area north of the Amatola Mountains was more densely populated because of more favourable living conditions.

During the early seventeenth century the Gonaqua Khoikhoi inhabited the Ciskeian coast and further inland along the Buffalo and Keiskamma rivers. During the winters they grazed their herds on the sweet grassveld on the dry and warmer lower slopes, migrating to the higher sourveld areas in spring.

The first wave of the southward migrating Xhosa-speaking peoples reached the Keiskamma River by the 1750s and the Gonaqua were either assimilated or driven out. They also grazed their cattle on the mountain slopes and called the impressive mountain range Amathola – "The Place of the Weaned Calves".

The great Xhosa split occurred in 1775 after Rharhabe tried to dethrone his father Phalo and then fled across the Kei River to settle at Izele near King William's Town. White traders and hunters began moving into the area during the early 1700s and in 1795 the Fish River was officially proclaimed the eastern boundary of the Cape Colony.

Disagreements over land ownership and stock theft led to considerable conflict and between 1779 and 1878 nine frontier wars were fought.

One name which will always be linked to the Pirie Forest is that of the famous warrior and chief, Sandile. He succeeded to the chieftainship of the Ngqika in 1829 at the age of nine after the death of his father Ngqika. Sandile came of age in 1841 and played a leading role in the frontier wars of 1846-47 (7th), 1850-53 (8th) and 1877-88 (9th). Because he was lame he never took part in the battles, but by his brave and shrewd tactics he became a thorn in the side of the British forces. In May 1878, pursued by British and colonial forces, Sandile hid in a deep cave at the foot of what subsequently became known as Sandile's Krantz. A few days later he was killed by Captain Lonsdale's renegade Mfengu in the Isidenge Forest. He was the only chief slain in the frontier wars.

The Pirie area takes its name from Dr Alexander Pirie, chairman of the Glasgow Missionary Society during the 1830s. During his term of office several mission stations were established, one of which, between Debe Nek and the Buffalo River, was named in his honour.

TRAIL DESCRIPTION

Day 1: Maden Dam to Evelyn Valley Hut

The trail starts at the information kiosk above the Maden Dam and, after a short while, passes a few cement foundations which is all that remains of Howse's sawmill. It then follows the old logging railway track for 4,5 km to Timber Square, gaining some 110 m in altitude, and along this section you will see the remains of a trestle bridge across the Hutchins Stream. The stream is named after David Hutchins, who was in charge of the Eastern Forestry Conservancy between 1883 and 1888. Other reminders of days gone by are a number of hand-hewn sleepers of lemonwood and hard pear, as well as a section of the original track.

At Timber Square the Pirie Walk continues to the right, while the Amatola Hiking Trail turns off to the left, passing the junction of the return route of the two-day circular trail a short way onwards. The trail now climbs steadily through beautiful unexploited indigenous forest, gaining some 400 m in altitude over 5,5 km to the top of the plateau behind McNaghton's Krans. The Hutchins Stream, a tributary of the Buffalo River, is again crossed along this section, but do not count on finding water here during the dry winter months. Before finally joining the gravel road leading to the Evelyn Valley Hut a delightful clearing with log seats and tables invites you to take a well-earned rest.

From here the trail follows a forestry road through pine plantations and patches of indigenous forest for a further 5 km to the old Evelyn Valley Forest Station. The old foresters' quarters have been converted into overnight accommo-dation equipped with bunks and mattresses. From the house you have a magnificent view over the Pirie Forest, Murray's Krans and the Rooikrantz and Maden dams some 600 m below.

Day 2: Evelyn Valley Hut to Dontsa Hut

Since this day's hike is 22 km long an early start is advisable and before setting off, remember to fill your water-bottle.

The first section of the day's hike follows the plantation road towards Isidenge over easy terrain. Ignore the turn-off of the Evelyn Valley Loop which is passed after about 4 km, continuing alongside pine plantations for about another 1 km. The trail then passes through a stretch of forest thicket before following an undulating course through the Abafazi Forest along the eastern slopes of Mount Kemp.

Further along, the route takes you through a patch of indigenous forest, the Mvulu Forest. Here, the steep cliffs force the route to descend to a tributary of the Bizana River before ascending steadily through the Dontsa Main Forest.

Shortly before reaching the turn-off to the Dontsa Forest Station you will cross the Dontsa Pass which was built in 1857 as a result of the initiative of a military chaplain, the Reverend George Dacre. The name is translated as "hard pull" and is probably a reference to the steep ascent which has to be negotiated when travelling from Keiskammahoek up the Dontsa Pass.

After crossing the Keiskammahoek/Stutterheim road the route winds through pine plantations, passing the turn-off to Dontsa Forest

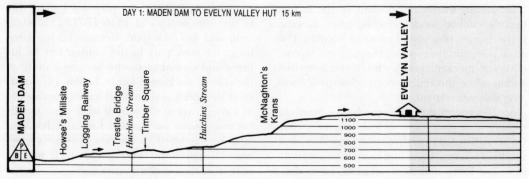

DAY 1: MADEN DAM TO EVELYN VALLEY HUT 15 km

FOREST EXPLOITATION

During the frontier wars trees were felled to provide timber for the construction of fortresses in King William's Town and the surrounding districts. The first recorded exploitation dates back to 1819 when trees were felled for the construction of Fort Willshire on the Keiskamma River. Exploitation by early woodcutters continued steadily until Captain Johann Baron de Fin was appointed the first Conservator of Forests in the eastern Cape in 1866. In 1879 the forests yielded 126 yellowwood logs with a volume of 554 m³ and a value of £368.

In 1897 Mr J E Howse was granted the sole concession to fell trees in the Pirie Forest and in 1910 he built a railway line and a timber chute. The railway line was 0,6 m wide and stretched over 4 km from Timber Square, where the engines were located, to Howse's Millsite. Lemonwood was used for railway sleepers and coffee bitterberry for the construction of the cantilever bridge over the Hutchins River. It has been estimated that some 400 000 m³ of wood from 16 500 trees was removed from the Pirie Forest between 1910 and 1917.

Station. Gubu Hut, the overnight hut on the Kologha Hiking Trail, is situated just on the other side of the watershed, about 2 km away.

With just over 5 km of the day's hike left the trail initially continues through plantations, but soon returns to the indigenous forest. The trail climbs steadily before dropping down to cross several streams with delightful waterfalls and pools in the Galarta Forest.

You then head up the Ngobazana River Valley, to reach Dontsa Hut about two to two and a half hours beyond the forest station. The hut, a three-sided structure with timber walls and a built-in stone fireplace, is situated among pine trees a short distance upstream of the Dontsa Falls. The magnificent pool between two waterfalls below the hut is irresistible and can be reached by taking the steep descent from the hut.

Day 3: Dontsa Hut to Cata Huts Since this is another long day (19,6 km) an early start is once again advisable. From the hut the trail follows the Ngobozana River Valley upstream, ascending steadily through the Mount Thomas indigenous forest. A magnificent 20 m-high waterfall is passed about 30 minutes after set-

ting off. Further along you will ascend steeply, passing another spectacular cascade before emerging into open fynbos on Mount Thomas. Over the next few kilometres you will gain some 350 m in height before descending to Cata.

Along this section you will have expansive views of the Keiskamma basin and among the features you should be able to identify are Keiskammahoek, where a military outpost was established in 1852. Keiskamma is a Khoi word which has been translated as "puffadder river" and "glistening water".

A short way past the 1 641 m beacon the trail zigzags steeply down to a basin carved by the headwaters of the Cata River. A series of pools at the bottom of the valley make for a good lunch stop and from here you have a choice of two routes.

The "high road" alternates between patches of pine plantations and indigenous forest, while the "low road" follows the river downstream to the Cata Forest Station before ascending through a magnificent indigenous forest. In fine weather the lower option is recommended because of the numerous cascades and pools.

Although the overnight stop is just less than 5 km from the forest station, you will gain some

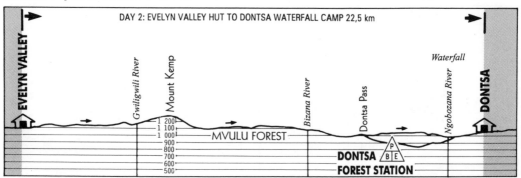

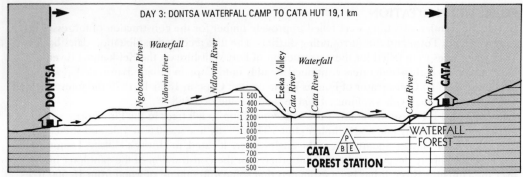

DAY 3: DONTSA WATERFALL CAMP TO CATA HUT 19,1 km

340 m in altitude and progress is slow with large boulders blocking sections of the path. The route takes you through the appropriately named Waterfall Forest where numerous cascading splendours will reward your effort. The overnight stop is situated at the foot of Geju Peak in a large amphitheatre and consists of three thatch-roof rondavels, a central cooking area or boma, as well as a shower and toilets.

Day 4: Cata Huts to Mnyameni Hut The first section of the day's hike ascends steadily alongside a tributary of the Cata River, passing a series of magnificent pools and going through small patches of indigenous forest. Near the top of the ascent you will have a choice of two routes, with the trail turning off to the left taking you along the edge of the cliffs. This route is much longer and since it winds close to the sheer cliffs, should be avoided in bad weather. Ignore the turn-off to the left in bad weather and head for the nek between the two Geju peaks instead.

The trail continues along the edge of the sheer cliffs of Geju for a while, rewarding you with magnificent vistas before crossing a nek. As you descend, the scenery to the north-west is dominated by the flat-topped Gaika's Kop (1 963 m), while the three Hogsback peaks are conspicuous to the south-west.

Over the next few kilometres the trail loses about 600 m in altitude and, on your way down, you will pass a viewpoint with breathtaking views into a deep gorge. The descent into the Mnyama River Valley zigzags steeply downwards and care should be taken here, especially after rains. A patch of forest where the trail meets a stream is an excellent lunch spot.

From here the trail once again descends steeply and at one point takes you through a crevice barely half a metre wide. Several waterfalls are passed along this section, each differing from the previous ones.

Once the bottom of the valley is reached the trail follows the course of the Mnyama River downstream, crossing it frequently, to reach the Mnyameni Hut 14,6 km after setting off from Cata. The distance is usually hiked in seven and a half to eight hours. Mnyameni is translated as "dark place" and is probably a reference to the dense, dark forests or the deep river valley – a most appropriate name. The overnight stop is on the banks of the Mnyama River in a valley between the Hogsback and Geju peak. It comprises a central "dining room" flanked on either side by the sleeping quarters. There is also a fireplace, a small "lapa", water and a toilet.

Day 5: Mnyameni Hut to Zingcuka Hut The day's hike starts with a steep climb through the

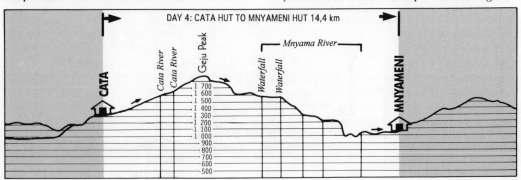

DAY 4: CATA HUT TO MNYAMENI HUT 14,4 km

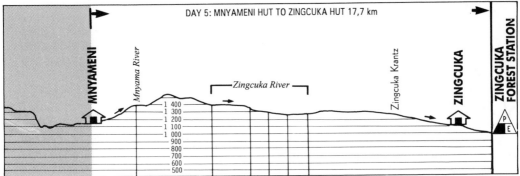

DAY 5: MNYAMENI HUT TO ZINGCUKA HUT 17,7 km

Heywood Forest, a small patch of indigenous forest, before emerging into fynbos along the slopes of the Hogsback Mountain. There are several explanations for the name Hogsback, one being that the first peak resembles the back of a hog, with the jagged rocks on the crest forming the spine. It has also been suggested that the name is derived from a Captain Hogg who was stationed at the nearby Fort Mitchell and who established a village here.

Over the next few kilometres you will gain about 200 m in altitude and after rounding the prominent ridge formed by the highest peak of the Hogsback you will reach the Upper Wolf Plateau. The trail passes a spongy area where the Zingcuka River rises, joining a stream a short way further on. Zingcuka means "place of the wolf" and the area was probably named after the abundance of hyaenas in years gone by. This section is characterised by numerous crystal clear pools which are especially inviting on a hot day. After following the stream, the trail leaves the river to skirt a ridge and then winds upstream along a tributary of the Zingcuka River.

From here the route traverses a spongy plateau and then descends steeply into the Wolf River Forest, losing some 100 m in altitude over a short distance. Shortly before reaching the overnight stop the trail to the Zingcuka Forest Station turns off to the left, while the track to the right continues to Zingcuka Lodge.

Zingcuka Lodge is a pleasant surprise. The hut is decorated with knotty pine with inlays of indigenous species of wood growing in the area. Other features of the hut include (solar-powered) electricity and flush toilets, as well as a hot shower once the water has been heated in the donkey boiler.

ALTERNATIVE ROUTES

It is possible to extend the trail by an additional day by continuing from Zingcuka Lodge to Hogsback, a distance of 16,5 km.

The Zingcuka Loop at the end of the trail is a two-day route over 36 km, starting and ending near Hogsback. The second day follows the last day of the linear route.

Another option is the two-day Evelyn Valley Loop at the start of the trail. From Evelyn Valley the trail returns to the starting point at Maden Dam, following the return leg of the original route. The total distance is 27 km.

At the time of going to press the following changes have been made to the Amatola Hiking Trail. The first day's hiking has been re-routed and hikers no longer overnight at Evelyn Valley, but hike 15,1 km to Little Mount Kemp where overnight accommodation is provided in a timber hut, Gwiligwili Hut. Although the first day's hike is now shorter, it is more strenuous than the original route, owing to the higher altitude of the Gwiligwili Hut. However, the second day's hike is now 19,1 km, allowing more time to appreciate the trail surroundings, waterfalls and pools.

KOLOGHA

This two-day trail in the Kologha Mountains is conveniently situated for hikers from the larger centres of the eastern Cape. It offers you the opportunity of walking through the beautiful indigenous forests of Isidenge, Barwa and Kologha and on the second day your efforts will be well rewarded with panoramic views of the surrounding countryside. The overnight hut is picturesquely situated on the edge of Gubu Dam where you stand a chance of seeing the Cape clawless otter as well as a variety of waterbirds.

TRAIL PLANNER

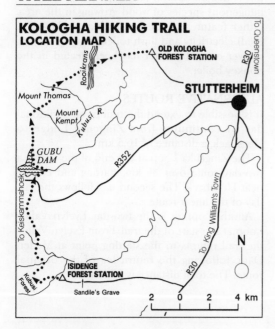

KOLOGHA HIKING TRAIL LOCATION MAP

Distance 34,6 km; 2 days

Grading B

Reservations The Regional Director, Tsitsikamma Forest Region, Private Bag X537, Humansdorp 6300, Telephone (0423) 5-1180, Fax (0423) 5-2745. Reservations are accepted up to a year in advance.

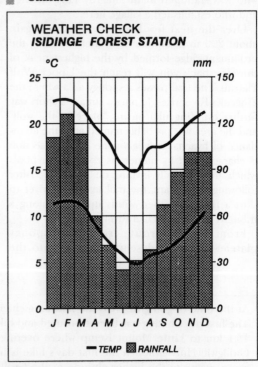

Climate

WEATHER CHECK ISIDINGE FOREST STATION

Group size Minimum 2; Maximum 30

Maps The trail is indicated on a photocopy of the 1 : 50 000 topographical map, which is forwarded with your receipt and trail permit.

Facilities The trail hut at Gubu Dam has four bedrooms, equipped with bunks and mattresses. A table and benches, sink, refuse bin, firewood and fireplace are provided in a spacious cooking shelter. There are also flush toilets and cold water showers.

Logistics Linear route, requiring two vehicles. Alternatively, the owner of the privately owned Kologha Campsite will assist hikers by dropping them off at the starting point. The campsite is conveniently situated at the end of the trail and arrangements can be made by telephoning (0436) 3-2474 or 3-1240. There are no overnight facilities at the start of the trail.

Relevant information
- Precautions against ticks are necessary.
- Although streams are crossed regularly, they could be dry during winter, making it advisable to set off each day with a full two litre water-bottle.

How to get there From King William's Town you must follow the R30 towards Stutterheim for about 26 km. Turn left onto the gravel road signposted Mount Kemp Sawmills, ignoring the turn-off to Isidenge after 3 km, to reach the Isidenge Forest Station about 10 km further on.

TRAIL ENVIRONMENT

Flora A highlight of this trail are the patches of beautiful indigenous forests, but the route also winds through pine plantations as well as brief stretches of grassland and fynbos.

The low-lying valleys are characterised by temperate high forests which are replaced by Dohne Sourveld at higher elevations.

The moisture-laden air blowing inland from the sea plays an important role in sustaining the forests. At the escarpment the warm air is forced upwards, resulting in frequent mist or rain.

The Outeniqua yellowwood is the dominant tree in the forest although the real yellowwood is also common. However, it should be borne in mind that large numbers of these trees were felled during the last century. Sawpits used to cut these forest giants into planks can be seen along the trail and serve as constant reminders of the large-scale exploitation. Other dominant species include white stinkwood, lemonwood, Cape chestnut and Cape beech.

Identifying trees in dense indigenous forest can often be frustrating for the layman. Among the more easily identifiable species is the knobwood with its distinctive bark studded with large conical knobs. The conspicuous rectangles, whorls and concentric rings on the bark of the lemonwood are distinctive features of this species. Some species again betray their presence by their flowers or fruit. A dense carpet of long, tubular red to orange or cream coloured flowers indicates the presence of the tree fuchsia, while the Cape chestnut has large, chestnut-like capsules.

Fortunately, though, some of the trees along the route have been marked according to the *National List of Indigenous Trees* and can be identified by referring to the list of 25 of the most common tree species which accompanies the trail map.

The undergrowth is dominated by white hazel and dwarf turkey-berry, while flowering plants of the forest floor include *Plectranthus* and *Clivia* species, as well as the mauve twin sisters *Streptocarpus rexii*.

Several factors have contributed to the reduction of these forests to relict patches. These include the regression of the tropical forests northwards, natural veld fires and exploitation by the early white settlers. It has also been suggested that local tribespeople contributed to the destruction of the forests because of their slash-and-burn method of agriculture. The grass which grew in abandoned areas was used for grazing instead of allowing the patches to revert back to bush and eventually forest.

At higher elevations the forest is checked by the increasingly cold, stony and less nutritious soil. At this level it is replaced by grasslands and mountain fynbos consisting of typical species such as proteas, ericas, bulbs and lilies, as well as several everlasting species. One of the everlastings, the golden guinea (*Helichrysum argyrophyllum*) tends to invade overgrazed grasslands, rendering them useless for grazing.

Conspicuous in places are black wattle (*Acacia mearnsii*), Australian blackwood (*Acacia melanoxylon*) and pine trees (*Pinus* spp.) which

The attractive white to pale pink flowers of the Cape chestnut create a spectacular display in summer

have been allowed to encroach along firebreaks, mountain grasslands and forest edges. These exotic fast-growing trees are grown commercially but have been allowed to spread unchecked, posing a serious threat to the indigenous vegetation.

Fauna The fauna is largely adapted to the forest habitat, and as a large percentage are smaller mammals you are unlikely to see them. The forests harbour species such as samango monkey and the tree dassie, while the forest floor is the habitat of bushpig, bushbuck, the diminutive blue duiker and porcupine.

Predators in the area include caracal and African wild cat, as well as large-spotted and small-spotted genets and the large grey mongoose.

Among the species which dwell underground are the Hottentot golden mole and the common molerat.

At edges of permanent water, such as Gubu Dam, you could see the vlei rat and the water mongoose. Also keep an eye out here for the Cape clawless otter.

The mountains are the habitat of rock dassie and chacma baboon, while the common duiker prefers dense undergrowth in fynbos, although seeking food and shelter on the forest edges.

Because you are hiking through changing habitats – indigenous montane evergreen forests, exotic pine plantations, open grasslands, fynbos, cliffs and mountains – bird-watching can be rewarding.

At the forest margins, be on the lookout for black cuckoo, which occurs between September and April, blackcollared barbet, cardinal woodpecker and barthroated apalis. Species favouring the dense undergrowth and the forest floor include terrestrial bulbul, as well as Cape and starred robins.

Birds to keep an eye out for in the upper elevations of the forests include rameron pigeon, Cape parrot, the elusive Narina trogon, redfronted tinker barbet and chorister robin.

A number of species occur in plantations and the indigenous forest. These include rameron pigeon, black cuckoo and cardinal woodpecker, as well as cinnamon dove, redbilled woodhoopoe, forktailed drongo and glossy starling, while the redchested cuckoo or Piet-my-vrou occurs from October to April.

Common quail and helmeted guineafowl can be seen in the open grasslands, while the Alpine swift, rock martin and stone chat are associated with the cliffs and mountains. Typical fynbos species include the Cape sugarbird and the malachite sunbird.

Gubu Dam attracts large numbers of water birds including whitebreasted cormorant, Egyptian goose, yellowbilled duck and redbilled teal, while the malachite kingfisher has also been recorded.

History The first white settlers in the vicinity of Stutterheim were Berlin missionaries who established the Bethel Mission close to a fort called Dohne Post in 1837. When the Crimean War in Europe ended, members of the British-German legion were invited to settle with their families in British Kaffraria. By March 1857 nearly 3 000 people, under the command of Major-General Carl Gustav Richard von Stutterheim, had been settled in the area. Those who settled around Dohne Post renamed it Stutterheim in honour of their commander.

The influx of these settlers resulted in a demand for wood for the construction of houses and *pludderwagens* ("German wagons"). Sneezewood was in especially great demand for fencing poles to enclose their small farms. The Kimberley mines also created a huge demand for timber and a local sawmiller, Mr J E Howse, established a mill in Stutterheim to prepare wood for the mines. Props a metre in circumference and nearly 7 m long were sold for the equivalent of between 20 and 40c each.

The first step to establish forestry control in

the Border region was taken in 1853 when all forested and deforested land in the triangle between Alice, Stutterheim and King William's Town was declared a Royal Forest Reserve. The proclamation did nothing to halt the destruction, however, as no effective control was exercised.

In 1866 Captain Johann Baron de Fin was appointed ranger of the Crown Forests. He was originally based at Stutterheim, but moved to Keiskammahoek in 1878. However, De Fin's concern for the forests was hampered by numerous obstacles such as insufficient control over the felling of trees, the lack of clear boundaries and official apathy. On his retirement in 1883 he was replaced by David Hutchins who began surveying the forests from Hogsback to Isidenge, as well as those closer to Stutterheim. Tighter control was effected when forest stations were established at Kologha, Isidenge and four other areas in the Amatola range.

Hutchins' most valuable contribution was his

effort to establish plantations. Although not very successful, it was significant in that it was the first systematic attempt to develop plantations in the Border region. However, the first exotic tree to be planted in the region, an oak, was planted in 1858, and it is passed on the first day of the trail.

In 1888 Hutchins was transferred and was succeeded by J Storr Lister. Lister reopened the indigenous forests for exploitation under a proper management system, but this was not successful owing to a lack of knowledge about forest ecology.

However when Lister left the region in 1904 some 3 590 ha of healthy plantations had been established. Those at Kologha and Isidenge were established in 1889. It was only in 1939 that all indigenous forests in South Africa were closed to woodcutters after the Woodcutters Annuities Act was passed by Parliament and woodcutters received a small state pension.

TRAIL DESCRIPTION

Day 1: Isidenge Forest Station to Gubu Hut

From the forest station the trail follows a gravel road gradually uphill for about 1 km before turning right into the indigenous forest. For the next 2 km the trail descends gently through the Isidenge Main Forest and along this section some magnificent Outeniqua yellowwoods, knobwoods and common cabbage trees can be seen.

After about 3 km you will reach the Isidenge picnic site where there are taps and toilets. On the far side of the picnic site is the De Fin oak tree which was planted by an unknown woodcutter in 1858. Although Baron De Fin did not plant the tree it was named after him in 1934 because of his efforts to protect these forests.

The approximate dimensions of the tree are: height 26,2 m, girth 3,6 m and crown spread 35,4 x 28,7 m.

The trail follows the road for a few hundred metres before returning to the indigenous forest and after 4,5 km joins a forestry road for about 0,5 km before turning right into the Barwa indigenous forest. After a fairly steep descent to a river, the route winds steadily upwards once more through beautiful forest scenery – with numerous tree orchids and clivias making it especially attractive.

Near the 7 km mark the trail leaves the indigenous forest and climbs gradually along a forestry road. Logs have been placed in a clearing close to the 8 km mark amid a small patch

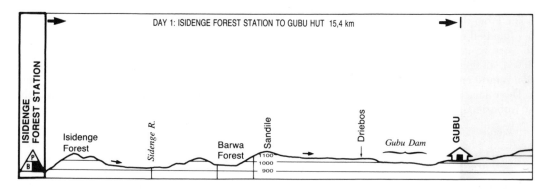

DAY 1: ISIDENGE FOREST STATION TO GUBU HUT 15,4 km

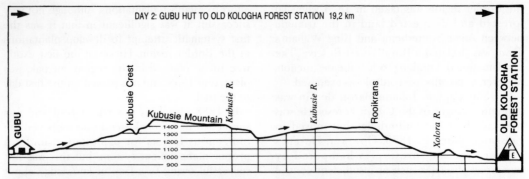

DAY 2: GUBU HUT TO OLD KOLOGHA FOREST STATION 19,2 km

of indigenous forest, making this an ideal lunch stop.

Over the next 2 km the trail continues through pine plantations until the Isidenge forestry boundary is reached.

After climbing over a stile, you will continue along a fence of the Fort Merriman grazing area for a few hundred metres before the trail swings left, shortly before reaching a stream. The route continues through a thicket of Australian blackwoods (*Acacia melanoxylon*) before emerging into short grassland and crossing a stream. You will then continue through the grassland until joining a gravel road and from here you will have a good view of Gubu Dam and the Kubusie Mountain.

After turning right the trail continues for a short while along the road before turning left onto the road signposted Kubusie Forest, Sawmills and Gubu Dam. After crossing the dam wall there is another stile and the trail skirts Gubu Dam for 2,8 km before reaching the hut. The wooden hut is situated on the western bank of the dam behind a row of oak trees and from the covered balcony you will have a splendid view of the dam.

Day 2: Gubu Hut to Kologha Forest Station

Before setting off, remember to fill water-bottles as the first water is only reached after about 6 km. From the hut you will follow a path for a few hundred metres before turning right onto a forestry road. Although the trail gains about 400 m in altitude over the next 5 km, this section is most enjoyable.

Three large logs provide comfortable seating at Kubusie Crest, near the end of the climb.

From here you have an expansive view and on a clear day you can see Gubu Dam and the Keiskammahoek Valley to the right, the radio mast on Mount Kemp, King William's Town and Berlin, some 70 km away.

The trail then continues upwards along a fire-break for a short distance before levelling out. For about the next 2 km a contour below the cliff face of Kubusie Mountain is followed and along this stretch you will reach an idyllic resting stop with steps leading down to a stream shaded by stunted yellowwoods. *Kubusie* is the Xhosa word for honey, a reference to the abundance of honey that used to occur in trees along the river of the same name.

From the fire-break the trail descends to a forestry road which is followed for about 5 km before branching off to the right. Before descending into the Kologha Forest, the trail follows the Rooikrans escarpment for about 1 km from where you will have panoramic views of the Stutterheim district and the Kologha Forest. Initially the trail descends steeply over the first kilometre, passing moss-covered tree trunks and glades of ferns.

Excellent specimens of yellowwoods, lemonwood and knobwood are seen along this section and after 14,5 km an old sawpit is passed. You will then join an old bridle path which traverses easy terrain, crossing several streams. Although some of these streams are indicated as water points on the map, they could be dry during the winter.

The trail ends at the old Kologha Forest Station with the Kologha Campsite on your right immediately after passing through the gates of the forest station.

TRANSKEI

The Transkei Wild Coast is one of the most beautiful coastal areas in the world. Stretching between Mtamvuna River Mouth in the north and the Kei River in the south, it is characterised by dramatic cliffs, rolling hills, tranquil lagoons, unspoilt beaches and fascinating rock formations. Each of the four trails which have been opened to date has a distinctive character and the scenery varies considerably from one trail to the next.

Aspects common to the three sections of the Transkei Hiking Trail included in this guide are discussed in this general introduction.

TRAIL PLANNER

Reservations Department of Agriculture and Forestry, Nature Conservation Section, Private Bag X5002, Umtata 5100, Telephone (0471) 31-2711 or 2-4322, Fax (0471) 31-2713. Reservations are accepted up to 11 months in advance.

Climate

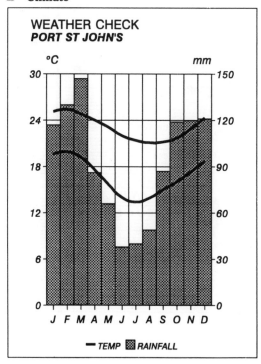

WEATHER CHECK
PORT ST JOHN'S

°C · mm

J F M A M J J A S O N D

— TEMP ▓ RAINFALL

Group size Minimum 2; Maximum 12

Maps Full-colour trail maps cover the three sections of the coast included in this guide. They contain useful information on the geology, flora and fauna of the coast and must be purchased separately.

Facilities Each overnight stop has two rondavel-type huts with triple bunks with mattresses, and a table and benches is provided in a third hut. Drinking water, refuse bins, firewood and fireplaces and toilets are also provided.

Relevant information
■ Be security conscious. Do not leave equipment unattended, even at the overnight huts, and arrange a night-watch system.
■ Be courteous to people living in the area and show the necessary respect for sacred sites and tribal life.
■ Archaeological and geological sites must not be disturbed.
■ Unlike other hiking trails, the trails along the Transkei coast are not clearly marked and you must follow the general direction indicated on the trail map.
■ Hikers should be on their guard against snakes, especially puffadders, where footpaths are covered by overhanging grass.

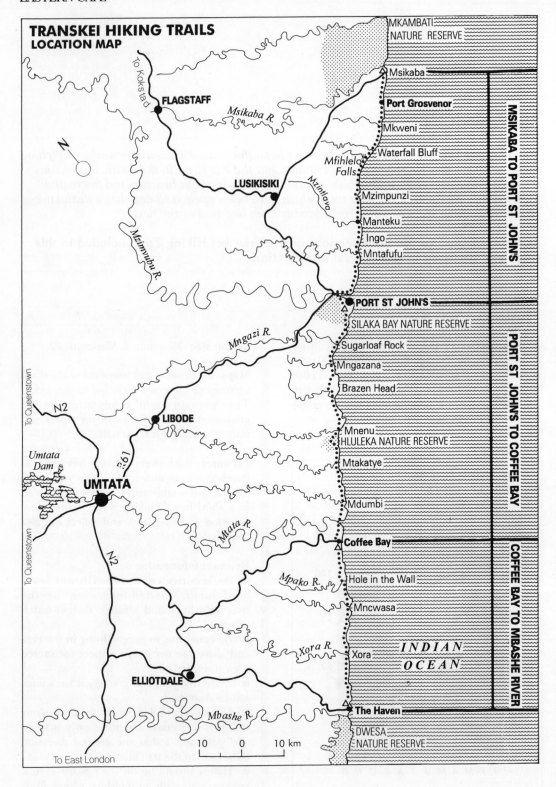

TRANSKEI HIKING TRAILS
LOCATION MAP

MKAMBATI NATURE RESERVE

Msikaba

Port Grosvenor

Mkweni

Waterfall Bluff

Mfihlelo Falls

Mzimpunzi

Manteku

Ingo

Mntafufu

PORT ST JOHN'S

SILAKA BAY NATURE RESERVE

Sugarloaf Rock

Mngazana

Brazen Head

Mnenu
HLULEKA NATURE RESERVE

Mtakatye

Mdumbi

Coffee Bay

Hole in the Wall

Mncwasa

Xora

The Haven

DWESA NATURE RESERVE

INDIAN OCEAN

MSIKABA TO PORT ST JOHN'S

PORT ST JOHN'S TO COFFEE BAY

COFFEE BAY TO MBASHE RIVER

To Kokstad

FLAGSTAFF

Msikaba R.

Mzintlava

LUSIKISIKI

Mzimvubu R.

Mngazi R.

To Queenstown

N2

LIBODE

Umtata Dam

UMTATA

R61

To Queenstown

N2

Mtata R.

Mpako R.

Xora R.

ELLIOTDALE

Mbashe R.

10   0   10 km

To East London

■ Several large rivers have to be crossed on all four sections of the Transkei Hiking Trail. Not all rivers have ferries and it is, therefore, advisable to carry a tide table and to plan river crossings for approximately 30 minutes after low tide.

■ Do not swim or wade across rivers with your pack on your back. Rather place it on an air mattress or in a survival bag and float your equipment across.

■ If there is no sandbar at a river mouth, try crossing further upstream. Select a straight, wide section of the river where the flow is usually slower. Beware of deep gullies along the inside bank of river and do not panic if you are suddenly washed downstream – keep paddling for the opposite bank which you will reach, just lower downstream.

■ Under no circumstances should you cross near a river mouth if there is a strong outgoing current.

■ Estuaries host sharks and a careful watch should be kept before and during river crossings.

■ Although most of the riverbeds are sandy, stonefish and stingrays can inflict painful stings so it is advisable to wear running or canvas shoes for river crossings.

■ Cuts sustained from rocks during river crossings are very susceptible to infection and should be treated with antiseptic immediately.

■ Limited drinking water is supplied at the huts, but it should be purified or boiled. Water obtained from streams and springs should also be boiled.

■ Watch out for ticks, especially during the winter months.

■ Carry cash in convenient denominations to pay for ferry trips, fish, "luxuries" available at the small general dealers and your bus or taxi trip back to your vehicle.

■ Some of the roads leading down to the coast can be treacherous after rain.

TRAIL ENVIRONMENT

Flora The vegetation of the Transkei coast varies from coastal grassland to coastal forest and patches of thornveld.

The extensive **coastal grasslands**, stretching down to the coast in places, consist largely of short grasses, dominated by buffalo grass (*Stenotaphrum secundatum*), redgrass (*Themeda triandra*) and wiregrass (*Aristida junciformis*).

Along the Pondoland Coast the veld has a typical park-like appearance with short grass and exposed sandstone "rock gardens". Among the flowering plants are red-hot pokers (*Kniphofia cooperi*), which favour damp areas, wild dagga (*Leonotis leonurus*), yellow tulips (*Homeria britteniae*), mountain bell (*Dierama igneum*), wild scabious (*Cephalaria oblongifolia*) and *Senecio* species.

Especially conspicuous on the hillsides south of Port St John's is the bitter aloe with its characteristic branched spikes of scarlet flowers during the winter months.

Remnants of the Cape flora are found in association with the sandstone formations of Waterfall Bluff and include everlastings (*Helichrysum*), silver sugarbush and *Leucadendron salignum*.

Three types of coastal forests occur along the coast. Numerous patches of **coast-belt forest**, with a total area of 75 000 ha, occur along the Transkei Coast. These forests are situated between the subtropical zone in the north and the temperate zone (Knysna forest types) in the south. Of the 385 Transkeian tree species 361 are found in Natal, while 24 temperate zone species have their northernmost limit in Transkei, giving the forests a closer affinity with the subtropical zone.

Typical forest trees include white stinkwood, umzimbeet, wild poplar, red beech and water berry. Between August and September the orange-scarlet flowers of the coast coral tree are unlikely to escape your attention. The coast coral tree is a medium to tall tree, favouring stream and river banks inside the forests and along the forest edges.

The **dune forest** is limited to extensive sandy areas of isolated beaches and is generally narrow. Among the pioneer species on recently formed dunes is the seeplakkie *Scaevola*, while the higher, more stabilised dunes are the habitat of dune string (*Passerina rigida*), metalasia (*Metalasia muricata*) and bush-tick berry.

The Natal wild banana, dune false currant

and coast silver oak are the most conspicuous forest margin species. Principal trees of the dune forest include coastal red milkwood, Natal guarri and quar.

The third coastal forest type, the **mangrove communities,** are described in the box below.

Fauna Most of the mammals recorded along the coast inhabit the coastal forest. Among these are bushbuck, blue duiker, bushpig, samango monkey and tree dassie. Other species include rock dassie, common duiker, vervet monkey, chacma baboon, caracal and African wild cat, as well as several smaller predators, hares and rodents.

Marine mammals you might spot include the southern right whale which frequently occurs close inshore, especially between May and November when it enters shallow water to calve. During these months you are also likely to observe schools of Indian Ocean bottlenosed and humpback dolphins.

More than 200 bird species have been recorded to date, including uncommon species such as the bald ibis, Delegorgue's pigeon and the Cape parrot, which is regularly seen in the forests at Mbotyi.

The forest species are well represented in the extensive patches of coastal forests and include Knysna lourie, redbilled woodhoopoe, trumpeter hornbill, sombre bulbul and southern boubou.

Among the species favouring the forest fringes and the grasslands are brownhooded kingfisher, forktailed drongo, blackeyed bulbul, spotted prinia, redshouldered widow and streakyheaded canary.

The mangrove canopies provide a convenient perch and vantage point for a wide range of birds including little and cattle egrets, grey, blackheaded and greenbacked herons, as well as pied, malachite and mangrove kingfishers.

At the lagoons, estuaries and larger rivers it is usually possible to spot African fish eagle, water dikkop and several kingfisher species, including giant and pygmy kingfishers.

Sea birds are not well represented because of the absence of offshore islands and the lack of

---

MANGROVES

Eighteen mangrove communities occur along the Wild Coast and the three dominant trees in the communities along the east coast of southern Africa south of Kosi Bay are the red, black and white mangroves. At many estuaries only one or two species occur, but at Mngazana, Mtata and Mntafufu all three species can be seen.

The mangrove community at Mngazana is considered the finest in southern Africa, but its future has been a cause for concern ever since the possible establishment of a harbour here was first mooted in October 1978. Other larger mangrove communities along the Transkei coast are found at the Mtamvuna, Mbashe and Kobonqaba rivers.

Each species has distinct habitat preferences. The white mangrove favours the outermost fringes and initially accumulates silt, creating a favourable environment, including shade, for the black mangrove. Watercourses develop in the mature swamps and appear almost man-made. Alongside these channels the mud is fine, thick and always wet, creating ideal conditions for the red mangrove. Adult trees are dependent on salt water and will die if the supply is cut off.

Although no animals are restricted to or exclusively associated with mangroves, a diverse animal population is supported by this finely balanced ecosystem.

One of the most interesting animals of the mangrove communities is the mud-skipper or skipping goby (*Periophthalmus*). This well camouflaged mottled grey-brown fish is about 70 mm long and is usually seen on a tree root or overhanging branch.

However, you are more likely to hear its characteristic splashing sounds as it takes cover in the water when it is disturbed than you are to actually see it.

When submerged, the mud-skipper breathes with gills, but on leaving the water air is gulped in and the gill chambers are sealed. In this unique way the gills are kept wet and supplied with oxygen, only needing periodic replenishment of air and water.

On land it is capable of moving slowly by using its pectoral fins to propel itself forward, rather like crutches. It is also capable of a fast skipping movement – a series of quick leaps made with an upward thrust of the pectoral fins. The mud-skipper can also skim across the water with most of the body submerged and just the large bulbous eyes protruding. The pectoral fins are then used for stability.

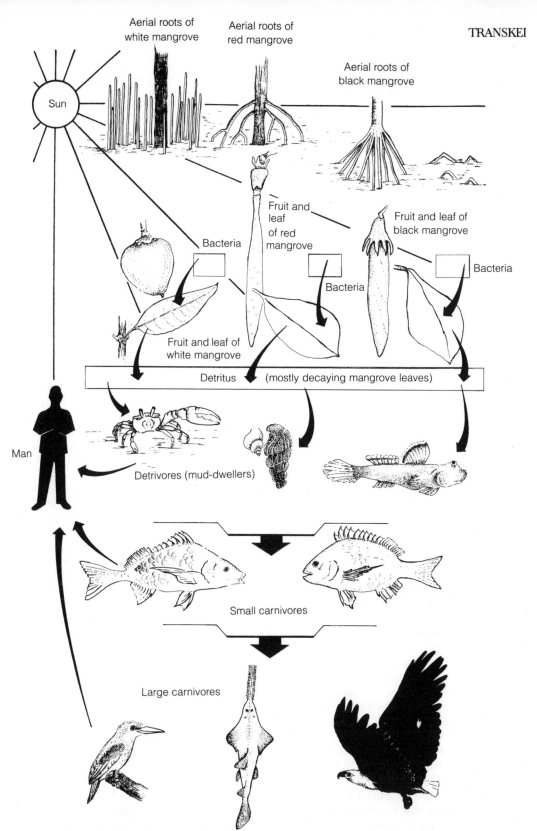

Aerial roots of white mangrove

Aerial roots of red mangrove

Aerial roots of black mangrove

Sun

Bacteria

Fruit and leaf of red mangrove

Fruit and leaf of black mangrove

Bacteria

Bacteria

Fruit and leaf of white mangrove

Man

Detritus (mostly decaying mangrove leaves)

Detrivores (mud-dwellers)

Small carnivores

Large carnivores

The complex inter-relationship of a mangrove community

protected bays and large shallow inter-tidal zones. However, you are likely to tick white-breasted cormorant, whitefronted plover, sanderling and common tern, while African black oystercatcher are frequently seen along rocky sections of the coast.

Birders will find Clive Quickelberge's *Birds of the Transkei* a useful guide to take along. It provides an ornithological history and annotated catalogue of 461 species recorded in the Transkei to date.

Both the green mamba (*Dendroaspis angusticeps*) and the black mamba (*D. polylepis*) occur along the coast, the Mzimvubu River marking the southernmost limit of their distribution.

The marine fauna of the Transkei coast is mainly characteristic of a warm temperate region with many endemic species.

Although much of the coastline is still relatively unexplored by conchologists, the Transkei coast is considered one of the best places in the world for shelling. Especially rewarding is the coast between Preslies Bay and Lwandile, Umtata River Mouth and the coastal area between Drew's Camp and Mbotyi. Although the distribution of shells is influenced by the tides, winds and swells, low spring tides, especially during the March and September equinoxes, are the best times to look for shells. Rock pools can also be interesting to explore, but shells still sheltering animals should not be disturbed.

The cone shape of the Conidae family is unmistakable and among the species you will probably come across is the white *Conus natalis* with its fine brown zigzag and a few darker brown bands. Also keep an eye out for *C. ebraeus*, which has distinctive black-brown markings and has its southern distribution limit at Port St John's.

The colourful, glossy cowrie shells will immediately attract attention. A few of the species reported from this coastline are *Cypraea tigris*, one of the largest cowries, *C. citrina*, an orange-brown shell with grey spots, the mauve, brown-spotted *C. lynx*, and *C. teres* which, after lying on the beach, is usually pale blue with brown herringbone patterns around it.

Those interested in shells will find Deidre Richards' *South African Shells – A Collector's Guide* a useful field guide.

The Wild Coast has long been regarded as a fisherman's paradise and you may want to supplement the usual trail diet with delicacies from the sea. Crayfish, line fish and oysters can sometimes be bought from the local people, although they are not as plentiful as in years gone by. Do not depend on this for your meals and no matter how tempting, undersized crayfish should be rejected.

Among the commonly caught line fish are cob (*Johnius hololepidotus*), elf or shad (*Pomatomus saltatrix*) and pignose grunter (*Lithognathus lithognathus*), while rock cod (Family Serranidae), galjoen or damba (*Coracinus capensis*) and black steenbras or poenskop (*Cymatoceps nasutus*) favour the rocky areas.

The east coast is famous for its annual sardine run when extensive shoals of mainly two- to four-year-old sardines (*Sardinops ocellata*) move up the south coast to Durban in June and July. After moving closer inshore from Port St John's they disappear north of Durban, possibly turning seawards to return to the Cape.

History Archaeological discoveries along the coast have confirmed the inhabitation of the coastline by Early and Middle Stone Age people for thousands of years. Groups of Khoisan people, loosely termed Strandlopers, began specialising in a marine shell economy along the southern Cape coast about 9 000 years ago. These people settled in the few coastal caves and at other suitable sites along the coast and well over 30 shell middens have been identified along the Transkei coast to date.

Archaeological research has shown that the coastal plateau was inhabited by pastoral Khoikhoi some 1 800 years ago. It has been suggested that the easternmost Khoikhoi group, the Gonaqua, were living in the Middle Keiskamma region about 900 years ago, migrating periodically as far east as the Mzimvubu River by 1450.

From historical evidence and the distribution of painting sites and rock shelters it appears that the San preferred the Kei basin, the hills forming the inland boundary of the Transkei and Griqualand East. However, recent discoveries of painted shelters along the north-eastern coast of Pondoland suggest that they also inhabited the coast, even if only periodically.

Early Iron Age pastoralists started settling along the southern parts of the Transkei coast nearly 1 500 years ago, followed by larger groups of migrants during the eleventh century.

New groups of people, the Southern or Cape Nguni, migrated into the Transkei from the north-east before 1500 and it appears that they were already well established in the coastal area between the Mzimkulu and Mzimvubu rivers by that date. It has been possible to reconstruct an account of their southward migration, based on the accounts of survivors of shipwrecks.

From the account of the survivors of the *Santo Alberto*, which ran aground in 1593 (there are varying accounts of it being wrecked near Hole in the Wall or along the Ciskei coast), it has been established that the Southern Nguni had already migrated as far south as the Mtata River by that date.

These pastoralists/agriculturalists lived in small clans which enjoyed political and economic autonomy. In the early seventeenth century some clans began subjecting neighbouring clans and in this way the Xhosa, Thembu, Mpondo and Mpondomise kingdoms were established.

Following the upheavals caused by the Difaqane wars, new groups of refugees settled in the Transkei during the early part of the nineteenth century. The most important group was the Mfengu, which comprised the Hlubi, Bhele and Zizi. Two other refugee tribes, the Bhaca and the Ntlangwini, also settled in the Transkei.

Until the late 1870s the area between the Mzimkulu and Mtata rivers was inhabited by the Mpondo. However, following the death of chief Faku in 1867, the Mpondo split into two independent groups. The Eastern Mpondo live in the area between the Mzimkulu and Mzimvubu rivers, while the area between the Mzimvubu and Mtata rivers is inhabited by the Western Mpondo.

Until 1878 Pondoland was regarded as an independent tribal state. The Mzimvubu River was navigable for several kilometres upstream, providing a convenient back door for gun-runners to smuggle arms and ammunition into the interior between the Cape Colony and Natal. At the same time merchandise could be smuggled duty-free to the interior of the two colonies.

In 1878 the Cape Colonial Government sent a commissioner to Port St John's to secure control of the river in an effort to end the smuggling. After negotiating with the paramount chief of Pondoland, the commissioner bought 15 km of the river upstream of the mouth, as well as an area of land on the southern side, for £2 000. While the arrival of the money was being awaited, a small naval force from Natal under the command of General Thesiger landed near Ferry Point and proclaimed the northern side of the river British territory. This anomalous situation existed until the British High Commissioner declared the areas on both banks British possessions. In 1884 the areas were incorporated into the Cape Colony and ten years later the whole of Pondoland was annexed by treaty with the paramount chief of Pondoland and incorporated into the Cape Colony.

Bomvanaland, the area south-west of the Mtata River, is inhabited by the Bomvana. Nguni chiefdoms settled in the area during the 1500s and some survivors from early shipwrecks along this section of the coast intermingled with the local inhabitants. One such group is known as the abeLungu or "white people".

The Bomvana originally lived in Pondoland, but during the late 1700s they were driven from their homeland. They appealed to the Gcaleka chief, Kawuta, and were accepted as serfs, settling north-east of the Mbashe River.

Following the resettlement of the Mfengu in Fingoland, hostilities between the Mfengu and Gcaleka increased and in 1877 war broke out between the two tribes. Many of the Gcaleka fled across the Mbashe River from the colonial forces commanded by Colonel Griffiths but the Bomvana, who decided to remain neutral, could not stem the tide of refugees.

As the war progressed it became necessary to keep the Gcaleka out of Bomvanaland and it was suggested that the Cape government take the territory into its custody. On 28 February the Bomvana were declared British subjects after their chief, Moni, agreed to such a step. In December of that year Bomvanaland, later the district of Elliotdale, and several other districts were united and proclaimed as the district of Thembuland. On 26 August 1885 the area was incorporated into the Cape Colony.

In keeping with the South African government's apartheid policy, the Transkei was proclaimed an independent state in 1976. It was never recognised internationally and in November 1993 the Negotiating Forum agreed to reincorporate Transkei and the other nominally independent states into South Africa.

COFFEE BAY TO MBASHE RIVER

The area between the Mtata and Mbashe rivers takes its name from the Bomvana people who live in the area. The terrain is not as rugged as that north of Coffee Bay and large areas are sparsely inhabited. The gentle hills of Bomvanaland make for a relaxing trail which takes you along long stretches of deserted beaches, across rolling hills and past beautiful estuaries and unspoilt lagoons. Hole in the Wall, one of the most fascinating rock formations along the Wild Coast, is a highlight of this trail.

Aspects common to all three sections of the Transkei Hiking Trail described in this guide are discussed in the general introduction, which should be read in conjunction with this chapter.

TRAIL PLANNER

Distance 44 km; 4 days

Grading B

Logistics Linear route, requiring two vehicles. Alternatively, you can arrange to leave your vehicle in Umtata and catch a bus to Coffee Bay. A bus leaves for Umtata from the Haven Hotel near the end of the trail between 06:00 and 07:00 in the morning. Huts are provided at the start of the trail at

Coffee Bay and at the Mbashe River where the trail ends.

How to get there The starting point is reached by turning onto the signposted road 18 km south of Umtata on the N2 and continuing for about 79 km. The Coffee Bay Huts are in the Department of Agriculture and Forestry campsite on the southern side of the lagoon, opposite the now derelict Lagoon Hotel.

TRAIL DESCRIPTION

Day 1: Coffee Bay to Mhlahlane Huts On leaving the campsite at Coffee Bay through the main gate, turn left and follow the road for a short distance before crossing the KuBomvu River. From here the trail follows an inland route over gently undulating terrain in order to avoid the coast, which is impassable. You can choose to follow a rough track or the footpaths used by the local people. After passing the village of Rini it is best to wind back gradually to the coast and you will join the road linking the coast with Umtata just before Hole in the Wall.

The popular seaside village of Hole in the Wall is situated above a small, secluded bay and is reached about two and a half to three hours after leaving Coffee Bay. If time permits you might want to stop for refreshments at the invit-

ing Hole in the Wall Hotel, but bear in mind that the Mpako River nearby is best crossed at low tide.

The well-known Hole in the Wall rock formation can be approached by continuing to the end of the road where you have to climb over a stile to gain access to the fenced forestry area.

Alternatively, you can ascend the coastal hills from where you will have a good view of the detached cliff standing in the sea at the mouth of the Mpako River like an island through which the pounding waves have eroded an enormous tunnel.

The Mpako River is normally easily crossed at low tide, but at high tide you might be in for a waist-deep wade or a swim. From here the coastline is once again too rugged to permit hiking and you will ascend the hills south of the

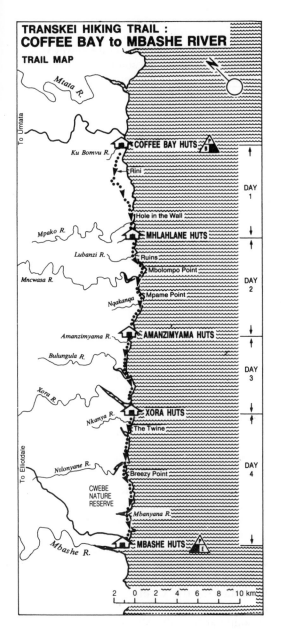

TRANSKEI HIKING TRAIL :
COFFEE BAY to MBASHE RIVER
TRAIL MAP

Dance of a Bomvana initiate – "Umtshilo abakhweta". This tradition is rapidly disappearing

Day 2: Mhlahlane Huts to Amanzimyama Huts Although the second day's hike covers 14 km and is the longest stretch of the trail, it is still relatively easy. From the huts the route first ascends to the crest of the hills, before descending along a disused track to the Lubazi River. You will then follow the rocky coastline, passing Mbolompo Point before reaching the beautiful Mncwasa Lagoon. You will continue along the wide open beach for about 1 km, and at the end of the beach have the option of rounding Mpame Point or cutting across the grassy hills to the Nqakanga River. The small, protected bay is bordered by a number of holiday shacks in a most idyllic setting.

From here the route continues along the coast for about 2 km before ascending to the crest of the coastal hills to avoid the rocky coastline. Once again you must be guided by the footpaths used by the local people and after traversing the crest of the coastal hills for just over 1 km, the trail descends steeply to the Amanzimyama River Valley. The huts are attractively situated alongside a patch of forest on the

Mpako River almost immediately after crossing the river. A short, but steep climb brings you to the crest of the hills from where you have magnificent side-on views of Hole in the Wall, as well as the Whale's Back and the Queen which form the prominent headland just north of Hole in the Wall.

The trail then drops down to the Mhlahlane River, where the first overnight huts are situated, about 2 km south of the Mpako River. The huts are well positioned on a grassy slope on the northern bank of the river, close to the beach.

HOLE IN THE WALL

The early Portuguese navigators named this spectacular landmark *Penedo das Fontes* or "The Rock of the Fountains". The name Hole in the Wall was given by Captain Vidal of the survey vessel *Barracouta* which was sent in 1822 by the British Admiralty to survey the south-east coast of Africa. According to Vidal they approached the coast to within 800 m of this very interesting spot "... where two ponderous rocks rose above the water's edge, upwards of 80 feet (24 m) above its surface, exhibiting through one of them the phenomenon of a natural archway ..." – which he appropriately named the Hole in the Wall.

The formation is known to the local Bomvana tribe as *esiKhaleni* – "The Place of the Sound". According to legend the passage of the Mpako was once blocked by the cliff, forming a great landlocked lagoon. One of the so-called "sea people" fell in love with a beautiful girl who lived in a village at the edge of the lagoon, but when her father found out about the relationship he forbade her to see her lover.

At high tide one night, a huge fish brought along by the "sea people" rammed a hole through the centre of the cliff with his enormous head and the "sea people" swarmed into the lagoon, singing and shouting. The great commotion caused the villagers to hide in fear and the girl was reunited with her lover and disappeared into the sea. It is said that on certain nights the "sea people" can still be heard singing and shouting as they stream through the hole.

northern bank of the river close to the mouth. The sheltered bay below the beach offers good swimming, but you should watch out for submerged rocks.

Day 3: Amanzimyama Huts to Xora Huts
This is the shortest section of the trail, enabling you to cross the Xora River at low tide and still have ample time in which to reach the overnight huts.

On leaving the huts prepare for a steep climb as the cliffs at Mbiza Point are extremely dangerous and the coast should be avoided. After climbing out of the Amanzimyama River Valley, the trail returns to the coast and after about 90 minutes of relaxed beach walking you will reach the Bulungula River. At high tide it might be necessary to wade or swim across the river, but otherwise the crossing is usually easy.

For the next 45 minutes the trail continues along the coast which is flanked by grass-covered slopes while the fascinating pools in the rock shelves exposed at low tide are well worth exploring. The final 1 km to the Xora River is along a magnificent stretch of beach.

At times it is possible to cross the Xora River near its mouth, but if the sandbar has been washed away or if there is a strong current it is best to walk a short way upstream. Here the river splits into two streams separated by a large tidal flat. After wading through the wide stream, the tidal flat is crossed to the smaller, but deeper stream which usually requires a short swim.

The southern bank of the river is well wooded, with the river euphorbia particularly obvious. This candelabra-shaped tree occurs from the eastern Cape northwards to southern Mozambique, favouring river banks and hills.

Set behind this woody fringe are a number of holiday cottages and, having crossed the river, you will follow a track southwards for about 1 km. The huts are situated on the landward side of a narrow strip of coastal forest.

Day 4: Xora Huts to Mbashe Huts The trail immediately follows the beach, passing three small lagoons which usually only flow into the sea after heavy rains. After about 90 minutes you will reach the Ntlonyane River which often blocked by a sandbar. However, should the river mouth be open, you might have to wade across if the tide is in.

About 30 minutes further south the northern boundary of the Cwebe Nature Reserve is reached. Covering 2 140 ha, the reserve stretches southwards to the Mbashe River which also forms the northern boundary of the Dwesa Nature Reserve. The trail leaves the beach here for a short distance to pass through the reserve gate. Once in the reserve you will continue past the cottages, ignoring the stile in front of the first row of cottages, and soon return to the beach.

The route continues along the coast, passing several delightful bays, and you will reach the Mbanyana Lagoon after about an hour. If you are tired of beach walking you can continue along the road to The Haven from the southern end of the lagoon. The road leads through fairly dense coastal forest, passing a few cottages, a lighthouse and, in about 30 minutes, The Haven Hotel.

The hotel has a restricted liquor licence and is only allowed to serve guests. You can, however, arrange to have a meal and make use of the bar facilities. The hotel requires a few hours' notice for large parties and none of the facilities should be used before making the necessary arrangements with the hotel management.

Continue past the hotel and after a while the road leading to the huts branches off to the left. The huts are tucked away in a clearing in the dense coastal forest and although the sea is not visible, you can hear its incessant murmur.

If you choose to continue along the coast you will pass Shelly Beach, a shell collector's paradise where several rare cowrie species have been collected. Further along Shark's Rock, a rocky outcrop also known as Sibebezulwini, is passed before you reach the Mbashe River. The river is followed upstream for about 500 m until you see a road heading off to the right through the forest. After following this road for a while, a track branching off to the right leads to the hut. A walk along the Mbashe River is always rewarding, especially for bird-watchers, while the small white mangrove community is also worthwhile exploring.

PORT ST JOHN'S TO COFFEE BAY

This trail provides a fine balance of natural scenery and Mpondo and Bomvana tribal life. The route mostly follows the coastline with its secluded beaches, unspoilt estuaries and patches of coastal forest. However, where the coastline becomes too rugged, footpaths are followed further inland. Here you will occasionally pass through Mpondo and Bomvana villages, adding another dimension to this scenic trail.

Aspects common to all three sections of the Transkei Hiking Trail described in this guide are discussed in the general introduction which should be read in conjunction with this chapter.

TRAIL PLANNER

Distance 60 km; 5 days

Grading B+

Logistics Linear route, requiring two vehicles. Alternatively, you can arrange to leave your vehicle in Umtata and catch a bus to Port St John's. There is also a regular bus service between Coffee Bay and Umtata. The first overnight stop is situated about 1 km from the start of the trail. Huts are also provided at Coffee Bay where the trail ends.

How to get there Port St John's is approximately 105 km from Umtata, the turn-off being at the intersection of Madeira and Sutherland streets on the eastern side of the town. The trail starts in the Silaka Bay Nature Reserve which is reached by following the tarred road to Second Beach and then crossing the Bulolu River, continuing up a steep gravel road to the reserve gate.

TRAIL DESCRIPTION

Day 1: Silaka Bay Huts to Mngazana River Huts The first overnight stop is in a small forested gorge carved by the Gxwaleni River, overlooking the small sandy cove at Third Beach.

From the huts you follow the coastline, passing Bird Rock which attracts large numbers of whitebreasted cormorants. At low tide it is possible to reach the island, which is just offshore, and the rock pools in the area are especially worthwhile exploring.

A short way onwards the trail ascends steeply to avoid the rocky coastline. It then descends to a small cove with a prominent rock formation aptly named Sugarloaf Rock. This well-known feature marks the southern boundary of the Silaka Nature Reserve which stretches northwards to Second Beach.

The trail then climbs steeply once again through grasslands dotted with bitter aloes, which add a splash of brilliant red-orange colour during the flowering season in June and July.

After traversing the coastal hills for about 3 km the route winds towards the coast shortly before reaching the Mngazi River and the Umngazi River Bungalows, one of the most popular resorts along the Wild Coast. As you descend towards the beach, keep an eye out for a clump of river euphorbia. Most of the trees in the Transkei are either used for medicinal pur-

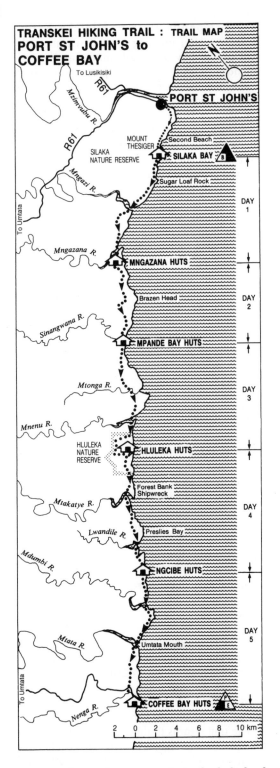

TRANSKEI HIKING TRAIL : TRAIL MAP
PORT ST JOHN'S to
COFFEE BAY

To Lusikisiki

R61

PORT ST JOHN'S

R61

Mzimvubu R.

MOUNT
THESIGER   Second Beach

SILAKA
NATURE RESERVE   SILAKA BAY   B

Sugar Loaf Rock

DAY 1

Mngazi R.

To Umtata

Mngazana R.

MNGAZANA HUTS

Brazen Head   DAY 2

Sinangwana R.

MPANDE BAY HUTS

Mtonga R.   DAY 3

Mnenu R.

HLULEKA
NATURE
RESERVE   HLULEKA HUTS

Forest Bank
Shipwreck

Mtakatye R.   DAY 4

Lwandile R.   Preslies Bay

Mdumbi R.

NGCIBE HUTS

DAY 5

Mtata R.   Umtata Mouth

To Umtata

COFFEE BAY HUTS   E

Nenga R.

2   0   2   4   6   8   10 km

ing parents the father will collect two plants from the veld and plant them in front of the hut. It is believed that the trees will protect the children from evil and that the trees and the children will influence each other throughout their lives.

You will reach the river about 90 minutes after leaving Silaka Bay and, depending on the tides and whether the river is sanded in, you can either cross without so much as getting your feet wet or wade across. At high tide and if the mouth has been washed open, it might be necessary to make arrangements with Umngazi River Bungalows for a boat to ferry you across. The Mngazi is named after the many fierce tribal battles which took place in the valley and the word means "River of Blood".

After crossing the river you have a choice of following a more inland route with superb views of the Mngazi River, before returning to the coast after about 30 to 45 minutes. However, it is also possible to continue along the coast, joining up with the inland route shortly after rounding a small rocky headland. The last 1,5 km of the day's hike follows a beautiful stretch of unspoilt beach before reaching the Mngazana River.

Despite the fact that the river is considerably larger than the Mngazi, its name is the diminutive form of Mngazi. This apparent contradiction is explained by the fact that although tribal fighting also took place in this river valley, less blood was spilled – hence the diminutive.

The Mngazana is a formidable obstacle at high tide, but fortunately the trading store on the southern bank of the river operates a ferry service. Provided you can attract the ferryman's attention, he will row you across for a small fee – well worth it though.

Once on the southern bank you will follow the river upstream for a short distance before reaching the huts, which are situated close to the finest mangrove community along the coast. Take some time to discover this fascinating ecosystem – its intricacies are not always obvious at first glance.

Day 2: Mngazana River Huts to Mpande Huts
From Mngazana the trail keeps inland because of the rugged coastline. The first section follows a rough gravel track which runs along the crest of the coastal hills. The track leads through cultivated fields planted with mealies, a small patch of forest and open grasslands, revealing a wide

poses or play an important role in the beliefs of the people, and the river euphorbia is one such species. When twins are born to Xhosa-speak-

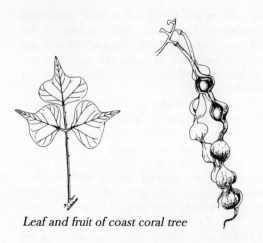

Leaf and fruit of coast coral tree

panorama with spectacular views of the sea and hills dotted with huts further inland.

The prominent headland on the left is known as Brazen Head, which is impassable at the coast. The crashing sound of the huge Wild Coast waves bashing against the cliffs has earned it the local name of Ndluzula and on a quiet day you can hear the waves thundering against it over a distance of several kilometres.

Further along you will reach the village of Luhlango and turn left, following a jeep track. A short way on the trail branches off to the right, following a well-marked route over Brazen Head before descending to the Ndluzula River. Along this section the trail winds through a patch of beautiful coastal forest and the forest corkwood is certain to catch your attention. The trees can easily be identified by their shiny, greenish-grey bark which sometimes peels off in characteristic paper-like flakes. Also to be seen here is the small knobwood with its conspicuous knob-thorn trunk.

From the Ndluzula River the trail climbs steeply out of the valley to the crest of the coastal hills and from here the Sinagwana River and Mpande Bay can be seen about 2,5 km away. The trail descends once again, this time following the course of a stream, and after passing along a rocky section reaches the beach.

Depending on local conditions and the tide, it is normally possible to wade across the Sinagwana. From the river you can either follow the more inland route indicated on the trail map or continue along the coast for about 1,5 km to the small bay at Mpande. The turn-off to the huts, which are situated behind a patch of dune forest, is a few hundred metres beyond the last holiday cottages you will pass.

Day 3: Mpande Huts to Hluleka Nature Reserve After crossing a small stream at the end of the bay, the trail immediately winds inland, following a disused jeep track. About 2 km from the start you will cross a gravel road leading towards the coast and then descend to the Mtonga River. The route crosses the river and leads up a short, steep hill. After passing through the village of Sikelweni, you will descend to the Mnenu River which is easily crossed provided the river mouth is sanded in.

The trail then continues along the coast, which in places is often several centimetres deep in shells. After about 1,5 km you will come to the boundary fence of Hluleka Nature Reserve where a noticeboard directs you inland, following the fence of the reserve. After passing through the northern entrance of the reserve, the trail winds back towards the coast for about 0,5 km before reaching the overnight stop.

When the trail first opened, hikers were accommodated in one flank of the reserve manager's house, a beautiful dressed stone dwelling with a magnificent view of the surrounding countryside. The overnight stop was subsequently moved to the bungalows close to the beach at Hluleka Bay.

The reserve covers about 772 ha and was proclaimed Transkei's second nature reserve in 1976. Bushbuck, bushpig, common duiker, rock dassie and Cape clawless otter occur naturally in the area, while eland, impala, blesbok, blue wildebeest, red hartebeest and Burchell's zebra have been introduced.

The birdlife is prolific and includes species such as the African fish eagle, osprey, Cape parrot, Knysna lourie and ground hornbill. Uncommon species to look out for include whitebacked night heron, longcrested eagle, African finfoot, green coucal and Knysna woodpecker.

Day 4: Hluleka Nature Reserve to Ngcibe Huts The trail leaves the reserve by means of the access road and just outside the reserve you can stock up with a few basic foodstuffs at the trading store at Hluleka village. Bread can sometimes be bought here.

The trail returns to the coast and after a while reaches Banana Bay, which is named after the abundance of the Natal wild banana. Although it belongs to the banana family, the three-lobed 5 to 7 cm-long woody capsule is not edible.

From here you will follow the coast to

UMTATA RIVER

There are several explanations of the origin of the name Mtata. One is that a clan of the Thembu tribe had the custom of interring their dead into the river with the words *mThathe Bawo* – "Take them, father". The noun Umtata is said to have evolved in this way. Another source suggests that the river acquired the name Umthata – "The Seizer" – because it claimed the life of at least one person each year when it came down in flood.

According to Palmer and Pitman, the name is derived from the abundance of umThathi or sneezewood trees growing along its banks. The name sneezewood is derived from the pungent smell of the wood when worked, which causes violent sneezing. The local people make snuff from it to relieve headaches, while the resin is applied to warts and can also be added to a dip to kill ticks on cattle. The trees reach up to 20 m in height, occurring in a variety of habitats from Port Elizabeth along the coast to Mozambique, as well as in the northern and eastern Transvaal.

Strachan's Bay, near the site where the British freighter *Forest Bank* ran aground and caught fire in 1958. The only reminder of this episode is a disused piece of machinery which was salvaged from the wreck. From this point you can either follow the track leading up the hill to the left or skirt the headland and cross further inland.

During outgoing tides the river flows swiftly into the sea and a crossing should not be attempted near the mouth. Conversely, during high tide the river mouth becomes a vast expanse of water and a crossing is not recommended either.

Sharks are a danger too and extra care should be taken. Should a crossing near the mouth be impossible it is best to continue upstream along the northern bank of the river for about 1,5 to 2 km. The river is fairly narrow and fordable opposite the Mtakatye trading store and although the detour adds about one hour to the day's hike, it is time well spent.

You will follow the beach to its end from where the trail leads up and over the hills and, looking back, there is a magnificent view of the Mtakatye River and Estuary. After about 1,5 km the trail joins a gravel road, leading past some

seaside shacks at Lwandile. Shortly after passing Lwandile you will cross the river of the same name and about 500 m further the Little Lwandile or Lwandilane is crossed. From Lwandilane there is a short, steep climb before the trail descends gently towards the huts at Ngcibe which are picturesquely situated along a small stream with a magnificent view of the coastline.

Day 5: Ngcibe Huts to Coffee Bay Huts
From Ngcibe the trail follows the coast as closely as possible for about 2,5 to 3 km before reaching the Mdumbi River. During high tide the river can be difficult to cross and is best negotiated about 500 m from the mouth.

After crossing the Mdumbi the trail continues along the coast, passing Tshani village and the small seaside resort of Umtata Mouth. Here you can quench your thirst at the Anchorage Hotel which used to be popular years ago, but is quite ramshackle now. From the village it is about 30 minutes' walk to the Mtata River, the last major river crossing.

There is usually a ferry to take you across the river into Bomvanaland, which stretches southwards to the Mbashe River. If a boat is not available to ferry you across you will most likely have a compulsory swim. Fortunately, though, the river is quite narrow at low tide and you will only need to swim a short distance.

The coast between the Mtata River and Coffee Bay is too rugged to follow, forcing you to continue along a rough vehicle track for about 3 to 4 km before joining the main Coffee Bay/Umtata Road. From here it is a short walk to the small holiday resort of Coffee Bay.

The huts at the end of the trail are on the southern bank of the Nenga River and unless the mouth is sanded in it might be necessary to follow the road to the low-level causeway which crosses the river higher upstream. The huts are situated among a patch of dune forest which has been set aside by the Department of Agriculture and Forestry as a camping area.

Coffee Bay is a well-known resort and used to boast two popular hotels, but both have become quite run-down over the years. The name is said to be derived from coffee beans which were washed ashore after a ship ran aground in the bay in 1863. According to a local tale, a trader by the name of Wilson and several of his friends travelled to the site of the wreck by oxwagon to salvage the cargo. After searching the area for survivors without success, they assumed that all on board the ship had perished. A raft was put to sea and after some difficulty the ship was boarded and the contents loaded onto the raft or dumped into the sea. The first barrel opened was found to contain rum and the salvage attempt was temporarily forgotten.

When the supplies ran out the ship was boarded again and more barrels were brought ashore. Much to the disappointment of the salvors it was found that some of the barrels contained chocolate, while others were filled with coffee beans. These barrels were abandoned and some floated up the Nenga River. Here the beans took root and tried to grow, unsuccessfully, for many years.

MSIKABA TO PORT ST JOHN'S

The coastline between Msikaba and Port St John's is often described as the wildest section of the Wild Coast. On this trail you will retrace the footsteps of hundreds of survivors shipwrecked along this rugged coastline. The trail leads through some of the most spectacular coastal scenery in the world – impressive waterfalls cascading into the sea, sea stacks, towering cliffs and unspoilt stretches of beach. The six-day hike between Msikaba and Port St John's is described here, but you also have a choice of a three-day hike between Mtamvuna River and Msikaba or you can hike the full nine-day route.

Aspects common to all three sections of the Transkei hiking trail described in this guide are discussed in the general introduction which should be read in conjunction with this chapter.

TRAIL PLANNER

Distance 65 km; 6 days (Msikaba to Port St John's)

Grading B

Logistics Linear route. Since there are no buses to Msikaba where the trail starts, two vehicles are essential. Overnight huts are provided at Msikaba where the trail starts and at Agate Terrace where it ends.

How to get there Approaching from the north along the N2, turn east onto the R61 about 13 km south-east of Kokstad. Pass through Flagstaff and continue to Lusikisiki, reached 112 km after leaving the N2. Just south of Lusikisiki take the gravel road branching eastwards and ignore the fork to the right 6 km further on, which is to Mbotyi. Although there are several roads branching off to the right, keep heading due east and about 36 km after the Mbotyi split you will reach South Sand Bluff at the mouth of the Msikaba River.

For hikers approaching from the south, take the R61 from Umtata to Port St John's. Turn onto the R61 to Lusikisiki 4 km west of Port St John's and continue for about 38 km. Just before entering Lusikisiki you will turn east onto the Magwa/Mbotyi road and continue as described above.

TRAIL DESCRIPTION

Day 1: Msikaba Huts to Port Grosvenor Huts
The huts at the starting point of the trail are situated on the southern bank of the Msikaba River, which is the southern boundary of the Mkambati Game Reserve.

If you have time in hand it is well worth exploring the impressive gorge carved by the Msikaba River. Another interesting alternative is to explore the "island" slightly offshore of the river mouth. The *Sao Bento*, which was original-ly thought to have been wrecked near Port St John's in 1554, ran aground off Msikaba. Cannons, fragments of Chinese porcelain and carnelian beads found here have also given rise to the theory that the HMS *Grosvenor* foundered here and not 12 km south of Port Grosvenor as is commonly believed.

South of Msikaba, which is also known as South Sands Bluff, the terrain consists of flat grasslands which make for easy hiking. Soon

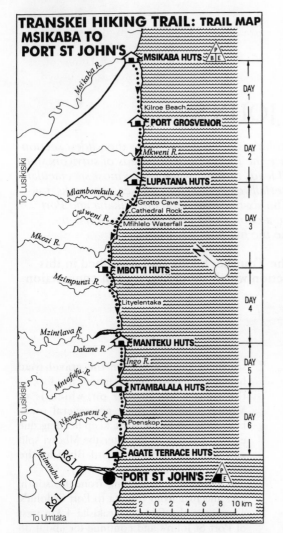

TRANSKEI HIKING TRAIL: TRAIL MAP
MSIKABA TO
PORT ST JOHN'S

past the holiday cottages at Port Grosvenor, continuing to the southern side of Lambasi Bay.

Day 2: Port Grosvenor Huts to Lupatana Huts When the trail was planned during the mid-1980s the area between Port Grosvenor and Lupatana had been set aside as a military zone, hence the long inland detour indicated on the original trail map.

The military zone is, however, no longer in operation and the trail now follows the coast-line. As a result, the day's hike is only about 8 km long and there is no need to rush.

The route traverses the short grasslands which extend right down to the rocky coast and after about 4 km the Mkweni River is reached. The small river is easily crossed and the trail continues through short grassland.

The coastline between Mkweni and Lupatana is characterised by flat rock shelves extending into the sea and are especially scenic during high tides when the spray of the pounding breakers shoots up to 15 m into the air. The huts are on the southern bank of the Lupatana River.

Day 3: Lupatana Huts to Mbotyi Huts From Lupatana the route continues along the low rock shelves past Top Hat, a flat-topped rock formation which resembles a top hat. About an hour after setting off you will reach Grotto Cave, a large rock overhang near the start of Waterfall Bluff. The Mlambomkulu Falls are reached a short way further on and are said to be one of four in the world that drop directly into the sea.

On account of the sheer cliffs south of the falls you will have to retrace your steps for a short distance in order to ascend to the coastal plateau. The river is crossed about 1 km inland where a series of inviting pools suggests an early morning dip. This is also an ideal breakfast stop and the large overhang on the southern bank of the river, a short way above a small waterfall, is a good place to brew up a cup of tea on a miserable day.

From here the trail winds back towards the edge of the cliffs and a short way beyond the river you will reach Cathedral Rock, a huge sea stack with breakers pounding through its arches. Along this section there are some incredibly beautiful views of the ocean some 80 m below. After about 1,5 km the 80 m-high Mfihlelo Falls, which also plunge directly into the sea, are

after setting off you will pass the 2 000 candle-power automatic lighthouse and about 5 km after setting off Kilroe Beach is reached. The lonely cottage on the beach was once the holiday home of the millionaire-herbalist Khotso Sethuntsa. Khotso's father worked as a groom for President Paul Kruger and is said to have helped transport the legendary Kruger Millions to their secret destination in the eastern Transvaal.

Port Grosvenor, where the British East Indiaman the *Grosvenor* was thought to have run aground on the night of 2 August 1782 is about 2,5 km further south. A few derelict buildings, the rusty remains of an old crane and a tunnel serve as reminders of numerous unsuccessful salvage attempts.

The overnight huts are reached by continuing

THE HMS *GROSVENOR*

The shipwreck of the *Grosvenor* gave birth to a legend that has refused to die, for the vessel was rumoured to be carrying gold and silver coins, as well as £1 314 000 in bullion. One of the many unanswered questions about the wreck is whether the ship was carrying the Peacock Throne of India, which was looted at more or less the same time. Only 15 of the company of 153 drowned, but only 18 of the crew survived the 2 000 km trek to Cape Town.

The first attempts to recover the treasures from the wreck were made by divers in 1842. They discovered a wrecked stern, but could not open the hatches. In 1880 Captain Sydney Turner recovered a box containing diamonds and gold coins worth about £ 6 000 from a wreck 4 m from the surface. On a second expedition he recovered small coins known as Star pagodas, Venetian ducats and Indian gold mohurs. On his third expedition he died without revealing the location of the wreck he had discovered.

Relics of the many attempts by treasure hunters to recover the treasures can still be seen at Port Grosvenor – abandoned ruins, rusty machinery and disused workings.

One of the earliest attempts by a syndicate to locate and salvage the treasures of the *Grosvenor* was the formation of the Grosvenor Recovery Syndicate by Alexander Lindsay in 1905. A steam-driven crane was used to scrape the seabed with a heavy chain and although a few hundred coins were recovered, the returns were insufficient and the syndicate went bankrupt. Two years later Lindsay formed another syndicate which planned to remove the sand, believed to be 2 m thick, from the wreck by using a suction dredger, but this scheme also failed.

In 1921 Martin Webster floated the Grosvenor Bullion Syndicate with the innovative idea of tunnelling to the wreck through the seabed. By November 1922 the tunnel was 122 m long, but like all previous attempts, the project ran out of money and in 1925 the tunnel collapsed.

Undeterred by the financial failures of several companies, various other schemes were subsequently planned, such as the building of a horseshoe-shaped breakwater around the wreck, using a grab-crane to hoist the wreck from its watery grave, and removing the sand from the wreck by means of water jets. Other attempts made in 1957, 1963, 1966 and 1970 also failed. Despite the poor success rate, the legend of the fabulous treasures of the *Grosvenor* lives on and for more than two centuries the sea has jealously guarded its spoils.

The only relics other than those recovered by Turner, coins dragged up by Lindsay's steam crane and an assortment of silver and gold coins discovered by individuals, are five cannons. One of these can be seen in the park at Port St John's, another is in the grounds of the Royal Hotel at Lusikisiki, two have been erected in front of the Umtata Town Hall, while the fifth is at the Old Fort in Durban.

reached. The Citadel, another sea stack, can be seen at the mouth of the Cutweni River about 1 km futher on. It is possible to scramble down a rather steep watercourse to the coast some 600 m before the Cutweni River. The descent is not recommended if you are afraid of heights and it is advisable to approach the Citadel at low tide when it is possible to explore the passages eroded into the stack by the waves. The large chunk of rock which has toppled sideways in one of the west-facing passages is known as the Fallen Idol.

Back on the plateau, the Cutweni River is crossed about 1 km inland to avoid the steep gorge at its mouth and after a steep descent a series of inviting pools awaits the weary hiker. The trail climbs steeply out of the gorge, returning towards the edge of the cliffs immediately. A few hundred metres further on a narrow but deep gorge is crossed by means of a natural rock bridge close to the cliff edge.

After descending Mgcagcama Hill you will reach Drew's Camp, situated at the end of a beautiful stretch of beach which offers excellent swimming. It is named after Dr Drew, who set up camp here to assist Professor Percival Kirby in his research into the Van Reenen expedition which was sent from Cape Town in 1790 to search for survivors of the *Grosvenor.*

From here the trail continues along the beach until the Mkozi River, which forms a small lagoon, is reached. A short way beyond the river the route follows a footpath across short grasslands just off the coast and the rock beds extending into the sea here are well worth exploring at low tide. The overnight huts are sit-

The African fish eagle can be spotted at the lagoons and estuaries

uated about 500 m before the small settlement of Mbotyi which consists of a number of holiday cottages, a trading store and the Mbotyi River Hotel which overlooks Mbotyi Lagoon.

The village is apparently named after the sea bean (*Entada gigas*), a leguminous plant which grows along river banks in the tropics. The seeds are carried from the Zululand coast and from Rodrigues, Madagascar, southwards by the warm Mozambique current and legend has it that the seeds come from a magical island. The sea bean is often worn by witch-doctors and is said to have great healing powers – owning such a seed will guarantee the owner popularity and success. It is, however, believed that a woman should not be in possession of the bean as it will cause infertility.

Day 4: Mbotyi Huts to Manteku Huts First thing in the morning you will have to cross the lagoon at Mbotyi, but this usually presents little problem. At low tide it is possible to follow the coastal route around the headland formed by Montshe or Shark's Point, but if the tide is unfavourable it is best to take the inland route. Follow the road past the trading store for about 100 m before turning onto a track leading off to the left which winds through the "Silent Forest".

About 2,5 km south of Mbotyi you will reach the Umzimpunzi River which is often sanded in to form a beautiful lagoon. The nearby sandy beach is a good place for a swim. The trail con-

tinues along the rocky coast, and prominent in the distance is a rocky outcrop known as Lityelentaka. The route skirts several bays, beaches and bluffs and after Lityelentaka you are forced to take a more inland route because of the rugged nature of the coast. The trail climbs a hill and from its crest a rewarding view of the coastline awaits you before you make your way down to a secluded bay.

A short way further on you are again forced to take to the hills to avoid the rocky headland of Mgoma and this time you will look down onto the lagoon at Manteku. At low tide the Mzintlava River is normally crossed about knee deep, but at high tide it is a compulsory swim. The huts are situated amongst a patch of dune forest on the southern bank, near the river mouth. Basic supplies can be replenished at the trading store at the top of the hill just behind the huts.

Day 5: Manteku Huts to Ntambalala Huts As happens so often on trails, the day commences with a stiff climb. Fortunately, the climb is fairly short and once you reach the trading store the road is followed for a short while before you branch off to the left. From here the trail follows a track through a fairly large village, descending steadily to a small secluded bay where the Dakane, a small stream, runs into the sea.

From Dakane the trail follows an easy route along the coastline for about 2,5 km. When you reach a fairly large bay, where the Ingo River runs into the sea, it is advisable to head slightly inland to avoid the rocky coast which is especially dangerous shortly before reaching the beach at Mntafufu.

After traversing the coastal hills for about 1,5 to 2 km, the trail descends to the beach, which is not only the longest stretch of beach along the trail, but also has some excellent coastal dune forests. The holiday village on the northern side of the river is tucked behind the dune forests and is not visible from the coast.

The Mntafufu River is reached after about 1,5 km of beach walking and is best crossed at low tide near the mouth. Like most rivers on the Wild Coast its depth varies seasonally and depends on the tide. The river can usually be crossed fairly easily at low tide, although a swim of a few metres cannot be ruled out. However, at high tide the river is a formidable obstacle.

The huts have been named after the

Pied kingfisher

Ntambalala Forest Station nearby and were originally situated about 2 km upstream, but new huts were subsequently built on the southern bank of the river close to the mouth. With time in hand it is a good idea to explore the magnificent mangrove community further upstream.

Day 6: Ntambalala Huts to Agate Terrace

The coastline is followed for about 1 km before the trail winds inland to avoid the treacherous coast. After descending to a small cove you are once again forced to ascend the coastal hills to avoid the dangerous cliffs of Dome Bluff before reaching the beach at Poenskop.

The trail descends to the beach and after about 1 km of beach walking the Nkodusweni River is reached. As it is normally sanded in, it is usually easily crossed.

Poenskop, a prominent headland, appears to have been named after the black steenbras (*Cymatoceps nastus*) which is also known in Afrikaans as the *poenskop*. They usually occur in rocky coastal areas where there is an abundance of shellfish and crustaceans.

From here the trail leads slightly inland, passing through several villages, and about 3 km further on you will find yourself looking down onto the beach at Agate Terrace. The name is derived from the antique Phoenician beads, known as agates, which are said to wash up onto the shore occasionally. After about 1,5 km of beach walking, the final overnight stop on the trail is reached.

Agate Terrace to Port St John's From Agate Terrace it is a brisk 45 minutes' walk to the Mzimvubu River where a regular ferry operates from Ferry Point. Mzimvubu means "Place of the Hippopotamus" – a reference to the abundance of hippos which used to occur here. Although they disappeared from the area more than a century ago, Huberta, the legendary hippo that wandered from St Lucia in 1928 to the Keiskamma River, stayed here for a while in 1930.

From the river you have an impressive view of the "Gates of Port St John's", which resemble an enormous gate to passing ships – opening and closing as they cruise past. The river originated on a broad flat plain above its present level and as a result of the uplift of the region between three and 15 million years ago, it was forced to cut its way through the hard resistant sandstone, carving a spectacular gorge.

OTHER EASTERN CAPE TRAILS

BEN MACDHUI

Distance 51 km; 3 days

Reservations Mr G van Zyl, P O Box 299, Barkly East 5580, Telephone (04542) 7021.

Group size Minimum 2; Maximum 24

Facilities At the starting point in Rhodes hikers are accommodated in a hall. On the trail hikers stay in an old farmhouse at the first overnight stop and a mountain hut at the second. Both overnight huts are equipped with bunks and mattresses, three-plate gas stoves, a kettle and pots as well as a coal stove for heating during the winter months. There is no hut at the start of the trail but hikers have a choice of private accommodation.

Description Situated north of Rhodes, this circular trail traverses the picturesque mountains of the north-eastern Cape. The first day's hike covers 16 km, following the course of the Bell River to the first overnight stop. On the second day the trail traverses the mountain slopes above the Kloppershoek River to the Lesotho border and then swings away to the overnight hut. An optional deviation is an ascent of Ben Macdhui, at 3 001 m the highest point in the Cape. The second overnight hut is situated at 2 535 m and said to be the highest hiking trail hut in South Africa. A highlight of the day's hike are the waterfalls in the Kloppershoek River. Shortly after setting off on the third day's hike of 17 km, hikers are rewarded with stunning views over Carlisleshoek.

BOSBERG

Distance 15 km; 2 days

Reservations The Reserve Manager, Somerset East Municipality, P O Box 21, Somerset East 5850, Telephone (0424) 3-1333.

Group size Minimum 2; Maximum 10

Facilities The overnight hut on the trail is equipped with bunks, mattresses, tables, benches, gas lamps and candles. Other amenities include fireplaces, water and toilets.

Description The first 2 km of this circular trail ascends steeply along the southern slopes of the Bosberg north of Somerset East before following an easier gradient to Slagbos. Massive dolerite rocks and shady trees here make for a welcome resting stop. About 3,5 km after setting off the trail swings westwards and then follows a gravel road to the overnight hut which has a commanding view of the landscape to the south. After following an easy route across the plateau, Bloukop – the highest point on the trail – is reached about 4 km after setting off on the second day's hike. From Bloukop the trail descends steeply before levelling out, with the final section passing through the game enclosure.

COMMANDO DRIFT

Distance 28 km; 2 days

Reservations The Officer-in-Charge, Commando Drift Nature Reserve, P O Box 459, Cradock 5880, Telephone (0481) 3925.

Group size Minimum 2; Maximum 6

Facilities The overnight hut is equipped with bunks, mattresses, a cold water shower and a fireplace.

Description The Commando Drift Dam is the focal point of the 5 890 ha Commando Drift Nature Reserve near Tarkastad and this circular trail mainly follows the edge of the dam. The terrain is dominated by low, undulating hills, but also includes Karoo plains, sandstone and dolerite cliffs, as well as dolerite hills. Some 150 bird species have been recorded to date and hikers might encounter animals such as Cape mountain zebra, black wildebeest, red hartebeest, kudu, blesbok, mountain reedbuck, steenbok and common duiker. The first day's hike covers 16,5 km and the hide close to the hut is ideal for game-viewing and bird-watching. The second day's hike follows the edge of the dam below Rooiberg, the highest point in the reserve.

DRIEKOPPE

Distance 29 km; 2 days

Reservations The Officer-in-Charge, Karoo Nature Reserve, P O Box 349, Graaff-Reinet 6280, Telephone (0491) 2-3453.

Group size Minimum 2; Maximum 10

Facilities The overnight hut at the end of the first day's hike is equipped with bunks and mattresses, while water, toilets, an outside fireplace and firewood are also provided. There is no accommodation at the start of the trail, but a wide range of options is available in nearby Graaff-Reinet.

Description This trail is situated in the eastern section of the 16 000 ha Karoo Nature Reserve surrounding Graaff-Reinet. From the starting point the trail gains about 500 m in altitude over 10 km to the overnight hut at Waaihoek. From the hut a 5 km circular route can be undertaken via the 1 482 m-high Hanglip, the highest point on the trail. The second day's hike winds past the prominent Driekoppe before joining the onward route of the first day's hike. Among the animals you might see are Cape mountain zebra, red hartebeest, kudu and mountain reedbuck, as well as smaller antelope species such as klipspringer, steenbok and common duiker.

EKOWA

Distance 41 km; 3 days

Reservations The Town Clerk, Elliot Municipality, P O Box 21, Elliot 5460, Telephone (045) 313-1011.

Group size Minimum 3; Maximum 10

Facilities An old farmhouse serves as accommodation at the start of the trail. Amenities include a limited number of mattresses, flush toilet and cold water. At the two overnight huts on the trail mattresses, fireplaces and firewood are provided as well as pit toilets and cold water.

Description This linear trail in the Cape Drakensberg, just north of Elliot, traverses an area dominated by Gatberg, a mountain through which the elements have eroded a hole, and magnificent sandstone formations. The trail winds mainly through grassveld interspersed with proteaveld and small patches of indigenous forest. Despite the relatively short distances covered (13 km on the first and third days and 15 km on the second) the trail is unsuitable for unfit hikers and those afraid of heights, on account of the steep gradients. However, hikers will be rewarded with expansive views of the north-eastern Cape landscape. Noteworthy bird species recorded in the area include Cape vultures, bearded vultures and crowned cranes.

GROENDAL

Distance Four circular routes, ranging in distance from 14 km to 38 km

Reservations The Officer-in-Charge, Groendal Wilderness Area, P O Box 445, Uitenhage 6230, Telephone (041) 992-5418.

Group size Minimum 3; Maximum 12

Facilities Since there are no overnight facilities in the wilderness area hikers have to sleep in caves and overhangs. Showers and toilets are available at the starting point.

Description This 30 000 ha wilderness area in the foothills of the Groot Winterhoek Mountains north-west of Uitenhage is characterised by forested ravines, deeply incised kloofs and impenetrable valley bushveld vegetation. Hikers have a choice of several circular routes: The Upper Blindekloof route is a moderate to strenuous 36 km circuit which traverses the watershed of the Groot Winterhoek Mountains before swinging back to the starting/ending point. The undulating terrain of the Dam route, a 38 km traverse around Groendal Dam, makes this a strenuous route which should only be undertaken by extremely fit hikers. The Emerald Pool route is a 32 km circular trail to the inviting pool of that name.

HOGSBACK

Distance 35 km; 2 days

Reservations The Regional Director,

195

Tsitsikamma Forest Region, Private Bag X537, Humansdorp 6300, Telephone (0423) 5-1180.

Group size Minimum 2; Maximum 18

Facilities Bunks, mattresses, fireplaces, firewood, water, cold/warm water showers, toilets and refuse bins are provided at the overnight hut.

Description Since the first day's hike of this circular trail, which starts at Hogsback, is 22 km long, an early start is advisable. The trail initially winds through indigenous forest to the Kettlespout Falls before gaining height to the Hogsback peaks. After traversing the upper slopes of two of the peaks the trail swings towards Bloemhof. The final 4 km of the day's hike to Gaika's Kop Hut winds through and alongside pine plantations. On the second day's hike the trail gains height towards Gaika's Kop and after traversing its slopes drops down through pine plantations to Tor Doone with its expansive view of Hogsback Village. Over the last 2 km the trail loses some 200 m in altitude, reaching the Hogsback Forest Station after 11 km.

KATBERG

Distance 50,8 km; 2 days

Reservations Contour, P O Box 186, Bisho 5608, Telephone (0401) 95-2115.

Group size Minimum 3; Maximum 12

Facilities The three overnight huts on the trail are equipped with bunks and mattresses. Fireplaces, firewood, water and pit toilets are also provided.

Description Stretching between the Mpofu Game Reserve and the Benholm Forest Station, the Katberg Hiking Trail traverses the slopes of the Didima Mountain, north of Balfour. The vegetation varies from valley bushveld in the low-lying areas to montane grasslands with patches of indigenous forest and pine plantations.
The first day's hike covers 17,3 km, ascending 600 m over the first 13 km, before descending to Diepkloof Hut. On the second day the route

ascends to just below the krantzes of Didima and a short way beyond Krantzkop the trail starts its 10 km descent to Readsdale Hut. The third day's hike of 16,7 km starts with a steady uphill slog for 6,5 km before the gradient becomes easier.

LAMMERGEIER

Distance 34 km; 3 days

Reservations Lady Grey Municipality, P O Box 18, Lady Grey 5540, Telephone (05552) 19.

Group size Minimum 2; Maximum 20

Facilities Hikers are accommodated in huts and farmhouses on the trail with basic sleeping, cooking and ablution facilities. There are no facilities at the start of the trail, but hikers have a choice of hotel accommodation, cottages and campsites in Lady Grey.

Description Named after the bearded vulture, also known as the lammergeier, this circular trail traverses the Lammergeier Conservancy in the Witteberg Mountains. From Lady Grey the first day's hike of 9 km follows an old Basotho trading route and after gaining height initially follows a contour path before dropping down to the first overnight hut at the old Helvellyn Police border post. Numerous mountain streams are crossed on the second day's hike, which follows farm roads and a cattle contour path. After crossing a plateau the trail loses height rapidly to reach the Burnet farmhouse 16 km after setting off. On the third day hikers have a choice of three routes – a 9 km hike along the main trail or two optional routes of 8 km and 14 km respectively.

OVISTON NATURE RESERVE

Distance No set distance; hikers can blaze their own trails.

Reservations The Officer-in-Charge, Oviston Nature Reserve, P O Box 7, Venterstad 5990, Telephone (0553) 5-0000.

Group size Minimum 2; Maximum 8 or 16, depending on overnight stops used

Facilities An old farmhouse equipped with 16 bunks, mattresses, cooking and eating utensils, fireplaces, toilet and bath is available. Alternative accommodation is available in a cottage which sleeps eight. Facilities include bunks, fireplaces, an outdoor shower and pit toilet.

Description Since there are no dangerous animals in this 13 000 ha nature reserve on the southern banks of the Gariep Dam near Venterstad, hikers are free to go wherever they like within the Goodlands section of the reserve, which is managed as a wilderness area. The typical Karoo plains are interspersed with dolerite hills which offer good vantage points for game-viewing. The reserve is renowned for its large numbers and diversity of game and among the species hikers could encounter are black wildebeest, red hartebeest, eland, kudu, mountain reedbuck, blesbok, steenbok and Burchell's zebra. With more than 140 bird species recorded to date, birding can be rewarding too.

PRENTJIESBERG

Distance 50 km; 3 days

Reservations North East Cape Forests, Regional Office, Private Bag, Ugie 5470, Telephone (045) 333-1044.

Group size Minimum 2; Maximum 12

Facilities A two-bedroomed hut equipped with bunks, mattresses and a small kitchen area is available at the start, while a house comprising three bedrooms, lounge, dining room and kitchen is provided at the end of the first day's hike. Amenities include bunks, mattresses, hot and cold water showers, a stove, fridge, cutlery and crockery. A cave with wooden floorboards, fireplaces, firewood and a toilet serves as accommodation at the end of the second day's hike.

Description This two- or three-day circular trail north-west of Ugie traverses the Prentjiesberg with its spectacular sandstone cliffs and caves with rock paintings. The 3 100 ha mountain is the property of North East Cape Forests and has been declared a Natural Heritage Site. Vegetation ranges from grassveld to proteaveld

and pockets of indigenous forest, and hikers might chance upon antelope like blesbok, grey rhebok and mountain reedbuck.

The first day's hike traverses the southern slopes of the mountain while the second day's route climbs steeply to the plateau and after an easy traverse drops down steeply to Craigmore Cave. Skirting the north-eastern side of the Prentjiesberg, the third day's hike gains height steadily to the plateau before descending to the starting/ending point.

SETHUZINI

Distance 60 km; 3 days

Reservations Sethuzini Trail, P O Box 64, Lady Grey 5540, Telephone (05552) 272.

Group size Minimum 4; Maximum 10

Facilities Hikers are accommodated in the Sethuzini Lodge at the start of the trail and, depending on the season, in rustic farmhouses or campsites along the trail.

Description This guided hike traverses the grassy hills and valleys of the Cape Drakensberg south of Lady Grey. The trail is on private farmland and winds past crystal clear streams, waterfalls, caves with rock paintings and the impressive Karringmelk Canyon. Animals occurring in the area include grey rhebok, mountain reedbuck and common duiker, while the rare bearded vulture has also been recorded. Also to be seen is the railways reverse system (one of only two in the world). Since all equipment is transported to the overnight stops, hikers only need to carry a day pack with lunch. The trail tariff is inclusive of breakfast, lunch and a three-course supper and hot water is available at each overnight stop. Horse-back trails are also conducted.

SHIPWRECK

Distance 64 km; 4 days

Reservations Contour, P O Box 186, Bisho 5608, Telephone (0401) 95-2115.

Group size No limit

Facilities The only campsite with facilities is at Hamburg, but camping is permitted anywhere along the coast. Alternatively, hikers can reserve accommodation at the Hamburg Hotel, Mpekweni Marine Resort or Kiwane Bungalows.

Description Stretching between the Great Fish and Ncera rivers on the Ciskei coast, this trail can be hiked in either direction. The coastline is characterised by forested dunes, unspoilt estuaries, long sandy beaches and small sandy bays, occasionally interspersed by rocky shores. Since there are no set overnight stops on the trail, hikers can set their own pace, stopping off along the trail for angling and shell-collecting. Bird-watching can be rewarding too, especially during summer when the number of resident species is swelled by migrants. Estuaries along the route are best crossed at low tide, but under no circumstances should you attempt to cross the Great Fish and Keiskamma rivers at their mouths.

STRANDLOPER

Distance 93 km; 4 days

Reservations The Officer-in-Charge, Cape Nature Conservation, P O Box 5185, Greenfields 5208, Telephone (0431) 46-3532 for permission to enter the Kwelera and Cape Henderson nature reserves.

Group size No limit

Facilities No camping is permitted on the beaches, but there are several hotels and other accommodation establishments, as well as formal campsites along the coast.

Description This coastal route south of the Kei River takes its name from the early coastal Khoisan people, commonly referred to as Strandlopers, who exploited the marine resources of the coast. The trail was initiated as a joint venture between the Border Branch of the Wildlife Society of Southern Africa and the Greater East London Publicity Association. Although there are several holiday resorts along the route, the scenery along the coast is spec-tacular. On the first day's hike the route takes hikers along the top of the spectacular Morbay Cliffs, just south of Morgan Bay. Further south the walking varies from long sandy beaches flanked by grassy hills and patches of indigenous forest to rocky bays. Several rivers and estuaries have to be crossed, adding to the adventure of the trail.

WOODCLIFFE

Distance 62 km; 4 or 5 days

Reservations Graham and Phyll Sephton, Woodcliffe Cave Trails, P O Box 65, Maclear 5480, Telephone (045) 323-1550.

Group size Minimum 3; Maximum 20 (arrangements can be made for groups of up to 30)

Facilities Four huts have been built inside Toks Cave at the start of the trail. Other amenities include fireplaces, firewood, barbecue grid, kettle, lamp and a cooking pot. Water is obtainable from a waterfall which cascades over the cave and there is also a toilet. At the three other overnight huts hikers are accommodated in four-roomed stone cottages equipped with three-plate gas stoves, lamps, kettle and pots. Sheepskins are provided for sleeping on.

Description Situated in the Joelshoek Valley near Maclear, this circular trail winds across a sheep and cattle farm with scenery ranging from steep grassy hills to sandstone cliffs and patches of indigenous forest. A high degree of fitness is required as the trail leads from the foothills of the Drakensberg to the escarpment and back. The first overnight stop, Toks Cave, is a short walk from the start. On the second day the trail gains some 800 m in altitude to the escarpment, while the third day's hike starts with a steep climb to the escarpment where hikers are rewarded with views of Woodcliffe and the previous day's route. From the Wide Valley Hut hikers have a choice of a 9 km walk down Woodcliffe Valley or extending their hike by another day by continuing to Termination Valley before returning to Woodcliffe.

KWAZULU/NATAL

THE NATAL DRAKENSBERG PARK

Stretching over some 200 km, from the Sentinel in the north to Bushman's Nek in the south, the Natal Drakensberg Park is one of the five largest protected areas in southern Africa. Covering 243 000 ha, the park consists of six game parks and reserves and six state forests. It is a world of spectacular sandstone cliffs, towering peaks – often snow-capped, waterfalls, soaring buttresses and the home of the bearded vulture. Little wonder then that it is South Africa's most popular backpacking and mountaineering area.

Aspects common to all trails in the Natal Drakensberg Park are discussed in this general introduction.

TRAIL PLANNER

Grading Depends on route, but generally moderate with some demanding (B+), difficult (C) or extremely difficult (C+) sections. All routes to the escarpment should be considered extremely difficult.

Climate

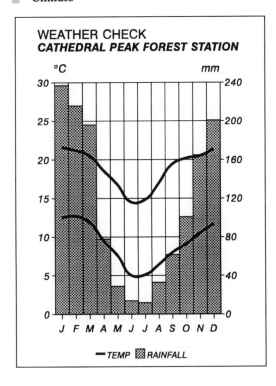

WEATHER CHECK
CATHEDRAL PEAK FOREST STATION

— TEMP ▨ RAINFALL

Frost occurs on about 150 nights a year, while snowfalls are recorded six to 12 times a year. Although snow can be expected any time of the year, it generally occurs between April and September. In the southern Berg snowfalls are generally more frequent and heavier than in the northern Berg. During summer the Little Berg and the summit are often blanketed by heavy cloud and mist which could last for anything up to two weeks before clearing.

Group size In wilderness areas groups are limited to a maximum of 12 people and the number of groups is also restricted. Groups should consist of at least three people.

Logistics In many instances circular routes are possible. However, when you tackle traverses, two vehicles are necessary because of the remoteness of some of the starting/ending points.

Relevant information
■ The Drakensberg is notorious for sudden weather changes and you should, consequently, always be prepared for adverse weather conditions.
■ Do not venture into the High Berg if you are unfamiliar with the area.
■ During recent years theft has become a problem, especially along the escarpment.

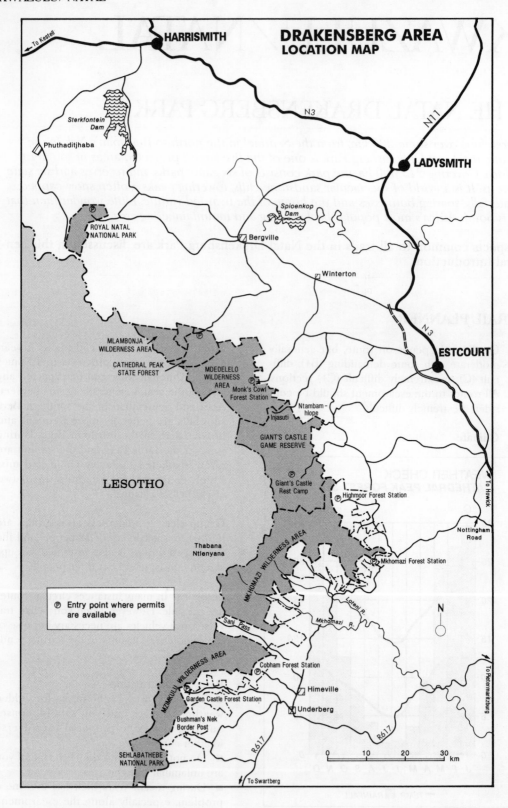

DRAKENSBERG AREA
LOCATION MAP

To Kestell

HARRISMITH

N3

N11

LADYSMITH

Sterkfontein
Dam

Phuthaditjhaba

Spioenkop
Dam

ROYAL NATAL
NATIONAL PARK

Bergville

Winterton

N3

ESTCOURT

MLAMBONJA
WILDERNESS AREA

CATHEDRAL PEAK
STATE FOREST

MDEDELELO
WILDERNESS
AREA

Monk's Cowl
Forest Station

Ntambam-
hlope

Injasuti

GIANT'S CASTLE
GAME RESERVE

To Howick

LESOTHO

Giant's Castle
Rest Camp

Highmoor Forest Station

Nottingham
Road

Thabana
Ntlenyana

MKHOMAZI WILDERNESS AREA

Mkhomazi Forest Station

Loteni R.

Mkhomazi R.

N

Sani Pass

To Pietermaritzburg

Ⓟ Entry point where permits
    are available

MZIMKULU WILDERNESS AREA

Cobham Forest Station

Himeville

Garden Castle Forest Station

Underberg

Bushman's Nek
Border Post

R617

R617

0   10   20   30
km

SEHLABATHEBE
NATIONAL PARK

To Swartberg

Do not leave equipment unattended and arrange a night-watch system.
■ Never pitch camp close to streams or rivers as flash floods are not uncommon after heavy thunderstorms.
■ A backpacking stove is essential, but stoves using butane or propane gas cartridges should be avoided as the gas is ineffective at high altitudes and low temperatures.
■ Also refer to **General Rules of Access to the Drakensberg** at the end of this chapter.

TRAIL ENVIRONMENT

Flora The vegetation of the Natal Drakensberg is dominated by extensive grasslands. On account of the variation in altitude from 1 280 to nearly 3 500 m there is a wide range of plant communities and three distinct vegetation belts have been identified.

Those accustomed to the rich floral wealth of the western Cape are often disappointed by the apparent absence of flowering plants. However, to date more than 1 600 flowering plants and 72 fern species have been recorded in the Natal Drakensberg. Many species are obscured by the grasslands or grow in protected places and are therefore easily missed. However, spring is full of surprises when the brown grass is brought to life with numerous plants bursting into flower.

The **montane belt** covers the vegetation from the valley floors to the lowermost basalt cliffs at the edge of the Little Berg between altitudes of 1 250 and 2 000 m. It consists mainly of grassland dominated by redgrass (*Themeda triandra*) with scattered protea stands which form protea savanna. The dominant species are common and silver sugarbushes, while the lip-flower sugarbush, *P. simplex* and *P. dracomontana* also occur.

Flowering species you are likely to encounter in the montane belt are the beautiful white *Anemone fanninnii*, the dark pink *Graderia scabra*, ox-eye daisy (*Callilepis laureola*), blue scilla (*Scilla natalensis*), watsonia (*Watsonia densiflora*) and various everlasting (*Helichrysum*) and *Agapanthus* species.

Yellowwood (*Podocarpus*) forests are limited to protected valleys and kloofs and south-, south-east- and east-facing slopes. The forests are mixed in character, comprising some 20 species. These include Outeniqua and real yellowwoods, as well as white stinkwood, white candlewood, red pear and assegai. Species occurring along the forest margins include oldwood, sagewood and tree fuchsia.

Oldwood and sagewood also form dense scrub communities in gullies and stream beds where they are protected from fires. A species characteristic of the area between the Clarens Sandstone and the lowermost basalt cliffs is the mountain cypress which grows between 3 and 4,5 m high. The Clarens Sandstone and the lowermost basalt cliffs are the habitat of the krantz aloe, Natal bottlebrush and the mountain cabbage tree.

The **sub-Alpine belt** extends from the edge of the Little Berg (approximately 2 000 m) to just below the Drakensberg summit. Five major grassland types have been identified in this belt with the redgrass (*Themeda triandra*) grassland being the most extensive.

Shrubs and trees of this belt consist mainly of

Leaf and flower of the Natal bottlebrush

mountain cypress, oldwood and sagewood.

The climax community of the sub-Alpine belt comprises fynbos dominated by *Passerina filiformis*, *Philippia evansii*, and mountain cypress. Other species occurring are *Protea dracomontana* and the lip-flower sugarbush. This community is best developed on the steep valley and escarpment slopes at the head of major rivers.

Flowering plants include *Albuca tricophylla*, *Aster perfoliatus*, the dainty *Nemesia denticulata* and the pineapple flower (*Eucomis*). A large number of orchids can be seen flowering in the summer. Among them you might spot *Satyrium longicauda* – one of the most common ground orchids, the pink-flowering *Disa versicolor* and the lime-green *Eulophia foliosa*.

The **Alpine belt** occurs above altitudes of 2 865 m and is dominated by ericas and helichrysums interspersed with grasslands consisting mainly of *Festuca*, *Danthonia* and *Pentaschistis* species.

The ground on the escarpment plateau is often boggy in the wet summer months, providing an ideal habitat for species such as the red-hot poker (*Kniphofia northiae* and *K. caulescens*), the Alpine iris (*Moraea spathulata*), the bell-shaped *Dierama igneum* and the yellow *Cyrtanthus flanaganii*. The alpine forbs are seen at their best between summer and early autumn

while several orchids can be seen flowering during January and February.

Donald Killick's *Field Guide to the Flora of the Natal Drakensberg* is a useful guide for identifying the 239 most common species occurring in the Berg. Also useful is Betty Hardy's *Drakensberg Flowers*, a pocket guide to 110 common flowers of the Little Berg.

Fauna Although very little remains of the large numbers of game which inhabited the Drakensberg in former times, game numbers are again increasing since virtually the entire Natal Drakensberg now enjoys protection.

The species you are most likely to come across is the grey rhebok which is probably the most common antelope in the Drakensberg. They prefer the more level areas of the Little Berg and are sometimes mistaken for the smaller mountain reedbuck. However, the latter usually occur on slopes where suitable cover – shrubs, rocks or boulders – is not far off.

Two other common animals which frequent the rocky areas of the Drakensberg and which you are likely to notice are the chacma baboon and the rock dassie.

You might also approach quite closely to eland on the Little Berg during spring and summer when the grasses here are palatable. During

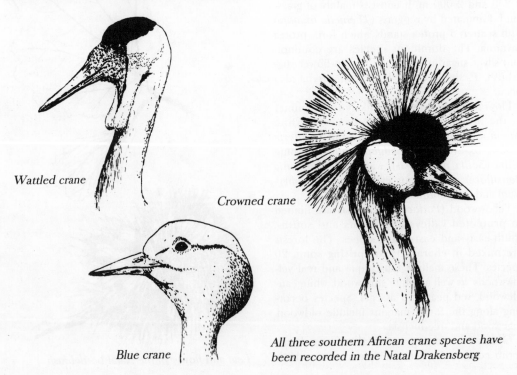

Wattled crane

Crowned crane

Blue crane

All three southern African crane species have been recorded in the Natal Drakensberg

winter, however, they move into the river valleys and forest patches where the vegetation is more nutritious.

Other large antelope occurring are blesbok, red hartebeest and black wildebeest. Smaller antelope include bushbuck, common duiker, oribi and klipspringer. The latter is confined to basalt krantzes between 2 400 and 2 700 m and is rarely seen.

Several predators occur, but on account of their nocturnal and secretive habits you are unlikely to see any. Predators recorded include the black-backed jackal, African wild cat, serval, caracal, Cape clawless otter, spotted-necked otter and several mongoose species. Leopards also occur, but since they inhabit remote and inaccessible areas they are rarely seen.

Of the 246 bird species recorded in the Natal Drakensberg Park to date, 213 species are either resident or occur regularly, while the remaining 33 species are considered vagrants or rare visitors.

One of the most interesting and rare birds of the Drakensberg is the bearded vulture. It has long, pointed wings and a wedge-shaped tail and is restricted to the upper elevations of the Drakensberg. Their numbers have been estimated at about 120 pairs.

Other birds of prey you might spot which are listed as *Red Data Species* are Cape vulture, cuckoo hawk and martial eagle.

The summit plateau and the slopes and rock-faces above 2 200 m are sparsely inhabited by species such as the white stork – a summer visitor – and the bald ibis. More commonly seen species include rock pigeon, whitenecked raven, sentinel rock thrush, familiar chat and red-winged starling.

In the open grassland keep an eye out for secretary bird, redwing francolin, common quail, ground woodpecker, orangethroated longclaw, bokmakierie and the pintailed whydah.

These species also occur in the proteaveld which, in addition, attracts birds such as Gurney's sugarbird, malachite and greater doublecollared sunbirds and fiscal shrike.

The patches of indigenous forest provide a suitable habitat for redchested cuckoo, cardinal woodpecker, blackheaded oriole, blackeyed bulbul and paradise flycatcher.

A large number of species are attracted to the riverine bush and scrub habitat, including the blackheaded heron, hamerkop, several kingfishers such as the pied, giant, halfcollared, mala-

chite and the brownhooded kingfishers and southern boubou.

The vleis, marshes and wetlands are sparsely distributed on flat ground. Typical species here are hadeda ibis, blue crane, marsh owl and long-tailed widow.

Birds of the Natal Drakensberg Park by R Little and W R Bainbridge gives a short description of the 246 species recorded to date, as well as information on their status, habitat, habits, voices and food. Diagrams are used to show their distribution and occurrence.

History Archaeological evidence indicates that the San lived in the caves and shelters of the Drakensberg for thousands of years before the arrival of the first wave of the Nguni people. It has been suggested that they inhabited the Drakensberg in the summer when game and food were plentiful, migrating to the Natal Midlands in autumn.

In terms of quantity and quality, the Drakensberg is considered one of the richest rock art areas in the world and to date more than 600 sites, with a total of more than 22 000 individual paintings, have been recorded. It has been estimated that the Drakensberg contains some 35 per cent of the total number of painted sites in South Africa.

The earliest known Nguni people to arrive in the foothills of the Drakensberg were the Zizi who settled between the Upper Tugela and the Bushman's rivers around 1700. It is, however, likely that groups of Iron Age people were already present in the Drakensberg foothills centuries earlier. Relations between the San and the new immigrants varied from absorption and acculturation to conflict.

The expansion of the Ndwandwe, the Ngwane and the Mthethwa chiefdoms and the rise to power of the Zulu kingdom under Shaka caused widespread destruction. In about 1818 the Ngwane under Matiwane were first attacked by Dingiswayo's Mthetwha and shortly afterwards by the Ndwandwe of Zwide. The Ngwane fled westwards, attacking the Hlubi and the Bele tribes. On reaching the Drakensberg they displaced the Zizi and settled in the vicinity of Mdedelelo. Peace was short-lived, though, for in 1822 the armies of Shaka swept as far south as the Umzimvubu River, destroying crops, razing entire villages and uprooting tribes. Tribes fell upon one another and some fugitives sought refuge in the caves and shelters of the Drakensberg where they clashed with the San. For one such tribe, the Duga clan under Mdavu, the situation was so desperate that they resorted to cannibalism. These events are known as the *Difaqane* or "forced migrations".

The first whites to see the Drakensberg were probably the survivors of the Portuguese vessel *Santo Alberto* which was shipwrecked along the Transkei coast on 24 March 1593. To avoid the wide river mouths along the coast they followed an inland route to Delagoa Bay (the present Maputo) and in the beginning of May they saw a range of snow-covered mountains to the west, which must have been the Drakensberg.

The first white man to explore the remote valleys of the Drakensberg was Captain Allen Francis Gardiner who travelled through the area in 1835. Gardiner was especially impressed by two peaks, naming them Giant's Cup and Giant's Castle. Both peaks were, however, subsequently renamed.

In October 1836 two French missionaries, Thomas Arbousset and Francis Daumas, reached the summit of the northernmost point of the Maluti Mountains and named it Mont-aux-Sources.

In December of the following year the Voortrekkers crossed the Drakensberg and settled in the area of the Upper Tugela Basin. Farms of 2 428 ha were allocated to Trekkers who had settled in Natal before 1840 and many settled in the area between the Tugela and Bushman's rivers.

Conflict soon arose between the Voortrekkers and the San. The influx of black refugees into Natal, land settlement arrangements and repeated raids by the San caused dissatisfaction among the Voortrekkers after Natal became a British colony in 1843. Large numbers of Voortrekkers crossed back into the Free State and it was only through the intervention of Sir Harry Smith that the remaining Trekkers were persuaded in 1848 not to leave Natal. The size of all farms was fixed at 2 428 ha and protection against the black tribespeople, as well as firm action against the San raiders, was promised. Many of the farms were laid out along the headwaters of the Tugela River and its tributaries which were sparsely populated.

Numerous English names such as Castle End, Castledene, Paiseley, Wilander Downs and Snowdon remind one of the farms established in the foothills of the Drakensberg by the English settlers who began occupying farms here around 1840.

Several locations were established in the foothills of the Drakensberg in 1849 to act as a buffer between the white farmers and the raiding San. The number of raids declined steadily and 20 years later, in July 1869, the last recorded San raid against a white farmer in Natal took place. A number of raids were carried out after this date on the black tribespeople, the last raid specifically attributed to San being in August 1872.

Some San continued their ancient way of life in the mountains of Lesotho. In 1878 a couple who visited the Tugela Valley came across what was thought to be the last group of San seen in the Drakensberg by whites. However, in 1925 a farmer with the name of Anton Lombard discovered a hunting outfit on a high ledge in Elands Cave – a shelter on the southern slope of the Mhlawazini Valley. A few days later the site was visited by another farmer, W Carter Robinson, who noticed sleeping quarters which were probably not more than six months old. It was presumed that these belonged to a lone San survivor.

Geology The scenery is one of the outstanding features of the Natal Drakensberg range and is among the finest in the world. The range is renowned for its sheer rock faces, spectacular free-standing peaks, towering buttresses, deeply eroded river valleys and fascinating sandstone formations.

The geological formations of the Natal Drakensberg belong to the Karoo Sequence which, from the base upwards, consists of the Upper Beaufort Beds of the Beaufort Group and the Molteno, Elliot, Clarens Sandstone and Drakensberg Basalt formations of the Stormberg Series.

The Upper Beaufort Beds are the older sedimentary formation and therefore the lowest. They were laid down some 200 million years ago under extremely wet conditions when much of South Africa was covered by swamps. They consist of several red, green and maroon shales overlain by yellow fine-grained sandstone with shales.

The Molteno Beds were deposited about 180 million years ago. They are recognisable as successive beds of sandstone, alternating with layers of blue and grey shales which accumulated in a vast inland lake. These sediments form the

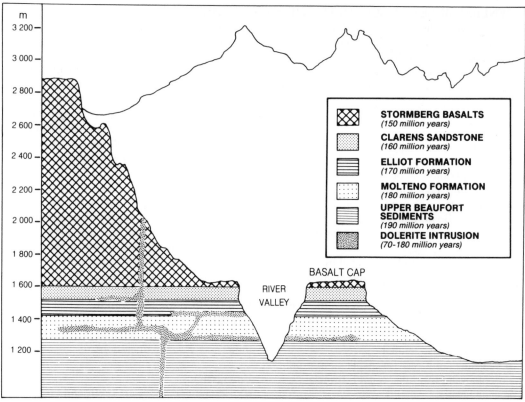

Profile of the geological structure of the Natal Drakensberg

terraces and ledges at the foot of the Little Berg and are best seen in the Southern Berg.

The Elliot Formation, formerly known as the Red Beds, was laid down about 170 million years ago and consists of alternating beds of red shales and fine-grained sandstone. This formation is rarely exposed and is best seen in the stream beds below the Clarens Sandstone Formation (formerly Cave Sandstone) and along paths. It forms the steeply vegetated slopes below the Clarens Sandstone Formation.

The Clarens Sandstone Formation is the most prominent of the sedimentary units exposed in the Drakensberg. The distinctive creamy-white cliffs are a characteristic feature of the Drakensberg foothills and the sandstone layer forms the Little Berg. These beds are about 160 million years old and were originally laid down as desert dunes in a very arid climate during the Jurassic Period. The formation originally took its name from the large number of caves and shallow overhangs occurring at the base of the thick sandstone layer.

The highest part of the Berg was formed by

lava flows, and is known as the Drakensberg Basalt Formation. Between the Middle Jurassic and early Cretaceous periods volcanic activity resulted in the flow of lava from fissures associated with the break-up of the supercontinent, Gondwana.

Individual flows have been traced for more than 32 km and the lava flows varied in thickness from 0,3 to 45 m and built up to a thickness of over 1 300 m, covering what is today known as KwaZulu/Natal. The dolerite dykes and sills associated with the Karoo rocks underlying the Drakensberg lavas represent magma (molten matter) that did not reach the surface to form basalt flows. These vertical sills and horizontal dykes have been exposed through subsequent erosion.

The present rugged landscape of the Drakensberg has been formed by headward erosion of the Great Escarpment following the break-up of Gondwana. The erosion has been aided by seaward tilting of the KwaZulu/Natal coastal area and four successive periods of continental uplift.

GENERAL RULES OF ACCESS TO THE NATAL DRAKENSBERG

On account of the rugged terrain and the weather, which can change extremely rapidly, the Drakensberg has claimed the lives of numerous backpackers. It is therefore essential to pay special attention to the general rules of access.

Permits

■ Access is by permit only and permit conditions must be strictly adhered to. The addresses where permits can be obtained are given in the relevant sections in this book.

■ Permits must be produced on demand by Natal Parks Board officers and any person not in possession of a permit is liable for prosecution.

■ Entry permits can be obtained by making a written or telephone reservation in advance or on arrival, provided the number of persons already in the area does not exceed the maximum capacity. The maximum group size is 12, but the number of groups permitted in a particular area is also limited.

■ Angling permits are available upon production of a valid Kwazulu/Natal Provincial angling licence.

■ A valid passport is required for excursions beyond the escarpment into Lesotho.

Equipment

■ Persons wishing to spend the night in the mountains may be refused a permit unless the following equipment is carried: tent, sleeping bag, adequate footwear and warm clothing, torch, candle and matches, camping stove and fuel, food – including sufficient emergency rations – and a first aid kit.

■ Sunglasses or sun-goggles are advisable in the event of snowfalls, when the glare can be damaging to the eyes.

Maps The entire Drakensberg from Mont-aux-Sources in the north to Sehlabathebe in the south is covered by a three-part recreational map series which is invaluable to backpackers.

The maps are printed to a scale of 1 : 50 000 on all-weather plasticised material, which is extremely durable. They provide a wealth of useful information on the Berg such as the location and maximum capacity of caves, perennial streams, dangerous river crossings, major and minor paths, ill-defined "Ways to Go", difficult sections where a rope may be required and approximate distances between path junctions.

A useful feature of the maps is the numbered intersections of footpaths. It has become standard practice for backpackers completing the mountain register to state the actual junction numbers of their intended routes. Another useful feature is the safety grid which enables you to pinpoint your position very quickly.

Rescue Register

■ It is compulsory to complete the mountain register upon entering any of the mountain areas. Do this as accurately as possible as this information will speed up assistance or rescue operations should these be necessary. The various mountain register points are listed under the relevant sections in this book.

■ It is imperative to record the actual time and date of your return in the rescue register to avoid being held liable for the costs of unnecessary rescue operations.

Emergencies

■ Rescue operations are costly and often extremely hazardous, especially when carried out in adverse weather conditions. You are therefore requested to take the necessary precautions and to avoid taking careless risks.

■ In the event of an accident or illness where the victim is immobile a Natal Parks Board official or the South African Police Services in charge of the area concerned must be contacted.

General

■ Firearms are not permitted in the Natal Drakensberg Park.

■ Littering is an offence. All litter must be carried out and should not be buried.

■ No open fires are permitted and it is an offence to collect firewood.

■ Sleeping is not permitted in caves with rock paintings, except those caves indicated as such on the recreational map series.

■ On arrival at the forest station, certain caves may be reserved for your party. However, this does not ensure exclusive occupation of the cave and in the event of inclement weather you will be obliged to share the cave with other backpackers.

GIANT'S CUP

This relatively easy trail is situated in the foothills of the southern Drakensberg and is an ideal hiking opportunity for those unfamiliar with the Berg. Stretching between Sani Pass in the north and Bushman's Nek in the south, the trail winds past eroded sandstone formations, across grassy plains and through spectacular valleys with inviting pools. Herds of eland can sometimes be seen, while raptors like bearded and Cape vultures are occasionally seen overhead.

Aspects common to the Natal Drakensberg Park are discussed in the general introduction which should be read in conjunction with this chapter.

TRAIL PLANNER

Distance 60 km; 5 days

Grading A+

Climate

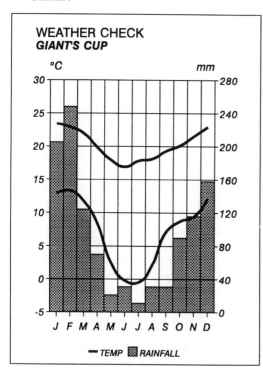

WEATHER CHECK
GIANT'S CUP

— TEMP ▓ RAINFALL

Reservations The Reservations Officer, Natal Parks Board, P O Box 1750, Pietermaritzburg 3200, Telephone (0331) 47-1981, Fax (0331) 47-1980. Reservations are accepted up to nine months in advance.

Group size Minimum 2; Maximum 30

Maps A full-colour trail map (waterproof or plain) with useful information on the history, flora and fauna on the reverse is available, but must be ordered separately.

Facilities The huts at the four overnight stops are equipped with bunks with mattresses, tables and benches, water, toilets and refuse bins.

Logistics Linear route without any public transport. Transport to the start or end of the trail can be arranged with Himeville Toyota Service Station at Himeville, Telephone (033) 702-1121 or Giant's Cup Motors, Telephone (033) 702-1615. There is no overnight hut at the start of the trail, but campsites with ablution facilities are available at the Himeville Nature Reserve which is conveniently situated close to the start of the trail. An overnight hut is provided about 1,5 km from the end of the trail.

How to get there The start of the trail is reached by turning left onto the Sani Pass road 3 km north of Himeville. The Sani Pass Hotel is passed after about 11 km and the start of the trail is about 5 km further on.

DRAKENSBERG HIKING TRAIL: Section GIANT'S CUP

LOCATION MAP

TRAIL DESCRIPTION

Day 1: Sani Pass to Pholela Hut The trail starts near the foot of the Sani Pass, the only road link between KwaZulu/Natal and north-eastern Lesotho. Over the first 4 km the trail rises gently to cross the ridge between the Mkhomazana and Gxalingena valleys. The name Gxalingena means "where one should not enter" and is said to have been given to the forest further downstream to which witch-doctors prohibited entry. After 5 km you will reach the Gxalingena River which is crossed by means of a log bridge at Ngenwa Pool. As the first overnight hut is only 8 km further (about three

hours) it is virtually compulsory to spend some time here to soak up the beautiful scenery.

From Ngenwa the trail climbs steadily uphill whilst skirting the eastern slopes of Ndlovini. A track branching off to the left near the 9 km marker follows the alternative route via Bypass Ridge. During rainy weather the Trout Beck, which has to be crossed several times on the main route, can be a problem, so it is advisable to follow the Bypass Ridge route after heavy rains.

The trail then descends to Trout Beck and shortly before reaching the river you will get a

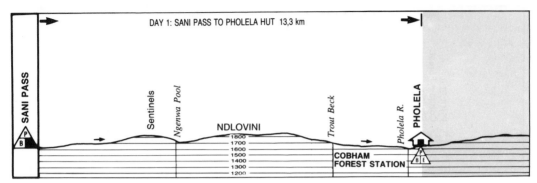

close-up view of a dolerite sill to the left of the trail.

Over the next 2 km the trail follows the course of the Trout Beck over fairly level terrain and as you enter the Pholela Valley, the peaks after which the trail has been named can be seen to the north-west. During his journey through the Drakensberg in October 1835 Captain Allen Gardiner recorded seeing a mountain with a "singularly indented outline" which prompted him to name it the Giant's Cup. The peaks were later renamed Hodgson's Peaks, a name which serves as a grim reminder of the fierce clashes which took place between the San and the early white settlers. Thomas Hodgson was a member of a punitive commando organised in 1862 to recover 67 cattle and 18 horses which were stolen by San cattle rustlers. Whilst giving chase, Hodgson was accidentally wounded in the thigh by one of his companions. He died the following day and was buried at the top of the pass. A cairn was erected on the site a year later.

Keep an eye out in the valley for eland which can sometimes be seen in large herds, especially during the winter months. Shortly before reaching the hut the trail crosses the Trout Beck by means of a suspension bridge. Pholela Hut was one of the original farmhouses in the valley and has been changed as little as possible to retain its character. It is a beautiful old house, built of dressed sandstone, and consists of three bedrooms, a large common room, a kitchen with a stove, and a shower and flush toilet.

Day 2: Pholela Hut to Mzimkulwana Hut

The second day's hut is only 9 km further on and takes about three hours to reach.

From Pholela the trail ascends gently towards the Tortoise Rocks, some interesting round, flattened rocks resembling prehistoric tortoises. From here the trail continues towards

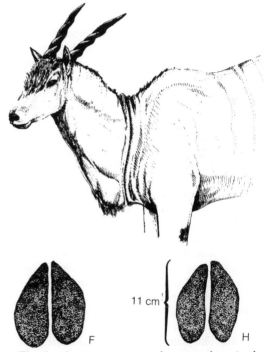

Eland – the most common large antelope in the Natal Drakensberg

Sipongweni Ridge and after 4 km reaches Bathplug Cave. After rain a small waterfall cascades over the opening of the cave, disappearing down a natural water drain-hole before emerging lower downstream – hence the name.

The cave contains several hundred small paintings of stick-like human figures in various positions – gesticulating, running and dancing – but there are no large paintings. The reason for this is that the cave is in the Molteno sandstone layer, and the coarse nature of the cave walls made it difficult to portray large images. In addition the cave is normally damp, causing lichens to grow on the walls. There are also several paintings of horses, some with riders and

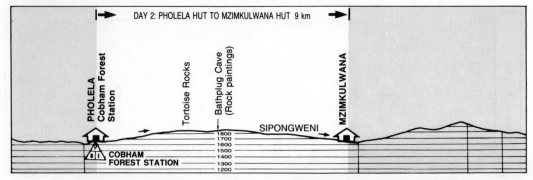

DAY 2: PHOLELA HUT TO MZIMKULWANA HUT 9 km

others without, as well as paintings of females showing the characteristic steatopygia.

Over the next 5 km the trail descends along the eastern and southern slopes of Sipongweni Ridge and on a clear day the Mzimkulwana Hut can be seen several kilometres away.

The hut is situated alongside a tributary of the Mzimkulwana River and consists of a row of six rooms, including a common room as well as ablutions, all under thatch. Nearby is a beautiful waterfall which cascades over a cave into a deep pool – an inviting spot on a hot day.

Day 3: Mzimkulwana Hut to Winterhoek Huts From Mzimkulwana the trail rises gently towards the Little Bamboo Mountains, named after the berg bamboo (*Thamnocalamus tessalatus*). It is the only bamboo indigenous to KwaZulu/Natal and grows in the montane belt where it occurs occasionally in moist areas with yellowwood forests.

After about 4 km the trail reaches its highest point at Crane Tarn, a natural pool on top of a plateau. The name is derived from the blue crane which migrates to the Little Berg to breed during the summer. Non-breeding birds congregate in large flocks, but breeding birds usually occur in pairs.

A short way beyond Crane Tarn the trail passes an interesting site where the remains of petrified trees can be seen in the exposed Beaufort Group. Do not expect to see a petrified forest in the true sense of the word, though, as the remains are scattered about and unless you have a closer look they look like ordinary rocks. Tempting as it might be, do not remove the smallest piece of petrified wood, but leave it untouched so that other hikers can also see it!

The trail continues along the lower western slopes of the Bamboo Mountains where the San recorded the entry of the white man into their domain. These sites are, however, not on the trail route.

You then follow Killiecrankie Stream and about halfway between the 5 km and 6 km mark there is another beautiful swimming pool beneath a massive boulder. From here the trail descends gradually and as on the previous day the huts can be seen several kilometres away. About 1 km beyond the pool you cross into private land and then follow the road to the Drakensberg Gardens Hotel for about 1 km before branching off to the left.

From here the route leads over a small koppie, with the Winterhoek Huts being reached about 1,5 km further on. The overnight stop is completely different from the others on the trail and consists of five rondavel-type huts, a cook-

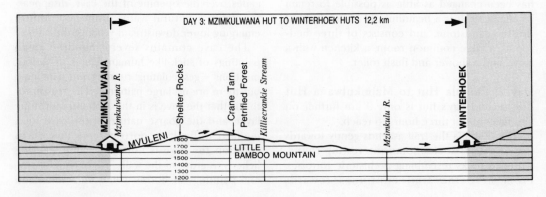

DAY 3: MZIMKULWANA HUT TO WINTERHOEK HUTS 12,2 km

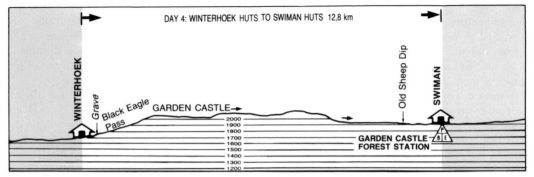

DAY 4: WINTERHOEK HUTS TO SWIMAN HUTS 12,8 km

ing hut and an ablution hut, all under thatch. The oak trees in the vicinity were probably planted towards the end of the 1800s or the early 1900s around the homestead of an early settler. A weir has been built in the stream which flows past the huts and it is possible to have a refreshing dip in the pool which is overlooked by the impressive Garden Castle.

Day 4: Winterhoek Huts to Swiman Hut

From the hut the trail climbs steeply up Black Eagle Pass on the northern slopes of Garden Castle for about 2 km before levelling out just above the 1 900 m contour.

Garden Castle was originally named Giant's Castle by Gardiner. Two days after seeing the Giant's Cup, Gardiner wrote that he was "quite startled at the appearance of a rugged mountain" which he named the Giant's Castle. In his *Narratives of a journey to the Zoolu Country in South Africa*, undertaken in 1835, Gardiner wrote: "Its resemblance to Edinburgh Castle, from one or two points, was so striking that, for a moment, I could almost fancy myself transported to Prince's Street." The name was later given to the peak known today as Giant's Castle and Gardiner's original name changed to Garden Castle.

After about 3 km the only semi-perennial water of the day's hike is reached, but do not count on finding water here in the dry winter months. The trail then follows the Mlambonja Valley more or less along the 2 000 m contour and further along you will find yourself looking down onto the Drakensberg Gardens Hotel. After about 8 km the trail descends steeply and at the 11 km marker you will pass an old sheep dip, a reminder of the pioneer farmers who farmed in the Drakensberg.

A short distance further on the trail joins the onward section of the last day's hike and about 2 km further you will reach Swiman Hut. The scenery in this area is magnificent and among the best in the Drakensberg. Large eroded sandstone outcrops dominate the lower Berg, while the escarpment is dominated by the appropriately named Rhino Peak (3 051 m).

Swiman Hut used to be a forester's house which was made available to hikers when a new house was built for the forester a short distance away.

Garden Castle Forest Station is frequently used as a base camp for backpacking trips to the escarpment and Rhino Peak via the Mashai Pass.

Day 5: Swiman Hut to Bushman's Nek Hut

After retracing your steps for about 1,5 km along the previous day's route the trail branches off to the right. From here you will follow an easy

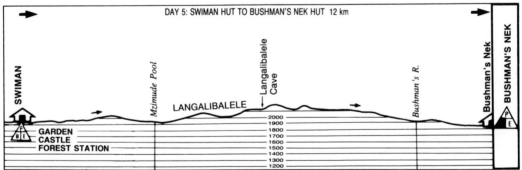

DAY 5: SWIMAN HUT TO BUSHMAN'S NEK HUT 12 km

route, ascending gently for about 2,5 km before descending steeply to the Mzimude River which is crossed by means of a suspension bridge.

Over the next 2 km you will gain some 200 m in altitude to Langalibalele Cave on the western slopes of the 2 270 m-high Langalibalele Peak.

A short distance past the cave a trail leading to the escarpment via the Mzimude Pass branches off to the right. The trail to Bushman's Nek Hut continues to the left and about 2 km further you will cross a jeep track. When the route was first laid out the trail followed the jeep track into the Bushman's River Valley, but now winds down the steep slope. From here you will enjoy a magnificent view of the Bushman's River Valley and over the final 2 km to the hut the trail loses about 300 m in altitude.

The Bushman's Nek Hut replaced the original Silverstream Hut which is situated about 1 km below the Bushman's Nek Police Post. From the hut it is roughly 1,5 km to the end of the trail and another 3 km to the Bushman's Nek Hotel.

MZIMKHULU

This 28 340 ha wilderness area in the southern Berg extends from Sani Pass in the north to Griqualand East in the south. It is characterised by spectacular sandstone formations, grasslands and numerous streams and rivers and those seeking to escape from the more popular areas further north will find Mzimkhulu a haven of tranquillity. Although the area lacks a well-defined contour path, it is traversed by an extensive network of footpaths.

Aspects common to the Natal Drakensberg Park are discussed in the general introduction which should be read in conjunction with this chapter.

TRAIL PLANNER

Distance 165 km of footpaths

Reservations The Forester, Cobham Forest Station, P O Box 168, Himeville 4585, Telephone (033722) 1831, or The Forester, Garden Castle Forest Station, Private Bag X312, Underberg 4590, Telephone (033) 701-1832.

Maps The area is covered by map 5 (Drakensberg South – Vergelegen, Cobham and Garden Castle) and map 6 (Drakensberg South – Garden Castle, Bushman's Nek and Sehlabathebe) of the Drakensberg Recreational Series.

Facilities In the wilderness area there are several shelters where you can overnight including Spectacle, Lakes, Venice, Wilson, Pillar, Sleeping Beauty and Thomathu caves.

Logistics A few informal campsites without any facilities are available at Cobham and Garden Castle forest stations, and advance bookings are advisable.

Relevant information
■ Mountain register points are at Cobham Forest Station, the Drakensberg Gardens Hotel (Garden Castle area) and at the South African Police Services border post at Bushman's Nek.

■ The Bushman's Nek border post is open between 08:00 and 16:00.

How to get there The main approaches are from Cobham Forest Station in the north, Garden Castle Forest Station in the centre and the Bushman's Nek border post in the south.

The Cobham access point is reached by turning right onto the D7 along the Underberg/ Himeville road just outside Himeville. The forest station is reached about 14 km further along this road.

The route to the Garden Castle access point and the Drakensberg Gardens Hotel is well signposted from Underberg. After following the Underberg/Swartberg road (R349) for about 4 km you must turn right onto a gravel road. The hotel is reached 29 km further on along this road, which ends a short distance further at the forest station.

From Underberg, the Bushman's Nek border post is reached by following the Swartberg road for about 5 km before turning right onto the Bushman's Nek road. After 25 km you will turn right, reaching the Bushman's Nek Hotel some 8 km further. The border post is situated a short way beyond the hotel.

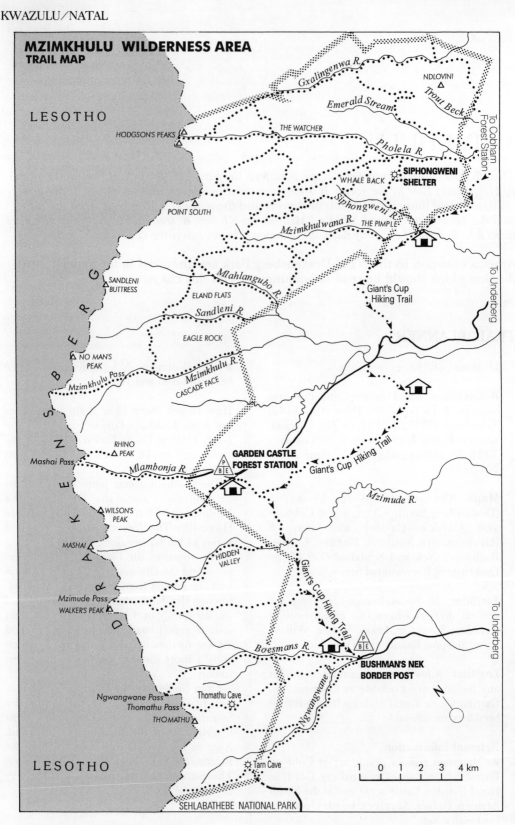

MZIMKHULU WILDERNESS AREA
TRAIL MAP

LESOTHO

Gxalingenwa R.

NDLOVINI

Emerald Stream

Trout Beck

To Cobham Forest Station

THE WATCHER

Pholela R.

HODGSON'S PEAKS

SIPHONGWENI SHELTER

WHALE BACK

Siphongweni R.

POINT SOUTH

Mzimkhulwana R.   THE PIMPLE

To Underberg

Giant's Cup Hiking Trail

SANDLENI BUTTRESS

Mlahlangubo R.

ELAND FLATS

Sandleni R.

EAGLE ROCK

NO MAN'S PEAK

Mzimkhulu Pass

Mzimkhulu R.

CASCADE FACE

RHINO PEAK

Mashai Pass

Mlambonja R.

GARDEN CASTLE FOREST STATION

Giant's Cup Hiking Trail

Mzimude R.

WILSON'S PEAK

MASHAI

HIDDEN VALLEY

Mzimude Pass

WALKER'S PEAK

Giant's Cup Hiking Trail

Boesmans R.

To Underberg

BUSHMAN'S NEK BORDER POST

Ngwangwane Pass
Thomathu Pass

Thomathu Cave

Ngwangwane R.

THOMATHU

LESOTHO

Tarn Cave

N

1 0 1 2 3 4 km

SEHLABATHEBE NATIONAL PARK

D R A K E N S B E R G

AREA DESCRIPTION

After stretching south-east for some 250 km, the escarpment swings sharply south-west at Sani Pass. Although the area lacks the prominent free-standing peaks of the Central and Northern Berg areas, several unusual buttresses and sandstone rock formations create impressive scenery.

Access to the greatest concentration of footpaths is from Cobham Forest Station – a convenient base for exploring areas such as Hodgson's Peaks, the Pholela River and Siphongweni Shelter and Rock.

Siphongweni Shelter is situated about 8 km from Cobham Forest Station and is reached by following the course of the Pholela River upstream for about 7 km before turning left. You will reach the shelter about 1 km further along this path. About two to three hours are required to reach the shelter which has been described as one of the best in the Drakensberg, taking into account the number of paintings, their good state of preservation and the interesting themes depicted. The reason for this is twofold: due to its remoteness the shelter was one of the last to be used by the San and for the same reason it has escaped the attention of vandals.

The shelter is perhaps best known for the scene depicting men spearing fish from small canoes. This painting is to the left of the cave and was much sharper when it was first pho-

tographed in 1907. The black pigment used by the San is, unfortunately, not as long-lasting as other pigments. This factor combined with exfoliation has resulted in the gradual fading and even disappearance of some of the paintings.

Routes and features to be explored from Garden Castle Forest Station include The Monk, the Hidden Valley and the Mashai Pass and Rhino Peak.

About 15 km south of Hodgson's Peaks is one of the most conspicuous peaks in the southern Drakensberg, the 3 051 m high Rhino Peak, which juts out approximately 2 km from the escarpment. Its Zulu name, *Ntabangcobo*, means the "rhino's horn peak". It is reached by following the well-defined Mashai Pass from Garden Castle Forest Station along the Mlambonja River Valley. About 2 km along this path you will reach Pillar Cave, which is often used as a base camp for excursions to the escarpment and can comfortably accommodate 12 people.

Over the next 3,5 km you will gain some 500 m in altitude, followed by another 400 m gain in height over the final 1,5 km. Once the escarpment is reached the path swings eastwards and about 2 km further on is Rhino Peak, which is easily ascended. To the south lie Wilson's Peak (3 276 m), Mashai (3 313 m), Walker's Peak (3 306 m), Thaba Ngwangwane (3 068 m), Thamathu (2 734 m) and the Devil's

Rhino Peak is a familiar landmark in the southern Drakensberg

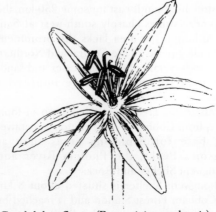

Candelabra flower (Brunsvigia natalensis)

Knuckles (3 028 m) which is also known as the Three Bushmen, Thaba-Ntsu or Baroa-Ba-Bararo.

From Garden Castle Forest Station to Rhino Peak you will gain some 1 200 m in altitude and, depending on your physical condition, about six hours are required for the ascent. The total distance is about 18 km and can be completed in a day, provided you make an early start.

South of Garden Castle the footpaths are restricted to a number of foot passes leading to the escarpment. They are the Mzimude, Ngwangwane and Thomathu passes.

The wilderness area borders on the north-western boundary of Lesotho's Sehlabathebe

National Park which can be reached along the Bushman's Nek Pass. The distance from the Bushman's Nek Police Post to Sehlabathebe Lodge is about 16 km.

The park has several rare and unusual features including weird sandstone formations, the *Aponogeton* waterlily, which is almost exclusively found in the rock pools of Sehlabathebe, and the Drakensberg minnow *(Pseudobarbus quathlambae)*, an endangered species which was rediscovered in 1970 in the Tsoelikane River after it was last seen in 1938. More than 60 rock painting sites have been recorded in the park and the stone shelters built in the natural recesses of overhangs by herdsmen are a familiar site in the park.

MKHOMAZI

This wilderness area in the central and southern Drakensberg stretches between Giant's Castle Nature Reserve in the north and Sani Pass in the south. Covering some 54 000 ha, it is traversed by deeply incised gorges and valleys that give the landscape a distinctly rugged appearance. The High Berg is not as accessible as other areas of the Berg and is consequently not as well known as the more popular areas further north.

Aspects common to the Natal Drakensberg Park are discussed in the general introduction which should be read in conjunction with this chapter.

TRAIL PLANNER

Distance The wilderness area is traversed by about 300 km of management paths with a further 165 km in adjoining areas.

Reservations The Forester, Highmoor Forest Station, P O Box 51, Rosetta 3301, Telephone (0333) 37240, or The Forester, Mkhomazi Forest Station, P O Box X105, via Nottingham Road 3280, Telephone (0333) 36444, depending on your point of entry.

Maps The area is covered by map 4 (Central Drakensberg – Highmoor, Mzimkulu and Loteni) and map 5 (Southern Drakensberg – Vergelegen, Cobham and Garden Castle) of the Drakensberg Recreational Series.

Facilities An informal campsite with a maximum of five sites, with basic ablution facilities, is situated at Highmoor Forest Station.

In the wilderness area there are several caves where you can overnight, including Caracal, Yellowwood, Ash, Runaway, Lotheni and Hlathimba caves, as well as Sinclair's Shelter.

Logistics Hutted accommodation outside the wilderness area is available at the Loteni and Vergelegen reserves. As accommodation at Vergelegen is limited, it is advisable to

book well in advance. Should you prefer to camp, this is possible at Loteni which has a campsite.

Enquiries for hutted accommodation should be directed to the Director, Natal Parks Board, P O Box 1750, Pietermaritzburg 3200, Telephone (0331) 47-1981, Fax (0331) 47-1980. Reservations for camping at Loteni must be made with the Camp Superintendent, Loteni Nature Reserve, P O Box 14, Himeville 4585, Telephone (033722) 1540.

Relevant information
■ Mountain register points are at the office in Loteni Reserve and at the Sani Pass Hotel. There are no registers at Highmoor Forest Station or Vergelegen Nature Reserve.

How to get there Highmoor Forest Station, the northernmost access point, is reached by following the signposted road from Rosetta to Kamberg Nature Reserve. About 30 km beyond Rosetta the route forks – keep to the right along the road which leads to Ntabamhlope. Almost immediately after this fork, you turn left. Continue along this road to Highmoor Forest Station, about 10 km further.

In the south the wilderness area can be approached from the Loteni and Vergelegen

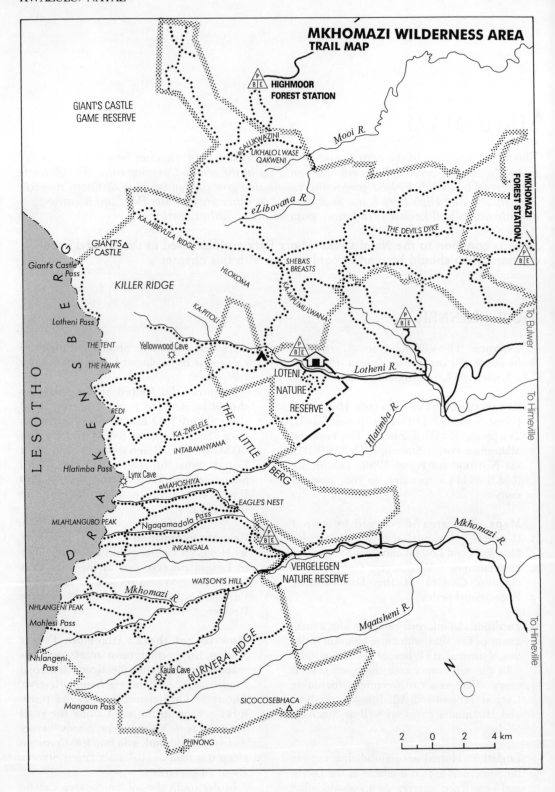

MKHOMAZI WILDERNESS AREA
TRAIL MAP

HIGHMOOR
FOREST STATION

MKHOMAZI FOREST STATION

GIANT'S CASTLE
GAME RESERVE

Mooi R.

eSALUKWAZINI

UKHALO LWASE
QAKWENI

eZibovana R.

THE DEVIL'S DYKE

KA-MBEVULA RIDGE

GIANT'S
CASTLE

Giant's Castle
Pass

KILLER RIDGE

HLOKOMA

SHEBA'S
BREASTS

Lotheni Pass

KA-PITOLI

KA-MPUMULWANA

THE TENT

Yellowwood Cave

THE HAWK

LOTENI

NATURE

RESERVE

Lotheni R.

REDI

KA-ZWELELE

iNTABAMNYAMA

Hlatimba R.

THE LITTLE BERG

Hlatimba Pass

Lynx Cave

eMAHOSHIYA

EAGLE'S NEST

MLAHLANGUBO PEAK

Ngaqamadola Pass

Mkhomazi R.

iNKANGALA

VERGELEGEN
NATURE RESERVE

WATSON'S HILL

NHLANGENI PEAK

Mkhomazi R.

Mgatsheni R.

Mohlesi Pass

BURNERA RIDGE

Nhlangeni
Pass

Kaula Cave

Mangaun Pass

SICOCOSEBHACA

PHINONG

LESOTHO

DRAKENSBERG

To Bulwer

To Himeville

To Himeville

N

2   0   2   4 km

nature reserves. The Loteni Nature Reserve is situated on the Nottingham Road/ Himeville road, the turn-off being signposted about 31 km north of Himeville and 63 km south of Nottingham Road. From the turn-off it is about 16 km to the rest camp.

Access to Vergelegen Nature Reserve is along the Nottingham/Himeville route. The turn-off to the reserve is about 15 km north of Himeville, the reserve being 34 km further along a well-signposted road.

AREA DESCRIPTION

Scenically the area is more rugged than the southern Drakensberg. The spurs of the Little Berg extend further east from the escarpment than they do further north and the area is characterised by numerous rivers which have carved deep valleys. Soaring buttresses and several unnamed peaks of over 3 000 m dominate the escarpment.

Despite the rugged nature of the area there are numerous footpaths, which are mainly restricted to the river valleys and the occasional spur. It is often necessary to boulder-hop up a valley to reach higher ground from where you can enjoy beautiful views of the escarpment. The main access routes to the escarpment are via the Hlatimba, Mlahlangubo, Nhlangeni and Mangaun passes.

Although the terrain lends itself mainly to one- or two-day hikes, it is possible to undertake a four-day traverse to Sani Pass.

The first day's hike initially takes you along the Lotheni River Valley which was used as early as 1847 by San stock raiders, who descended from Lesotho via the Hlathimba Pass and raided farms in the foothills of the Berg. To escape their pursuers they then drove their booty up the tributaries of the Lotheni River.

A painting in the upper reaches of the Lotheni River depicts a commando of 22 horsemen and from the close resemblance between this scene and historic documents it has been suggested that the artist was depicting the Harding Commando, which pursued a group of San up the valley in January 1847.

After following the Lotheni River upstream for about 5 km you will take the left-hand path which ascends along the Ka-Mosihlengo River to the contour path, passing Yellowwood Cave. Follow the contour path for 4 km to a four-way intersection just below Redi Pass where there is a suitable overnight spot. The day's hike covers 14 km and you will gain some 850 m in altitude.

The second day's hike continues along the contour path for about 5,5 km before ascending steeply along the Hlatimba Pass to the escarpment.

The pass was the site of the historic Langalibalele "Rebellion" of 1873. Following the refusal of the Hlubi chief, Langalibalele, to register his people's firearms and to report in Pietermaritzburg, the Natal Government decided to seal the passes over the Drakensberg to prevent him from fleeing to Basutoland.

Major Anthony Durnford of the Carbineers was detailed to ascend the escarpment via Giant's Castle Pass, but he took the Hlatimba Pass by mistake. When they arrived at the head of the Bushman's River Pass on the morning of 4 November 1873 the Hlubi were already in possession and in the ensuing skirmish three Carbineers and two black helpers were killed.

From the top of the pass you will follow the escarpment in a southerly direction for about 1 km to Lynx Cave, which can accommodate six people. The second day's hike covers 8,5 km and you will gain nearly 500 m in altitude.

On the third day you will follow the escarpment in a south-westerly direction to reach the head of the Mlahlangubo Pass after about 1 km. The route takes you down the pass and you will lose some 600 m in altitude before joining the contour path. Turn right and, less than 1 km further on, right again, following a winding path below Mlahlangubo Peak for about 2 km before crossing the first Ngaqamadolo Pass. About 1 km onwards the second pass is reached, but you will continue along the footpath in a westerly direction, passing the Rock Arch and crossing numerous streams below The Saddle. Ignore the turn-off to the Mkhomazi River 4 km later and continue for another 2 km to the Mkhomazi Pass which is reached 14 km beyond Lynx Cave. Depending on how fit you are you can either pitch camp here or continue to the Nhlangeni River which is another 5 km further.

If you opt to camp at the Mkhomazi River junction, Kaula Cave is probably the best spot

Fruit and male catkins of (left) the Outeniqua yellowwood and (right) the real yellowwood

to break the remaining 25 km into two more manageable days.

From the Nhlangeni River you will head for a sulphur spring which is reached 2 km further on and you will no doubt find the thermal water very therapeutic. Continue up the ka-Ntuba River Valley for 3 km before turning left to reach the Burnera Ridge junction 5 km further. Turn right here and, after about 1 km turn left,

following a path below The Pillars to reach Koko Tabagi Ridge 4 km beyond the previous junction. Here you will cross into the Mzimkhulwana Nature Reserve and after traversing below the Twelve Apostles for about 6 km you will cross the Mkhomazana or Little Mkhomazi River shortly before joining the Sani Pass road. The junction is about 4 km beyond the South African Police Services post.

GIANT'S CASTLE

The pristine beauty of this Central Drakensberg reserve can only be appreciated on horseback or on foot. Situated on a grassy plateau among deep valleys below the sheer cliffs of the Drakensberg, Giant's Castle Game Reserve is a backpacker's paradise. The reserve is criss-crossed by a network of paths and riding trails, providing both the serious backpacker and the casual day walker with numerous options. You might be fortunate enough to spot the rare bearded vulture or one of the large herds of eland, while the numerous rock paintings are another attraction.

Aspects common to the Natal Drakensberg Park are discussed in the general introduction which should be read in conjunction with this chapter.

TRAIL PLANNER

Distance The reserve is traversed by about 285 km of footpaths.

Reservations The Officer-in-Charge, Giant's Castle Game Reserve, Private Bag X7055, Estcourt 3310, Telephone (0363) 2-4617.

Maps The area is covered by map 3 (Central Drakensberg – Injasuti to Highmoor) of the Drakensberg Recreational Series.

Facilities There are four mountain huts as well as a few caves in the reserve where backpackers can overnight. The huts are equipped with bunks, a gas stove, pots and a flush toilet. Reservations for the mountain huts and caves should be made with the Officer-in-Charge of the reserve.

Accommodation at Giant's Castle Camp consists of self-contained cottages and bungalows. Visitors must supply their own food which is prepared by a cook assigned to each hut. Hutted accommodation and camping facilities are available in the Injasuti Camp in the northern section of the reserve, while camping is also permitted at Hillside, some 30 km from the main camp. Hutted accommodation must be reserved with the Reservations Officer, P O Box 1750, Pietermaritzburg 3200, Telephone (0331) 47-1981, Fax (0331) 47-1980.

Campsites at Injasuti and Hillside must be reserved through the Camp Manager, Injasuti Camp, Private Bag 7010, Estcourt 3310, Telephone (036) 488-1050 or The Warden, Hillside, P O Box 288, Estcourt 3310, Telephone (0363) 2-4435.

Relevant information
■ Mountain register points are located at Injasuti Camp and the warden's office at Giant's Castle Camp.
■ Fires are not allowed at the huts or caves and you must carry a backpacking stove.
■ A daypack is useful if you use the Giant's Castle Hut as a base for a day hike to Giant's Castle.

How to get there The reserve can be approached from either Estcourt or Mooi River. From Estcourt you follow the signpost to Ntabamhlope, turning left at the White Mountain Resort after about 35 km. Continue for another 12 km until the Mooi River/Giant's Castle Road is reached. Turn right and continue for 19 km to the reserve office.

From Mooi River you take the road signposted to Giant's Castle. After about 37 km turn right onto the Ntabamhlope/Kamberg Road which you follow for about 12 km to the turn-off to the Giant's Castle Game Reserve. From here it is 19 km to the reserve office.

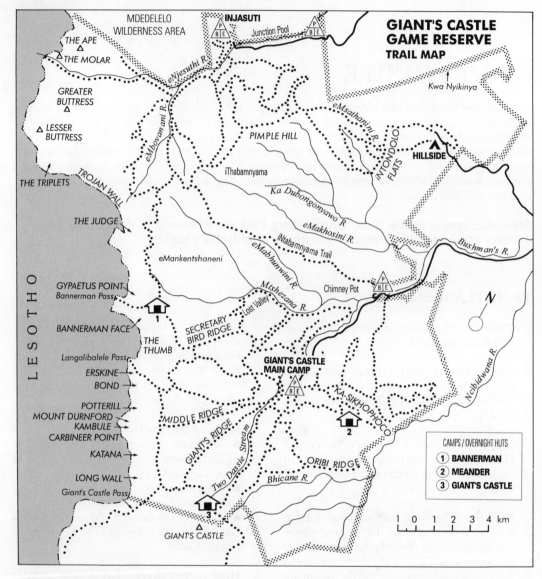

GIANT'S CASTLE
GAME RESERVE
TRAIL MAP

TRAIL DESCRIPTION

A four-day circular route, incorporating two of the mountain huts, is described here, but this can be varied, depending on the time available.

Day 1: Giant's Castle Rest Camp to Giant's Castle Hut via Two Dassie Stream From the camp you must follow the path signposted to Main Caves and after about 1,5 km the path winds downhill to an outcrop of boulders. The boulders mark the spot where a detachment of the 75th Regiment of Foot, commanded by Major Anthony Durnford, established a base camp in 1874 while they were engaged in blow-

ing up the entrances to the passes between Oliviershoek and Giant's Castle. These passes were used by cattle rustlers and raiders and for a long time were a thorn in the flesh of the Natal Government. The figure 75 was carved into one of the boulders, reputedly by the cook of the 75th Regiment.

The path crosses a footbridge and rises steeply to the Main Caves Museum which has been fenced off. A game guard is on duty between 08:30 and 16:30 and a small entry fee is payable to view the paintings. A tape recorded commentary on the San, their paintings, culture and history is played hourly. Displayed in the museum is a realistic model of the way of life of the San, as well as replicas of artefacts and a stratigraphical reconstruction of the excavations of a hearth-site.

Considering the quality and quantity of rock paintings occurring in the reserve, it has been suggested that it is one of the richest rock art areas in the world. To date more than 50 sites, with a total of more than 5 000 individual paintings, have been recorded in the reserve. The Main Caves contain more than 540 individual paintings.

From the caves a path leads down to the Main Caves Forest, where you will pass through a small patch of forest and join the Giant's Castle route. Two Dassie Stream is crossed several times before you cross over to the right, where you will remain until the stream splits. Although the first section of the route is level and fairly easy going, you will nevertheless appreciate the few inviting pools for cooling off. Several boggy areas then have to be crossed, making the going difficult, and as a result of the intervening ridges your view will be limited.

After the stream splits you have a fairly steep climb ahead of you and you'll gain some 250 m in altitude before the path levels off just before joining the contour path. Giant's Castle Hut, a beautiful stone hut with a thatched roof, is situated in unsurpassed surroundings a short distance to the west along the contour path. The total distance covered is about 10 km.

Looming behind the hut is the prominent Giant's Castle (3 314 m), which is known to the Zulu as iNtabayikonjwa. There are several explanations of the meaning of the name, one being that pointing at the mountain is disrespectful and that the mountain will respond by bringing bad weather.

Day 2: Giant's Castle Peak Day Hike Giant's Castle Hut is ideally situated if you intend to climb the peak. The total distance covered is about 18 km and you should allow eight to nine hours.

From the hut you will follow the contour path for about 2 km, initially in a northerly and then in a westerly direction before it is joined by the Giant's Ridge path. Another 2 km further on the contour path brings you to the foot of the Giant's Castle Pass which was probably the route followed by the party of six who made the first recorded ascent of the Giant in 1864. You will continue up the pass for about 2 km, gaining some 770 m in altitude. The final section of the pass is steep and you must be careful of landslides. Avoid gullies branching off to the left as they are impassable.

From the top of the pass you will gain some 230 m in altitude to the summit of Giant's Castle which lies about 2,8 km east of the pass. You will return along the same route to Giant's Castle Hut.

Day 3: Giant's Castle Hut to Bannerman Hut
From Giant's Castle it is about 17,5 km to Bannerman Hut. The contour path traverses the reserve at an altitude of about 2 300 m and except for crossing numerous mountain streams where the terrain becomes more demanding, the walk is fairly easy.

After leaving Giant's Castle Hut, the foot of Giant's Castle Pass is reached after 4 km and the contour path then swings in a north-westerly direction. Several streams have to be crossed and this may slow you down. Take your time, though, and enjoy the superb scenery.

To the left of the path several prominent peaks tower above the escarpment. The Long Wall (3 114 m) is the first to be passed, followed by Katana (3 072 m), Carbineer Point (3 154 m), Kambule, Mount Durnford, Potterill (3 159 m), Bond (3 153 m) and Erskine. Far below you in the foothills several other landmarks can be distinguished, including World's View, Oribi Ridge and the Chimney Pot.

About 7 km after setting off the contour path is joined by the Middle Ridge route and about 2,5 km further on you will reach the base of Langalibalele Pass. At least six hours should be allowed for the ascent and descent of the pass, which is about 3 km long, rising almost 700 m over this distance. A simple stone cairn at the top of the pass marks the graves of Erskin, Bond and Potterhill and two local blacks, Kambule and Katana. It was here that Major Durnford's forces were put to flight by Chief Langalibalele's Hlubi on 4 November 1873. Five of the peaks passed earlier were named in honour of the men killed during the skirmish.

You will continue along the contour path for a further 1 km, where it is joined by the direct route between Giant's Castle Main Camp and Langalibalele Pass. About 2,5 km further on you will pass another junction, reaching a tarn 0,5 km onwards. The path then traverses below the Thumb and Bannerman's Face, which, as its

BEARDED VULTURE

Gypaetus Point, north of Bannerman Pass, is named after the bearded vulture. The bristly "beard" of black feathers on the chin gave rise to the common name of the vulture as well as the species name *barbatus*. The bearded vulture is easily recognised by its wedge-shaped tail. It has a wingspan of 2,5 to 3 m and is extremely powerful on the wing with gliding speeds of around 105 km per hour.

Close-up of head of bearded vulture showing "beard"

Historically they occurred from Cape Town along the mountains of the east coast and the Drakensberg as far as Lydenburg in the eastern Transvaal. In southern Africa the total population is only about 630 birds, while the number of breeding pairs is estimated at just over 200. Some 122 breeding pairs have been recorded in Lesotho and 37 in the Natal Drakensberg, with smaller numbers occurring in Transkei, Griqualand East and the eastern Orange Free State. Their decline is due to several factors such as better stock management which has resulted in a shortage of carcasses, poisoned meat put out by farmers to eradicate jackal and other problem animals and persecution by local tribesmen.

Bearded vulture also occur in Kenya, Ethiopia, Egypt, the Sinai Peninsula, southern Arabia, Spain, Greece, the Balkan states and eastwards as far as western China. Breeding populations of the European race have been exterminated completely in the Swiss Alps, Bavaria and the Carpathian Mountains.

These highly evolved specialist birds have features of both eagles and vultures and as such have defied classification for a long time. The beak is like that of an eagle, while the long curved claws are vulture-like. Unlike vultures, however, there is no evidence of a large crop for the storage and transport of food, despite the fact that they feed almost exclusively on carrion.

The major part of their diet consists of bone and they are able to swallow bones as large as the thigh-bone of a lamb. Large bones are dropped onto rock slabs - known as ossuaries - from a height of 30 to 40 m, with drops of over 100 m having been recorded. This accounts for the Greek name *ossfractus* - "the bone breaker".

Marrow is extracted from the bones with their specially adapted tongues. Unlike other birds of prey, for example the owl, they digest all their food with exceptionally strong gastric juices and no indigestible lumps are regurgitated.

---

name suggests, resembles the profile of Sir Henry Campbell-Bannerman, British Prime Minister from 1905 to 1908.

The hut is situated at the foot of Bannerman Pass, which is about 3 km long and the ascent requires about two and a half hours. The path is generally well defined with cairns indicating the route in the more difficult places, but boulder scree makes the ascent tricky in the steepest section. From the top of the pass (3 050 m) a short walk along the escarpment brings you to the cairn marking the top of Bannerman Face (3 070 m).

Day 4: Bannerman Hut to Giant's Castle Main Camp From Bannerman Hut you can either continue along the contour path to the Injasuti Valley, roughly 18 km further, or you

can return to Giant's Castle Main Camp. Transport arrangements usually dictate the latter option, which is described here.

Set off by retracing the previous day's hike. After 4 km you will reach a turn-off at a small tarn. You can turn left here, in which case you will descend along Secretary Bird Ridge for 3 km to a T-junction where you turn right. Over the next 5,5 km you will lose some 280 m in altitude to the Bushman's River and after crossing the river it is only a short walk back to the rest camp.

A more direct route is to continue along the contour path for 0,5 km beyond the Secretary Bird Ridge turn-off. Turn left here to reach the Bushman's River 6 km further on. The rest camp is a short distance further on.

MDEDELELO

This 29 000 ha wilderness area takes its name from the Zulu name for Cathkin Peak. The area is characterised by deep valleys and imposing peaks with familiar landmarks such as Champagne Castle, Gatberg and the Dragon's Back – an impressive range of free-standing block-shaped peaks. A contour path links the wilderness area in the north with Ndedema Gorge with its wealth of rock paintings, as well as Cathedral Peak State Forest, and in the south with Giant's Castle Game Reserve.

Aspects common to the Natal Drakensberg Park are discussed in the general introduction which should be read in conjunction with this chapter.

TRAIL PLANNER

Distance The wilderness area is traversed by about 185 km of footpaths.

Reservations The Forester, Monk's Cowl Forest Station, Private Bag X2, Winterton 3340, Telephone (036) 468-1103 or The Forester, Cathedral Peak Forest Station, Private Bag X1, Winterton 3340, Telephone (036) 488-1880, depending on your starting point.

Maps The area is covered by map 2 in the Drakensberg Recreational Series: Drakensberg North – Cathedral Peak to Injasuti.

Relevant information
■ There are mountain register points at Injasuti Camp, Mike's Pass Gate (Cathedral Peak) and Monk's Cowl Forest Station.

Facilities At Monk's Cowl there is a pleas-ant campsite with ablution facilities. Access to the campsite remains open until 18:00 on Fridays to accommodate late arrivals.

In the wilderness area you may camp in the Twins, Nkosazana, Stable and Cowl caves which can be reserved on arrival at Monk's Cowl for the exclusive use of a party.

How to get there The main access point is from Monk's Cowl, but it is also possible to enter from Injasuti in the south and Cathedral Peak to the north.

From Bergville you must turn right onto the road signposted Cathedral Peak shortly after crossing the Tugela River, east of the town. After about 14 km the Cathedral Peak turn-off is reached but you will continue for another 13 km until turning right onto the road signposted Cathkin Peak, Dragon Peaks, Champagne Castle. The Monk's Cowl Forest Station is reached after roughly 21,5 km.

AREA DESCRIPTION

One of the most popular routes onto the Little Berg from Monk's Cowl Forest Station is via the Sphinx and Verkykerskop. This is the usual route onto the contour path and hence also to the higher peaks and passes.

Dominating the scenery is Cathkin Peak (3 149 m), from which the area derives its Zulu name, Mdedelelo. The name is translated as "make room for him" and refers to the prominent position of Cathkin which seemingly

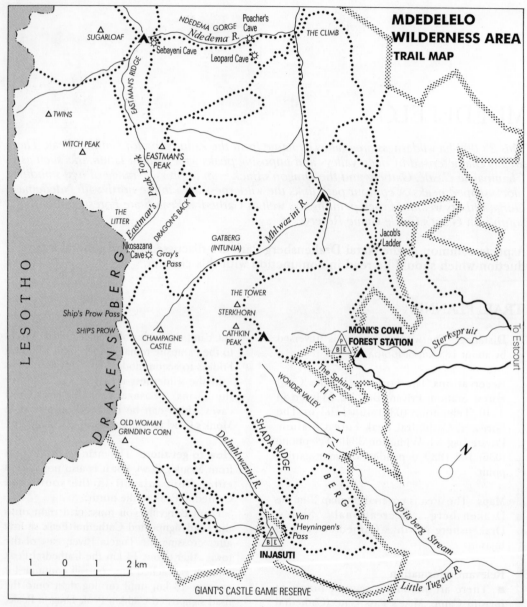

MDEDELELO WILDERNESS AREA
TRAIL MAP

pushed the other peaks aside to make room for itself.

To the north of Cathkin is another well-known peak, Sterkhorn (2 973 m), also known as Mount Memory. Further north is The Tower (2 670 m) and the Amphlett (2 620 m). Although Champagne Castle (3 377 m) can lay claim to being the second highest peak in South Africa, it is almost completely obscured by Cathkin Peak when approached from this direction.

The contour path is reached about 5,5 km from Monk's Cowl Forest Station and provides

access to either the south-eastern parts of Mdedelelo or the north-western parts of the wilderness area. Construction of the contour path to link the Cathkin and Cathedral Peak areas began in 1937 under the guidance of Mr J van Heyningen, the forester-in-charge of Monk's Cowl at the time. The path was subsequently extended.

By following the path to the left you can backpack to Injasuti, some 21 km to the south-east. The right-hand route leads to Ndedema Gorge and further afield to the Organ Pipes and to just below Cathedral Peak. Hlatikulu Nek is

The Cathkin Range. Cathkin Peak (on the left) is also known as Mdedelelo

reached after 2,5 km and here you can turn right if you wish to explore the north-eastern part of Mdedelelo. This area offers several options, including the Mhlwazini River Valley, the Valley of the Pools in the Nkwazi River and Eland Cave which has the largest number of paintings of any cave in the Drakensberg.

The cave is not indicated on the map and you will have to obtain the necessary directions from the forester at Monk's Cowl. The cave takes its name from the group of eland near the centre of the frieze which contains more than 1 600 individual paintings. A large eland, measuring nearly 1 m in length, was superimposed on human figures, as well as a roan – an animal rarely portrayed in rock paintings. Other paintings include bushpig, running human figures, two figures with the appearance of winged buck and what is thought to be a beehive with bees.

Should you continue along the contour path, the turn-off to Gray's Pass is reached on your left 1,5 km further on. This path brings you to Keith Bush Camp, a beautiful campsite surrounded by cliffs on three sides at the head of the Mhlawazini River, about 4 km beyond the turn-off. Between Monk's Cowl Forest Station and Keith Bush Camp, a distance of approximately 13,5 km, you will gain some 870 m in altitude and, depending on your physical condition, about six to seven and a half hours will be required.

Gray's Pass is the most popular route to the escarpment in the area and, although it is only 2,5 km long, you will gain roughly 700 m in altitude. The ascent starts a short distance above the camp and as you gain height you will have your first uninterrupted view of Monk's Cowl (3 234 m). It is one of the most challenging peaks in the Drakensberg with some G-grade rock climbs and it was not until 1942 that it was successfully scaled.

Nkosazana Cave near the top of the pass is a good place to spend the night on the escarpment. It is situated next to a perennial stream which sometimes flows through the cave in summer, limiting accommodation to about four people. During winter the cave can accommodate up to 10 people, but could be iced up after heavy snowfalls.

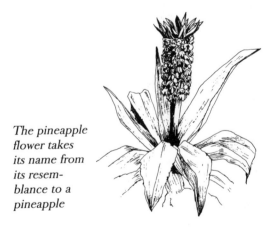

The pineapple flower takes its name from its resemblance to a pineapple

From the top of the pass it is an easy walk of about 3 km to Champagne Castle (3 377 m). You can either return via Gray's Pass, or descend along Ship's Prow Pass, south of Champagne Castle. The descent immediately south of Champagne Castle is extremely dangerous and should not be used under any circumstances. Continue heading south instead for about 1 km where the easier descent of about 4,5 km to the contour path commences.

Another backpacking option is to follow the contour path to Ndedema Gorge, which is about 28 km from Monk's Cowl Forest Station. An impressive sight along this route is Gatberg – a peak with an enormous hole through its base. The Zulu name of this unusual formation, *Intunja*, is translated as "the eye of the needle" and "the hole in the mountain through which the shepherds can creep".

The gaping hole through the basalt has a diameter of about 9 m. Also conspicuous is the Dragon's Back, a spur of free-standing, block-shaped peaks extending from the escarpment and Eastman's Peak and Ridge.

Although a contour path is theoretically followed, this is a strenuous walk which takes you through the Mhlawazini and Nkosazana river valleys with long downhills followed by steep ascents. Some 400 m in altitude are lost over the last 4 km to Ndedema Gorge.

CATHEDRAL PEAK

The Cathedral range, with its numerous free-standing peaks and magnificent mountain scenery, is one of the most favoured parts of the Berg for backpacking and rock-climbing. Bordered in the north and north-west by the Upper Tugela Location and in the south by the Mdedelelo Wilderness, the area is dominated by the spire-like Cathedral Peak after which it is named. Popular routes include Cathedral Peak itself, the Organ Pipes and Ndedema Gorge with its wealth of rock paintings.

Aspects common to the Natal Drakensberg Park are discussed in the general introduction which should be read in conjunction with this chapter.

TRAIL PLANNER

Distance You have a choice of roughly 120 km of footpaths in the Cathedral Peak State Forest and the Mlambonja Wilderness Area.

Reservations The Forester, Cathedral Peak Forest Station, Private Bag X1, Winterton 3340, Telephone (036) 488-1880.

Maps The area is covered by map 2 in the Drakensberg Recreational Series: Drakensberg North – Cathedral Peak to Injasuti.

Facilities A campsite with ablution facilities is situated a short way below the Cathedral Peak Forest Station.
  The following rock shelters can be reserved upon arrival: Ndumeni, Barker's Chalet, Bell, Ribbon Falls, Schoongezicht, Xeni, Zunkels, Drip, Leopard, Sherman's and Outer Horn caves.

Relevant information
■ The mountain register point is at Mike's Pass Gate near the Cathedral Peak Forest Station.
■ The Cathedral Peak Hotel is out of bounds to backpackers unless you have reserved accommodation.

How to get there Approaching from Bergville, turn right onto the road signposted Cathedral Peak shortly after crossing the Tugela River, east of Bergville. About 14 km further, turn right again, continuing for about 30 km to the Cathedral Peak Forest Station and campsite.

AREA DESCRIPTION

The scenery of this area is dominated by the massive Cathedral range, also known as the Ridge of the Horns. This 4 km-long row of free-standing peaks includes some of the most spectacular peaks in South Africa such as Cathedral Peak (3 004 m), Bell (2 930 m), Outer Horn (3 005 m), Inner Horn (3 005 m) and the Chessmen. Two other well-known spectacular free-standing peaks, the Column (2 926 m) and Pyramid (2 914 m) are situated south-west of Cathedral Peak Forest Station.
  The peaks of the escarpment here are all over 3 000 m and include names like Ndumeni Dome (3 206 m), Castle Buttress (3 053 m),

229

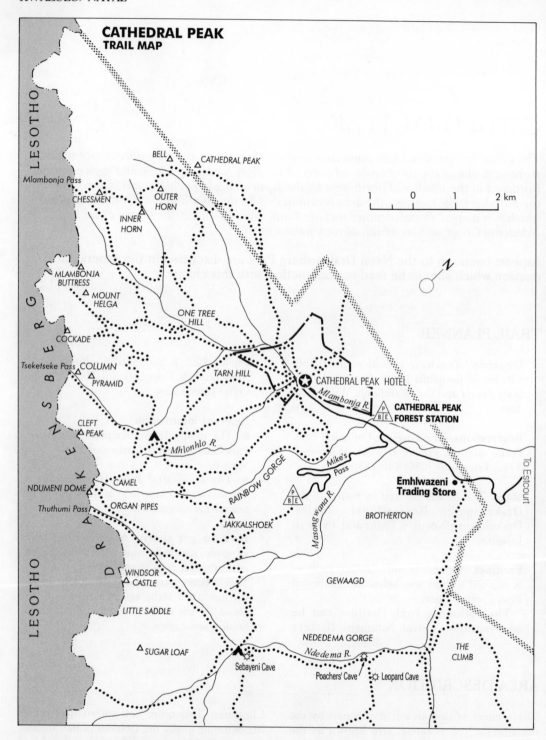

CATHEDRAL PEAK
TRAIL MAP

LESOTHO

Mlambonja Pass

BELL

CATHEDRAL PEAK

CHESSMEN

OUTER
HORN

INNER
HORN

1 0 1 2 km

MLAMBONJA
BUTTRESS

MOUNT
HELGA

ONE TREE
HILL

COCKADE

Tseketseke Pass COLUMN

PYRAMID

TARN HILL

CATHEDRAL PEAK HOTEL

Mlambonja R.

CATHEDRAL PEAK
FOREST STATION

CLEFT
PEAK

Mhlonhlo R.

Mike's
Pass

NDUMENI DOME

CAMEL

RAINBOW GORGE

ORGAN PIPES

Thuthumi Pass

JAKKALSHOEK

Masongwana R.

Emhlwazeni
Trading Store

BROTHERTON

WINDSOR
CASTLE

LITTLE SADDLE

GEWAAGD

THE
CLIMB

SUGAR LOAF

NEDEDEMA GORGE

Ndedema R.

Sebayeni Cave

Poachers' Cave

Leopard Cave

LESOTHO

DRAKENSBERG

To Estcourt

Cleft Peak (3 281 m), Cockade (3 161 m), Elephant (3 109 m) and Mlambonja Buttress (3 007 m). Access to the escarpment is along any of a number of passes, the more popular being the Organ Pipes, the Camel and the Thuthumi passes.

One of the most popular excursions in this part of the Berg is an ascent of Cathedral Peak.

Approximately eight to nine hours should be allowed for this fairly strenuous round trip of about 18 km. The final section involves a C grade scramble and is, therefore, not recommended for inexperienced backpackers. On a clear day the view from the summit is magnificent with Cathkin Peak in the south and Eastern Buttress in the north clearly visible. Immediately below you, to the south-east, the scenery is dominated by the deep valley carved by the Mlambonja River.

Cathedral Peak is the only Berg area where you can drive to the top of the Little Berg, bringing you much closer to the escarpment. Access to the Little Berg is via Mike's Pass, a 10,5 km-long jeep track which was built between 1947 and 1949 by an Italian road engineer, G R Monzali. The pass, which climbs some 500 m, ends at the Arendsig gate and was named after Mike de Villiers, the forestry research officer at the time who played a major role in establishing the Cathedral Peak research station and having the pass built. The Arendsig Gate is the starting point of routes to the renowned Ndedema Gorge, the Organ Pipes and the escarpment.

The head of the Ndedema Valley is about 10 km from the Arendsig Gate along easy terrain. The gorge has been described by the international authority on rock art, the late Harald Pager, as the richest rock art area in the world. During his survey of the area, Pager recorded over 3 900 individual rock paintings in 17 shelters and published his research findings and lifelike tracings in the classical work *Ndedema*.

Sebayeni Cave is the first shelter in the sandstone band on the southern side of the valley. It is the largest of the painted shelters in the gorge, containing more than 1 100 individual paintings, a large number of which have unfortunately faded. The site was first discovered by the Frobenius expedition in 1929 but was "lost" for a number of years before it was "rediscovered" by the late Alex Willcox, an authority on the rock art of South Africa.

One of the most interesting scenes in the shelter is that of 30 antelope-headed figures. It was initially suggested that they represented "foreigners" from the Mediterranean, but it is now believed that these paintings depicted the visions of medicine people, or *shamans* in trance. Several hundred human figures are also depicted, including running figures, most of them with bows, a white animal superimposed

Sebayeni Cave is renowned for its rock paintings

on a row of women and two strange beings with animal ears.

Ndedema means "place of reverberations", a likely reference to the thundering noise caused by the river when in flood. A footpath follows the upper edge of the gorge for about 5 km, giving you splendid views of the extensive yellowwood forests on the south-facing slope. The footpath then descends into the forest and in this vicinity there are two shelters, Poacher's Cave and Leopard Cave, with rock paintings where backpackers may overnight.

Poacher's Cave on the southern slopes of the gorge contains more than 200 individual paintings and is one of the few shelters in the Berg depicting reclining rhebok. Other paintings include a swarm of bees, some of them in two colours, and numerous human figures in various poses, including a hunting scene.

The turn-off to Leopard Cave, which can sleep about 12 people, is reached shortly before you start descending into Ndedema Gorge. After turning right you will continue for about 1 km before reaching the cave, which faces south-west. The cave takes its name from a painting which depicts a man being chased by a cat-like figure, presumably a leopard. There are well over 100 paintings, mainly of human figures but also of eland, bushbuck and rhebok, but unfortunately they are mainly fragmentary.

Another popular route is to ascend the escarpment via the Organ Pipes Pass, the start of which is signposted some 2,5 km before you reach Ndedema Gorge. Over the next 6,5 km you will gain more than 900 m in altitude, passing an assembly of spires and buttresses known to the Zulu as *Qolo la Masoja*, the "Ridge of the Soldiers". It has been suggested that the name could be a reference to the fluted columns which could conjure up visions of a regiment of soldiers standing to attention or could be derived from a tradition which associated it with military action. The columns echo when you shout or yodel and this natural phenomenon was used to maintain contact between the Zulu and the Basotho. One such instance was in 1823 when the Basotho sought the help of Shaka.

49 The rockslide passed on the first day of the Mountain Zebra Hiking Trail, part of which can be hiked as a day walk
50 The second day's hike of the Mountain Zebra Hiking Trail leads past massive sheets of dolerite

▲ 49

50 ▼

51 Log footbridge on the first leg of the Amatola Hiking Trail
52 Historic Doornhoek farmhouse on the last day of the Mountain Zebra Hiking Trail
53 Hiking along a forestry road through pine plantations on the Amatola Hiking Trail
54 Hole in the Wall, seen on the first day's hike of the Transkei Hiking Trail between Coffee Bay and Mbashe River

▲ 51   52 ▼

▲ 55

55 Beach walking between Coffee Bay and Mbashe River, Transkei Hiking Trail
56 Crossing the Xora River on the third day of the Coffee Bay to Mbashe River section of the Transkei Hiking Trail
57 The section of the Transkei Hiking Trail between Port St John's and Coffee Bay leads past numerous small rural villages
58 The Transkei Hiking Trail takes hikers along unspoilt beaches and secluded bays
59 Crossing a small stream on the Msikaba to Port St John's section of the Transkei Hiking Trail

▲ 56   57 ▼

◀ 60   ▲ 61   62 ▼

60 Rugged coastal scenery from Waterfall Bluff, Transkei Hiking Trail
61 The Mlambomkulu Waterfall, one of only a few waterfalls in the world which cascade directly into the sea
62 Pholela Hut, the first overnight stop on the Giant's Cup Hiking Trail

▲ 63

63 Bathplug Cave on the Giant's Cup Hiking Trail
64 Typical scenery in the foothills of the southern Drakensberg – Giant's Cup Hiking Trail

64 ▼

▲ 65   66 ▼

65 The 3 314 metre high Giant's Castle dominates the scenery in the central Drakensberg
66 Dragon's Back, a prominent range of block-shaped peaks in the Mdedelelo Wilderness Area

▲ 67   68 ▼

▼ 69   70 ▶

67 Rock paintings, Sebayeni Cave, Cathedral
Peak State Forest
68 Cathedral Peak Range − left to right, Inner
Horn, Outer Horn, Bell and Cathedral Peak
69 Natal bottlebrush, Natal Drakensberg
70 Backpacking on the contour path in the
Mdedelelo Wilderness Area

◀ 71

72 ▲

73 ▲

71 The Tugela Falls as it cascades 850 metres down the Drakensberg escarpment
72 Pools in the Tugela River just before the river plunges over the sheer cliffs of the Amphitheatre
73 Scaling the chain-ladder which give access to the top of the Amphitheatre and Mont-aux-Sources
74 The indigenous forests of Ntendeka are rated among the most beautiful in Zululand

◀ 74

▲ 75

▲ 76

77 ▼

75 Strangler Fig, Ntendeka Wilderness Area
76 Waterfall on the first day of the Koranna
Hiking Trail
77 Hiking through grasslands on the Koranna
Hiking Trail in the eastern Free State
78 Salpeterkrans, the largest overhang in the
southern hemisphere, is one of the highlights of
the Brandwater Hiking Trail
79 The fourth day's hike of the Brandwater
Hiking Trail partly follows the course of the Little
Caledon River

▲ 78   79 ▼

80 The second day's route of the Rhebok Hiking Trail leads to Generaalskop, the highest point in the park
81 The Mushroom Rocks – one of the many outstanding rock formations in the Golden Gate National Park

MZIKI

This trail in the Greater St Lucia Wetland Park is named after the Zulu word for the reedbuck and winds through one of the most remarkable areas in Africa. Situated at the southernmost limit of the true tropical zone, it boasts a wealth of plant and animal life from both the tropical and the subtropical regions. The route winds through a rich variety of vegetation types such as open grassland and coastal forests and offers splendid views of the Indian Ocean and the St Lucia Complex.

TRAIL PLANNER

Distance 38 km; 3 days

Grading A

Reservations The Reservations Officer, Natal Parks Board, P O Box 1750, Pietermaritzburg 3200, Telephone (0331) 47-1981, Fax (0331) 47-1980. Reservations are accepted up to nine months in advance.

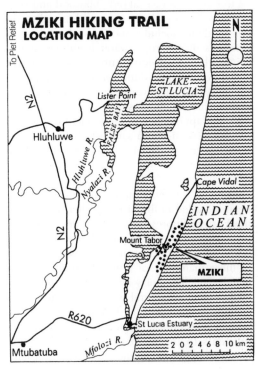

Climate

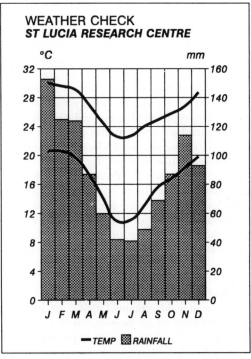

Group size Minimum 2; Maximum 8

Maps A sketch map of the trail is included in the trail pamphlet which is forwarded with your receipt and permit.

Facilities Accommodation at Mount Tabor Base Camp is provided in a stone hut equipped with bunks with mattresses, a table, benches, lamps, a two-plate gas cooker and eating utensils. Water is provided, as well as a primitive shower and a toilet.

Logistics Three day walks are undertaken from the base camp. Mount Tabor is about 2 km from the Mission Rocks Outpost where vehicles are left, and all equipment and food must be carried to the base camp.

Relevant information

■ You must report to the Trails Officer at the Mission Rocks Outpost between 14:00 and 16:00 on the day for which you have made a reservation.
■ You are advised to take anti-malaria precautions.
■ Swimming and wading is not permitted

in the lake owing to the presence of crocodiles and sharks.
■ During high tide it is extremely difficult to hike along the coast and the two trails which return to Mount Tabor along the coast should ideally be hiked at low tide, making a tide table useful.

How to get there The trail starts at the Mission Rocks Outpost in the Eastern Shores Nature Reserve of the Greater St Lucia Park. The starting point is reached by turning north onto the Cape Vidal/Mission Rocks road at the T-junction near the entrance to St Lucia village. After approximately 14 km the Mission Rocks outpost is signposted to the right, with the outpost being a short distance further along the road.

TRAIL ENVIRONMENT

Flora The vegetation of Lake St Lucia consists of coastal forest and thornveld and the trails wind through four vegetation communities. Some of the trees along the trail have been marked with the *National List of Indigenous Trees* numbers and interesting information on these trees is provided in the trail pamphlet.

The **grassland** and **Umdoni parkland** consist of open, rolling grassland which constitutes the major vegetation type of the Eastern Shores Nature Reserve. As the Zulu name implies, the *Umdoni* or water berry is the most dominant species. Other species occurring among the occasional clumps of lala palms and trees are the common coral tree, marula and the Lowveld mangosteen. This habitat is of particular importance as a feeding ground for hippo and also supports a high reedbuck population.

Swamp forests are found along the edge of the lake and the streams feeding the lake and are characterised by large-leafed trees such as the swamp fig, which play an important role in reducing evaporation. Other species include the powder-puff tree, water berry and wild frangipani.

The **dune vegetation** can be subdivided into three zones. The pioneer zone immediately above the high water mark of the Indian Ocean comprises species such as seeplakkie (*Scaevola*), sea pumpkin (*Arctotheca populifolia*) and *Gazania rigens*. The steep seaward dune slopes

and strong winds have resulted in the vegetation being less developed than elsewhere along the KwaZulu/Natal coast. The dune scrub zone occurs on the higher, more stabilised dunes and supports species such as gonnabos (*Passerina rigida*), dune myrtle, bush-tick berry, and stunted trees such as coastal red milkwood and coast silver oak. The dune forest blanketing the coastal dunes includes species such as the conspicuous thorny rope, water ironplum, poison olive, white milkwood and the small-leaved jackal-berry. These dune forests are said to be the tallest in the world, reaching heights of almost 200 m above sea level. Although they have the appearance of large hills they actually consist of wind-blown sand which has accumulated on the underlying rock bed during the past 12 000 to 20 000 years.

Fauna Of the 59 mammal species which have been recorded in the St Lucia area, 47 occur in the Eastern Shores Nature Reserve. St Lucia is primarily a hippopotamus reserve and is the home of the world's southernmost population of these mammals, of which there are approximately 700. They play an important role in the lake ecology in several ways. By disturbing the bottom sediments of the lake the fertility of the lake is maintained, while their dung provide nutrients to the plant plankton. In addition, they also help to keep the grass short on islands

Large numbers of reedbuck occur in the area through which the Mziki Trail winds
Above right: *spoor*

where birds nest in large numbers and their paths provide easy access for crocodiles to and from the lake shores.

With a population of between 4 000 and 5 000 reedbuck, the reserve supports one of the largest concentrations of this species in Africa. They prefer the dense patches of reeds and open vleis, occurring singly or in small groups of five or six pairs. When alarmed, they emit a sharp whistle and in flight display a rolling, rocking-horse gait showing the white underside of their tails.

Ten other large mammal species occur, namely leopard, cheetah, bushpig, warthog, buffalo, waterbuck, impala, bushbuck, kudu and black rhinoceros.

The smaller antelope include red duiker, common duiker, steenbok and suni, while the smaller predators are represented by black-backed jackal, serval and three mongoose species. Three primates also occur, namely samango monkey, vervet monkey and thick-tailed bushbaby.

Close on 370 bird species have been recorded at St Lucia, while some 245 species have been recorded at Cape Vidal to date. Species which are likely to be of particular interest to birders are Rudd's apalis, brown robin and Woodwards' batis.

Forest species you could tick include tam-bourine dove, Knysna lourie, white-eared barbet, goldentailed woodpecker and squaretailed drongo. These birds, as well as sombre bulbul, Natal robin, wattle-eyed and bluemantled flycatchers and forest weavers often form large bird parties.

About one-third of the total number of species recorded in the Greater St Lucia Park are waterside birds which inhabit the open waters of the lake, reed beds, mudflats and swamps. Large numbers of white pelicans breed on the islands in the lake which also attracts greater and lesser flamingos.

During the summer months several waders can be seen along the lake edge, including ringed and grey plovers, turnstone, marsh and curlew sandpipers, little stint and blackwinged stilt.

Since more than 50 per cent of the St Lucia Complex is covered by water, the aquatic life of the lake is of special interest. The St Lucia System is considered to be the most important prawn habitat in South Africa, a species which is of fundamental importance in the food cycle. Five species have been recorded, of which the white prawn, *Penaeus indicus*, is the most common.

To date some 120 fish species have been recorded, including four shark, one stingray, one sawfish and six freshwater fish species.

The large population of Nile crocodile (*Crocodilus niloticus*), estimated at about 1 000 crocodiles of 1 m or longer, plays an important role in maintaining the aquatic ecology of St Lucia. By preying on sick and weaker fish, the crocodiles not only control the fish population, but also ensure a healthy population. They occur throughout the lake environment, but during the winter months when the salinity of the lake increases, they tend to concentrate around the rivers feeding the lake.

Another noteworthy reptile found here is the Gaboon adder (*Bitis gabonica gabonica*), which is one of the most beautiful snakes. Although it can easily be identified by its geometric buff, black, grey and pastel purple and yellow patterns, the Gaboon adder is rarely seen as it blends in extremely well with the leaf litter of the forest floor. In South Africa it is restricted to the coastal forest from St Lucia northwards to Kosi Bay and is considered vulnerable. Its venom is highly toxic and potentially lethal, but fortunately it is very placid and bites are rare.

Thirty-seven amphibian species have been

(a) (b)

The bill of the greater flamingo (a) is pink with a black tip, compared with the dark red bill of the lesser flamingo (b). The latter species is considerably smaller and pinker than the greater flamingo

recorded from the Lake St Lucia area, while the reptiles are represented by 61 species, including the parti-coloured sea snake (*Pelamis platurus*), which is found in the sea along the Eastern Shores, and the loggerhead (*Caretta caretta*) and leatherback (*Dermochelys coriacea*) turtles, which nest along the coast.

History Archaeological evidence from a site near St Lucia Bay has confirmed inhabitation of the area by Early Iron Age people from around the fourth century. It has been suggested that these people were the ancestors of the Nguni, who comprise the Xhosa-speaking people, the Zulu, Swazi and Southern Ndebele.

The Nguni settled in a large number of politically and economically independent communities between the coast and the escarpment.

During the mid-eighteenth century some of the clans began expanding their power by incorporating neighbouring clans. One such clan was the Ndwandwe, who lived north and east of the Black Umfolozi River.

This period also saw the rise of the Mthethwa kingdom of Dingiswayo in the early 1800s, and in 1818 the Ndwandwe defeated the Mthethwa. The period between 1820 and 1830 saw large areas of southern Africa torn apart as a result of inter-tribal conflict and witnessed the rise of the powerful Zulu kingdom under Shaka. During this period the area west of the lake was inhabited by two small Nguni clans, the Msane and the Ncwangeni.

To the north of the Nguni lived the Tsonga. During the sixteenth century the Nyaka kingdom developed into one of the principal Tsonga states south of present-day Maputo, expanding its control as far south as St Lucia. The seventeenth century saw the rise of another Tsonga kingdom, the Tembe, who subjected the Nyaka and controlled elephant hunting as far south as St Lucia. Through their control of the ivory trade the kingdom increased its wealth and power, but towards the end of the eighteenth century the kingdom disintegrated as a result of civil war.

The name St Lucia dates back to 1575 when the Portuguese explorer Manuel Perestelo arrived at the lake on the feast of St Lucia and named it in honour of the saint. He recorded the lake as being quite shallow, while in 1849 it was reported to be navigable.

The bay and its shores were proclaimed British territory on 18 December 1884 after HMS *Goshawk* arrived there a few days before a German warship. Annexation was possible because of a treaty made in 1843 with the Zulu king, Mpande.

Realising the need to conserve the unique beauty and ecology of the lake, the Natal Government proclaimed the lake's water surface and islands a game reserve on 16 April 1897. St Lucia shares the honour of being one of Africa's oldest game reserves with Hluhluwe and Umfolozi.

TRAIL DESCRIPTION

The hut at Mount Tabor serves as a base camp from where you have a choice of three routes. It was constructed during World War II to serve as a radar observation post for the Catalina aircraft which provided air cover for Allied vessels, especially against attacks by German submarines. The St Lucia base was originally manned by the Royal Air Force, but in 1943 the personnel were replaced by members of the South African Air Force. It was closed in February 1945.

Route 1 From the base camp the trail heads south, alternating between open hillsides, pine plantations and indigenous dune forest. Initially the trail follows the same route as the Mfazana Pan route before branching off to the left. The first pine plantations in the area were established in 1954 and since 1978 the emphasis has been on the production of pulp wood.

Of interest along this route is an information marker next to a prospecting beacon. An application for prospecting leases in the area was made during the 1970s and in 1983 and 1986 Richards Bay Minerals acquired prospecting rights on two leases in the Eastern Shores. In 1989 the company applied to have the Kingsa-Tojan lease, over a 17 km-long strip of dunes covering 1 200 ha, changed to a mining lease.

The prospect of mining caused a public outcry and over 300 000 people signed the "Save St Lucia" petition. As a result, the government ordered an environmental impact assessment (EIA) in September 1989 and in March 1993 the *Report on Mining and Ecotourism Options for the Eastern Shores of Lake St Lucia* was released. Among the conditions recommended by the EIA if mining goes ahead are that no mining should take place closer than 400 m from the high water mark, and no mining should take place within 800 m of the lake.

In December 1993 the St Lucia Dune Mining Review Panel announced that there should be no mining of the area and the final decision by the government was still pending by December 1994.

Shortly after crossing a fire-break you will cross the road to Mission Rocks Outpost and after about 2 km the trail descends steeply through dune forest to the beach at Rangers Rocks. From here the route follows the coast northwards with most of the coastline being rocky with occasional sandy beaches. These rocks consist of sea sand which was cemented by calcium carbonate derived from sea shells about 80 000 years ago and provided the base on which the coastal dunes developed. Large tracts of this sandstone rock base, which also forms the offshore coral reefs, are exposed along the coast.

Since the day's hike is only 10 km long, you will have ample time to explore the tidal pools. Bear in mind, however, that this section is best hiked at low tide.

After about 2 km of beach walking the trail

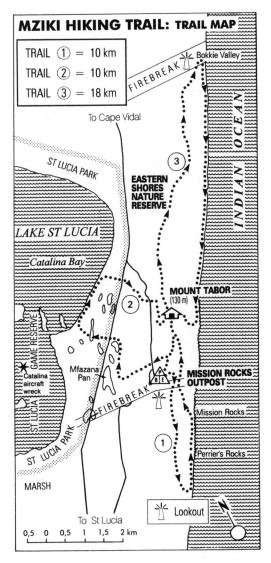

MZIKI HIKING TRAIL: TRAIL MAP

TRAIL ① = 10 km
TRAIL ② = 10 km
TRAIL ③ = 18 km

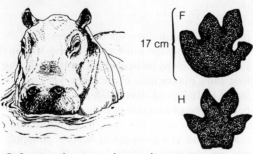

17 cm

F

H

*St Lucia is home to the southernmost
population of hippo in the world*

turns inland at Mission Rocks, ascending
through the dune forest back to the base camp.

Route 2 This route covers about 10 km and
winds through a mosaic of forest, grassland and
wetlands. After following the road to the Mission
Rocks outpost for about 1 km the route turns
off to the right, meandering through tall coastal
forests. Immediately after crossing the road to
Cape Vidal the trail returns to the forests and
about 2 km after setting off you will come to a
track turning off to the left. This track ends at a
hide overlooking a small pan, while the main
route continues to a hide overlooking the
Mfazana Pan.

The Mfazana Pan forms part of the extensive
network of pans and vleis which are characteristic of the low-lying plains of the Eastern Shores.
These pans and vleis are filled by rainwater
which seeps through the coastal dunes and they
are an important supplementary source of water
for the lake, especially during dry years.

A short way beyond the Mfazana Hide the
trail crosses the old main road to Cape Vidal
and heads through grasslands to the shore of
Lake St Lucia. Along this section the route follows a hippo path and, once you reach the edge
of the lake, the trail passes through a forest
where there is a possibility of encountering
hippo. During the day they often rest in patches
of forest like this and you are warned to keep a
sharp lookout. In the event of being confronted
by an aggressive hippo, the trail brochure advis-
es hikers to retreat as fast as possible or to
climb a decent sized tree and not to return to
the forest. If the hippo doesn't appear to be
aggressive, however, it is best to stand still and
to withdraw quietly.

If this sounds too nerve-racking for you there
is an alternative route to the right of the forest
which meets up with the trail along the lake
shore about 500 m further. Although the likelihood of encountering hippo here is reduced
considerably you should still keep an eye out
for them.

After following the lake edge for about 1,5 km
the trail swings away from the lake, ascending
gradually through grassland and parkland to the
Mount Tabor base camp.

Route 3 From Mount Tabor the trail follows
the dune ridge before descending into Bokkie
Valley, which takes its name from the high concentration of reedbuck found here.

Trees numbered along this route include the
common coral tree, marula, Lowveld mangosteen and the water berry. Known as the *umDoni*
in Zulu, the water berry is the most dominant
tree of the grassland and Umdoni Parkland.

The final 4 km of the inland leg of the trail
winds through indigenous forest and the unique
dune forest with its dense undergrowth. The
trees provide an ideal habitat for several ferns
and epiphytic orchids such as the beautiful
white *Mystacidium venosum*, which flowers from
April to July. Among the mammals you could
chance upon are the red squirrel and the
samango monkey.

The climax dune forest reaches a height of up
to 20 m, but on leaving the forest you will
notice a change in the vegetation of the seaward
dunes. Here the vegetation is lashed by the salt-
laden onshore winds, giving them a stunted
appearance, and there are fewer species than in
the climax forest.

After descending to the beach the trail follows
the unspoilt coastline southwards for about
8 km, alternating between sandy beaches and
rocky shores, before climbing steeply to Mount
Tabor.

OTHER KWAZULU/NATAL TRAILS

AMANZIMNYAMA

Distance 39 km; 4 days

Reservations KwaZulu Bureau of Natural Resources, 367 Loop Street, Pietermaritzburg 3201, Telephone (0331) 94-6698.

Group size Minimum 2; Maximum 10

Facilities Hutted accommodation is provided at Nhlange where the trail starts and at Bhanga Nek camp, while tented accommodation is provided at the two other overnight stops. Beds, mattresses, pots and a kettle, a two-plate gas cooker, lamps, water and ablution facilities are provided at the four overnight stops.

Description This guided trail in the north-eastern corner of KwaZulu/Natal leads through one of southern Africa's most fascinating ecosystems. The trail winds around the Kosi Bay Lake system, passing through pristine coastal forests, delicate swamp forests and raffia palm forests, as well as along unspoilt beaches. Some 250 bird species have been recorded to date, including Pel's fishing owl and the rare palmnut vulture. Hippos and crocodiles occur in the lakes and, depending on the time of the year, trailists might also be lucky enough to see loggerhead turtles. Trailists will also gain an insight into local tribal customs and how the traditional fishing kraals work. The Kosi Bay estuary is one of the best places in southern Africa for snorkelling and snorkelling gear is recommended.

BALELE

Distance 25 km; 2 days

Reservations Utrecht Municipality, P O Box 11, Utrecht 2980, Telephone (03433) 3041.

Group size Minimum 2; Maximum 12

Facilities Accommodation at the start is provided in an old farmhouse equipped with beds, mattresses, a coal stove, hot and cold water

showers and toilets. Other amenities include a fireplace, firewood, pots, pans, kettle, a gas lamp and lanterns. At the overnight stop hikers are accommodated in two beehive huts with dung floors. Amenities include mattresses, fireplaces, firewood, pots, pans, as well as toilets. Drinking water is also supplied, but washing is in the nearby stream.

Description The Enhlanzeni Valley in the Langalibalele Mountains provides an ideal setting for this trail on the outskirts of Utrecht. The first day's hike covers about 10,2 km to the hut where packs can be left to explore the nearby waterfall. On the second day trailists explore the two waterfalls higher upstream in the valley before returning to the hut. The return leg follows an easier route back to Weltevrede, joining the onward route at the suspension bridge over the Dorps River. Highlights of the trail include historical sites such as the old Voortrekker road and an irrigation furrow which dates back to the 1860s. Interesting rock formations, spectacular views and inviting rock pools add to the attraction of this trail.

BURNERA

Distance No set distance; 7 to 14 days

Reservations The Secretary, Wilderness Leadership School, P O Box 53058, Yellowwood Park 4011, Telephone (031) 42-8642.

Group size Up to 9 people

Facilities The course is conducted from an old farmhouse, equipped with all the necessary facilities. The trail fee is inclusive of transport from Durban, food and equipment except sleeping bags and daypacks.

Description Burnera is the name of an old farmhouse in the southern Drakensberg which is used by the WLS as a base for its Wilderness Education Programme. This programme focuses mainly on training and offers outdoor and wilderness skills courses for anyone wishing to learn more about the various aspects of wilderness travel. The course curriculum includes the following subjects: wilderness awareness and environmental ethics, outdoor living skills and minimum impact camping, outdoor travel techniques, leadership and expedition dynamics, safety and rescue procedures.

CANNIBALS

Distance 32 km; 2 days

Reservations Jacana Country Homes and Trails, P O Box 95212, Waterkloof 0145, Telephone (012) 346-3550.

Group size Minimum 2; Maximum 30

Facilities At the Kalwerfontein base camp hikers are accommodated in a shed equipped with beds and mattresses. Other amenities include a lapa with fireplaces, firewood, pots, potjies, pans, a kettle, a gas stove and electric fridge. The modern ablution block has hot and cold showers and flush toilets.

Description Situated in the Biggarsberg Mountains in northern KwaZulu/Natal, the Cannibals trail network consists of two one-day hikes which can be undertaken from a base camp. The trail traverses four farms in the Helpmekaar Conservancy south-west of Dundee and is named after those unfortunate people who were forced to resort to cannibalism in the wake of the Difaqane. Evidence of their kraals and shelters can be seen on the 20 km Cannibals trail, as well as the ruins of a fort dating back to the Anglo-Boer War. More than 200 bird species have been recorded and the large dam offers excellent opportunities for birding.

Trailists will enjoy sweeping views along the 12 km Black Eagle trail, with a good chance of spotting the birds after which the trail is named. Kudu, impala and mountain reedbuck may also be sighted.

DUGHANDLOVU

Distance 17 km; 2 days

Reservations The Reservations Office, Natal Parks Board, P O Box 1750, Pietermaritzburg 3200, Telephone (0331) 47-1981.

Group size Minimum 2; Maximum 16

Facilities The overnight hut is equipped with beds and mattresses. Eating utensils, pots, paraffin lamps, drinking water, cold water showers, toilets, fireplaces and firewood are provided.

Description
Novices and families with children will find this trail in the False Bay Park, which forms part of the Greater St Lucia Wetland Park, ideal because of the short distances covered. The trail initially winds through woodlands and thickets and then follows the lake shore to reach the overnight camp 8,5 km after setting off. The rustic camp overlooks the Hluhluwe River and floodplain and during favourable conditions large flocks of waterbirds, including white and pinkbacked pelicans, African spoonbill and greater flamingo are attracted to the floodplains. Several species can be seen breeding here between December and April. The same route is followed back to the start of the trail.

GEELHOUT

Distance 21 km; 2 days

Reservations Mr D J T Esterhuyze, P O Box 1901, Newcastle 2940, Telephone (03435) 640.

Group size Minimum 2; Maximum 10

Facilities Hikers are accommodated at the start of the trail in a hut equipped with beds, mattresses, a fridge and a stove. Other amenities include a lapa with fireplaces, electricity, hot and cold water showers and flush toilet. The hut at the overnight stop is equipped with beds and mattresses and there is also a toilet.

Description This trail traverses the foothills of the northern Drakensberg, 50 km south-west of Newcastle. The circular trail is on a farm which has been managed as a private wilderness area for many years and leads through beautiful indigenous forests and across sparkling streams. Trailists stand a chance of spotting blesbok, black wildebeest, mountain reedbuck, bushbuck and oribi. The first day's hike to Geelhout Hut is 10 km long, while the return route of 11 km initially leads to the plateau before winding down through a magnificent indigenous forest. Among the trees and shrubs occurring commonly along the trail are Outeniqua and real yellowwoods, Natal bottlebrush, red pear, pompon trees and mountain cabbage trees.

ITALA

Distance Guided wilderness trail, no set route or distance; 3 days/4 nights

Reservations Central Reservations Office, Natal Parks Board, P O Box 1750, Pietermaritzburg 3200, Telephone (0331) 47-1981.

Group size Maximum 8

Facilities Hikes are undertaken from a rustic base camp consisting of tents, an eating area, hot and cold water showers and toilets.

Description The 29 653 ha Itala Game Reserve in northern KwaZulu/Natal is renowned for its undulating grassy hills, deep river valleys and steep cliffs. Trailists are transported by vehicle to the base camp from where day hikes are undertaken into the reserve's wilderness area under the guidance of a trails officer and a game guard. The reserve is a sanctuary to giraffe, kudu, eland and klipspringer, while white and black rhinos, elephant and buffalo also occur. Some 200 bird species have been recorded to date. Trails are conducted between March and October and participants must provide their own food as catering is not included in the trail fee.

LAKE

Distance Guided wilderness trail; no set route or distances; 4 or 5 days

Reservations The Secretary, Wilderness Leadership School, P O Box 53058, Yellowwood Park 4011, Telephone (031) 42-8642.

Group size Maximum 8

Facilities The trail fee is inclusive of all equipment, including sleeping bags and backpacks, food and transport from Durban.

Description The Lake Trail is conducted in the wilderness area on the eastern shores of Lake St Lucia and offers trailists the opportunity to explore the largest complex of its kind in southern Africa on foot or by canoe. St Lucia is a haven for bird-watchers and to date more than 370 species have been recorded, of which about one-third are waterbirds. The lake supports large populations of hippo and crocodile, while the adjacent land areas are the habitat of reedbuck, waterbuck, kudu, impala and bushbuck, as well as black rhino, leopard, cheetah and a host of smaller mammals.

MKHAYA

Distance 24 km; 2 days

Reservations Mrs M de Swart, P O Box 734, Pongola 3170, Telephone (03841) 4-1076.

Group size Minimum 2; Maximum 18

Facilities Accommodation at the start of the trail is provided in rondavels while huts are available at the end of the first day's hike. The rondavels and huts have beds and mattresses, while fireplaces, firewood, hot and cold water showers and toilets are also provided.

Description Situated between Vryheid and Pongola, this circular route winds through the bushveld of northern KwaZulu/Natal on a private farm. Places of interest on the first day's hike include the site where Dingaan is said to have slept when he fled to Swaziland, stone cairns and the underground granaries of the early Zulu inhabitants. Also of interest is the Wonderboom, a paperbark thorn tree with a crown of 30 m, believed to be the largest specimen of this species in South Africa. The trail ascends to the 951 m-high KwaVundla Mountain with its commanding view over the surrounding countryside before descending to the overnight camp. On the second day the trail drops down into the low-lying valley carved by the Mkhaya River after which the trail is named.

MONKS

Distance 21 km; 2 days

Reservations Jacana Country Homes and Trails, P O Box 95212, Waterkloof 0145, Telephone (012) 346-3550.

Group size Minimum 2; Maximum 14

Facilities A stone rondavel with beds, mattresses, hot/cold water, a bathroom and toilet serves as accommodation at the start. Other amenities include fireplaces, firewood, pots, pans, a kettle and a potjie. The overnight stop is a renovated dormitory with the following facilities: beds, mattresses, fireplaces, firewood, a pan, pots and a potjie, as well as a toilet.

Description Named after the Trappist Monks who established a mission at the foot of the Biggarsberg in the late 1880s, this circular trail starts on the farm Gartmore between Ladysmith and Newcastle. The first day's hike of 13 km ascends to a plateau of the Biggarsberg and offers a detour to the top of Hlatikulu Mountain, the highest peak in the Biggarsberg range. The trail then descends to the Maria Ratchitz Mission where hikers are accommodated. The second day's hike is a short 8 km back to the start. Much of the trail passes through grassveld with a rich diversity of flowering plants. More than 250 bird species are known to occur in the area and animals include mountain reedbuck, grey rhebok, impala, oribi and steenbok.

NGELE

Distance 36 km; 2 days or 40 km; 3 days

Reservations The Forester, Weza State Forest, P O Weza 4685, Telephone (039452) 24.

Group size Minimum 2; Maximum 30

Facilities Either of two overnight huts on the two-day hike can be used as the starting point, while the Blackwater hut serves as the starting point on the three-day loop. Two other huts are also provided on this loop. Amenities at the huts include bunks, mattresses, tables, benches, wood stoves (except at KwaShwili where a lapa is provided), firewood and toilets.

Description The two loops of the Ngele Hiking Trail in the Weza State Forest near Harding in the Griqualand East region passes through the largest plantation in South Africa, grasslands displaying a gay array of flowers and patches of indigenous forest. Highlights of the two-day route include impressive views over Weza from the Umsilo Ridge, the Ngele Forest and the Lower Stinkwood Forest, two relict patches of indigenous forest. The three-day loop winds through plantations and the Mpetsheni Forest on the first day. A highlight of the second day's hike, which is mainly through grassveld, is the Fairview Falls, while the third day's hike is mainly through pine plantations. Weza has a large population of bushbuck, while common duiker is also plentiful. Other species hikers might spot include mountain reedbuck, grey rhebok, samango and vervet moneys and chacma baboon.

NTENDEKA

Distance 25 km; 2 or 3 days

Reservations The Forester, Ntendeka Wilderness Area, Private Bag X9306, Vryheid 3100, Telephone (0386) 7-1883.

Group size Minimum 2; Maximum 12

Facilities A campsite near the forest station with ablutions, fireplaces and firewood is the only facility available to hikers. Camping is not permitted in the wilderness area.

Description Ntendeka – the Place of Precipitous Heights – is a wonder-world of spectacular cliffs, tropical indigenous forests and grasslands. The 5 230 ha state wilderness area east of Vryheid in northern KwaZulu/Natal is traversed by a network of trails which can be explored as day walks from the campsite. Among the numerous places of interest are several old sawpits, a cave where the Zulu king Cetshwayo took refuge in 1879, an old stone oven and a large stone cairn. The forest is considered one of the most beautiful in Zululand and is the habitat of more than 60 fern species, 19 ephipytic orchid species and the giant-leaved streptocarpus which has leaves of up to one metre long. Close on 200 bird species, including several rare and endangered species, have been recorded.

ORIBI

Distance 29 km; 2 days

Reservations Jacana Country Homes and Trails, P O Box 95212, Waterkloof 0145, Telephone (012) 346-3550.

Group size Minimum 2; Maximum 24

Facilities Hikers are accommodated in a barn at the start of the trail, equipped with beds, mattresses, electricity, a bathroom and toilet. Fireplaces and firewood, as well as potjies, pans and pots are also provided. A farmhouse equipped with beds, mattresses, stove, hot and cold water bath and flush toilet serves as accommodation at the end of the first day's hike. Other amenities include fireplaces, firewood, a potjie, pans, pots and a two-plate gas cooker.

Description By combining this two-day circular trail with the Monk's Trail, hikers can extend their exploration of the Biggarsberg in northern KwaZulu/Natal to four days. The area is rich in archaeological and historical sites and trenches and forts dating back to the Anglo-Boer War can be seen along the trail. Starting off from Gartmore Farm, the trail ascends Vungashi Mountain and then passes a lovely kloof with a waterfall and swimming pool. Further along the trail passes through a yellowwood forest and at Inkruipberg hikers will enjoy expansive views of the Sundays River Valley and the distant Drakensberg. The second day's hike covers 12 km and after crossing Inkruipberg descends to Up George farm. The route then traverses the southern slopes of Vungashi before swinging back to the starting/ending point.

ST LUCIA

Distance Guided wilderness trail, no set route or distance; five days/four nights

Reservations Central Reservations Office, Natal Parks Board, P O Box 1750, Pietermaritzburg 3200, Telephone (0331) 47-1981.

Group size Maximum 6

Facilities Accommodation at the base camp is in tents equipped with mattresses and bedding. Other amenities include a kitchen, and ablutions with hot and cold water showers and toilets. Tented accommodation is also provided at the bush camps, but cooking is over an open fire and ablution facilities are basic.

Description The St Lucia Wilderness Trails are conducted in one of the most unusual ecological areas in southern Africa. Trails are guided by a trails officer, accompanied by a game guard, and the emphasis is on discovering the environment. Two nights are spent in the base camp at Bhangazi Lake near Cape Vidal, while two nights are spent in a bush camp in the wilderness area. In addition to unspoilt coastal scenery, trailists can also explore sections of Lake St Lucia by canoe. Birdlife is prolific and among the animals that can be seen along the trail are reedbuck, red duiker and black rhino. The lake is the habitat of hippo and crocodile. Trails are conducted between April and September and the tariff is inclusive of all meals.

UMFOLOZI

Distance Guided wilderness trail, no set route or distance; three days/four nights

Reservations Central Reservations Office, Natal Parks Board, P O Box 1750, Pietermaritzburg 3200, Telephone (0331) 47-1981.

Group size Maximum 8

Facilities Tented accommodation equipped with mattresses and bedding is provided at the base camp and the bush camps. Showers and toilets are available at the base camp, while bucket showers and basic toilet facilities are provided at the bush camps.

Description The Umfolozi Game Reserve in Zululand is considered one of the finest conservation areas in southern Africa. These guided trails are conducted in a 25 000 ha wilderness area and groups are accompanied by a trails officer and a game guard. Game-viewing is generally rewarding and in addition to white rhino, trailists might also have close-up views of blue wildebeest, impala and Burchell's zebra. Other species of game occurring in the reserve include elephant, buffalo, giraffe and nyala, as well as lion, leopard and cheetah. The first and last night of the trail is spent at the Mndindini base camp, while two more nights are spent in tented camps in the wilderness. Trails are conducted from March to November only and the fee is inclusive of all meals.

WATERHOEK

Distance Two trails of six to eight hours and four hours; 2 days

Reservations Jacana Country Homes and Trails, P O Box 95212, Waterkloof 0145, Telephone (012) 346-3550.

Group size Minimum 2; Maximum 20

Facilities Two thatched cottages equipped with beds, mattresses, electricity, pots, pans and utensils serve as a base camp. Other amenities include hot and cold water, a bathroom with an outside shower and flush toilets. Fireplaces and firewood are also available.

Description Situated near Mooi River in the scenic Natal Midlands, this trail offers expansive views of the Drakensberg, the Natal Midlands and the spectacular Mooi River Valley. Hikers need not carry a heavy backpack as both trails are undertaken from the base camp on the farm Waterhoek.

The first day's trail leads to the breathtaking Harleston Falls and passes close by two breeding colonies of bald ibis. This route is hiked in six to eight hours. The second day's hike follows an easier route and is normally completed in four hours. Among the animals you might spot are mountain reedbuck, bushbuck and oribi, while bushpig also occurs.

WHITE RHINO

Distance Guided wilderness trail, no set route or distance; 4 or 5 days

Reservations The Secretary, Wilderness Leadership School, P O Box 53058, Yellowwood Park 4011, Telephone (031) 42-8642.

Group size Maximum 8

Facilities The trail fee is inclusive of all equipment, food and transport from Durban.

Description The White Rhino wilderness trails are conducted in the Umfolozi Game Reserve in Zululand, one of the oldest proclaimed conservation areas in South Africa. The area is steeped in the legends and traditions of the Zulu people and the reserve is renowned for its large population of white rhino. Other species of game include black rhino, blue wildebeest, Burchell's zebra, buffalo and giraffe, as well as impala, waterbuck, reedbuck, nyala and kudu. The vegetation of the 47 753 ha reserve is dominated by mixed acacia woodlands. The trails are conducted in the 25 000 ha wilderness area in the south of the park.

FREE STATE

KORANNA

Rising some 400 m above the surrounding plains, the Korannaberg is like an island amongst a patchwork of farmlands and a hike here will dispel any illusions that the Free State has only flat, monotonous grasslands. It is ideal hiking country with varied scenery ranging from well-wooded kloofs to waterfalls, interesting sandstone formations and grasslands. The trail is in the Koranna Conservancy, the first conservancy in the Free State. It was established in 1986 by nine farmers who jointly manage 7 000 ha.

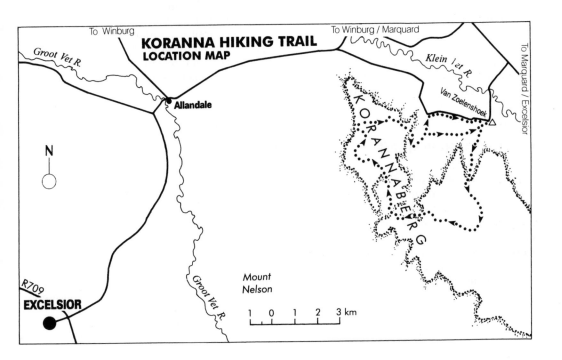

TRAIL PLANNER

Distance 32 km; 2 days

Grading B

Reservations Jacana Country Homes and Trails, P O Box 95212, Waterkloof 0145, Telephone (012) 346-3550, Fax (012) 346-2499. Reservations are accepted up to 12 months in advance.

Group size Minimum 2; Maximum 15

Relevant information
■ Since the first day's hike is fairly long with steep upgrades an early start is advisable.
■ Use the stiles provided and close gates which you find closed and leave those which you find open.

■ A torch is essential for the detour through Magul se Gat on the second day.
■ Wood is not supplied at the overnight stop, making a backpacking stove essential.
■ Be prepared for extremely cold conditions during the winter.

How to get there If travelling from the south, turn off the N1, 65 km north of Bloemfontein, onto the R709. Travel for 40 km to Excelsior where you take the Marquard road. The turn-off to the Koranna Conservancy on your right is signposted 21 km further on. It is a further 9 km to the Van Zoelenshoek farmhouse. Travelling from the north, turn off the N1 at Winburg and carry on south for 43 km until you join the Excelsior/Marquard road. Turn left here and continue for 9 km to the Koranna Conservancy gate.

Maps A sketch map is included in the information leaflet on the trail which is forwarded with your receipt and permit.

Facilities At the overnight stop hikers sleep in a large overhang. Amenities are limited to a pit toilet, while water is available about 200 m from the overhang. No firewood is provided here.

Logistics Circular route. Accommodation is provided in a farmhouse at Van Zoelenshoek where the trail starts. Amenities include beds with mattresses, a kitchen, bathroom and toilet, as well as an outside fireplace.

Climate Summer days are hot with temperatures of up to 30 °C not uncommon. During winter the daytime temperatures are generally pleasant, but early mornings and evenings can be cold, with minimum temperatures dropping to below 0 °C in midwinter. Frost is not unusual in winter.

The trail lies within the summer rainfall area and most of the average annual rainfall of 500 mm is recorded between January and March, usually as thunderstorms in the afternoons.

TRAIL ENVIRONMENT

Flora The vegetation of the plains and plateaus is dominated by short, dense grassveld comprising mixed and sour grass species. Among the flowering species are watsonias, amaryllis, wild dagga (*Leonotis leonurus*) and pig's ears (*Cotyledon* spp.), while an extremely rare fern species (*Psilotum nundum*) has also been recorded in the area.

The river valleys are dominated by indigenous forest and impressive stands of wild olive trees can be seen along the route. Other common species are oldwood, karree, common wild currant and blue guarri, while white stinkwood, Cape holly, sagewood and tree fuchsia also occur.

Species which have the limit of their distribution further east but occur in isolated populations in the Korannaberg include mountain cypress, wild peach and red pear.

Stands of wild olive trees can be seen along the route

Mountain reedbuck – a species which favours bushy slopes

Some of the trees along the route have been marked in accordance with the *National List of Indigenous Trees* to assist hikers with their identification.

Also conspicuous, especially near the end of the first day's hike and the first few kilometres of the second day's route, are the patches of brilliant yellow (almost luminous) lichens which create a colourful spectacle.

Fauna The plains surrounding Korannaberg were once home to large herds of black wildebeest, springbok, blesbok and Burchell's zebra, as well as other species of game. With the arrival of the Voortrekkers in the area in the late 1830s, however, virtually all the larger game species were exterminated. Predators posed a threat to the livestock of the Voortrekkers while antelope were shot for their meat as well as their skins.

The only antelope species you might encounter along the trail is the mountain reedbuck, while chacma baboon and smaller mammals such as rock dassie, ground squirrel and hares are seen from time to time. Porcupine, caracal and several smaller predators, as well as a number of rodents also occur, but are seldom seen.

Although a comprehensive bird checklist has not yet been compiled, the number of species occurring in the area is estimated at around 150.

In rocky areas you can expect to see ground woodpecker, familiar chat, bokmakierie and rock bunting. The grasslands are the habitat of greywing and redwing francolins, as well as four lark species – rufousnaped, clapper, redcapped and pinkbilled.

Other grassland species include Richard's and yellowbreasted pipits, while the moist grasslands attract redcollared and longtailed widows. The black korhaan reaches the easternmost limit of its distribution here.

Species to keep an eye out for in the forested kloofs include olive thrush and Cape robin, while neddicky and fairy flycatcher favour scrubveld.

Several species are attracted to the dams and streams in the area. Among these are hamerkop, yellowbilled and African black ducks, spurwinged goose, as well as giant and malachite kingfishers.

Birds of prey you might tick include blackshouldered kite, black and martial eagles, steppe and jackal buzzards and rock kestrel.

History Rock paintings on the walls of caves have provided evidence of the inhabitation of the area by the last of the Later Stone Age people, the San.

Prior to the arrival of the Sotho, the north-eastern Free State was inhabited by the Zizi, who migrated from the Tugela during the 1500s. Sotho-speaking migrants began settling in the north-eastern Free State during the late 1700s or early 1800s.

They included the Tlokwa and Kwena, who settled in the north-east, and the Lihoja and Taung in the north-west. Groups of Fokeng were scattered throughout the area.

The Korannaberg takes its name from the Khoi-speaking Kora, also known as the Korana and Koranna, and the mountain fortress was one of their last strongholds in the north-eastern Free State. They settled in the area in the mid-1770s after having driven the Sotho people further east.

White trekboers began settling in the area during the second half of the 1830s and land claims and stock theft gave rise to conflict between them and the Sotho, as well as the Kora who lived in the Koranna Mountains under their chief Gert Taaibosch.

The years between 1840 and 1871 were extremely volatile and were marred by numerous clashes and two wars between the whites and the Basotho. One of these clashes took place at the Korannaberg in March 1858. During this period the boundaries of Basutoland were constantly redrawn. The 1843 boundary drawn by Napier excluded the Korannaberg from Basutoland, but in terms of the Warden Line of 1849 and the First Treaty of Aliwal North of 1858, the area became part of Basutoland. After the Treaty of Thaba-Bosiu in 1866, the area became part of the Free State once again.

As a result of clashes between the settlers and the Kora it was decided to flush the Kora from their stronghold, Magul se Gat, but because of the layout of the terrain it was difficult to surprise them. It was then decided to frighten the Kora away by blowing up part of the rock directly above the overhang. Having seen no Kora leaving the cave during the night, the farmers stormed the overhang. Much to their surprise they found no Kora, but discovered a tunnel through which the Kora had escaped during the night. Magul se Gat is visited on the second day of the trail.

TRAIL DESCRIPTION

Day 1: Van Zoelenshoek Hut to Overhang

The first 2,5 km of the day's hike is over easy terrain through tall grassland interspersed with dense stands of wild olive and karree. After about an hour the trail crosses over to the right-hand side of the river, just above a small waterfall – an excellent breakfast stop.

The ascent now becomes considerably steeper with the trail crossing the river several times. The final section in Boskloof follows the river course and stretches of boulder-hopping make this section demanding. About two and a half hours after setting off a magnificent waterfall is reached and from here it is about 15 minutes to the top of the kloof.

A short way on the trail winds its way through beautiful rock formations and then passes some ruins before climbing steadily for about 40 minutes. Along the base of the cliffs you will pass through dense clumps of bush to reach a waterfall after about 20 minutes. The waterfall cascades over the lip of a large overhang and you might meet up with hikers here doing the Red Trail, which starts at Merriemetsi.

After lunch a moderate climb awaits you before the trail drops down to the site where a Zulu with the unlikely name of Jonas van Tonder lived in an overhang during the last century. The orange, lemon and pear trees which he planted have survived up to this day.

A short way beyond Jonas van Tonder you will pass the wreck of an old car and after descending gradually to cross a stream you will join a disused jeep track. Along this section you are rewarded with magnificent views of the Maermanshoek Valley and Wonderkop straight ahead.

After rounding Wonderkop the trail descends to a basin where the route passes through Olienhoutbos, named after the abundance of large wild olive trees. The trail then ascends steeply to the plateau and, after following a riverbed with patches of luminous yellow-green lichens, emerges into grassland.

The overnight stop is a large overhang consisting of two chambers connected by a natural arch. Natural rock was used to build stone walls in the recesses of the larger chamber. Water is obtainable from a spring about 200 m from the overnight stop.

Day 2: Overhang to Van Zoelenshoek

The second day's hike starts with an easy traverse through short grassland. To the left of the trail the scenery is dominated by a large outcrop and straight ahead you will look down onto the farmlands surrounding Korannaberg. Also conspicuous are the lichens which form mottled yellowish-green patches on the rocks.

After a short descent the trail reaches Magul se Gat which is situated just below the cliffs. Packs can be left at the turn-off, but remember to take a torch along. At the far end of the overhang you will find the tunnel which becomes progressively narrower until you are forced to crawl underneath a chockstone. You will then find yourself in a wide chimney where you must clamber up some large rocks before emerging into the open. Before continuing, explore the roof of the cave where the holes caused by the explosions to frighten the Kora from their stronghold can still be seen.

Shortly after setting off again, you will pass a water point and about 25 minutes beyond Magul se Gat the trail joins a farm track which is followed for the next 5 km. The road initially traverses the grassy plateau, passing several huge round boulders, reminiscent of a giant's marbles

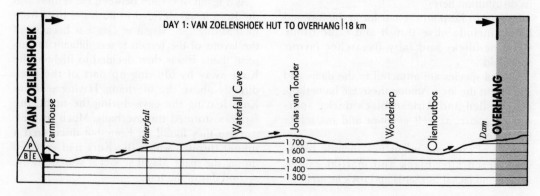

DAY 1: VAN ZOELENSHOEK HUT TO OVERHANG | 18 km

VAN ZOELENSHOEK — Farmhouse — Waterfall — Waterfall Cave — Jonas van Tonder — Wonderkop — Olienhoutbos — Dam — OVERHANG

1 700
1 600
1 500
1 400
1 300

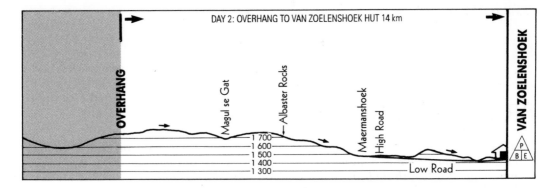

DAY 2: OVERHANG TO VAN ZOELENSHOEK HUT 14 km

- hence the name Albaster Rocks. The road then descends steeply to the Maermanshoek Valley where you will head in a northerly direction.

After a short while you will have a choice of following the high road or to continue to the low road. Although slightly more demanding, the high road is more interesting than the low road which follows the access road to Van Zoelenshoek.

After winding across a level stretch of land, the high road ascends steadily, gaining some 100 m in altitude, to cross the spur separating the Boskloof and Maermanshoek valleys. The final section of the trail is a short descent to the end.

BRANDWATER

This five-day trail in the north-eastern Free State will soon correct any preconceived ideas that the Free State is flat and uninteresting. The trail winds through grasslands and beautiful mountain kloofs, with their natural vegetation still intact, as well as past white sandstone cliffs and green meadows. Steep climbs reveal views of the Maluti Mountains forming the border with Lesotho. There are several large overhangs along the trail and Salpeterkrans, reputed to be one of the largest overhangs in the Southern Hemisphere, is visited. Four of the nights on the trail are spent in large sandstone overhangs.

TRAIL PLANNER

Distance 72 km; 5 days, or 26 km; 2 days

Grading B+

Reservations Rev J Mostert, P O Box 24, Fouriesburg 9725, Telephone (058) 223-0050.

Group size Minimum 2; Maximum 20

Maps The trail is marked on a photocopy of the 1 : 50 000 topographical map (section numbers 2828 AC, 2828 AD, 2828 CA and 2828 CB) that is forwarded on confirmation of a reservation.

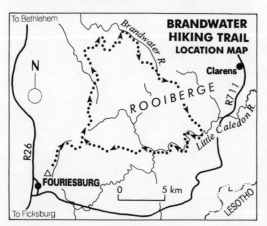

Facilities Caves provide shelter on the first, second and fourth nights, while an old sand-

stone barn serves as shelter on the third. Water and a toilet are available at each overnight stop, but a refuse bin is provided only at the third stop.

Logistics Circular route. Vehicles can be parked at the Meiringskloof Nature Park. There is no hut at the start/end of the trail, but campsites and fully equipped chalets can be rented at Meiringskloof Nature Park. Reservations should be addressed to Meiringskloof Nature Park, P O Box 101, Fouriesburg 9725, Telephone (058) 223-0067.

Relevant information
■ The first day's hike is the most difficult, so an early start is advisable.
■ Since fires are not permitted along the trail, a backpacking stove is essential.
■ Extremely cold temperatures and snow can be expected in winter, while the higher altitudes are often covered in mist during the summer months, making it advisable to have at least one experienced hiker in the party.
■ It is important to remember that if it had not been for the co-operation of private landowners, this trail would not have been accessible.
■ Use the stiles provided and remember to close gates which are found closed, while gates found open should be left open.

Climate

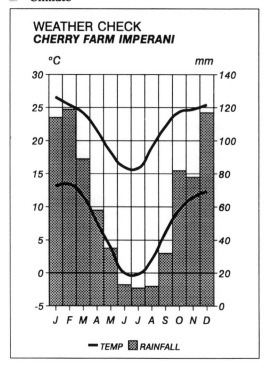

WEATHER CHECK
CHERRY FARM IMPERANI

°C   mm

— TEMP ▨ RAINFALL

■ Hikers should not make a nuisance of themselves when passing farmsteads, especially at the third overnight stop which is adjacent to a farmhouse.

■ Despite regular inspection of the trail, route markers are sometimes removed, making it possible to lose your way. Keep the trail map handy and refer to it as soon as you notice that a route marker has not been seen for a while.

■ Salpeterkrans is of great religious significance to many people and should be accorded the necessary respect. If the cave is occupied, ask permission to pass through and do so quietly.

■ Be on the lookout for ticks.

How to get there From the centre of Fouriesburg turn right into Robertson Street. Half a kilometre further on, turn left into Commissaris Street which leads into a gravel road to the right, signposted to Meiringskloof. About 2,5 km further you will enter the Meiringskloof Nature Park.

TRAIL ENVIRONMENT

Flora The vegetation of the mountains is dominated by sour grassveld with patches of scrub forest in the river valleys and on the valley slopes.

Among the numerous flowering plants of the grassveld are red-hot pokers (*Kniphofia*), scabiosa, nemesias and at least three gazania species, while agapanthus occur in rocky areas. Also favouring rocky areas is *Xerophyta viscosa*, which has beautiful pinkish flowers between December and April.

A number of everlastings (*Helichrysum*) occur, while the ericas are represented by the red fire

The leaf of the oldwood tree

heath (*Erica cerinthoides*) and *E. woodii* with its red to pink urn-shaped flowers. Scattered stands of common sugarbush are encountered near the end of the second day's hike.

An unusual plant, which resembles a round termite mound but is green, is seen on the first day's hike. This is *Euphorbia clavarioides*, a succulent with a convex "cushion" which has a height of up to 300 mm and a diameter of up to 600 mm. It has an underground stem, while the cushions are formed by the tips of the tightly packed branches. In this way the smallest possible surface is exposed to heat and wind, reducing transevaporation. It occurs from Graaff-Reinet and other Karoo areas to the north-eastern Free State and Lesotho, as well as in parts of KwaZulu/Natal and Transvaal. Other succulents occurring include the pig's ear (*Cotyledon orbiculata*) and several crassula species.

Dense stands of oldwood occur along stream banks along with wild olive and sagewood, while broom karree, karree and bladder-nut grow on the rocky valley slopes.

The bearded vulture is classified as rare

Also much in evidence along river valleys and at farmhouses are two exotics which have become part of the north-eastern Orange Free State landscape, poplar trees (*Populus*) and the weeping willow (*Salix*). Another exotic is the Scotch thistle (*Cirsium vulgare*) with its reddish-purple flowers. You are also sure to notice the pink flowering roses along the Little Caledon River on the fourth day of the trail.

Fauna Although typical montane species such as blesbok, grey rhebok and black wildebeest occurred in the area in historical times, very few animals, other than cattle and sheep, are likely to be seen along the trail.

The birdlife of the area is typical of the highlands of the eastern Orange Free State. The bearded vulture has been recorded here and watching this rare species gliding effortlessly along high in the sky will undoubtedly be a highlight for many hikers. Your best chances of ticking this species is on the third day's hike when the trail reaches its highest point.

Among the typical montane species you can expect to see on the rocky slopes are buff-streaked chat and rock pipit. Other species to be seen here are rock pigeon, ground woodpecker and redwinged starling. Cape and sentinel rock thrush, as well as orangebreasted rockjumper, occur at high altitudes.

Keep an eye out in the grasslands for stonechat, orangebreasted longclaw, golden bishop and pied starling – a species also attracted to cultivated lands.

Species recorded on dams along the trail include blackheaded heron, hadedah ibis, Egyptian goose, yellowbilled duck and red-knobbed coot.

History The numerous overhangs of the north-eastern Free State definitely served as homes to the San for thousands of years before the arrival of Later Iron Age people in the foothills of the Malutis about 1 500 years ago.

During the early 1800s the area was inhabited by the Tlokwa under Sekonyela. As a result of the Difaqane, however, they were displaced by the Hlubi, settling south of the Witteberge towards the end of 1823.

The Voortrekkers began settling in the area in 1837 and various border disputes soon arose, resulting in several border demarcations. However, conflict also arose between Sekonyela and Moshoeshoe I who laid claim to the Caledon and Little Caledon river valleys. In 1853 Moshoeshoe conquered the Tlokwa area after defeating Sekonyela.

Border disputes between the Voortrekkers and Moshoeshoe culminated in the First Basotho War in March 1858. The war ended inconclusively and two border demarcations failed to solve the dispute, resulting in the Second Basotho War in June 1865.

In 1868 Basutoland was annexed by Britain and in terms of the Treaty of Thaba Bosiu (1866) the areas of Fouriesburg, Clarens, the Little Caledon River and Witsieshoek were awarded to the Orange Free State. Fouriesburg was founded in 1892 on the farm Groenfontein and named after the first owner, Christoffel Fourie. Following the occupation of Bloemfontein by the British forces in March 1900, the Brandwater Basin became the last refuge of some 8 000 Boer fighters. A provisional government was established at Fouriesburg which also became the headquarters of the Boer forces.

On the night of 15 July 1900 General Christiaan de Wet, President Marthinus Steyn and a commando of over 2 000 men evaded the British forces and escaped from the Brandwater Basin. By blocking five of the six passes giving access to the Brandwater Basin the British forces cut off the retreat routes of the Boers and after a two-week campaign General Marthinus Prinsloo and over 4 300 men surrendered. However, since the British did not have enough forces the Golden Gate was left unguarded and General J H Olivier and 1 500 men escaped through the poort.

TRAIL DESCRIPTION

Day 1: Meiringskloof to Waterfall Cave

From the rest camp, continue up the valley along a path popular with day walkers. Soon after setting off a weir takes you across the Meiringskloofspruit to the right-hand side of the valley. A short uphill follows through the well-wooded kloof and, as the valley narrows, you will pass an enormous sandstone overhang, measuring about 100 m long and 30 m deep.

Some 10 minutes later you will reach one of the highlights of the first day's hike – a long narrow chasm shaped on one side like a tunnel, with ferns and mosses clinging to the dark, damp walls. After rains the stream flowing through the narrow chasm could present a problem.

A short way further on the gorge comes to an end, leaving you with no option but to climb up a chain ladder. At the top of the ladder you will turn right and skirt the dam to join a farm track on its north-eastern side. Shortly after joining the track an ingenious bridge spans a deep river chasm. On closer inspection you will notice how the pioneering farmers constructed it by blocking the chasm halfway down with large boulders and then filling it with smaller rocks and gravel.

For the next two hours you will remain mostly on the track, gaining height steadily to the old farmstead at Ventersberg where water is available at a drinking trough. This is the last water before the overnight stop, so check the level of your water-bottle.

A steep half-hour ascent follows through grasslands to a nek where your efforts are rewarded with magnificent views. To the west the Witteberg and the conspicuous Visierskerf are clearly visible, and to the south the Malutis form a formidable barrier to the highlands of Lesotho.

From the nek it is 20 minutes of easy walking to the turn-off of the two-day route. Along this section you have a bird's-eye view of the cultivated lands stretching to the Malutis. For the next few kilometres the route winds in and out of several kloofs and although mainly downhill or level, it takes longer than you will expect to get to the lunch stop marked on the map.

Tucked away in a well-wooded kloof, the lunch spot offers a welcome respite from the midday sun. A short uphill stretch follows to a nek and after passing a large overhang you will descend to a grassy plain which could become boggy after rain.

About an hour's walk beyond the nek you will descend into a badly eroded gully and after crossing a river it is only a short, steep climb to the overnight stop, an enormous, almost semi-circular sandstone overhang. Before the trail was opened the cave was used by herders who took shelter here with their cattle during inclement weather. Water is obtainable from the waterfall cascading over the lip of the cave. About seven hours are required to hike this section.

Day 2: Waterfall Cave to Protea Ridge Cave

Soon after setting off the trail ascends, easing off some 25 minutes later to skirt cultivated lands. After passing the abandoned farmstead at Rocklands, you will keep to a track through cultivated fields until a large overhang is reached less than two hours after setting off. This is an ideal shelter for a tea stop in windy conditions.

Over the next half hour the trail climbs gently, then descends, ascends and finally descends steeply, crossing a stream which has carved a narrow furrow with small potholes into the sandstone. A farm road is followed down the valley where sheep and cattle frequently graze

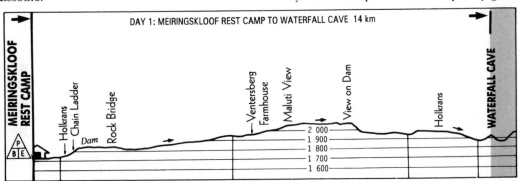

DAY 1: MEIRINGSKLOOF REST CAMP TO WATERFALL CAVE 14 km

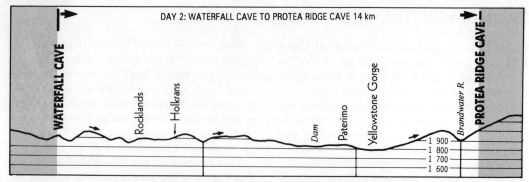

DAY 2: WATERFALL CAVE TO PROTEA RIDGE CAVE 14 km

in the adjacent pastures. About 20 minutes after joining the road you will join another farm road, passing a dam where you might see blackheaded heron, Egyptian goose, yellowbilled duck and redknobbed coot.

A little way further on you will pass a graveyard dating back more than 70 years and the old Paterimo farmhouse. As with most other old buildings in this area, dressed orange sandstone rock was used to build the house, and the barn and stables are particularly eye-catching. Since water is available here this is the most suitable lunch stop.

After crossing the Brandwater River the trail continues along a valley characterised by rows of sandstone outcrops which are reminiscent of a miniature Yellowstone. A steep climb through proteaveld must however be negotiated to the overnight shelter, which is reached about an hour after passing the Paterimo farmhouse.

Although water can sometimes be obtained from a seep just below the cave, it might be necessary to walk to the stream in the valley.

Day 3: Protea Ridge Cave to Lushof Barn
Since there is no water along the route until you reach the Little Caledon River, be sure to set off with a full water-bottle. The day's hike starts with a strenuous 40-minute climb up the Snymanshoekberg before the trail eases off, tra-

versing the mountain slopes for half an hour. After crossing to the southern side of Snymanshoekberg at a nek, the Maluti Mountains are once again visible and in fine weather this is an excellent breakfast or tea stop.

From the nek you descend initially gradually and then steeply along a ridge before traversing a grassy plateau. In the distance you will notice the cliffs of the Salpeterkrans, which you are heading for. As you approach the Little Caledon River, an alternative route – indicated with a black vertical bar on a yellow background – branches off to the right. This route, which runs along the edge of the cliffs overlooking Salpeterkrans, is recommended if the Little Caledon River is in flood.

A steep descent takes you down to the Little Caledon River which is usually easily crossed by boulder-hopping. After a short uphill stretch you will reach Salpeterkrans, said to be one of the largest caves in the Southern Hemisphere.

Salpeterkrans is still used for ancestral rituals and you may well find the cave occupied by a sangoma or other worshippers, in which case you should request their permission before proceeding.

The inside of the cave is neatly maintained and a path leads past numerous stone enclosures, some containing household goods such

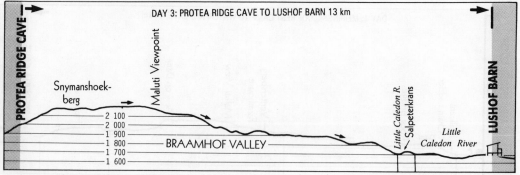

DAY 3: PROTEA RIDGE CAVE TO LUSHOF BARN 13 km

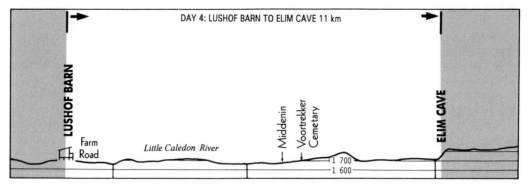

as pots, pans and blankets. At the far end of the cave the path descends to the river, which you may have to wade across. A well-defined path is joined on the opposite side of the river and here you may come across offerings such as maize, cigarettes and snuff left for the ancestral spirits. The remainder of the day's hiking continues along the river bank, initially passing through a poplar grove. Less than an hour after leaving the cave you will reach the overnight stop, an old thatched barn built from sandstone.

Day 4: Lushof Barn to Elim Cave The morning commences with an easy stretch along a gravel road before turning right onto a path which leads down to the Little Caledon River – reached about 40 minutes after setting off. The river, which is icy in winter, has to be crossed here and you are unlikely to find it narrow enough to merely leap across. For about an hour you will remain on the left bank, passing below some magnificent sandstone cliffs.

The final crossing of the Little Caledon River usually does not present a problem and once again there is an alternative route if the river is flowing too strongly. The trail now leaves the river valley and passes through a meadow at the end of which you will cross a small stream and join a farm road. The short stretch along the road is followed by a fairly steep ascent which gradually eases off and reveals a tapestry of farmlands. Forty minutes after crossing the stream you will reach the crest of a hill overlooking the valley at the head of which the overnight shelter is situated.

From here you will traverse some rock slabs and descend into the valley through a delightful poplar grove. The next hour is quite a struggle and if the trail has not been maintained for some time you will have to battle through wild roses, brambles and thickets of oldwood trees. Shortly before ascending to the overnight cave a stream is crossed, so fill up your water-bottles here.

Day 5: Elim Cave to Meiringskloof The final day commences with a short but steepish climb followed by an easy walk along the edge of cultivated fields to a farmhouse. Here a steep cement road is followed for 20 minutes before branching off to the left. A short while later a split is reached with the trail continuing uphill. After quite a slog the nek overlooking the Ventersberg farmstead is reached. A short descent follows and at the old farmstead the outward route of the first day is joined. Two hours later the chain ladder is descended and within a few minutes you will be back at Meiringskloof.

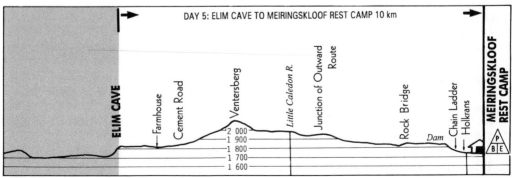

RHEBOK

This two-day trail in the Golden Gate Highlands National Park in the north-eastern Free State is situated in the foothills of the Malutis. The trail winds through open grassland, passing impressive sandstone buttresses which are especially attractive in the late afternoon when they are transformed from pink and yellow to a glowing golden colour. You will also have views of the Drakensberg to the east and the Malutis, as well as the Caledon and Little Caledon river valleys. There is also a possibility of seeing several species of game on foot.

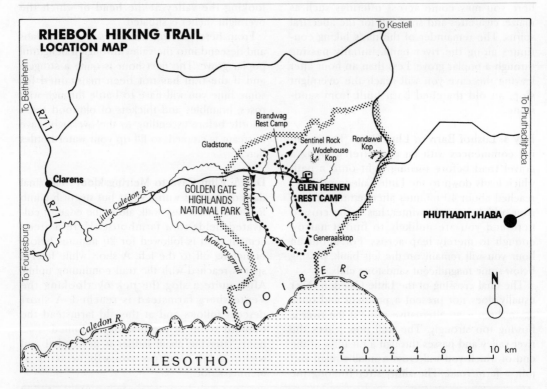

TRAIL PLANNER

Distance 30 km; 2 days

Grading B+

Reservations The Director, National Parks Board, P O Box 787, Pretoria 0001, Telephone (012) 343-1991, Fax (012) 343-0905 or P O Box 7400, Roggebaai 8012, Telephone (021) 22-2810, Fax (021) 24-

6211. Reservations are accepted up to a year in advance.

Group size Minimum 2; Maximum 18

Maps A sketch map is included in the information leaflet on the trail which is forwarded with your receipt and permit.

Climate

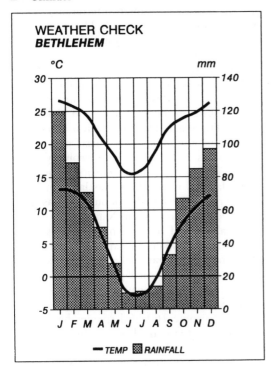

WEATHER CHECK
BETHLEHEM

TEMP ■ RAINFALL

Facilities The overnight hut consists of three rooms equipped with bunks with mattresses and a kitchen with a paraffin stove. There is also a lapa with a fireplace and

sandstone seats, two flush toilets and a shower. Firewood, paraffin lamps and a blanket for each bed are also supplied.

Logistics Circular route. There is no overnight hut at the start of the trail, but facilities at the two National Parks Board rest camps range from campsites and huts at Glen Reenen to hotel-type accommodation and fully equipped chalets at Brandwag Camp. There is a shop and filling station at Glen Reenen, while Brandwag has a licensed restaurant.

Relevant information
■ Lightning poses a danger during summer, so it is advisable to make an early start to ensure that you are not on the high peaks during the early afternoon.
■ In winter it can become extremely cold, especially when the mountain slopes are covered in snow. Sufficient warm clothing must therefore be packed.

How to get there From Bethlehem take the R49 to Harrismith for about 8 km before turning right onto the R711 to Clarens. From Clarens it is another 22 km to Glen Reenen Rest Camp. You can also approach the park via Fouriesburg in the south or Kestell in the east.

TRAIL ENVIRONMENT

Flora The sour grassveld habitat of the Golden Gate Highlands National Park has been identified as one of the park's main national assets and is, consequently, a conservation priority. The vegetation is dominated by dense montane sour grasslands with a colourful variety of bulbous plants and herbs. About 65 grass species have been identified, including red grass (*Themeda triandra*).

Plantlife is similar to that of the sub-Alpine and Alpine belts of the Natal Drakensberg and over 200 flowering plants have been recorded. In mid-summer several striking plants such as agapanthus (*Agapanthus campanulatus*), pineapple flowers (*Eucomis bicolor*), berg lilies (*Galtonia candicans*) and red-hot pokers (*Kniphofia triangularis*) add a splash of colour to the grasslands.

Fynbos relics are represented by species such

as everlastings (*Helichrysum*) – at least 20 species have been recorded in the park – ericas, *Cliffortia* spp. and *Stoebe vulgaris*.

Where the trail passes through humid marshy areas you could see the star-like white to cream, yellow and salmon flowers of *Sebaea grandis* between February and June. *Diascia intergerrima*, which bears pinkish, bell-shaped flowers between September and May, favours damp sheltered areas on lower mountain slopes.

Trees and shrubs are scarce and are dominated by oldwood, which takes its common name from the usually gnarled, twisted trunk which makes even young trees appear old. It is a member of the rose family and grows as a shrub or multi-branched tree of up to 7 m high. The woody vegetation is largely restricted to the Little Caledon River Valley, sheltered ravines and sandstone crevices where oldwood forest and mixed forests of wild peach and mountain sage are dominant. Other species you are likely to see are silver sugarbush, mountain cabbage tree, wild olive and tree fuchsia.

An interesting feature of the sandstone cliffs are the characteristic "ink lines". Until recently it was assumed that these black lines were caused by water run-off containing vegetable colouring, minerals and other dissolved substances. However, after closer investigation it was found that the lines are caused by a variety of lichens, algae and bacteria and can be formed within 30 months.

The age of some of the lichens clinging to the rocks at Golden Gate has been estimated at more than 500 years and research has shown that some lichen species contribute to the weathering process of the sandstone rocks.

Although the willow trees (*Salix babylonica*) growing along the Little Caledon River Valley are exotic, they are both aesthetically and historically important to the park and have not been eradicated.

Fauna This trail takes its name from the grey rhebok which you are likely to see along the trail. However, more often than not you will only become aware of this medium-sized antelope with its shaggy grey coat when a sharp alarm cough is emitted before they bound away. In flight they can easily be identified by their rocking-horse gait and the white flash under the bushy tail. The rhebok is endemic to southern Africa and is restricted to areas of the southwestern Cape to the central Transvaal.

When the park was proclaimed in 1962 the only ungulates occurring were rock dassie, grey rhebok and steenbok. Several species which

The grey rhebok is mainly found on mountain plateaus

occurred in the area historically, but disappeared because of human interference, were subsequently reintroduced. These include Burchell's zebra, eland, mountain reedbuck, blesbok, springbok and oribi.

Between 1963 and 1968 a total of 83 black wildebeest were reintroduced from the Willem Pretorius Game Reserve and private farms at Odendaalsrus in the Free State and Makwassie in the Transvaal. The population expanded rapidly and the park today boasts one of the largest herds of this species in the country.

A species to keep an eye out for is the oribi which favours open, short grassland on fairly even terrain. The founder population was reintroduced from Greytown in Natal.

The absence of any large predators has made it possible for hikers to explore the park on foot. However, several smaller predators such as black-backed jackal, small grey mongoose, aardwolf, caracal and African wild cat have been recorded.

To date some 160 bird species have been identified in the park. These include the bald ibis, which breeds in the park, and the rare bearded vulture which sometimes soars overhead. Other birds of prey to keep an eye out for include Cape vulture, black eagle and jackal buzzard.

The grassy patches near streams are the habitat of grassbird, while orangethroated longclaw occur in short grassland. Cape bunting can be found in the valleys and small groups of greywing francolin occur on grassy hillsides at higher elevations.

Species you may see on the rocky slopes are buffstreaked chat and rock pipit, while sentinel rock thrush and orangebreasted rockjumper occur in the uppermost elevations.

The cliffs provide a habitat for several species and those most likely to be seen here are rock pigeon and redwinged starling, as well as black, whiterumped and Alpine swifts.

Species you might see at Langtoon Dam include grey heron, hamerkop and African black duck, while Egyptian goose, yellowbilled duck and spurwinged goose occur occasionally.

A bird checklist can be obtained from the reception office at Glen Reenen.

The park has a surprising diversity of butterflies, considering the montane grassland vegetation, and to date some 78 species have been identified. The butterflies of Golden Gate are typical of those occurring in Lesotho and are

GIANT GIRDLED LIZARD

An interesting lizard you might see in flat or gently sloping grasslands is the giant girdled lizard (*Cordylus giganteus*). Also known as sungazers because of their habit of gazing into the sun for hours, this species is endemic to the north-eastern Free State, western KwaZulu/ Natal and south-eastern Transvaal.

In 1990 several hundred lizards threatened by farming operations on a farm near Harrismith and developments at the Thsiame area in QwaQwa were successfully relocated to the park.

Particular attention was paid to their habitat requirements and holes which resembled their natural tunnels as closely as possible were drilled for each lizard. Ten months after the relocation it was found that 60 per cent of the lizards had survived the move.

best viewed from late December until the end of February. The top of Brandwag Buttress is the habitat of the endemic Brandwag brown (*Pseudonympha paragaika*) and the Golden Gate widow (*Torynesis orangica*), a species which has been recorded in the park and in the vicinity of Clarens. The only population of the Basuto blue (*Lepidochrysops lerothodi*) in South Africa occurs on Wodehouse Peak, while the Basuto copper (*Poecilmitis pelion*) is to be found at the top of Generaalskop.

History Stone implements, ancient middens and paintings indicate that the San lived in the area for thousands of years before the ancestors of the Southern Sotho settled in the foothills of the Malutis about 1 500 years ago.

During the early 1820s the Difaqane wars spread westwards of the Drakensberg, displacing the numerous small Sotho chiefdoms on the Highveld and the north-eastern Free State.

When the Voortrekkers began settling in the vicinity of Golden Gate in 1837, the area south of the Witteberg was inhabited by the Tlokwa under Sekonyela. After several clashes between Sekonyela and Moshoeshoe, the Tlokwa were finally defeated in 1853 by Moshoeshoe, who became the ruler of the former Tlokwa territory.

The volatile situation on the Orange Free State/Basutoland border gave rise to conflict between the Voortrekkers and the Basotho, and in 1858 the Orange Free State Republic declared war on them. The attack against the Basotho failed, however, and it was agreed that the area conquered by Moshoeshoe from Sekonyela in 1853 (including Golden Gate) be incorporated into Basutoland.

In 1864 the boundary between the Orange

Free State and Basutoland was demarcated by the governor of the Cape, Sir Philip Wodehouse. Beacons were erected at regular intervals along the Rooiberge – the first of these on Wodehousekop and the second on Bakenkop. The area south and east of the Rooiberge was allocated to Moshoeshoe and Golden Gate remained Basotho territory.

The Voortrekkers declared war against the Basotho again in June 1865, conquering large areas, including Golden Gate. In terms of the 1866 Treaty of Thaba Bosiu the conquered territories were incorporated into the Orange Free State.

During the Anglo-Boer War of 1899-1902 almost the entire fighting force of the Orange Free State retreated into the Rooiberge. Realising that they could capture the Boers by sealing off the four major passes, the British forces occupied three of the passes on 23 July 1900 with little difficulty. After the Scots Guards took possession of the position abandoned by Commandant Marthinus Prinsloo at Noupoort Nek the Boers retreated to the only unguarded exit – the route via Golden Gate to Witsieshoek.

A plea for a four-day armistice was turned down and Prinsloo surrendered. Some 1 500 men however, escaped through Golden Gate, while nearly 4 300 surrendered.

Golden Gate was proclaimed South Africa's sixth national park on 7 September 1962. The original park covered an area of 4 792 ha and consisted of seven farms – Wilgenhof, Melsetter, Eldorado, Wodehouse, Glen Reenen, Zuluhoek and Gladstone – which were bought by the Executive Committee of the Orange Free State and donated to the National Parks Board. In

1981 the park was further enlarged when Noord-Brabant, a farm of about 1 500 ha, was incorporated and in 1988 the size of the park was nearly doubled when the Board acquired a further ten farms.

Geology The park is underlain by the upper part of the Karoo Sequence which, from the base upwards, consists of the Beaufort group and the Molteno, Elliot, Clarens and Drakensberg formations.

The most outstanding feature of the park is the striking buttresses and formations, which are especially spectacular in the late afternoon when the pink and yellow cliff faces and rocky outcrops turn a glowing orange colour. The sandstone cliffs were formed by fine, windblown sand which was deposited in a huge basin when the climate became increasingly dry during Karoo times. Originally named Cave Sandstone, the Clarens Sandstone Formation is characterised by an abundance of caves and overhangs.

These formations were shaped by a combination of several processes, including the calcification of the sandstone at different levels, resulting in differences in resistance to weathering. Another process is salt weathering, which takes place when salt solutions crystallise when they seep out near the base of the cliffs and gradually scale off the rock surfaces. In addition, groundwater is forced to seep out near the base of the sandstone when it reaches the impermeable mudstone, undermining the base of the sandstone. One of the most spectacular examples of sandstone weathering in South Africa is Cathedral Cave, which takes its name from the dome-shaped roof which is reminiscent of that of a cathedral. Although the cave is not on the trail it is well worth a visit. The cave can only be visited in the company of a Parks Board official and if you plan on visiting it the necessary arrangements must be made with the park staff in advance.

Also conspicuous is the Drakensberg Formation which reaches a thickness of 600 m at Ribbokkop. The formation was formed some 190 million years ago when vast flows of lava covered large parts of southern Africa. The lava subsequently solidified to form thick layers of basalt which are today the high mountains in the park.

Palaeontology Several fossils have been discovered in the park, mainly in the Elliot Formation and the lower part of the Clarens Formation. The most exciting discovery to date has been a clutch of six dinosaur eggs which provided the first record of fossil eggs of the Upper Triassic age (185 to 195 million years ago). The eggs were discovered at Rooidraai in 1987 and subsequent research revealed that they show a transition from reptile to bird eggs. Other discoveries include fossils of a sauropod, a small thecodont, a bird-like dinosaur, an advanced cynodont and parts of a fossilised crocodile.

TRAIL DESCRIPTION

Day 1: Glen Reenen Rest Camp to Rhebok Hut The first day's hike covers roughly 16 km and takes about six to seven hours. The start is at the footbridge over the Little Caledon River in the Glen Reenen Caravan Park and the trail gradually ascends towards the impressive Sentinel Rock. Ignore the turn-off to Echo Ravine which is passed shortly after setting off, as well as the turn-off to Boskloof a little further on. Beyond the Boskloof turn-off the trail ascends steeply, passing over a bare rocky section where a chain has been anchored to assist hikers up the slope. From the Sentinel there is an impressive view of the Little Caledon River Valley and Brandwag Rest Camp some 130 m below.

Many hikers will undoubtedly remember the exhausting climb which followed, but fortunately the route was changed in 1991. The gradient is now more gentle and from the Sentinel you will ascend gradually up the mountain slope overlooking Brandwag Rest Camp.

After skirting the Boskloof Valley for a short while, the trail swings in a north-easterly direction with Wodehouse Peak (2 438 m) dominating the scenery to the east and Spitskop commanding the view to the north.

After crossing Boskloof the trail joins up with the original route, passing behind Tweelingkop before descending steeply to the Wilgenhof Youth Complex, which can accommodate up to 60 people.

From Wilgenhof you will follow a gravel road

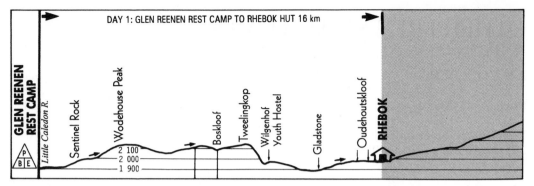

DAY 1: GLEN REENEN REST CAMP TO RHEBOK HUT 16 km

before crossing the access road to Glen Reenen. Looking towards the east, you will see an impressive sandstone cliff that so resembles the profile of William Gladstone, a former British prime minister, that it was appropriately named Gladstone's Nose. The route passes the visitors' centre and if you have any questions you can drop in here.

The final 3 km of the day's hike follow a gravel road to the overnight hut which is situated in Oudehoutskloof, named after the abundance of oldwood trees in the valley.

Day 2: Rhebok Hut to Glen Reenen Rest Camp

The second day covers roughly 14 km and requires about six to seven hours to complete.

From the hut the trail ascends gradually up the Ribbokvallei which is the favoured habitat of the park's eland population, while black wildebeest and blesbok also occur. About an hour after setting off the trail winds past interesting rock crevices where centuries of water from the Ribbokspruit carved passages up to 6 m deep. The route continues to climb and about 30 minutes later you will reach an impressive waterfall cascading into a beautiful pool.

Over the next 3 km the trail follows the watershed between the Little Caledon and Caledon rivers, gaining almost 200 m in altitude. From the viewpoint you can enjoy an expansive view of the Caledon River to the south and the rugged countryside surrounding you.

The trail then follows the eastern boundary of the park to Generaalskop (2 732 m), the highest point in the park. On a clear day this is a good place to stop for lunch to admire Mont-aux-Sources to the south-east and the impressive Malutis towering in the distance. There is, however, an optional route which skirts Generaalskop.

With only about two and a half hours to Glen Reenen, the trail descends steeply along a spur and here you will be rewarded with dramatic views of the Little Caledon River Valley and the spectacular Mushroom Rocks.

The slopes above Langtoon Dam are frequented by several game species and there is a good possibility of seeing black wildebeest, Burchell's zebra and blesbok. From the dam it is a short walk over the koppies to the rest camp. Shortly before reaching Glen Reenen you will pass a pool with a natural rock slide which is especially appreciated on a hot day.

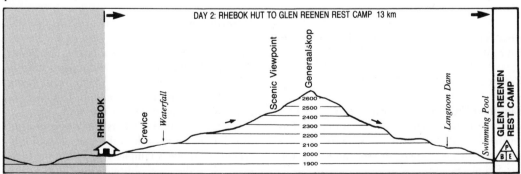

DAY 2: RHEBOK HUT TO GLEN REENEN REST CAMP 13 km

OTHER FREE STATE TRAILS

AASVOËLBERG

Distance 34 km; 2 days

Reservations Jacana Country Homes, P O Box 95212, Waterkloof 0145, Telephone (012) 346-3550.

Group size Minimum 2; Maximum 12

Facilities The overnight huts at Smitshoek are equipped with bunks and mattresses, while fireplaces, firewood, water, toilets and refuse bins are also provided.

Description Much of this moderately difficult trail in the Aasvoëlberg Conservancy in the south-eastern Free State is through unspoilt natural surroundings. The circular route starts in Zastron and is characterised by interesting rock formations, sandstone caves and forested kloofs. Highlights of the first day's hike over 18 km include the Mushroom Rock, the Face Rock and Die Oog, an impressive rock arch. On the second day's hike you will gain about 400 m in altitude to Kranskop before making your way back to the starting/ending point. Cape vultures are often seen and mammals you stand a chance of spotting include grey rhebok, mountain reedbuck, chacma baboon and rock dassie, while a host of smaller mammals have also been recorded.

BOESMANGROT

Distance 25,5 km; 2 days

Reservations Mr H Venter, P O Box 29, Fouriesburg 9725, Telephone (058222) 1702.

Group size Minimum 2; Maximum 30

Facilities Accommodation is provided in a variety of huts, rondavels and prefabricated dormitories equipped with beds, mattresses, a kitchen with gas burners, showers and flush toilets. Fireplaces and firewood are also provided.

Description The trail network on this farm just south of Fouriesburg consists of three circular routes which can be undertaken as day hikes from a base camp. The scenery is dominated by sandstone cliffs and overhangs, while the abundance of rock paintings adds an interesting dimension. Highlights of the 16,5 km Hoenderkop Trail include a chain ladder, the half-finished castle on Hilltop and magnificent views from the slopes of the 1 938 m Hoenderkop. The Old Fort Trail is a 6 km circuit which leads past caves with rock paintings and a fort dating back to the Anglo-Boer War. The Bird Trail is a short, 3 km walk along a kloof that, as its name implies, offers excellent opportunities for birding.

BOKPOORT

Distance 15 km; 2 days

Reservations Jacana Country Homes and Trails, P O Box 95212, Waterkloof 0145, Telephone (012) 346-3550.

Group size Minimum 2; Maximum 24

Facilities Hikers are accommodated in an old sandstone barn, equipped with beds, mattresses, paraffin lamps, hot and cold water showers and flush toilets. There is also a covered kitchen area with fireplaces, potjies, a skottel braai and a kettle. Facilities at the mountain huts are basic and hikers must provide their own ground sheets or closed-cell mattresses, as there are no beds. Fireplaces and firewood are provided.

Description This short, circular two-day trail near Clarens in the north-eastern Free State winds through spectacular Clarens Sandstone scenery. Highlights of the first day's hike of 7 km include a tyre ladder which assists hikers up a steep sandstone section and "Die Oog", an impressive tunnel carved by the wind.

On the second day hikers can either take the direct 4 km route back to the start or opt for an ascent of George's Pimple, at 2 540 m the highest peak in the area. Although the climb is fairly steep, this option is highly recommended on account of the breathtaking views over Lesotho and the Malutis. The route descends along a bridle path through grasslands to reach the starting/ending point after 8 km.

FIKA PATSO

Distance 23 km; 2 days

Reservations QwaQwa Tourism and Nature Conservation Corporation, Private Bag X826, Witsieshoek 9870, Telephone (058) 713-4444.

Group size Minimum 2; Maximum 24

Facilities Amenities at the start of the trail are limited to a hut equipped with gas lights, hot and cold water and toilets, while bunks, mattresses, toilets, fireplaces and firewood are provided at the overnight hut.

Description Starting at the Fika Patso Resort in a valley west of the Witsieshoek Mountain Resort in QwaQwa, this two-day circular trail winds through magnificent scenery ranging from dense kloof forests to proteaveld and interesting rock formations. The trail has been laid out around the Fika Patso Dam with a connecting route to the Mountain Resort. The first day's hike traverses the mountain slopes west and south of the dam before joining the connecting route which gains some 400 m in altitude to the Witsieshoek Hut. On the second day the route retraces the connecting route for about 5 km and then traverses the mountain slopes to the east of the Fika Patso Dam.

KAMEELKOP

Distance 23 km; 2 days

Reservations Jacana Country Homes, P O Box 95212, Waterkloof 0145, Telephone (012) 346-3550.

Group size Minimum 2; Maximum 15

Facilities Accommodation is provided at Kameelkop base camp and Oranjezicht overnight hut at the end of the first day's hike. Amenities include beds with mattresses, bathroom, toilet and fireplaces, while firewood is also provided.

Description Situated in the 12 000 ha Banke Conservancy east of Marquard, this two-day circular trail winds through an area with an interesting geology and history. The trail is named after the resemblance of the 1 903 m-high Kameelkop near the end of the trail to the profile of a camel's head.

The first day's hike covers 12 km and after winding through a magnificent kloof the trail winds across Petra Koppies with its panoramic view of the eastern Free State and the Malutis. After passing the Mushroom Rock the route follows a kloof and then ascends to the overnight stop. Highlights of the second day's route include Warden's Tower, which served as a beacon of the Conquered Area demarcated by Major Henry Warden, a dolerite dyke which extends across the conservancy and Zwawelkrans, a magnificent sandstone overhang.

KIEPERSOL

Distance 40 km; 2 days

Reservations Municipality of Bethulie, P O Box 7, Bethulie 9992, Telephone (051762) 2.

Group size Minimum 2; Maximum 10

Facilities The overnight hut is equipped with bunks and mattresses, while water, braai places and toilets are also provided. Self-contained cottages are available at the Bethulie Dam Resort where the trail starts.

Description This circular route on the outskirts of Bethulie in the southern Free State traverses kloofs, rocky ridges and hills, leading past interesting rock formations.

The first day's hike covers 16 km and after ascending Moroccokop, the highest point on the trail, hikers are rewarded with expansive views of the Gariep Dam. Further along the vegetation is characterised by enormous wild olives and cabbage trees (kiepersol), after which the trail has been named. The second day's hike winds up Broekspoort Mountain with its expansive views before winding along the spectacular Sleutelpoort Canyon, ending at the Bethulie Dam Resort, 17 km after setting off. Hikers could chance upon blesbok, eland, grey rhebok and steenbok.

KLIPSTAPEL and ORANGE RIVER

Distance 28 km; 2 days

Reservations The Principal Nature Conservator, Tussen die Riviere Game Farm, P O Box 16, Bethulie 9992, Telephone (051762) 2803.

Group size Minimum 2; Maximum 40

Facilities Accommodation at the Spes Bona base camp is in an old barn. Amenities include water, cold water showers, a lapa with fireplaces and a pit toilet. No beds, mattresses or firewood are provided.

Description The trail system on the Tussen die Riviere Game Farm, 20 km south-east of Bethulie, consists of two routes which can be undertaken as day hikes from a central base camp. A highlight of the 12 km Klipstapel route, which winds through small ravines and dry rivulets and over hills, are the piles of dolerite rocks balancing neatly on top of each other. The 16 km long Orange River Hiking Trail partly follows the course of the Orange River. The reserve is well stocked with game and hikers stand a chance of seeing kudu, eland, gemsbok, mountain reedbuck, springbok, common duiker and white rhinoceros, while 255 species of birds have been recorded to date.

KUTUTSA

Distance 28 km; 2 days

Reservations Jacana Trails, P O Box 95212, Waterkloof 0145, Telephone (012) 346-3550.

Group size Minimum 2; Maximum 30

Facilities The first night is spent in a shearing shed with hay beds, hot/cold water showers, toilet and fireplaces. Kututsa Cave, the overnight stop along the trail, is in a magnificent setting. Facilities include a rock pool where hikers can cool down, fireplaces and toilets.

Description Situated in a valley on the western side of the Witteberg range between Ficksburg and Fouriesburg, this trail traverses one of the most picturesque and interesting areas of the eastern Free State. The first day's hike covers

about 17 km. Among the many interesting features encountered are a 300 m-long manmade stone wall, a handmade sandstone sheep dip, a "hidden" valley where cattle rustlers once hid stolen cattle, and corbelled huts. You might spot blesbok, springbok, grey rhebok, mountain reedbuck and blue wildebeest. A highlight of the second day's hike, which is a mere 8 km long, is an area scattered with semi-precious stones. The trail is named after the sandstone cave Kututsa, which means "cave" in Sotho.

LESOBA

Distance 28 km; 2 days

Reservations Mrs A Viviers, 62 Nerina Street, Gardeniapark, Bloemfontein 9301, Telephone (051) 22-8659.

Group size Minimum 2; Maximum 22

Facilities The base camp is equipped with mattresses, a kitchen with a fridge, hot and cold water showers, toilets and fireplaces.

Description This trail in the mountains between Clarens and Fouriesburg has been laid out in a figure eight formation, enabling trailists to hike the two routes without the burden of a heavy backpack. The name Lesoba means "hole in the mountain" in Sotho. Attractions along the trail include well-known sandstone formations such as Queen Victoria and the Kerkdeur (Churchdoor), rock paintings and fossils. The stiff hike to the crest of the mountain is rewarded with expansive views of the Lesotho lowlands and the Maluti Mountains. The trail passes through an interesting diversity of vegetation which is especially eye-catching in spring.

MERRIEMETSI

Distance 28 km; 2 days

Reservations Jacana Country Homes and Trails, P O Box 95212, Waterkloof 0145, Telephone (012) 346-3550.

Group size Minimum 2; Maximum 31

Facilities Merriemetsi Barn is equipped with

beds, mattresses, a gas cooker, pots, kettle, fire-places, firewood, hot/cold water showers and pit toilets. Merriemetsi Lodge is furnished with two double and five single beds, a fridge and gas stove, while cutlery and crockery are also provided. Other amenities include fireplaces, a kettle, pots and pans, as well as a hot/cold water bath and flush toilets.

Description The Merriemetsi trail network in the Korannaberg Conservancy, east of Excelsior, enables trailists to explore one of the most interesting mountains in the eastern Free State from a base camp. The three one-day walks follow sections of the two-day Koranna Hiking Trail and have been designed to cover virtually the entire Korannaberg. The Green and the Blue routes both cover 10 km and can be hiked in four and six hours respectively, while the White Route is 8 km and takes between four and six hours to complete. Highlights of the trails include an interesting variety of plants, including the voetangel (*Euphorbia pulvinata*), interesting rock formations, historical sites such as Magul se Gat and spectacular views.

METSI MATSHO

Distance 31 km; 2 days

Reservations QwaQwa Tourism, Private Bag X826, Witsieshoek 9870, Telephone (058) 713-4444.

Group size Minimum 2; Maximum 20

Facilities The Metsi Matsho Hut is equipped with beds and mattresses, while fireplaces, firewood and toilets are also provided. At Witsieshoek hut facilities are limited to gas lighting, hot/cold water and toilets.

Description Starting from the Witsieshoek Mountain Resort in QwaQwa, this trail winds across grassy slopes and past beautiful sandstone formations. The trail initially follows the watershed between the Free State and KwaZulu/Natal with stunning views of the Royal Natal National Park, the Natal Drakensberg and the Maluti Mountains. At Cold Ridge the route veers away from the escarpment and descends along a ridge to the Metsi Matsho River, to reach the overnight hut near the Metsi Mathso Dam about 15 km after setting off. The first 3 km of the return leg follows a different route before joining the outward route, gaining about 300 m in altitude to Witsieshoek.

OUMA'S KRAAL

Distance 24 km plus various day routes of up to 8 hours

Reservations Jacana Country Homes and Trails, P O Box 95212, Waterkloof 0145, Telephone (012) 346-3550.

Group size Minimum 2; Maximum 16

Facilities A stone hut with 10 bunks and mattresses, gas cooker, kettle, fireplace, firewood and pit toilet is available at De Rots where the trail starts/ends. The Ouma's Kraal hut is equipped with 16 beds and mattresses, gas cooker, kettle, donkey-fired geyser for hot water and pit toilets.

Description Bordering on the Golden Gate National Park east of Clarens, this trail is situated in the 20 000 ha Clarens Conservancy, an area renowned for its spectacular scenery and stunning views. Starting at De Rots, the trail heads towards Mamkhanfu Mountain, passing behind George's Pimple before joining the circular Angel's Wing route. The trail then descends to Ouma's Kraal, which is reached 12 km after setting off. Hikers have a choice of three circular routes from Ouma's Kraal, which serves as a base camp for day hikes. The Angel's Wing route gains some 400 m in altitude and takes between 6 and 8 hours to hike. The Cheche Bush Traverse, hiked in about 5 hours, initially follows the Angel's Wing route and then traverses the western slopes of Langkrans. A third option is the shorter Ouma's Kraal Circular Route.

PLATBERG

Distance 26 km; 2 days

Reservations Harrismith Municipality, P O Box 43, Harrismith 9880, Telephone (058) 613-0895.

Group size Minimum 2; Maximum 18

Facilities Boshuis, an old forestry house at the start of the trail, is equipped with beds, mattresses, a gas fridge, stove, gas lamps, hot and cold water showers, toilets, fireplaces and firewood. The first overnight stop, Badenhorst Hut, has all the necessary facilities like bunks, mattresses, hot and cold water showers, fireplaces and firewood. Amenities at Die Skerm, a small Zulu village, comprise a lapa, hot and cold water, gas lamps, fireplaces and toilets.

Description Starting at the Harrismith Botanical Gardens, this two-day circular trail winds through the 5 000 ha Platberg Game Reserve. The first day's hike of 12 km leads to the top of the Platberg with its expansive views over the Free State, Sterkfontein Dam, the Natal Drakensberg and the Malutis, before descending to the overnight stop. The second day's hike leads back up the mountain and traverses the plateau before descending along One Man Pass to Die Skerm. From here it is a two-hour walk to the ending point through the botanical gardens and past an old blockhouse built by British soldiers during the Anglo-Boer War. The reserve has been stocked with 11 species of game including eland and blesbok, while more than 100 bird species have been recorded.

PORCUPINE

Distance 24 km; 2 days

Reservations Ms J Moffett, Porcupine Hiking Trail, P O Box 25, Gumtree 9731, Telephone (05192) 3959.

Group size Minimum 2; Maximum 25

Facilities Accommodation at the base camp ranges from a stone farmhouse to a rondavel and a cottage dating back to 1871. Bunks with mattresses, showers, toilets and fireplaces are provided.

Description This trail has been laid out in the form of a figure eight along and below Mount Denniston in the Gumtree Conservancy between Ficksburg and Clocolan. Highlights on the first day's hike include 45 steps hewn into a sheer rockface in 1925, a lookout post dating

from the Anglo-Boer War and rock paintings. Among the interesting features on the second day's hike of 14 km are the ruins of a Basotho village and rock paintings in a large overhang, while good views of the Maluti Mountains can be enjoyed.

ROOIHAAS

Distance 21 km; 2 days

Reservations Venterskroon Central Reservations Service, 66 Tom Street, Potchefstroom 2520, Telephone (0148) 294-8572.

Group size Minimum 2; Maximum 26

Facilities Accommodation at the start is provided in restored houses at the historic Venterskroon village. Amenities include electricity, a fridge, stove, hot and cold water, bath and fireplaces. Accommodation at the overnight stop comprises a rondavel and two chalets and an ablution block.

Description The Vredefort Dome provides the setting for this trail, which traverses private property in the northern Free State. In addition to the interesting geology of the Vredefort Dome, the trail also passes through an area with Iron Age settlements and relics of the goldmining days of the 1880s. The first day's hike covers 15 km, mainly across hilly terrain, with several short detours to places of interest and viewpoints. However hikers will be rewarded with panoramic views of the Vaal River Valley. The second day is a short, easy 6 km walk, ending at the farmhouse where the well-known Afrikaans poet Totius once lived. The trail takes its name from the abundance of red rock rabbits occurring in the area.

SENTINEL

Distance 10 km; 2 days

Reservations QwaQwa Tourism and Nature Conservation Corporation, Private Bag X826, Witsieshoek 9870, Telephone (058) 713-4444.

Group size Minimum 2; Maximum 50

Facilities There are no facilities at the start of the trail or on the plateau and a tent is essential on overnight trips.

Description This is essentially a day hike which can be extended into an overnight trail if an ascent of Mont-Aux-Sources is included. From the car park at the end of the Mountain Road you will gain about 550 m in altitude in just under 4 km. Two chain ladders at the end of the contour path provide access to the top of the escarpment. Those with a fear of heights are, however, advised to ascend along The Gully. From the top of the Amphitheatre you will enjoy spectacular views of the Eastern Buttress, Devil's Tooth and the Inner Tower, as well as the Tugela Falls. Mont-Aux-Sources lies about 2,5 km south-west of the Guard Hut and nearly 300 m in altitude is gained to the top of this peak. In case of sudden weather changes and snowfalls waterproof gear, warm clothing and emergency food rations are essential, even on a day trip.

SKIP NORGARB

Distance 22 km; 2 days

Reservations Mr V Moffett, Kannabos Farm, P O Box 261, Ficksburg 9730, Telephone (05192) 4542.

Group size Minimum 2; Maximum 25

Facilities The base camp is equipped with beds, mattresses, a kitchen with a wood stove and a bathroom with toilet and shower. Other amenities include fireplaces, firewood, two potjies and a kettle.

Description This figure-eight shaped trail north of Ficksburg takes hikers through valleys and along unspoilt kloofs with beautiful indigenous vegetation. The trail also ascends the surrounding mountains which offer dramatic views of the Maluti Mountains in Lesotho, the Witteberg range and the patchwork farmlands far below. Other interesting features along the trail include old Basotho kraals, interesting rock formations and rock paintings. The trail network consists of two day-hikes covering 14 km and 8 km. Since the base camp is located at the junction of the two routes there is no need to carry a heavy backpack.

SPHINX

Distance 24,4 km; 2 days

Reservations Jacana Trails, P O Box 95212, Waterkloof 0145, Telephone (012) 346-3550.

Group size Minimum 2; Maximum 22

Facilities The old farmhouse at Moolmanshoek is equipped with bunks and mattresses, stove, fridge, hot and cold water showers, toilets and a lapa with braai facilities. Facilities at the Sphinx overnight hut include bunks and mattresses, cold-water showers, toilets and a lapa with braai.

Description This trail is named after a prominent peak which resembles a sphinx. The first day's hike ascends the Witteberg range from Moolmanshoek, east of Ficksburg. Highlights of the first day's hike include two magnificent swimming pools and an optional 4 km ascent of Visierskerf. The route then winds past The Sphinx along the slopes of Jacobsberg, passing Kiepersoltuin and through dense indigenous forest to reach the Sphinx Hut after 10,5 km.

On the second day's hike the trail traverses the slopes of the two Pyramid peaks, passing a large overhang, with an optional 1,4 km ascent of Pyramid Mountain. The Sphinx Hiking Trail can be extended to a 33 km trail over three days by following the first day and a half of the Waterkloof Hiking Trail and then continuing with the Sphinx Hiking Trail.

STERRETJIES

Distance 25,5 km; 2 days

Reservations The Chief Conservator, Sterkfontein Dam Nature Reserve, P O Box 24, Harrismith 9880, Telephone (058) 612-3520.

Group size Minimum 2; Maximum 20

Facilities A campsite with running water and toilets is provided at the start of the trail at Boschkloof.

Description Situated in the south-western corner of the Sterkfontein Dam Nature Reserve near Harrismith, this trail winds mainly through grasslands with constant views of the Sterkfontein Dam. The first day's route covers

13 km, ascending steadily to Die Venster where hikers can enjoy panoramic views over KwaZulu/Natal, before levelling out and dropping down to the overnight spot. Except for the initial climb the second day's route is gently undulating. The route winds past an enormous overhang, sandstone cliffs and along the banks of the dam. The trail is named after the abundance of *Hypoxis* species, known in Afrikaans as sterretjies. During summer the yellow flowers create a spectacular display in the grasslands.

STEVE VISSER

Distance 16 km; 2 days

Reservations Ladybrand Municipality, P O Box 64, Ladybrand 9745, Telephone (05191) 4-0656.

Group size Minimum 2; Maximum 40

Facilities The base camp hut is equipped with beds, mattresses, a gas stove, fireplaces, firewood, cold water showers and flush toilets.

Description The short distances and easy terrain make this trail with its figure-eight design ideal for novices and families with children. The overnight hut is close to the Leliehoek Resort on the outskirts of Ladybrand and serves as a base camp for day hikes. The first day's hike traverses the upper slopes of Platberg, returning along a lower level, while the second day's hike leads to Die Stalle, a 30 m-high crevice which was reputedly used by the Boers as a stable during the Basotho War in the late 1850s. The trail passes through a rich variety of indigenous trees and shrubs, plantations and grassveld with panoramic views of the Maluti Mountains.

STOKSTERT

Distance 26 km; 2 days

Reservations Mrs M Pretorius, P O Box 67, Smithfield 9966, Telephone (05562) 2411.

Group size Minimum 2; Maximum 30

Facilities Hikers are accommodated in a restored farmhouse equipped with beds, mat-

tresses, showers, toilets and fireplaces at the start of the trail. The Thaba Total overnight hut has beds, mattresses, showers, solar lighting, pit toilets and fireplaces while charcoal is provided.

Description This circular trail follows an interesting route alternating between ridges, cliffs and ravines in the Caledon River Conservancy between Smithfield and Wepener. From the start at Sunnyside the trail ascends to Burnet's Kop, the highest point in the area, where an expansive view over the surrounding area can be enjoyed. The Thaba Total overnight hut is usually reached by midday and after lunch hikers can explore a 6 km loop which partly follows the course of the Caledon River, winding along the spectacular Diepkloof, one of the highlights of the day's hike. Early on the second day the trail passes close by the historic Beersheba Mission Station before following the winding course of Arendkloof, reaching the starting/ending point after 12 km.

VENTERSBERG

Distance 25 km; 2 days

Reservations Rev J Mostert, P O Box 24, Fouriesburg 9725, Telephone (058) 223-0050.

Group size Minimum 2; Maximum 20

Facilities A large overhang serves as overnight accommodation at the end of the first day's hike. Amenities are limited to water from the nearby stream and pit toilets. Campsites and self-contained bungalows are available at the Meiringskloof Resort where the trail starts.

Description The two-day circular route offers a shorter variation of the Brandwater Hiking Trail near Fouriesburg in the eastern Free State. Starting at the Meiringskloof Resort, the first day's hike follows the same route as the Brandwater Hiking Trail until the halfway mark where it splits off, descending to the overnight shelter. The second day's hike follows the same route as the last day's route of the Brandwater Hiking Trail. Much of the trail is through montane grassland, occasionally alternating with unspoilt kloofs. Hikers will also enjoy panoramic views over the Maluti Mountains and the Lesotho lowlands.

VINGERPOL

Distance 27 km; 2 days

Reservations Mrs C De Beer, P O Box 6, Paul Roux 9800, Telephone (05847) 230/1.

Group size Minimum 2; Maximum 15

Facilities The base camp at Waterskraal and the overnight hut at Witnek consist of three rooms, equipped with bunks and mattresses. Other amenities include a lapa with firewood, hot and cold water showers and a toilet.

Description The trail, south of Paul Roux, is named after the conspicuous Vingerpol (*Euphorbia clavarioides*), which is abundant on the mountain slopes. The first day's hike covers about 15 km and starts with a steep climb to the crest of the Witteberg where the hiking becomes easier. Looking southwards, hikers are rewarded with far-reaching views of the Brandwater Basin. The trail then descends to the overnight hut at Witnek, where a skirmish took place during the 1914 Boer Rebellion. The second day's hike of 12 km traverses the mountain slopes below the sandstone cliffs and is, therefore, less demanding. A highlight along this section of the trail is a large overhang where women took refuge during the Anglo-Boer War.

VREDEBERG

Distance 25 km; 2 days

Reservations Mrs J Roux, 36 De la Rey Street, Hobhouse 9740, Telephone (051982) 71.

Group size Minimum 2; Maximum 16

Facilities Accommodation at the start of the trail is provided in a clubhouse, while an old house at the end of the first day's hike is available to hikers. Amenities include running water, fireplaces and firewood.

Description From Hobhouse in the southeastern Free State the route follows the course of the Leeu River before swinging west, ascending steadily. The trail then doubles back down an unspoilt kloof and gains height once more along a kloof to Vredeberg with its panoramic views of the surrounding countryside and Lesotho. The final leg of the first day's hike is a downhill stretch to the overnight stop, an old farmhouse. The second day's hike continues in an easterly direction to the confluence of the Leeu and the Caledon rivers before swinging north to Hobhouse.

WATERKLOOF

Distance 23 km; 2 days

Reservations Jacana Trails, P O Box 95212, Waterkloof 0145, Telephone (012) 346-3550.

Group size Minimum 2; Maximum 30

Facilities The Waterkloof base camp is equipped with beds, mattresses, a two-plate gas stove, pots, kettles and a potjie, bathrooms with hot/cold water showers and baths, as well as flush toilets. Fireplaces and firewood are available. Amenities at the overnight cave include straw mattresses, fireplaces, firewood, a kettle and cast iron pots, as well as pit toilets. There are also three traditional wattle-and-daub rooms.

Description This two-day circular route is situated in the Moolmanshoek Conservancy in the Ficksburg district, immediately south of the Sphinx Hiking Trail. The first day's hike follows a beautiful unspoilt kloof where wooden ladders help hikers reach the top of the kloof. The route then follows a contour below the cliffs, with the option of climbing the 2 312 m high Sikonjelashoed Peak. An inviting rock pool in a kloof before descending to the Barolong overnight stop suggests itself as an ideal lunch spot. The second day's route initially winds along the cliffs with an option of ascending the highest point in the Witteberg range, 2 410 m-high Visierkerf, before winding down to starting/ending point.

WOLHUTERSKOP

Distance 23 km; 2 days

Reservations The Resort Manager, P O Box 551, Bethlehem 9700, Telephone (058) 303-5732.

Facilities The overnight hut on the trail is equipped with bunks, mattresses, a kitchen with a gas stove, cutlery (but no pots), hot/cold water showers, toilets, fireplaces and firewood.

Description From the Loch Athlone Holiday Resort just south of Bethlehem the trail gains some 200 m in altitude to Wolhuterskop with its expansive views of the Wolhuterskop Nature Reserve, the surrounding farms and the Maluti Mountains further afield. Further along the trail

meanders around the Gerrands Dam and then makes a wide loop before doubling back along the edge of a pine plantation to reach the hut 15 km after setting off. The second day's route is a mere 8 km. The trail winds mainly through grasslands with interesting rock formations while sections pass through pine plantations. Game to be seen in the 1 200 ha reserve includes eland, blesbok, impala, red hartebeest and Burchell's zebra.

NORTH-WEST, GAUTENG AND EASTERN TRANSVAAL

RUSTENBURG

This trail, which is close to Johannesburg, allows you a weekend escape from city life to enjoy the tranquillity of the Rustenburg Nature Reserve in the North-West Province. Hikers are accommodated in rustic thatch-roofed huts and an added attraction of this easy trail through open savanna and grassveld is the possibility of spotting game. You might even see Cape vultures soaring overhead. The diminutive but beautiful Frithia pulchra, a succulent which flowers in summer, will delight hikers fortunate enough to notice it.

TRAIL PLANNER

Distance 20,6 km; 2 days

Climate

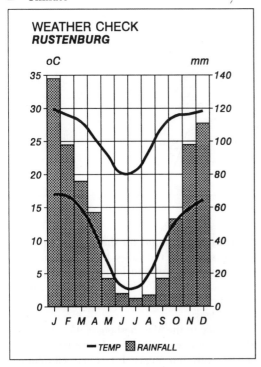

WEATHER CHECK
RUSTENBURG

Grading A+

Reservations The Officer-in-Charge, Rustenburg Nature Reserve, P O Box 511, Rustenburg 0300, Telephone (01421) 3-1050. Reservations are accepted up to six months in advance.

Group size Minimum 2; Maximum 10 Only one group is permitted on the trail at any given time.

Maps A sketch map is included in the information leaflet on the trail, which is forwarded with your receipt and permit.

Facilities The two trail huts comprise two bedrooms, each with five beds and mattresses, and a central sitting/eating area with a table and benches. An outside fireplace, firewood, two three-legged pots, a water bucket, two paraffin lamps and a dustbin, as well as a pit toilet, are also provided.

Logistics Circular route. The first overnight hut is situated at the start of the trail.

Relevant information
- Be prepared for extremes of temperature, during both winter and summer.
- Since there is very little overhead cover,

it is important to make an early start during the summer months.

■ Although distances are relatively short, it is advisable to carry two litres of water per person during the dry winter months.

How to get there From Rustenburg the

start of the trail is reached by following Wolmerans Street and then continuing along Maroela Street to the northern gate. The approach route along Boekenhout Street provides access to the reserve office and information centre only.

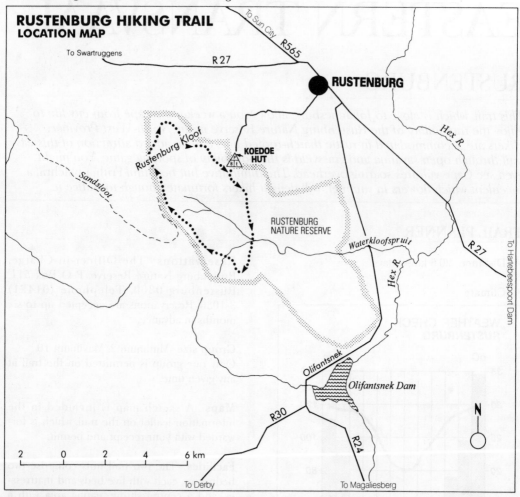

RUSTENBURG HIKING TRAIL
LOCATION MAP

To Swartruggens

R 27

To Sun City R565

RUSTENBURG

Hex R.

Rustenburg Kloof

KOEDOE HUT

Sandsloot

RUSTENBURG NATURE RESERVE

Waterkloofspruit

Hex R.

R 27

To Hartebeespoort Dam

Olifantsnek

Olifantsnek Dam

R30

R24

N

2 0 2 4 6 km

To Derby

To Magaliesberg

TRAIL ENVIRONMENT

Flora The vegetation of the reserve is sourish mixed bushveld and within the reserve several vegetation communities have been identified. These range from woodlands on the northern slopes to grasslands on the plateau.

The wooded areas of the northern foothills and slopes, as well as the higher-lying mountain valleys, are dominated by acacia and bushwillow (*Combretum*) species, while white stinkwood, Natal fig and Transvaal red milkwood occur in the sheltered kloofs.

Proteaveld is found on the plateau and the middle slopes of the valley basin and includes common sugarbush and honey-scented protea. Transvaal beech is dominant in the open savanna, while Transvaal milkplum occurs along rocky ridges.

Endemic to the Magaliesberg is *Aloe peglerae*, which produces striking red tubular blooms between July and August. It favours well-drained positions and is found on rocky slopes, usually with a northern aspect. The species was first dis-

FRITHIA PULCHRA

Among the rare plant species occurring in the reserve is *Frithia pulchra*, a succulent which grows in shallow soil with only the leaf tips exposed. This species is restricted to the Magaliesberg range, occurring from Pilanesberg in the west to Pretoria in the east, with isolated populations as far east as Witbank. The specific name means "beautiful" while the genus was named after Mr Frank Frith, who first brought the existence of these plants to the attention of botanists.

Each plant has five to seven finger-like leaves and during the summer it grows to a height of between 10 and 25 mm. The violet to white flowers vary from 20 to 25 mm in diameter and sometimes cover the plant completely. The flowers are seen at their best between November and February. When the plant is not in flower it is easily overlooked and during winter only 1 mm is exposed above the ground.

An interesting feature of this species is that the upper ends of the leaves are translucent, allowing light to penetrate to the subterranean inner parts.

covered near Rustenburg in 1903 by Ms Alice Pegler, after whom it was named.

Fauna When the reserve was proclaimed in 1967 the only antelope occurring naturally in the area were common duiker, klipspringer and mountain reedbuck. However several species have been introduced, including sable, black wildebeest, blesbok, impala, red hartebeest, springbok, kudu and Burchell's zebra. Oribi and reedbuck were subsequently also reintroduced.

The sable is the emblem of the reserve, an appropriate choice since the first sable ever recorded for science was shot in this vicinity by the traveller Captain Cornwallis Harris in December 1836. The specimen was sent to the British Museum with a description, and the antelope was initially known as the Harris buck.

Although once considered endangered, the sable is now listed as a vulnerable species. They prefer dry woodlands or mixed bush and grasslands and their distribution covers Zimbabwe, northern Botswana and the savanna woodlands of the Transvaal.

Carnivores in the area are brown hyaena, aardwolf, caracal, black-backed jackal and leopard. The primates are represented by three species – chacma baboon, vervet monkey and the lesser bushbaby.

A total of 234 bird species have been recorded in the reserve and the Magaliesberg range provides an ideal habitat for several bird of prey species.

Among the colourful species you might spot are Meyer's parrot, lilacbreasted roller, paradise flycatcher, crimsonbreasted shrike and shaft-tailed whydah.

Eleven thrush and chat species have been identified, while all four bunting species occur in the reserve. You are also likely to hear the loud, drawn-out, nasal "kwe" or "go way" call of the grey lourie and the loud ringing song of the bokmakierie.

Other species with distinctive calls include the diederik cuckoo, blackheaded oriole and the Cape robin with its characteristic "Jan-Fred-erik" call, from which its Afrikaans name is derived.

History The healthy climate, abundance of water, wild fruit and wildlife of the Magaliesberg have attracted people for hundreds of thousands of years and archaeological evidence indicates that the range was inhabited by Early Stone Age people some 250 000 years ago.

Around the middle of the fifth century Early Iron Age people settled in the area and no less than 481 settlements have been identified between Seekoeihoek and Olifantsnek.

CAPE VULTURE

Keep an eye out overhead for Cape vulture, which are seen in the reserve from time to time. Two of the 11 Cape vulture breeding colonies in the Transvaal are situated in the Magaliesberg and the total number of breeding pairs here is estimated at about 370. One of the colonies, Olifantshoek, lies a few kilometres south-east of the reserve.

About 150 to 200 years ago the Cape vulture was the most common vulture in South Africa, occurring throughout the country as well as in Namibia, Botswana, western Mozambique and southern Zimbabwe. Over the last few decades, however, numbers have declined drastically and today this species occurs in only a fraction of its former range.

The most important reasons for the decline are a shortage of carrion, improved stock farming practices, deliberate poisoning and shooting and indiscriminate use of poison by stock farmers in combating predators. Other causes are electrocution while they are perched on electricity pylons and increased juvenile mortality as a result of calcium deficiencies.

In more recent times the area was inhabited by the Tswana who crossed the Zambezi River in about the eleventh or twelfth century. Several independent tribes established themselves in the Transvaal, the area around the Magaliesberg being settled by the Kwena chiefdom, who were also known as the People of the Crocodile.

Towards the autumn of 1825 Mzilikazi invaded the Kwena territory and two months later reached the Rustenburg district. The Kwena offered little resistance and by early 1826 Mzilikazi had completed his campaign against them.

Robert Schoon, a hunter and trader from Grahamstown who undertook an expedition to the western Transvaal in 1829, gave a spine-chilling description of the devastation he found there. Survivors were found living in tree huts to escape marauding lions and hyaenas who had become accustomed to human flesh.

The missionary Robert Moffat made a sketch of one of these trees and in 1967 an old red-leaved fig, believed to be the one illustrated by Moffat, was located on a farm in the Boshoek district.

TRAIL DESCRIPTION

Day 1: Koedoe Hut to Rooihartebees Hut
From Koedoe Hut the trail winds gradually uphill through bushwillow (*Combretum*) and protea woodlands for about 2 km to the summit of the northern slopes. Once you reach the summit of the ridge there is an impressive view over Seringvlakte and Rietvallei below and the Magaliesberg range further east. Keep an eye out for clumps of honey-scented proteas as you descend through grassveld. They are sporadically dispersed over the western, southern and eastern Transvaal with isolated populations also occur-

ring in Natal. They grow up to 1 m tall and produce untidy, cream-white flowers in summer. Shortly before crossing the tarred road, the trail passes through a clump of wild seringa trees.

After crossing the tarred road which leads to the visitors' centre the trail crosses the Waterkloofspruit at a weir. Swimming is prohibited here, but fortunately Whitewater Pool is only 2,5 km further on. From here the trail continues along the northern and western slopes of the valley which are dominated by Transvaal milkplum shrublands.

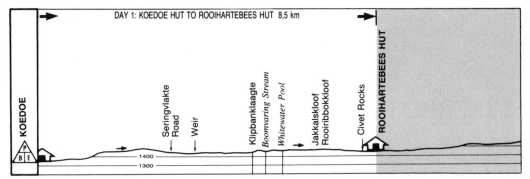

The slopes are characterised by numerous small kloofs and weathered quartzite rock formations. Just beyond the 5 km mark you will pass Boekenhoutsknop, named after the Transvaal beech which is known in Afrikaans as boekenhout. A short way on you will cross Boomvaringstroom, named after the common tree fern, and then reach Whitewater Pool – a popular resting place, judging by the flattened grass on the banks of the stream.

From here the trail crosses two more kloofs which are unlikely to have water during the winter months, gaining altitude gradually until the Little Matopos are reached.

The final section is close to the south-western boundary of the reserve and the Rooihartebees Hut is reached within about three hours after setting off. The hut is similar in design to Koedoe Hut, but water has to be fetched from a nearby stream, for which water-buckets are provided.

Day 2: Rooihartebees Hut to Koedoe Hut
The second day's hike covers 12,1 km and at a relaxed pace can be completed in four hours.

You will set off from the hut, ascending gently through protea woodlands for about 2 km before emerging into montane grasslands. A stream is crossed at the 2 km mark and it is advisable to fill water-bottles here. Continuing to climb towards Hoogstepunt (1 690 m), you will gain some 120 m in altitude over the next 2 km.

Shortly after the 3 km mark you will have an excellent view of the western Transvaal along a section of the trail which winds close to the vertical cliffs on the western side of the Magaliesberg.

From Hoogstepunt the trail skirts Waterkloof, ascending gently until the turn-off to Zebra Dam, which is situated a few hundred metres off the main track, is reached. The plateau is the favoured habitat of several game species including Burchell's zebra, red hartebeest and sable, so walk quietly and keep an eye out.

After crossing a stream, the trail gains altitude gradually towards Hartebeesrug and you will follow the ridge for a while before descending to a viewpoint overlooking the densely wooded Boskloof. A short way beyond Rock Fig Gully the trail joins Oom Jannie se Pad, one of the service roads in the reserve, which is followed for the last 3 km. Over this section the trail descends steeply to Koedoe Hut, losing about 350 m in altitude.

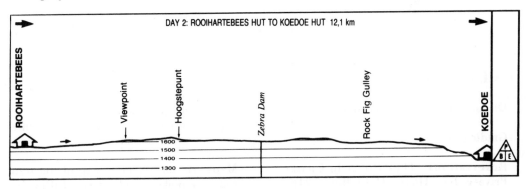

SUIKERBOSRAND

The Suikerbosrand Hiking Trail is within easy reach of the densely populated Gauteng, providing an easy escape for those who need a break from city life. The short distances between trail huts and the easy terrain make this an ideal trail for beginners and families. Various trail options are possible, allowing you to plan a hike to suit your particular needs. The trails wind through contrasting flora – from aloe veld in the west to proteaveld in the east – and you can also do some game spotting.

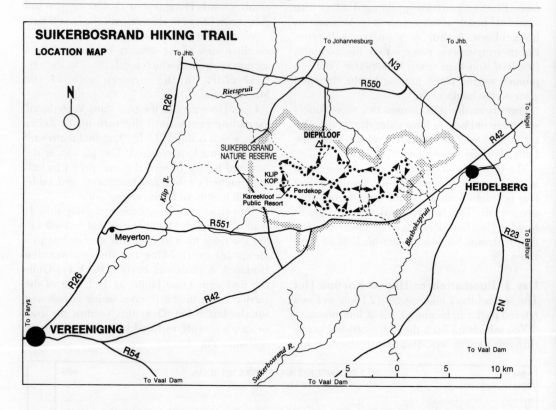

TRAIL PLANNER

Distance 66 km; Various combinations

Grading A+

Reservations The Officer-in-Charge, Private Bag H616, Heidelberg 2400, Telephone (0151) 2181. Reservations are accepted up to six months in advance.

Group size Minimum 2; Maximum 10 Huts are restricted to one party, irrespective of size.

Maps A rough sketch map of the trail routes is available and is forwarded to you with your receipt and permit.

276

Climate

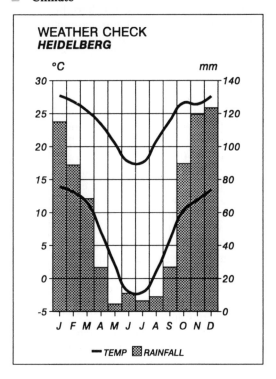

WEATHER CHECK
HEIDELBERG

°C   mm

J F M A M J J A S O N D

— TEMP   ▨ RAINFALL

Facilities Facilities at the six overnight huts on the trail include beds with mattresses, an outdoor cooking area, refuse bins, firewood, water, gas lamps and toilets.

Logistics Circular route. Although there are

no overnight facilities at Diepkloof, two of the huts – Springbok and Blesbok – are less than two hours from the start/end.

Relevant information

■ During the summer months thunderstorms occur virtually daily and lightning can be dangerous. An early start is recommended to ensure that you reach your destination before the thunderstorm sets in, usually early afternoon.

■ Water should be carried between huts, especially during the dry winter months.

■ Although the route is well marked, care should be taken at intersections because of the large number of options available.

■ Before commencing your hike do call in at the visitors' centre. The exhibits of the ecology, geology, early history and flora and fauna of the reserve will enhance your trail experience considerably.

How to get there The start of the trail in the Suikerbosrand Nature Reserve is reached by taking the R550 off-ramp on the N3 between Johannesburg and Durban signposted Kliprivier/Nigel. On the off-ramp you must turn right, following the road marked Kliprivier to reach the turn-off to the reserve about 6 km further on. The entry gate is reached 4 km further, while the start of the trail is at the northern end of the parking area at the visitors' centre.

TRAIL ENVIRONMENT

Flora The vegetation consists of false grassveld with patches of woodland and shrubland, generally known as Bankenveld – a name given to the low bench-like hills by the early white settlers on the Witwatersrand. To date some 650 plant species, including 61 tree and 115 grass species, have been recorded in the reserve.

Four major plant communities have been identified: those on the north-facing slopes, south-facing slopes, low-lying plains between 1 500 and 1 650 m and the plateau between 1 700 and 1 850 m.

The effect of climate on the vegetation of north- and south-facing slopes is particularly noticeable. On the north-facing slopes the average temperature and the evaporation rate are higher, while the moisture content of the soil is

lower. General climatic conditions are also more variable than on the south-facing slopes. Consequently, the northern slopes have a shrubby vegetation and large trees, while woody vegetation is abundant in the valleys and on rocky outcrops. Among the trees growing here are common wild currant, which forms dense thickets, baboon grape, mountain cabbage tree, blue guarri and velvet rock alder.

The wooded kloofs are the habitat of Karoo, Natal and Transvaal blue bushes, wild olive and traveller's joy (Clematis brachiata). Dense stands of oldwood occur in open grasslands, on rocky slopes, along several krantzes and especially in kloofs.

By contrast, the cool southern slopes support almost pure stands of grassland, although

The common sugarbush after which the area has been named

the common sugarbush also occurs on these slopes.

The low-lying plains and the plateau also support stands of pure grasslands, occasionally interspersed with common hook-thorn and mountain cabbage tree.

Typical tree species of the valleys are white stinkwood, lemon thorn and tree fuchsia.

Among the flowering plants are the pineapple flower (*Eucomis autumnalis*), paintbrush (*Scadoxus puniceus*) and tumbleweed (*Boophane disticha*), which flowers between September and October. Other flowering species include *Eulophia ovalis*, an orchid with cream-coloured flowers, wild gentian (*Chironia purpurascens*), *Berkheya* and the small harrowbreaker (*Erythrina zeyheri*), a small herb which has bright scarlet flowers between October and January.

Flowering plants of the steep slopes and cliffs include the meelplakkie (*Kalanchoe thyrsiflora*), an erect member of the crassula family which looks as if it has been dusted with flour (meel) and the pig's ear (*Cotyledon orbiculata*), while *Streptocarpus vandeleurii* seeks the shade and protection of rock crevices and boulders.

Fauna When the reserve was established only a few larger mammals such as grey rhebok, mountain reedbuck, common duiker and steenbok, as well as a large number of smaller mammals, occurred naturally. They have been supplemented with species which historically occurred in the area and to date some 43 mammal species have been recorded in the reserve, while a further 23 may occur here.

The reserve is a sanctuary to more than 2 000 antelope of 12 different species, of which more than a third are blesbok. Other dominant antelope include springbok, red hartebeest and black wildebeest, while kudu, mountain reedbuck, grey rhebok, steenbok, common duiker and reedbuck also occur. Keep an eye out in the open grasslands for oribi, a species which is considered vulnerable.

Until the mid-1980s the reserve boasted one of the largest herds of eland in South Africa, but in 1986 it became necessary to reduce their numbers from nearly 500 to about 350.

Among the predators in the reserve are cheetah, which were reintroduced from farms where they were in danger of being exterminated. Eight animals were originally introduced in 1975, but their numbers increased to nearly 40 by the early 1980s. This population explosion had a negative effect on the game populations, resulting in the translocation of most of the cheetah to the Eastern Shores at St Lucia, the Timbavati Game Reserve in the eastern Transvaal and the Rolfontein Nature Reserve in the northern Cape.

Other predators include the aardwolf, brown hyaena, leopard, black-backed jackal and Cape fox.

Forty-one reptile species, including 26 snake species, and 13 amphibian species have been recorded in the reserve.

To date approximately 250 bird species have been recorded and those interested in birdwatching can obtain a checklist from the visitors' centre.

Anteating chat and stonechat occur in the open grassveld, while the mountain, familiar and mocking chats prefer rocky outcrops and boulder-strewn hillsides.

In the short grasslands the cat-like mew of the orangethroated longclaw is unlikely to escape your attention.

The grassland at higher elevations is also the ideal habitat for greywing francolin, which favour short, dense cover, while redwing francolin occur on slopes with sparse, but longer grass.

Both the yellowbilled and black kite have been recorded while black eagle breed on the south-facing cliffs. Other birds of prey include blackshouldered kite, African hawk and martial eagles and the black sparrowhawk.

Species to look out for in the wooded kloofs include speckled, whitebacked and redfaced mousebirds, hoopoe, blackcollared and crested barbets, redeyed bulbul and Cape robin. Other species you could tick here are malachite, greater doublecollared and black sunbirds.

Nearly 20 per cent of the birds are associated with dams, vleis, marshes or streams and are, therefore, seasonal visitors unlikely to be ticked during the dry winter months. They include whitebacked and yellowbilled ducks, redbilled teal, grey, blackheaded and purple herons, as well as the blackcrowned night heron.

History The hills of Suikerbosrand were once used as a refuge by Stone Age hunter-gatherers who hunted the plentiful game here. They were displaced between 1600 and 1800 when the first large-scale settlement of the Transvaal Highveld took place by the descendants of the Early Iron Age Sotho-Tswana people who had established communities in the Transvaal around 300 AD. Radio-carbon readings obtained from Late Iron Age sites close to the reserve have been dated at between 1640 and 1845.

Early in 1825 Mzilikazi, leader of the Matabele, moved his stronghold at Steelpoort to the Apies River near Pretoria, bringing destruction to the Sotho people living on the Highveld.

After crossing the Vaal River in 1836, the Voortrekkers initially settled at Potchefstroom, but later spread to Suikerbosrand, Magaliesberg, Pretoria and Zeerust where they formed commando centres. At the end of October 1837 a commando of 330 men was mounted at Suikerbosrand to attack Mzilikazi. After a nine-day battle, from 4 to 12 November, Mzilikazi was defeated at his stronghold in the western Transvaal and he and his followers fled northwards across the Limpopo River.

The old farmhouse below the visitors' centre dates back to the 1850s when a farmer, Jan Gabriel Marais, settled on the slopes of Suikerbosrand. The entire complex has been restored to its original form.

The Suikerbosrand Nature Reserve was established primarily through the initiative of a former director of the National Veld Trust, Mr T C Robertson, and a former mayor of Johannesburg, Mr J F Oberholzer. Both men saw the need for outdoor recreation and a nature reserve near the vast Gauteng urban complex and their ideals became a reality in 1969 when the Transvaal Executive Committee agreed to undertake the development of the Suikerbosrand Project.

The project received the enthusiastic support of 22 Rand municipalities and the Board for the Development of Peri-urban Areas, which pledged to contribute nearly R86 000 a year for 30 years. The council of Heidelberg donated the Heidelbergkloof area, part of which was incorporated into the reserve.

Nine farms, covering more than 13 337 ha, were expropriated at a cost of nearly R3,2 million. The first animals were reintroduced in 1971 and three years later the reserve was officially proclaimed.

TRAIL DESCRIPTION

Unlike most other routes, the trail network can be hiked in any direction. A typical four-day trail description is given here which will prove to be particularly suitable for beginners or families with small children. This route can, however, be covered fairly easily in two days or extended to three days by incorporating the eastern section of the reserve into your hike.

Day 1: Diepkloof to Springbok Hut Since this section is only about 6 km long, it can easily be hiked after lunch. After reporting at the Diepkloof visitors' centre, head for the northeastern corner of the parking area where the trail starts. Take care not to follow the road turning off to the right which leads to the Kiepersol Group Camp. Almost immediately you will cross a usually dry river bed where a footbridge is provided. There is a short, gentle climb over Baboon Ridge before reaching the second trail beacon which directs you to the right-hand route. This route ascends gently along the eastern slopes of Baboon Ridge through grasslands.

About 2 km beyond the turn-off the trail passes a wall and you will notice a forested kloof to the left. The wall was built by the early white settlers to divert the water trapped by the dolerite dyke into the side valley.

The tarred game-viewing drive is crossed about 1 km further on and you will find yourself at the highest point of the day's hike (1 880 m) with good views of the surrounding reserve.

From here the trail skirts Kiepersolkloof, named after the abundance of mountain cabbage trees, descending through grasslands and a patch of acacia bushveld. Along this section you will pass a large stone-walled kraal, dating back to the Late Iron Age, shortly before reaching Springbok Hut which is tucked away in a dense patch of kloof and krantz forest.

Day 2: Springbok Hut to Eland Hut Initially the trail continues through the well-wooded Koedoeskloof, passing a number of good specimens of wild olive trees and eventually ascending into the grasslands. After about 1,5 km the walking becomes easier and along this section the pink flowers of *Aloe davyana* brighten up the yellow-brown grass in June and July.

Looking to the south-east the Kareekloof Resort and the access road to the resort can be seen in the densely wooded Kareekloof, which is named after the karree tree. Shortly after the 3 km mark the trail swings sharply westwards at Blind Man's Corner and continues along a short level section before turning into Luiperdkloof, descending along Doringbospad which has been named after the abundance of acacia species dominating the valley.

Soon after the 7 km mark you will cross the road to Kareekloof Resort which is about 2 km further on. After crossing the road, the trail immediately climbs up through the Aloe Forest where you will feel dwarfed by the tall mountain aloe. Older specimens can grow up to 6 m high, although the average height is 2 to 3 m. The yellow-orange candelabra flowers add cheerful colour to the winter landscape from July to September although their usual flowering time is from April to July.

After about 1,5 km the trail returns to open grasslands, passing over the 1 875 m-high Perdekop. The trail then descends gradually along Swartwildebeestrug where wildebeest middens can be seen. After about 1 km the trail loses some 100 m in altitude to a forested kloof where it turns sharply right to reach Eland Hut

less than 1 km further on. The water-tank and toilet are well concealed amongst the trees a short way beyond the hut.

Day 3: Eland Hut to Blesbok Hut Two options are available from Eland Hut to Blesbok Hut – a short, direct route (6,5 km) or a longer route of 16,8 km. The longer route is described here as you have the whole day at your disposal and the next day's hike is fairly short.

On leaving the hut, first retrace the previous day's steps a little way up the valley before branching off to the right. The trail continues to climb for about 1 km until it more or less follows the 1 800 m contour. After about 45 minutes an optional route to Steenbok Hut turns off to the right. This route is about 2 km longer, so continue to head for Springbokvlakte, an open grassy plain where herds of springbok, black wildebeest and Burchell's zebra are likely to be seen. At beacon number 9 the shorter route to Blesbok Hut continues straight on while the longer circuit turns right, following the route indicated to Steenbok Hut.

For about 0,5 km the path zigzags fairly steeply down the valley. Looking around you will notice that the kloof forest extends high up the sides of the valley until it is checked by the steep white cliffs, which are conspicuous because of their apparent lack of vegetation. The descent takes about 30 minutes and from trail beacon 8 it is about 1,5 km to Steenbok Hut with most of the route leading through kloof forest. At times you might feel hemmed in by what appears to a jumble of seemingly dead trees. Steenbok Hut is usually reached after about two and a quarter hours and on account of the availability of water is a good brunch or tea stop. If the hut is occupied, however, you will have to continue past.

From the hut the trail meanders through

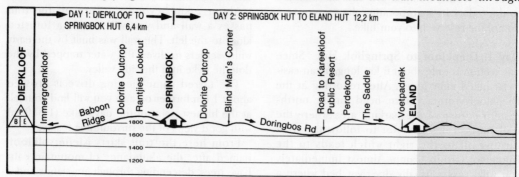

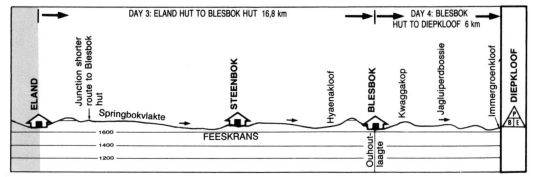

kloof forest for a short while before emerging into open grassland. From the path you will look down onto Elandsvlakte where you might be able to spot some game, especially black wildebeest and large herds of blesbok. The trail remains on a level course through grasslands, and 2 km after leaving Steenbok Hut heads off into a more northerly direction. This section of the trail looks down onto Hartebeesvlakte, where large numbers of red hartebeest can usually be seen. Soon after crossing the game-viewing road the trail swings westwards up Hyaena Kloof where common and silver sugarbushes, as well as mountain cabbage trees, are scattered together on the lower slopes. Mountain aloe can be seen higher up on the rocky outcrop to the left. Be on the lookout for eland here as they seem to favour this type of habitat. They are difficult to spot, though, as they often remain motionless amongst the vegetation.

As you ascend along the kloof the vegetation becomes more dense, and you will pass gnarled and surprisingly large specimens of oldwood. The trail soon crosses to the right-hand side of the kloof, leaving the cover of the trees, and after a short level section comes a gradual descent to Ouhoutlaagte, named after the abundance of oldwood trees in the valley. At the T-junction about 1 km after leaving Hyaena Kloof you will turn left and head up the valley to reach Blesbok Hut less than 0,5 km further on.

Once again the hut is situated in a valley, surrounded by trees, so there are no spectacular views. It is a bird-watcher's delight, however, as a large variety of birds are attracted to the wooded valley.

Day 4: Blesbok Hut to Diepkloof The 6 km to the end of the trail should not take more than two to two and a half hours, giving hikers who still have to drive home ample time. Begin by returning along the previous day's route for about 0,5 km to the T-junction where the trail turns left. You will cross over a grassy ridge with rocky outcrops before descending into a valley where the stream has been dammed with two weirs.

The trail continues down this valley, heading for the reserve fence which is reached about 3 km after leaving the hut. From here you will follow a vehicle track which winds gradually uphill along the fence for about 1 km. At the crest of the hill the remains of an old Iron Age settlement can be seen. The walls of the kraals were built wide enough so that the Tswana could walk along them when checking their cattle and goats in the kraals. It seems likely that this site was chosen because of the excellent vantage it afforded its inhabitants.

Continuing along the track downhill, the trail crosses the tarred road leading to the Protea Group Camp and then joins a path through grassland. About 0,5 km after crossing the road, trail beacon 2 (where you turned off to Springbok Hut on day 1) is reached. Less than 1 km remains and after a short ascent up Baboon Ridge the trail winds down to Diepkloof.

UITSOEK

This two-day trail in the south-eastern Transvaal takes the hiker from the foothills of the Transvaal Drakensberg to the eastern Transvaal escarpment and back, traversing deep valleys and high mountains, offering magnificent views. The route alternates between montane grasslands, pine plantations and beautiful indigenous forests. It was the first National Hiking Way Trail constructed with the active involvement of hiking clubs, especially the Roodepoort Hiking Club.

TRAIL PLANNER

Distance 29,5 km; 2 days

Grading B+

Reservations The National Hiking Way Board, Private Bag X503, Sabie, 1260, Telephone (01315) 4-1058 or 4-1392, Fax (01315) 4-2071. Reservations are accepted up to a year in advance.

Group size Minimum 3; Maximum 12

Maps The trail is indicated on a photocopy of the 1 : 50 000 map included in the trail brochure which contains information on the geology, flora and fauna of the area. It is forwarded with your receipt and permit.

Climate

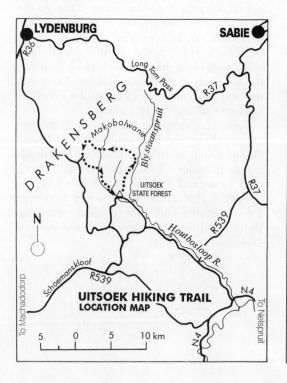

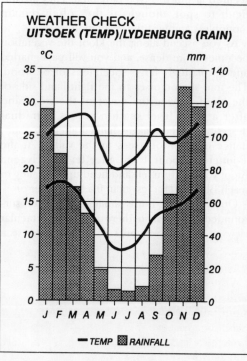

282

Facilities Lisabon Hut accommodates 12 people and is equipped with bunks and mattresses, water and a chemical toilet.

Logistics Circular route. Uitsoek Hut at the start accommodates 36 people and is equipped with bunks with mattresses, electricity, braai facilities, firewood, hot water and cooking utensils.

Relevant information
■ No firewood is provided at Lisabon Hut and hikers must, therefore, carry a backpacking stove.
■ During summer ticks can be a problem and it is advisable to take the necessary precautions.

■ Mist is common during most of the year, so take rain gear and waterproof your pack.
■ From Uitsoek Hut it is also possible to hike the Beestekraalspruit and Bakkrans day walks, both 11 km long.

How to get there Travelling along the N4 between Witbank and Nelspruit, turn left onto the R36 to Lydenburg just before Waterval-Boven. Continue along the R36 for 16 km before turning right onto the Schoemanskloof road (R359). About 26 km further you must turn left at the Weltevreden sign, continuing for 7,5 km to a T-junction. Take the road to the right, turning left onto the road signposted Uitsoek 3 km further.

TRAIL ENVIRONMENT

Flora The vegetation of the low-lying areas in the south of the Uitsoek State Forest is characterised by Lowveld sour bushveld, while patches of semi-deciduous forest also occur here. Above 1 200 m the vegetation consists of north-eastern mountain sourveld, although much of it has been afforested with pine plantations.

Among the tree species found here are Transvaal and broad-leaved beech, as well as wild teak, while oldwood is especially conspicuous at higher elevations on the second half of the first day's hike.

Grassveld flowers of interest include the dwarf red poker (*Kniphofia triangularis*) and the pineapple lily (*Eucomis humilis*). At least eight *Disa* species have been recorded in the area to date. Among these are *D. stachyoides* with its purple flowers and *D. patula* var. *transvaalensis*, which has small, pinkish-white flowers. Another species, *D. cooperi*, is restricted to altitudes between 1 800 and 2 000 m and has large white to cream flowers with a lime-green lip. All three species can be seen flowering between December and February.

Fynbos species such as *Erica woodii*, wild rice-bush (*Cliffortia linearifolia*) and everlastings (*Helichrysum*) occur on rocky outcrops.

A species of particular interest is *Encephalartos humilis*, a cycad which is restricted to the mountains of the Lydenburg, Carolina and Nelspruit areas. The specific name means "lowly", a reference to its small size (30 cm) and the fact that it is a grassland species usually growing between rocks. The 80-ha Flora Nature Reserve which lies to the east of the first day's hike has been set aside for the protection of this species.

Clivia caulescens – *a forest lily which bears striking red flowers between October and December*

Extensive patches of montane forest have survived in the Houtbosloop and Beestekraalspruit valleys and about 120 tree species have been recorded in the area. Dominant trees at higher elevations include white candlewood, forest waterwood and false cabbage tree, while white stinkwood, lemonwood, common wild quince and wild peach are common at lower elevations. Other trees include forest beech, red pear, assegai and Cape beech.

A noteworthy species is the forest lavender tree which is endemic to the south-eastern Transvaal and Swaziland. This usually small (3 to 8 m) tree favours forested ravines and riverine forests and is recognisable by its dull drooping foliage. It is especially abundant in the Houtbosloop, with excellent specimens occurring in the north-western parts of the Houtbosloop Valley.

The forest lily (*Clivia caulescens*) occurs in damp areas in the forest, while dense stands of bracken fern (*Pteridium aquilinum*) also grow in cool, damp places. Another characteristic species of the forest floor is the wild iris (*Dietes iridioides*) with its white flowers which are characterised by a yellow spot on the three outer petals.

Fauna Although the mammals are similar to those occurring elsewhere in the eastern Transvaal, you may see two antelope with a restricted distribution. The red duiker favours forests and dense thickets, while the oribi is attracted to short, open grassland. On the grassy slopes and plateaus you stand a chance of spotting grey rhebok and mountain reedbuck, while klipspringer occur in rocky areas. Common duiker occur in a wide range of habitats while bushbuck and bushpig favour forested areas.

The only large predator occurring in the area is the leopard, while the smaller predators are represented by serval, caracal, small-spotted genet and striped mongoose. Primates include chacma baboon and vervet monkey.

To date some 100 bird species have been recorded in the area. Species to keep a lookout for are white stork, Narina trogon and buff-streaked chat.

Birds of prey recorded in the area include blackshouldered kite, longcrested eagle, steppe and jackal buzzards, as well as rock kestrel.

Among the inhabitants of the rocky areas and cliffs are rock pigeon, Cape rock thrush and redwinged starling. Grassland species you might

tick include kurrichane buttonquail, fantailed cisticola and orangethroated longclaw.

History Archaeological research indicates that the area was inhabited hundreds of years ago by Iron Age people who grazed their livestock in the valleys and the grassy hills.

During more recent times the region was inhabited by the baNaqonane and the Mbayi, while the Swazis lived to the south-east. The baNaqonane inhabited the Lowveld between the Lomati River in the south and the Sabie River in the north, while the Mbayi, a group of Bapedi origin, lived in the foothills and mountains of the Transvaal escarpment.

During the first half of the 1800s, the baNaqonane and Mbayi were subjugated by the Swazis under King Sobhuza I, who conquered the lowveld and the escarpment between the Crocodile and Olifants rivers. To escape the periodic raids of the Swazis, the Mbayi took refuge in the forests and remnants of the structures they built in the forests can still be seen.

In 1846 the areas conquered by Sobhuza were ceded to the Voortrekker republic of Ohrigstad and two years later the first whites started settling in the area. The forests in the higher-lying areas were a ready source of timber for the settlers who needed wood for their wagons and for construction. The north-western part of the Houtbosloop Valley was, however, declared a public timber resource – the first state forest in the Transvaal.

At the time the government at Lydenburg was known as the Kantoor, hence the name Kantoorbos. Exploitation of the 12 different kloofs in the upper Houtbosloop Valley was controlled by a forestry office which was situated in the centre of the forest – the ruins of which can still be seen today.

In 1849 the valleys of the Uitkyk plateau were subdivided into farms, but malaria took a heavy toll and many farmers moved back to the Highveld. When the seat of the Zuid-Afrikaansche Republiek (Transvaal Republic) was moved to Pretoria in 1860 more farmers moved out of the area and by the 1870s large areas were abandoned.

Following the discovery of gold in the eastern Transvaal in 1872, gold was also discovered in the south-eastern Transvaal. Although prospectors undoubtedly explored the hills in the area, mining activities were centred on Barberton and Kaapsehoop.

During the late 1870s and early 1880s, horses and mules were in short supply and zebras were bred and trained as draught animals at the farm Beestekraal. The remains of the stone-wall stables can still be seen here.

During the 1930s two gold mines were opened in the Uitsoek area, the Uitsoek Mine on the slopes of the Blystaanspruit and the Rocky Ridge Mine in the Mynrug area.

TRAIL DESCRIPTION

Day 1: Uitsoek Forest Station to Lisabon Hut

From the forestry station the trail ascends steadily along the eastern slopes of the Beestekraalspruit. About 2,5 km after setting off you will cross a stream and since the next water is some 6 km further on it is advisable to fill your water-bottle here.

A little further you will join a forestry road and over the next 5 km you will gain 400 m in altitude, ascending steeply near the 8 km mark. Shortly after the 8 km mark the headwaters of the Beestekraalspruit are crossed and the trail then more or less follows the 1 800 m contour along the southern slopes of Makobolwane. This section passes through the Mokobulaan Nature Reserve which covers an area of 1 200 ha in the catchment areas of the Houtbosloop, Beestekraalspruit and Blystaanboschspruit. It was declared the 20th nature reserve in state forests in September 1992.

Just beyond the 10 km mark the trail skirts the upper reaches of the Kwagga River and about 1 km further on descends steeply into Clivia Gorge, where the Houtbosloop originates. It is worthwhile persevering to this shady kloof for lunch.

From Clivia Gorge the trail ascends steeply to the escarpment, gaining some 180 m in less than 1 km. The trail then follows an easy route across a rocky hill, passing close to a fire lookout tower. Keep an eye out here for *Aloe chor-*

toloroides, while the coral-red flowers of the krantz aloe create a spectacular display between May and July.

Situated on a small rise, Lisabon Hut is reached after a short climb and has a commanding view of the surrounding countryside. Built from natural stone, the hut consists of two bedrooms equipped with six bunks each and a central dining area. Water is pumped from a nearby stream.

Day 2: Lisabon Hut to Uitsoek Forest Station

After a short uphill stretch through grassland, the trail passes through pine plantations before winding close to the escarpment edge.

Near the 3 km mark the trail drops into Grootkloof, making its way down the near-vertical cliffs before following a zigzag course along the slopes and following a tributary of the Houtbosloop. In just over 3 km you will lose about 500 m in altitude to the Houtbosloop Valley, passing through beautiful indigenous forest.

You will then follow the course of the Houtbosloop through the original Kantoorbos, criss-crossing the Houtbosloop countless times. Many of the wooden bridges were built by members of the Roodepoort and other hiking clubs who assisted with the construction of the trail. Between 1987 and 1989 some 100 club members spent more than 400 hours helping to

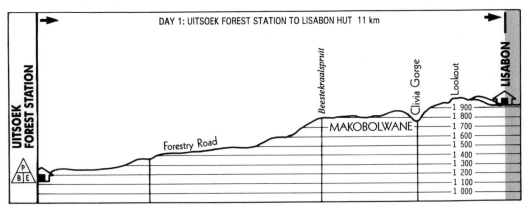

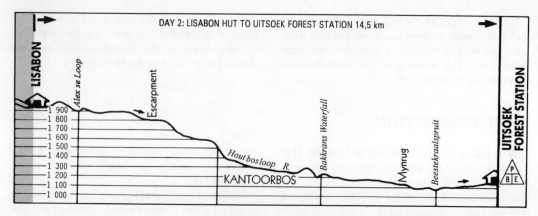

build the trail and the three routes at Uitsoek probably have the largest number of bridges in any trail area.

Shortly before the 9 km mark the trail makes a detour to the Bakkrans Waterfall which is tucked away in dense vegetation. With less than 6 km remaining to the end, the waterfall with its

large pool is an excellent lunch stop. From here the trail continues to follow the course of the Houtbosloop and after running along a contour, the Beestekraalspruit is crossed at Elandsdrif. The final section of the trail winds gradually uphill through protea grassveld to reach Uitsoek after 14,5 km.

FANIE BOTHA

The Fanie Botha Hiking Trail was the first National Hiking Way Trail and was officially opened during the Green Heritage Year in 1973. Located on the Drakensberg escarpment in the eastern Transvaal, the trail alternates between pine plantations, patches of indigenous forest and grassland, offering many splendid views of the Lowveld. Several of the popular tourist attractions of the eastern Transvaal, including Mac-Mac Falls, the Pinnacle and God's Window, are seen on this route.

TRAIL PLANNER

Distance 79 km; 5 days (shorter options, including two 2-day circular routes are possible)

Grading C

Reservations The National Hiking Way Board, Private Bag X503, Sabie 1260, Telephone (01315) 4-1058 or 4-1392, Fax (01315) 4-2071. Reservations are accepted up to a year in advance.

Climate

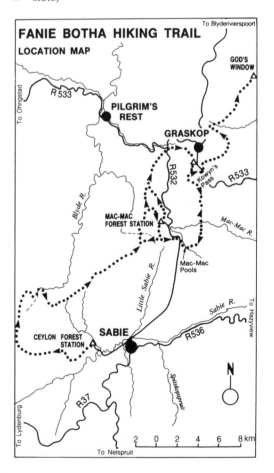

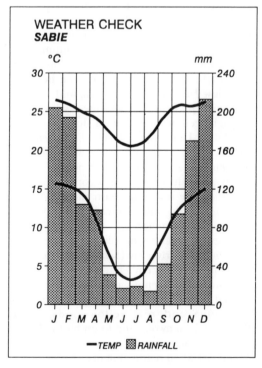

287

Group size Minimum 2; Maximum 30

Maps A full-colour trail map with useful information on the history, flora and fauna of the area on the reverse is available and is forwarded to you with your permit and receipt. One map is supplied for every six adults.

Facilities The six trail huts are equipped with bunks with mattresses, cooking pots, firewood, fireplaces, water, refuse bins and toilets.

Logistics Linear route, requiring two vehicles. Although there is no public transport it is usually fairly easy to hitch a lift between God's Window and Sabie. The first overnight hut, Ceylon Hut, is at the start of the trail, while the President Burgers Hut at Mac-Mac Forest Station is also conveniently situated. There is no overnight hut at God's Window where the trail ends.

Relevant information
■ It is advisable to set off with a full water-bottle from each hut, especially between May and September, when little water is available.
■ Water at the huts must be used sparingly.

How to get there From Sabie the starting point at Ceylon Forest Station is reached by turning left into Lydenburg Street. Turn onto the road signposted to the Bridal Veil Falls 3 km further to reach the forest station about 3 km past the turn-off to the falls.

TRAIL ENVIRONMENT

Flora The trail is primarily through plantations, but some sections traverse grassland and indigenous forest. The mountain sourveld vegetation is dominated by redgrass (*Themeda triandra*), russet grass (*Loudetia simplex*) and toothbrush grass (*Rendlia altera*). A large variety of flowering plant species such as red-hot pokers (*Kniphofia*), pineapple flowers (*Eucomis*) and gladioli grow in the grassveld. Especially attractive during late summer and early autumn are the clumps of pink *Watsonia transvaalensis* on the Hartebeestvlakte. Also to be seen here are the yellow *Helichrysum acutatum*, wild verbena (*Pentanisia prunelloides*) and the *Hypoxis* with its bright yellow, star-shaped flowers. Ericas include the Drakensberg heath (*E. drakensbergensis*) which bears attractive white flowers between January in July and *E. woodii* which usually grows in ravines. Also common in the grassveld is the silver sugarbush and the African white sugarbush, with its creamy white flowers prolific in mid-summer.

Alongside streams you will notice tree ferns, while the scarlet river lily (*Schizostylis coccinea*) flowers between December and February.

Patches of indigenous montane forest have survived in the kloofs and ravines and include Outeniqua and real yellowwoods, white stinkwood, lemonwood and forest bushwillow to mention a few. Some 57 trees occurring along the trail are listed on the trail map.

You will be able to identify many of the plants seen on the trail by carrying Jo Onderstall's *Wild Flower Guide to the Transvaal Lowveld and Escarpment* which illustrates about 350 species.

The first known commercial planting of trees in the area took place as long ago as 1876, when J Brooke Shires planted eucalyptus and wattles for mining timber. As a result of the change from alluvial to reef working in 1881 the demand for timber increased and the indigenous forests were soon exhausted.

In 1878 a patch of eucalyptus was planted at Elandsdrif and 25 years later the Transvaal Gold Mining Estates planted the first eucalyptus and wattle plantations at Driekop near Graskop.

The then Department of Forestry followed suit and established its first pine plantations at Mac-Mac in 1906. Between 1929 and 1932 vast afforestation schemes were launched by the government in this region to provide work for the thousands of farmers who were forced off their farms during the 14 years of drought and the depression.

Today plantations in the eastern Transvaal cover over 257 000 ha and supply about 50 per cent of South Africa's sawn timber requirements.

Fauna Very little has remained of the wildlife which once made the area attractive to hunters.

BLUE SWALLOW

The blue swallow is restricted to the grasslands of the mist-belt along the eastern escarpment of the Transvaal and in south-central KwaZulu/Natal from Greytown southwards to Ixopo. It is considered endangered and in 1994 the total population of breeding pairs in South Africa was estimated at just over 50. The main reason for their decline is commercial afforestation, which has reduced their foraging grounds, and the loss of suitable breeding sites.

They occur either singly or in small groups of up to nine birds. The nest, a half-cup of mud mixed with fine grass, is built in potholes in subterranean streams, dongas and antbear holes.

This species can be identified by its metallic blue-black plumage and long outer tail feathers. Unlike most *Hirundo* species, it lacks red in the plumage and white spots in the tail feathers. Since it is an intra-African migrant it is usually only seen between late September and April.

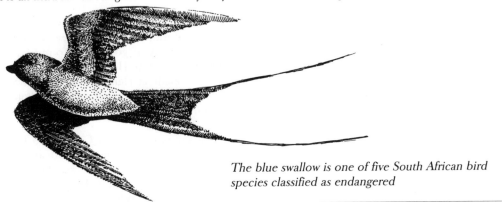

The blue swallow is one of five South African bird species classified as endangered

Today the wildlife is restricted to the forested gorges, the grassveld of the mountains and, to a lesser extent, the plantations.

Hartebeestvlakte takes its name from the red hartebeest which used to roam on these plains, but disappeared in the 1930s. However, after an absence of more than 60 years the plain could live up to its name again in 1991 when two red hartebeest escaped from an adjoining farm and settled on the plain.

Klipspringer, grey rhebok, mountain reedbuck and oribi favour the grassveld, while common duiker occur in open, bushy country, but feed on the forest fringes. Bushbuck occur in the forests and plantations, which are also the habitat of bushpig.

Chacma baboon and rock dassie are common and are usually encountered near rocky ridges. Several other mammal species such as leopard, caracal, serval, Cape clawless otter, honey badger and black-backed jackal, as well as other smaller predators, also occur, but because of their shy, secretive behaviour they are unlikely to be encountered.

Because of the variety of both vegetation and terrain, the region is rich in birdlife. Two species which have been recorded on Hartebeestvlakte and are likely to be of particular interest to birders are the blue swallow and the broadtailed warbler.

Among the birds of prey favouring stony sites and krantzes are black eagle, jackal buzzard and rock kestrel. Other species to look out for here include rock pigeon, Cape rock thrush and redwinged starling.

The open grassveld attracts species such as Swainson's francolin and helmeted guineafowl. Gurney's sugarbird is usually found near stands of proteas, while the stonechat is generally seen perching on the tips of dry twigs or grass stems.

Species to be seen in the plantations include the rameron pigeon which is conspicuous by its yellow bill and feet, while the plaintive call of the diederik cuckoo can be heard from late September to March.

The indigenous forests and kloofs are the favoured habitat of the Knysna lourie, redchested cuckoo and sombre bulbul. Malachite and scarletchested sunbirds are attracted to the nectar of flowering species such as aloes which often cling to rockfaces of kloofs.

Along or near watercourses you could tick blue crane, rock martin, longtailed and Cape wagtails, masked weaver and red bishop.

History Until the arrival of the Early Iron Age

pastoralists around the fourth century, the area was inhabited by the San and to date more than 100 Later Stone Age sites have been located in the Transvaal, a number of them in the eastern Transvaal.

During the 1500s large areas of the Transvaal, including the eastern Transvaal, were settled by the Sotho-Tswana, while the Ndebele were one of the first Nguni groups to settle in the Transvaal. They are known to have settled in the Randfontein area around 1550 and later moved to the area north of Wonderboom.

After a dispute over the chieftainship, the younger son Ndunduza and his followers settled in the upper reaches of the Olifants River. These people are today known as the Southern Ndebele and their brightly coloured and patterned houses are a familiar sight on the Highveld.

The 1600s saw the arrival of a Sotho chieftaincy, known as the Pedi, in the northern Transvaal and they incorporated the Sotho clans into an empire in the central Transvaal area known as Sekukuniland.

During the Difaqane or "forced migrations", the Matabele of Mzilikazi caused widespread destruction among the Sotho and virtually destroyed the Pedi during a campaign in 1826. The Swazi also regarded the eastern Transvaal as their territory and raided the Pedi and other Sotho groups and it was not until 1864 that they were finally defeated during the battle of Moholoholo.

The battle took place at Mariepskop, named after Chief Maripi who chose the nearby Moholoholo ("The Very Great One") as a sanctuary for himself and his followers.

Between 1835 and 1840 the eastern Transvaal experienced an influx of Tsonga people from Mozambique, northern Zululand and the north-eastern Transvaal following raids by a Nguni clan under Chief Soshangane. Those who refused to submit to their Zulu ruler are still known as Tsonga, while tribes who accepted Zulu rule and adopted Nguni customs and traditions became known as Shangaan, after Chief Soshangane.

The numerous springs and the Sabie River were popular camping and resting places and the early white hunters and explorers knew the area by its African name, Sabielala or the "Sabie Sleeping Place". The name Sabie is said to be derived from the Shangaan word meaning "Sand".

The history of the eastern Transvaal is inextricably linked with that of man's search for gold. The first traces of gold were found east of Lydenburg in 1869. However, more promising finds were made at Hendriksdal south of Sabie in 1873 and shortly afterwards at Spitzkop and Geelhoutboom, resulting in a gold rush to the eastern Transvaal.

For many years Thomas Glynn, who bought the farm Grootfontein in 1880 and later renamed it Sabi (later Sabie), searched in vain for gold in the area until in 1895 it was discovered – by accident. While camping in the upper reaches of the river, Glynn and some friends engaged in target shooting when a stray bullet struck a rock and exposed what appeared to be a gold-bearing reef. The Glynns-Lydenburg Gold Mining Company was floated and between May 1897 and July 1950 the mine milled 3,4 million tons of ore and extracted 1,2 million oz of gold, making a profit of £ 2,1 million.

Between 8 and 10 September 1900 fierce fighting took place in the mountains south of Sabie when the Boers put their Long Tom cannons into action against the pursuing British forces of General Redvers Buller. Several reminders of this battle, including the last position of the Long Toms and a Long Tom shell-hole, can be seen along the Long Tom Pass between Lydenburg and Sabie.

TRAIL DESCRIPTION

Day 1: Ceylon Hut to Maritzbos Hut From the Ceylon hut the trail follows a road through pine plantations lined with turpentine trees (*Syncarpia glomulifera*), gaining some 300 m in altitude over the first 3 km. After descending for a short distance (during which time you lose 200 m in altitude) the trail levels out and further along crosses the Lone Creek – Sabie's domestic water supply.

Here the trail splits, ascending gently on either side of a grove of match poplars (*Populus deltoides*) with the path to the right following the course of the Lone Creek. These poplars are native to the southern and south-eastern

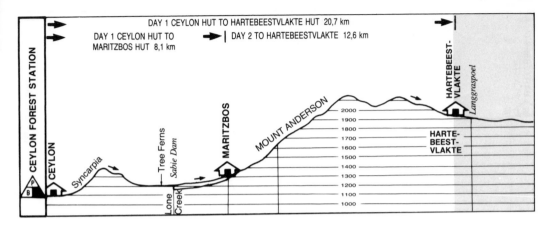

regions of the United States and the first record of their cultivation in South Africa was in 1878. As the common name suggests, they are especially suitable for the manufacturing of matches and skillets for match boxes.

Maritzbos Hut is usually reached in about three hours and is conveniently situated for hikers setting off after lunch. It was built a few years after the trail was opened to shorten the long first day (20,7 km) to Hartebeestvlakte Hut. The indigenous forest here was named after a certain Maritz, a woodcutter who exploited the forest in the 1800s for mining timber.

Day 2: Maritzbos Hut to Hartebeestvlakte Hut

Although the day's hike is a mere 12,6 km, you will gain more than 800 m in altitude and it is advisable to start early and to take your time. There is a choice of two routes: you can either take the plantation route or you can follow the course of the Lone Creek through Maritzbos. The Maritzbos route is, however, impassable after heavy rains.

The route through Maritzbos winds through a patch of beautiful indigenous forest of yellowwoods, white stinkwood and lemonwood, to mention but a few of the typical high forest species. Keep an eye open for the cabbage trees, which are especially striking in Maritzbos. The route zigzags through the forest, frequently crossing the Lone Creek, and at Tarka Falls and Piper Pools you can brave the crisp, refreshing water of the river. It is advisable to fill your water-bottle at one of these streams as there is no water until Hartebeestvlakte Hut. After leaving the indigenous forest there is a steep climb through pine plantations before the trail joins the alternative route from Maritzbos Hut.

If you take the plantation road, fill your water-bottles at Maritzbos Hut and use the water sparingly as there is no water along this route. From the hut the trail ascends steeply along a forestry road through pine plantations. Where the two trails join you will have to negotiate a rather steep section, but fortunately it is short.

After passing through a patch of pines the trail emerges into grassveld, following a jeep track along the eastern slopes of Mount Anderson (2 277 m), the second highest point in the Transvaal. In the mid-1800s the old wagon road to Delagoa Bay (Maputo) used to cross here, hence the old name Delagoosberg.

The trail continues to ascend steadily, reaching a height of some 2 150 m before descending to a ridge which affords magnificent views of the Spekboom and Blyde rivers. After a final uphill section the trail descends to Hartebeestvlakte Hut, an old farmhouse with pine trees serving as a windbreak.

Day 3: Hartebeestvlakte Hut to Mac-Mac Hut

The section between Hartebeestvlakte Hut and Mac-Mac Hut covers just over 19 km and takes about seven hours to complete.

Initially the trail descends gently through grassveld and after about 1 km reaches Langgraspoel, which makes a pleasant breakfast stop. From here you will carry on descending through grassland past the Blyde Falls and at the 2 km mark you join a gravel road through pine plantations.

After about 4 km you will reach Tweehekke where the alternative shorter route to Ceylon Forest Station branches off to the right. This route reaches the Bridal Veil Falls after 6,5 km and the final stretch to the forest station follows the outward route of the Lourie Nature Walk.

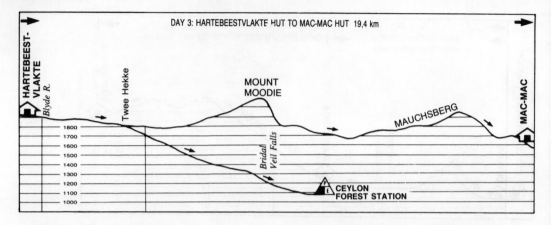

The trail to Mac-Mac Hut continues along the edge of the pine plantation to reach the turn-off to the Tweehekke Pools a short way further. The pools are situated some distance off the trail, but as there is no water further along the trail it is advisable to fill water-bottles here.

Skirting the edge of the pine plantation, the trail winds up to Mount Moodie (2 078 m) and you will have a magnificent view of Sabie some 1 000 m below and Graskop further along the valley. The trail descends steeply from the summit of Mount Moodie, losing nearly 300 m in altitude, and continues along a ridge of Mauchsberg. This mountain was named after a German explorer, Karl Gottlieb Mauch, who first predicted in the late 1860s that gold would be discovered in the area.

After following a route alongside a beautiful patch of montane forest, the trail swings towards Mauchsberg Peak (2 115 m), climbing gently to its eastern edge before losing height rapidly at first and then more gently, passing through open grassveld to the overnight hut.

Day 4: Mac-Mac Hut to Graskop Hut There is a choice of two routes – a 22 km route via Mac-Mac Pools or a 13 km route via The Bonnet.

Mac-Mac Pools Route
From the hut the trail descends through pine plantations, reaching the supplementary route starting at the Mac-Mac Forest Station after 3 km. Continue along the right-hand route and about 3 km further you will cross the Sabie/Graskop road to reach the Mac-Mac Falls a short way onwards. The area was originally known as Geelhoutboom because of the abundance of yellowwood trees.

Following the discovery of gold in the area in 1873 large numbers of foreign prospectors, a great many of them Scotsmen, flocked here and by March 1873 about 180 diggers were living there. When President F T Burgers of the Zuid-Afrikaansche Republiek (Transvaal Republic) visited the diggers in August that year, he renamed it Mac-Mac after the many Scotsmen who were introduced to him.

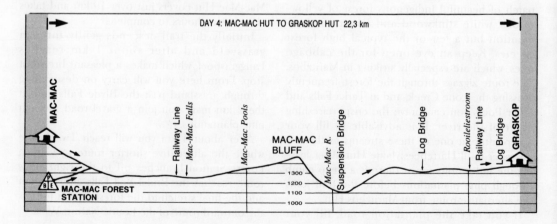

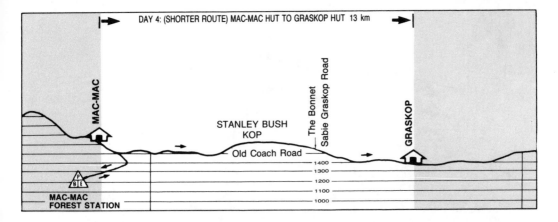

The 65 m-high falls were originally a single waterfall, but in 1873 miners blasted the crest of the falls in search of gold, splitting the stream in two.

The trail ascends gently through open grassveld for about 3 km before it reaches Mac-Mac Pools. The pools were created by trapping the river behind a succession of weirs just below the small waterfall. The picnic site nearby is popular with tourists which somewhat detracts from the feeling of being away from it all.

After ascending along Mac-Mac Bluff the trail drops sharply to the Mac-Mac River where a suspension bridge takes you across the river. The route then ascends through indigenous forest before following an easy route through pine plantations interspersed with a stretch of grassveld to Graskop Hut.

The Bonnet Route
From the hut the trail follows an undemanding route through pine plantations, passing a swimming pool after about 2,5 km before it is joined by the Prospector's Hiking Trail which begins at

Mac-Mac Forest Station. The two trails follow the same route for about 1 km before the Prospector's trail branches off to the left to continue to Pilgrim's Rest.

The Fanie Botha trail continues along the eastern slopes of Stanley Bush Hill, passing mine excavations and partly following an old coach road. At The Bonnet you will cross the Sabie/Graskop road and follow a route leading alongside and through pine plantations to the hut 4 km further on.

Day 5: Graskop Hut to God's Window The final section covers 14,5 km and is normally completed in four hours of very easy walking. Along this section you will have some magnificent views of the Lowveld, but unfortunately the last 4,5 km of the trail runs close to the tarred road. Not only will you hear the traffic roaring by, but meeting up with tourists at viewpoints is something of an anti-climax.

From Graskop the trail heads south-east, crossing the railway line and, a little further, the road to Bosbokrand. After skirting the Graskop

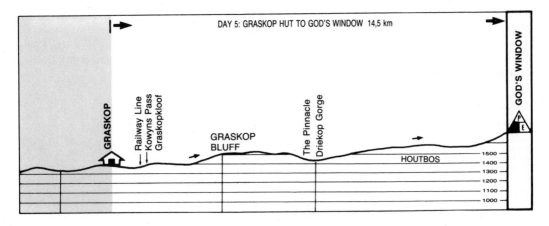

The Pinnacle, which is passed on the final day of the Fanie Botha Hiking Trail

Gorge the route ascends through open grassveld and lichen-clad weathered rock formations up Graskop Bluff before dropping down to the Driekop Gorge. The 30 m-high Pinnacle rock formation at the head of the gorge is reached shortly before the 9 km mark. Looking down the densely wooded gorge, a magnificent patchwork view of the plantations of the Lowveld stretches as far as the eye can see.

The remaining 6,5 km winds close to the edge of the escarpment, ascending gently, with more splendid views of the Lowveld some 1 500 m below. The route ends at the parking area at God's Window, which is also the start of the Blyderivierspoort Hiking Trail.

ALTERNATIVE ROUTES

From Ceylon Forest Station it is possible to do a two-day circular route (26,4 km) via Hartebeestvlakte.

The trails in the vicinity of Mac-Mac Forest Station have been changed to allow two-way traffic, making it possible to do a two-day circular trail (42 km), starting and ending at Mac-Mac Forest Station. The route takes you from Mac-Mac Forest Station to Graskop Hut via The Bonnet, returning via Mac-Mac Pools on the second day.

The President Burgers Hut at Mac-Mac Forest Station is conveniently situated for trailists undertaking this two-day hike.

PROSPECTOR'S

On this trail, which traverses the Transvaal Drakensberg in the scenic eastern Transvaal, you will follow in the footsteps of the early miners. The trail winds past deserted goldmines, along old coach routes and through the historic mining village of Pilgrim's Rest. This little town is a reminder of the heady days after the discovery of gold when men ordered footbaths of champagne and lit cigars with £ 5 notes. The historic atmosphere is enhanced by the authentic miner's cottage on the outskirts of Pilgrim's Rest, which is the first overnight stop.

TRAIL PLANNER

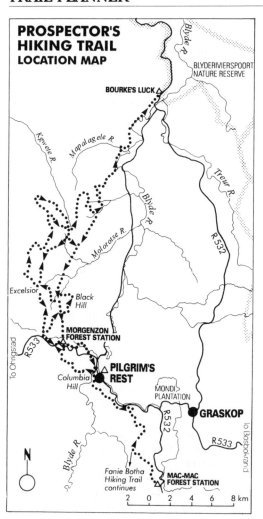

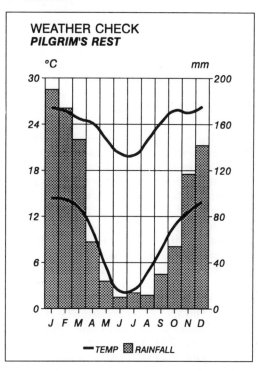

Climate

Distance 69 km; 6 days (shorter options possible)

Grading B

Reservations The National Hiking Way Board, Private Bag X503, Sabie 1260,

Telephone (01315) 4-1058 or 4-1392, Fax (01315) 4-2071. Reservations are accepted up to a year in advance.

Group size Minimum 2; Maximum 30

Maps A full-colour trail map with useful information on the history, flora and fauna of the area on the reverse is forwarded to you with your receipt and permit. One map is supplied for every six adults.

Facilities The trail huts are equipped with bunks with mattresses and there are also fireplaces, firewood, water, refuse bins and toilets.

Logistics Either circular or linear. The linear route ends at Bourke's Luck on the R532 between Graskop and Blydepoort and it is usually fairly easy to hitch a lift back to Mac-Mac. Hikers using Mac-Mac Hut as their first overnight stop must depart from Mac-Mac Forest Station before 15:30 in winter and 16:00 in summer to reach the hut before dark. Alternatively, reservations

should be made for the President Burger's Hut at the forestry station.

To accommodate late arrivals the route between Morgenzon Forest Station and Morgenzon Hut, and between Mac-Mac Forest Station and Mac-Mac Hut, is indicated with illuminated footprints, so keep a torch handy.

Relevant information

■ It is advisable to set off with a full water-bottle from each hut, especially between May and September when little water is available.

■ The gates at Bourke's Luck are open from 07:00 to 17:00 daily and no entries or departures are permitted after hours. Hikers ending at Bourke's Luck are required to pay entrance fees to enter the Blyderivierspoort Nature Reserve and must produce the cash register slip when collecting their vehicle.

How to get there The trail starts at Mac-Mac Forest Station, situated a short distance from the Mac-Mac Falls on the R532 between Sabie and Graskop.

TRAIL ENVIRONMENT

Flora The vegetation of the area is dominated by open, sour *Themeda* grassveld, but large areas have been converted into pine plantations. Although the grasslands are brown and unattractive during winter, a wide variety of lilies, orchids and irises can be seen in full flower during spring and summer.

Elements of the Cape flora include a number of proteas and ericas. Among the proteas occurring here are the common, African white, silver and the Transvaal mountain sugarbushes, as well as the Transvaal rambling protea (*Protea parvula*). This species occurs naturally along the eastern Transvaal escarpment from Mariepskop and the Blyde River Canyon to the Lydenburg and Dullstroom areas. It grows from an underground root-stock and seldom exceeds 16 cm in height. The attractive greenish-white to pink flowers are reminiscent of waterlilies when open between mid-December and mid-March.

Ericas include the striking red fire heath (*Erica cerinthoides*) and *Erica woodii* which produces beautiful pink, bell-shaped flowers between February and July.

Common tree ferns occur generally along streams in the grassveld, while krantz aloe, red-leaved fig and Transvaal milkplum favour rocky outcrops.

In some of the more inaccessible valleys and kloofs relict patches of indigenous forest have survived. Among the species you can expect to see here are Outeniqua and real yellowwoods, lemonwood, common wild quince, knobwood, common cabbage tree, assegai, Cape beech and common wild elder. Especially eye-catching here are masses of forest lilies (*Clivia caulescens*).

Fauna The animal life of the trail area is similar to that which you are likely to see elsewhere along the Transvaal Drakensberg. Keep an eye out for oribi, one of the most graceful small antelope, especially on Oribivlakte between the Excelsior and Sacramento Creek huts. They occur in pairs or small family groups in short grassland and are often confused with the steenbok from which they can be distinguished by the white rump, the striking black-tipped tail and the gold-coloured coat. When alarmed they give a sharp whistle and start off briskly, bounding stiffly into the air. The oribi is listed as vulnerable, mainly because of the degradation of its habitat as a result of agriculture, afforestation and bush encroachment.

Other antelope species to keep an eye out for on the grassy plains include grey rhebok and mountain reedbuck, while klipspringer occur in rocky areas. The rocky areas also provide a habitat for rock dassie and chacma baboon. In the plantations and forest patches you might chance upon red duiker, bushbuck and bushpig.

Among the predators occurring are leopard, serval, civet, caracal, black-backed jackal and small-spotted genet. Smaller mammals include vervet monkey, porcupine, Cape clawless otter and honey badger.

The birdlife of the area is similar to that of the Fanie Botha Hiking Trail and is therefore not described here. Refer to p 289.

History The history of the area is closely related to the frantic search for gold during the 1800s and numerous reminders of this era can still be seen along the trail. The search for gold in the Zuid-Afrikaansche Republiek (Transvaal Republic) began in 1853 when a prospecting concession was awarded to Piet Marais. Marais never reported any discoveries, however, and it was Karl Gottlieb Mauch who reported the first finds in the Spekboom River near Lydenburg.

Diggers and fortune-seekers streamed to the area and first settled at Mac-Mac after some commercially viable finds were made there. According to legend, Alec "Wheelbarrow" Patterson decided to leave the busy goldfields at Mac-Mac and discovered gold at Pilgrim's Rest in 1873. He was given this nickname because of his habit of roaming through the eastern Transvaal with a wheelbarrow containing all his possessions. He decided to keep his discovery to himself, but was soon followed by

The oribi, a vulnerable species which favours short grassland. Right: *spoor*

another digger, William Trafford. Trafford was apparently so impressed by the place, which he believed meant the end of his pilgrimage, that he called it Pilgrim's Rest.

After Trafford had registered his claim, news about his discovery spread like wildfire and the Pilgrim's Rest valley soon became the centre of goldmining in the eastern Transvaal. More than 1 500 diggers rushed to the valley, prompting the Gold Commissioner, MacDonald, to move his offices from Mac-Mac to Pilgrim's Rest in 1874.

In the following year the exploitation of alluvial gold reached a peak at Pilgrim's Rest. The town soon became famous for the number of large gold nuggets that were discovered – the largest of which was said to weigh 11,3 kg (400 oz).

The miners were hard-working, but Sunday was considered a day of rest and, to protect their claims at night, no one was permitted to work after sunset. Anyone found on a claim after dark was heavily fined. Towards the end of 1875 the town consisted of 21 shops, 18 bars, three bakeries and a variety of other buildings.

THE MORGENZON WILD HORSES

There has been much speculation about the origin of the wild horses of Morgenzon. It has been suggested that they are the descendants of horses which were abandoned by prospectors during the gold rush of the 1880s or that they belonged to Boer or British soldiers who were killed in the Anglo-Boer War.

The population of about 46 animals consists of a main herd of 26 animals, two smaller herds and three bachelor herds.

Mortality among foals is nearly 40 per cent, while several horses have been killed by lightning. The only sign of inbreeding which has been detected so far has been a mare with deformed hooves.

Mining activities were brought to a halt temporarily during the (First) Anglo-Boer War of 1880-81. At the end of the war D H Benjamin obtained a concession for the mining rights on which Pilgrim's Rest was situated.

By this time most of the alluvial gold was already worked out and the high cost of reef mining and the formation of Benjamin's Transvaal Gold Exploration Company in 1882 effectively put an end to individual mining operations. On 29 July 1896 the Transvaal Gold

Mining Estates Company was formed and it remained active at Pilgrim's Rest until 1971 when the mine became unprofitable.

Towards the end of the Anglo-Boer War of 1899-1902, the Boers took the town without resistance and the State Mint in the Field was established west of Pilgrim's Rest. Banknotes were printed on pages of schoolbooks, while 986 veldponde were minted from gold obtained from the Pilgrim's Rest Reduction Works and the Mint in Pretoria.

TRAIL DESCRIPTION

Day 1: President Burger Hut to Pilgrim's Rest Hut
The first 8 km of the route winds steadily uphill through pine plantations. Shortly before the 7 km mark the path joins the section of the Fanie Botha Hiking Trail which winds via The Bonnet to Graskop Hut and then crosses the Burgerspas.

The two trails run concurrently for about 1,5 km before the Fanie Botha Trail branches off to the right. The Prospector's Trail branches off to the left onto an old coach road which ascends gradually along the western slopes of Stanley Bush Hill.

The trail then descends towards The Bonnet Pass, passing the Desiré Mine and a grave before joining a plantation road immediately above the tarred road to Pilgrim's Rest. The descent is followed by a gentle ascent and at the 14 km mark another old mine is passed. Shortly afterwards you will pass the headgear of an old cable station which used to convey ore down to the river. The trail finally drops down to the Pilgrim's Rest Hut, an authentic miner's cottage on the outskirts of the town.

Day 2: Pilgrim's Rest Hut to Morgenzon Hut
The second day's hike covers a mere 8,3 km, but as it gains about 400 m it will take you about three hours to reach Morgenzon Hut. The trail winds through the centre of Pilgrim's Rest and you will find the pamphlet *Ramblers Guide to Pilgrim's Rest*, which contains interesting information on the main attractions, useful.

Don't miss the opportunity of visiting the Diggings Museum, which is situated close to the hut. Daily demonstrations of the methods used by the early diggers are given at a reconstructed mining camp.

The museum in the Miner's House depicts the home of a mineworker during the period 1910-20. Also well worth visiting is the Reduction Works where guided tours are conducted at 10:30 on weekdays.

After crossing the Joubert Bridge which was built in 1896 and named after the Mining Commissioner at the time, the trail turns off to the left for a short distance before ascending steadily up Columbia Hill. After passing the Columbia Mine the trail levels out for the next

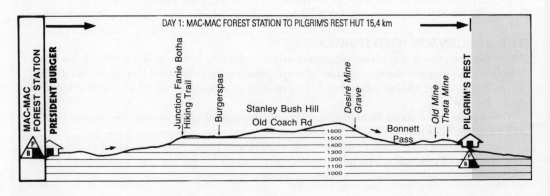

DAY 1: MAC-MAC FOREST STATION TO PILGRIM'S REST HUT 15,4 km

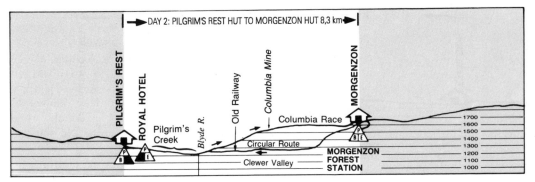

2 km, following a water race that used to carry water for several kilometres to the Columbia Mine.

With just over 1 km left to the hut, the trail winds through a small but delightful patch of indigenous forest with perennial water. Another short climb brings you to the Morgenzon Hut which was sponsored by the Gencor Mining Company.

Day 3: Morgenzon Hut to Excelsior Hut

From Morgenzon Hut the trail passes through pine plantations and after about 1,5 km crosses the provincial road to Lydenburg. The route to Morgenzon Forest Station and the circular route to Pilgrim's Rest branches off to the right here, while the route to Excelsior Hut continues straight ahead. The trail ascends steadily through pine plantations parallel to the provincial road for just over 1,5 km before swinging north-east along a forestry road.

Along this section you will follow the route of the original Morgenzon Hiking Trail, which was opened as a two- or three-day trail in 1975. Towards the end of 1981 it was incorporated into the Prospector's Hiking Trail which links the Fanie Botha and Blyderivierspoort hiking trails.

Shortly before the 4 km mark you will notice a track branching off to your left. This is the direct route to Excelsior Hut via Cliviabos, a delightful patch of indigenous forest with a profusion of forest lilies (*Clivia caulescens*), orchids, ferns and young yellowwoods. The 6 km route was originally designed as a one-way return route from Excelsior Hut to Morgenzon Forest Station, but can now be hiked in both directions.

If you opt to take the longer route you still have about 11 km ahead of you. About 6,5 km from the start the trail crosses a stream and shortly afterwards leaves the road. From here you will climb steadily up the eastern slopes of Black Hill through pine plantations, crossing the return route between Black Hill Hut and Morgenzon Forest Station near the 8 km mark before emerging into the open. Black Hill Hut was originally used as a lookout for fires, but in 1992 the house was converted to accommodate hikers doing the circular route between Sacramento Creek Hut and Morgenzon Forest Station.

Shortly after the 9 km mark you will reach a viewpoint and, with a height of 2 079 m, this is the highest point along the trail. As the song says "on a clear day you can see forever" – below lies Pilgrim's Rest, with Graskop in the distance and, looking north, it is possible to see the Wolkberg.

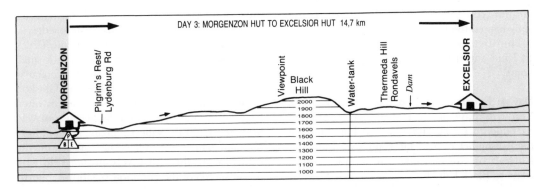

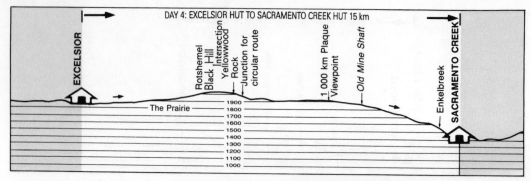

DAY 4: EXCELSIOR HUT TO SACRAMENTO CREEK HUT 15 km

EXCELSIOR
Rotshemel
Black Hill
Intersection
Yellowwood
Rock
Junction for
circular route
1 000 km Plaque
Viewpoint
Old Mine Shaft
Enkelbreek
SACRAMENTO CREEK

The Prairie — 1900 1800 1700 1600 1500 1400 1300 1200 1100 1000

Along this section the trail winds through lichen-clad, weathered quartzite formations along the edge of Black Hill before descending through a patch of fynbos vegetation. Just beyond the 11 km mark you will pass a water-tank and cross the Sacramento Creek/Black Hill return route once again. After crossing a stream, the trail climbs gently through pine plantations before reaching a fire-break.

A notice here informs you that this section winds over private property and it is important to bear in mind that the future of trails passing over private property depends on the co-opera-tion of hikers. You will pass a dam and although it might be tempting to take a quick dip, this is not permitted as the dam is a source of drink-ing water for the private resort nearby.

Shortly after the 13 km mark the trail winds westwards across open grassland where grey rhebok can sometimes be spotted.

After following a gravel road for a short dis-tance the trail passes through a pine plantation for about 1 km before rejoining the access road to Excelsior Hut.

The hut is a complete surprise – a very mod-ern looking double-storey house which was used as a holiday cottage before the area was incorporated into the Morgenzon State Forest. Additional accommodation is available in a hut adjacent to the house. Looking northwards from the hut, you will see the wide open expanse aptly named the Prairie.

The distance covered on this section is 14,7 km and it is normally hiked in five to six hours.

Day 4: Excelsior Hut to Sacramento Creek

You will have a choice of two routes to Sacramento Creek Hut – a 14,5 km route via the Rotshemel, or a 21 km route over Eldorado Ridge – or you can take the circular return route to Black Hill Hut.

The direct route to Sacramento Creek and the Excelsior/Black Hill loop follows a jeep track over easy terrain to reach the turn-off to the Black Hill Hut 4,6 km from the start. About 3,7 km further the trail joins the Sacramento Creek/Black Hill loop and from here it is another 8,1 km to Black Hill Hut. However, if you are heading for Sacramento Creek, ignore the turn-off to Black Hill to reach the junction with the Eldorado Ridge Loop less than 2 km onwards.

The route via Eldorado Ridge winds along the western edge of the Prairie, passing through spectacular rock formations. Shortly before Aalwynrug the trail once again winds its way through sculptured rock formations. The ridge takes its name from the profusion of krantz aloes which create a blaze of colour among the grey rocks during July. From the ridge there is a superb view of the Nooitgedacht Valley and the mountains to the east. Along this section you might still see herds of South Africa's only population of wild horses.

Close to the 8 km mark you will reach a shortcut which will reduce the day's hike by about 4 km or you can continue along the Eldorado Ridge Loop. About 2 km beyond the turn-off to the shortcut the trail passes the site of an old prospector's camp.

The trail then doubles back along the edge of more lichen-clad sandstone rock formations, joining the direct route at the eastern edge of Oribivlakte. Here the trail to Sacramento Creek turns off to the left and after crossing a small knoll continues along a ridge with spectacular views of Sacramento Creek below and Graskop in the distance. Unfortunately the view is often hazy during the winter months because of veld fires. Several of the valleys flanking the trail have remnant patches of indigenous forest, with the trail passing through lovely protea veld with dense stands of the common sugarbush. Shortly

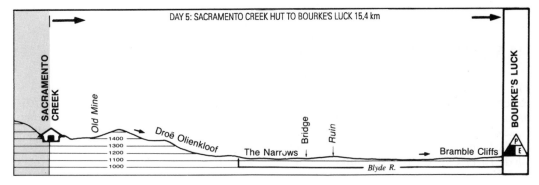

after the 9 km mark you will cross a stream and, as this is the last water before you reach the hut, it is advisable to fill your water-bottle.

A short way on a detour leads to a viewpoint near a cluster of large broad-leaved waxberry trees and a plaque commemorating the completion of 1 000 km of National Hiking Way Trails. At the viewpoint you are met by a breathtaking view over the Blyderivierspoort Canyon and the Lowveld.

The remaining 4 km of the trail is all downhill. Just beyond the 11 km mark the trail passes an old mineshaft and then loses altitude rapidly along a section known as Enkelbreek – so proceed carefully!

Sacramento Hut, a stone shelter situated in a small forested kloof, was donated to the National Hiking Way Board by Transvaal Gold Mining Estates. It consists of two large rooms with an outside cooking shelter with a fireplace.

Day 5: Sacramento Creek Hut to Bourke's Luck

On the last day the trail climbs the hill immediately behind the hut and then descends to cross a tributary of the Sacramento Creek. Shortly before the 2 km mark you will pass an old mine and a little way further on you will come to another stream. As the next water is about 6 km further it is advisable to fill your water-bottle here.

The trail continues to ascend from here and about 0,5 km further passes into land owned by Transvaal Gold Mining Estates. Shortly before the 4 km mark the trail drops into Droë Olienkloof, which was named after the wild olive.

The remaining 9 km of the trail follows an easy route over level terrain, passing through several gates. Shortly after the 6 km mark you will reach the Blyde River, but since the water is polluted it is not advisable to drink it. The trail

then follows the road between Pilgrim's Rest and Ohrigstad for about 1,5 km along the Narrows. About 8,5 km beyond Sacramento Creek a tributary of the Blyde River, the Mapalageli, is passed and here you can fill up your water-bottle.

From here the trail skirts around Granite Hill, following a route past Bramble Cliffs, and after passing through three more gates you will reach Bourke's Luck after 15,4 km. The distance is normally completed in about five hours.

ALTERNATIVE ROUTE

Sacramento Creek Hut to Black Hill Hut

This route was opened in August 1992 to eliminate the transport problems hikers encounter on the linear route. Hikers can now start at the Pilgrim's Rest Hut or the Morgenzon Forest Station and do a circular route ranging from two to five days. On the first half of the 17,9 km loop linking Sacramento Creek and Black Hill, the trail passes through a magnificent patch of indigenous forest where relics of the gold rush era of the 1870s are much in evidence. Reminders of this era include the stone ruins of what was probably a gold-digger's shed or house and a rather impressive stone bridge. The trail is, however, mainly through open grassveld and numerous mining shafts and excavations can be seen on the mountain slopes.

The intersection with the Excelsior/Black Hill Loop is reached after 9,8 km. The remaining 8,1 km to Black Hill Hut is mainly through pine plantations and is usually covered in about three hours.

The hut once served as a forestry lookout post and has a commanding view over the surrounding countryside, Graskop and the Lowveld. From the hut it is a mere 8,8 km to the Morgenzon Forest Station, or a 17,5 km hike if your final destination is Pilgrim's Rest.

BLYDERIVIERSPOORT

The Blyderivierspoort Hiking Trail winds mainly through the Blyderivierspoort Nature Reserve and takes the hiker through an area with landscapes varying from mist forests to montane grasslands. Stretching from God's Window on the escarpment to Swadini in the Lowveld, the relatively easy terrain makes this an ideal trail for beginners. Features include God's Window, with its stupendous views of the Lowveld, Bourke's Luck Potholes and the Blyde River Canyon, one of southern Africa's greatest natural wonders.

TRAIL PLANNER

Distance 65 km; 5 days (shorter options possible)

Climate

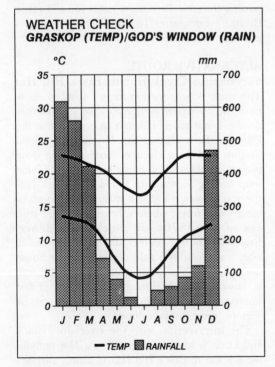

WEATHER CHECK
GRASKOP (TEMP)/GOD'S WINDOW (RAIN)

— TEMP ▒ RAINFALL

Grading A

Reservations The Officer-in-Charge, Blyderivierspoort Nature Reserve, Private Bag X431, Graskop 1270, Telephone (01315) 8-1216. Reservations are accepted up to six months in advance.

Group size Minimum 2; Maximum 30

Maps A full-colour trail map with useful information on the history, flora and fauna on the reverse is available, but must be purchased separately.

Facilities Facilities at the four trail huts include bunks with mattresses, water, showers, flush toilets, fireplaces, firewood and refuse bins.

Logistics Linear route, requiring a two-car party. It is usually fairly easy to hitch a lift between God's Window and the Blydepoort Resort, but from Swadini it is more difficult. Although there is no overnight hut at the start of the trail, Watervalspruit Hut is a mere 5,8 km from the start. Accommodation at Aventura's Swadini Resort, where the trail ends, ranges from self-contained chalets to campsites. There is also a swimming pool, shop and a licensed restaurant. The central reservations telephone number is (012) 346-2277.

Relevant information
■ Precautions should be taken against ticks.
■ Hikers ending at Swadini are advised to take precautions against malaria, especially during the summer months.
■ To protect the sensitive Treur River system from pollution you should under no circumstances use soap in or near rivers. For this reason showers are provided at all huts.

■ The water between Old Mine Hut and Blydepoort is unfit for drinking and water should be carried along this stretch.

How to get there From Graskop, the start of the trail is reached by following the R532 to the signposted turn-off 3 km north of the town. You then turn right onto the God's Window Loop road which is followed for about 7 km to the God's Window viewpoint.

TRAIL ENVIRONMENT

Flora As a result of the variations in altitude, temperature and rainfall a rich variety of plants and trees is to be found along the trail.

The high-lying southern part of the reserve is dominated by open, sour grassveld with patches of dense mist forests. Trees include real yellowwood, Cape beech and coast silver oak, while forest lilies (*Clivia caulescens*) are abundant on the forest floor.

The grassveld is generally devoid of any tall trees except for the occasional Transvaal beech, while common tree ferns can often be seen lining stream banks.

The vegetation of the centre of the reserve consists of several acacia species, as well as sickle bush, buffalo-thorn, common wild pear and several bushwillow species.

The northern part of the reserve is characterised by Lowveld sour bushveld. Trees and shrubs occurring include Transvaal beech, wild pear, cabbage trees and the Transvaal milkplum. This area is also the habitat of a number of fynbos species such as *Cliffortia*, seven members of the erica family, seven species of the protea family and no less than 18 everlasting (*Helichrysum*) species.

Among the proteas found in the reserve is the Blyde sugarbush, which was discovered in 1970 by Mrs L Davidson. The discovery prompted her to name it after the Blyde River and the specific name (*laetans*) is translated as "rejoicing". Only a few hundred of these plants, which grow up to 5 m high, occur in the reserve. Between April and May, their brilliant carmine flowers present a beautiful display. Other proteas found here include common sugarbush, African white sugarbush, silver sugarbush, Transvaal mountain sugarbush, cluster-head sugarbush and *P. parvula*.

A single *Leucospermum* species, *L. saxosum*, also grows in the reserve and can be seen alongside the trail in the vicinity of Fann's Falls on the third day's hike. It is the pincushion with the most northerly distribution and the only one

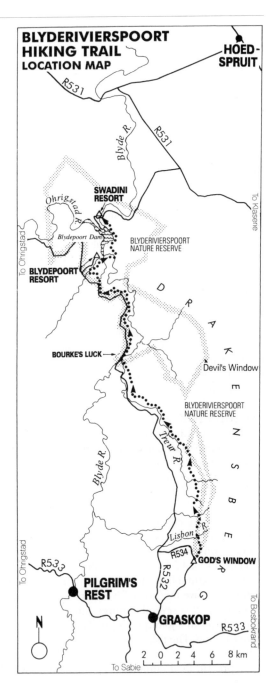

303

occurring in Zimbabwe and Mozambique. The yellow-orange flowers are seen at their best between September and December.

The reserve is also the habitat of four cycads endemic to the Transvaal, namely the Lydenburg, Kaapsehoop and Barberton cycads and *Encephalartos cupidus.*

The vegetation of the Swadini area consists of arid Lowveld. Typical species here include large-leaved rock fig, round-leaved teak, mountain seringa, velvet corkwood, tamboti, leadwood and several bushwillow species.

Some of the trees along the trail have been numbered according to the *National List of Indigenous Trees* and by referring to the trail map you will be able to identify some of the more than 100 species listed.

Fauna Because of the patchwork vegetation of the reserve the animal populations, which are dependent on the different plant communities, are more varied than they are abundant. The reserve is one of the few places where all five South African primates (excluding man) occur. Chacma baboon are found mainly on the rocky mountain slopes and, even if you do not see them, you are likely to hear their loud barks. Vervet monkeys occur over a wide area, but seem to prefer the more wooded areas. The rare samango monkey is limited to the evergreen forest of the Blydepoort and can be identified by its piercing call. The thicktailed bushbaby occurs in the montane and riverine forests, while the lesser bushbaby inhabits the savanna areas of the reserve.

The forests are the natural habitat of bushbuck, kudu, red duiker and bushpig. Common duiker favour open, bushy country, but often feed on the forest fringes. Animals of the more rocky and higher-lying areas include klipspringer and grey rhebok respectively.

Some 227 bird species have been recorded in the reserve, including 25 raptors.

Species you can expect to tick in the mountain grassland with rocky outcrops include striped flufftail, Cape rock thrush, buffstreaked chat and wailing cisticola.

The cliffs of the escarpment and the Blyde River Canyon provide a habitat for black stork, black eagle, rock pigeon, several martin and swallow species, mocking chat and redwinged starling.

From the Old Mine Hut it is sometimes possible to watch the bald ibis when they return to their roosting sites in the krantzes. Some 37 breeding colonies, with a total population of about 1 500 birds, have been recorded in the Transvaal and their total numbers in southern Africa are estimated at 1 250 breeding pairs.

Species to keep an eye out for in the indigenous forest include rameron pigeon, Knysna lourie, emerald cuckoo, sombre bulbul, chorister robin, paradise flycatcher and olive bush shrike, while green pigeon and purplecrested lourie occur along the forest fringes.

History Monochrome rock paintings in the reserve provide proof that the last of the Stone Age people, the San, inhabited the region. Between 1 200 and 200 years ago the area was

---

TREUR RIVER BARB

In 1958 an endemic species of minnow (small freshwater fish) was discovered in the Treur River near Bourke's Luck, ironically during an investigation into the suitability of the river for rainbow trout. This small minnow, which is about 9,5 cm long, was named the Treur River barb (*Barbus treurensis*) after the river in which it was first discovered. Ten years after its discovery, it no longer occurred in the Treur River and was thought to be extinct due to the rainbow trout and smallmouth bass which had been introduced into the river.

In 1970 a Treur River barb population was discovered in the upper reaches of the Blyde River in a section which passes through the property of South African Forest Investments. In 1976 the nature conservation section of SAFI initiated a research project and found that the minnows were confined to a 4,5 km stretch of the Blyde River bound on either side by a waterfall.

These natural boundaries prevented trout from invading this stretch, thus playing a vital role in helping to save the Treur River barb from extinction.

Early in 1994 several hundred minnows were transferred from the upper Blyde River to the Treur River in a joint project of Transvaal Nature Conservation, Mondi Paper and the Olifants River Forum. The fish were transported some 30 km by road in a 200-*l* tank maintained at river temperature.

At present their numbers are estimated at over 20 000 and they are considered vulnerable.

also inhabited by Iron Age people and their descendants. The remains of their settlements can be seen on the Guinea Fowl Trail above the Kadishi Valley.

In 1840 the Voortrekker leader Hendrik Potgieter set out from Potchefstroom to open a route to the sea. After an easy journey across the Highveld, the sheer escarpment prevented the trek from travelling further. However, Potgieter and a party of men decided to continue on horseback to Delagoa Bay (present-day Maputo), while the rest of the party camped alongside the Sefogwane River, a short way downstream of Clearstream Hut.

When Potgieter failed to return after some time it was assumed that he and his men had perished and the river was renamed the Treur River ("River of Mourning"). The remainder of the party set out to return to Potchefstroom but had not travelled far when they were overtaken by Potgieter and his party. The meeting took place just as they were about to cross another stream and this they named the Blyde River ("River of Rejoicing").

Like the surrounding areas of the eastern Transvaal, the area through which the trail winds was also overrun by prospectors and fortune-seekers in search of gold. Near Bourke's Luck Potholes disused mines, an old crane wheel and ruins bear witness to the fortunes made and lost in the area. In the foothills of the mountains in the southern corner of the reserve a herd of wild horses can still sometimes be seen. They are said to be the descendants of horses that belonged to the gold diggers, who used them to draw ore trolleys out of the mines.

TRAIL DESCRIPTION

Day 1: God's Window to Watervalspruit Hut

Since this section is only 5,8 km long you can use the morning to make transport arrangements or to discover the many scenic attractions in the area.

From the parking area the trail winds up to Quartzkop where you will pass through a magnificent mist forest dominated by young yellowwoods and masses of clivias. A short detour to the edge of the escarpment will reveal all the glory of the eastern Transvaal some 500 m below.

The route continues close to the escarpment edge, winding through interesting quartzite rock formations shaped by the forces of erosion to reach the Wonder Viewpoint a short distance further on. The trail then winds down to Paradise Pool, traversing typical treeless mountain grassveld punctuated with occasional common tree ferns along stream banks. These are the headwaters of the Lisbon River, which cascades 92 m over a waterfall further downstream.

Over the next 1,5 km the trail ascends gently and as you start descending you will see Watervalspruit Hut, which is well concealed against a slope, part of which has been excavated to provide shelter against the wind. The hut consists of a row of rooms and there are also two covered outside fireplaces with benches, tables and large cast-iron cooking pots.

Day 2: Watervalspruit Hut to Clearstream Hut

The second day's hike initially winds through rocky quartzite outcrops which have

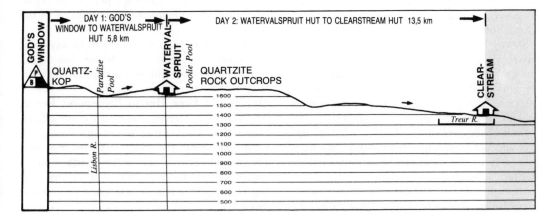

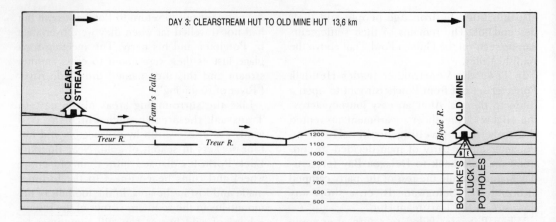

been eroded into interesting shapes and are mottled yellow, white and red-brown from the lichens which grow on them. Trees to be seen on this section include real yellowwood, mountain cypress and Transvaal milkplum.

After about 4 km the trail descends to the Treur River Valley and then ascends along the edge of a pine plantation for about 2 km. The final 4,5 km of the route winds through grassland with spectacular rock formations to the right of the trail.

Clearstream Hut is similar in design to the Watervalspruit Hut. It consists of two stable-like buildings in natural stone and blends in well with its surroundings. It is usually reached after four or five hours of easy walking and boasts one of the most beautiful pools on any trail. For the remainder of the afternoon you can enjoy the inviting pool, explore the waterfall further upstream or ramble about the interesting rock formations in the vicinity of the hut.

Day 3: Clearstream Hut to Old Mine Hut

The trail follows the Treur River closely for a while before passing the site from which Potgieter's reconnaissance party is believed to have set off.

Shortly before reaching Fann's Falls the trail passes close by the remains of a prospector's hut. Only a few crumbled walls and a large hole remains as the prospector apparently buried dynamite under the floor boards and during a veld fire in 1977 the hut was blown up.

Fann's Falls are situated roughly 1 km off the trail and although you will probably pass here too early in the morning for a swim, it is a worthwhile detour.

You will continue to follow the course of the Treur River for about 2 km and along this sec-

tion there are some beautiful pools for an early morning dip. Near the 5 km mark the trail briefly swings away from the river before skirting the Goedgeloof plantation. There are several side tracks in the vicinity of the sawmill, but you must not deviate from the main trail.

The remainder of the trail to Bourke's Luck was the scene of a frantic rush after gold was discovered in the eastern Transvaal in the 1870s.

A short way above the potholes the trail passes a beautiful waterfall and then crosses the gorge at the confluence of the Treur and the Blyde rivers where the famous Bourke's Luck Potholes are situated. The cylindrical potholes, some of which are up to 6 m deep, were formed by the erosive action of water and water-borne stones which ground into the soft layers. The potholes were named after a certain Tom Bourke, who predicted that gold would be found in the vicinity. Ironically, Bourke's nearby claim turned out to be unproductive.

Do not miss the opportunity of calling at the visitors' centre which forms part of the Bourke's Luck complex. It consists of a permanent exhibit of natural and cultural-historic aspects of the reserve.

The Old Mine Hut, reached a short way on, is a beautiful stone and thatch house dating back to the mining days, with an outside cooking area.

Day 4: Old Mine Hut to Blydepoort Resort

The trail dips steeply down to Bourke's Luck Ghost Mine where active goldmining took place until 1955. Until the early 1970s small quantities of gold were still mined here and it is interesting to note that very little of the heavy mining equipment was removed when production ceased.

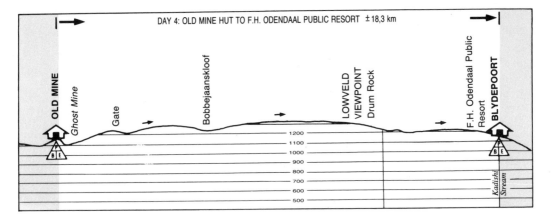

The climb to the edge of the canyon is one of the longest ascents of the trail. From here you will skirt the edge of the canyon, following sections of the old mail-coach road, which ran from Bourke's Luck to the Ohrigstad River Valley and the Lowveld. Along this section there are splendid views of the Belvedere Valley and the canyon itself.

Unfortunately the trail is fairly close to the tarred road here, but this is necessary to keep within the boundaries of the reserve. The vegetation along this section consists mainly of grassveld interspersed with Transvaal milkplum and cabbage trees, as well as a number of species of the Cape flora, such as everlastings (*Helichrysum*), ericas and proteas.

Several viewpoints along this way afford splendid views of the canyon twisting some 500 m below and shortly before the 17 km mark you will pass the Three Rondavels viewpoint. Between September and December the summit of one of the Three Rondavels is covered with the dark pink flowers of one of the Transvaal's most beautiful proteas, the Transvaal mountain sugarbush. They can be seen in the same locality as the rare Blyde sugarbush by taking a short detour to the Three Rondavels viewpoint, where they grow on a rocky ledge below the viewpoint.

After crossing the road to the Three Rondavels viewpoint, the trail traverses open grassveld dotted with proteas in a northerly direction for about 1 km. It then swings west to the hut which is situated alongside the Kadishi Stream. The hut was sponsored by Gencor and replaces the original hut which was situated just below the caravan park in the Blydepoort Resort. Although the map gives the distance as 18,3 km, be prepared to walk another kilometre.

Day 5: Blydepoort Hut to Swadini The last section of the trail covers 13,8 km and is hiked in four to five hours. It is not only the most spectacular section of the trail, but also the most difficult and over the first 6 km you will lose some 500 m in altitude. To reach Swadini before dark you are advised to make an early start, which will give you time to appreciate the

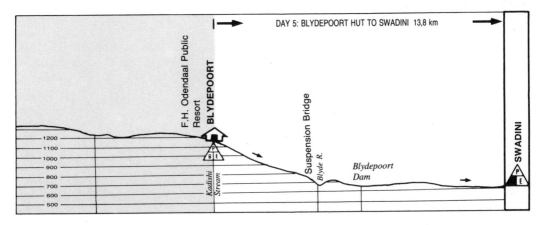

The Three Rondavels, a familiar landmark of the eastern Transvaal

dramatic change in vegetation and climate between that of the escarpment and the Lowveld.

From the hut the trail heads north-east, passing through proteaveld for about 2 km before reaching the gallery forest. The route will take you below the Three Rondavels Viewpoint, descending steadily and at one point there is a ladder to assist you in negotiating a difficult spot. Before crossing the Blyde River there is a short, steep descent to the river where a suspension bridge takes you to the opposite bank. The bridge is normally reached after three to four hours and you should heed the warning that no more than three people should use it at a time.

The warning to beware of hippos and crocodiles should not be taken lightly, especially in the late afternoon when the hippos leave the water to graze on the banks. If you are not for-tunate enough to spot the hippos, you will possibly hear their loud snorts. The 51 km stretch of river from the Blydepoort Dam to the confluence of the Blyde and Olifants rivers supports a healthy hippo population and several are resident in the dam.

After a steep climb out of the Blyde River Valley the trail continues for about 3 km through gallery forest passing between Thabaneng, also known as "The Sundial", and the Three Rondavels, before levelling out along the eastern side of the dam.

As you emerge from the shady, moist gallery forest you will be struck by the dramatic change in the vegetation. Shortly after passing the dam wall the trail reaches the official exit point where it joins the road leading to the visitors' centre. The resort is reached by turning right here and following the road for about 2 km.

OTHER NORTH-WEST, GAUTENG AND EASTERN TRANSVAAL TRAILS

NORTH-WEST

MARICO

Distance 30 km; 2 days

Reservations Omega Game Farm, Telephone (014288) 502 or 364.

Group size Minimum 2; Maximum 20

Facilities The overnight hut is equipped with bunks, mattresses, fireplaces, firewood, cold water showers and toilets.

Description Situated conveniently close to Gauteng, this circular trail has been laid out on the Omega Game Farm near Groot Marico. The farm has been stocked with 12 antelope species, including gemsbok, red hartebeest, waterbuck and kudu, while some 103 bird species have been recorded to date. The trail winds mainly through mixed bushveld vegetation while sections of the first and second day's route follow the winding course of the Marico River with its inviting swimming pools.

PILANESBERG

Distance Guided wilderness trail, no set route or distance; 3 to 5 days

Reservations The Secretary, Wilderness Leadership School, P O Box 87230, Houghton 2041, Telephone (011) 455-6805.

Group size Maximum 8

Facilities The trail price is inclusive of equipment, food and transport from Johannesburg.

Description This guided wilderness trail is conducted in the Pilanesberg National Park, an area with some of the most fascinating geology in southern Africa. The area boasts more than 320 bird species and the extinct volcano is home to a large diversity of mammals, including the third largest population of white rhinos in the world. Also occurring are black rhino, elephant, mountain reedbuck, red hartebeest, blue wildebeest, Burchell's zebra and giraffe. The scenery is superb with steep slopes, impressive mountain peaks and rolling plains, while the vegetation varies from savanna to open grassland and densely wooded valleys.

THABA

Distance Variable; 2 days or longer by arrangement

Reservations Jacana Country Homes and Trails, P O Box 95212, Waterkloof 0145, Telephone (012) 346-3550.

Group size Minimum 2; Maximum 12

Facilities A rustic base camp consisting of twin-bedded tents, a reed kitchen, showers and flush toilets is provided. All meals, plus tea and coffee, are provided.

Description These guided trails are conducted from a bush camp on the Thaba Lodge Game Farm in the Rustenburg/Brits area. The emphasis is on environmental education and activities are planned to suit the requirements of the group. Groups are guided by a qualified game ranger and activities include early morning and/or late afternoon game walks, game-viewing and bird-watching, as well as night game drives. Specialist guides can be arranged for groups with a particular interest. Birdlife is prolific and to date over 180 bird species have been recorded.

GAUTENG

GEMSBOK

Distance 23 km; 2 days

Reservations Zemvelo Game Park, P O Box 599, Bronkhorstspruit 1020, Telephone (01212) 2-5728 or 2-2211.

Group size Minimum 2; Maximum 32

Facilities Sixteen people can be accommodated in each of the two hikers' huts. Amenities include bunks, mattresses, a gas fridge, two-plate stove, gas lamps, fireplaces, showers and toilet. The three family huts accommodate six people each and, in addition to the facilities provided at the hikers' huts, are equipped with cooking and eating utensils.

Description This trail is in the Zemvelo Game Park, 20 km north-east of Bronkhorstspruit. It winds through a rich diversity of vegetation and among the tree species occurring are common cabbage tree, Transvaal milkplum, wild peach, mountain silver oak, cheesewood and wild elder. Species of game hikers might encounter are eland, kudu, impala, blesbok, red hartebeest, black wildebeest, waterbuck and springbok. Several archaeological sites such as old ruins and graves can also be seen along the trail.

KLIPKRAAL

Distance 27 km; 2 days

Reservations Jacana Country Homes and Trails, P O Box 95212, Waterkloof 0145, Telephone (012) 346-3550.

Group size Minimum 2; Maximum 20

Facilities Hikers are accommodated at the Strydfontein base camp in a restored old farmhouse, equipped with beds, mattresses, a hot and cold water shower and toilets. There is also a three-plate gas cooker, kettle, pans, cast-iron pots and two lapas with braai facilities.

Description Situated in the hills extending southwards from the Suikerbosrante, the trail winds through typical Highveld scenery. The first day's hike covers 15,5 km and for most of the way the Vaal Dam remains in view. On the second day's hike of 11,5 km the trail passes an enormous rock which is considered sacred by the local people. Of historic interest are the Late Iron Age ruins, including a 5 km stone wall, dating back to the 1600-1700s. A wide variety of waterbirds are attracted to the dams in the area and hikers may also see steenbok, grey rhebok and blesbok. The easy terrain, combined with the fact that the route consists of two one-day hikes obviating the need for a heavy backpack, makes this trail ideal for novices and families.

EASTERN TRANSVAAL

BABOON

Distance 20 km; 2 days

Reservations Cycad Hiking Trail, P O Box 1326, Middelburg 1050, Telephone (0132) 43-1040.

Group size Minimum 2; Maximum 40

Facilities At Scheepersdal accommodation is provided in an old farmhouse, while the Ravine and Mountain huts are rustic reed and thatch huts. Amenities at the overnight huts include water, fireplaces, firewood and toilets.

Description This circular trail traverses private farmland north-west of Middelburg. The first day's hike of 9 km is along the Olifants River with its steep cliffs, rapids and inviting rock pools. From the overnight stop the trail initially continues along the Olifants River and then follows the course of the Little Olifants River until the Tarentaal Trail is reached. From here the trail ascends steeply along a farm road to the Mountain Huts where the Cycad Trail starts. Scheepersdal is a short way on along farm roads or alternatively you can follow the 9 km Cycad Trail. Highlights on this route include dense stands of Olifants River and Waterberg cycads, as well as magnificent views of the Olifants River Valley.

BOSCHHOEK

Distance 21 km; 3 days

Reservations Mr A Erlank, P O Box 191, Lydenburg 1120, Telephone (01323) 8-0061.

Group size Minimum 2; Maximum 24

Facilities The base camp can accommodate 24 people and facilities include bunks, mattresses, a fridge, freezer, pots, electricity, fireplaces, firewood, hot and cold showers and flush toilets. The mountain huts at the two overnight stops sleep 12 people each and are equipped with bunks, mattresses, pots, lanterns, fireplaces, firewood, hot and cold water and flush toilets.

Description The trail network on the farm Boschhoek, about 20 km south-east of Ohrigstad, offers an option of a three-day circular hike over 21 km or four one-day hikes ranging from 10 to 13 km. The trail winds through spectacular mountain scenery with numerous streams, inviting natural pools and waterfalls. About 550 m in altitude is gained between the Mantshibi River near the base camp and Loodkop, the highest point on the trail, but the view makes the slog more than worthwhile. Much of the trail network follows mountain tracks through montane grassland dotted with proteas, while krantz aloes, mountain cabbage trees and Transvaal milkplum are encountered in rocky areas. The 2 500 ha farm is well stocked with game and among the species you could encounter are eland, blesbok, blue wildebeest, red hartebeest, Burchell's zebra and giraffe.

BROOK

Distance 21,5 km; 2 days

Reservations Lothair District Office, H L & H Timber, P O Box 75, Lothair 2370, Telephone (017) 845-3024.

Group size Minimum 2; Maximum 20

Facilities The hut at the base camp is equipped with bunks, mattresses, a kitchen with a stove, tables and benches, showers and baths, as well as toilets. There is also an outside fireplace.

Description This trail west of Carolina in the eastern Transvaal traverses the edge of the Transvaal Drakensberg escarpment, crossing numerous streams and brooks. The trail is on the property of one of the largest private forestry companies in South Africa, H L & H, and some adjacent farms, and consists of two routes which can be explored without a backpack from a base camp – a 16 km trail and a 5,5 km route. The long route leads through a variety of landscapes, ranging from grasslands and massive boulders to patches of indigenous forest and an impressive ravine with a series of pools. A highlight of the short option is the aptly named Boulder Canyon, an impressive canyon with beautiful pools.

BUSHMAN'S

Distance Guided wilderness trail, no set route or distance; 2 days/3 nights

Reservations National Parks Board, P O Box 787, Pretoria 0001, Telephone (012) 343-1991, or P O Box 7400, Roggebaai 8012, Telephone (021) 22-2810.

Group size Maximum 8

Facilities The base camp is equipped with beds, mattresses and bedding. Other amenities include cooking bomas, bush showers and toilets.

Description Situated in the south-western corner of the Kruger National Park, this guided wilderness trail is conducted in an area which boasts more than 90 rock art sites, as well as numerous Stone and Iron Age sites. The generally hilly terrain is interspersed with granite outcrops which afford trailists magnificent views of the area. Among the mammals trailists might encounter are white rhino, mountain reedbuck, kudu, klipspringer, Burchell's zebra and giraffe. Trailists meet at the Berg-en-Dal rest camp, from where they are transported to the base camp which is close to the Wolhuter trails camp.

ELAND

Distance 24 km; 2 days

Reservations Botshabelo Historic Village, P O Box 14, Middelburg 1050, Telephone (0132) 43-5020.

Group size Minimum 2; Maximum 12

Facilities Two overnight huts, each accommodating six people, are available at the end of the first day's hike. Mattresses, firewood, cast-iron pots and a braai grid are provided.

Description Starting at Botshabelo village, some 12 km north of Middelburg, this circular trail winds through an area rich in history and the culture of the South Ndebele. The trail traverses magnificent scenery and groves of the Olifants River cycad are a highlight. After initially traversing the slopes above the Klein Olifants River the trail makes a wide loop around Aasvoëlkrans and continues to the overnight hut after crossing the Klein Olifants River. The second day's hike follows an 8 km route along the Klein Olifants River, leaving ample time to explore the South Ndebele open-air museum and the Site Museum comprising the fort, two churches, the Merensky House Museum and several other buildings. The nature reserve has been stocked with eland, blesbok, springbok, red hartebeest, black wildebeest and oribi.

ELANDSVALLEI

Distance 22,5 km; 2 days

Reservations Jacana Country Homes and Trails, P O Box 95212, Waterkloof 0145, Telephone (012) 346-3550.

Group size Minimum 2; Maximum 20

Facilities The "Old Skooltjie" (Old School) base camp and Cheeky's Place mountain hut are equipped with bunks, mattresses, toilets and hot and cold water showers. There is also a lapa with a fireplace, firewood and a cooking area supplied with a kettle, pots and a potjie.

Description This trail in the Elands River Valley between Ngodwana and Nelspruit winds

through grassveld and indigenous forests. The first few kilometres of the trail follow an easy route alongside the Elands River, where hikers stand a chance of seeing hippo, before ascending steeply to the Sugar Loaf. The trail then passes several caves and rewards hikers with spectacular views. Highlights of the second day's hike include an old mine, the site of a cannon emplacement and a stone wall from where Elandshoek was bombarded by the Boers during the Anglo-Boer War. From the plateau the trail descends steeply to a kloof to reach the starting/ending point just over 7 km after setting off. About 250 bird species occur in the area.

JOCK OF THE BUSHVELD

Distance Guided wilderness trail, no set route or distance; 3 to 5 days

Reservations The Secretary, Wilderness Leadership School, P O Box 87230, Houghton 2041, Telephone (011) 455-6805.

Group size Maximum 8

Facilities The trail price is inclusive of equipment, food and transport from Johannesburg.

Description The Jock of the Bushveld Trail is conducted in the privately owned Timbavati Game Reserve and samples the wealth and beauty of the unspoilt Transvaal Lowveld. Situated adjacent to the Kruger National Park, Timbavati is home to most of the big game animals, including elephant, rhino, buffalo, lion and leopard, while some 240 bird species have been recorded to date.

KAAPSCHEHOOP

Distance 29 or 36 km; 2 days, and 41 km; 3 days

Reservations The National Hiking Way Board, Private Bag X503, Sabie 1260, Telephone (01315) 4-1058 or 4-1392.

Group size Minimum 2; Maximum 30

Facilities At the Berlin Forest Station hikers

82 The Vingerpol Hiking Trail derives its name from *Euphorbia clavariodes*
83 Views of the Olifants River, Baboon Hiking Trail
84 God's Window – ending point of the Fanie Botha Hiking Trail and starting point of the Blyderivierspoort Hiking Trail

▲ 82

▲ 83

84 ▼

▲ 85

85 Mac-Mac Falls on the Fanie Botha Hiking Trail
86 Facilities on the Blyderivierspoort Hiking Trail are excellent and include covered cooking areas outside the Clearstream Hut
87 Bourke's Luck Potholes, a well-known feature on the Blyderivierspoort Hiking Trail, is also the ending point of the Prospector's Hiking Trail

▲ 86

88 Viewpoint on the Blyderivierspoort Hiking Trail overlooking Blydepoort Dam
89 The Prospector's Hiking Trail leads through the historic village of Pilgrim's Rest

◀ 87

▲ 90   91 ▼

90 Both sections of the Magoebaskloof Hiking Trail wind through magnificent indigenous forest

91 Accommodation at Excelsior Hut on the Prospector's Hiking Trail is provided in what used to be a holiday cottage and in an adjacent rondavel

92 A ladder assists hikers up a difficult section on the Grootbosch section of the Magoebaskloof Hiking Trail

93 Grootbosch Lapa on the Grootbosch section of the Magoebaskloof Hiking Trail offers basic shelter for hikers

94 Indigenous forest, Grootbosch section of the Magoebaskloof Hiking Trail

95 View of the Devil's Knuckles and Kruger se Kop in the Wolkberg Wilderness Area

▲ 92

▲ 93

◀ 94

▲ 95

97 ▲

◀ 96

96 Klipdraai Waterfall, a magnificent tufa waterfall in the Wolkberg Wilderness Area
97 Ground hornbill, one of about 495 species
of birds trailists chance ticking on the guided
wilderness trails in the Kruger National Park
98 Accommodation for trailists undertaking the
Mapulaneng Nature Trails is provided in comfortable self-contained log cabins
99 Burchell's zebra, a common species seen by
trailists undertaking one of the guided wilderness
trails in the Kruger National Park

▲ 98   99 ▼

100 Forest scenery along the trails laid out in the Welgevonden Forest Station, Mapulaneng Nature Reserve

are accommodated in an old train coach, while the overnight huts are equipped with bunks, mattresses, fireplaces and firewood. Toilets and refuse bins are also provided.

Description The trail network of the Kaapschehoop Hiking Trail in the Berlin State Forest, south-west of Nelspruit, consists of two circular two-day hutted routes. The Wattles Circle (northern loop) traverses easy terrain through and alongside pine plantations with magnificent views over the Elands River Valley and the Starvation Creek Nature Reserve. The second day's hike covers a mere 9 km and passes several points of geological interest. The Coetzeestroom Circle (southern loop) covers 37 km over two days and rewards hikers with spectacular views of the indigenous forest of the Coetzeestroom. On the second day's hike the trail winds alongside and through pine forests and skirts Blouswawelvlakte, which has been set aside as a breeding site for the endangered blue swallow.

METSI-METSI

Distance Guided wilderness trail, no set route or distance; 2 days/3 nights

Reservations National Parks Board, P O Box 787, Pretoria 0001, Telephone (012) 343-1991, or P O Box 7400, Roggebaai 8012, Telephone (021) 22-2810.

Group size Maximum 8

Facilities The base camp is equipped with beds, mattresses and bedding. Other amenities include cooking bomas, bush showers and toilets.

Description This guided wilderness trail is conducted in the wilderness area east of the Nwamuriwa Mountain near Tshokwane in the Kruger National Park. The trail is named after the Metsi-Metsi River, whose name is translated as "water-water". Game occurring in the area includes white and black rhino, elephant, buffalo, lion and several antelope species, while hippo are to be found in the Nwaswitsontso River. The area is characterised by rolling hills dominated by knobthorn and marula trees. Trailists depart from Skukuza to the base camp,

which is situated at the foot of the Nwamuriwa Mountain in a hilly area.

NAPI

Distance Guided wilderness trail, no set route or distance; 2 days/3 nights

Reservations National Parks Board, P O Box 787, Pretoria 0001, Telephone (012) 343-1991, or P O Box 7400, Roggebaai 8012, Telephone (021) 22-2810.

Group size Maximum 8

Facilities The base camp is equipped with beds, mattresses and bedding. Other amenities include cooking bomas, bush showers and toilets.

Description The base camp of this guided wilderness trail in the south-western part of the Kruger National Park is situated at the confluence of the Mbayamiti and Napi rivers between Pretoriuskop and Skukuza. The rolling landscape is characterised by savanna and trailists might chance upon white rhino, elephant, buffalo, sable, kudu and reedbuck, while black rhino are also encountered occasionally. Predators such as lion, leopard and wild dog also occur in the area. Trailists meet at Pretoriuskop from where they are transported to the base camp.

OLIFANTS

Distance Guided wilderness trail, no set route or distance; 2 days/3 nights

Reservations National Parks Board, P O Box 787, Pretoria 0001, Telephone (012) 343-1991, or P O Box 7400, Roggebaai 8012, Telephone (021) 22-2810.

Group size Maximum 8

Facilities The base camp is equipped with beds, mattresses and bedding. Other amenities include cooking bomas, bush showers and toilets.

Description The base camp of this guided wilderness trail in the centre of the Kruger

National Park is situated on the southern bank of the Olifants River, 4 km west of its confluence with the Letaba River. Game is plentiful and species to be seen include elephant, giraffe, blue wildebeest, waterbuck, Burchell's zebra and lion, while hippo and crocodile abound in the river. The landscape in the area is diverse, ranging from plains to the foothills of the Lebombo Mountains, while the narrow ravines with their fascinating potholes a short way upstream from the camp are a scenic highlight. Trails depart from the Letaba rest camp.

PROTEA

Distance 38 km; 4 days

Reservations The Officer-in-Charge, Blyderivierspoort Nature Reserve, Private Bag X431, Graskop 1270, Telephone (01315) 8-1216.

Group size Minimum 2; Maximum 10

Facilities The Hikers' Huts at Bourke's Luck are equipped with beds, mattresses, flush toilets and showers. Amenities at the overnight huts on the trail include beds, mattresses and flush toilets. Fireplaces and firewood are provided at the Hikers', Muilhuis and Eerste Liefde huts. At Muilhuis and Eerste Liefde water has to be fetched from the nearby streams.

Description Starting from Bourke's Luck Potholes at the confluence of the Treur and Blyde rivers, this circular trail affords hikers an opportunity to escape into the heart of the Blyderivierspoort Nature Reserve. The first day's hike traverses the upper slopes of the Belvedere Valley to reach Muilhuis after 12,5 km. On the second day the trail ascends steadily to the escarpment, passing through the Yellowwood Forest before reaching The Divide. A short deviation to the Devil's Window reveals spectacular views of the Lowveld some 1 000 m below and the Op De Berg Hut is reached after a short 6,5 km hike. About 9 km is covered on the third day's hike to Eerste Liefde, alternating between montane grassland and montane forest. The final day's hike covers 11 km and follows the same route as the return route of the Yellowwood Hiking Trail.

RATELSPRUIT

Distance 27 km; 2 days

Reservations Mr and Mrs L Mostert, P O Box 27, Dullstroom 1110, Telephone (01325) 4-0821.

Group size Minimum 2; Maximum 12

Facilities The base camp hut is equipped with bunks, mattresses and a small kitchen with a coal stove. There is also an ablution block with hot/cold water showers and toilets, as well as a lapa with fireplaces and firewood.

Description The trail network on this farm north-east of Dullstroom consists of two circular day routes which are undertaken from a base camp. Highlights of the 15 km route include spectacular cliffs, waterfalls and deep ravines, while the 12 km route traverses grassveld with interesting features such as old stone kraals and unusual rock formations, locally known as the "Langklippe". Typical trees and shrubs occurring along the trail include cabbage trees, Natal bottlebrush, proteas and common tree ferns, while numerous plants can be seen in bloom during the summer months. Animals you could spot include grey rhebok, chacma baboons and honey badgers, as well as a wide variety of birds.

RIBBOK

Distance 20 km; 2 days

Reservations The Town Clerk, Lydenburg Town Council, P O Box 61, Lydenburg 1120, Telephone (01323) 2121.

Group size Minimum 2; Maximum 12

Facilities The overnight hut at the end of the first day's hike consists of two bedrooms, each equipped with six beds and mattresses. Fireplaces, firewood and kettles are provided.

Description This circular trail on the outskirts of Lydenburg traverses the 2 200 ha Gustav Klingbiel Nature Reserve. Hikers cover 10 km on each day, allowing ample time for game-viewing and bird-watching. The reserve is stocked with several species of game, including eland, impala, blesbok, blue wildebeest, kudu, Burchell's zebra and oribi. Over 200 bird species have been recorded to date and the vulture restaurant at the foot of Vyekop is of special interest to birders. Other features along the route include remnants of terraces, stone walls and the remains of homesteads dating back to the Iron Age, as well as old forts used by the retreating Boers during the Anglo-Boer War.

SALPETERKRANS

Distance 25 km; 2 days

Reservations Jacana Country Houses and Trails, P O Box 95212, Waterkloof 0145, Telephone (012) 346-3550.

Group size Minimum 2; Maximum 24

Facilities Accommodation at the base camp comprises two huts each equipped with 12 beds and mattresses. Other amenities include a lapa with a fireplace, firewood, hot/cold showers, paraffin lamps and toilets.

Description This trail traverses the Salpeterkrans Mountains west of the Steenkampsberg range at Dullstroom. Since both days' hike start and end at a base camp, only daypacks need to be carried.

On the first day's hike of 15 km the trail ascends the Salpeterkrans Mountains before dropping down to the Klip River where hikers can cool off in the inviting pools before heading back to the base camp. The second day's hike begins with a steady ascent up Perdekop and on the return leg hikers pass a natural rock bridge in the Klip River, an ideal stop for a swim. The trail surroundings are especially attractive between October and January when masses of yellow arum lilies provide a blaze of colour. Of particular interest to birders is the possibility of seeing all three crane species – blue, crowned and wattled.

SONGIMVELO

Distance Guided wilderness trail, no set route or distance; 3 to 5 days

Reservations The Secretary, Wilderness Leadership School, P O Box 87230, Houghton 2041, Telephone (011) 455-6805.

Group size Maximum 8

Facilities The trail price is inclusive of all equipment, food and transport from Johannesburg.

Description The Songimvelo Game Reserve is situated on the north-western border of Swaziland and nestles in the Barberton Mountain range. The vegetation ranges from montane forests to bushveld and riverine forest which provide ideal wilderness trailing areas. Rhino, elephant, giraffe, Burchell's zebra, blue wildebeest, various antelope and an abundance of birdlife can be seen on this trail. The Komati River meanders through the 65 000 ha game reserve. Archaeological sites between 2 200 and 2 400 years old add an interesting dimension to this scenic reserve.

STEENKAMPSBERG

Distance 29 km; 2 days

Reservations Dullstroom Village Council, P O Box 1, Dullstroom 1110, Telephone (01325) 4-0151.

Group size Minimum 2; Maximum 12

Facilities Campsites with ablution blocks are available at the Dullstroom Dam where the trail starts, while amenities at the overnight stop comprise a rondavel (without any facilities), a chemical toilet and a weir in a stream where hikers can cool off.

Description Situated at an altitude of 2 000 m, the Steenkampsberg lies at the north-eastern extremity of the Highveld. On account of its sub-alpine climate the mountain boasts a remarkable variety of flora with more than 200 species of flowering plants having been identified. To date some 150 bird species have been recorded in the area, which is the last stronghold of the wattled crane in Transvaal. The first day's hike ascends the Steenkampsberg, passing an overhang and a magnificent waterfall before reaching the overnight stop after 17 km. The second day's hike winds back up the plateau before descending to Dullstroom.

STERKSPRUIT

Distance 30,6 km; 2 or 3 days

Reservations The Town Clerk, Lydenburg Town Council, P O Box 61, Lydenburg 1120, Telephone (01323) 2121.

Group size Minimum 2; Maximum 10

Facilities The three overnight huts are equipped with bunks, mattresses, a table, saucepan and kettle. Running water and firewood are provided at Rooikat base camp, but at the two overnight stops hikers must gather firewood and collect water from the nearby streams.

Description This circular trail traverses the 10 080 ha Sterkspruit Mountain Catchment Area south-east of Lydenburg. Much of the trail winds through and alongside plantations, while stretches pass through grassveld. The first day's hike covers either 9,6 km or 16,6 km, passing an old gold mine and affording hikers magnificent views of Kaapsehoop and Swaziland. Hikers can either overnight at the Oribi Hut or continue for 7 km to the Klipspringer Hut. Shortly after setting off from the Klipspringer Hut, hikers are once again treated to an expansive view while several spectacular waterfalls and pools are encountered further along. The finals section of the trail winds through grassveld, passing relics of the Lydenburg goldmining days.

SUIKERBOSCHFONTEIN

Distance 18 km; 2 days

Reservations Jacana Country Homes and Trails, P O Box 95212, Waterkloof 0145, Telephone (012) 346-3550.

Group size Minimum 2; Maximum 20

Facilities The farmhouse at the start of the trail is equipped with bunks, mattresses, hot/cold water, toilets and showers, as well as fireplaces and firewood. Amenities at the

overnight camp consist of four huts, showers, toilets, fireplaces and firewood. Cooking utensils at both overnight facilities include a kettle, potjie, pots and pans.

Description Each leg of this circular two-day trail on the farm Suikerboschfontein, 20 km north-east of Carolina on the Highveld covers about 9 km. The first day's hike meanders across grassveld and through a yellowwood forest before descending into a basin with an inviting swimming pool. The final section of the day's hike to the overnight stop at Rooikrans winds past interesting rock formations. The second day's hike descends along a kloof to the Mooifontein Waterfall and further along there is a spectacular view of Rooikrans and Suikerbosrant. The trail then crosses into Gladdekloof where swimming can be enjoyed in the inviting pools.

SWENI

Distance Guided wilderness trail, no set route or distance; 2 days/3 nights

Reservations National Parks Board, P O Box 787, Pretoria 0001, Telephone (012) 343-1991, or P O Box 7400, Roggebaai 8012, Telephone (021) 22-2810.

Group size Maximum 8

Facilities The base camp is equipped with beds, mattresses and bedding. Other amenities include cooking bomas, bush showers and toilets.

Description This trail is conducted in the wilderness area south-west of the Nwanetsi rest camp in the Kruger National Park. The base camp is named after the Sweni Spruit and is situated in an area characterised by grassy plains with scattered knobthorn and marula trees. A species of particular interest is the ilala palm which grows on the floodplains of the Sweni Spruit.

Game attracted to the bush savanna includes buffalo, blue wildebeest, Burchell's zebra and impala, while predators such as leopard and lion also occur. Trailists are met at the Orpen rest camp, from where they are transported to the base camp.

VLAKVARK

Distance 20 km; 2 days (both routes)

Reservations Mr G Stemmet, P O Box 226, Ohrigstad, Telephone (01323) 8-0413.

Group size Minimum 2; Maximum 12

Facilities At the base camp accommodation is provided in a two-roomed park home, sleeping a total of 24. Amenities here include electricity, as well as hot and cold water showers. The base camp and the overnight huts on the two routes are equipped with bunks, mattresses, fireplaces, firewood, a three-legged pot and a large kettle.

Description Situated on the farm Nooitgedacht, east of Ohrigstad, the two two-day circular routes wind through typical bushveld vegetation. The first day of the original Vlakvark Hiking Trail follows an easy route past a lookout down to a river where the pools and waterfall suggest an ideal rest stop. From here the trail winds up to the plateau to reach the Bergsig Hut which overlooks the valley 10 km after setting off. On the second day the trail winds down to the river where another waterfall is encountered. After ascending to a viewpoint the trail returns to the river which is followed for a while before the route branches off to the base camp. Among the mammals hikers could spot are warthog, after which the trail has been named, bushpig, bushbuck, kudu and chacma baboon, while leopard also inhabit the kloofs.

WELBEDACHT

Distance Various options, ranging from 2 km to 20 km, are available

Reservations Jacana Country Homes and Trails, P O Box 95212, Waterkloof 0145, Telephone (012) 346-3550.

Group size Minimum 2; Maximum 32

Facilities The two houses at the starting point are equipped with beds, mattresses, hot/cold water showers and flush toilets. Paraffin lamps, pots, pans, a kettle, fireplaces and firewood are also provided. Fernkloof Hut on the trail is equipped with beds, mattresses, pots, pans, a kettle, fireplace and firewood. Water is obtainable from a nearby stream and there is also a cold water shower and pit toilet.

Description A network of trails covering about 40 km traverses the Welbedacht farm on the edge of the Transvaal escarpment, south-west of Lydenburg. Scenery ranges from the Crocodile River Valley to grassy mountain slopes and the escarpment, while some of the most unspoilt indigenous forests in the eastern Transvaal are also encountered. The difference in height between the base camp and the highest point of the trail is over 600 m, but hikers will enjoy expansive vistas of the Steenkampsberg, the Lowveld, the mosaic of farmlands in the valley below the escarpment and several waterfalls. Some 160 bird species have been recorded and bird-watching hides have been erected along the Crocodile River.

WOLHUTER

Distance Guided wilderness trail, no set route or distance; 2 days/3 nights

Reservations National Parks Board, P O Box 787, Pretoria 0001, Telephone (012) 343-1991, or P O Box 7400, Roggebaai 8012, Telephone (021) 22-2810.

Group size Maximum 8

Facilities The base camp is equipped with beds, mattresses and bedding. Other amenities include cooking bomas, bush showers and toilets.

Description This trail honours the legendary Harry and Henry Wolhuter, the father and son who were in control of the southern section of the Kruger National Park for many years. It was the first guided wilderness trail in the Kruger National Park and trails are conducted in the area between Pretoriuskop and Berg-en-Dal. The vegetation varies from open broad-leaved species to red bushwillow veld and among the game favouring this area are mountain reedbuck, white rhino, sable, impala, giraffe, blue wildebeest and lion. Trailists must report at the Berg-en-Dal rest camp, from where they are transported to the base camp situated on the banks of the Mavukane River.

YELLOWWOOD

Distance 25 km; 2 days

Reservations The Officer in Charge, Blyderivierspoort Nature Reserve, Private Bag X431, Graskop 1270, Telephone (01315) 8-1216.

Group size Minimum 2; Maximum 10

Facilities The Hikers' Huts at Bourke's Luck and the overnight stop at the end of the first day's hike, Salma Hut, are equipped with bunks and mattresses, as well as a cooking shelter with firewood provided. At Bourke's Luck tap water is provided, but at Salma hikers have to fetch water from the nearby stream.

Description This circular trail in the Blyderivierspoort Nature Reserve winds through a variety of vegetation types ranging from montane grassveld to gallery forest. From Bourke's Luck the trail descends steeply to the old hydro-electric power station at the confluence of the Blyde River and Belvederespruit. The trail then gains some 400 m in altitude, passing initially through forest before emerging into grassveld, and then descends gradually through gallery forest to the hut alongside the Belvederespruit. The second day's hike covers 11 km and initially follows an old wagon road before traversing the slopes above Belvedere Creek. At Belvedere Lodge the trail joins up with the first section of the previous day's hike, ascending steadily to Bourke's Luck.

NORTHERN TRANSVAAL

MAGOEBASKLOOF

The forests of Magoebaskloof are among the most beautiful indigenous forests in South Africa, resembling a fairytale wonderland. Large masses of clivias cling to tree branches, the striking Knysna lourie glides between trees and the usually nocturnal bushpig is sometimes surprised during the day. The Magoebaskloof Hiking Trail consists of two sections, Grootbosch and Dokolewa, and although both wind through indigenous forest and pine plantations each one has its own attractions.

Aspects common to both sections of the Magoebaskloof Hiking Trail are discussed in this general introduction.

TRAIL PLANNER

Climate

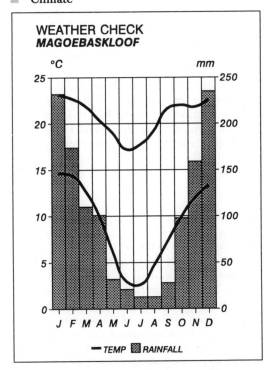

Reservations The National Hiking Way Board, Private Bag X503, Sabie 1260, Telephone (01315) 4-1058 or 41392, Fax

(01315) 4-2071. Reservations are accepted up to a year in advance.

Group size Minimum 2; Maximum 30 (Dokolewa) and 12 (Grootbosch)

Maps A full-colour trail map with information on the history, flora and fauna on the reverse is available and is forwarded with your receipt and permit. One map is supplied for every six adults.

Logistics Circular routes. Overnight huts at the start of both trails.

Relevant information
■ Precautions against ticks and malaria are necessary.
■ Some of the water points indicated on the map might be dry during the winter months, making it advisable to set off with a full 2-litre water-bottle each day.
■ No soap may be used in any of the streams.
■ Vehicles may only be parked at De Hoek.
■ Due to the strenuous nature of the Grootbosch route, children under 12 are not permitted on this section.

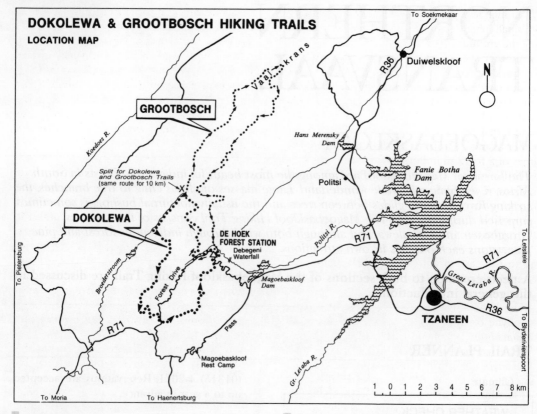

DOKOLEWA & GROOTBOSCH HIKING TRAILS
LOCATION MAP

- After heavy rains the access road to and from De Hoek can become very slippery.

How to get there Both trails start/end at the De Hoek Forest Station which is reached from Pietersburg by taking the R71 to Tzaneen. About 79 km beyond Pietersburg you must turn left onto a gravel road signposted Debengeni Falls and De Hoek Forest Station and continue for 7 km to the huts at the start.

Approaching from Tzaneen, you must leave the town on the R36, travelling 5 km before turning onto the R71 to Pietersburg. The turn-off onto the gravel road to De Hoek is reached 10 km further on.

TRAIL ENVIRONMENT

Flora The vegetation of the area has been classified as north-eastern mountain sourveld and consists mainly of indigenous evergreen high forest, while the former grasslands have been planted with pines.

Covering some 4 600 ha, Grootbosch is the largest indigenous forest in the Transvaal. The forest covers the northern slopes of the Woodbush State Forest and the south-eastern escarpment of Woodbush, as well as the catchment area and the numerous valleys of the Dokolewa River.

Among the dominant forest species are Outeniqua and real yellowwoods, white stinkwood, lemonwood, forest bushwillow and ironwood. A checklist of 72 of the more common tree species in the area is available.

You are likely to be struck by the near-absence of yellowwoods on the first day's hike. Most of these magnificent forest giants were felled by early woodcutters − a few half-covered sawpits being evidence of the wanton destruction. It has been estimated that about 4 000 mature yellowwood trees were felled in these forests by the early woodcutters.

A species you are likely to identify easily is the red stinkwood with its characteristic rough, peeling bark. It is a medium to tall tree of 10 to

24 m high and between September and January its small, pinkish-brown fruit can be seen littering the ground.

Another species which is easy to identify by its bark is the Transvaal plane which has a smooth, pale grey-brown trunk that flakes off in thin layers to reveal a distinctive mottled reddish to olive underbark. It occurs from the southern Cape along the east coast, growing either as small shrubs or small to medium-sized trees of 2 to 12 m in height. The tree derives its specific name, *o'connorii*, from Alexander O'Connor, the first professional forestry officer in the northern Transvaal region. O'Connor was responsible for establishing many plantations in the region.

Among the species which are mainly restricted to the eastern and north-eastern Transvaal are the wild quince, Transvaal white ash, bastard onionwood and matumi.

The Woodbush area is the home of several epiphytic orchids. These include the charming *Mystacidium caffrum*, with 12 crispy-white flowers between September and January, and *Tridactyle tricuspis* which bears up to 30 small, pale greenish-cream flowers on each stem during autumn.

Attractive flowering species to look out for on the forest floor are the forest montbretia (*Crocosmia aurea*) which produces between five and eight brilliant yellow-orange flowers between January and April, and the showy *Streptocarpus parviflorus* with its striking white to light pink flowers, decorated with one yellow and between three and seven purple lines. Other forest species include *Impatiens duthieae* which bear delicate pink to mauve flowers between October and March and forest clivia (*Clivia caulescens*) which is especially prolific on tree branches.

Between July and November the scarlet, bell-shaped flowers of the Transvaal bottlebrush are likely to catch your attention. This species reaches up to 5 m in height and favours rocky outcrops on the margins of forested ravines and gullies. Also favouring the forest margins is the curry bush, a bushy shrub which grows up to 3 m high. It has a characteristic curry smell and bears attractive yellow flowers throughout the year.

The Woodbush State Forest was established in 1917 and with an area of almost 7 700 ha it is the largest state forest in the Transvaal. About 2 400 ha are under plantation, while another 1 000 ha have been turned into plantations in the adjoining De Hoek State Forest.

To meet the growing demand for furniture wood, plantations of tropical hardwood species such as East African mahogany (*Khaya nyasica*) and Indian mahogany (*Chukrasia tabularis*), as well as yellowwood, were established at De Hoek during the late 1970s. Some of these plantations are seen on the drive up to the overnight hut at De Hoek.

Fauna   The forests of the north-eastern Transvaal are the habitat of three rare mammal species; namely red duiker, leopard and samango monkey. The distribution of the red duiker is limited to coastal bush in north-eastern KwaZulu/Natal and isolated forests in the Transvaal.

Leopard are unlikely to be seen as they are primarily nocturnal, lying up in dense cover during the day. Favouring forests, they also occur in mountainous areas, but avoid grasslands.

Troops of samango monkey also inhabit the forests, but because of their habitat they are difficult to see. More often, though, they can be identified by their call which can easily be confused with that of the Knysna lourie. The most common call, a loud repeated "nyah" often followed by a series of chuckles, is used by adult males, while other members of the troop emit a more high-pitched call. The smaller vervet monkey occurs in areas adjacent to the De Hoek Forest Station, but ventures only occasionally into the montane forest edge.

Provided you walk quietly, there is a good possibility of seeing bushbuck and bushpig in the forest. Although bushpigs are mainly nocturnal, they are often seen in Grootbosch during the daytime when they are not disturbed.

The curry bush occurs at high altitudes in open grasslands, at forest margins and along streams

The bushpig is mainly nocturnal, but is often seen foraging in the Magoebaskloof forests during the day

Also occurring in the area are common duiker, which favours more open, bushy areas, caracal and porcupine.

Although it is unlikely to be seen, the Woodbush forest is the habitat of Gunning's golden mole – one of 15 species of golden moles occurring in southern Africa. It was discovered in Woodbush in 1908 and was thought to be endemic to this area until 1974 when it was also collected in the New Agatha Forest Station.

Birdlife is prolific with some 309 species having been recorded in the De Hoek and Woodbush areas. Grootbosch is one of the best places in South Africa to tick the blackfronted bush shrike, but as this species is difficult to see you will need patience. Two other worthwhile species you might tick are chorister and starred robins, which are restricted to the narrow belt of evergreen montane forest from Port Elizabeth north-eastwards to the northern Transvaal. The brown robin is also mainly restricted to this area and can be spotted in clearings on the forest floor, while the Cape robin is likely to be ticked in the forest edge and wooded kloofs.

The black-eyed bulbul and the small, highly vocal Cape white-eye are found at all levels in the forest, while the yellowthroated warbler prefers the middle to upper strata. Yellowstreaked bulbuls are occasionally seen in mixed bird parties in the forest canopy.

Keep an eye out for the blackcrowned night heron which has been spotted in treetops in the late evening near Broederstroom and Woodbush huts.

Birds of prey include crowned eagle, forest buzzard and African goshawk, while the longcrested eagle is occasionally seen in the vicinity of marshy areas.

The indigenous forests of Woodbush are the habitat of several interesting and unusual reptiles. Methuen's dwarf gecko (*Lygodactylus methueni*) is endemic to Woodbush, while the Woodbush flat gecko (*Afroedura pondolia multiporus*) and the Woodbush legless skink (*Acontophiops lineatus*) were considered vulnerable until recently when populations were discovered on the Wolkberg. Also occurring here is an isolated population of the Swazi rock snake (*Lamprophis swazicus*), which is restricted to the Transvaal escarpment further south and Swaziland. The African rock python (*Python sebea natalensis*) has also been recorded here.

History Archaeological research has revealed that the north-eastern Transvaal was inhabited by Early Iron Age man during the late third or early fourth centuries.

These early inhabitants were not only pastoralists, but they also cultivated crops, mined and manufactured pottery. They preferred the open grassy areas where they lived in fairly large settlements. Today it is commonly accepted that they were the ancestors of the Sotho people with whom the whites made contact when they began settling in the area in the 1870s.

One of the earliest finds of gold in the area was that of C F Haenert, who discovered gold at the foot of the Iron Crown in the Strydpoort Mountains. The mining activities required large quantities of timber and during the 1870s woodcutters began exploiting the indigenous forests and established Houtbosdorp.

The invasion of the area by miners, prospectors and woodcutters was bitterly resented by the Tlou, a Sotho tribe who inhabited the present-day Magoebaskloof. Their chief, Magoeba, instructed his followers to destroy mining beacons and after refusing to pay tax and ordering the white intruders out of his territory, he was arrested on 2 November 1888, but was later released.

The Haenertsburg goldfield was disappointing, though, and most of the miners turned their attention to the Murchison fields further east where richer deposits were discovered in 1888.

Relations between the whites and Magoeba remained uneasy. Tribesmen were continually harassing the woodcutters, miners and government officials and uprooting claim pegs and in 1894 outlying buildings and farmhouses were attacked and set alight.

Nearly 800 men of various commandos and

70 men of De Staats Artillery, armed with three cannons, were dispatched to deal with the recalcitrant chief. The commandos were further strengthened by several hundred Swazis and Shangaans. Magoeba and his warriors retreated into the forests and defied attempts to dislodge them for almost a year. On one occasion he was surrounded in the vicinity of Pypkop in the De Hoek Forestry area, but under cover of darkness the men escaped.

The Boer commando found their task, which was continuously hampered by the dense forest, mist and rain, so unpleasant that they named the forest Helsche Bosch.

In June 1895 a strong force was mounted and in the main action the forest was shelled by the artillery. Magoeba's kraal was captured on 4 June and the chief was taken prisoner four days later by Swazi mercenaries and, according to legend, beheaded.

DOKOLEWA

This trail in the northern Transvaal leads through aromatic pine plantations and evergreen montane forests which were perhaps best described by John Buchanan, author of Prester John and Greenmantle. In an article which appeared in Blackwoods Magazine in December 1902, Buchanan wrote of the Woodbush Forest: "Here was a true park ... so perfectly laid out that one could hardly believe that it was not the work of a man ...". Fairly short distances are covered each day, allowing you ample time to appreciate the forests.

Aspects common to both sections of the Magoebaskloof Hiking Trail are discussed in the general introduction which should be read in conjunction with this chapter.

TRAIL PLANNER

Distance 36 km; 3 days

Grading B

Facilities All three trail huts are converted forestry houses and amenities include coal stoves, showers/baths (with hot water after the stove has been stoked up) and electric lighting. Bunks with mattresses, fireplaces, firewood, pots, pans, kettles and refuse bins are also provided.

TRAIL DESCRIPTION

Day 1: De Hoek Hut to Broederstroom Hut
Initially the trail follows a plantation road which is flanked by a few indigenous trees. Some of the trees have been numbered, making it easy to identify them, especially as you have a clear view of their growth form. This first section is very easy walking, as it is mostly level or gradually downhill.

After turning off the Forest Drive the trail remains level for a while before ascending steeply, but fortunately the route is shaded by tall pines which filter the often harsh sunlight. A short way beyond the 4 km mark you will enter the indigenous forest and, after climbing gently for about 1 km, join a contour path before ascending steadily through magnificent indigenous forest. A number of old saw pits can be seen close to the path after the 5 km mark. Although you will remain on the contour path for about 3,5 km, there is an occasional break in the forest, allowing you a glimpse of the indigenous forest and the Lowveld. Forest lilies

(*Clivia caulescens*) are prolific along this section, many of them growing as epiphytes in the forks of trees, and clusters of forest tree ferns also attract attention.

After about 8,5 km you will emerge onto the dry western slopes, continuing on more or less the same contour. The scrub-like vegetation here contrasts sharply with the lush indigenous forest and the trail traverses across some large rock slabs for about 1 km before entering pine plantations. Just after the 10 km mark you will reach a forestry road where a sign indicates that the Dokolewa Section continues to the left while the Grootbosch Section continues in the opposite direction. The park-like setting under the pines is an ideal tea or lunch spot.

Follow the road for about 1 km until the trail branches off to the right and crosses the Broederstroom, where a few large trees create a shady resting spot. For the remainder of the day's hike, you will follow the course of the stream, crossing it several times.

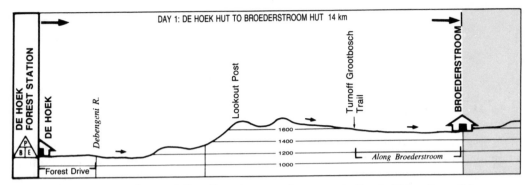

DAY 1: DE HOEK HUT TO BROEDERSTROOM HUT 14 km

The last section is a short uphill pull to the hut which is an old forestry house, overlooking the Broederstroom Valley. A causeway below the hut has formed a fairly deep pool which offers some relief during the hot summer months.

Day 2: Broederstroom Hut to Woodbush Hut

After an early morning climb along an aromatic footpath covered by pine needles, the trail joins a gravel road and continues through pine plantations, until it turns right to pass through a delightful indigenous forest after about 1,5 km. Close to the 2 km mark you will reach the escarpment and follow plantation roads once again, except for about 1 km which passes through indigenous forest. Shortly after the 6 km mark the trail emerges from the indigenous forest at a small waterfall, an ideal resting spot.

Over the next 2 km there are good views over the Dokolewa Valley and at the 8 km mark you will cross a gravel road leading to Houtbosdorp. The trail continues along a forestry road through pine plantations for about another 2 km and then passes through the Helpmekaar Forest for about 1 km. Shortly after the 11 km mark you will turn right and pass through a plantation which boasts the tallest *Eucalyptus*

saligna trees in South Africa. One of these trees, which was planted in 1905 or 1906, has a diameter of 114 cm and is no less than 82,6 m in height.

The final kilometre to the hut takes longer than expected, but you will eventually get there! The hut, an old forestry house, is situated on the edge of the Woodbush Arboretum which was established in 1907 by the first professional forestry officer in the northern Transvaal, Mr J A O'Connor. Various northern and central American trees were planted here to determine their suitability for timber production.

Day 3: Woodbush Hut to De Hoek Hut

Soon after leaving the hut you will pass a memorial to Mr O'Connor. At first the trail mainly follows forestry roads through pine plantations and along this section you will notice some stone mule stables to the left of the trail. These stables probably date back to the 1920s and were built of soapstone, hence the Afrikaans name Seepsteenstalle. The residence of the first forester in the area was also built in this area.

Further along, the trail enters the indigenous forest and in this section some magnificent specimens of wild quince, Transvaal plane and forest waterwood can be seen.

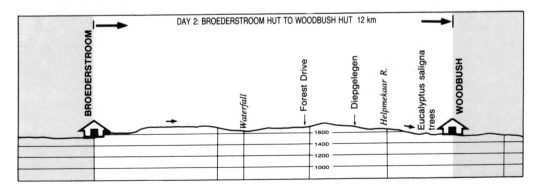

DAY 2: BROEDERSTROOM HUT TO WOODBUSH HUT 12 km

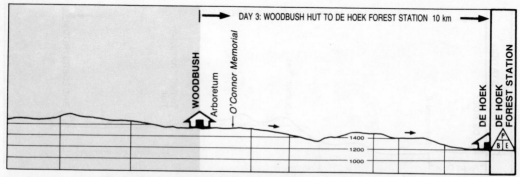

Shortly before the 4 km mark the trail descends to a tributary of the Politsi River and, after a short, steep ascent, reaches another pine plantation.

One kilometre further the trail once again leaves the pine plantations, following a fairly level route through indigenous forest along the northern slopes of Magoebaskloof. Several tributaries of the Debengeni River have their origin here and the trail crosses numerous streams. During winter the streams are likely to be dry and the waterfalls referred to on the trail map are easily overlooked. Good specimens of forest fever-berry, assegai and forest elder are seen along this section.

Just before the 8 km mark the trail once again emerges into a pine plantation. After a short

while the route joins a forestry road which takes you through indigenous forest. Then, quite suddenly and unexpectedly, you will find yourself back at De Hoek.

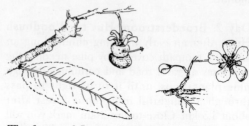

The fruit and flower of the Transvaal plane, which is seen in the indigenous forests of Magoebaskloof

GROOTBOSCH

This magnificent three-day trail in the north-eastern Transvaal leads through pine planta-tions and the largest evergreen forest in the Transvaal. The verdant high forests are charac-terised by masses of forest lilies, lichen-clad tree trunks, mosses and tree ferns. The trail caters for hikers preferring less sophisticated accommodation and is the first National Hiking Way Trail where bunks and mattresses are not provided. With fairly long distances over demanding terrain, this trail is for the seasoned hiker.

Aspects common to both sections of the Magoebaskloof Hiking Trail are discussed in the general introduction which should be read in conjunction with this chapter.

TRAIL PLANNER

Distance 50 km; 3 days

Grading C

Facilities Facilities at the Grootbosch Hut at De Hoek include a fireplace, firewood, pots and pans, bunks and mattresses, water, refuse bins and toilets. No bunks and mat-tresses are provided at the other two overnight shelters and amenities are limited to fireplaces, firewood, a toilet and water.

Relevant information
■ Since the nearest water is about 300 m from both overnight stops on the trail, extra water-bottles or expandable containers will be useful.
■ During and after heavy rains the trail is extremely slippery, making footwear with a good grip essential.
■ Use firewood sparingly and do not rely on finding firewood at the shelters on the trail as some hikers burn up more than their fair share. It is, therefore, advisable to carry a backpacking stove.
■ Since the Grootbosch Lapa only sleeps eight, it is advisable to carry a tent when the trail is fully booked. A cleared area is pro-vided near the lapa for tents.

TRAIL DESCRIPTION

Day 1: Grootbosch Hut to Grootbosch Lapa
The first 10 km follows the same route as the first day of the Dokolewa section. A plantation road is reached shortly before the 10 km mark and here you must turn right − the route to the left being to the Broederstroom Hut on the Dokolewa Route.

The route initially passes through pine plan-tations before alternating between stretches of pine plantations and indigenous forest. Near the 12 km mark the trail branches off to the right and a short while later there is a detour to the left to the Huilklip, a large oval-shaped rock

positioned on a few smaller rocks. When it is struck with a stone it resonates with a metallic sound and it has been suggested that it was used by the early Sotho inhabitants for ritual purposes.

After hiking for about 5 km along plantation roads, the trail branches off to the left, following a footpath through the Grootbosch. Good specimens of red stinkwood, forest fever-berry and water berry can be seen along this section.

Shortly after the 16 km mark the trail descends, crossing a tributary of the Kudu River, and about 10 minutes later another tributary is

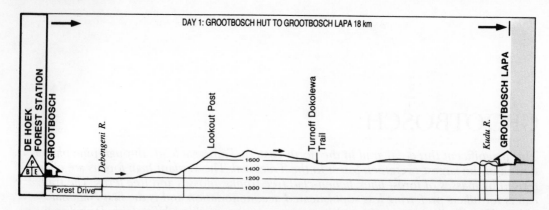

DAY 1: GROOTBOSCH HUT TO GROOTBOSCH LAPA 18 km

crossed. Keep an eye out here for some impressive forest figs, also known as strangler figs because of their characteristic growth form of strangling their hosts. A few minutes later you

The lovely Knysna lourie is likely to be seen in the forests of Magoebaskloof

will cross another tributary of the Kudu River. Remember to fill your water-bottles here before the final short but steep ascent to the overnight stop. Grootbosch Lapa is a circular hut built from natural stone in a clearing. There is also a fireplace and a table and benches.

Day 2: Grootbosch Lapa to Berg-en-Dal Lapa Since you have an 18 km hike ahead of you an early start is advisable. The trail immediately disappears into the cool indigenous forest and soon after setting off you will pass an enormous Outeniqua yellowwood lying next to the path. It is worth taking a break here to admire this centuries-old forest giant which was uprooted during a storm in December 1982. It used to tower about 31 m above the forest floor, with a trunk 2,16 m in diameter.

About 2 km after setting off the trail winds along a ridge, affording you glimpses over the Lowveld, the Tzaneen Dam and the Mooketsi Valley. The trail winds up to a beacon which, at just over 1 600 m, is the highest point on the trail. In winter, however, the view is often obscured by the smoke of veld fires.

The trail returns to the indigenous forest and

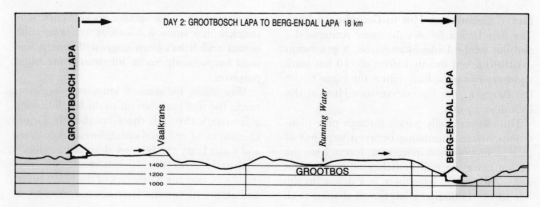

DAY 2: GROOTBOSCH LAPA TO BERG-EN-DAL LAPA 18 km

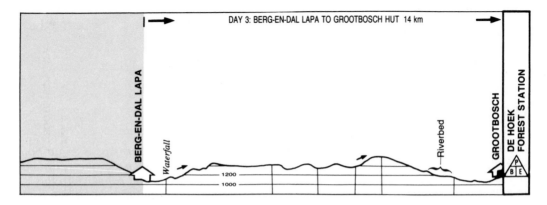

DAY 3: BERG-EN-DAL LAPA TO GROOTBOSCH HUT 14 km

you will now head in an easterly direction, descending steeply before swinging in a southerly direction. Along this section the gradient becomes less steep and near the 6 km mark you will cross a stream by way of a bridge. About 10 minutes later an old saw pit is seen to the left of the trail.

Shortly before the 10 km mark you will look down onto the Westphalia Estate and then continue along a fire-break for about an hour before returning to the indigenous forest. During and just after the rainy season numerous small streams with delightful waterfalls are passed on this section, one such spot being between the 13 and 14 km marks. These streams eventually find their way into the Hans Merensky Dam, named after the renowned South African geologist who discovered several important mineral deposits as well as the Alexander Bay diamond deposits.

Once again water has to be carried to the lapa as the last stream is crossed about 300 m before you reach the hut. Berg-en-dal Lapa is a rather uninspiring corrugated iron structure, which is difficult to appreciate even in heavy rain. With time in hand you can freshen up in the pool some 500 m from the lapa along the next day's route.

Day 3: Berg-en-Dal Lapa to De Hoek Forest Station
From the lapa the trail descends to a tributary of the Mabitse River which is followed

upstream for a short way, reaching a beautiful waterfall about 500 m after setting off. Although it is usually too early for a dip, fill your water-bottle here because a fairly steep climb awaits you over the next 3 km. Over this stretch you will gain some 400 m in altitude but the enchanting forest scenery will distract your attention from the slog! At one point a short wooden ladder has been provided to help you overcome a boulder obstructing the way.

Further along, you will follow the 1 400 m contour and for the next few kilometres you will cross numerous tributaries of the Mabitse River, which has its origin here. This section is especially attractive after the summer rains, but if you are caught in a thunderstorm, care should be exercised since the trail can become dangerously slippery. However, do not count on finding water here in the winter months and top up your water-bottle whenever you have the opportunity.

Shortly after the 8 km mark the trail gains about 200 m in altitude and after a short level section starts to descend, affording you views of the expansive pine plantations, tea estates and the Magoebaskloof Dam.

With about 4 km of the day's hike remaining De Hoek Forest Station comes into view, but it appears deceptively close. After descending along a fire-break for a short while, the trail continues along plantation roads to the end where a final short but steep ascent awaits you.

WOLKBERG

The Wolkberg, forming an arc in the northern extension of the Drakensberg, is an unspoilt area of deep ravines, indigenous forests and high mountain peaks which are often covered in a fine mist during the summer months, lending an air of mystery and romance to this area. It abounds in myths and legends, and John Buchanan was inspired to use it as a back-drop to his classic adventure story, Prester John. *Harry Klein, too, came under its spell and immortalised it in his books* Valley of the Mists.

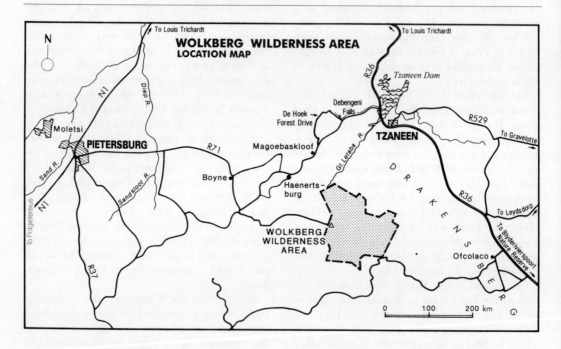

TRAIL PLANNER

Distance Depends on the route chosen

Grading B to C+ options are possible

Reservations The Officer-in-Charge, Serala Forest Station, Private Bag X102, Haenertsburg 0730, Telephone (015272) 1303. Reservations are accepted up to three months in advance.

Group size Groups are limited to a maximum of 10 persons, while the total number

of people allowed to overnight in the wilderness area is restricted to 60.

Maps A sketch map and an information booklet is forwarded with your receipt and permit. It is essential to obtain the 1 : 50 000 topographical map sections 2330CC and 2430AA.

Facilities No facilities are provided in the wilderness area and you are free to camp wherever you choose.

Climate

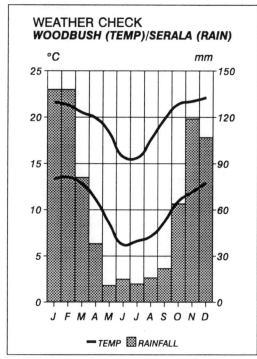

WEATHER CHECK
WOODBUSH (TEMP)/SERALA (RAIN)

— TEMP ▨ RAINFALL

Rainfall in the wilderness area varies from 500 mm in the south-west to 1 350 mm in the higher lying areas in the north-east, the months between November and February being the wettest. Mist occurs on average 147 days a year at an altitude of 1 200 m and higher and is most common during the summer rainy period.

Logistics Access to and from the wilderness

area is only from Serala Forest Station where you can overnight at a small campsite with showers and toilets.

Relevant information

■ A backpacking stove is essential as fires are not permitted in the wilderness area.
■ The use of soap and detergents in rivers and streams is strictly prohibited.
■ Always carry a tent as rain and mist can be expected in summer and extremely cold temperatures in winter.
■ Be prepared for rain during summer by waterproofing your pack and keeping rain gear handy.
■ The paths are often indistinct and you need to have at least one competent mapreader/navigator in your group.
■ Ticks can be a nuisance.

How to get there From Pietersburg take the R71 highway and after passing through Zion, about 40 km further, turn right onto a gravel road. Some 9 km onwards you will reach a four-way intersection where you must carry on straight. The Serala Forest Station is reached 25 km further on. Ignore the two roads deviating to the right, the first after 7 km and the second to Ashmole Dales about 5 km from the forest station.

Approaching from Tzaneen, travel to Haenertsburg from where you must take a gravel road on the south-western edge of the town. Keep left at the fork 14 km further and turn left 6 km onwards at the four-way intersection mentioned above.

TRAIL ENVIRONMENT

Flora The vegetation of the Wolkberg Wilderness Area varies from montane grassland to semi-deciduous indigenous forest and evergreen montane forest.

The vegetation consists mainly of North-eastern mountain sourveld dominated by redgrass (*Themeda triandra*). Be on the lookout here for the Transvaal mountain sugarbush, which is restricted to the mistbelt from near Lydenburg in the Drakensberg escarpment to the Wolkberg. It grows as a small gnarled tree or shrub, although it can reach up to 8 m in areas with high rainfall and frequent mists. Brilliant, rosy-pink flowers are produced in spring. Other

proteas recorded in the wilderness area include the common, African white, silver and clusterhead sugarbushes. The common tree fern occurs alongside streams.

Flowering plants include the pink to mauve *Gladiolus varius*, blue quills (*Scilla natalensis*), the unobtrusive *S. nervosa* and little stars (*Hypoxis filliformis*). Also occurring here are *Kniphofia coralligemma*, which bears yellow-orange flower spikes between January and April, everlastings (*Helichrysum*) and *Gnidia kraussiana* with its clusters of round flowers between August and November.

In the southern part of the wilderness area

Growth form, leaf, and female and male cones of the Modjadji cycad, which takes its name from the legendary Rain Queen of the Lobedu

adjacent to the Mohlapitse River the vegetation is characterised by Lowveld sour bushveld consisting of sour grassveld with bushveld species such as Transvaal beech, wild and round-leaved teak, marula and large-fruited bushwillow.

Patches of evergreen montane forests are found in the deep valleys and on the higher southern and south-eastern slopes and comprise about 40 tree species. Typical forest species such as Outeniqua and real yellowwoods, common wild fig, lemonwood, forest bushwillow, forest waterwood, Cape beech and tree fuchsia occur.

It is estimated that about 4 000 Modjadji cycads occur in the appropriately named Cycad Valley – a very steep valley at the western end of the Devil's Knuckles. The Modjadji cycad is the largest of the 17 South African cycads, reaching an average height of between 5 and 8 m,

although they occasionally reach up to 13 m. The leaves reach a length of up to 2,5 m, while the female cones can weigh as much as 37 kg. The popular name is derived from the Mujaji or Rain Queen of the Lobedu, who lives in the vicinity of Duiwelskloof.

The hill overlooking her kraal is covered with several thousand of these cycads and the cycad forest here is among the largest in the world. The forest enjoyed the protection of succeeding generations of the Rain Queen and was proclaimed a national monument in 1936.

Fauna The most common antelope are bushbuck and common duiker, but you might also spot grey rhebok, klipspringer and reedbuck. The primates are represented by vervet monkey, lesser bushbaby, chacma baboon and the samango monkey. Predators include leopard, caracal, brown hyaena, Cape clawless otter, African wild cat, black-backed jackal and genets. Bushpig inhabit the forests.

To date some 157 bird species have been recorded for the area. The more uncommon species you might be fortunate to spot include the bat hawk, martial eagle and the blackfronted bush shrike which breeds in the Wonderwoud. The bat hawk is listed as rare in the *South African Red Data Book – Birds* and only two breeding pairs have been recorded in the north-eastern Transvaal. Other raptors include black-shouldered kite, black eagle, forest buzzard, peregrine and lanner falcons.

Other interesting species to look out for are the Goliath heron, striped flufftail, yellow wagtail and the crested guineafowl, which can be distinguished from the more common helmeted guineafowl by the tuft of feathers on the crest.

The numerous rivers and streams of the area are the habitat of species such as Egyptian goose, yellowbilled duck, black crake and moorhen. In riverine bush, look out for Burchell's coucal, brownhooded kingfisher, southern boubou and glossy starling.

In the wooded savanna and grassland you might spot secretary bird and redcrested korhaan. Among the other species occurring in the wilderness area are speckled mousebird, lilacbreasted roller, clapper lark, blackeyed bulbul, longtailed wagtail, Marico sunbird and swee waxbill.

History Archaeological finds in the north-eastern Transvaal have provided abundant evidence that the region was already inhabited by Early Iron Age man during the late third and early fourth centuries.

These early inhabitants, the ancestors of the Sotho, were not only pastoralists but also cultivated crops, worked metal and manufactured pottery. They preferred the open, grassy areas where they lived in fairly large settlements.

Stone walls in the wilderness area and names like Mampa's Kloof, which was named after a local Sotho chief, serve as reminders of the Sotho-speaking people who inhabited the area. Other Sotho chiefs who lived in the area when the whites started settling there included Motshutli, Tsolobolo, Magoboya and Mamathola, after whom the 3 011 m-high peak towards the south-east of the wilderness area was named. Further west lived the Tlou tribe of Chief Magoeba.

Whites began taking an interest in the area after traces of gold were discovered in the Murchison range south-east of Tzaneen in 1870. The earliest find of gold was the discovery of Ellen's Fortune Reef at the foot of the Iron Crown (2 126 m) by C F Haenert in 1887. A town was established in the same year and named after him (Haenertsburg).

However the Woodbush Gold Fields, as they were known, were disappointing and after the discovery of richer deposits in the Murchison range the miners turned their attention eastwards. In 1890 the mining settlement south of the Murchison range was proclaimed a town and given the name Leydsdorp after the then State Secretary of the Transvaal Republic, Dr W Leyds. The government administrative centre for the goldfields was originally situated near Thabina in the Lowveld. It was named Agatha, after the wife of Dr Leyds. The site was badly chosen, however, and malaria and bilharzia forced the settlers to relocate the centre in the foothills of the mountains. The new centre was named New Agatha, a name that still exists today.

The hotel at New Agatha was originally a coach house on the route between Pietersburg and Leydsdorp. The coach service was run by the coaching firm of C H Zeederberg which, after the discovery of gold in the eastern Transvaal, moved its headquarters from Pietermaritzburg to Pretoria. It was a four-and-a-half day journey from Pretoria to Leydsdorp with passengers sleeping over en route first at Nylstroom, then Pietersburg, followed by Haenertsburg and finally, Thabina – now New Agatha.

The coach eventually arrived at Leydsdorp at noon on the fifth day, a Saturday. For this journey of roughly 500 km the single fare was £ 15. Mules were mainly used to haul the coaches, although the Zeederbergs became well known for the domesticated zebras which were also employed!

The more recent history of the area is closely linked to that of Orrie Baragwanath who in the early 1900s settled in the highlands, known as the Downs, south of the wilderness area. He and his ex-hunting partner, Frank Lewis, bought land from the government and began farming sheep and seed potatoes. No roads led into the mountains until Baragwanath and Lewis constructed a track up the Asberg from the Mohlapitse River and later a route down the northern face of the mountains was surveyed.

On 28 October 1977 the Wolkberg was declared South Africa's seventh proclaimed wilderness area. It covers some 17 390 ha and is renowned for its spectacular mountain scenery and beautiful indigenous forests.

TRAIL DESCRIPTION

Like other wilderness areas, the Wolkberg allows you to create your own experience. No trails are laid out but backpackers have a choice of management paths and jeep tracks to follow. A four-day route giving you a good orientation for a first visit is described here.

Day 1: Serala Forest Station to Ashmole Dales River From the Serala campsite you will follow a jeep track bordered on the right by a pine plantation. The walking is easy, mainly level or downhill, and after 40 minutes the track splits. Keep right here continuing downhill to reach the Klipdraai River 30 minutes later. From here the track starts climbing but take your time and identify some of the features across the valley – Serala Peak (2 050 m) and Krugerkop, which resembles the profile of Paul Kruger with the forest at the foot of the dome forming his beard.

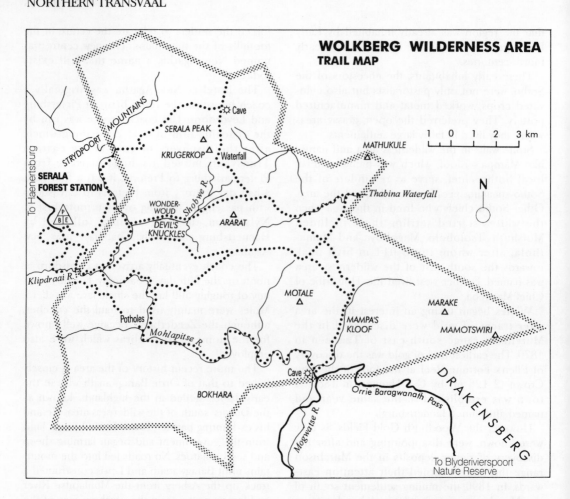

After about an hour the jeep track commences a lengthy zigzag descent, levelling out after an hour and a half. Here a grassy patch alongside the jeep track with the Ashmole Dales River close by is an ideal campsite. Covering about 14 km, this is a pleasant day's backpacking if you have made a mid-morning start.

Day 2: Ashmole Dales River to Mampaskloof
Continuing along the jeep track the walking is easy and after 15 minutes you will reach the Mohlapitse River, a tributary of the Olifants River. You will remain close to the river for the rest of the morning. The jeep track crosses the river many times and you will admire the determination of Orrie Baragwanath, who crossed the river no less then 45 times in one day between Haenertsburg and the Downs when he first explored the area. Along this section you will reach the lowest point of the wilderness area – 795 m compared to 2 050 m of Serala

Peak. The scenery surrounding you will again demand a slow pace. Dry, steep slopes to the west are punctuated with mountain aloe and common tree euphorbia, while there is also an enormous tufa formation which is no longer active.

Numerous inviting swimming places are passed in the first few hours of walking and, as this day of backpacking is short, enjoy yourself. The bird-watching in the riverine scrub is also rewarding.

Gradually the valley becomes wider and after crossing the river at least 20 times, about four hours' (excluding breaks) walking from the campsite, there is a split. Turn left here onto the route leading up Mampaskloof (the main route continues to the Downs) and follow the jeep track which winds through rank grass. About an hour beyond the split you will reach a small stream which suggests itself as a good camping spot.

Lesser bushbaby – a nocturnal inhabitant of the indigenous forest of the Wolkberg

Day 3: Mampaskloof to Wonderwoud With a strenuous day ahead an early start is advisable. Set off with full water-bottles as there is not much water along the way. Less than 10 minutes after leaving the overnight camp the jeep track seems to end and a path leads off to your left. You will gain altitude rapidly, soon emerging into grassveld dotted with proteas. Falling away steeply to your left is a forested kloof and looking backwards (south-east) you will identify the Marake and Mamotswiri peaks.

You will continue to climb for the next few hours, before descending into a wide valley about four hours after setting off. The stream running through the valley usually has water and this is a good spot for an early lunch. Remember to refill water-bottles before continuing.

From the stream you will ascend the opposite slope of the valley along an interesting rocky pass. Less than an hour after setting off you will be at the top of the pass, standing in a large amphitheatre formed by the Devil's Knuckles, also known as Tandberg and Ararat. The Devil's Knuckles, a row of quartzite cliffs, initially face north-east for about 2 km but then swing west for about 6 km, ending in the Mohlapitse Valley. This barrier can only be crossed in one place and this is at the highest knuckle (1 853 m). Do not attempt to descend anywhere else!

A stone beacon has been packed on the highest knuckle and although you may not be able to distinguish it immediately, make your way across the flat grassy basin in a north-westerly direction towards the bend in the barrier. More likely than not you will not be able to find a path but as you approach the Devil's Knuckles scan them with binoculars and you should be able to pick up the beacon on the highest knuckle to guide you in the correct direction.

Once on top of the knuckle you have a 360-degree view and it is worth taking a break here, not only to enjoy the view but also to orientate yourself. You will notice a small flat area cleared of rocks which just accommodates a tent and, depending on your timing, you could decide to overnight here as the view is so magnificent. Water supplies usually dictate that you continue down into the Wonderwoud, however.

The route down the "knuckle" is clearly visible and although it is a little tricky in places, chains have been secured to assist you. From the top of the Devil's Knuckles the descent will take about 30 minutes and, once in the grassy valley, you will turn left towards the forest. Do not continue to Serala Plateau via Kruger's Nose.

A large part of the Shobwe catchment area is clothed by the most extensive indigenous forest (500 ha) in the wilderness area – the Wonderwoud. Here you will be impressed by the towering yellowwoods, some with a trunk circumference of 5 m. About an hour after entering the forest a stream is crossed and there are many suitable campsites here.

Day 4: Wonderwoud to Serala Forest Station Depending on how long you continued before setting up camp, about two hours of forest walking remain. On leaving the forest you will join a jeep track where you must turn left, to continue down the Mohlapitse River Valley. At this junction there is another idyllic campsite shaded by a large tree. Judging from the flattened grass this is a popular site and also close to water.

Continuing along the jeep track which snakes through the valley, you will cross the river several times but the pools are not as inviting as on the second day. About an hour after joining the jeep track you will pass a shady campsite on your left, but it is worthwhile continuing to a magical waterfall tucked away in a wooded kloof. At the junction of the Klipdraai River you will continue along the jeep track and after ascending through scrublike bush for about 15 minutes you will notice a deviation to your right. Take the detour and follow the path to one of the most perfect lunch or overnight spots on any trail. Here you can spend hours in the tranquil setting, watching the broad band of white water gushing over a tufa formation into a delightful pool.

Backtrack along the path to rejoin the jeep track which continues uphill to intersect with the jeep track along which you descended on the first day. You must turn right here and unfortunately the homeward stretch is all an uphill slog.

GIRAFFE

This two- or three-day trail in the Hans Merensky Nature Reserve in the Lowveld is over extremely easy terrain, making it ideal for beginners, families or those who simply want a relaxing hike. Distances are short and an added bonus is the possibility of encountering several species of game on foot, while birding can also be rewarding. Facilities at the base camp are amongst the best offered by hiking trails in southern Africa.

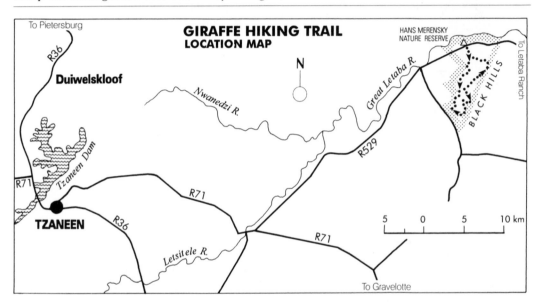

TRAIL PLANNER

Distance 32 km; 2 or 3 days

Grading A

Reservations The Officer-in-Charge, Hans Merensky Nature Reserve, Private Bag X502, Letsitele 0885, Telephone (0152) 3-8632. Reservations are accepted up to six months in advance.

Group size Minimum 2, during peak periods 3 Maximum 12. Only one group is permitted on the trail at any given time.

Maps A sketch map is included in the information leaflet on the trail, which is forwarded with your receipt and permit.

Facilities The overnight camp consists of three thatched A-frame huts equipped with four bunks and mattresses each. There is also an eating area under thatch with a table and benches, a fireplace, drinking water, refuse bins, a flush toilet and cold water showers. Firewood is supplied for cooking only.

Logistics Circular route. There is no trail hut at the start/end of the trail, but Aventura's Eiland Resort near the northern periphery of the reserve offers a choice of fully equipped rondavels and caravan/campsites. Amenities include a mineral bath, shop, butchery, bottle store and licensed restaurant. The central reservations telephone number is (012) 346-2277.

Climate

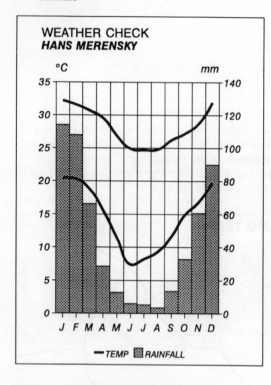

WEATHER CHECK
HANS MERENSKY

°C   mm

— TEMP ▨ RAINFALL

Relevant information

■ The trail is shaped like a figure eight and has been designed as a three-day route. The full route can, however, be covered in two days, or hikers can opt to do the first and third sections only.

■ Precautions against malaria as well as mosquitoes and ticks are necessary.

■ Water is only available at the starting point and at the overnight camp. Water encountered along the trail should not be drunk.

■ With temperatures rising up to 40 °C during summer, you should take precautions against the sun, such as a hat and sunscreen.

■ During summer lightning is a hazard.

■ Carry a daypack for the loop on the second day.

How to get there From Tzaneen, take the R71 signposted Letsitele and turn left onto the R529, signposted Eiland, about 31 km after leaving Tzaneen. Continuing on this road, the Hans Merensky Nature Reserve is some 29 km further on.

TRAIL ENVIRONMENT

Flora The vegetation of the reserve consists mainly of mopane woodlands and variations of round-leaved teak, red bushwillow and silver cluster-leaf woodlands. Patches of open knobthorn woodlands and silver cluster-leaf woodlands are scattered in the reserve.

White seringa scrubland is found in the Black Hills region. With its sparse foliage and almost flat crown, it is one of the most striking trees of the northern and eastern Transvaal. Also to be seen on the Black Hills are some impressive Transvaal candelabra trees.

The mopane varies from a multi-stemmed shrub to trees of up to 15 m high and its most characteristic features are the leaves, which resemble the wings of a butterfly. During the heat of the day, the leaflets close up and turn sideways-on to the sun to reduce transevaporation. In arid areas the leaves are a vital source of food for species such as kudu, eland, impala and giraffe. The grey to blackish bark is characterised by deep, vertical fissures and flakes in narrow strips.

The red bushwillow is a multi-stemmed,

scraggly, small to medium-sized tree. Clusters of small, yellow to creamy-green flowers are borne between September and January and these later form the characteristic red-brown, four-winged fruits.

Another tree with winged fruit is the silver cluster-leaf, which is conspicuous by its silvery to grey-green leaves. It usually grows to between 4 and 10 m high and produces flat, buff-pink, two-winged fruits.

The round-leaved teak is spectacular when in flower and the strongly scented deep yellow flowers usually appear with the first summer rains. It grows as a medium to large tree with an average height of between 10 and 15 m.

Other tree species include sickle bush, tamboti, marula and the black monkey orange.

Several epiphytic orchids occur in the Letaba area, of which *Ansellia gigantea* is fairly common in the reserve. This species is among the largest of the South African epiphytic orchids and its cluster of pale yellow, brown-flecked flowers can usually be seen before the start of the summer rains.

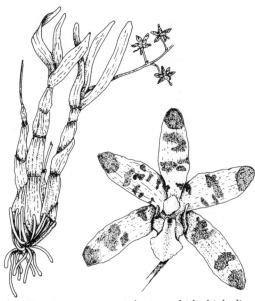

Ansellia gigantea, an epiphytic orchid which displays a variety of flower shapes and blotching

If you are hiking between May and September, the showy white to pale pink flowers of the impala lily, with pink to dark red borders, are unlikely to escape your attention. The greyish-white stems arise from a large underground rootstock and although the trees sometimes reach up to 2 m in height, those in the reserve are small and stunted.

Fauna The reserve is the home of some 80 mammal species, 75 per cent of which are smaller mammals such as rodents, small carnivores, bats and shrews.

Of the 11 antelope species occurring in the reserve the impala is the most numerous, numbering about 500. Other antelope are bushbuck, kudu, common duiker, waterbuck, reedbuck, blue wildebeest, klipspringer, steenbok and Sharpe's grysbok. Also watch out for sable, which are bred here for trans'-ation to other reserves.

You are almost certain to catch a glimpse of the comical warthog which occurs in large numbers, while there is also a possibility of seeing Burchell's zebra. The northern boundary of the reserve is formed by the Letaba River, which is the habitat of hippos.

The primates are represented by chacma baboon, which occur in the vicinity of the Black Hills, lesser bushbaby, thick-tailed bushbaby and vervet monkey.

Among the 17 species of small carnivores are caracal, African wild cat, bat-eared fox, side-striped jackal and black-backed jackal. Brown and spotted hyaenas, as well as leopard, occur permanently in the reserve, while wild dog and lion pass through occasionally.

To date some 280 bird species have been recorded, including openbilled stork, hooded vulture, Pel's fishing owl and whitebreasted cuckoo shrike.

The mopane woodlands provide an ideal habitat for Arnot's chat, a species which reaches the southern limit of distribution in the eastern and north-eastern Transvaal. The throat and the bend of the wing of the female are white, while the crown and the bend of the wing are white in the male. The remainder of these birds, which occur in pairs or small groups, is jet black.

Among the commonly seen species are grey lourie, redbilled hornbill and forktailed drongo, often confused with the black flycatcher which also occurs in the reserve.

Conspicuous species include scimitarbilled woodhoopoe, the blackheaded oriole with its liquid call, and arrowmarked babbler, which can usually be seen clambering about the lower stratum of thick bushes.

Species likely to be ticked at the dams include grey and blackheaded herons, hamerkop, Egyptian goose and pied kingfisher. The saddlebilled stork, with its slightly curved red and black bill with a yellow saddle, is also often ticked.

Some 29 birds of prey have been recorded and although some are only occasional visitors, martial eagle, brown snake eagle and African fish eagle are resident.

Nile crocodile (*Crocodilus niloticus*) and water monitor (*Varanus niloticus*) occur in the Letaba River, while the veld monitor (*Varanus exanthmaticus*) prefers the dry land.

Despite the low rainfall, amphibians are well represented and to date five toad and 16 frog species have been recorded. Toads include the leopard toad (*Bufo pardalis*) while the frogs include the bullfrog (*Pyxicephalus adspersus*) and striped grass frog (*Ptychadena porosissima*).

History The earliest Bantu-speaking inhabitants of the north-eastern Transvaal were the Early Iron Age ancestors of the Sotho people. One of the oldest Iron Age sites in South Africa, Silverleaves, which is 16 km east of Tzaneen, was

GIRAFFE

Giraffe are bred here for translocation to other provincial reserves in the Transvaal and there are about 100 in the reserve. They are active mainly during the day, with some nocturnal movements. During the heat of the day, however, they rest in the shade, either standing or lying down. Their movement is not restricted by the availability of water as sufficient moisture is obtained from the vegetation they eat. Although they occur in a variety of habitats ranging from scrub to woodland, they prefer acacia woodlands and do not seem to feed in pure mopane woodlands.

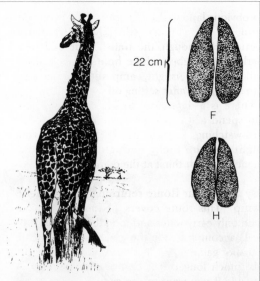

Trailists are likely to encounter giraffe in the acacia woodlands

occupied in the late third century or early in the fourth century.

Some 50 km further east, Eiland has produced numerous archaeological sites, including Early Iron Age smelting works and salt-works. The oldest pottery from these sites dates back to the third century and has features similar to those found at Silverleaves. Two other distinct pottery types have been identified, while about 50 000 potsherds were discovered at the salt-works.

In the mid-1830s the northern and eastern Transvaal were used as a refuge by large numbers of Tsonga, who fled from Mozambique. From the mid-sixteenth century these people, together with the Chopi and Tonga, inhabited Mozambique and northern Zululand.

In 1819 the Ndwandwe of north-eastern Zululand were defeated by Shaka and two Ndwandwe generals, Zwangendaba and Soshangane, began raiding the surrounds of the present Maputo soon afterwards. By subjecting the Tsonga kingdoms, Soshangane established the Gazankulu kingdom which he named after his grandfather, Gaza.

Although the followers of Soshangane adopted the Zulu military system, they largely retained their language and culture and became known as the Shangaans. Those Tsonga who did not submit to their new ruler fled to the northern and eastern Transvaal. After the death of Soshangane the Shangaan dynasty was weakened by a succession dispute and the Shangaans in turn were conquered by the Portuguese. Large numbers subsequently fled to the Transvaal where both groups live in Gazankulu.

TRAIL DESCRIPTION

Day 1: Visitors' Centre to Overnight Camp

From the visitors' centre in the reserve, you will initially follow the same route as the 11 km-long Waterbuck Trail. After ten minutes you will come to a game fence which encloses the portion of the reserve south of the main road passing through the reserve. The fence is crossed by means of a stile and after another five minutes the Waterbuck Trail splits off to the left. A yellow marker with a green giraffe indicates the route to the overnight camp. Winding through mopane woodland the path follows an easy, level route, leading past trees with epiphytic orchids, the easily identifiable knobthorn and the deciduous marula. You will also pass several large termitaria (termite mounds).

On account of the dense vegetation there are

no obvious landmarks and after a while you will tend to lose your sense of direction. Fortunately, though, the trail is wide and well marked. After about three hours of easy, level walking the overnight camp suddenly comes into view, 9 km after setting off.

There is a dam close to the camp and you can spend a rewarding afternoon doing some bird-watching. Towards the late afternoon you might also be lucky enough to spot game quenching their thirst at the dam.

Day 2: Circular Route returning to Overnight Camp This route covers 11 km and as you need only carry water and food for the day, it is easily accomplished in three hours. Of course, if you spot game or do some bird-watching, it will take much longer. It is best to start as early as possible if you want to see game because most animals are inactive during the heat of the day.

Once again the trail leads through mopane woodland, but red bushwillow becomes more dominant after a while. The red bushwillow belongs to the combretum family, which is characterised by its winged fruit.

After about 45 minutes you will reach the Black Hills at the eastern boundary of the reserve. Most of the soil in the reserve is of granitic origin except in the Black Hills, where a dolerite dyke forced its way through the granite. The trail leads to a viewpoint at the top of the Black Hills – 542 m above sea level – which offers the only panoramic view on the trail.

A conspicuous species here is the Transvaal candelabra tree which belongs to the euphorbia family. It reaches a height of up to 5 m and the branches consist of five to six-angled heart-shaped segments which are strung together.

The route does not continue along the ridge and you will have to retrace your steps down the ridge before branching off to the left. After a while you will pass a waterhole which is often dry towards the end of winter. About 30 minutes after leaving the Black Hills the trail passes a fairly large dam which you would have noticed from the Black Hills. It is a good idea to rest under one of the large trees near the water as a variety of birds are attracted to the area and there are not many other suitable shady places along the route.

From the dam it is about one and a half hours of easy walking back to the overnight camp. Before heading north, the trail winds in a westerly direction and you are most likely to

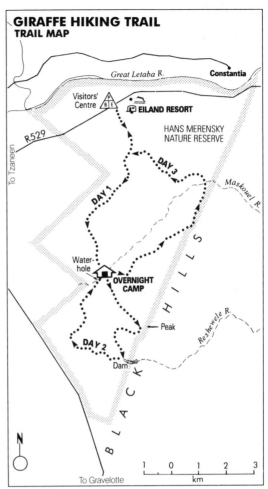

GIRAFFE HIKING TRAIL
TRAIL MAP

spot game in the few open grassy areas along this section.

Another large dam is passed about 20 minutes before reaching the overnight camp.

Day 3: Overnight Camp to Visitors' Centre This section covers 12 km and winds in a north-easterly direction to reach the Black Hills after about an hour. The route runs parallel to the hills for a short distance and along this section the distinctly different vegetation growing at the base of the hills is particularly obvious. Dominant species here include white seringa and the marula with its characteristic mottled trunk.

After a short while the trail swings west and eventually joins up with the first day's route. A short distance further you will pass the Waterbuck Trail turn-off to your right and once the stile is crossed it is just a few minutes' walk to the visitors' centre.

HANGLIP

This trail follows part of the route of the original Soutpansberg Hiking Trail with the scenery dominated by Hanglip, translated as "hanging lip", with its exposed cliffs. The route takes you along the southern slopes of the Soutpansberg through indigenous forest with trees draped in old man's beard, dry scrub forest as well as pine and bluegum plantations.

TRAIL PLANNER

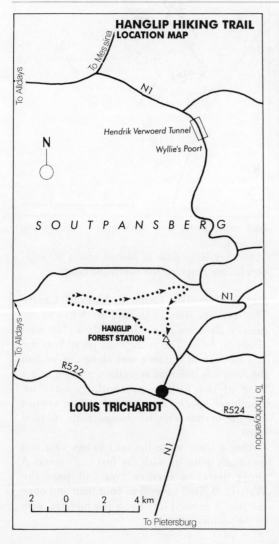

Distance 21 km; 2 days

Grading B

Reservations The National Hiking Way Board, Private Bag X503, Sabie 1260, Telephone (01315) 4-1058 or 4-1392, Fax (01315) 4-2071. Reservations are accepted up to a year in advance.

Climate

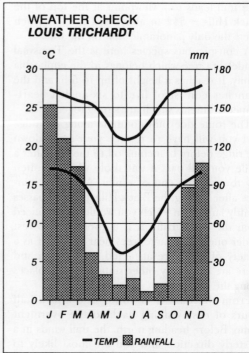

Group size Minimum 3; Maximum 30

Maps A full-colour trail map with useful information on the history, flora and fauna of the area on the reverse is available and is forwarded with your receipt and permit. One map is supplied for every six adults.

Facilities The trail huts are equipped with bunks with mattresses, cooking pots, firewood, fireplaces, water, refuse bins and toilets.

Logistics Circular route. The first overnight hut, Zoutpansberg, is about 1,3 km from the Hanglip Forest Station. To accommodate late arrivals, the route is indicated with illuminated footprints, so keep your torch handy.

Relevant information
■ Water should be used sparingly at the overnight stops as it has to be carted to the huts.
■ Precautions should be taken against malaria, ticks and bilharzia.

How to get there From Louis Trichardt continue along Krogh Street to Forestry Road at the northern end of the town. Turn left here and continue for about 3 km to the Hanglip Forest Station.

TRAIL ENVIRONMENT

Flora The vegetation of the area has been classified as north-eastern mountain sourveld, ranging from scrub forest and bushveld to high indigenous forest.

Small patches of indigenous high forest have survived in protected valleys and kloofs below Hanglip and in the Entabeni State Forest. These forests are dominated by real yellowwood, lemonwood, forest bushwillow, forest waterwood and Cape beech.

Other species to be seen here include knobwood, Cape chestnut, Transvaal plane, assegai and forest elder.

Particularly interesting on the section between Ou Entabeni and Entabeni Forest Station is the Stamvrugwoud on the eastern slopes of Entabeni Peak. The forest is named after the Transvaal milkplum, which favours rocky outcrops and has an average height of 2 m. The specimens here are unusually tall, forming a dense forest.

To protect the few remaining areas of indigenous forest, three nature reserves have been set aside in the Entabeni State Forest. In 1992 two of these reserves, Entabeni and Matiwa, covering 522 ha and 179 ha respectively, were consolidated into the Entabeni Nature Reserve. Covering some 56 ha, the Ratombo Nature Reserve in the south-western corner of the State Forest was declared to protect the semi-deciduous indigenous forest of that name.

The trail emblem, the common coral tree, is especially attractive during the winter months when its brilliant scarlet flowers brighten the landscape. It is a small to medium-sized deciduous tree, favouring scrub forest and woodland.

Some of the trees have been marked according to the *National List of Indigenous Trees* numbers and by referring to the numbers on the reverse of the trail map some 59 species can be identified.

Many of the lower slopes of the Soutpansberg have been planted under pine and other exotic trees. Afforestation at Entabeni dates back to 1914 and initially three separate plantations were established. Entabeni is the largest afforested state forest in the northern Transvaal, but in 1988 nearly half of the 5 500 ha under plantations was burnt down after an uncontrolled fire spread into the area. Production at the Entabeni State Forest concentrates on pine sawlogs for structural timber and poles for telephone and powerlines. Forest hardwood species such as toon tree (*Cedrela toona*), East African mahogany (*Khaya nyasica*) and Indian mahogany (*Chukrasia tabularis*) are also grown at Entabeni to meet the demand for furniture wood.

Two uncommon aloe species grow in the Entabeni area, but as the trails do not pass through their habitats you will not see them. *Aloe vossii* grows among rocks and grass of the southern slopes of the mountain. It grows 40 to 50 cm high and the bright scarlet or deep pink flowers can be seen during February and March. *Aloe vogtsii* is restricted to high altitudes where

SAMANGO MONKEY

The samango monkey occurs from the eastern Cape northwards along the coastal strip to northern Zululand, as well as along the Transvaal Drakensberg escarpment, the Soutpansberg and the Blouberg. It is restricted to evergreen high forests and lives in family parties or troops of ten to 25. They have an overall length of 1,3 m and their weight varies between 9 kg for males and 7 kg for females. Their diet is mainly vegetarian, consisting of leaves, young

The indigenous forests of Entabeni provide an ideal habitat for the samango monkey

shoots, berries, flowers and fruit. Bushbuck are attracted to troops of samango monkeys feeding in the hope of finding discarded fruit. A single young is usually born between September and December.

During the late 1960s the samango monkeys in the northern Transvaal began damaging especially young *Pinus taeda* trees, apparently to get to the sweet inner bark. Trees were either ringbarked or only part of the bark was removed, causing trees to die or resulting in smaller logs of poorer quality.

A research project was initiated in 1979 to investigate the problem and to find suitable measures to reduce or prevent the damage, estimated at R400 000 a year. Since the samango monkey is classified as rare it was decided to relocate some of the 1 150 monkeys living in the Entabeni State Forest. The National Parks Board offered to resettle monkeys in the Pafuri area of the Kruger National Park where they were last recorded in 1959. The first group was released in June 1982 and, since then, close on 100 animals have been released in the northern parts of the Kruger Park, while some 250 monkeys have been resettled in the Makuya National Park in Venda.

mist frequently occurs. It grows up to 75 cm high and the bright scarlet flowers can be seen between February and April.

Fauna The herds of large game which once roamed the plains of the northern Transvaal have long since disappeared and only a few species have remained. Five leopards were released in a remote part of the forest station a number of years ago after they were trapped elsewhere by the Transvaal Directorate of Nature Conservation. Although they are hardly ever seen, it appears that all five animals are still alive.

Among the antelope species are bushbuck, klipspringer, oribi, common duiker and an isolated population of red duiker. Three primate species occur in the Soutpansberg – chacma baboon, vervet monkey and samango monkey.

Because of the variety of habitat types, the area supports over 400 bird species. Interesting species you stand a chance of ticking in the Entabeni State Forest include African broadbill, grey cuckooshrike, which occurs in the forest canopy, longtailed wagtail and blackfronted bush strike, while black stork breed on the cliffs at Hanglip.

The patches of indigenous forest are the

habitat of Knysna lourie, Narina trogon, chorister and starred robins, as well as olive bush shrike, while crested guineafowl inhabit the forest margins.

Birds of the exotic plantations frequently overlap with those of the indigenous forest. Among the species found here are black sparrowhawk and redeyed dove, as well as Cape and forest canaries. You might also be fortunate to tick longcrested and crowned eagles in the plantations. Since they play an important role in keeping the rodent population under control, nesting trees as well as a number of surrounding trees are left undisturbed when plantations are felled. In addition, special perches have been erected in open areas and among young trees, providing excellent vantage points for these birds.

The rocky ridges and krantzes are the preferred habitats of several other raptors such as black eagle, lanner falcon and rock kestrel. Other species you can expect to see in this habitat type include rock pigeon, Cape rock thrush, mocking chat and redwinged starling.

An interesting reptile species which is endemic to the area is the Soutpansberg flat lizard (*Platysaurus relictus*). It occurs from Vivo eastwards to Entabeni, favouring rocky north-facing slopes. The body of the males is coloured blue to green, reaching a maximum length of 83 mm. This species was described for the first time as recently as 1967. Another interesting reptile of the Entabeni area is the African rock python (*Python sebae natalensis*). Since 1984 more than 70 pythons have been released in the Entabeni State Forest, mainly in areas planted with trees cultivated for furniture timber. These pythons were rescued from areas where they were in danger of being exterminated.

History Early Iron Age immigrants first crossed the Limpopo River some 2 000 years ago. It is likely that these early black people passed through the Soutpansberg near Wyllie's Poort. Pottery from Matakoma in the Soutpansberg has been dated to the fourth century.

The origins of the Venda remain obscure, but it is thought that they migrated from the Great Lake region of central Africa. By the end of the twelfth century the foremost group had crossed the Limpopo and named their new home Venda – The Pleasant Land.

At first the Venda lived in harmony with the San in the area, but the increase in the numbers of new immigrants resulted in friction between the two groups. As their numbers grew the Venda began to dominate the area and subjugated the original inhabitants, including the Stone Age Ngona.

A major wave of immigration took place in the eighteenth century, with the Vhasenzi and the Vhalemba being the last groups to arrive. The Lemba were descendants of Arab traders who originally settled on the east African coast and the Venda culture was greatly influenced by these people, who had many Semitic traits. They practised circumcision and did not eat pork, or the meat of any other animal unless its throat had been cut in a kosher manner. From their ancestors they learnt to trade and were skilled craftsmen, potters and weavers.

The Vhasenzi settled on the slopes of Lwandali and established their capital, Dzata I, about 35 km west of Sibasa. While on a hunting expedition their chief was trapped when a cave collapsed and after unsuccessful rescue attempts he asked to be left there to die. The name was then changed to Tsiendenla, meaning "grave". A second capital, in the Nzhelele Valley and about 19 km south of Dzata I, was then established under Thohoyandou, whose name means "the head of the elephant".

After the mysterious disappearance of Thohoyandou his sons, Mpofu, Raluswielo and Ravhura abandoned Dzata II and founded settlements at Hanglip, Depene and Makonde. Although each chief ruled independently, Mpofu was the most senior chief.

During the Difaqane the Venda took refuge in the caves originally occupied by the San, escaping annihilation because of their inaccessibility and the decentralised monarchy which made it difficult for all the Venda chiefs to be subjugated.

The mountain range takes its name from the salt pan known to the Venda as Letshoyang – "The Place of Salt". The name Soutpansberg probably dates back to the 1820s and it has been suggested that the name was given to the range by the children and followers of Coenraad de Buys. After fleeing the Cape in 1795, De Buys and his clan eventually reached a large salt pan at the base of the mountain. Shortly afterwards De Buys abandoned his clan, never to be seen again, but his followers remained in the area, naming the range the Soutpansberg.

In 1836 the Voortrekkers under Louis Tregardt established a camp near the present town of Louis Trichardt, from where exploratory journeys were undertaken. In the same year Tregardt was instrumental in instating Ramabulana as Mpofu's successor after one of his younger brothers had also laid claim to the position.

Zoutpansbergdorp was established by Andries Hendrik Potgieter in 1848 and initially the Boer settlement was welcomed by Ramabulana. After Potgieter's death in 1852 the town came under the control of Stephanus Schoeman, who renamed it Schoemansdal. The brisk trade in ivory soon made it the largest and most prosperous settlement in the interior of southern Africa. By 1855 some 200 people had settled there and ivory exports totalled £ 200 000.

Arms and ammunition were supplied indiscriminately to the Venda to obtain ivory and a tense situation developed after misunderstandings arose about, among other things, the introduction of tax. In 1867 the town was evacuated and subsequently destroyed by the Venda.

Rumours of the Venda being supplied with rifles, ammunition and even a cannon by white renegades began to cause concern and in September 1898 resulted in a campaign against Mphephu.

On 17 October 1898 General Piet Joubert's commando pitched camp at Rietvlei at the foot of Hanglip and erected a portable iron fort. On the day before the attack on Sunguzwi (Hanglip) General Joubert held a church service and made a covenant that a church would be erected on the site if the campaign was successful. The Venda became the last independent tribe in the Transvaal to be subjected by the whites when they were attacked from three sides simultaneously on 16 November 1898.

Mphephu's royal village, Luatame, was burned down, forcing him and his followers to flee across the Limpopo River into Zimbabwe.

A town was established on the farms Rietvlei and Bergvliet in 1898 and named Trichardtsdorp, which was subsequently changed to Louis Trichardt.

After the defeat of the Zuid-Afrikaansche Republiek in the Anglo-Boer War of 1899-1902, Mphephu was allowed to re-establish himself at Nzhelele.

TRAIL DESCRIPTION

Day 1: Zoutpansberg Hut to Hanglip Hut

Zoutpansberg Hut was officially opened in July 1989 and consists of a complex of five pre-fabricated huts sleeping six hikers each. From the hut the trail ascends rather steeply through pine plantations along a forest track for nearly 5 km and you will gain some 300 m in altitude.

Shortly before the 6 km mark you will pass through a chain gate and the trail enters a beautiful indigenous forest where large specimens of knobwood can be seen. Just over 1 km further on the trail passes through a patch of pine plantations before doubling back to ascend once again through indigenous forest. The section of the route along Bobbejaanskrans winds its way through a jumble of fascinating rock formations and is an excellent mid-morning stop.

After another short interlude through pine forest the trail returns to the indigenous forest, continuing along the lower slopes of Hanglip (1 719 m), gaining altitude gradually. Just beyond the 12 km mark a road leading to a pic-

Close-up of trunk and fruit and leaves of knobwood

nic spot turns off to the right. This is the start of the Veteran Route, a 1 km walk to the hut.

With less than 1 km of the day's hike remaining, you will pass through plantations and then descend through mountain grassland to the hut. Situated amongst a natural rock garden featuring krantz aloes and colourful lichens, the hut overlooks Hanglip, one of the highest peaks in the Soutpansberg range. After good rains it is

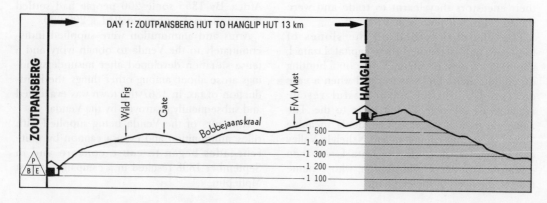

DAY 1: ZOUTPANSBERG HUT TO HANGLIP HUT 13 km

ZOUTPANSBERG

Wild Fig

Gate

Bobbejaanskraal

FM Mast

HANGLIP

1 500
1 400
1 300
1 200
1 100

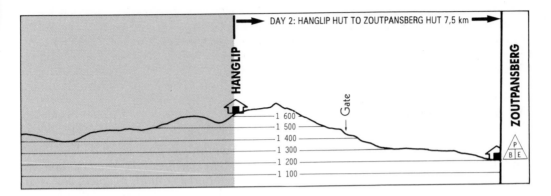

possible to cool down in the nearby natural pool, but do not count on freshening up here in the dry winter months.

Day 2: Hanglip Hut to Hanglip Forest Station From Hanglip Hut the trail ascends steadily through rock formations for about 1 km to a small hill. Here the route emerges into scrub forest and along this section you will have expansive views of Louis Trichardt, the surrounding farms and the Albasini Dam which supplies water to Louis Trichardt and Levubu.

Shortly after the 3 km mark the trail swings in a south-westerly direction. The original Soutpansberg Hiking Trail, which was opened in 1975, used to continue eastwards to Sandfontein Hut. However, this 93 km trail gained the reputation of being over-strenuous and was consequently under-utilised.

Continuing to descend, you will enter a plantation after the 6 km mark. The final 1,5 km descends steeply through plantation.

The information provided under 'Trail Environment' relates to the Hanglip and the Entabeni sections of the Soutpansberg Hiking Trail. However, since the Entabeni section was closed at the time of going to press, some of the information is no longer relevant.

MABUDASHANGO

This circular hiking trail in the Soutpansberg takes you through pine-scented plantations and dank, unspoilt indigenous forests. The area is rich in legends of the Venda people, with the trail winding through the Thathe Forest, the sacred burial grounds of chiefs, and you will also have a glimpse of the sacred Lake Fundudzi. Various vantage points afford splendid views of golden-green tea plantations, interlocking pine plantations and indigenous forests, as well as of typical Venda villages.

TRAIL PLANNER

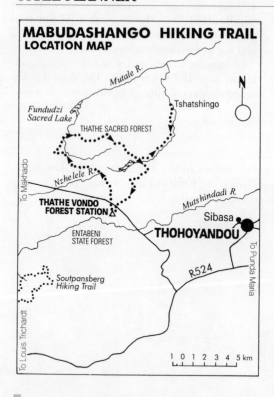

MABUDASHANGO HIKING TRAIL
LOCATION MAP

Distance 54 km; 4 days

Grading B+

Reservations The Director General, Department of Agriculture and Forestry, Private Bag X2247, Sibasa, Venda, Telephone (015581) 3-1001, extension

2167 or 2290. Reservations are accepted up to a year in advance.

Climate

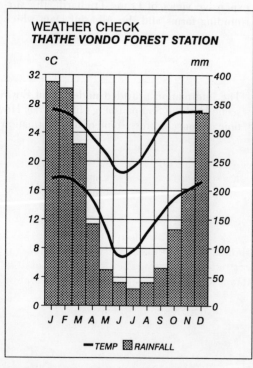

WEATHER CHECK
THATHE VONDO FOREST STATION

— TEMP ▨ RAINFALL

Group size Minimum 2; Maximum 30

Maps The trail is indicated on a photocopy of the 1 : 50 000 topographical map that is forwarded to you with your receipt and permit. It is essential to obtain topographical map section 2230 CD.

Facilities The two overnight stops on the trail consist of a basic thatched open shelter, a toilet, refuse bins, firewood and water.

Logistics Circular route. A forestry house at the Thathe Vondo Forest Station can be used before and after the trail. Twelve bunks and mattresses are supplied, as well as a cold water shower, flush toilet and refuse bins.

Relevant information
■ Precautions are necessary against ticks, mosquitoes and malaria. Water in the running mountain streams is bilharzia-free.
■ During summer heavy rains can be experienced, making river crossings difficult,

especially on day three. Care should also be taken in sections of indigenous forest which can become slippery.
■ During summer it is usually unnecessary to carry water but in winter streams along the trail could be dry.

How to get there Travelling from Louis Trichardt, the starting point at Thathe Vondo Forest Station is reached by following the R524 signposted to Thohoyandou and Punda Maria. After travelling for about 66 km turn left into Thohoyandou at the road sign to the Venda Sun Hotel. Continue to the four-way stop in Sibasa (about 4,5 km) and turn left. Continue along this road for about 15 km until a sign on the left – Department of Forestry and Bruply Sawmills – indicates the turn-off to the start of the trail.

TRAIL ENVIRONMENT

Flora The vegetation consists of mountain sourveld and the trail alternates between pine plantations, small patches of woodland and high indigenous forests.

Some of the trees along the trail have been marked according to the *National List of Indigenous Trees* and it is useful to take a copy of this handy booklet along to familiarise yourself with the trees occurring here.

Among the trees that can be seen on the first day's hike are broom cluster fig, Natal fig, lemonwood, Cape holly, common onionwood and tree fuchsia, to mention but a few.

A species unlikely to escape your attention is the forest fever tree with its unusually large leaves reaching up to 1 m in length. This species, which grows up to 30 m in height, has a limited distribution in southern Africa, being restricted to north-eastern and south-eastern Transvaal and isolated patches in Zimbabwe and Mozambique.

At higher elevations the trail leads past dense stands of Transvaal wild banana and the large-leaved dragon tree, a soft-wooded shrub or much-branched small tree which reaches 2 to 4 m in height. At the upper margins of the forest, Transvaal milkplum can be seen growing amongst the rocky outcrops.

Keep an eye out for epiphytic orchids, especially the attractive *Mystacidium braybonae*

which is endemic to the mistbelt of the Soutpansberg. This species only occurs on wild fig (*Ficus*) trees, producing one to three sprays of white flowers in November.

Trees to be seen in the Thathe Sacred Forest include real yellowwood, lemonwood, forest ironplum, Transvaal pock ironwood, common wild elder, wild loquat and red bird-berry.

The common tree fern is found in forest margins, wooded kloofs and along streams in grasslands

Common species of the undergrowth of the indigenous forests include wild pepper (*Piper capense*), the exquisite forest bell bush (*Mackaya bella*) with its pale lilac flowers which can be seen between September and December, the spindly Zulu bead-string and various fern and moss species.

On the third day's hike magnificent common tree ferns, some of which are up to 5 m high, as well as common coral trees are seen along the trail. You are also likely to spot the conspicuous flat-crown along forest margins. This species occurs from the eastern Cape northwards along the east coast and is also widespread in large areas of the Transvaal. In winter the rectangular leaves are shed, forming a dense leaf carpet.

Species of the open grassy woodlands include jacket-plum, seen amongst rocks and along riverine fringes, while the forest silver oak grows along the margins of the evergreen forests.

Fauna Among the animals occurring in the forests are bushbuck, bushpig, samango monkey, leopard and red duiker. The forest fringes are the habitat of vervet monkeys while chacma baboon are attracted to the rocky mountain areas, as well as the forests. Common duiker prefer open, grassy areas while mountain reedbuck also inhabit the area. Numerous smaller mammals also occur here, but they are unlikely to be spotted.

The birdlife of the area is exceptionally prolific, with some 400 species having been recorded in the Soutpansberg range. Among the less common species found here is the crested guineafowl which is restricted to the eastern part of the country, occurring from Durban northwards to the Soutpansberg.

Birds you might tick in the forests are emerald cuckoo, grey cuckoo shrike and olive bush shrike, while starred robin occur between September and February.

The forest edge is the habitat of species such as crowned hornbill, blackheaded oriole, barthroated apalis, paradise flycatcher and southern boubou. While the Knysna lourie is mainly confined to the evergreen forests, the purplecrested lourie favours riverine forests and dry forest thickets.

The streams and rivers attract species such as hamerkop, whitefaced duck, Burchell's coucal and both the Cape and the more sparsely distributed longtailed wagtails. While the Cape wagtail prefers small, slow-flowing streams, the longtailed wagtail is confined to well-wooded, fast-flowing rivers and streams. Your best chance of ticking this species is in the vicinity of the Tsatshingo Falls.

Birds of prey include crowned eagle and African goshawk, both of which are to be seen in the indigenous forests, as well as black eagle and rock kestrel which favour the rocky cliffs and krantzes.

The Soutpansberg is the habitat of several rare reptiles including the Transvaal mountain lizard (*Lacerta rupicola*). This blackish, white-banded lizard was first described in 1933 by the renowned herpetologist Dr V F M FitzSimons after a specimen was found at Lake Fundudzi. Sixteen years passed before it was "rediscovered" by Dr G R McLachlan in 1949 on a mountain peak above Louis Trichardt. Some 30 years later another specimen was found at Fundudzi, while three more have subsequently been recorded.

History The history of the area is similar to that of the Hanglip Hiking Trail and is therefore not repeated here. Refer to p 345.

TRAIL DESCRIPTION

Day 1: Mabudashango Hut to Fundudzi Camp Initially you will follow a track alongside pine plantations for about 15 minutes before crossing the tarred road between Sibasa and Wyliespoort. The trail then ascends steeply along plantation roads for another 20 minutes before branching off to the right into an indigenous forest. For the next 45 minutes you will continue to climb through indigenous forest until you emerge onto a plateau, a short distance east of the forestry lookout. The trail then continues to the right and after a short while reaches a viewpoint which offers splendid views of the Tshivhase Tea Estate, which was established in 1973, the Vondo Dam behind the forest station, and Lwamondo Kop. According to

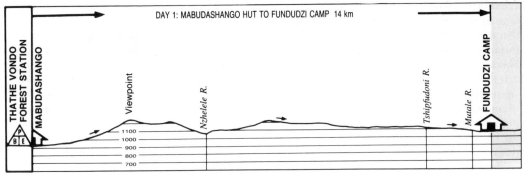

DAY 1: MABUDASHANGO HUT TO FUNDUDZI CAMP 14 km

legend, the baboons inhabiting the mountain used to warn the people in the village below of an enemy's approach. The villagers could then clamber to the top of the mountain to roll rocks down the slopes onto the enemy. Understandably, therefore, the baboons of Lwamondo were never killed.

After hiking a short distance along the edge of a pine plantation you will join a forestry road and proceed along it for a little way before deviating onto a path to the left. The turn-off is easily missed so do watch out for it. After crossing some open grassveld the trail descends steeply to another forestry road. Turn left and follow the road for a short distance until the trail branches off to the right. Once again you should take care not to miss the turn-off. The trail then climbs through beautiful indigenous forest and after about 90 minutes it levels out below the cliffs of the uppermost plateau. From here you will look down onto the Nzhelele River catchment area.

The trail winds through another patch of indigenous forest which is markedly drier than the forest in the valley. Here the observant hiker will notice epiphytic orchids clinging to the trees. After a short while the trail emerges into plantations and the remainder of the day's hike is along forestry roads through pine plantations.

After leaving the indigenous forest it is roughly another two hours' walk to Fundudzi Camp, beautifully situated alongside the Mutale River which forms an inviting pool. A table and benches have been ingeniously constructed by binding thin branches together and add to the charm of the site.

Day 2: Fundudzi Camp to Mukumbani Camp

This day hike starts by following the river through indigenous forest before the trail joins a fire-break after about 45 minutes. Here you will have your first glimpse of the Fundudzi Sacred Lake which has been referred to as the real heart of Venda.

Surrounded by a ring of mountains, the lake plays an important role in Venda traditions and folklore. It was created by a landslide across the Mutale River at the eastern end of the lake.

The area below the fire-break is fairly densely populated, but the nature of the terrain conceals the huts and at times the only indication of human habitation is the occasional lazy jingle from a cowbell. The trail continues along a road, passing a small school, and remains on the road until it joins another fire-break.

After a short climb you will turn left, crossing to a narrow path running parallel to the fire-break. Shortly thereafter the trail deviates to the

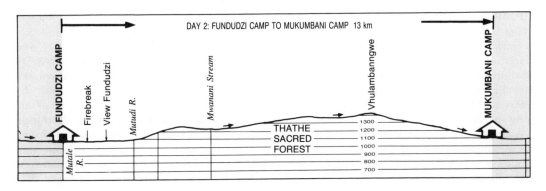

DAY 2: FUNDUDZI CAMP TO MUKUMBANI CAMP 13 km

LAKE FUNDUDZI

One of the beliefs of the Venda people is that the water from Lake Fundudzi does not mix with that from the Mutale River, but that the water of the Mutale "swims" over the lake, escaping through an underground passage in the Tshaphwidzi Ridge which blocks the eastern side of Fundudzi.

It is also believed that the south-western bank of the lake (the bank seen from the trail) is the "spirit gardens" where spirits still cultivate their crops. The large stones in the shape of Venda drums, known as *Ngoma-dza-Vhadzimu*, at the extreme western end of the lake, are said to be the place where the spirits gather for celebrations. Offerings are still made at the rocks stretching into the lake at the eastern side each year at harvest time so that the spirits may taste what has been reaped.

There are numerous fascinating legends surrounding the lake, one of which relates the story of the flight of Thohoyandou and his followers from Dzata to Fundudzi where they were all made immortal. According to this legend, voices and laughter followed by Venda *shikona* dances can be heard coming from the lake on certain cool evenings. It is also said that Venda baskets (*mifaro*) have been seen floating across the lake, as if carrying food to the immortals. Calabashes filled with foaming beer would follow the baskets and ceremonies associated with royal feasting could be heard.

One explanation regarding the origin of the name of the lake is that it is derived from the words *fundu*, (to bend) and *dziba* (large pool), the reference being to people who pay respect to the lake by bowing with their backs to the water and looking at the lake through their legs.

---

left into scrubby woodlands and about an hour's walk beyond the school the Mwanani Stream, a well-earned resting spot, is reached.

For the next 45 minutes you will climb steadily through pine plantations to the Thathe Sacred Forest. The forest was originally named Nethathe, which can be roughly translated as "the chaser" or "the owner of the Thathe area". Being a magician, Nethathe transformed himself into a lion at times and would not allow anyone to collect fruit or berries in the forest. The human-lion features in a Venda poem: "... hair closes the lion's eyes but when they open all animals are frightened away into the trees, caves, holes in the ground or out of the forest by its powerful roar and the simultaneous lashing of its tail. In the silence which follows the roar the only sound is the wind in the leaves of the wild quince".

In 1949 the Thathe Forest was saved from being felled by the Department of Forestry because it is the traditional burial ground of chiefs of the Netshisivhe family. Ancestors are worshipped here and the forest is, therefore, sacred to the Venda. Special permission is necessary to enter the forest, to collect wood or plant specimens.

A gravel road through the forest is followed for about 20 minutes and the huge trees all around you create a mysterious, almost eerie atmosphere.

After leaving the forest, the trail branches off to the right, passing through beautiful indigenous forest before ascending to the beacon at Vhulambanngwe (1 438 m), the highest point on the trail. Below, patches of indigenous forest and pine plantations stretch out as far as the eye can see. Mukumbani Dam, where the overnight camp is situated, can also be seen some 350 m below. The trail then descends steeply through unspoilt indigenous forest where wooden ladders assist hikers in difficult sections. This section is soon over and the trail then joins a fire-break for a short distance, descending steeply once more.

The remainder of the route is along forest roads through pine plantations until a turn-off to the left is reached which leads through a patch of indigenous forest to the overnight stop above Mukumbani Dam.

The camp is in a picturesque setting – a rectangular clearing surrounded by indigenous forest just above the dam. In the morning and evening the raucous "haaa" or "ha-ha-hadeda" of hadedah ibis can be heard as they leave and return to their roosts.

Day 3: Mukumbani Camp to Tshatshingo Potholes and back The trail descends to the dam where you will turn left and continue through indigenous forest where numerous young yellowwoods can be seen. After about 25

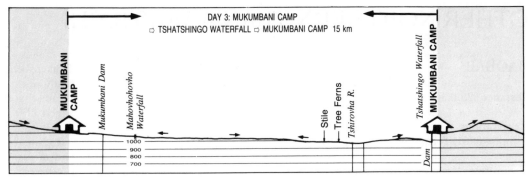

minutes there is another steep descent to the Mahovhohovho Waterfall and for the next 90 minutes you will follow forestry roads through pine plantations.

After crossing a stile there is a short walk through open countryside before the trail enters a dry forest where some impressive common tree ferns – some of which are up to 5 m tall – can be seen. About 25 minutes after crossing the stile the Tshirovha River is crossed and a short while later it is crossed again. The trail continues through dry 'scrub and you will have occasional glimpses of small Venda settlements. Roughly 45 minutes after crossing the river for the first time, the trail joins a road which is followed for a short distance before leading off to the right to the Tshatsingo Potholes.

Over the ages, the Tshirovha River has eroded two huge potholes in the flat rock slabs in the river course. The river cascades about 4 m into the first pothole where the swirling water resembles a cauldron of boiling water. Several metres lower downstream the water reappears in a smaller pothole and continues down a ravine. During winter when the level of the river is low, you can cross just above the potholes to explore the potholes and the ravine. Great care should be taken, however.

A pleasant lunch break can be enjoyed here before returning to the Mukumbani Camp along the same route.

Day 4: Mukumbani Camp to Thathe Vondo Forest Station After crossing the Mukumbani Dam wall, the trail ascends steeply along a jeep track to the lookout on Murangoni (1 230 m), where you can pause to enjoy a magnificent view over Venda. From here the trail descends steeply along a fire-break, passing briefly through pine plantations, before entering an indigenous forest, descending all the time.

Although the dense forest obscures any view, village sounds are usually faintly audible, a sign that a settlement is not too far away. Eventually, though, you will reach an opening where there is a view over the fairly extensive settlement below. To the left you can see the Mukumbani Tea Estate which is irrigated from the dam at the overnight camp.

The trail descends towards the village which is passed about 90 minutes after setting off. You will skirt the village before swinging right into pine plantations. The remainder of the trail leads along forest roads through pine plantations for about two hours. Once the tarred road is crossed, it is a short walk to the exit point at the forest station.

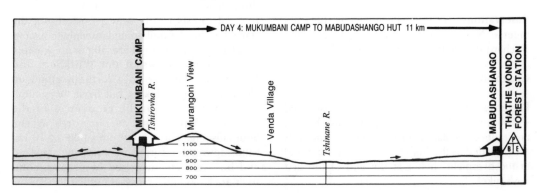

OTHER NORTHERN TRANSVAAL TRAILS

BAOBAB

Distance 25 km; 2 days

Reservations The Resort Manager, P O Box 4, Tshipise 0901, Telephone (015539) 724.

Group size Minimum 2; Maximum 12

Facilities The hut at the end of the first day's hike is equipped with bunks, mattresses, cast iron pots and a kettle. There is also a fireplace and firewood, water and a toilet. Accommodation at the resort varies from a hotel to fully equipped rondavels.

Description Aptly named after the abundance of baobab trees, this trail meanders past numerous baobabs, including a giant with an estimated age of 4 000 years. The two-day circular route starts at Aventura's Tshipise Resort, south of Messina, and winds through mopane woodlands in the 2 200 ha Honnet Nature Reserve. The reserve has been stocked with several species of game and hikers may see giraffe, Burchell's zebra, sable, eland, kudu, impala, waterbuck and nyala. The trail winds across plains, along usually dry river courses and over boulder-strewn ridges. The generally easy terrain makes this route ideal for inexperienced hikers and families. The first day's route covers 12 km, while the return leg covers 13 km.

LEKGALAMEETSE

Distance 44 km; 3 days

Reservations The Officer-in-Charge, Lekgalameetse Nature Reserve, Private Bag X408, Trichardtdal 0890, Telephone (0152302) 15.

Group size Minimum 2; Maximum 24

Facilities The huts on the trail are equipped with bunks and mattresses, as well as showers and toilets. Fireplaces, firewood, kettles and pots are provided at the hut at the starting point and at the overnight shelter at the end of the first day's hike.

Description Where the Transvaal Drakensberg drops away to the Lowveld, 60 km south-west of Tzaneen, the Lekgalameetse Mountains have created spectacular scenery – jagged cliffs, waterfalls and crystal clear streams.

The 19 500 ha Lekgalameetse Nature Reserve is ideal hiking country and offers a choice of a two-day linear route or a three-day circular route. The reserve is the habitat of over 180 bird species, while game include Burchell's zebra, eland, waterbuck, mountain reedbuck, bushbuck and klipspringer. More than 1 200 plant species, including several rare plants, have been recorded and the reserve also boasts the second largest Outeniqua yellowwood in South Africa.

LEOPARD

Distance 22 km; 2 days

Reservations Duivelskloof Village Council, P O Box 100, Duivelskloof 0835, Telephone (0152) 309-9246.

Group size Minimum 2; Maximum 12

Facilities The stone overnight shelter at the end of the first day's hike is equipped with bunks, mattresses, a water tank, rudimentary shower and a toilet. There is also a fireplace, but wood is not always available.

Description On this circular route, which traverses the mountains above Duivelskloof, hikers are rewarded with far-reaching views and magnificent forest scenery. The trail passes mainly through indigenous forests, ranging from subtropical forests to dry acacia bush. From the starting point the trail ascends steeply to a viewpoint on Piesangkop where hikers are greeted by panoramic views of the Wolkberg and Mariepskop. Further on a tortuous climb up Helshoogte awaits hikers, but from the summit expansive views can be enjoyed over the Mooketsi Valley and as far north as the Soutpansberg. The second day's hike of 10 km winds down the escarpment, traversing grassland and bushveld characterised by acacias, coral trees, rock figs and Transvaal bottlebrush.

MAPULANENG

Distance 45 km; 3 days

Reservations The Head, Nature Conservation, Department of Agriculture and Environmental Conservation, Private Bag X01, Chuniespoort 0745, Telephone (015) 632-4145.

Group size Minimum 2; Maximum 16

Facilities Accommodation at the base camp is provided in three luxury, self-contained log cabins with six beds, fridge, stove, hot/cold water shower and a flush toilet. Bedding is provided.

Description Since the trails in the Mapulaneng Nature Reserve radiate from a base camp hikers need only carry a daypack. The start of the trails is near the Welgevonden Forestry Station, north-east of Bushbuckridge, and the longest of the three routes, the Trogon Trail, covers some 16 km. From the base camp the route winds southwards through magnificent indigenous forest, ascending steadily towards Matleloge (1 787 m). The final few kilometres follow the onward route. The Red Duiker Trail initially winds northwards, ascending steeply up the slopes of Makapane. The trail then descends along a spur to join up with a plantation road and the remainder of the day's hike is mainly through pine plantations. The Swimming Pool Trail leads to a delightful natural pool. The route covers 14 km, with the onward and return routes being along the same trail.

NYALALAND

Distance Guided wilderness trail, no set route or distance; 2 days/3 nights

Reservations National Parks Board, P O Box 787, Pretoria 0001, Telephone (012) 343-1991, or P O Box 7400, Roggebaai 8012, Telephone (021) 22-2810.

Group size Maximum 8

Facilities The base camp is equipped with beds, mattresses and bedding. Other amenities include cooking bomas, bush showers and toilets.

Description The Nyalaland Guided Wilderness Trail is conducted in the Punda Maria region in the north of the Kruger National Park. The base camp is situated among sandstone koppies 8 km south of the confluence of the Mutale and Luvuvhu rivers, alongside the Madzaringwe Spruit. This area has the richest variety of flora and fauna in the park and several bird species occur only in this corner of South Africa. The trail is named after the nyala, which is seldom seen in the south of the park but occurs in significant numbers here. Other species of game trailists might chance upon include elephant, buffalo, Burchell's zebra and impala. A characteristic tree of the area is the baobab which grows in extensive "forests" here.

SABLE VALLEY

Distance 26 km; 2 days

Reservations Mr J Klopper, P O Box 19279, Pretoria West 0117, Telephone (012) 327-0442.

Group size Minimum 2; Maximum 20

Facilities The Sable Valley Camp at the start of the trail and the first overnight stop, Tierkloof Camp, have beds, mattresses, showers and toilets. Braai facilities, firewood and a scullery are also available.

Description This circular trail traverses the 2 000 ha farm, Naauwpoort, south of Naboomspruit, alternating between savanna and valleys, as well as deeply incised kloofs with crystal clear pools and waterfalls. Patches of indigenous forests with species such as yellowwood, bladder-nut, tree fuchsia and cheesewood are also encountered and hikers will enjoy panoramic views of the Waterberg to the west. Antelope occurring in the area include mountain reedbuck, reedbuck, kudu and klipspringer.

TAAIBOS

Distance 19 km; 2 days

Reservations Taaibos Hiking Trail, P O Box 185, Vaalwater 0530, Telephone (0147552) 222 (evenings).

Group size Minimum 2; Maximum 30

Facilities Accommodation at the start of the trail is provided in two beautiful thatched huts equipped with bunks, mattresses, flush toilets and a hot and cold shower. Fireplaces, firewood, a kettle and iron pots are also provided. At the Krematart huts bunks, mattresses, fireplaces, firewood, a kettle and pots are provided. Water is available in the nearby river.

Description The first day's hike of this circular trail which is situated on a farm west of Vaalwater covers 12 km. After passing through a magnificent water berry forest the trail winds to the top of a krantz before dropping down to the Taaibosspruit. The route then ascends steadily before making its way down a kloof to the Taaibosspruit which is followed to the overnight hut. The second day's route starts with a climb to the krantzes and then drops down to the Bobbejaankrans where rock paintings can be viewed. More rock paintings are encountered further on while the weir built by Italian prisoners of war during the early 1940s is an ideal place to cool off. From here it is a mere 600 m to the end of the trail.

TRIPLE B

Distance 26 km; 2 days

Reservations Jacana Country Homes and Trails, P O Box 95212, Waterkloof 0145, Telephone (012) 346-3550.

Group size Minimum 2; Maximum 20

Facilities Hikers are accommodated in restored farmhouses equipped with bunks, mattresses, flush toilets and showers. A gas cooker, pots, cast iron pots and pans, as well as fireplaces and firewood are also provided.

Description Situated north of the Waterberg, this circular trail on a farm near Vaalwater takes hikers through an area where the Kalahari sands and the Waterberg sandstones meet. A rich diversity of plantlife occurs on the farm – over 800 plant species have been recorded. Birders are unlikely to be disappointed as an estimated 300 species occur in the area. The trail meanders up and over the koppies of a vast Bonsmara cattle ranch where maize and tobacco are also cultivated. Approximately 13 km are covered on each day. Horse-riding trails are also conducted and can be combined with the hike either before or after the trail.

WATERBERG-STAMVRUG

Distance 17,3 km; 2 days

Reservations Jacana Country Homes and Trails, P O Box 95212, Waterkloof 0145, Telephone (012) 346-3550.

Group size Minimum 2; Maximum 20

Facilities The Kloof Hut is equipped with 20 beds and mattresses. Other amenities include bathrooms, outside showers, a kitchen with a fridge and stove, as well as a communal lounge and fireplace. Pots, cast iron pots, fireplaces and firewood are provided at the two lapas. At the Stamvrug Hut bunks, mattresses, a kitchen with pots and pans, showers and toilets, as well as two lapas with braai facilities and firewood are provided.

Description This two-day circular route is situated on two farms between Warmbaths and Nylstroom. The trail traverses a plateau at the foothills of the Waterberg, meandering amongst koppies, and is named after the dense concentrations of Transvaal milkplum, known as stamvrug in Afrikaans, occurring here. The trail can be started either at Kloof Hut or Stamvrug Hut. The Kloof route is 10,5 km long, with an option of a 3 km shortcut, while the Stamvrug route is 6,5 km long, with an optional 3 km loop. Some 250 bird species are thought to occur in the area and among the animals hikers might encounter are blesbok, kudu, reedbuck, klipspringer, chacma baboon, vervet monkey, bushpig and warthog.

REFERENCES

GLOSSARY

ENVIRONMENTAL TERMS

Aquatic – living in water

Arboreal – living in trees

Browser – an animal that feeds on the leaves and shoots of trees and shrubs

Carnivore – flesh-eating animals, can be predators or scavengers

Carrion – the decaying flesh of dead animals

Diurnal – active mainly during the day

Ecology – study of the interactions and relationships between living organisms and their habitat

Ecosystem – any area, large or small, that encompasses all interactions between living (animals and plants) and non-living (soil, water, sun) components

Endemic – a plant or animal that is restricted to a particular area

Epiphytic – a plant that grows on another plant or object (stone) without being parasitic

Estuary – a river mouth where fresh and sea water mix

Family – a grouping used to classify several genera of plants or animals together; similar families are grouped together in an order

Fauna – all animal life

Floodplain – usually a grass- or reed-covered fringe alongside a river which is seasonally inundated

Flora – all plant life

Fynbos – the richly varied fine-leaved bush vegetation of the south-western Cape which is mainly composed of ericas, proteas, reeds and rushes

Genus – a group of closely related animals or plants, e.g. all zebras are grouped in the genus *Equus*

Gestation period – the time from conception to birth in animal species

Grazer – an animal that feeds on grass

Gregarious – living in groups or flocks

Habitat – the surroundings in which an animal or plant lives

Herbivore – a plant-eating animal

Indigenous – occurring naturally in a particular area, but not necessarily restricted to that area

Intra-African migrant – birds that migrate seasonally within Africa

Lagoon – an area of water partly or completely separated from the sea by a sand-spit or sandbar

Lichen – a primitive plant consisting of a fungus and an algae co-existing in symbiosis

Migrant – animals that move seasonally

Monocotyledon – flowering plant that has only one leaf arising from the seed, bulb or corm; it has long leaves with parallel veins

Nocturnal – active mainly during the night

Omnivorous – eating both animals and plants

Palaearctic migrant – birds that migrate seasonally from the northern hemisphere

Perennial – a plant living for more than two years; alternatively, a stream or river which can be expected to contain water throughout the year

Predator – an animal that kills and feeds on other animals

Raptor – diurnal bird of prey, i.e. one that hunts and feeds during the day

Riparian – of or on a river bank

Savanna – grassland containing scattered trees, shrubs and scrub vegetation

Species – the most basic unit of classification; members of the same species are identical in structure and are capable of reproducing within the group

Tarn – small lake surrounded by mountains

Terrestrial – living on land

Wader – collective name for nine bird families of the sub-order *Charadrii*, including plovers and sandpipers; however, the term is often used very generally when referring to all wading birds, i.e. birds which wade in search of food

Woodland – vegetation type characterised by trees with a well-developed but not completely closed canopy

GEOLOGICAL TERMS

Archaean rock – rocks formed in the oldest era in geological history, which ended 1 850 million years ago; the earliest sandstones were transformed by heat into the basement complex

Basalt – a fine-grained, dark grey igneous rock

Basement – *see Archaean*

Conglomerate – a sedimentary rock containing fragments of other rocks that have been cemented together by clay and finer material

Dolerite – a coarse-grained, light coloured rock of volcanic origin occurring in dykes and sills and containing quartz and feldspar

Dyke – a vertical or steeply inclined wall-like sheet of dolerite that is only exposed during subsequent erosion

Fault – a fracture along which the rocks on one side have been displaced relative to those opposite

Feldspar – a white or pink crystalline mineral found in rocks

Gabbro – a coarse-grained crystalline igneous rock formed at great depths

Gneiss – white and black banded rock containing the same minerals as granite, which have undergone a metamorphosis by heat and pressure

Granite – a common, hard and coarse-grained igneous rock, consisting mainly of quartz and feldspar; it is exposed when the overlying rocks are worn away and its colour ranges from pink to grey, according to the colour of the feldspar

Igneous rock – formed from molten material, either on the earth's surface from lava becoming volcanic rocks or underground magma forming plutonic rocks

Inselberg – the more resistant land surfaces which have remained, despite erosion, to form isolated mountains

Lava – molten material that appears on the surface during volcanic eruptions, cooling to form basalt

Magma – molten material that does not reach the earth's surface during a volcanic eruption, but is sometimes subsequently exposed through erosion

Metamorphic rocks – igneous or sedimentary rocks that have undergone a metamorphosis because of temperature, pressure and chemical reactions

Quartzite – a sedimentary, metamorphic rock formed from silica and sandstone

Sandstone – the second most common, but most familiar sedimentary rock, forming about one-third of the sedimentary rocks exposed on the earth's surface; it consists of rounded grains of sand and usually quartz cemented together; the colour varies according to the mineral make-up

Scree – loose fragments of rock covering a slope

Sedimentary rocks – eroded material transported by either wind or water and deposited with the sediments accumulating to eventually form firm rocks after a cementation process has taken place

Schist – a metamorphic rock which is much coarser than gneiss and flakes easily

Shale – the most common sedimentary rock, forming nearly half of the exposed sedimentary rock; grey, purple or black in colour, it is arranged in distinct layers of fine silt and clay

Sill – magma which has been forced between layers of sedimentary rocks subterraneously; when the magma hardens, it forms near-horizontal sheets of igneous rock which is exposed through subsequent erosion

Talus slope – slope consisting of loose rock fragments (scree) caused by the weathering of a cliff face

Tufa – calcium deposits formed when carbon dioxide is extracted by moss from flowing calcium-rich water; usually associated with waterfalls

AFRIKAANS WORDS

Baai – bay

Berg – mountain

Bos – bush

Bosveld – (bushveld) when referring to the Lowveld of the eastern Transvaal, the term is used to describe the vegetation type

Drift – a ford; usually natural but could be artificial

Drostdy – Dutch name for the residency of the landdrost (magistrate)

Fontein – fountain or spring

Gat – hole

Hoëveld – (Highveld) the high-lying area (approximately 1 830 m above sea level) which covers large areas of South Africa; the vegetation consists of treeless grassland

Klip – stone or rock

Kloof – gorge, ravine or narrow gully

Koppie – hillock

Kraal – cluster of huts occupied by indigenous people

Krans – cliff

Mond – river mouth

Nek – col, saddle between two high points

Poort – a narrow passage through a range of hills or a mountain

Rant – ridge

Rondavel – round African hut

Rug – ridge

Sloot – ditch or furrow

Sneeu – snow, often used to refer to snow-capped mountains (Sneeuberg)

Spoor – tracks, usually of animals but also of man; including scent, droppings and urine

Spruit – a stream that is usually almost dry, except after rains

Stroom – stream

Tafel – table; used to refer to flat-topped mountains

Veld – open country with natural vegetation

Vlakte – plain

Vlei – a low-lying area into which water drains during the rainy season, usually smaller than a lake

BIBLIOGRAPHY

The following sources have been consulted and will prove useful if you wish to obtain more detailed information. They are divided into categories for easy reference and periodicals and brochures are listed after the books.

Hiking – general
Books
Burman, J 1980. *Trails and Walks in the Southern Cape.* Cape Town: Human & Rousseau.
Changuion, L 1977. *Met Rugsak en Stewels.* Johannesburg: Perskor.
Hennig, H 1983. *The South African Backpacker.* Cape Town: Centaur.
Levy, J 1993. *Complete Guide to Walks and Trails in Southern Africa.* Cape Town: Struik.
Steyn, A 1982. *Backpack for Pleasure.* Pretoria: Intergrafix.

First Aid
Books
Jackson, J (ed) 1976. *Safety on Mountains.* Manchester: British Mountain Council.
Mitchell, D 1979. *Mountaineering First Aid.* Seattle: The Mountaineers.
Pitchford, R J 1976. *Bilharzia: Beware.* Pretoria: Department of Health.
Reitz, C J 1978. *Poisonous South African Snakes and Snakebite.* Pretoria: Department of Health.
The South African First Aid Manual – Emergency Procedures for Everyone at Home, at Work or at Leisure (The Authorised Manual of the St John Ambulance and the South African Red Cross Society) 1986. Cape Town: C Struik.

Conservation – general
Books
Greyling, T & Huntley, B J (eds) 1984. *Directory of Southern African Conservation Areas.* South African National Scientific Programmes Report No. 98, Pretoria: CSIR.

Periodicals
Ackerman, D P 1977. "Nie-Kommersiële Aktiwiteite van die Departement van Bosbou." *South African Forestry Journal* 103, 1-4.
Ackerman, D P 1979. "The Reservation of Wilderness Areas in South Africa." *South African Forestry Journal* 108, 2-4.
Bands, D P 1977. "Planning for a Wilderness Area." *South African Forestry Journal* 103, 22-27.
National Committee for Nature Conservation: Register of Permanent Conservation Areas in South and South West Africa. 1974. *Koedoe* 17, 85-119.

Southern Africa – general
Books
Andersson, C J 1974. *Lake Ngami* (Facsimile reprint). Cape Town: Struik.
Duggan, A (ed) 1983. *Game Parks and Nature Reserves of Southern Africa.* Cape Town: Reader's Digest.
Gardiner, A F 1966. *Narrative of a Journey to the Zoolu Country in South Africa* (Facsimile reprint). Cape Town: C. Struik.
Gordon, R & Bannister, A 1983. *The National Parks of South Africa.* Cape Town: Struik.
Leigh, M 1986. *Touring in South Africa.* Cape Town: C Struik.
Oberholster, J J 1972. *The Historical Monuments of South Africa.* Stellenbosch: The Rembrandt van Rijn Foundation.
Raper, P E 1972. *Streekname in Suid-Afrika en Suidwes.* Kaapstad: Tafelberg.
Raper, P E 1987. *Directory of Southern African Place Names.* Johannesburg: Lowry Publishers.
Steyn, A (ed) 1987. *Off The Beaten Track – Selected Day Drives in Southern Africa.* Cape Town: Automobile Association of South Africa.

Namibia
Books
Jankowitz, W J 1975. *Aloes of South West Africa.* Windhoek: Division of Nature Conservation and Tourism, Administration of South West Africa.
Joubert, E. *Meesterplan: Namib-Naukluftpark – 'n Verslag met beleid ten opsigte van doelstellings, sonering en benutting van die*

Naukluft-Bergkompleks en aangrensende gruisvlaktes, insluitende Sesriem en Sossusvlei. Windhoek: Suidwes-Afrika Administrasie, Afdeling Natuurbewaring en Toerisme.

Muller, M A N 1984. *Grasses of South West Africa/Namibia.* Windhoek: Directorate of Agriculture and Forestry.

Periodicals

Broekhuysen, G J; Broekhuysen, M G; Winterbottom, J M and Winterbottom, M G 1966. "Birds Recorded from Ai-Ais, Fish River, South West Africa." *The South African Avifauna Series* 42. Cape Town: Percy Fitzpatrick Institute of African Ornithology.

Giess, W 1971. "A preliminary Vegetation Map of South West Africa." *Dinteria* 4.

Kinahan, J 1987. "Archaeological sites in the Fish River Canyon, southern SWA/Namibia." *Madoqua* 15 (1), 17-19.

Simpson, E S W & Hywel Davies, D 1957. "Observations on the Fish River Canyon in South West Africa." *Transactions of the Royal Society of South Africa* 35 (2), 97-108.

Vrey, T 1983. "A hike into the unknown." *Custos* 12 (8), 4-5.

Northern and Western Cape

Books

Andrag, R H 1977. Studies in die Sederberge oor (i) Die Status van die Clanwilliam Seder (*Widdringtonia cedarbergensis*) (ii) Buitelugontspanning. M.Sc Thesis, University of Stellenbosch.

Balchin, B K 1980. *Birds of the Wilderness-Knysna Lakes Area.* Sedgefield: Published by the author.

Bristow, D 1991. *Western Cape Walks - A practical guide to hiking along the coast and in the mountains.* Cape Town: Struik Publishers.

Burman, L and Bean, A 1985. *Hottentots Holland to Hermanus - South African Wild Flower Guide 5.* Cape Town: Botanical Society of SA.

Cape Bird Club. *A Guide to the Birds of the S W Cape.* Cape Town: Cape Bird Club.

Carter, N 1977. *The Elephants of Knysna.* Cape Town: Purnell & Sons.

Day, J; Siegfried, W R; Louw, G N and Jarman, M L (eds) 1979. *Fynbos Ecology: a preliminary synthesis.* South African National Scientific Programmes Report No. 40, Pretoria: CSIR.

Hall, A V and Veldhuis, H A 1985. *South*

African Red Data Book: Plants - Fynbos and Karoo Biomes. South African National Scientific Programmes Report No. 117, Pretoria: CSIR.

Le Roux, A and Schelpe, E A C L E 1988. *Namaqualand and Clanwilliam - South African Wildflower Guide 1.* Cape Town: Botanical Society of SA.

Lundy, M 1992. *Weekend Trails in the Western Cape.* Cape Town: Human & Rousseau.

Moriarty, A 1982. *Outeniqua, Tsitsikamma and Eastern Little Karoo - South African Wild Flower Guide 2.* Cape Town: Botanical Society of SA.

Skead, C J 1982. *Historical Mammal Incidence in the Cape Province, Volume 1: The Western and Northern Cape.* Cape Town: Department of Nature and Environmental Conservation of the Cape Provincial Administration.

Skead, C J 1987. *Historical Mammal Incidence in the Cape Province, Vol 2: The Eastern Half of the Cape Province, including the Ciskei, Transkei and East Griqualand.* Cape Town: Chief Directorate Nature and Environmental Conservation of the Cape Provincial Administration.

Von Breitenbach, F 1974. *Southern Cape Forests and Trees.* Pretoria: Government Printer.

Von Breitenbach, F 1985. *Southern Cape Tree Guide - with a leaf key to 116 indigenous tree and tall shrub species of Outeniqualand and the Tsitsikamma.* Pretoria: Department of Environment Affairs.

Periodicals

Anon. 1987. "Fynbos islands in the Knysna Forest Sea." *Forestry News* 4/87, 12-13.

Kluge, R L 1983. "Biological control of *Hakea sericea.*" *Forestry News* 2/83, 7-10.

Kruger, F J 1983. "The Hottentots-Holland Nature Reserve." Directorate of Forestry of the Department of Environment Affairs, Pamphlet 316.

Luckhoff, H A 1980. "The Sederberg Wilderness Area." Directorate of Forestry and Environmental Conservation, Bulletin 60.

Midgley, J J and Bond, W J 1990. "Knysna Fynbos 'Islands': Origins and Conservation." *South African Forestry Journal* 153, 18-21.

Mostert, V 1976. "Die Sneeuprotea." *Veld & Flora* 62 (4) 21 & 22.

Rautenbach, I L; De Graaff, G and Schlitter, D A 1979. "Notes on the mammal fauna of the

REFERENCES

Augrabies Falls National Park and surrounding areas with special reference to regional zoo-geographical implications." *Koedoe* 22, 157-75.

Slabbert, M J and Malherbe, S J 1983. "Die invloed van Nate op die loop van die Oranjerivier in die omgewing van die Augrabieswaterval Nasionale Park." *Koedoe* 26, 1-7.

Stuart, C and Stuart, T 1991. "A Leopard in the Wilderness." *African Wildlife* 45 (5), 251-4.

Tapson, W 1973. *Timber and Tides - the Story of Knysna and Plettenberg Bay.* Cape Town: Juta & Co.

Taylor, H C 1976. "Notes on the Vegetation and Flora of the Cedarberg." *Veld & Flora* 62 (4), 28-30.

Werger, M J A and Coetzee, B J 1977. "A phytosociological and phytogeographical study of the Augrabies Falls National Park." *Koedoe* 20, 11-51.

Winterbottom, J M 1970. "The birds of the Augrabies Falls National Park." *Koedoe* 13, 171-80.

Eastern Cape

Books

Butchart, D 1989. *A Guide to the Coast and Nature Reserves of the Transkei.* Durban: Wildlife Society of Southern Africa.

Ciskei Tourist Board. *Ciskei Hiking Trails.* Bisho, Ciskei: Ciskei Tourist Board.

Courtney-Latimer, M; Smith, G G; Bokelman, H and Batten, A 1967. *The Flowering Plants of the Tsitsikamma Forest and Coastal National Park.* Pretoria: National Parks Board.

Darrow, W K 1975. *Forestry in the Eastern Cape Border Region.* Bulletin 51. Pretoria: Department of Forestry.

Derricourt, R M 1977. *Prehistoric Man in the Ciskei and Transkei.* Cape Town: Struik.

Gledhill, E 1981. *Eastern Cape Veld Flowers.* Cape Town: Department of Nature and Environmental Conservation of the Cape Provincial Administration.

Grobler, H and Hall-Martin, A. *A Guide to the Mountain Zebra National Park.* Pretoria: National Parks Board.

Moriarty, A 1982. *Outeniqua, Tsitsikamma and Eastern Little Karoo - South African Wild Flower Guide 2.* Cape Town: Botanical Society of SA.

Page, D (ed) 1982. *Strategy and Guidelines for the Physical Development of the Republic of Ciskei.* Stellenbosch: Institute for Planning Research, University of Stellenbosch.

Quickelberge, C D 1989. *Birds of the Transkei - An ornithological history and annotated catalogue of all recorded species.* Durban: Durban Natural History Museum.

Rycroft, H B 1980. *Trees of the Tsitsikamma National Park.* Pretoria: National Parks Board.

Saunders, C & Derricourt, R M (eds) 1974. *Beyond the Cape Frontier - Studies in the History of the Transkei and Ciskei.* London: Longman.

Tietz, R M 1974. *Tsitsikamma Shore.* Pretoria: National Parks Board.

Von Breitenbach, F 1974. *Southern Cape Forests and Trees.* Pretoria: Government Printer.

Von Breitenbach, F 1985. *Southern Cape Tree Guide - with a leaf key to 116 indigenous tree and tall shrub species of Outeniqualand and the Tsitsikamma.* Pretoria: Department of Environment Affairs.

Wildlife Society of Southern Africa 1977. *A Preliminary Survey of the Transkei Coast Undertaken to Identify Nature Conservation Priorities and High Density Recreation Areas.* Linden: Transvaal Wildlife Society of Southern Africa.

Periodicals

Allen, J E 1989. "Indigenous orchids often overlooked." *Custos* 18 (6), 32.

Anon. 1982. "The Pirie Forest and Pirie Walk." *Forestry News* 1, 18-20.

Bowland, A and Hanekom, N 1989. "Rare blue duiker - Food may limit population growth." *Custos* 18 (6), 12-13.

Brown, C 1991. "Terrestrial birds of the Alexandria dunefield." *African Wildlife* 45 (3), 133-35.

De Graaff, G 1976. "Mountain Zebra in their natural habitat." *Custos* 5 (6), 58-62.

De Graaff, G and Nel, J A J 1970. "Notes on the smaller mammals of the Eastern Cape National Parks." *Koedoe* 13, 147-9.

De Graaff, G 1989. "Dertien walvisspesies by Tsitsikamma opgemerk." *Custos* 18 (6) 40-41, 43.

Fourie, A 1976. "Hakea enemies released in Tsitsikamma." *Custos* 5 (4), 9-12, 41-3.

Fourie, J A 1976. "The Tsitsikamma Forest National Park." *Custos* 5 (7), 5-7, 12-13.

Grobler, H 1983. "Haven for the Mountain Reedbuck." *Custos* 11 (9), 31-2.

Hanekom, N 1992. "Cape Clawless Otter – Tsitsikamma can maintain a viable population." *Custos* 20 (12) 32-5.

Illenberger, W K 1988. "Past and present coastal dunefields in the Algoa Bay area." In: Macdonald, I A W and Crawford, R J M. Long-term data series relating to southern Africa's renewable natural resources. *South African National Scientific Programmes Report* No. 157, 389-95.

Illenberger, W and Rust, I C 1992. "Duneland – wasteland or wonderland." *Conserva* 7 (6), 13-15.

Johnson, C T 1983. "The forests and trees of Transkei." *Veld and Flora* 69 (1), 26-7.

Millar, J C G 1968. "The Mountain Zebra." *Wildlife of southern Africa series.* Mammalogy Seminar, University of Pretoria.

Mostert, S C 1989. "De Vasselot – Rich in natural beauty and wildlife." *Custos* 18 (2), 26-31.

Nel, J A J and Pretorius, J J L 1971. "A note on the smaller mammals of the Mountain Zebra National Park." *Koedoe* 14, 99-110.

Penzhorn, B L 1970. "A checklist of flowering plants in the herbarium of the Mountain Zebra National Park." *Koedoe* 13, 131-46.

Penzhorn, B L 1979. "Social organisation of the Cape Mountain Zebra *Equus z. zebra* in the Mountain Zebra National Park." *Koedoe* 22, 115-56.

Poduschka, W 1982. "Extinction at work." *Custos* 10 (12), 10-11.

Rudner, J 1971. "Painted burial stones from the Cape." *Supplement to the South African Journal of Science*, Special issue No. 2, 54-61.

Skead, C J 1965. "Report on the Bird-life of the Mountain Zebra National Park, Cradock, C.P." *Koedoe* 8, 1-54.

Skead, C J and Liversidge, R 1967. "Birds of the Tsitsikamma." *Koedoe* 10, 43-62.

Toerien, D K 1972. "Geologie van die Bergkwagga Nasionale Park." *Custos* 15, 77-82.

Van der Walt, P T 1975. "The Tsitsikamma Forest of today." *Custos* 4 (5), 22-3.

Van der Walt, P T 1980. "A Phytosociological Reconnaissance of the Mountain Zebra National Park." *Koedoe* 23, 1-32.

Van der Zee, D 1989. "Cape clawless otter – Tsitsikamma's inquisitive wanderers." *Custos* 18 (6), 66-8.

Vlok, J 1984. "*Mimetes splendidus* – 'n bedreigde spesie." *Bosbounuus* 3/84, 16-17.

Von Gadow, K 1977. "100 Indigenous Trees of the Eastern Cape Border Region – A Leaf Key." *Department of Forestry Pamphlet* 195.

Wilson, M L and Van Rijssen, W J J 1990. "The Coldstream Stone – A unique artefact in the South African Museum Collection." *Sagittarius* 5 (1), 6-8.

Woodehouse, H C 1968. "The Coldstream burial stone: painting of a prehistoric painter." *South African Journal of Science* 64, 341-4.

KwaZulu/Natal
Books

Ackhurst, J; Irwin, D and Irwin, P 1980. *A Field Guide to the Natal Drakensberg.* Durban: Natal Branch of the Wildlife Society of Southern Africa.

Bristow, D 1988. *Drakensberg Walks: 120 graded hikes and Trails in the 'Berg'.* Cape Town: C Struik Publishers.

Dodds, D 1975. *A Cradle of Rivers – The Natal Drakensberg.* Cape Town: Purnell & Sons.

Killick, D 1990. *A Field Guide to the Flora of the Natal Drakensberg.* Johannesburg: Jonathan Ball.

Little, R M and Bainbridge, W R 1992. *Birds of the Natal Drakensberg Park.* Durban: Natal Branch of the Wildlife Society of Southern Africa.

Moll, E 1981. *Trees of Natal.* Cape Town: University of Cape Town, Eco-Lab Trust Fund.

Pager, H 1971. *Ndedema – a documentation of the rock paintings of Ndedema Gorge.* Graz, Austria: Akademische Druck-u Verlagsanstalt.

Pearse, R O 1978. *Mountain Splendour – The Wild Flowers of the Drakensberg.* Cape Town: Howard Timmins.

Pearse, R O 1989. *Barrier of Spears.* Johannesburg: Southern Book Publishers.

Taylor, R 1991. *The Greater St Lucia Wetland Park.* Pietermaritzburg: Parke-Davis for the Natal Parks Board.

Vinnicombe, P 1976. *People of the Eland – Rock Paintings of the Drakensberg Bushmen as a Reflection of their Life and Thought.* Pietermaritzburg: University of Natal Press.

Willcox, A R 1984. *The Drakensberg Bushmen and Their Art – With a Guide to the Rock Painting Sites.* Winterton: Drakensberg Publicity Association.

Periodicals and brochures

Brown, C J 1992. "Distribution and status of the Bearded Vulture *Gypaetus barbatus* in southern Africa." *Ostrich* 63 (1), 1-9.

REFERENCES

Cawe, S 1992. "The coastal forests of Transkei." *Veld & Flora* 78 (4), 114-7.

Cooper, K H 1991. "The Transkei Wild Coast." *Veld & Flora* (77) 4, 108-10.

Day, D H 1974. *Giant's Castle Game Reserve.* Pietermaritzburg: Natal Parks Board.

Ivey, P 1991. "The Battle for the Eastern Shores – Part 1." *Veld & Flora* (77) 4, 118-19.

Ivey, P 1992. "The Battle for the Eastern Shores – Part 2." *Veld & Flora* 78 (1), 22-3.

Killick, D J B 1963. "An Account of the Plant Ecology of the Cathedral Peak Area of the Natal Drakensberg." *Memoirs of the Botanical Survey* No 34.

Lubke, R 1991. "The Eastern Cape Coast." *Veld & Flora* (77) 4, 105-7.

Luckhoff, H A 1983. "The Natal Drakensberg wilderness areas." *Forestry News* 3, 21-24.

Natal Parks Board. *St Lucia.* Pietermaritzburg: Natal Parks Board.

Natal Parks Board. *Royal Natal National Park.* Pietermaritzburg: Natal Parks Board.

Vincent, J 1980. "The ecology of Lake St Lucia." *Environment RSA* 7 (1), 4-6.

Free State

Periodicals

Groenewald, G 1988. "Katedraalgrot – wonder van water en rots." *Custos* 17 (6), 34-5.

Groenewald, G 1992. "New home for threatened lizard." *Custos* 21 (1), 45-6.

Immink, R J 1976. "Golden Gate." *Custos* 5 (6), 70-2, 75-6.

Penzhorn, B L 1975. "The Lammergeyers of Golden Gate." *Custos* 4 (2), 11-12, 29-33, 36.

Rautenbach, I L 1976. "A summary of the mammals occurring in the Golden Gate Highlands National Park." *Koedoe* 19, 133-43.

Roberts, B R 1969. "The vegetation of the Golden Gate Highlands National Park." *Koedoe* 12, 15-28.

Van Rensburg, A P J 1968. "Golden Gate – die geskiedenis van twee plase wat 'n park geword het." *Koedoe* 11, 83-131.

Van Zyl, L 1982. "Golden Gate's Cathedral Cave." *Custos* 11 (6), 23, 25.

Wessels, D C 1990. "Golden Gate se inkstrepe." *Custos* 19 (9), 42-6.

Wessels, D and Wessels, L 1990. "Eeu-oue ligeen verweer sandsteen." *Custos* 19 (2), 46.

Woodhall, S 1992. "Butterflies of Golden Gate." *Custos* 21 (4), 28-9.

North-West, Gauteng, Eastern Transvaal and Northern Transvaal

Books

Bulpin, T V 1974. *Lost Trails of the Transvaal.* Cape Town: T V Bulpin.

Cartwright, A P 1980. *Valley of Gold.* Cape Town: Howard Timmins.

Germishuizen, G and Fabian, A 1982. *Transvaal Wild Flowers.* Johannesburg: Macmillan.

Klein, H 1972. *Valley of the Mists.* Cape Town: Howard Timmins.

Onderstall, J 1984. *Transvaal Lowveld and Escarpment Including the Kruger National Park – South African Wild Flower Guide 4.* Cape Town: Botanical Society of South Africa.

Rautenbach, I L 1982. *Mammals of the Transvaal.* Pretoria: Ecoplan.

Ryan, B and Isom, J 1990. *Go Birding in the Transvaal.* Cape Town: Struik.

Transvaal Provincial Library and Museum Service. 1980. *Pilgrim's Rest – A Pictorial History.* Pretoria: Transvaal Provincial Library and Museum Service.

Van Gogh, J and Anderson, J 1988. *Trees and Shrubs of the Witwatersrand, Magaliesberg and Pilanesberg.* Cape Town: Struik.

Van Wyk, B and Malan, S 1988. *Field Guide to the Wild Flowers of the Witwatersrand and Pretoria region including the Magaliesberg and Suikersbosrand.* Cape Town: Struik Publishers.

Von Breitenbach, F 1990. R*eports on indigenous forests, Part 1: Introduction and methods – South-eastern Transvaal forests, Kaapsehoop forests, Uitsoek forests.* Pretoria: Department of Environment Affairs, Forestry Branch.

Periodicals

Allan, D 1988. "The Blue Swallow: In with a Chance." *Quagga* 22, 5-7.

Anon. 1981. "Entabeni se samango-ape onder soeklig." *Bosbounuus* 1/81, 14-15.

Anon. 1992. "Fokus Op: Bosstreek Noord-Transvaal – Bewaring is hier geen modewoord". *Bosbounuus* 3/92, 16-7.

Anon. 1992. "Fokus Op: Bosstreek Oos-Transvaal – Land se enigste wilde perde gedy op vlakte." *Forestry News* 4/92, 18-9.

Benson, P C; Tarboton, W R; Allan, D G and Dobbs, J C. "The breeding status of the Cape Vulture in the Transvaal during 1980-1985." *Ostrich* 61 (3 & 4), 134-42.

Dearlove, T W 1978. "Bushveld Open to Hikers." *Custos* 7 (6), 6-11.

Dearlove, T W 1980. "A Third Wilderness Trail for Kruger National Park." *Custos* 9 (8), 5-8.

Dearlove, T W 1983. "New hiking trail for Kruger Park." *Custos* 12 (4), 7-9.

Esterhuyse, C J 1986. "The Wolkberg Wilderness Area." *Forestry Branch of the Department of Environment Affairs, Pamphlet 361*, Pretoria.

McC Pott, R 1981. "The Treur River barb – a rare fish in good company." *African Wildlife* 35 (6), 29-31.

Netshiungani, E N; Van Wyk, A E and Linger, M T 1981. "Thathe – holy forest of the Vhavenda." V*eld and Flora* 67 (2), 51-2.

Oates, L 1978. "Suikerbosrand." *African Wildlife* 32 (3), 36-8.

Publications Division, Venda. 1981. *Welcome To Venda.* Sibasa: Department of Information and Broadcasting.

Publications Division, Venda. 1989/90. *Venda Travelogue.* Sibasa: Department of Information and Broadcasting.

Venter, F 1983. "*Frithia pulchra.*" *Fauna and Flora* 40, 19-20.

Viljoen, P J 1984. "Red-list monkeys re-established at Pafuri." *Custos* 13 (6), 29-30.

Flora
Books

Berjak, P; Campbell, G K; Huckett, B I and Pammenter, N W 1977. *In the Mangroves of Southern Africa.* Durban: Natal Branch of the Wildlife Society of Southern Africa.

Coates Palgrave, K 1992. *Trees of Southern Africa.* Cape Town: Struik.

Harrison, E R 1981. *Epiphytic Orchids of Southern Africa.* Durban: Natal Branch of the Wildlife Society of Southern Africa.

Palmer, E and Pitman, N 1972/73. *Trees of Southern Africa* (3 vols). Cape Town: A A Balkema.

Reynolds, G W 1970. *The Aloes of Southern Africa.* Cape Town: A A Balkema.

Rourke, J P 1980. *The Proteas of Southern Africa.* Cape Town: Purnell & Sons.

Schumann, D; Kirsten, G and Oliver, E G H 1992. *Ericas of South Africa.* Cape Town: Fernwood Press.

Stewart, J; Linder, H P; Schelpe, E A and Hall, A V 1982. *Wild Orchids of Southern Africa.* Johannesburg: Macmillan.

Vogts, M 1982. *South Africa's Proteaceae – Know Them and Grow Them.* Cape Town: Struik.

Von Breitenbach, F 1974. *Southern Cape Forests and Trees.* Pretoria: Government Printer.

Von Breitenbach, F 1986. *National List of Indigenous Trees.* Pretoria: Dendrological Foundation.

Von Breitenbach, F 1989. *National List of Introduced Trees.* Pretoria: Dendrological Foundation.

Periodicals

Acocks, J H P 1975. "Veld Types of South Africa." *Memoirs of the Botanical Survey of South Africa* 40.

Gibbs Russell, G E et al 1984. "List of Species of Southern African Plants." *Memoirs of the Botanical Survey of South Africa* 48.

Smith, C A 1966. "Common Names of South African Plants." *Memoirs of the Botanical Survey of South Africa* 35.

Fauna
Mammals: Books

Skinner, J D and Smithers, R H N 1990. *The Mammals of the Southern African Subregion.* Pretoria: University of Pretoria.

Smithers, R H N 1986. *South African Red Data Book – Terrestrial Mammals.* South African National Scientific Programmes Report No 125, Pretoria: CSIR.

Smithers, R H N 1986. *Land Mammals of Southern Africa – A field guide.* Johannesburg: Macmillan.

Periodicals

Lloyd, P H 1984. "The Cape Mountain Zebra." *African Wildlife* 38 (4), 144-5, 147, 149.

Penzhorn, B L 1971. "A summary of the introduction of ungulates into South African national parks (to 31 December 1970)." *Koedoe* 14, 145-59.

Birds: Books

Berruti, A and Sinclair, J C 1983. *Where to Watch Birds in Southern Africa.* Cape Town: Struik.

Brooke, R K 1984. *South African Red Data Book – Birds.* South African Scientific Programmes Report No 97, Pretoria: CSIR.

Chittenden, H 1992. *Top Birding Spots in Southern Africa.* Johannesburg: Southern Book Publishers.

Maclean, G L 1993. *Roberts' Birds of Southern*

Africa. Cape Town: The Trustees of the John Voelcker Bird Book Fund.

Newman, K 1993. *Newman's Birds of Southern Africa.* Johannesburg: Southern Book Publishers.

Periodicals

Brown, C J and Rennie, S E 1981. "Vulture or Eagle?" *African Wildlife* 35 (4), 12-14.

Reptiles and amphibians: Books

Branch, W R 1988. *South African Red Data Book - Reptiles and Amphibians.* South African National Scientific Programmes Report No 151, Pretoria: CSIR.

FitzSimons, V F M 1970. *A Field Guide to the Snakes of Southern Africa.* London: Collins.

Visser, J and Chapman, D 1981. *Snakes and Snakebite.* Cape Town: Purnell & Sons.

Fish: Books

Salomon, M G 1978. *Freshwater Fishing in South Africa.* Johannesburg: Chris van Rensburg Publications.

Skelton, P H 1993. *A Complete Guide to the Freshwater Fishes of Southern Africa.* Johannesburg: Southern Book Publishers.

Skelton, P H 1987. *South African Red Data Book - Fishes.* South African National Scientific Programmes Report No 137. Pretoria: CSIR.

Periodicals

Jubb, R A 1972. "Disappearing river fishes." *African Wildlife* 26 (2), 48-52.

Scott, H A 1982. "The Olifants River System - Unique Habitat for Rare Cape Fishes." *Cape Conservation Series* 2, Cape Town: Cape Department of Nature and Environment Conservation.

Marine fauna: Books

Richards, D 1981. *South African Shells - A Collector's Guide.* Cape Town: Struik.

Archaeology, history and anthropology

Books

Cameron, T and Spies, S B (eds) 1986. *An Illustrated History of South Africa.* Johannesburg: Jonathan Ball Publishers.

Inskeep, R R 1978. *The Peopling of Southern Africa.* Cape Town: David Philip.

Levitas, B 1983. *Ethnology - An Introduction to the Peoples and Cultures of Southern Africa.* Cape Town: Oxford University Press.

Miller, P 1979. *Myths and Legends of Southern Africa.* Cape Town: T V Bulpin Publications.

Muller, C F J 1980. *500 Jaar Suid Afrikaanse Geskiedenis.* Pretoria: Academica.

Parsons, N 1982. *A New History of Southern Africa.* London: Macmillan Education Ltd.

Phillipson, D W 1977. *The Later Prehistory of Eastern and Southern Africa.* London: Heinemann Education Books.

Willcox, A R 1976. *Southern Land - The Prehistory and History of Southern Africa.* Cape Town: Purnell & Sons.

Willcox, A R 1984. *The Rock Art of Africa.* Johannesburg: Macmillan.

Wilson, M and Thompson, L (eds) 1982. *A History of South Africa.* Cape Town: David Philip.

Geology

Books

Mountain, E D 1968. *Geology of Southern Africa.* Cape Town: Books of Africa.

All available trail literature was also consulted. These publications are too numerous to list and we suggest that those interested make enquiries to the relevant authorities.

INDEX

In view of the large number of possible entries a select index has been compiled. The same sequence is followed in the book in respect of flora, fauna, history and geology of each area, making a comprehensive index superfluous. Entries in the index are limited to instances which have received more detailed description than a mere mention.

Aasvoëlberg Hiking Trail 262
Adder
    Gaboon 235
    plain mountain 156-7
Agate Terrace 193
Ai-Ais 43, 45, 48
Alexandria Hiking Trail 147-153
Algeria Forest Station 68
Aloe
    fan 85
    mountain 280
Aloe peglerae 272-3
Amanzimnyama Hiking Trail 239
Amatola Hiking Trail 160-67
Amatola Mountains 160
Anglo-Boer War (1899-1902) 68, 252, 259, 290, 298
Arangieskop Hiking Trail 119
Attaquaskloof Hiking Trail 119
Augrabies Falls National Park 50
    proclamation of 53

Baboon Hiking Trail 310
Backpack, packing 12-14
Backpack
    packing of 12
    selection of 8-9
Backpacking trail, definition of 4
Bain, Andrew Geddes 80
Bain, Thomas 79, 99, 102, 129
Bain's Kloof Pass 80
Balele Hiking Trail 239
Bankberg 154, 158
Baobab Hiking Trail 354
Barb
    Border 163
    chubbyhead 59
    Namaqua 53
    Treur River 304
Ben Macdhui Hiking Trail 194
Besemfontein Hiking Trail 120
Bilharzia 19
    map of distribution 21

Bites 19
Blisters 19
Blossom tree 95, 131
Bloukrans River 130, 140-41
Bloupunt Hiking Trail 120
Bluebuck, extinct 90
Blyderivierspoort Hiking Trail 302-308
Blyderivierspoort Nature Reserve 302
Boesmangrot Hiking Trail 262
Boesmanskloof Hiking Trail 120
Bokpoort Hiking Trail 262-3
Boland Hiking Trail, introduction 74-7
Bomvanaland 179, 180
Bontebok 90
Bontebok National Park 90
Boosmansbos Wilderness Area 121
Boots, *see* footwear
Bosberg Hiking Trail 194
Boschhoek Hiking Trail 311
Bottlebrush (*Greyia*), Transvaal 321
Bottlebrush (*Mimetes*), Kogelberg silver 74
Bourke's Luck 306
Brandberg Backpacking Area 49
Brandvlei Dam/Kwaggakloof Hiking Trail 121
Brandwater Hiking Trail 250-255
Brook Hiking Trail 311
Bruises 19
Buchu 66, 84-5
Buffalo 25, 130
Burnera Wilderness Education Programme 239-40
Burns 19
Bush tea 132
Bushman's Hiking Trail 311
Butterflies, Golden Gate 258-9

Candelabra tree, Transvaal 341
Cannibals Hiking Trail 240
Cape Floral Kingdom 74-5
Catfish, sharptooth
Cathedral Peak, Drakensberg 229, 230
Cathkin Peak, Drakensberg 225
Cedar tree 66

INDEX

Cederberg Wilderness Area 63-73
    proclamation of 68
Champagne Castle, Drakensberg 226
Chat, Arnot's 339
Cheetah 278
Clothing, trail 11
Coffee Bay 188
Cogmanskloof Hiking Trail 120
Coldstream, burial stones 138
Commando Drift Hiking Trail 194
Cramps 19
Crocodile, Nile 235
Crystal Pool, Cederberg 68-9
Cwebe Nature Reserve 182
Cycad, Modjadji 332

Dassie, tree 162
Dassieshoek Hiking Trail 121
Day walks 4
De Finn, Captain Johann Baron 151, 165,
    171
De Vasselot de Régné, Count M 68, 108, 115,
    129
Devil's Knuckles, Wolkberg 335
Diarrhoea 19
Difaqane 179, 203-4, 252, 259, 290
Dinosaur fossils, Golden Gate 260
Dinosaur tracks, Waterberg 28
Dislocation 19-20
Dokolewa Hiking Trail 324-6
Drakensberg see Natal Drakensberg Park and
    Transvaal Drakensberg
Driekoppe Hiking Trail 195
Dughandlovu Hiking Trail 240
Duiker, blue 136
Dune forest, St Lucia 234
Dunefield, Alexandria 151
Du Toit's Kloof Pass 79

Ear infections 20
Earthworm, giant 162
Ekowa Hiking Trail 195
Eland 278
Eland Hiking Trail 312
Elandsberg 142
Elandsvallei Hiking Trail 312
Elephants, Knysna 107, 115
Emergency blanket 10
Emergency situations 17-8
Encephalartos humilis 283
Entabeni Hiking Trail 347
Equipment 7
Ethics, trail 16-7
Exhaustion 20

Eye infections 20
Eye injuries 20

Fanie Botha Hiking Trail 287-294
Fever 20
Fika Patso Hiking Trail 263
Fires 16-7
First aid 17-22
First aid kit 18
Fish River Canyon Backpacking Trail 41-8
Fish River Canyon, proclamation of 45
Flash floods 14
Flooded rivers 14
Food, trail 5
Footwear 7
    care of 8
Forest fever tree 349
Forest lavender tree 284
Forests, exploitation of
    Southern and Eastern Cape 108, 115-6, 129,
        131, 151, 165, 170-1
    South-western Cape 90
Franschhoek Pass 87
Frithia pulchra 273
Frog
    Hewitt's ghost 144
    Hogsback 162-3
Fundudzi Sacred Lake 351, 352
Fynbos, description of 74
Fynbos islands 106, 115

Gamka Hiking Trail 121-2
Gecko
    Hawequa flat 77
    Methuen's dwarf 322
    Woodbush flat 322
Geelhout Hiking Trail 240-41
Gemsbok Hiking Trail 310
Genadendal Hiking Trail 122
Generaalskop, Golden Gate 261
Geology
    Alexandria 151
    Augrabies Falls 53
    Drakensberg 204-5
    Fish River Canyon 45-6
    Golden Gate Highlands National Park 260
    Naukluft 36
    Waterberg Plateau Park 27-8
Giant's Castle, Drakensberg 223
Giant's Castle Game Reserve 221-4
Giant's Cup Hiking Trail 207-212
Giraffe 340
Giraffe Hiking Trail 337-341
God's Window 294, 305

Gold, discovery of
  Eastern Transvaal 290, 292-3, 305, 306
  Knysna forests 108, 109, 110, 111
  North-eastern Transvaal 322, 333
  Pilgrim's Rest 297-8, 301
  South-eastern Transvaal 284-5
Golden Gate Highlands National Park 256
  proclamation of 259-60
Golden mole
  giant 162
  Gunning's 322
Gonaqua Hiking Trail 142-6
Greater St Lucia Wetland Park 233
Groendal Wilderness Area 195
Grootbosch 320
Grootbosch Hiking Trail 327-9
Grootvadersbos 121
Groot Winterhoek Wilderness Area 122
Groundpad 10
Guided wilderness trail, definition of 4

Hakea 128
Hanglip Hiking Trail 342-7
Hans Merensky Nature Reserve 337
Harison, Christopher 108, 115, 129
Harkerville Hiking Trail 113-7
Harris, Captain Cornwallis 272
Heat exhaustion 20
Heat stroke 20
Hiking Federation of South Africa 4
Hiking trail, definition of 4
Hints, useful hiking 14-16
Hippopotamus 234, 238, 308
Hluleka Nature Reserve 186
Hogsback Hiking Trail 195-6
Hole in the Wall 182
Horses, wild, Morgenzon 297, 300
Hottentots-Holland Hiking Trail 82-95
Hottentots-Holland Nature Reserve 74, 82
Huilklip, 327
Hypothermia 20-1

Ibis, bald 304
Impala lily 339
Interpretative trail, definition of 4
Itala Guided Wilderness Trail 241

Jock of The Bushveld Guided Wilderness Trail
  312

Kaapschehoop Hiking Trail 312-3
Kameelkop Hiking Trail 263
Karoo National Park 123
Katberg Hiking Trail 196

Keurboom, see Blossom tree
Kiepersol Hiking Trail 263
Kitlist 13
Klipkraal Hiking Trail 310
Klipspringer 52
Klipspringer Hiking Trail 50-55
Klipstapel Hiking Trail 264
Knersvlakte 61
Knysna forests, see Southern Cape forests
Kologha Hiking Trail 168-172
Kologha Mountains 168
Königstein, Brandberg 49
Koranna Hiking Trail 245-9
Korannaberg 245
Kranshoek Falls 117
Kristalkloof Hiking Trail 122
Kruger National Park Guided Wilderness Trails
  311, 312, 313-4, 316, 317, 355
Kubusie Mountain 172
Kututsa Hiking Trail 264

Lake Guided Wilderness Trail 241
Lake St Lucia 234, 235, 236, 237, 238
Lammergeier Hiking Trail 196
Langalibalele 219
Langeberg Mountains 88, 92, 94, 119, 121, 122,
  123
Lekgalameetse Hiking Trail 354
Leopard, sanctuary 67
Leopard Hiking Trail 354
Lesoba Hiking Trail 264
Leucospermum saxosum 303
Lichens 24-5, 258
Limietberg 80
Limietberg Hiking Trail 78-81
Lizard
  red-tailed rock 52
  Transvaal mountain 350
Lung infections 21
Lwamondo Kop 350-1

Mabudashango Hiking Trail 348-353
Mac-Mac Falls 292-3
Magaliesberg 272, 273
Magoebaskloof 319
Magoebaskloof Hiking Trail, introduction
  319-323
Magoebaskloof: Dokolewa Section 324-6
Magoebaskloof: Grootbosch Section 327-9
Malaria 21
  map of distribution 21
Maltese Cross, Cederberg 72
Mangroves 176, 177, 185, 183
Mapulaneng Hiking Trail 355

Marico Hiking Trail 309
Marine fauna
  Otter Hiking Trail 136-8
  Transkei Hiking Trail 178
Marloth Nature Reserve 88
Mauchsberg 292
Mdedelelo Wilderness Area 225-8
Menu, trail 6
Merriemetsi Hiking Trail 264-5
Metsi Matsho Hiking Trail 265
Metsi-Metsi Guided Wilderness Trail 313
Millwood 109, 111
Mimetes, silver, *see also* Bottlebrush (*Mimetes*)
Minnow, Drakensberg 216
Mist 14
Mkhaya Hiking Trail 241
Mkhomazi Wilderness Area 217-220
Moffat, Robert 274
Mokobulaan Nature Reserve 285
Monkey, samango 344
Monks Hiking Trail 242
Monk's Cowl, Drakensberg 227
Mont-Aux-Sources, Drakensberg 267
Moshoeshoe I 252, 259
Mountain Zebra Hiking Trail 154-9
Mountain Zebra National Park 154,
  proclamation of 157
Mud-skipper 176
Mziki Hiking Trail 233-8
Mzilikazi 274, 279, 290
Mzimkhulu Wilderness Area 213-16

Napi Guided Wilderness Trail 313
Natal Drakensberg Park 199-206
  access rules 206
Naukluft Hiking Trail 31-40
Ndedema Gorge, Drakensberg 231-2
Ngele Hiking Trail 242
Nosebleeds 21
Ntendeka Wilderness Area 242
Nutrition 6-7
Nyalaland Guided Wilderness Trail 355

Oldwood 257
Olifants Guided Wilderness Trail 313-4
Olifants River System, fish of 59
Oorlogskloof Hiking Trail 56-62
Oorlogskloof Nature Reserve 56
  proclamation of 59
Orange River Hiking Trail 264
Orange View Hiking Trail 118
Orchids, epiphytic 321, 338-9, 349
Organ Pipes, Drakensberg 232
Oribi 296-7

Oribi Hiking Trail 243
Otter 137
Otter Hiking Trail 134-141
Ouma's Kraal Hiking Trail 265
Outeniqua Hiking Trail 104-112
Outeniqua Mountains 105, 108, 124
Oviston Nature Reserve 196-7

Pain 21
Palm Springs, Fish River Canyon 46-7
Parrot, Cape 162
Pilanesberg Guided Wilderness Trails 309
Pilgrim's Rest 297
Pincushion, rocket 65
Pinnacle 294
Plane, Transvaal 321
Platberg Hiking Trail 265-6
Pofadder Hiking Trail 118
Pondoland 179
Porcupine Hiking Taril 266
Port St John's 179
Prentjiesberg Hiking Trail 197
Prospector's Hiking Trail 295-301
Protea
  honey scented 274
  mountain 76
  snow 65, 72-3
  strap-leaved 98
Protea Hiking Trail 314

Rain gear, *see* waterproof garment
Ratelspruit Hiking Trail 314
Redwood, Californian 116
Reedbuck 235
Reedbuck, mountain 156
Resurrection bush 33
Rhebok, grey 258
Rhebok Hiking Trail 256-261
Rhinoceros, black 25-6, 51
Rhinoceros, white 25
Rhino Peak, Drakensberg 215
Ribbok Hiking Trail 314-5
River crossing, precautions 14, 175
Rock paintings
  Brandberg 49
  Drakensberg 209-10, 215, 216, 219, 222-3,
    227, 231-2
  Kruger National Park 311
  Sehlabathebe National Park 216
Rooibos tea 66
Rooihaas Hiking Trail 266
Rooiwaterspruit Hiking Trail 123
Rustenburg Hiking Trail 271-5
Rustenburg Nature Reserve 271

Sabie 290
Sable 273
Sable Valley Hiking Trail 355
Salpeterkrans 254
Salpeterkrans Hiking Trail 315
Sandfish, Clanwilliam 59
Sawfin 59
Sea bean 192
Seekoeirivier Hiking Trail 118
Sehlabathebe National Park 216
Sentinel Hiking Trail 266-7
Sethuzini Hiking Trail 197
Shipwreck Hiking Trail 197-8
Shipwrecks
    Forest Bank 187
    HMS *Grosvenor* 189, 190, 191
    Santo Alberto 179, 204
    Sao Bento 189
Silaka Nature Reserve 184
Sinclair Nature Reserve 113
Skeleton Coast Park 49
Skink, Woodbush legless 322
Skip Norgarb Hiking Trail 267
Sleeping bag
    care of 9
    types of 9
Snakebite 21-2
Snake, Swazi rock 322
Sneeuberg, Cederberg 72-3
Songimvelo Guided Wilderness Trail 315
Southern Cape forests 105-6
Soutpansberg 342, 345, 348
Soutpansberg Hiking Trail, *see* Hanglip Hiking
    Trail
Sphinx Hiking Trail 267
Sprains 22
Springbok Hiking Trail 123
St Lucia Complex 234-6
St Lucia Guided Wilderness Trail 243
Steenkampsberg Hiking Trail 315-6
Sterkspruit Hiking Trail 316
Sterretjies Hiking Trail 267-8
Steve Visser Hiking Trail 268
Stings 19
Stinkwood, red 320-1
Stokstert Hiking Trail 268
Stove, backpacking 10
Strains 22
Strandloper Hiking Trail 198
Strandveld Hiking Trail 123-4
Sugarbush
    Blyde 303, 307
    Transvaal mountain 331
Suicide Gorge 86

Suikerboschfontein Hiking Trail 316
Suikerbosrand Hiking Trail 276-281
Suikerbosrand Nature Reserve, proclamation of
    279
Sunstroke 20
Swallow, blue 289, 313
Swartberg 96
Swartberg Pass 99
Swartberg Hiking Trail 96-103
Swellendam Hiking Trail 88-95
Sweni Guided Wilderness Trail 316

Taaibos Hiking Trail 355-6
Tafelberg, Cederberg 70-71
Tent 11
Tern, Damara 150
Thaba Guided Trails 309
Thathe Sacred Forest 352
Three Rondavels 307, 308
Throat infections 21
Thunberg, Carl 95, 108
Tickbites 22
Tierkop Hiking Trail 124
Toad, Amatola 162-3
Transkaroo Hiking Trail 119
Transkei Hiking Trail, introduction 173-9
Transkei Hiking Trail
    Coffee Bay to Mbashe River 180-183
    Msikaba River to Port St John's 189-193
    Port St John's to Coffee Bay 184-8
Transkei Wild Coast 173
Transvaal Drakensberg 282, 287, 295
Tree fern 350
Triple B Hiking Trail 356
Tshatsingo Potholes 353
Tsitsikamma forests 114, 126, 127-8
Tsitsikamma Hiking Trail 125-133
Tsitsikamma Mountains 125
Tsitsikamma National Park, proclamation of 138
Tugela Falls 267

Ugab River Guided Wilderness Trail 49
Uitsoek Hiking Trail 282-6
Umfolozi Guided Wilderness Trail 243-4
Umtata River, origin of name 187

Van Stadensrus Hiking Trail 124
Ventersberg Hiking Trail 268
Vingerpol Hiking Trail 269
Vingerpol (*Euphorbia clavarioides*) 251, 269
Vlakvark Hiking Trail 317
Vomiting 19
Vredeberg Hiking Trail 269
Vulture

Bearded 224
Cape 26, 274

Wagon tree 66, 98
Waterberg Guided Wilderness Trail 49
Waterberg Hiking Trail 23-30
Waterberg Plateau Park 49
  proclamation of 27
Waterberg-Stamvrug Hiking Trail 356
Waterfall Bluff 190-91
Waterhoek Hiking Trail 244
Waterkloof Hiking Trail 269
Waterproof garment 10, 15
Wattle, weeping 25
West Coast National Park 123
White Rhino Guided Wilderness Trail 244
Wild banana, Cape 114
Wild Coast, *see* Transkei Wild Coast

Wilderness trail, definition of, *see* Guided
  wilderness trail
Wildebeest, black 258
Wolfberg Arch, Cederberg 71
Wolfberg Cracks, Cederberg 71-2
Wolhuter Guided Wilderness Trail 317
Wolhuterskop Hiking Trail 269-70
Wolkberg Wilderness Area 330-336
  proclamation of 333
Woodcliffe Hiking Trail 198

Yellowwood Hiking Trail 318
Yellowfish, Clanwilliam 59

Zebra
  Burchell's 157
  Cape mountain 156
  Hartmann's mountain 34, 44, 156